JUDITH PARIS
A NOVEL

JUDITH PARIS

A NOVEL

BY

HUGH WALPOLE

MACMILLAN AND CO., LIMITED
ST. MARTIN'S STREET, LONDON

1933

PRINTED IN GREAT BRITAIN
BY R. & R. CLARK, LIMITED, EDINBURGH

FOR
J. B. PRIESTLEY

A PREFATORY LETTER

My dear Jack,

There is in general no reasonable excuse for burdening a novel with a Preface or any sort of statement; a novel should show in itself its purport without outside emphasis. But, after the publication of *Rogue Herries*, I saw that with the next ' Herries ' volume there must be a note of explanation. And for these reasons:

First: when a reader sees another instalment of Herries history he may think it necessary that he should read the first in order to understand the second.

Secondly: after *Rogue Herries* had made some friends it was in some places assumed that ' *now*, of course, I would write a sequel.'

And thirdly: the principal criticism of *Rogue Herries* was on the ground of its diffuseness.

I must explain then that, firstly, the story of *Judith Paris* may be followed without any knowledge of her father or curiosity as to her descendants. Then, far from considering a sequel to *Rogue Herries* for the first time *after* its publication, I must here confess that I had, more than twenty years ago, the plan of writing the history of an English family that should cover two

hundred years and that should have, throughout, the same English scene for its centre.
This was, I think (although Mr. Galsworthy
may correct me), before the later Forsytes were
thought of, or any suspicion of Sagas hung in the
literary air.

Thirdly, I hope that when any who are interested realise (possibly with dismay and indignation) that there are to be, in all, four volumes
of Herries history, certain details and characters
will not seem so unnecessary, nor certain scenes
so diffuse.

I would like, very modestly, to defend the fact
that I write, and must write, from my own point
of view. I can see that the Herries family
offers, in its history, subject-matter for every
kind of historian. But my view of the Herries in
these volumes is frankly a romantic one.

Every historian, whether of a country or a
family, is compelled by his temperament to his
own individual vision. I can see that there is a
Herries history that is realistic, one that is comic,
one that is scientific. Any of these might be
more broadly convincing than my own, but I
must mix my own colours and stand by the result.

As to diffuseness, compression in such a
scheme as this is not easy. I might have written
a novel, a long one too, only about Jennifer.
Even with Judith I have been compelled to
squeeze ten years of her life into one chapter.
Those ten years could well be the subject of
another novel. The Rockages at Grosset fasci-
nate me, but my theme compels me to keep them

minor. And how much more I know about Georges Paris in London or Charlie Watson in Watendlath than I have space to tell!

Every scene and character has been deliberately chosen by me because of the book's continuous theme. At the awful word 'Theme,' however, I feel that I am growing altogether too serious and solemn.

My intention is simply to record scenes from the life of an English family during two hundred years of English change and fortune, and beyond that to pay a tribute to a part of England that I dearly love.

Judith Paris may be read as a quite independent novel, but the four books are seen together in my mind as a piece of gaily-tinted tapestry worked in English colours.

Affectionately yours,

HUGH WALPOLE

I have kept my faith, though faith was tried,
To that rock-born, rock-wandering foot,
And the world's altered since you died,
And I am in no good repute
With the loud host before the sea,
That think sword strokes were better meant
Than lover's music—let that be,
So that the wandering foot's content.

W. B. YEATS

CONTENTS

PART I

PAGE

ROGUE'S DAUGHTER 1

Forechapter 3

Life at Uldale 10

Stone Ends 31

Sunwoods in Cockermouth . . . 51

Fireworks over the Lake 73

The Fugitive 96

Death of David 128

Quarrel and Flight 152

Madame Paris 173

PART II

WATENDLATH 199

Francis rides over 201

The Crimson Bird 230

Happiness in London 259

The Herries Ball, May 17, 1796 . . 289

The Hanging 321

The Clipping 347

The Old Man of the Sea . . . 369

Tumble Downstairs 393

PART III

PAGE

THE BIRD OF BRIGHT PLUMAGE . . . 407
    Family Papers 409
    Uldale Again 439
    Paying a Call on Mrs. Southey . . . 458
    Gone to Earth 486
    Ghostly Idyll 510
    Will Herries dines at Westaways . . 530
    Judith in Paris 558
    Palais-Royal 581

PART IV

MOTHER AND SON 601
    The Hills 603
    Judith returns to Uldale . . . 626
    Round of the Moon . . . 648
    Francis in London, Spring 1821 . . 674
    Money 692
    Mob 714
    The Choice 744

PART I

ROGUE'S DAUGHTER

FORECHAPTER

THE old woman and the new-born child were the only living things in the house.

The old woman, Mrs. Henny, had finished her washing and laying-out of the bodies of the child's father and of the child's mother. She had done it alone because she had been afraid to leave the house with no one alive in it save the new-born child. Now she was exhausted and, in spite of her labour, fearfully chilled, for the snow, although it fell now more lightly, was piled high about the doors and windows as if, with its soft thick fingers, it wished to strangle the house.

She was very cold, so she drank some gin, although it was not as a rule her weakness. The bodies of Mr. and Mrs. Herries lay, the eyes decently closed, the pale hands folded, each in its proper bed.

A fine heat burnt through Mrs. Henny's old body. The gin was good. Then her head fell forward and she slept.

The old house rattled and squealed in the wind that was rising up now that the snow had almost ceased to fall. Feet seemed to creep up and down the stairs, fingers were at the windows, but the dead and Mrs. Henny slept on.

3

Then, in the room where the old woman, the child, and its mother were, from the window a piece of glass, very old and dark green like weeded water, was loosened with the wind and fell tinkling to the boards.   The snow blew in like a live thing and the room was icily chilled.

The child that had been sleeping felt the cold and began to cry, a shrill cry on one note.   But Mrs. Henny heard nothing, the gin holding her fast.

Squire Gauntry—little Tom Gauntry—riding along the Borrowdale path just below the house on the farther side of the little bridge, heard the cry.   It was strange that from so weak a creature the cry should be so clear.   He heard it, and he pulled up his horse; the six hounds who were with him stopped also.   The snow had but just ceased to fall and for the first time that day.   It was so unusual in that country for there to be so heavy a fall that he halted and looked about him in wonderment.   The roofs of Rosthwaite, all the hills, the fields were buried in the white smooth covering, and now, for the first time, light began to break through.   The grey stuff of the snowy sky was torn and a faint green field spread over the dim hills, and the snow began shyly to sparkle. The wind blew the top of the snow into little smoking spirals.   Some rooks flew, like black leaves, cawing, breaking the sacred silence.   The green field spread.

Herries, the house, raised on its little hill, to Gauntry's right, seemed to be overwhelmed by the snow, huddled, shapeless, helpless, and out of that white shapelessness this thin, desolate, tiny cry continued.

Gauntry was eager to be home; his high black riding-coat was heavy with snow, he was weary and chilled, but there was something in that cry that moved him. A hard-bitten little man, leading always his own life and telling everyone else to go to the devil, nevertheless he was sentimental too: so he turned his horse, crossed the bridge over the stream, and, followed by the six hounds, guided the animal through the snow, and, striking with his whip on the gate of the courtyard, holloaed three times.

There was no answer at all. The silence settled down again. There was no sound but the thin persisting cry. He hesitated as to his next step. He had met Herries once and again, but had no intimacy with him. Indeed, no one had. He was said to be a queer customer, one not easy to deal with, one who would not thank you for uninvited interference.

Gauntry was just like that himself, and, for that very reason, had always felt a sympathy with Herries. He liked a man who told the world to go to the devil: it was what the world was meant for. Nevertheless, he was tired, cold, thirsty. Why should he put himself about for a man who would only curse him?

Then something about the stillness of the house hit his attention. The place was but a ruin in any case; under the snow he could fancy how the boards creaked and the chimneys rocked.

He dismounted from his horse, pushed wide

the old, grumbling gate, the snow falling thickly from it, then, followed in silence by the hounds, crossed the courtyard.

The house-door was unbarred. The iron handle turned easily. He entered, to be met by two rusted suits of armour stationed at the foot of the stairs. Still there was silence everywhere, save for the lament of the child.

How cold the house was! He shivered, drawing his cloak tighter about him. Then again he holloaed. No answer. Where the devil were they hiding? Not a sound, not even a clock-tick. Up the creaking stairs he went, the dogs padding after him.

He came to a room hung with faded brown tapestries; there was a portrait of a wicked-looking old man in the dress of Elizabethan times, dead ashes in the stone fireplace, remains of a meal, bread, a mutton bone, on the table.

He called again: 'Herries! Herries!' but this time softly. Something in the place constrained him. Lord! how cold the house was!

A narrow wooden stair led higher, so on he went, the hounds following, crowding one another on the stair but making no sound.

At the stair-head there was a room. He pushed the door, entered, then stood there looking.

First he was aware that the snow was blowing in through a broken window, and then that a child lay in a wooden cradle. It was the child's cry he had heard. Then he saw that in a chair near the bed an old woman was asleep, and at her side was a bottle, tumbled over, spilling its contents on the floor. Then, stepping forward, he saw farther. On the bed a woman was lying. He saw at once that she was dead. Her red hair was spread about the pillow, her eyes were closed, and in her face there was a look of great peace and contentment.

Mrs. Herries! He had heard of her many a time, but had never seen her. She had been a gipsy girl when Herries married her. She had run away from him, and then returned. Herries' second wife, the only woman, they said, whom he had ever loved. Gauntry bent forward and touched reverently the cold, thin hands. Yes, she was dead. Where, then, was Herries? Roughly he shook the old woman by the shoulder, but she would not stir. Only her old head rolled. He called softly ' Herries! ', then went to the cradle, and the infant, who must be but newly born, at once ceased to cry.

He went to the door and listened, then seeing a room close by pushed softly into it. Herries himself was lying in bed there. Going closer Gauntry saw that he, too, was dead—an old man, his face scarred, but he, too, seemed to smile in great contentment and happiness.

Both, then? Both dead? He turned back to the other room, again shook the old woman, but saw that the drink held her fast. He stood there wondering what he should do, while the hounds sat on their haunches by the door and watched him.

Through the dusk the snow sparkled like diamonds, and somewhere a solitary bird began its chirping. The infant did not cry, but seemed to watch him.

'Old woman!' he cried. 'Wake up! Wake up!'

But she would not wake. What must he do? The child must not be left here in this bitter cold: he could see that it was very warmly wrapped. Every preparation had been made for its coming. Poor woman! Poor Mrs. Herries! Died in childbirth maybe, and Herries himself dying in the next room. Strange end to a strange life!

A tenderness seized him as he looked at that thin childish face, those thin delicate hands! What lovely hair she had! Herries had loved her, they said, almost to madness.

Well, someone must be told. Herries' son, David Herries, at Uldale must be told. Someone in Rosthwaite village must be fetched. But he could not leave that child there to start its melancholy cry so soon as he was gone. No, he could not. Very delicately for so dried and rough a little man he picked up the child, wrapping round it its warm bedding. Were it warm enough it would not suffer. They were hardy children in Gauntry's world. He was pleased that the child did not cry, but lay there in his arms contentedly.

Then he went out, down the stairs, across the courtyard, led the horse with one hand, and so, followed by the hounds, crossed the little bridge.

He knocked on the first cottage-door in Rosthwaite. An old, wrinkled woman opened it. He told her of what he had found. She exclaimed something incoherently of witches and warlocks; another woman came, they chattered together. Two men joined them.

After many wonderings, forebodings and murmurs they started off up the hill to the house, in a group together as though they were afraid.

He stood there, considering. He did not wish to leave the child. It would be late when he was home. He would take it to his own place, Stone Ends, that night, and the family at Uldale should have it in the morning.

Yes, he did not want to leave it. Poor baby; it trusted him and seemed to watch him lest he should go away. Both dead in the one hour! He was helped to his horse, the child lifted to him by a village girl, then he called to the hounds and rode away. The infant, warm under the thick wrapping, uttered no sound.

LIFE AT ULDALE

In the autumn of the year 1785 David Herries was sixty-six years of age, his wife Sarah forty-seven, his children, Francis twenty-five, Deb twenty-three and Will fifteen; his little half-sister, Judith Herries, was eleven.

They all lived at Fell House, Uldale. Uldale is on the farther side of Skiddaw and looks over the moor to the Solway Firth. The sprawling flanks of Skiddaw spread between Uldale and the town of Keswick.

In 1785 Marie Antoinette was playing hide-and-seek with her ladies in the gardens of Versailles, William Pitt was Prime Minister of England, Jane Austen was ten years old, and a Keswick boy of sixteen had just been hanged for stealing a leg of mutton. Nevertheless, this is a poor way of reckoning history, especially at Uldale, where the crops mattered and cock-fighting mattered and old Mrs. Monnasett had only this very moment died.

History, of course, begins anywhere and everywhere. For Judith Herries it began, perhaps, when little Tom Gauntry found her squealing under the closed and lifeless eyes of both her parents. She never reckoned it so; she reckoned

that it began on this autumn day when, after looking at Mrs. Monnasett's corpse, she was whipped
by her half-brother David.

This at once shows the ludicrousness of her
position.   She was eleven years old, and yet was
sister to David Herries, who was sixty-six, and,
yet more absurd, aunt, or at any rate half-aunt, to
Francis, who was twenty-five, and Deb, who was
twenty-three.

To make the matter more complicated yet
and surely most improper, she was in love with
her nephew Francis.   For excuse you may say
that she loved and hated alternately everyone
around her a hundred times a day.

One of the disgraceful colours to this first
notable event in Judith Herries' life was that
Mrs. Monnasett was but just dead and lying
in state in the Blue Room.   It was, indeed, because Mrs. Monnasett lay there that the trouble
began.

Fell House was a pleasant building, square-
shaped, its brick rose-coloured, a walled-in garden,
many fruit trees, the farm buildings with all the
animals and the odours, a Gothic temple beyond
the lawn, pigeons in the loft, swelling downs
stretching almost to the sea, Skiddaw against the
windows, and the road where the coaches ran not
so far away that you could not hear the horses.

Life for Judith should have been agreeable there.
They all wished to love her, and there was nothing
in the world that she liked better than to be loved,
but it had all been spoilt for her from the very
beginning because she preferred so infinitely the

life at Stone Ends, where Uncle Gauntry drank, hunted, beat her, loved her, taught her to ride, to hunt, to prepare the birds for cock-fighting and to learn everything there was to learn about men and women.

She was only eleven, but she knew more, far more, about everything than her half-niece Deb, who was twenty-three, or that other Deborah, her half-sister, who was married to a clergyman at Cockermouth and had two grown sons.

Uldale was by far too tame for her, and yet she loved them all and yearned for them all to love her. She knew, though, even at this age (she had known it long ago), that they could not really love her, for her mother had been a gipsy woman taken by her father off the fells and married by him when he was already an old man. She knew that David and Deborah, his children, had been ashamed of this marriage and had despised him for it. (They had not despised him for it. She would learn that one day.) Oh yes, they could not love her at Uldale, because she was the daughter of a gipsy and had been found one day dancing naked on the roof and could swear most horribly. But at Stone Ends they did not mind whose daughter she was and allowed her to do whatever she pleased.

Now on this afternoon in October they had but just finished dinner, Mrs. Herries, Deb, Will and Judith. Mr. Herries and Francis had ridden to Newlands to see about a piece of land. Mrs. Monnasett was to be buried the following day. The house was quite still. Mrs. Herries went to the China Room to write a letter to her sister-in-

law, Mrs. Sunwood of Cockermouth.   Deb was
for the dairy, Will away on some secret purpose
of his own.   No one needed Judith.   She stood,
listening to the stillness of the house, half-way up
the staircase, her fingers in her lip, considering.
She was an odd little creature, even as odd little
creatures go.   She was very small, although made
in excellent proportion, save that her red hair,
which hung in ringlets, seemed weighty for her
head.   Her complexion was pale and would always
be so: she had the horse-features of all the
Herries, prominent nose and cheek-bones.   She
was, in fact, no beauty, but there was very much
character in her bright and challenging eyes, the
resoluteness of her mouth.   When she smiled
she could be very winning.   She could also look
exceedingly impertinent, and, when angry, with
her red hair, her pale face, and perfectly balanced,
lightly swinging body, she could seem a flying
fury.   She had tiny hands and feet; of these
already she was boastfully proud.

She was dressed in a red bodice with silver
buttons and a small orange hoop.   She wore red
shoes.   This was her best dress, bought for her
in Carlisle on a birthday by David Herries, who
alternately loved and hated her.   She was supposed to wear this grand dress only on very
special occasions; she put it on most days of the
week, but although she wore it so often it was as
fresh as when it was new.   She had, from the
first, that gift of being as clean and spotless in all
her circumstances as a piece of china.   That was
a dirty age, but Judith had always a passion for

washing; no water was too cold for her; she was so hardy that nothing ever ailed her. One out of every three children at this time died before it was four years of age. Judith had never known an ache or a pain. They said that it was because Tom Gauntry had carried her on the very day that she was born through all the snow and ice from Borrowdale to Stone Ends. If that hadn't killed her, nothing would.

She stood, swinging a red shoe, sucking her thumb, and considering. She had intended to go to the corner of the road and watch for the return of Mr. Herries and Francis. She loved Francis madly, passionately, although he was her nephew. She loved his thin delicate body, his pale austere face with the dreaming eyes, the soft gentle voice. He should have been a woman, people said, and that was why so few understood him, but Judith understood him and she would willingly (she thought) die for him. She would not, of course, in reality die for anyone, having now and always a fierce and tenacious hold on life. But she fancied that if he said (in his soft dreaming voice) ' Judith, pray jump from yonder window and break all your bones,' she would jump. The fact that he considered her very little, scarcely ever thought of her, made no difference. She loved him only the more fiercely. He and Uncle Gauntry were the gods of her fiery, agitated, dramatic world.

As she stood there the stillness of the house forced itself ever more upon her attention. She had intended to go to the road, but what an opportunity this was to creep in and look at Mrs.

Monnasett! She had seen dead people before.
There was the boy in Bassenthwaite village
who had been beaten by his master and had
suddenly (most ungratefully) died; she had been
walking with Will and they had come on him
lying against the Cross on the Common. There
had been the beggar who came to their door one
summer night to ask for food, and he had fallen
dead while walking away up the hill. She was no
stranger to death, and thought, in a general way,
little of it. But Mrs. Monnasett was different.
Judith had known her all her life. She had been
nurse and tyrant and friend to all the children.
She had been, there for years, ever since Francis
and Deborah were born, and what a strange woman
she had been, with the hairy mole on her cheek, the
strange stories that she used to tell, the songs that
she used to sing, the ghosts she had seen and the
witches she had known, and, more than all, the
little gold box that she carried with the charm of a
snake's skin and the queer-smelling foreign root;
would she have that little box with her yet, even
though she were dead?

Judith had thought that the charm would prevent her from ever dying. She would live for ever.
But no, she had not. She was dead now and the
worms would eat her. Had she the little box yet
with her? Judith considered. She and Will had
been forbidden to go near the room, but that forbidding only made the matter more charming.
She would have a whipping, but she had had many,
and when David Herries whipped her she had
only to sob in a certain strangling way and he was

always sorry for her and would kiss her and let
her have a pinch of snuff out of his box.   Yes, the
risk was nothing.   Softly she stole up the stairs.

As it happened, Mrs. Sarah Herries was at
that same moment writing of Judith to her sister-
in-law, Mrs. Deborah Sunwood.   She sat in the
China Room, pleasant and sunny, the low windows
looking across to Skiddaw.   The room was handsomely furnished with some pagodas and vessels
of Chelsea china, in which were set coloured sprigs
of artificial flowers.   The walls were hung with
a Chinese wallpaper and, to quote an old Herries
journal, ' A looking-glass, enclosed in a whimsical
frame of Chinese paling, stood upon a Japan table
over which was spread a coverlet of the finest
chintz.'   Yes, a pretty room, burnished now with
the last orange glow of the setting sun, for it
was after five, and Sarah Herries must light the
candles.

She stood there a moment watching the
trembling flame, a handsome woman in a rose-
coloured hoop, wearing her own hair, a fine bosom,
and the face stout a trifle, but kindly, good-
humoured and patient.

She was thinking, perhaps, as she held the
snuffer in her hand and glanced at her broad
figure in the looking - glass, that her life had
been cast in pleasant places since that day so
many years ago when David had snatched her
out of Wasdale and fought her uncle on the Stye
Head Pass.

She was thinking of that and of her Will, whom
she adored, and her Francis, whom she adored

not quite so much, and of her fat good-natured
Deborah, whom, because she took a trifle after herself, she loved a little less . . . yes, ever so little
less.   And then her thoughts turned, as they
always did were they given any freedom at all,
to her beloved, worshipped David, the fire, the
heat, the passion of her happy life, still the most
handsome of all human creatures although he
might be stout now, still the best of all humans
although he might on occasion drink himself under
the table or lose at faro with Squire Osmaston
and the others the money that he had put aside for
the purchase of Brandon's field.   Her eyes were
wet a trifle, the candle-flame danced mistily as she
sat herself down in the dark Irish Chippendale
chair to write to her sister Deborah.

There was nothing in the world that she liked
better than to write to Deborah, for she understood so precisely the importance of everything
that Sarah thought important, was interested in all
the cures that Sarah practised on the children,
thrilled to the heart when she heard that wicked
Cousin Pelham, now nearly seventy and old enough
to reform (but he never would), had sent Sarah
all the way from London by coach and carrier a
Chippendale bookcase with a Gothic design in the
cornice and rosettes on the lower panels.

Yes, Deborah understood everything, and most
especially did she understand about Judith.

This, then, was the letter's first part, the candle-
flame trembling, the China paper dancing, the
outer world fading to a silver star and the white
tone of the climbing road.

My dearest Sister—I hope that you were not disappointed of your lodgings in Kendal and that the boys took care for you.   I can give but little account of these last days for, as you know, we have had Kate Morris's children with us while the house in Keswick was set to order. Their visit had like to have been fatal to me for they not being acquainted with the Semblance of Manners nor trained indeed to anything but having their own Way perfectly in all things that were bad enough without our Judith's added wickedness to excite them.

There is also now Mrs. Monnasett dead in the House and last Tuesday the new Coachman that we had from Mr. Newsom of Newlands was drunk returning Home from Penrith and the postillions also and like to have overturned us on a gallop against a Post coming through Threlkeld.

However, dearest Deborah, you are aware that my Nature is both Tranquil and Harmonious and that if I might but be sure that the Beneficient Creator is not on occasion busied with His Attention in other more interesting Directions I would not trouble for drunken Coachmen or anything else.

Mrs. Monnasett is to be buried to-morrow forenoon.

I am happy that I consider nothing more disagreeable than Learning in a Female for Mr. Huxtable the Tutor of Kate's children has been here a week and found us all Savages save Francis.

With him he must talk Greek and all the Indian Languages and has Mr. Young's *Night Thoughts* at his Finger End and Mr. Pope's *Essay on Man* sprouting from his Eyeballs—a Man heavy of figure and such a Comedy on a Horse that it would do you good to see.   But Judith who must always carry everything too far put a Cracker under his Chair and a Mouse in his Wig for which David whipped her, but not I fear so severely as she merited. But Mr. Huxtable showed no Impatience, reminding us that Alexander the Great and Diogenes were Characters alike for their indifference to Trifles the one holding the

World as his Tub, the other his Tub as the World or some
such Nonsense.

And now in Seriousness, my dearest Sister, I have been
so gravely disturbed over Judith that last Tuesday I was
blooded and on two occasions my throat has been excoriated.

For the Child has a Devil that there's no exorcising.
She is now high and now low and not altogether bad;
David indeed swears that she is not bad at all and has as
good a Heart as anyone in this house, which may be in
Truth enough save that if she has a Heart she has also a
Temper and a Disposition to Evil that I swear poor child
is as great a Trouble to Herself as it is to Us.

I have no doubt as I have often said to you before but
that it had its commencement in Mr. Gauntry's love
for her as a Baby. We have forbidden her his Place for
the Present. I have no Need to tell you, Sister, of the
scandalous Conduct now current in Stone Ends. It is
the Talk of the Countryside. The last Time Judith was
there they had been wanting to make her drink with
him and I must not be ingreateful to the Squire when I
acknowledge that he will not have her contaminated and
in any Case she can with a marvellous Discretion for a
child of her years manage the whole Establishment at
Stone Ends that she has under her little finger. It is
Managing that she is always after and has been from a
Baby. All the satisfaction that I have is that she has not
yet learnt the Fashion of managing me nor ever will,
but to see that Chit of a Child with her red hair and
Herries Nose giving orders to my Will and Deb is so
Unnatural as to be only partly Decent. Monnasett
could deal with her and would have it that her Temper
was from her Consciousness of and Uneasiness at her
unlikely Parentage, but I have not seen her so Sensitive
but have found again and again a brutal insensibility to
the wants and opinions of others.

For the present she is in a Pretty Tantrum because
she is forbidden Mr. Gauntry's and if we do not watch
her she will be over there in a trivet. She has found out,

I fancy, that I am not to be feared although I am not yet assured that she has found out that I am to be loved. But am I indeed? She is too odd a changeling for either David or myself to be certain of our Hearts towards her. It was the same with her mother, poor Mirabell, who as you will well remember, dearest Sister, never loved me because I was too Settled a Wife and Domestic a Woman for her. And this Child also could be in her turn Domestic when she wished. She is in fact of a Mixture so odd that it needs a more perceiving Woman than myself to fathom her only it is Plain enough that she must have her Way in everything and Dominate all those around her. Then, granted her Desires, she will let her Heart speak and has a Generosity that is not to be checked. Nevertheless I am filled with Fears for the future. As she grows her Nature becomes more clear with every hour and this house is in a Turmoil over her. . . .

As to your Complaint, gentle purging is to be advised; no vomits but if your stomach flags four to eight drops of Elixir of Vitriol is excellent and if feverish three spoonfuls of a decoction of the bark by boyling one ounce and a half in a quart of water to a pint. I must tell you, dearest Deborah, that since the days that Cupid set Hercules to the distaff he has not had a nobler conquest than mine over the straightening of the cupboard-room in the new . . .

The remainder of this letter has nothing for our purpose.

It is Herries history, however, that at the moment when Mrs. Sarah Herries was doing her best to place Judith upon paper, the same Judith was with the utmost gentleness and caution opening the door of the Blue Room where Mrs. Monnasett was lying.

Entering, she was both pleased and sensually alarmed by the dim candle-fluttering light that

hung about the room, making the blue pagodas
on the wallpaper, the high tallboy, seem of infinite
mystery, and the blue tester hangings and overlay
of the bed sway in some dimly felt stirring of the
breeze. Not that she was frightened. Judith did
not know now, did not, for many years, know what
it was to be afraid. The day would come, and in
a room not unlike this present one, when, hearing
her beloved Francis enter the hall below, she would
know, but that was not yet.

She approached the bed; it was one that had
always most especially attracted her with its reeded
and fluted columns, delicately carved with acanthus
leaves. There were very few things, even at this
early age, that she did not notice. The candles
were standing at the bed-head, and Mrs. Monnasett, very yellow against the white of the pillow,
her black hair spread, her large strong hands
neatly folded, lay there, her lips curved in a sar-
donic smile. So, Judith reflected, often in real
life she had smiled as though she knew more, far,
far more than anyone around her. And so, indeed,
Judith was very sure that she did. If she had not
been an actual witch she had been as near to it
as not to matter. Judith had known that all the
domestics and hands about the farm had thought
her one. Yes, she had known everything, and
now what did she know? Did Death tell you
anything more? She looked as though, behind
those closed eyelids, she were seeing a thousand
things. A fire burned in the room. It was hot,
and there was a faint cloying smell of corruption.
Judith came very close, stood on her toes because

the bed was high, and touched with her warm
fingers the dead hand. It was not only cold
like iron but hard like iron. Where was Mrs.
Monnasett now? With God? Asking God questions? Telling Him, perhaps, things that He did
not know. But, above all, had she the little gold
box with her? Judith did not intend to steal it,
only to see whether they would bury it with her.

She looked about the dim dark room, sniffing
the faint decaying odour like a little dog. The
heavy curtains at the windows fluttered, the blue
pagodas on the wall seemed to run a race, the fire
crackled and sputtered, mice would be behind
the wainscot, but none of these disturbed Mrs.
Monnasett, who lay there, growing surely with
every moment more yellow, and the mole black
upon her cheek, smiling her secret smile because
of the things she knew that others didn't. But
had she the little gold box with her? Had she?
Had she? Judith must know.

She stood at her tallest, leaned over and, with
a shiver of excitement at her daring, felt with her
hand, under the clothes, in the hollow of Mrs.
Monnasett's breasts.

She had scarcely touched that chill flesh when
there was a voice at the doorway, a voice of horror
and disgust.

She nearly lost her balance and, half tumbling,
started away from the bed to see Mrs. Herries,
holding high a lighted candle, in the doorway. The
child assumed at once the attitude that she always
had when she was set for trouble. She flung her
head back, held her hands behind her and waited.

'Judith! Come out of here.'

She followed Mrs. Herries from the room. In the passage she stood by the door like some small wild animal ringed about with enemies.

'What were you doing there?'

'Nothing.'

'Nothing! That is a lie!'

'I wasn't doing anything.'

'You wicked child! You had been forbidden to enter the room.'

'Yes, ma'am.'

'You confess your disobedience?'

'Yes, ma'am.'

'And at the bed you were touching——'
Sarah Herries' voice broke in her disgust and revulsion.

'I wished to look at Mrs. Monnasett—and bid her farewell.'

Sarah Herries sighed. This strange child! But there was feeling there, tenderness. The child had heart. And all would have been well had not that odd impulse to absolute honesty that would, throughout Judith's life, force from her such inconvenient avowals burst from her now:

'I wished to see whether Mrs. Monnasett had yet with her the gold box with the charms.'

'You wished to see—what?'

'Whether she had yet the little gold box with the charms.'

'You would see . . .' Mrs. Herries broke off. Her nature was kindly, wise, tolerant, but she did not understand this child any better than in the earlier days she had understood the mother.

And just as then elements would arise that sickened some sound English normality in her, so now with Judith there would be often moments when she hated this child, in reality hated her so that she wished her out of her house and her family, a thousand miles away, never to return.

She felt this revulsion now, a sort of sickness. To search the corpse for a gold box—a child of eleven. She was afraid of what she might do, so she said: ' Go to your room and wait there until I come to you.'

Judith, without a word, turned and went.

Her room was a small one under the roof. From her window she could see the road, the hills, the woods that stretched towards Bassenthwaite. Here she had her treasures—a candlestand that Francis had given her, a china jar, old and cracked, but with lovely orange flowers on it, that she had begged from Mrs. Monnasett, two ' babies '—rag dolls from her own baby-hood—a fox's brush that Tom Gauntry had sent her, a piece of China silk, a faded and stained battle-piece in a black frame that she had found in a cellar, a treatise on cock-fighting, and a Bible that Reuben Sunwood had presented to her last Christmas-time. Here she would sit on a small oak-panelled arm-chair and watch from the window the outside world that she so desperately loved.

Now she banged the door behind her, kicked off her red shoes and stood scowling. She hated Fell House and everyone in it save Francis. She knew that she had been wrong to

go and look at Mrs. Monnasett, and more wrong
still to touch her. Her immaculate honesty
forbade her to blame Mrs. Herries for any injustice. She had been right to be angry, the
punishment that would follow would be just.
She was so much wickeder than all the others, as
she very well knew. Here was no portrait of a
poor, ill-treated little girl. They tried to love
her ; it was her own fault that they could not.
But with every breath that she drew she was
longing for Tom Gauntry—the odd, rambling,
ill-shaped house with the smell of dogs and
horses and drink and dung and cooking food and
musty curtains, with the noise and laughter and
songs, with the freedom and airy indulgence as
though all the doors and windows were for ever
open—that was her life, that the place into which
she had been taken on the very first day of her
existence, and Uncle Tom with his twisted brown
face and twisted brown body, his funny bow-legs
and his hoarse whisper and his cry to the hounds
and his oaths and angers—*he* understood her as
no one else in the world did. . . . And then,
cutting across that picture, as so often it did, was
another one, quite opposite, that made her understand the Herries decency of Uldale, made her,
in certain moods, finely handy about the place, in
the store cupboards, the dairies, so that she could
sew and bake and clean with the best of them,
and understood too when Will (for whom she
did not really care) would tell her, with all the
gravity of a grown man, of how he would advance
the Herries family and have money in all the banks

and buy land everywhere—all this she could understand and believe in.

Yes, but at this precise moment she was a little girl of eleven in one of her hellish tempers, one of her incoherent rages, so that she could swear in proper Cumberland just like any of the girls or men about the place, so that she was mad to be out of the house and over the fells, sniffing the peat, hearing the water of the mountain-streams run and the tug of the sheep at the grass and the sharp bark of the sheep-dogs. . . .

She turned, her eyes furious and her little feet stamping, at the sound of the open door. Francis Herries had come in.

At the sight of him she forgot for a moment all her trouble. He was still in his riding-clothes. He must have come straight to her after his arrival. His face was so beautifully peaked and serious under his brown wig, his legs in their riding-boots so handsomely shaped and his eyes so far away, so mysterious. . . .

She drew her breath sharply as she always did when she saw anything that seemed to her beautiful. How she loved him! And he, from his great height, looked down gravely to the odd little figure with the defiant mouth and the red hair and rebellion in every inch of her.

He slapped his whip against his thigh.

'Father is coming shortly to beat you. I thought I'd best prepare you.' Then he smiled, a lovely winning smile which, in anyone more self-conscious, must have been artificial. But

Francis Herries, as he never thought of himself,
never thought of his smile either.

'I know.' Her eyes devoured him. 'I don't
care as long as you've come.'

'What have you done, you little devil?
Why can't you be good?'

'I can't be good,' she answered defiantly,
'because my father married a gipsy. And I'm
happy he did,' she added.

This was an old familiar statement of hers.
She was always dragging in the gipsy. It seemed
to Francis to be in bad taste, so he said again:

'What have you done this time?'

'I went in to see Mrs. Monnasett.'

The thought and image of death, so familiar
as to be less than nothing at all to the men and
women of his time, always affected Francis Herries with a queer tremor of mystery and horror.
It seemed to him revolting that this child should
have been in Mrs. Monnasett's room.

'Why must you do that?' he asked.

'To see if she had her little gold box.'

'What box?'

'A box of spells that she had.'

He said nothing and turned to the door.

With a little tremor in her voice she said:
'Please punish me.'

He turned back. 'Punish you?'

She broke out passionately, an unusual passion
for so young a child.

'I didn't know that it was wrong, but if you
had told me not I would never have gone. Punish
me and you will see. I will do anything you

tell me, stand in icy water or let the rats in the cellar gnaw me or sleep in the stable.'

He looked at her, met the intense absorbed devotion of her eyes, and was greatly touched. When he could come out of his dreams and notice human beings he loved them, loved all humanity. He was humble also, and found it strange that anyone should care for him. This small child, standing there, in her stockinged feet and coloured hoop, adoring him, moved him. They were friends from that moment, although neither realised that it was just then that their long alliance was formed. He spoke lamely enough:

'Punish you? No. Why should *I* punish you?'

They could say no more because at that moment David Herries came in. He carried a riding-whip, was in his riding-clothes, looked exceedingly sheepish. He had been always of great size and immense strength. Now, at sixty-six, he was beginning to be corpulent, had a red face and something of a belly, but looked very much the same kindly, obstinate, unimaginative boy who had, nearly thirty years before, carried his Sarah away from the dark house in Wasdale.

He looked sheepish because he hated this business. Francis went out. Judith bent over the chair and he whipped her. Neither said a word until it was over. She replaced her little clothes, then stood, her lip trembling, because she was very near to tears but would not cry, near the window.

Her stockings were crooked, which seemed to David very pathetic, and without knowing it she had her hand on her back where it was sore.

He filled the room with his great bulk, and his red face was creased with kindliness. He scratched his bare head, pushing his wig a little awry. He talked because he saw that she was near to tears.

' Now, Judith, why must you do such a thing? 'Tisn't decent to be in the death-chamber, and it was against all orders, as you very well knew. Now, then, it is over, isn't it? Never to be spoken of again. . . .'

He went and picked her up and kissed her. Had he known it (and it had been always one of David's weaknesses that he was not clever at perceiving things), this was, of everything that he could do, the thing that she detested most.

To be picked up, like a tiny baby, to be dangled in the air, to be held close to this huge man and feel his bristly cheek and smell the odour of liquor and horses, to have her neck pricked by the sharp buttons of his coat, and, worst of all, to have his great heart hammering in her ear, this was the final ignominy!

She stayed passive, only when he would kiss her mouth she turned her head aside. He put her down with a grunting sigh. She was a problem, this child, just as her mother Mirabell had been before her. He did not understand her at all.

He looked at her, smiled an awkward, clumsy smile, muttered, ' We shall say no more about the thing,' and stumped away.

She stood there, considering. She did not want to see any of them ever again, save Francis. Somewhere a clock sounded six. A cart rattled down the Fell road. She went to the window and looked out. It was almost dark; the hills were shadows against shadow.

Then she smiled.

She knew what she would do.

STONE ENDS

SHE was so made that once a plan came to her nothing in the world was ever going to stop her, and every pulse of her body beat to that one purpose.

She flung back the narrow diamond-paned window, found a cloak and a shawl, left the red shoes for thick country ones. No time was wasted, and as she worked for her purpose her small mouth was set, her chin was out. Nothing was to stop her in such a mood. She didn't think of consequences (she was never to think of them as she should do), recked little that this second disobedience in one evening meant trouble for her more serious, perhaps, than any that she had yet encountered.

She had been out of that window before. There was still light enough for her to see the old crooked water-pipe that jerked an arm round the farther end of her casement, then there was the water-butt, then the stone passage leading to the stable. But she had a long descent on that pipe. She clung to it with hands and feet, her chin and nose rasped by its casing. Her small legs trembled, the shawl blew against her face, she felt (or imagined that she felt) spiders' thread

31

in her hair, then her feet found the water-butt, she held her body together and jumped.

She fell on her hands and knees, and the black cat, Solomon, ran from under her very feet, scrambling up the monkey-tree. Her knees were bleeding, her hoop under her cloak was torn. But she stood, holding her breath like a proper conspirator, to hear whether the noise had made any stir. There was no sound but the owl hooting. It seemed that a breath of light had blown back again into the sky. Over the garden wall, the Caldbeck fells were outlined as though a row of candles were lit behind them.

It was the moon; later that moon would strengthen, and the freshening wind would blow the stars up. All the garden scents were crowding the night air. She was very cheerful indeed, and, pulling the cambric tight about her face again, stepped across the irregular paving of the yard, called very softly, 'Barnabas! Barnabas!' At once the little black horse with the white star on his forehead put his head over the paling. In another moment she had unbarred the door and was leading him out, stroking his nose.

Barnabas understood perfectly what she wanted. She mounted the black outside the gate and, her legs spread very wide, her hair flying, was away up the road. A mile later, the first delirium of freedom passed, she began to consider ghosts, witches and warlocks. She was not afraid, but there was the man with the face like a rat, the woman with two heads, the lost soul of Judas that whimpered like an infant, the old woman with a rat on her shoulder, the lovely lady on the skeleton horse, the old woman with three beards, the soldier who had lost his head in the wars and carried it in his handless arms, the coach with the eight devils and the fiery horses, the lady of Caldbeck who walked searching for the child that she had murdered.

And worse, perhaps, in actual fact, than any of these, the highway robber who had been hung in chains on the path between Thistlebottom and Whelpo, although there were now only his bones remaining.

She was not afraid of any of them, but she repeated aloud to herself the Lord's Prayer and so much of the Creed as she could remember, and then the names of the places near her home —Ireby, Snittlegarth, Binsey, Aughertree, Nevin Tarn, Orthwaite, Over Water, Braefell, Branthwaite. It comforted her that Barnabas trotted comfortably along as though he knew precisely his destination, but it comforted her yet more when she met a cheerful gang of pack-horses, the bell-horse first with his pleasant noise. They were carrying peat from the moors in halts, old-fashioned wicker-baskets that were very soon now to give way to carts.

Judith called out to the men as she passed them, waving her hand, and they talked that night about the witch that had greeted them (on a black horse) and had waved in the air hands shining with flame.

Stone Ends, Tom Gauntry's place, was a mile

C

beyond Caldbeck. She made no further encounter. The clock of Caldbeck Church struck seven as she trotted through the deserted little street.

On the dark road beyond Caldbeck she met two drunken soldiers who stood in the road and waved at her. They had a lantern; one had a wooden leg. She leaned forward on to Barnabas' mane and cursed them in good Cumbrian. She called them 'Hulkers' and 'Lubbers' and 'Dummle-heads.' She told them that they gave her 'a nasty dwallow taste in her mouth' and that they'd better 'jump up and knep a daisy.' She must have astonished them, perched on the horse, her red hair flying about in the uncertain circumference of the lantern that waved in their drunken hands. At any rate, they did nothing, and stood aside to let Barnabas by.

So she arrived at Stone Ends. This was a rough-cast building of no height, with an outside gallery and stair. There were mullioned windows, great trees overhanging the mossy slates and round thick chimneys. There was a garden with a clipped hedge, the fells everywhere beyond, a rough plot of flowers, some outbuildings, a sundial, a little stream.

Lights burnt in the windows, but Judith did not need a light. This little place had been familiar to her since her babyhood, her only true home. She tied Barnabas to the gate and went cautiously to the porch. She was not certain how she would be received. Old Gauntry was not always the perfect host, especially when taken unawares. Riding Barnabas so soon after the

beating had not improved the soreness of her seat.
She did not want another whipping, nor to be sent
directly back to Uldale again. So, with her ear
to the heavy door, she listened. Little listening
was needed. The chorus of revelry was clear
enough. They would have been hunting, she
decided, and were now in process of becoming
drunk as soon as possible. *That* did not frighten
her. She had heard often enough: ' Now this is
a fine fox we've killed and it munna be a dry one.'
The important thing was to ascertain the *stage* of
drunkenness at which they had arrived. She knew
that between the first and second hour they would
all be in a state of exceeding friendliness.

She was, however, given no time to consider.
The door opened and Wull shoved his hairy head
out. Wull (or William Flint as was his proper
name) stood to Tom Gauntry as the Fool stands
to his King. Judith would never forget the agitation with which she had first beheld him. In her
babyhood she had been told that he was the Hobthross, the Brownie who lurks in old houses—
works all night for the family to whom he has
attached himself, stretches himself before the fire,
churns the milk for the girls, and can be heard
singing at his tasks. A kindly spirit, but wild to
look at, with his shock of hair, his broad ugly face,
his misshapen limbs. Just so was ' Wull,' and
when she was an infant he would love to pull faces
at her until she howled with rage. She was never
frightened of him, but only angry. Later he became her friend, then her warm ally. He poked
his ugly head out at her now.

' Wull! Wull! ' she whispered.

Sometimes he was a complete fool, sometimes
most intelligent. He would tell her about himself with a broad grin: ' Ah'm nobbut a bit
goffish.' It was probable that he was not ' goffish '
at all, but knew exactly what he was doing. When
he saw who it was he let her in. The house-place
was filled with dogs and smelt like a midden.
Judith did not mind the smell in the least. The
dogs were everywhere; every kind of dog. They
ran at her when they saw her, barking and tumbling all over her. Some of the hounds were bigger
than she. They all knew her. One, a spaniel
bitch, Clara, adored her, had followed her once
almost all the way back to Uldale.

When Clara saw her she was in an ecstasy of
happiness, springing up and down, yapping on a
shrill high note, her beautiful large eyes beaming
with joy. Judith asked Wull how many gentlemen there were in there. He didn't know; about
twenty maybe. They had had a grand day's
hunting and had killed over by High Hesket.
He cuffed the dogs and quieted them, but the
noise had been heard. The room door opened
and Tom Gauntry came out. He stood with his
funny crooked legs straddling. He was very fairly
drunken. When he saw Judith he gave a loud
' Yoicks! Yoicks! Tally-ho! Tally-ho! ' and they
came crowding to the door. Judith recognised
a number she knew—young Osmaston, Squire
Watson, old Birkmyre, Statesman Peel—also two
ladies.

Gauntry came over to her and picked her up

and carried her shoulder-high into the room where
they were dining. Oddly enough, what she hated
in David Herries she liked in Uncle Tom.

' And why the hell have you come? ' he asked
her.

' Because I wanted,' she answered.

From her height she looked over the scene,
which was for her no new one.   The room was not
large.   They were crowded about the round table
upon whose shining surface the candles guttered
grease.   Food was piled everywhere—mutton,
beef, puddings; wine was spilt on the table, and
almost the first thing that Judith noticed was the
naked head of old Dunstable, robbed of its wig,
lying forward in a puddle of wine.   He had succumbed already.

Most of them had not.   Sitting now, sharp-
eyed, on a chair beside Uncle Gauntry, she saw
very quickly that there were two boys there, boys
of about her own age.   It was not unusual that
boys should be there, and one of them she knew,
little Johnny Peel, two years younger than herself.
It would later be said of him that he was ' lang
in the leg an' lish as a lizard,' and someone in
the *Gentleman's Magazine* was to record that ' he
seems to have come into this world only to send
foxes out of it.'   He was of Caldbeck village, but
there was no hunt already that he wasn't attending
within any radius from Penrith to Cockermouth,
Cockermouth to Carlisle.   It was said of him
already that he could do thirty miles in the day and
not be tired of it; later on it was to be fifty.   But
Judith knew that boy before; he didn't interest

her.   The other was another matter.   She had
not hitherto allowed her young life to be much
encumbered with boys.   On the whole she despised them; of late especially her real worship of
Francis Herries had veiled her sight.

But this boy struck through to her deep consciousness. How often afterwards she was to look
back to this moment when, as she sat perched up
on the chair beside Tom Gauntry, her little sharp
eyes flashed across to the table to the equally sharp
eyes of that small, black-haired, bullet-headed
urchin, who was grabbing any food that he could
see. Very characteristic that Judith's first vision of
him should be of greedy rapacity!   But (also how
characteristic of him!) it was not merely greed.
While he snatched at meat and bread and the thick
pastry of the beef-pie his little black eyes were
flashing about him, humorous, contemptuous, but
as alive as fire-balls!

'Who's that?' Judith asked of Gauntry.   He
was, as she had hoped, at the cheerful side of his
drinking, singing a catch, shoving food into his
mouth, exchanging bawdy stories with all and
sundry.

'That!' he laughed, following her eyes.
'That's the Frenchy! There's his mama!'
pointing a chicken-bone at a lady farther along
the table.   There were only two women here,
one of them the wife of young Squire Osmaston,
a flaxen-haired, broad-bosomed, opulent lady at
the moment chucking Sam Newton under the
chin. This other was different. She sat upright
like a maypole and was black as a raven.

Marvellous black eyes, she had, a lovely shapely bosom, and silver ornaments in her dark hair, which was her own and unpowdered. You could see, Judith decided, that she was the little boy's mother. They would be French then. Judith had heard of Paris, where silks and brandy came from. She had seen a print of the French Queen dancing in a great hall lit with flambeaux. This lady looked as though she could be a queen were she given the opportunity.

The noise and confusion now were very great. Old Dunstable had slipped beneath the table.

Wilson of Ireby was standing on his chair proposing healths; fat Dick Conyngham of Penrith and a thin young man with a crooked nose were embracing. Voices rose and fell, then suddenly the chorus, everyone joining together:

> Then chink and clink your glasses round
> And drink to the Devil below the ground.
> The more you drink the better you be
> And kiss the lasses upon your knee.
> > Chink, clink!
> > Chink, clink!
> The Devil himself can't drink like me.

Then young Drayton of Keswick, whose sweet tenor was famous for miles around, stood up and sang the song of 'Beauty Bathing':

> Beauty sat bathing by a spring
> > Where fairest shades did hide her;
> The winds blew calm, the birds did sing,
> > The cool streams ran beside her.
> My wanton thoughts enticed mine eye
> > To see what was forbidden:

But better memory said, fie!
    So vain desire was chidden:
        Hey nonny nonny O!
        Hey nonny nonny!

Into a slumber then I fell,
    When fond imagination
Seemèd to see, but could not tell
    Her feature or her fashion.
But ev'n as babes in dreams do smile,
    And sometimes fall a-weeping,
So I awaked as wise this while
    As when I fell a-sleeping:
        Hey nonny nonny O!
        Hey nonny nonny!

The beauty of the words, of the voice, seemed for a moment to sober them.

        Hey nonny nonny O!
        Hey nonny nonny!

they sang, and down the fat cheeks of Dick Conyngham drunken tears were coursing.

No one appeared to think it strange that the child should be there.   Most of them knew her; she seemed to belong to the place, and for many of them that happy time was now approaching when nothing anywhere seemed strange, when the candles on their silver stalks swam like gold roses in a shimmering haze, and the moon, now delicately rising beyond the uncurtained windows, was quadrupled in its pure serenity; now, through the open door, the dogs were coming in to pick up what trifles they might from the scattered floor, and a thousand clocks were ticking their friendly

chatter on a thousand walls.   No one thought of
the child, not even Gauntry himself; only Clara,
the spaniel bitch, coming in with the rest, had
found her and was sitting behind her chair.

Judith ate very little and drank nothing.   It
was no unusual thing at that time for a child to be
drunk.   The children of the poor lay in the gutter
drowned with gin.   In the back parts of Keswick
town Judith herself had seen them.   But something in her, connected possibly with her immaculate personal cleanliness, had made her, so long as
she could remember, detest liquor.   When she
was only a baby some friend of Gauntry's had tried
to make her drink Madeira, and she had screamed,
beaten his face with her hands, torn his nose with
her nails.   She didn't like the smell of it very
much, but in a scene like this the stench of wine
and heat and unwashed human bodies, dogs and
horses, candle-grease and cooked meats, was so
familiar to her that she never thought of it.

What she did think of, though, was that when
the drinking and rioting had reached a certain
pitch she would leave them, for they were then
no longer of any use to anybody.

It neither shocked nor distressed her that they
should lie about the floor with their heads in
puddles of wine.   She preferred in fact the rough-
and-tumble riot here to the orderly drunkenness
at Fell House, and she had on several occasions
watched while Wull and Andy and Matthew
had stripped Uncle Gauntry and laid him in his
naked bed.   What she did mind was that they
were all so stupid when they were ' gone.'   She

was quickly developing that passion, afterwards to be so strong in her and so irritating to her acquaintances, of hating to waste a single moment! Her restless energy was, later, never to leave her for an instant alone. They were a waste of time, these stupid hours when they all lay about, dribbling and drabbling, with the moon high, the wind fresh, blowing the stars about the sky. She might as well be in her bed, which was where, indeed, she *would* be had she remained at Uldale.

Her bright eyes searched the room. She saw one thing, that the French lady was absorbed by Mr. Drayton, who had sung 'Beauty Bathing.' He was a good-looking màn, Mr. Drayton, slender and straight, with yellow hair like a blazing candle, and he wore a beautiful flowered waistcoat. There were gold buckles on his shoes. The French lady liked him, that was plain. They stood, the handsome pair of them, gravely by the window, away from the litter, noise and mess; quite suddenly Mr. Drayton took the French lady's hand. Now was the time, then, for Judith to speak to the little French boy.

She stepped off her chair and, followed by the spaniel, came round to where the French boy was sitting. She touched his shoulder. He turned round and smiled at her.

' Come out,' she said.

He came at once, making a last grab at a handful of raisins before he went. They ran hand in hand, as though they had known one another for ages, into the dark hall, where the fire was blazing, and the dogs, as though they owned the house and everyone in it, were moving about, snapping at one another, yawning, lying down to sleep, climbing the stairs, gnawing bones, scratching for fleas.

The two children sat close together beside the fire.

' I know.   You're French,' Judith said.

He spoke without an accent, as though he were English.   He gave her, rather reluctantly, some raisins.   The truth is, she took them.

' I was born in London,' he told her.

' Oh, I want to see London! '

' Is your hair in truth that fine colour? ' he asked, pulling it.

She slapped his face, not lightly but with genuine feeling.   He got up, his eyes blazing. He stood there, his sturdy little body trembling with anger.   It seemed that he would kill her. But he thought better of it.   His hand to his cheek he sat down again.

' Because you are a girl I won't hurt you,' he said.

' Hurt me! '   She was indignantly scornful. ' No one can hurt me! '   Then she went on: ' I was whipped this noon.'

They were friends again.   She, taking more of his raisins, asked him how it was if he were French he had never been in France.

' My papa and my mama are French born,' he told her.

She asked him his name.

' Georges.'

And his other name.

' Georges Paris.'

'But Paris is a town.'

He told her there were people called Paris too.
He told her then (he always from the very earliest
time loved to talk about himself) that his father
was dead, that his mother liked England to live
in, that they lived for the most part in the village
of Hampstead, near London. Hampstead was
on a hill, and at night you could see all London
lit up from their window. Judith wanted to
tell him something about herself. Her name was
Judith Herries, her mother had been a gipsy,
she lived with her half-brother at Fell House
in Uldale. She could ride and swim, had a
horse called Barnabas (it wasn't in fact her horse
at all, but it made it grander to say so), could
stand on her head, train a bird for fighting, and
so on, and so on. Mrs. Monnasett was dead and
would be buried to-morrow. She had run away
and would be whipped on her return.

But he wasn't interested. He could do nothing but look at her hair. He had never seen
anything like it in his life before.

Then her mind ran away from him. The
place where they were was lovely to her, with
the leaping fire, the moonlight, the dogs. She
thought of Statesmen and farmers and boys and
horses—all friends of hers. She liked to hear
the men singing in the distance. All her troubles
were far away; to-morrow, the whipping, Fell
House. In an impulse of general happiness that
had little to do with the boy she put her arm
round his neck, drew his head towards her and
kissed him. He did not mind that at all and

pulled her hair—but gently. And she did not, this time, smack his cheek.

Dreamily she went on: 'Maybe when I'm grown I shall marry you. But I must have dogs and horses, and we must have our house near to this. But you must not be drunken.' Then, pushing his head away from her, she asked sharply: 'But what shall our children be—French or English?'

'French,' he answered her quickly.

'No, they shall not. English.'

'French.'

'No, English.'

'Then I'll not marry you.'

She pinched him in the place where it hurt the most. In another moment they were fighting, rolling on the floor, all the dogs yelping. But they were interrupted by a greater agitation, for the door suddenly swung open, there was a shout and clatter, and into the hall came fat Dick Conyngham riding Judith's Barnabas. Poor Barnabas was in any case overweighted by the huge body that rode him; he was frightened also. He came kicking into the hall, the dogs setting up an infernal din.

'The stairs! The stairs! I'll ride him to the attic!' and Conyngham drove the little horse towards the staircase, waving his fat arms like a madman.

They all came pouring in out of the other room, those of them who could stand, to see Barnabas kicking with his hind legs and Judith raging like a mad thing.

She rushed to little Gauntry, catching him by

the arm: ' 'Tis my Barnabas. . . . He has no
right . . . He'll break his knees!' and Gauntry, who had been singing the tail-end of some
chorus, was suddenly, in the manner of drunken
men, in a terrible rage and rushed at Conyngham.
The fat man drove the horse at the stairs, but in
a moment they had him on the floor and were
kneeling on his stomach.

Barnabas, wild now with the lights, the dogs,
the fire, began to prance madly hither and thither;
and Judith, fearing nothing, had caught him,
was carried off her feet as she hung to his mane,
crying ' Barnabas! Barnabas! Dear Barnabas!
They shall not touch you!' The little horse
knew her hand and voice. He snorted, pawing
the wood floor with his hoofs; he looked wildly
around, then he suffered her to lead him away.

She took him this time to one of the outhouses. She stood there in the soft moonlight
wondering whether after all she would not ride
home again. Not far from her was the lower end
of the garden that held a little pond with a statue
of an armless lady. The little pond was like a
curved shell of ivory, and the lady was green in the
moonlight.

A moment later they all rushed past her, a
shouting and singing rabble. Fat Conyngham
was to be ducked in the pond for that he had
taken a lady's horse without her permission.
They were not like men at all, but shadows that
the moon had made. They were stripping him;
a moment he escaped and ran, a ridiculous pink
figure, bald-headed, across the grass. They

chased him around the sundial, caught him; there was a splash, and she could see a spray of water dazzle the air.

She rubbed her nose in Barnabas' mane. Should she go home? She was lonely, a little frightened. They had never been so wild before in this place. The house did not seem to be her friend any longer, only the quiet fells that stretched beyond it, with the boggy peat, the sheep cropping, the eternal sound of running water.

It seemed of a sudden comforting to have Sarah Herries' arm around her. She was a child again. She was not *truly* frightened. She had never been frightened. She would not be frightened now. But in absolute truth it would be pleasant to be in her bed with the cherry curtains, to hear the owl hooting and Deborah Herries snoring not too far away.

Then, because she would never grant to either God or Man that she could be afraid of anyone or anything, she threw up her head defiantly at the moon, stroked Barnabas on the nose, whispered to him that she would not be long away and went back to the house.

They were still dancing and singing round the pond. The garden had a fantastic air like a witches' sabbath. The house was now deserted and empty. The dogs were for the most part away, the moonlight stained the floor, the fire was low. No sign of the French boy, no sign of anyone. She peeped through the door, and there were two men, asleep, with their heads on the table. The candles guttered.

She herself felt a fearful weariness. She was aching for sleep. She staggered on her little feet. Her shoes hurt her, her beautiful dress was torn, the place where she had been whipped was smarting. She would find the room upstairs that was generally hers. The thought of sleep was so delicious as to be incredible.

She sat down half-way up the stairs, and with her head in her hand dreamily considered herself. She had learnt to do this early in life, because, observing things and people, she had realised that if you do not consider yourself no one else is going to. But when she began to think of herself it was always to her mother and father that she was led.

Years ago she had persuaded Tom Gauntry to take her, pillion-fashion, to see the house where she was born. They had ridden into the heart of the valley of Borrowdale, and there, on a little hill above the village of Rosthwaite, was standing this strange tumble-down house. She could not credit her own sharp eyesight when she saw it. They had tied the horse to the gate and walked in the grass-grown courtyard. It was late April, and the smaller daffodils were blowing under the wind. A storm was coming up over Glaramara, and flashes of sun glittered in cold sharp gleams and were gone again. Under the wind and the hurrying cloud the house looked desolate enough. Judith, used to the noise and vitality of Stone Ends, the luxury and comfort of Uldale, could not believe that this was where her father had lived for so many years. Some peasant lived there now. Two very dirty children, sucking their thumbs,

lurked in the doorway.   Behind the house a
waterfall glistened against rock.   There was the
sound of running water everywhere.   It looked
as though one ' fuff ' of wind would blow the place
down.

That day ' Uncle Tom ' told her to the smallest
detail of how he had found her, the snowstorm,
her wailing cry, her father and mother dead.   But
he would never tell her enough about her father.
He had not known him, he said.   Neither would
David and Sarah tell her much, although he had
been David's father, and so David must know
everything.   David would tell her only the grand
things, how passionately through many years he
had loved her mother, how tall he was and strong,
how noble he was, and went his own way whatever
people might say.   ' Whatever people might say
——'   Judith nodded her head over that.   People
had said a good deal, no doubt.   She only wished
that she could have been there, standing at her
father's side, to tell those people what she thought
of them.   To tell those people what she thought
of them——   Her head was nodding, and had
not the moon been shining straight into her eye
she would have fallen into deep slumber.   As it
was she was suddenly awake.   She would find the
room and the bed. . . .

She climbed the stairs, looked out of the window
on to the outside gallery and the fell beyond,
pushed back a door.   She stood there.   Her heart
seemed to stop its beating.   The almost bare
room, with only the yellow-curtained bed, two
chairs, a chest, was sunk in moonshine.   In the

middle of the moonlit pool the French lady was standing quite naked. Behind her, her clothes were piled on the boards. She stood, her legs together, her arms raised above her head, her black hair loosened about her shoulders. Her breasts were full and firm. She was smiling.

At her feet, clad only in his shirt, young Drayton was kneeling, his hands about her naked waist, his eyes raised in an ecstasy to her face.

They never spoke nor moved. Judith saw that something glittered sharply in the light—the diamond buckle of her shoe, lying on top of her clothes.

Then the child heard him speak:

' Oh, how beautiful you are! Oh, how beautiful you are! '

But the French lady only smiled.

Judith turned away. Her shoes made clop-clop on the boards. She sat down on the top of the stairs.

What had she seen?

Something that she would never forget, something that hurt her.

She began to cry very softly, lest anyone should hear her. She cried and cried. She wanted to go home. She wanted someone to care for her.

Huddled up, now only a baby lost and bewildered, crying and sobbing, there with her head against the banister she fell fast, fast asleep.

SUNWOODS IN COCKERMOUTH

DEBORAH HERRIES, the daughter of Francis
Herries, sister of David Herries and half-sister
of Judith, married, early in 1761, the Reverend
Gordon Sunwood, a clergyman who lived in the
town of Cockermouth. Mr. Sunwood had no particular cure, but after his marriage published two
admirable works—one *A Treatise on the Magnificat*,
the other *The Hope of Grace to Come*, or *Sinners at
the Feet of Jesus*. This second work had a very
real sale throughout the North of England. He
was in considerable request as a preacher. In
1765 his aunt, Miss Mercia Sunwood, died in the
town of Exeter, bequeathing him a very reasonable
fortune.

They had two boys, twins, born in the year
1763, Reuben and Humphrey.

Deborah Herries had been always, unlike her
sister Mary and brother David, of a quite un-
ambitious disposition. For the first half of her
life she had lived quietly with her father at Herries
in Borrowdale, perfectly content to care for him
and offer him as much love and affection as he was
willing to accept.

After his second marriage, however, which
occurred when he was well on in years, she con-

sidered that she was no longer needed by him (which was perfectly true), left him and married her clergyman in Cockermouth. She had loved Mr. Sunwood from the first moment of seeing him at a ball in Keswick, and he was indeed exactly suited to her, being as kindly, well-disposed, un-enterprising and equable as she. She differed from him greatly in her perceptions; she had a good deal in her of her father's poetry, very much more than had her brother David, who had, how-ever, been always much closer to their father. She had been kept from her father by a sort of terror of him, being never very comfortable with persons who were scornful or sarcastic, or liable to sudden temper or indignation.

Mr. Gordon Sunwood had been a rest and refreshment to her after her life with her father, for, as his rotund body, snow-white hair and kindly rosy face portended, he could with the greatest difficulty be angry with anyone or anything, and then only for a moment at a time. Methodists, Wesleyans, Quakers, Dissenters of any kind—these were almost the only animals who could rouse him to any sort of genuine indignation.

Marriage with Deborah excited him to a kind of mild ambition, and it is quite certain that he would never have written, or, having written, would never have published his two books had she not stirred his faculties.

Having published them he exhibited a natural pride very evident in most authors, who have, from time immemorial, found it difficult to conceive that theirs are not the only shining fish in the literary ocean.

When Deborah's twins were born the cup of her joy was full. And, as is not the case with all optimistic parents, her joy continued, for as the boys grew in physical stature so also they grew in kindliness of nature and obedience to their parents.

They were, one is happy to record, by no means angels, but their vices were mild ones, and their faults just sufficient to keep them properly human. Humphrey had by far the easier disposition of the two. Tall, slender and flaxen-haired, life was for him one long adventure. He was as restless as he was merry, so popular at the Cockermouth school that it was entirely to his credit that he should wish to be constantly with his parents.

Everyone spoke well of him, and it is not, perhaps, altogether to be wondered at that his charm became his principal asset and an easy substitute for hard work and diligence. His parents succeeded in affording him his residence at St. John's College, Cambridge, and, if he did nothing there but secure the pleasant good wishes of his fellow-men, that was more than many others succeeded in securing.

After Cambridge the question was what should be done with him. He would hear of nothing but London, and to a lawyer's office there he went. On this bright afternoon in early November of the year 1785 his proud mother was excitedly occupied in reading his first letter from the Metropolis.

Humphrey's twin brother Reuben had quite

another history. They had only small resemblance to one another whether in character or in physical appearance. And yet the bond between them was almost fantastic. From their first conscious moments they had been all in all the one to the other; theirs, indeed, was a love that nothing in life would be able to influence. Humphrey, volatile, restless, and woman-lover as he was, yet knew no emotion so unyielding and passionate as this for his brother. For Reuben, Humphrey was always and ever in a world apart. Reuben was unlike Humphrey in that he was stout, clumsy and plain. He was not uncleanly in his person, but his clothes never fitted him, nor could he be brought to consider the practical details of daily life. His eyes were good and faithful, his mouth, although too large, kindly and tolerant, but his nose was ludicrously ill-shaped, his hair wild and of a dingy colour, his limbs uncouth and ill-disciplined. From his very early years he had been of an intensely religious mind. It had been always understood that he would be a clergyman. At the age of sixteen he joined the religious society of St. Bees, but was there for a year only, finding that he could not come to the same mind with the authorities.

He returned to his parents' house in Cockermouth, and to their considerable grief had in the last five years shown little progress in anything; his favourite occupation was to walk the hills for days on end by himself, and he could be seen striding along the roads, talking aloud and snapping his fingers in the air.

He was devoted to his parents, amiable and docile. There had, however, been strange rumours of late concerning him, not of any immorality or cock-fighting or gambling, but of something that was, in his father's eyes, very much worse: a suspicion that he was concerting with the Methodists. A well-known Wesleyan itinerant, Mr. Jeremy Walker, had been seen in his company. There was a rumour that he had taken part in some sort of outdoor meeting. His father had not yet dared to ask him whether there was any sort of truth in this. He knew well his son's honesty, but Mr. Sunwood was grievously disturbed in his mind.

Their home on the outskirts of Cockermouth was a pretty place, looking out to the fields and woods, having a garden filled with sweet-williams and pinks and hollyhocks in their due season, and an arbour and a trellis for roses. In the parlour there was a rosy chintz and some fine pieces of mahogany, in Mr. and Mrs. Sunwood's bedroom a grand four-poster and a dressing-chest with a lattice of Chinese decoration. At the corner of the stair there was a round-faced clock of Irish Chippendale. There were spindle-backed chairs, a Bury settee and a fine Turkey carpet in the dining-room. These things were the very pride of Mr. and Mrs. Sunwood's hearts. There was a maid-servant called Rebecca, a cat, Timothy, and a boy, who worked (when he felt inclined) in the garden, named Jacob. Deborah herself cared for the preserving, pickling and daily cooking. She and Rebecca kept the little house as clean and shining as a new saucepan. They were, both of them, so proud of it that they dreamt of it at night.

Deborah had but seldom any time for rest and reflection; she did not, indeed, desire it. On this particular afternoon, however, she was expecting her sister-in-law, Sarah Herries, and some members of her family to dinner at four o'clock; they would remain for the night and return to Fell House on the following day. Everything was ready for them, the Guest Room prepared, the dinner preparing. All day she had had with her Humphrey's letter. Only now was she free to settle herself and read some of it. Her excitement was as intense as though Humphrey himself had made a sudden unexpected appearance.

Mr. Sunwood came in from tending a pig, who led (unwitting his destiny) a greedy and contented life in a sty at the back of the house; close together on the settee, his hand resting often on her plump shoulder, they read the letter. Humphrey began with loving messages to everyone. Then he had many things to tell of London: the eating-house where he had paid a shilling for his dinner of meat and pudding, the Thames with its fine bridges and noble arches, the hackney coaches, the dangers of the streets where the coaches and carts crowded so closely that there was scarcely room to move, and the noise so fierce that you must step into the quiet of a shop if you wanted to converse with a friend, a ship on land near the Tower that was a trap for pressing simple people into being sailors, the signs outside the shops with

' Children educated here,' ' Shoes mended here,'
' Foreign spirituous liquors here,' the general
drunkenness, so that the common people were always far gone in gin and brandy. He had visited
Vauxhall with the son of his master, Mr. Hodges,
and had much to say about the paintings and
statues, the rotunda and the orchestra therein.

The most exciting news to his parents, however,
was that he had taken dinner with his mother's
cousin, Sir Pomfret Herries, who had a fine house
in Kensington: Pomfret was the son of Deborah's
first cousin Raiseley, who had once owned a
fine house in Keswick but was now with God.
Deborah's memory flew back to her cousin
Raiseley, a sickly and arrogant youth who had been
for ever at war with her brother David. It had
seemed that there would be a family feud there,
but when Raiseley had in later years moved to
London, and the Keswick house was sold, com-
munication had altogether dropped.

It seemed, however, that this child Pomfret,
whom Deborah remembered as a little stout boy
beating David's big black horse with a toy whip,
now a man of thirty-four or so, had done well
for himself in the City, married a clergyman's
daughter, and begotten of her body two healthy
children.

Well, feud or no feud, Pomfret Herries had
been kind to her boy, and for that she would
forgive him all old scores. Young Humphrey
described the splendour of the Kensington house,
the garden with its fountain and statues, the many
servants, the rich food and wine. Cousin Pomfret

was large and stout ('like his poor grandfather before him,' sighed Deborah, with a sudden desire to go somewhere and be kind to that poor old man with his red face and pimples, suffering so sadly from gout, sitting alone and deserted in the Keswick house by the Lake). And now there was this new Pomfret with his children and handsome wife sitting in his grand Kensington house, forgetting no doubt that he had ever had a grandfather. Time flies, thought Deborah, and this is a modern world that we are in. Those old days are gone for ever! There was indeed a certain moment's melancholy in this excited acceptance by her son of this new life. She had lost him! —he who only a moment ago had been rolling naked on this Turkey carpet while she turned the tunes in the music-box—and, her eyes a little tearful, she placed her chubby hand on her husband's chubby arm that she might feel securely that he, at any rate, was still with her.

Mr. Sunwood loved his son, but so confusing is this modern life that there were four things in his head all obscuring and dimming the things that Humphrey had to tell him. That was the worst of these days: you never had a moment's peace. There was his friend Mr. Forster, who wanted a midshipman's place for his boy, and hadn't Mr. Sunwood some interest; there was his own wickedness in sitting up almost all night at cards two days back at Mr. and Mrs. Donne's, and although he had lost but a shilling in all it was a habit that must not grow on him; and there was the funeral of Mrs. Hardacre to-morrow and

he must see that his black silk hatband had its
proper white love-ribband; there was their own
dinner, too, this very day. Sarah and David
Herries were accustomed to good fare. Deborah
had told him that there would be a couple of
rabbits smothered in onions, a couple of ducks
roasted and an apricot pudding. He himself
had seen to the wine, punch and beer. And
what was that that Deborah was reading to him?
' A girl staying in the house, Nancy Bone, has a
lovely figure, and we laughed and joked much
together. I sat beside her when we played For-
feits, and I have bought her to-day a purse made
of morocco leather. For dinner we had a turkey
roasted, a boiled chicken, blancmange, tarts, a
damson cheese. . . .'

Deborah, her eyes shining, said: 'If it should
be a match between our Humphrey and this
Nancy . . .' upon which, throwing to the wind
all the other concerns that had been plaguing
him, and realising only her, the best wife God had
ever given to man, he put his arm around her
broad shoulders, kissed her on the lips and pinched
her ear for an audacious matchmaker.

He was about to ask ' And where is Reuben?'
when they heard the clatter of the horses on the
cobbles. A moment later and there in the doorway were Sarah, David and their youngest boy.

Everyone was very happy; they were sitting
in the parlour, and little Rebecca, looking her best
in her fresh cap and ribbons, was offering wine
and cake, and Jacob was caring for the horses.

Mr. Sunwood, although he would acknowledge

it to no man, was always a little shy of his brother-in-law, David Herries. He was always hoping that this hesitation would shortly be conquered and had even prayed to God about it, but on every fresh occasion the shyness was there. For one thing David Herries was now a great man in the county, his influence everywhere felt, and men said that one of these days he would be knighted. Mr. Sunwood could never feel perfectly assured that David had not a little despised his sister for marrying a simple clergyman. Then David was a great man physically too, enormous he looked now as he spread about the settee with his snow-white wig, which he still occasionally wore, his round red face, his full-skirted blue coat and silver waistcoat, his immense thighs and legs in their riding-boots, his silver spurs.

But no one could have been kinder than David was to his brother-in-law. There was no condescension in his heart to anyone, he had no pride anywhere in his heart save that he was a Herries and had done something to raise his branch of the Herries family in the world. It was strange indeed to see how, the moment that David and Deborah his sister were together again, the Herries family feeling was suddenly everywhere.

The house, the furniture, the cake, the wine, Rebecca and the cat, little Mr. Sunwood himself, all became adjuncts of the Herries Family, whether they would or no. That was a way that the Herries people had.

Nevertheless David and his brother-in-law discussed the affairs of the nation in quite a broad general spirit. David had a great deal to say about the recent rejection of Pitt's Reform Bill. He was glad indeed that it had been rejected. If ever there was a true Tory in the world it was David Herries, and Mr. Sunwood agreed with him, being as Tory in Church as David was in State. David's voice had a way of rising to a regular boom when his feelings were roused, and they were roused now. He could not himself see that there was anything wrong with Parliamentary Representation. He would have things left as they were. For all that he could see, this was nothing but a plot on the part of the Yorkshire freeholders to put a check on the authority of their good and wise King. He shook his great head over these new times. Why couldn't we leave things as they were? This discontent of the lower orders boded no good. What was this chatter about their Rights? When he had been a boy they had had no Rights and were contented enough. He recalled the admirable behaviour of a servant his father had had, Benjamin he had been called. The more you whipped him the better he was pleased, and he had died in his father's arms. David never perceived the incongruity of his remarks in that he himself could never beat anyone and was notorious for over-indulging his servants. Mr. Sunwood, however, agreed cordially and sighed over these new times, and was afraid that there were many fresh changes coming.

Sarah and Deborah meanwhile were talking together as eagerly as any two women will who

are very old friends and have not seen one another
for a while. Sarah, although she did not at
present declare it, was paying this visit because,
above everything, she wished to discuss with
Deborah the urgent matter of Judith. Deborah,
on her side, was longing for the moment when
she might begin about Humphrey's letter and his
visit to the Pomfret Herries.

Sarah had the greatest opinion of Deborah's
sound common sense. Judith's escape to Tom
Gauntry's on the evening of her whipping had
had most momentous consequences. David had
ridden over to Stone Ends and brought her home.
From then until now her nature was changed.
She was obedient, docile, with flashes of fiery
temper, strange impetuous affections; Sarah,
whose nature was equable and always under
control, could not understand her at all: she felt,
too, that she was alone in this, for David had not
the art of understanding temperaments. Francis
could do what he liked with the child, but would
not, so there you were. . . .

Meanwhile one member of the household was
in his attic room drumming with his fingers on
the window. This was Reuben. He could not
decide to go down. He had seen them arrive.
The one of them that interested and touched him
most was not there—Judith. She came in his
heart after his brother and his mother, and so
warm, so almost passionate, were his affections
that she would have been surprised indeed had
she known of them. As yet she never thought

of him; she had seen him but seldom, and he was no figure to appeal to a child, with his lanky hair, his stout ill-shapen body and his untidiness.

But if she had been there he would have come down. He would have endured his awkward distrust of himself before his grand uncle and his discomfort before the sharp critical eyes of young Will his cousin. Had Judith been with them he could have sat and looked at her lovely hair, and perhaps done her some little service.

But he knew what they thought of him. He could hear his uncle ask why he was not at some work, saving his parents their charges. He had seen his uncle stand by the horse, give his riding-coat to Jacob, revealing the splendid clothes. Why was he never to be like that? Why was everything in him just so turbulent and disordered, as though he heard from a great distance some Call to the obeying of some Order, and yet could not distinguish what that Call might be—and why, oh, why, was something driving him now towards a step that must enrage his father and make his brother grieve?

It had been only a year ago that Mr. Walker had given him an ill-written, exceedingly ill-printed *Life of John Wesley*, and this book had been for him, since then, almost his Gospel. Everything related in it had seemed to grow into his own nature. When he read that Wesley wore his hair flowing loose upon his shoulders to give the money that would be spent in caring for it to the poor, that seemed to him a divine action. When he read Wesley's words: ' I would as soon expect to dig happiness out of the earth, as to find it in riches, honour, pleasure (so called) or indeed in the enjoyment of any creature. I know there can be no happiness on earth, but in the enjoyment of God, and in the foretaste of those rivers of pleasure which flow at His right hand for evermore. Thus by the Grace of God in Christ I judge of happiness. Therefore I am in this respect a new creature': his soul thrilled within him; it was almost as though he saw God Himself standing before him and the light of His Countenance shining upon him.

When he read of how Whitfield on the afternoon of Saturday, February 17, 1739, stood upon a mound, in a place called Rose Green, his 'first field pulpit,' and preached to the Kingswood colliers, he felt that he would have given all that he had might he but have stood at his side on that great occasion.

He read how Wesley preached at Gwenap, in Cornwall: ' I stood on the wall, in the calm still evening, with the setting sun behind me; and almost an innumerable multitude before, behind and on either hand. Many likewise sat on the little hills, at some distance from the bulk of the congregation. But they could all hear distinctly while I read " The disciple is not above his Master," and the rest of those comfortable words which are day by day fulfilled in our ears.'

Oh, those comfortable words! Why had he not too been there on that beautiful evening, following that great man's counsel?

Above and beyond all there was the necessity

for the New Birth. ' One will ask with all assurance, " What! Shall I not do as well as my
neighbour?" Yes; as well as your unholy neighbour, as well as your neighbours that die in their
sins; for you will all drop into the pit together, in
the nethermost hell. You will all lie together in
the lake of fire, " the lake of fire burning with
brimstone." Then at length you will see (but
God grant you may see it before!) the necessity of
holiness in order to glory, and, consequently, of
the new birth; since none can be holy, except he
be born again.'

None can be holy except he be born again! So
he was not holy. No, indeed, he was not. He
was filled with a loathing and hatred of himself,
of his body, but far more of himself, his character
and true person. He knew himself for a glutton,
a coward, an idler, filled with vanity, sensual
thought, ingratitude.

But it was worst of all that he should not know
which way he should go. He had seen during
the last year something of Mr. Walker and his
friends; he had been to some of their meetings and
was not happy there. There was something of
his father in him, more than he knew; something
perhaps of the Herries blood of his mother. The
violence and hysteria in the meetings repelled and
silenced him. And they, too, felt that he was not
with them. What he wanted he could not tell,
save that he must serve God, and must in himself
bring about some entire change. Poor Reuben!
He was just now the loneliest young man in the
world.

D

He leaned from his window and listened to the
sounds of the little world about him.   Some horse
was impatiently pawing the cobbles, a pedlar
sharply cried his wares, a flock of sheep came
hurrying under the window, pressing together
with their wide, startled, stupid eyes; the shepherd,
an old man, with a white shaggy beard, wearing a
wide black hat, called shrilly and with an absent
mind to his sheep-dog.   Beyond these movements
the wood lay in dark shadow, motionless as though
painted on the silver sky.   Every fibre in him
responded to this lovely world.   He must get out
into it.   He would not go down to his aunt and
uncle.   He would see them later in the evening.
Had little Judith been there——!   And at the
thought of her, although he had no sensual feeling
for her (was she not, ludicrous thought, his aunt?),
he became quite suddenly disturbed by consideration of women.   They flocked, like a covey of
bright shining birds, about him, settling on his
head, his shoulders, his hands, ruffling their
feathers, crimson and silver and gold, with their
sharp beaks pecking at his cheeks, smiling at him
out of their hard bright eyes.   His body was
burning, his heart roughly beating.   The Devil
himself was with him in the room, which had
become hot and airless.   The sun was sinking,
and the wood, as though stricken by the hand of
God, was ebony.   The silver sky was a camping-
ground for tents of crimson; shadows of approaching evening stole across the brightness of the field.
His room was evil and filled with temptation.
Not realising that he was hurrying to the turning-

point of his life, he hastened softly down the stairs, along the passage, into the path before the house.

The little town was embraced by the rosy light of approaching evening. Fresh breezes from the sea ruffled the hair and wigs of the citizens; not far away the kindly hills caught the light. The streets were narrow, ill-paved and of a certain odour, but it was the time when the labours of the day are drawing to a close, many were at their dinner, children ran playing from door to door.

At the door of Jacob Hilton's Library young Mr. Clementson, flour-dealer, was having a pleasant word with Mr. Fletcher of the 'King's Arms,' and here was the Carrier coming in from Workington.

They all knew young Reuben Sunwood well enough and greeted him kindly, but he had the sense (perhaps with some truth) that they regarded him oddly and avoided too plain a recognition of him for the Methodist company he was keeping.

So he turned off the main street up a dark and narrow way, thinking of his own troubles, his evil temptations, his loneliness, his perplexed opinions, and found himself, almost without knowing it, in the coach-yard at the back of the 'Black Bull.'

He had been attracted here, it might be subconsciously, by the shouts and laughter of a pushing, pressing crowd. He was among them before he knew. He stood there watching. In the middle of the yard there was a cleared space

and in the cleared space a post. Chained to the
post was an old, ragged and exceedingly weary
bear. Near to the bear, held in the arms of two
stout young men, was a small brown-faced man,
his forehead streaked with blood. It seemed
that he was a foreign pedlar of some kind from
his long black hair, his brown complexion, a torn
jacket of crimson with a silver chain. It was
soon clear that he was a foreigner, for he jabbered
ceaselessly in a strange tongue, words pouring
from him in a tangled, agitated flow. Once and
again he would raise his little body as though he
would break away, and then his voice jumped into
a shrill scream of protest that roused bursts of
laughter from the onlookers.

Kneeling on the ground were two men who
held in leash a bulldog and a small terrier, and
these two dogs were madly straining to be free
that they might get at the bear.

Everyone was hurling bets into the air, and
close to Reuben a short thick-set man sucking a
straw was taking bets down in his book. The
excitement was intense; it was months, a tall
farmer near Reuben told him, since there had
been a bear to be baited.

Above the hubbub and bustle, clouds of saffron
sailed tranquilly over the sky that was now white
as moonlit water. Two children hung between
the balusters of the inn balcony, laughing at the
little pedlar.

At first it seemed to Reuben that he was not
concerned in the matter. The bustle and noise,
the friendly stomach of the large farmer against

which he was pressed, the general air of goodwill
and happiness was a relief to him after his own
silly and selfish perplexities. There was very
much of the child in him, and he liked above
all to have happy people around him. To see
animals baited was no fresh thing to him; he
had been accustomed to such sights since he was
a baby. The cruelty of his time was natural to
his time and so was no cruelty. He pushed
himself forward that he might see the better.

Then he encountered the face of the bear.
An encounter it was, as though the pale sky, the
crowd, the inn buildings had been swept into
lumber and only he and the bear remained. The
bear raised its old sad wrinkled face and looked
at him. Age was there, bewilderment was
there, but what was there, beyond all else, was
Reuben himself. Reuben looked at Reuben.

The bear was fastened to the post by a rusty
chain that went round his middle and his foot.
His body was chafed in a number of places, where
life had been hard on him. The long brown
shaggy hair of his body was tangled with mud and
dirt, and above his left eye there was a deep cut
from which blood dripped.

It was this that Reuben first saw, how he
raised his paw clumsily, slowly, as though he
were resolved to be cautious, and wiped the blood
that trickled down his nose. From under his
thick tangled brows his eyes looked out, melancholy, slow and brooding. It was these eyes that
seemed at first to be exactly Reuben's own. He
knew how often his gaze had been fixed upon

himself and the world in which he moved with exactly that same perplexity and sadness. The bear's loneliness was his own loneliness.

Then the bear began quietly to realise that he was in the middle of his enemies. Carefully, with that same caution, he moved his head to look for his master, and when he saw him held with his coat torn and his brown breast bare he began to be angry. (Just, Reuben thought, as he would himself slowly, in the middle of his enemies, begin to be angry.) But with his anger there rose also slowly his sadness and his bewilderment. He shuffled with his feet; his paw rose and fell again. He began to roll his head. Then he tried to break from his chain, and when he found that he could not, he jerked his head towards his master. Then again rubbed the drops of blood from his nose.

Something very grand entered into him, the grandeur of all captured and ill-treated things. He lifted his head and stared from under his jutting brows at the crowd, and was at once, with that single movement, finer than all of them. He was no longer Reuben. Reuben had been left behind and was now one of the crowd.

Then a large fat man without a hat, his hair tied with a brown ribbon, in red faded breeches, strode forward and undid the chain. Everyone shouted. The bear, bewildered, hesitating, rubbed his nose again, then, like a man in bedroom slippers, shuffled towards his master.

At the same moment the two dogs were loosed. Everyone began to shout together. It seemed to Reuben that it was towards himself that the dogs were running.

The bulldog instantly attacked the bear, caught his leg and hung on there. The smaller dog stayed back, whining.

The world was pandemonium. Men were laughing, yelling, moving, so that the crowd rocked like a wave. But the bear stood doing nothing; he only raised his paw and stroked his nose. He was a very old bear, who had been travelling for an infinity of years; he was very weary and did not understand why things were as they were.

The bulldog loosed his hold, sprang at the bear's throat, missed and rolled over. The bear sank on all fours, and, rolling his head with a blind gesture, seemed to be asking of them all what they were about.

It was then that Reuben, pushing violently his way, broke into the centre and ran to the bear. Then everything happened swiftly and, for the crowd, comically. A bear or a man, it was the same to the crowd. The bulldog bit Reuben's leg. Something struck his face. There were shouts and cries. Lightning broke from heaven, and the multitude of men, faces, heads of hair, hands, rose in a swirl like a shifting canopy of black flies and carried him sky-high. Then he fell, fell into a pit that was black, that had the mouth of a fish, opening, shutting, opening again. But as he fell somewhere, triumph, joy, freedom —things that he had never known—broke like silent fireworks in his heart. . . .

Many generations after, he was sitting in a chair in the parlour of Mr. Candlish the bellman. He knew him well, a short pursy fellow with a wart on his nose. Mrs. Candlish had bound his head. One eye was closed. A little crowd in the doorway surveyed him. Someone held a candle. He smiled feebly on them all, climbed to his feet, found that he could walk, although his body ached and blood trickled from under the bandage.

He said that he would go home now, thank you. No one stayed him. They were silent when he limped past them, and stared after him in silence as he hobbled down the street. He did not know at all why he was happy, but he was.

He had not far to go. Every step was an agony. He opened his house-door and pushed into the parlour, where they were at dinner. With his one eye from under his bandage he saw his uncle David, shining in splendour, his father pouring wine, his mother—her face suddenly springing into terror at the sight of him—his aunt, and his little cousin Will, who watched everything and missed nothing that anyone said.

He saw the table piled with food, the candles that danced in their silver holders and the harpsichord in the corner. Someone cried out; he swayed in the doorway, tried to ask for some wine, could not, fell fainting at his mother's feet. As he tried to catch her hand he smiled.

He was the bear, and none of them knew it.

FIREWORKS OVER THE LAKE

For the evening of June 23, 1787, Mr. Joseph Pocklington of Vicar's Island announced that there would be fireworks discharged from his own ground *if* the weather were fine.

If the weather were fine! How that phrase beat its anxiety in a thousand hearts, for not only was it a question of the fireworks, but the band, organised by Mr. Peter Crosthwaite of Crosthwaite Museum, would play airs from Haydn and Mozart, and there would be dancing in Crow Park, to say nothing at all of the boats that there would be on the Lake itself, the Chinese lanterns, and the dark recesses of the water hidden from the inquisitive glances of the moon.

Would there be a moon? Yes, there would be a moon. Mr. Crosthwaite himself, who, after serving his country for twenty years in the Navy, had but recently returned to his native place with a most interesting collection of curiosities, promised that there should be a full and lustrous moon.

It mattered little where you went on that early morning of June 23. Every riser had the same idea; night-cap after night-cap might be seen hanging from the window, sniffing at the weather.

From the windows of the 'Royal Oak' and the 'Queen's Head,' from John Powe's where the Old Club for so many years held its meetings, from the attics of the 'Shoulder of Mutton,' from the Excise Officer at the 'George and the Dragon,' from Abel Graves the hairdresser's and Mr. Lancaster the patten-maker's, from the toll-gate at Brow Top —yes, and much farther afield than these . . . right around the Lake, from Stable Hill and Burrow and Low Low Door, High Low Door and Grange, Borrowdale Common and Manesty Nook, Mutton Pye Bay and Branley, House End and Water End, Finkle Street and Portinskill. Yes, and beyond these again, from Newlands and Rosthwaite, Stonethwaite and Watendlath, Braithwaite and Bassenthwaite, even to Buttermere and Uldale and Caldbeck and Threlkeld—even to Penrith and Grasmere, to Patterdale and Ambleside, the news had run and the night-caps were at all the windows, whether of mansion or Statesman's farm, of shop, of meeting-house or humble cottage.

For these nights on the Lake, *if* only the weather were fair, were nights to stir the poets to song, and they *did* stir the Keswick poets to song. Are not those poems to be found in Keswick archives to this very day?

Mr. Pocklington himself loved to give pleasure to the people of Keswick, and the people of Keswick loved to have pleasure given them. And was not Mr. Pocklington a fine man, seeing that he owned so much land around the Lake and had his place on Vicar's Island and at Ashness and at Fall

Park, and had set up a wonderful Druid's Circle
in the pleasantest imitation of the real one above
Keswick?

If only the sun would shine, everyone and
everything was in favour.   And the sun *did* shine.
It rose above a curtain of mist that cut the Lake
into half, turned the islands into clouds of emerald,
touched Skiddaw with rose and the sharp edges of
Blencathra with ebony.

All the gardens of Keswick—and at that time
Keswick was filled with gardens—glittered in the
sun.   Then as now, no gardens in England could
grow sweet peas and pinks and stock better than
the Keswick gardens.   On a summer day, such as
this one, Keswick smelt of flowers, save only in the
slums, behind Main Street, where the odour was
quite another one.   But here dwelt only gipsies
and whores and smugglers from St. Bees and
Ravenglass, and they didn't matter to anyone.

So the day lengthened; the air was balmy,
Mr. Crosthwaite took out his flute and tuned
it, Miss Evins the schoolmistress practised
her dancing-steps privately in her bedroom; the
'Royal Oak,' the 'Queen's Head,' the 'Shoulder
of Mutton' prepared for an infinity of custom; all
the children were beyond human discipline, Mr.
Pocklington's gardeners guarded the fireworks,
and from distant silent valleys the horses had set
out, the ladies riding pillion as happy as though
there were not a heartache in the world.   All the
Herries would be there.   It was a proud day
for the Sunwoods, for their Reuben was but just
returned from France, where he had been these

last two years; and all the Herries from Uldale
—David and Sarah, Francis, Deborah, Will and
Judith—rode out in the forenoon and had dinner
in state at the ' Royal Oak.'

William Herries, now seventeen years of age,
small, short, spindly-legged, an arrogant nose in
the proper equine Herries style, a thin rather tight
mouth that could, and often did, break into a very
charming smile, and clothes neat, correct and
most unobtrusive, this William Herries was, as
he always had been, exceedingly old for his age.

He himself knew that this was so; he had
realised for the last ten years at least that he was
quite the oldest of them all. Without any sense
of condemnation, without any outward show of
superiority, he had long felt a very real contempt
for all the other members of his family—for his
mother because she was jog-trot, his father because
he was conservative, his brother Francis because
he was a dreamer (here was his severest contempt),
and Judith (could she be reckoned as one of the
family) because she was mad and had no control
of her emotions. (Strangely, though, here he recognised in Judith some spirit of mastery closely
akin to his own.)

He recognised that he was superior to every
member of his family but chiefly in this: that he
knew so exactly what he wanted to do with his
life and how he would do it.

His father, poor man, had a kind of notion that
Will would follow himself in his trading business,
would work in Liverpool for a while, travel in the
East for a while, and finally, having doubled the

value of everything, settle down as Squire of Fell House.

Some of this prophecy was, indeed, correct. Will *would* follow his father in the business, would in truth double it and more than double it, but *not* from Liverpool. It was in London that Will Herries intended to make his career. It was not at all that Will objected to business; that was not the kind of snob that he was. Now, with all England's glorious foreign conquests, with the India Trade, the China Trade and the rest, now was the very time to make a fortune. But it was to be a fortune made in the grand manner, made in the very heart of the universe, made against the very strongest opposition, and made—here was the fount and crown of the whole ambition— made for the HERRIES' glory.

Will was nothing if he was not Herries, and Herries practical, material, of the earth earthy. He was sentimental about nothing; he was most certainly not sentimental about this. He did not know in what distant childish dreams this ambition had not had its birth, to make a fortune and with that to take his place at the head of the Herries family. So that men everywhere might say: ' That is a Family, that is. It has houses and barns, gardens and fields, ships and horses and sheep and cattle. *That* is what a Herries can do.'

He saw neither poetry nor romance in this ambition. It seemed to him a perfectly practical logical plan. He would not mind if, at the end of it, one day he returned to Uldale as its master. He cared for this North Country if he cared for any country at all. There was something in its bleak spaces, its coldly blowing winds, its little stone walls running like live things about the fells, its glancing, shining waters, its cleanliness and strength and honesty, that was akin to his own strong unfaltering purpose.

He had, of course, the defects of his qualities like all of us, and it was one of his defects that he made no allowance for the poetic, incalculable quality in human nature. He thought, even now at the young age of seventeen, that he could always calculate with perfect safety. He knew exactly what his father and mother would do and say. His father with his large hearty good-nature, his simple laughter, his ability for seeing what was under his nose, and his stupidity in thinking that that was all that there was; his common sense that stopped just short of real knowledge; his senti-mentality (Will, like many another practical man and woman, mistook for sentimentality quite deep and genuine feeling), his boisterous physical life, love of food, of drink, of hunting, of horses, of cock-fighting and card-playing and wrestling and football; his kindliness and satisfaction with small material things. Will knew that most of the business was now left to Mr. Metcalfe and his son, his father's partners in Liverpool, and he despised his father for so leaving it. He had a good-natured regard for his father and he despised him thoroughly.

He really loved his mother; it was perhaps the strongest human feeling that he had, and this was chiefly because he thought that she managed the

house very well, ruled the servants and had everything in order, but she was always doing what
seemed to him silly sentimental things.

For his elder brother Francis he felt a contempt
that was almost savage.   Francis stood for everything that he despised; he did nothing, but hung
in idleness about the house, reading, dreaming,
saying absurd, ridiculous things, seeing poetry in
everything, liking to be alone, simply cumber-
ing the ground.   He had not even the natural
passions of drinking, wenching, gaming.   He
was nothing, nothing at all.

From them all, with a self-control that argued
well for his future success in the world, he completely hid his scorn.   To them all he appeared
a quiet, obedient, studious boy, who did what he
was told and gave no trouble.

Francis possibly had some suspicion of the iron
will and determined purpose that was developing
there, but no one knew what Francis thought about
anything.   The only other person who had any
accurate knowledge of Will was Judith.   His own
attitude to Judith was a peculiar one.   He had to
confess that Judith perplexed him.   He had to
confess regretfully enough that to sum her up as
wild and foolish was not sufficient.   She was, it
was true, all of these things, but she appeared to
be something else besides.

The relation between them was exceptional.
Judith was now approaching thirteen years of age.
She, like himself, was older than she looked, except
that, at times, she looked old enough to be eighty.
She had all the colour, all the oddness, all the

uncertainty, irresponsibility, that he distrusted and condemned. It was natural enough, he considered, when you thought of her mother. But besides this was her desire to dominate everyone with whom she came in contact, and this was like his own desire except that she wanted it for other reasons. She wanted power because of *people*, he wanted it because of *things*. He had sensual feeling like anyone else, and had had already two experiences. She had sensual feeling too, but it was quite different from his, because whenever she cared for anybody (and she cared for fifty different people a week) she threw herself into it as though this were the only affection of her life, while he always knew that people were nothing, that no one ever cared for anyone else very long.

And he told himself this, although right before his eyes were his own father and mother who had loved one another for so many years and would do so to the end. But his father and mother had so much ridiculous Sensibility—and very little Sense at all.

Nevertheless it remained to him puzzling, this relation of his with Judith. Defensive or offensive? She wished to dominate him as well as the rest of her world. It amused him sometimes to allow her to think that she did.

So he remained, this young man of seventeen, watching, waiting, calculating all his chances.

The night was enchantingly warm. They went down to the Lake in a body—David in his fine rose-coloured coat, wearing his own hair

clubbed and powdered (an increasing fashion);
Sarah in a fine hoop of silver with little roses;
Deborah, red in the face with pleasure and happiness ('blowzy,' Will thought her); Judith, a
fascinating little hat on the side of her red hair and
a little hoop with silver ships painted on it; Will,
very soberly dressed in brown, demurely in the
rear; Francis, slim, aloof.

Mr. and Mrs. Satterthwaite of Bassenthwaite
village walked down with them. Mrs. Satterthwaite's talk was all of servants, a new one, Mary
Benson, recommended by Mrs. Blane, five pound
a year, tea twice a day, good at cookery and understanding her needle. Well, we hope, don't we,
that it will turn out for the best? But they begin
so well, don't they, up so early, ready to milk the
cow, and then, where are you? A month later,
already in child from the cowman or drunk on the
parlour floor. Yes, where are you? All the sky,
milky now with golden fleece before the sun's
setting, is crowded with maids flying like witches,
mocking their mistresses, and men, bare as they
were born, down the wind after them. Do what
you will, it is all Nature, and what do you say to
Mr. Bradby, the new schoolmaster in Keswick?
A sensible and good-natured man, unmarried—and
at once Mrs. Satterthwaite's two daughters, single
and plain, poor things, always left to their own
thoughts at every dance in the neighbourhood,
staying in Carlisle at this very instant with an
aunt to see whether *she* couldn't do something
about it, filled the scene and checked the conversation.

Not for Judith. She was so happy that she must dance along the path as she went, chattering to Francis, although she knew that he was listening to nothing that she had to say.

Everywhere, on every side of her, people were moving forward to the Lake, and all of them as happy as she. She loved that people around her should be happy; she was to love that as long as she was alive. If only they were happy and *also* did what she told them, she asked nothing more of life.

And to-night, everything was perfection. She had had her own way in everything, was wearing the clothes that she wanted, there would be dancing under the trees and they would be in a boat on the Lake, the moon would rise, and then, best of all, there would be Fireworks—Fireworks, of all things in life that she loved best! Could she have seen Mr. Joseph Pocklington, she would have flung her arms around him and kissed him. She did not mind what she did when she was happy. Her soul and body surrendered then completely to the emotion of the moment. Nothing existed for her except that moment.

Even Will, who thought it foolish, indeed, when you were a little short thing with a pale face and so many people around you, to dance along so that all must notice you, was forced to acknowledge to himself that her happiness was infectious. He himself hoped to have his arm around some feminine waist before the evening was over.

When they gained the lakeside it was beautiful

indeed.   The Lake, whose waters scarcely moved, only a trembling shudder of pleasure once and again mysteriously stirring, had caught flakes and scatterings of gold from the last rays of the sun as it fell behind Cat Bells.   Vicar's Island lay like a dark hand upon the water.   Under the trees there were booths with many things to buy. Someone was playing a fiddle.   Everywhere boats floated, and the oars plashed like music through the air.

Happiness? Happiness? Where is it? Where is it? Here, now, this very moment, with the movement of the people under the trees, the fiddle and the soft distance of the orchestra on the Meadow, before one's eyes the silver stretch of water spreading to the hills that lay like friendly elephants (thought Judith, who had never seen an elephant) humped against the sky.   Yes, here is Happiness, because here is Mystery and promise of Adventure.   One cannot quite see who is moving beneath the trees.   One step and whom may one not encounter?

Two boats were waiting for the Herries family in the charge of old John Blacklock, who was so broad in the waist and thick of the leg that he was like one of the sights at the Fair, two bodies with one head.   This head and face, too, were so thickly covered with hair that his eyes shone out like a friendly animal's from a bush.   Judith always talked Cumberland to him.

She greeted him now with: ' Noo than what, John? ' which pleased him greatly.   In his opinion she was a ' gay fewsome lass.'   When the weather was bad, he would come out to Uldale and work in the garden for a week or more.

But there was at once a real excitement for her, because Reuben was there. They were waiting for them—little Mr. Sunwood, very neat in his best parson's clothes; Deborah, always so kind and comfortable; and Reuben, a trifle neater for his two years' sojourn in France, but otherwise very little changed. She liked Reuben, in part because of the power she had over him, in part because of his modesty and warm-heartedness. She even understood his shyness, although it was so far from anything in herself. It was, indeed, part of her character that she should care more for Francis and Reuben, so unlike her in temperament, than any other of her relatives.

And at once her power for having things as she wanted them was apparent. A child of less than thirteen, she was in five minutes seated under an oak tree; the Lake spread in front of her, and settled around her were Reuben, Francis and Will. It was true that they were there to take a breath and look about them before the activities of the evening began for them, and were scarcely conscious, perhaps, that Judith was there, or it was Reuben only who was conscious. Will, as usual, had his sharp eyes fixed on everything at once and was absorbed in considering how he should turn things to his own advantage, and of what Francis was thinking no one could tell, but very quickly Judith had fastened her personality upon all of them and was taking the lead.

So they talked, the background of the fading

evening, the faintly rustling trees, the moving people, voices, music forcing from all of them a gentle comfort and well-being that drew them all together in general friendliness. In after days these voices of the lost and ghostly past of this moment would visit them again.

For Judith, as she sat perched on the bole of the tree, a cloak over her shoulders, her shoes shining in the dusk, it seemed to her, as it had seemed to her a thousand times already, that life was at this very moment beginning. She was so happy that she should have been afraid, but she was never afraid when she was happy.

'Reuben, tell us about France. Did you see the King and Queen?'

But Reuben had very little to tell about France. Something about Lourdes, where there was a castle on a rock; state prisoners were sent there by *lettres de cachet*. Here they died of despair and misery. At Pau he had been shown the cradle of Henry IV., which was the shell of a tortoise. At Bordeaux he had seen Dauberval the famous dancer. He had visited Versailles and had seen men walking in rags of the direst destitution. There was a wonderful botanical garden there. In the Castle at Chambord he had been shown the room where Marshal Saxe had died. It was said that he had been run through the heart by the Prince of Conti in a duel. And so on. And so on. Little things, unalive, related by him in his shy, hesitating voice so that, Will thought impatiently, he turned everything to dullness. But how could it be other? How could he, in this quiet homely comfortable scene, tell them of the things that had been burning in his heart—the filth, oppression, cruelty, suffering? Tell them of the man whom he had seen in Tours beaten to death before his eyes, because he had taken a log from the Seigneur's wood, or the two girls ravished by the son of the Lord of the Manor, one of them within a week of her wedding, or of the horde of starved creatures that he came upon on the road outside Paris, scarecrows, their bodies shivering in the bitter wind? The bear again, lodged now close in his heart, he the protector of it; how could he speak of that to Will or Francis Herries? So his voice died away, and he felt the scornfulness of Will's eyes.

'When I am grown,' Judith cried, ' I shall go to France. I shall see the French Queen and dance in Versailles. I shall see India and China and the savages of the West Indies. What will you do, Will? '

He smiled. It was always his way to be courteous and friendly to everyone. Besides nothing in the world interested him so greatly as to think of what he would do when he grew up, a time that was very near to him already.

' I shall build the Herries fortunes,' he said in that voice, a little mocking, a little ironical, so that if anyone objected to what he said he could declare that he had never meant it. ' I shall have a larger fortune than any other Herries, and then, when I have accumulated it, I will

tour the globe and return to make another
fortune.'

'And will you not marry?' asked Judith
greatly interested.

'I shall marry,' said Will gravely, 'and so
increase the Herries stock. I shall have six
children,' he added mockingly.

To their surprise an angry voice broke on
the scene—surprise because it was the voice of
Francis, who seemed never to be disturbed nor to
wish to join in their childish conversations. But
he was disturbed now, and at the sight of his
disturbance two fish-shaped clouds above Vicar's
Island joined hurriedly together the better for
self-protection.

'There, Will; that's your fancy. It's you,
yourself. Money-bags, children, more money-
bags. God, what ambition!'

It was a sharp interruption and rather frightened all of them. Francis was twenty-seven
years of age and so in another world from their
own. He had never mingled with them; he was
like a ghost to them with his thin handsome face,
his cold blue eyes that could on a sudden so
strangely burn, the severe suit of grey and silver
that he so generally wore. Will might despise
him, but there was fear mingled with that scorn.

And now suddenly he was standing, all
shadows around him, his voice that had been
always so chill and reserved beating with emotion.

'You shall have your money-bags if you want
them. What is easier? And getting them you
will have nothing. And is that all life is to you?

Are you so blind that you can see no ghosts behind the money-bags and ghosts behind them again? Have you only your physical parts to cram food into your swelling belly?'

('I have no swelling belly,' Will thought complacently. 'I have an admirable figure.')

Francis went on, coming close to them, standing over them. His anger was gone as soon as it had come. He spoke now gently.

'When I was small I had a dream of a grand white horse breaking from an icy pool and breasting the rocks, tossing its mane. I have not dreamt that for a long while, but I know that that dream is more real to me than all the chairs and sofas, the mutton-pies and shoe-buckles. How can you not tell that that only is real in this world, that vision of ice and strength breaking it, and if we have not seen that we have seen nothing? Who can tell what is Reality? But this at least I know, that I shall never know happiness until I have seen more than you will ever see, Will, my young brother.'

'Thank you for nothing, Francis,' Will answered, looking up at him and smiling. 'I prefer my money-bags to your white horses.'

'Aye, I know what you think,' Francis broke out passionately. 'What you all think. That I loaf at home and take what my father gives me. . . . Wasting . . . wasting.' His voice broke. 'Our grandfather was so. He was searching all his days and never found anything. . . . Forgive me, I have been absurd. This world itself is absurd to me, but behind it . . . behind it

. . . there are Wonders.   Forgive me . . . forgive me,' and to their utter surprise he turned
and vanished into the trees.

For a moment they were all in a great discomfort.   It was so agreeable an evening.   They
had not the slightest notion of Francis' meaning
and they did not wish to spoil his pleasure.
Judith, who loved him, would have wished to
have run after him, to have taken his arm and
comforted him.   But to have comforted him for
what?   She could not tell.

And at that moment, fortunately, the first fireworks broke like a sigh in the darkening heaven.
Everyone said 'Ah!' and then 'Ah!' again, just
as a hundred years after, and a hundred years after
that again, they would sigh with pleasure and
strain their eyes upwards.   So now they gazed.
Everywhere they were gazing, in the little flower-
scented streets of Keswick, lovers waiting among
the Druid stones, shepherds on Blencathra,
watchers by the Watendlath Tarn, children
gathered by the cottages in Newlands and under
Castle Crag and by the waving reeds of Bassenthwaite.

A star broke into a silver cluster, another into
points of blue, another showered drops of gold.
In the hills the echo called and answered.   For a
flash all the faces were lit with a white radiance, the
dancers paused in the Meadow, the trees on the
Island were fiery and then the darker for their flame.

For Judith it was a moment of sheer ecstasy.
She sat, her head back, her hat behind her neck,
her legs uptilted, and at every rush as of wings, at

every gentle crackle of sound, at every fresh
miracle of blue and gold she murmured, her hands
tightly clasped. She forgot everything and everyone in that beauty. A star burst, and showers of
silver flecked the sky.

She sprang up and ran to the Lake edge.
Others were crowding there, and she stood with
them, her head bare, gazing upwards. Three
rockets burst together, and the sky was scattered
with stars. 'Bravo!' 'Bravo!' 'Bravo!' everyone
shouted. She clapped her hands; everyone was
clapping with her. Again the hills called and
answered. Then the pause came, a sudden deep
and mysterious silence. The Lake was now infinite. Far, far away, where the hills were packed
together, a faint radiance was gathering, the
coming moon. Real stars began to twinkle.

Out of this dark lovely world a voice spoke to
her: ' It is better in a boat.'

She knew the voice well; in the last two years
she had thought of it very often. It was the
French boy of Tom Gauntry's.

The lanterns had been lighted and were swaying from the trees. She could see him quite
plainly. He was just the same, only taller, in a
very grand coat and breeches with gold braid.
Under his hat his hair was as black as ever, and
his eyes as black. His mouth was just as impudent. She grinned at him, a childish grin.

' Fetch me a boat then.'

What would Sarah think? It would mean
perhaps another beating. She had been ordered
not to go near the boats until they told her.

The thought of being alone with the French boy was most exhilarating. She watched him while, without another word, he was in a boat, had pushed it towards her and, like a grown man, with fine ceremony, handed her in. As she stepped in she glanced about her to see whether any of the family were near. No sign of any of them. She fancied that she heard Sarah's voice, and in a sudden panic pushed from the shore. Many other boats were now moving, and, in the distance, they were singing.

' Quickly,' she cried, with delight, ' or they will see us.'

They floated away: the oars touched very gently the water as though they were whispering to it their pleasure in the evening. As they moved, the shore behind them came out, with all the dark figures, the lights like jolly smiling faces among the trees, and shadows dancing on the Meadow to a thin faint tune that was reedy like wind through wallpaper.

' Where have you been? '

' In London with an uncle.'

' And your mother? ' She saw the room, the beautiful naked woman, her arms raised, the diamond buckle shining.

' My mother is dead.'

Dead? And at the moment a firework broke in the sky again, this time a circle of fierce rasping flame that whistled with the hiss of an angry cat.

Dead? Judith shivered. Then for these two years the picture that had transformed her, that had

changed her from a thoughtless baby into something, something very different . . . that picture
had been for nothing, of a dead woman.

'Why did she die?'

'What is it? I cannot hear.' He had leaned
forward on the oars.

'Why did she die?'

'She died of the smallpox.'

'When was it?'

'A year back.' He spoke quite indifferently.

'Did you not care?'

'No. She was unkind to me.'

'She must have been very gracious; a beautiful lady. Her hair was so dark.' Judith shivered
again. She wanted to return to the shore, to be
with her own people. And surprisingly something else dominated almost every other feeling,
that she wanted to kiss the French boy. Hateful,
when his mother, his beautiful mother, had for
her, at any rate, only this moment died.

'How old are you now?' he asked her.

'Twelve—nearly thirteen.'

'I am sixteen.'

'What are you doing here? Why are you not
with your uncle?'

'My uncle is in Carlisle. I am with Gauntry
until he fetches me. I like this country. Soon
I shall come to live here.' Then he added, laughing: 'Is your hair yet the same colour? I have
thought of your hair often.'

Because she wanted to kiss him and because
she mustn't, because she was only twelve and he
sixteen, she flipped water in his face. He laid

down his oars in the boat, moved near to her and
roughly kissed her, cheeks, eyes, mouth. She
pulled her head free and smacked his face just as
she had done two years before. But he did not
move. He sat quietly beside her, his hand at her
waist. She did not move either. Fires were
burning now on Vicar's Island, the set-pieces of
the fireworks. A trellis-work of flame ran like
live things from tree to tree. All the Lake near
the Island glowed, but in the distance it was very
dark, with a smoky sheen on it, the first fore-
shadowing of the moon.

She sat there in perfect happiness. She hoped
that he would kiss her again. He did so. Then
she returned his kiss.

' I shall be whipped if they know about it.'

' My mother whipped me, but my uncle dare
not. When my mother was angry she could
kill a man.'

' Was she long ill of the smallpox? '

' No. A month. I was glad when she died.
Do you love me? '

' No.'

' Later you will. You are only a baby. In
two years I will write you a letter, and perhaps you
will come to London.'

' Will you want to marry me? '

' Perhaps. You have such beautiful hair.'

Judith considered. In two years she would
be nearly fifteen. She could marry soon then and
leave Fell House and live in France.

' If I married you should we live in France? '

' Maybe.'

'Will you have money and a house and horses.'

'Yes. Of course.'

'And we will have children?'

'Yes. Of course.'

'We will have six children, and I want to see the French Queen dance in Versailles.'

'I want to live in this country and have dogs and horses.'

'But will you not take me to France for a visit?'

'Maybe.'

They kissed again. She kissed him like a child, just as she kissed Francis. Then quite suddenly she knew that she must return to the shore. At once, at once! She was afraid of him and of the Lake that seemed dark now because the fireworks had died away.

She told him to take her to the shore.

'No. We will stay here.'

Then he saw another Judith. She stepped from him, and, the boat rocking under them, went to the oars and began to row. She could do anything with a boat or a horse.

'If you leave me now I will never see you again,' he said to her fiercely. She made no answer, and a moment later had scrambled over the boat's edge and had landed.

That was the last she saw of him, standing up very dimly against the dark water.

She ran in to the trees and, quite breathless, tumbled straight into Reuben and his mother.

'I was lost,' she said. 'Where are they?'

She put her hand under Reuben's arm and smiled at him so sweetly that he was enraptured. She looked such a baby with her pretty hat crooked, a little breathless.

'We will go and find them,' he said.

THE FUGITIVE

How does a house first know that changes are coming to it? or does a house know? Are we not attributing to it emotions, fears, agitations that are not its real property? The answer depends on yourself. What you see, hear and feel is for yourself alone.

It is certain in any case that in that winter of 1788–1789 Sarah Herries, just arrived at her fiftieth birthday, knew that some change was at hand. It was the first unhappy winter for her since—since when? Since she had lived with David at Herries.

Had she cared for wider issues she might have realised that the change was not only here, but in all the civilised world. She did not, however, care for wider issues, had never done so. It had never meant anything to her that the American rebels had thrown tea into Boston Harbour, that old Chatham had the gout, that Fox made an unholy alliance with North, that young Pitt pored over *The Wealth of Nations* at Cambridge, that men were trampled to death by the horses of noble carriages on the roads outside Paris, that Necker sat up all night biting his thumbs over the impossible business of turning twice two into five. If she had known of these things she would not have cared.

But she did perceive that nothing now went right in the house, that doors swung on their hinges and refused to close, that the Chinese figures in the Blue Room tumbled, through nobody's fault, and were broken to pieces, that the cows gave no milk and the horses went lame.

Twenty years earlier she would have hunted for witches. Now she could only discover that David was becoming an old man, that she herself was fifty and that everyone in her family was at odds. She was a sensible woman, who refused to surrender to superstition, but things were going wrong, and as she lay at night awake in the big four-poster beside David she could hear the wind come whispering down from Skiddaw and must listen, do what she would, to a hundred steps creeping about the stairs and mysterious voices behind the curtain.

But there were unhappy evidences more material than steps and voices.

The first trouble was on the day after the firework evening on the Lake. At dinner Will had suddenly said to Judith:

' Well, miss, you enjoyed, I trust, your pleasant trip in the boat last night.'

No one knew why he said it. He did not care for Judith, but he bore her no especial malice. He did not himself, perhaps, know why he said it. It came no doubt from his deep restless love of power. He was only a boy, but he could turn them any way he wished.

E

All might even then have been saved had it not been for Judith's implacable honesty.

' You were in a boat? '

' Yes, ma'am.'

' With whom? '

That she would not say: with a gentleman, yes. For a brief period, to see the fireworks better. David beat her. The child said nothing, only afterwards alone with Will she told him that she would not forget his kindness.

' I wanted to see how it would go,' he told her quite honestly. He admired her then, such a little thing, standing on her toes to make herself seem taller. She bore him apparently no grudge.

' It shall not be for long,' she said, nodding her head like a woman of forty. She turned on her toes, pirouetting. ' I'll be a woman very shortly.'

But for the moment, as the consequence of this indiscretion following many others, she was in great danger of the one and only thing that she dreaded—of being sent to Miss Macdonald's Academy at Carlisle.

She had heard something of this school from Margaret and Hetty Worcester of Threlkeld, who attended this place for a time, and she did not like what she had heard. They rose at six winter and summer, ate a piece of bread and then had an hour's schooling. Then there was ' Punishment Hour,' wherein, it seemed, the Misses Macdonald indulged in an orgy of whipping, six stripes of the rod for a small offence, and a ' proper whipping ' meant that you fetched the rod, kissed it, and then, before the school, were stripped, ' mounted ' on another girl's back and beaten till the blood came. Hetty Worcester gave an admirably detailed description of it. Judith knew well that before she suffered that ignominy there would be a murder done. Not that Hetty thought much of it, for in her home everyone was whipped, the maids and the grooms, the dairy girls and even the tutor. Nevertheless, Judith knew that a week in Miss Macdonald's Academy and she would be a vagrant loose upon the world, and for that she was not yet ready.

While her fate hung thus in the balance the relations between Sarah and Judith developed uncomfortably. Judith bore her sister-in-law no grudge, she knew herself to be a difficult illdisciplined child, but the difference between their ages was so great and their characters were so ill-suited that, as Judith grew, trouble was bound to come.

Sarah in her heart cared for nothing at the last resort but David. She loved her children, but David was her adoration. She could not endure to see him vexed, even for a moment, and now she realised that Judith was constantly vexing him. He understood her as little as did Sarah. He was too kindly-natured to exercise his authority sufficiently. Judith was for ever escaping him. After all she was not his child, but his half-sister. There were many times when she seemed to him her mother come alive again.

He was a great deal at home now; went to Liverpool very seldom. He trusted the Metcalfes for everything, and soon Will would be in Liverpool. Therefore he was much at Uldale. He loved every stick and stone of it, and he could be seen, his body casting a vast shadow, pottering over the sunny lawn, looking up as a great hurrying cloud flung its shadow over the Fell, examining the horses, watching the maids working in the dairy, going over accounts with Mr. Matcham the agent, or simply leaning on the stone wall and gazing across the white road at the low sprawling shape of Skiddaw.

So, being at home thus, he was always tumbling upon Judith and Francis; Judith, her ringlets flying, riding Barnabas or sliding down the banister of the great staircase, or, in another mood altogether, standing motionless, watching, waiting—what was the child about and why did she look so damnably like her mother?

Or Francis, twenty-eight years of age now, always so slim, elegant, apart, silent—and doing nothing. Twenty-eight and doing nothing! For you could not call reading Cowley or Milton or Shakespeare anything, or roaming aimlessly the countryside (and greeting no one as he went) anything. His father would catch him writing in a book and when he would ask him of it he would close the book and, secretly, deep in himself, would answer the question by saying:

' Nothing, sir.'

Once David lost his temper, and only once.

' I'll not keep you here idling.'

An hour later Francis came down the stairs
in his riding-coat, Andrew the boy carrying his
valise. He was going away, and David knew that
it was for ever. David found then how deeply
he loved him. Afterwards he pleaded with him:
why were they drifting so far apart? Could they
not open their hearts to one another? And Francis
answered: 'Oh, sir, would to God I could!
Something silences me. I will work, father, anywhere you place me . . . in your Keswick office
. . . I will do all I can.'

What an echo of ghosts was here! For had
not David's father once, in the dead years, said
the same? For a moment Francis Herries the
Elder stood there, that same ironical twist to his
lip that his grandson had.

So Francis went to work in the Keswick office,
and he was useless. All he cared for was to read
poetry and philosophy. Poetry and philosophy!
So, loving one another deeply, they drifted
farther and farther apart.

But Judith was a greater mystery for poor
David, who would sit back in his arm-chair before
the fire, his legs spread, his great bulk at ease, but
his honest friendly face twisted with perplexity.

He wanted to do what was right by the child.
She was his own father's daughter; but the truth
was that neither he nor Sarah felt that she had anything to do with him at all. At one moment she
was a child of her proper age, at another almost
a woman, ordering the men and maids in the
place as though she commanded it. She had a
good heart, he could tell that, but when she

couldn't get her own way she was a devil, not raging nor crying but her sharp, pale, little face cold and savage under her red hair. And he sometimes thought that she hated Sarah. They didn't forbid Gauntry's to her any more. What was the use? She would simply go there, and one day, if they were not careful, she would never come back, and what a scandal that would be! Besides, there was no harm in little Gauntry, and he loved the child like his own daughter.

So David went over all his perplexities, feeling perhaps, as Sarah did, that changes were coming. When things were too difficult for him he would ride over to Worcester's or Osmaston's and play cards all night or get drunk and be carried up to bed.

Meanwhile he clung to Sarah, his wife, ever more deeply. She was his real friend, had always been. He loved Deborah, his daughter, but in his heart found her a little dull; he was a little afraid of Will, who always knew better than he himself did; Francis, whom he loved best of his children, was a mystery. So he stayed with Sarah and was only truly happy when she was by.

In March of the new year they decided that Judith should pay a visit to the Sunwoods in Cockermouth. Maybe they would manage her. Judith was very happy to go. She was very happy to go, but never dreamt before going that when she was there she would be so happy to stay.

She had visited a number of times at the little house, but had had no notion that it would suit

her so perfectly to live in it.   It was the very
size that she liked, small, compact, comfortable.
Everything in it went on under her very nose; she
could have her fingers in every pie, in Deborah's
cooking and preserving, sewing and cleaning, in
the dealings with the pig, in all the little affairs of
the town, the gossip, the tea-parties, the expeditions on fine days, the cosy conferences round the
fire on wet ones.   In five minutes she had Mr.
Sunwood entirely under her control, he would
read his sermons to her, she would listen to his
accounts of his Quadrille parties, enjoy by proxy
the first piece of roasted swan that he had tasted
at a grand party at the Castle, and even advise
him as to the right time to take a good dose of
rhubarb.

But the element that made this visit so enchanting was her quite unexpected friendship with
Deborah. Deborah was nearly sixty-six years of age
and Judith only fourteen, yet the difference in their
ages seemed to make no division between them
at all.   Judith was hungering for affection with
all the ardour and excitement of her temperament.
She was separated from Francis and also (although
of this she tried to prevent herself thinking) from
Georges, the French boy.   So she was ready, in
any case, to throw herself upon Deborah and
Reuben.   But she soon discovered that she had
never been brought into contact before with
anyone at all like this stout, soft-eyed, soft-voiced,
gentle-hearted woman.   The people whom she
had hitherto known had not (save for Reuben, and
he had been two years away) been gentle-hearted

—not Gauntry, nor Sarah, nor Will, nor even Francis.

The first thing that drew her to Deborah was that Deborah let her do anything that she wished, and the second thing was that Deborah told her so much that was new and exciting about her father.

They sat together beside the fire, Deborah sewing and Judith leaning forward, her chin cupped in her hands, and Deborah recovered for the child her own childhood. This gave Deborah herself a surprising happiness and pleasure. No one in her own family had asked her questions about those days. It was her husband's belief that he had rescued her from some wild sort of savagery and the less said about it the better, and her sons had never shown any curiosity. But this strange child with her ardent, eager, impetuous spirit brought her father back to her as though he were with them in the room. *Her* father! *Their* father! And at the thought that they had, both of them, she nearing the end of her life, the child only beginning hers, the same father, a bond of affection was formed and remained. She soon discovered that she herself loved to recall that long-ago time, the wild Borrowdale valley, so cut-off and remote, the old house rocking to every wind, the death of her mother and her own fear at being left alone with her father, although she loved him. Her devotion to her brother David, such a wonderful boy, the strongest boy and man in the valley (different, she was forced to confess, from the stout, rather lazy monarch of Uldale),

the old witch, Mrs. Wilson, who lived with
them and was drowned in the Derwent by the
villagers, her own lonely thoughts, love of natural
things, shyness—then the ball in Keswick and
the little clergyman coming to sit beside her and
make love to her, her father's strange marriage
to Judith's mother, and then the unhappiness of
that odd woman, her flight, her father's loneliness
and madness and search, and always the tumble-
down house and the isolated valley behind and
through it all.

She let Judith ask as many questions as she
wished and answered all that she asked.   Judith
recovered the personalities of her father and
mother as she never had done before.   They
became alive to her.   She saw Francis, her father,
the scar marring his face, tumbling the villagers
down the stairs after the wedding.   She saw
Mirabell, her mother (it was part of her oddness
that she should have a man's name), breaking her
heart because the man she had loved had been
murdered under her eyes in Carlisle.   She saw
Francis, her father, setting out in search of her,
wandering over England looking for her, at last
capturing her again, and then the two of them
dying together in that lonely house.

Something grew in her as these two ghosts
were drawn to her side.   *Her* ghosts and only
hers.   No one alive in the world had the right
to both of them as she had.   She was never,
after this, to lose the fancy that all her life long
there were three of them moving about together
through the world.

E 2

' Oh, if but I had been there,' she cried.   ' I
could have made them so happy ! '

And Deborah, in her turn, recovering thus her
young days, felt her heart warm in her for her
dear, lost father.   Only she and David in all the
world thought of him any more—and now this
child.   How could she but love her?

Judith was easy enough to love in such a case.
She asked nothing better than to love and be
loved in return: it was only when someone was
an enemy, or she thought was an enemy, that her
fierce hostility flamed out.   Even then she could
be generous and large-hearted.   She wished Will
no evil because he had betrayed her about the
evening on the Lake.   She could not be mean nor
spiteful about little things.

They were both large-hearted, she and Deborah.

Then something more drew them together.
Judith discovered that Deborah was very unhappy.   For eight months she had had no word
from her son Humphrey.   Mr. Sunwood pooh-
poohed the whole business.   The boy would
write when he had leisure; the Post was a very
uncertain affair; he, himself, would soon make a
journey to London and see the boy.

But none of this could comfort Deborah.
They had heard nothing, either, from his master.
The last news had been a year ago.   At first the
boy had written frequently.   He had been last
home a year and a half ago and had been well and
merry, but, even at that, she had fancied that he
had said too little about his work.   It was all

his pleasure, his visits to Vauxhall, how he had
seen the good King and Queen, been to a picnic
in Twickenham, travelled down the river with the
Pomfret Herries, and so on, and so on. But of his
work very little. And that was a year and a half ago.

As Judith listened to all this her impatience
leapt into flame. But why didn't someone go to
London? Why didn't Mr. Sunwood or Reuben?
She would go herself. Why should not she and
Deborah go? It was a shame to leave it in this
uncertainty. . . . She jumped up and ran about
the room, tossing her red ringlets in the air.

But Deborah, smiling, shook her head. It
wasn't so easy to go to London, a very long journey. Mr. Sunwood felt no alarm, why should
she? Reuben had his work at Mr. Stele's the
solicitor's. Oh, it was all right. She was sure
that all was well. Humphrey was such a good
boy. Any day there would be a letter. And she
would look across the room at the little bottle-
green window and shake her head, and her eyes
would swim in tears.

So Judith went to Reuben. Reuben was
changed by his two years in France, more remote.
He was tidier, but alas! little cleaner. It was not
at that time important that you should be clean,
and Judith was peculiar in wishing for cleanliness.
When Mr. Sunwood came in from attending to the
pig he was not very clean and would sit down to
his dinner without thinking of it. But Reuben's
linen, his small-clothes, oh, they wanted a deal
of attention! His hair was not brushed and fell
untidily about his shoulders. His shoes were

often caked with mud. In his attic there was always a close stuffy smell, terrible untidiness, his bed where he used to lie, his hands behind his head, looking up at the attic roof, staring and thinking, sadly tumbled. Judith never came into the room but she longed to set about it with a scrubbing brush and a pail of water. But she loved him none the less, his fat loose body, his kindly, large, wondering eyes. He was generous and soft-hearted like his mother, but so often like something that had lost its way. He moved at times as though he were blind. He was a dreamer like Francis, but what an incongruous comparison he made with that slim, elegant, severe figure! And he had told her once that if he were afraid of anyone in the world it was of Francis.

Then one evening she came up to his attic and found him lying on his bed, his coat off, his shoes off, his stockings half-way down his legs, and he was talking to himself, while a long drunken candle guttered on a chair beside the bed.

She herself held a candle. She stood for a moment listening to him:

'Oh, Lord! Oh, Lord!' he was saying, 'I am a sinner. I have no courage in my heart. I am a poor wretch. Oh, damnation! Damnation! I long in my heart after women and go the way I should not! Oh, Lord, Lord! . . .'

She stopped this peroration by crying in a very solemn voice: 'I am the Devil and have come for your soul, O Reuben!' and he, hearing her, jumped from the bed and stood blinking at her like an owl.

'Do you truly long after women?' she asked
him a little later, when they were both sitting
on the bed close together, the candles throwing
great shadowy shapes on the wall.

'Yes, I do.'

'Well, then, you should marry.' She nodded
her head, swinging her little legs and wishing
for the thousand-thousandth time that they were
longer.

'No woman would have me.'

'No, not while you are so untidy in your
clothes. Why don't you brush your hair and
have a new ribbon for it? And there is a hole in
your stocking.'

'I hate Mr. Stele and his office,' he said
suddenly. 'I was so happy the day I saw the
bear. That was a sign, and I did not follow it.'

'They sent you away to France,' she said, 'because of the bear.'

'Yes.' He nodded his head. 'And one day in
the road beyond Tours—a hot glaring day—I saw
Jesus Christ standing there. He stood right in
my path; the sun was shining in His hair. He
looked at me so kindly and said: "Reuben,
feed my Lambs." And I have done nothing,
nothing.'

'For how long did He stay there?' she asked.
She had a very practical mind and no sense of
religion at all. She could not help that. She
wished to have it, but she found it very difficult to
believe in anything that she did not see.

Reuben pulled up his stockings. He was
always aware that she disliked his untidiness.

She herself looked so neat now in her little orange hoop and brown shoes.

'He did not stay long,' Reuben sighed. 'It was the second time. He came to me once at St. Bees.' He put his hand timidly and took one of hers.

'Judith,' he said. 'You are so brave. Show me what to do.'

'Yes, I will show you,' she answered, coming close to him. 'Go to London and see Humphrey.' She felt him tremble.

'I dream about Humphrey,' he answered her, 'every night. I know that he is in great trouble. One of us always knows when the other is in trouble. I know that mother also is grieving, but I am afraid to go to London. I am afraid of everything. I would not know how to behave in London nor what to do. They would all laugh at me, and I cannot bear to be mocked. London is so vast, and there is so much noise there. . . .' He broke off, plucking with his fingers at his clothes.

'No, but you must go,' she answered. 'I will never speak to you again if you do not. It is your duty to your mother. Do you love me, Reuben?'

'Of course.'

'Then go to London or I will never see you again.'

She began then eagerly to speak of what he would do and just where he should go. She seemed to know everything about London, although she had never been there. His cheeks

kindled, there was light in his eyes.   Yes, he
would go.   He would ride into Kendal and take
the coach there.   He would speak to his father.
. . . And then he shrank back.   But all the
people, so many strangers, the lighted streets, he
would be lost.

'Well, if you do not go, I am finished with
you.'

She stood in the middle of the floor, her head
up, scorning him.   And at that moment some of
her strength entered into him, entered into him
never to leave him again.   He went to the window
and looked out across the darkness.   Then he
looked back into the lighted room and saw her
standing there.   He cried out in a kind of frenzy:

'I'll go!   I'll go!   I'll go!'

How often in other places, in later times, he
remembered that scene!   And then she danced
about the room like a mad thing, caught his hands
and made him dance too.   She ended by tying his
hair with a new ribbon and finding another pair
of stockings for him.   She hoped that he would
find a woman in London to make him happy, and
she also hoped that he would not, because she
wanted to have him all to herself.

Howbeit, events moved faster than Reuben.
Before he could speak to either his mother or his
father something very terrible occurred.

Years and years afterwards Judith would remember that March afternoon and its sudden
storm sweeping her off her feet into an adventure
that would have its consequences for all her life.

She and Deborah had been shopping in the

town. It was market-day and proper March, with a sky that was here pale green, there pale blue, while little busy clouds like torn sheets of grey paper flew and scattered under cross tugs of wind. The sky was swept with streams of light that flooded out into glory, throwing sheets of pale silver colour on to field and wood.

It was one of those days when everyone in the little town was conscious of the near neighbourhood both of the mountains and the sea. The wind had begun with little anticipatory gusts, as though it were trying its forces to see whether they were strong and sound, then, as everything went well, it increased its power, began to find pride in its strength, and soon, doubtless, would be bellowing with vainglory. You could see in your mind's eye Ennerdale, that was not far away, ruffling into little flakes of foam, its waters chocolate-coloured, while the sky above the hills was all busy with its traffic, sending clouds hither and thither, flashing light now on, now off, under order of the March gale. All the hills, black and grim, gathered like conspirators close about the waters. On the other side of the town there was the sea, the wind tugging at St. Bees Head, and all the shipping tossing maliciously in Whitehaven Bay.

The booths of the market were creaking and cracking, cloths blowing about, the pedlar forced to cover his wares, ropes straining, doors rattling, everyone clinging to their hats and wigs.

Then with a shriek of whistling fun the wind and the rain came, driving straight up the street, sweeping the trestles and boards away, carrying the whole town with it as though it would toss it into Ennerdale.

Judith and Deborah went scurrying home, hats, wigs, pieces of cloth, fragments of wood, dogs, cats, shrill voices, laughter, all hurrying through the air, it seemed, with them.

Safe in the little house again, panting for breath, wet, blown, laughing, they looked about them, while the rain rattled on the windows crossly because they had escaped it.   They stared under wet eyelashes about them, and the first thing that Judith saw was a letter, lying innocently on the table: it was addressed ' Miss Judith Herries.'

She snapped it up.

' A letter? ' asked Deborah.

' Yes.'

' From Uldale, I warrant.'

' Yes,' said Judith.   It was not a lie because she had not yet looked at it.   It lay warm in her wet hand.   She thought it would be from Sarah, summoning her home.   Who had left it there? Had David perhaps ridden over, or Francis?   It might be that they would spend the night.   But she wouldn't go back to Uldale.   She was too happy where she was.   She wouldn't go back until she had seen Reuben safely away to London. . . . She had got thus far.   She was climbing the stair to her room.   She saw what it was.   It was from Georges Paris.   He was in Cockermouth.   He asked her to meet him in the parlour of the ' Grey-hound,' five o'clock that evening.   He would wait until six.

Her first thought was of his impertinence, then

that he should have the spunk to leave the letter
at her very door where anyone might read it, then
that she wouldn't go, nothing should induce her,
then that she would greatly like to see him again
just to tell him what she thought of him, then
that she would take Reuben with her (it would be
so amusing to see Georges' face of disappointment), then that this would be the first time of
seeing him since the evening on the Lake, then
that she would not go but would send a letter by
Reuben, then that perhaps she *would* go just to see
what he was like now. . . .

By this time she was in her room and laughing at the thought of an adventure. For it *was*
an adventure. Georges was always an adventure.
She would wear her orange hoop. . . . But in
this weather with the streets swimming in water!
She heard the maid calling her to dinner. Three
o'clock. There would be plenty of time before
five. . . .

By the end of the meal she was uneasy. She
was always uneasy when she thought of Georges.
She determined that she would take Reuben with
her.

Behind the parlour there was a little room with
nothing much in it but a large yellow globe, a
powder-stand and a shaving-table. It could
be turned into a guest-room at a crisis. She
pulled Reuben in there after her. The little
windows looked out on to a narrow crooked path
that ran through fields to a shaggy wood, on fine
days a pleasant prospect, but this afternoon you
could see nothing but the storm that swung in

sheets of rain across the scene, the drops on the panes in the windows rattling like little pellets from a shot-gun. From a side-door of this room there was a short passage and another door opening on to the field.

When she had Reuben in the room with her, she suddenly thought—no, after all, she would not tell him. Why should she not go alone? Georges could not harm her. They would be in a public place. She was not afraid to smack his face again if need be. She was not afraid of Georges nor of anyone. So when she saw Reuben, still wiping his last draught of ale from his mouth and smiling in that uncertain way that he had when he was not sure how she was going to use him next, she burst out laughing.

' Reuben——' she said, and then she paused.

' Yes,' he said obediently.

' It's raining.'

' Yes,' he said again, wondering.

' But I am going out into it.'

He said nothing.

' And no one is to know. I shall go by this door.'

He looked at her in perplexity. She could always do as she liked with him, but after all she was but a child. Her small stature and something innocent in her wide-open eager eyes always made her younger than her age, just as the resolved dominating lines about her mouth made her older. Nevertheless, she was young to be going out into the town alone, and in this weather, and what could she be going for but to see a man?

At the thought his heart beat thickly, his stout cheeks coloured, he plucked at his coat.

'You shall not go alone,' he said. 'I shall accompany you.'

'Oh no, you will not!' she answered laughing. 'You shall stay here and keep them quiet. If they ask where I am you shall say I am busy working—and so I shall be.'

'Busied at what?'

She stood on her toes, pulled his head down, and kissed him.

'Never you mind. I am your aunt.'

'I shall accompany you,' he said firmly.

She looked at him. Would it be better perhaps, after all, that he should? She was *not* safe with Master Georges. She remembered a moment in the boat when, in an instant, at a touch of his hand, she had been warned.

Many visits to Stone Ends had acquainted her with life. Children were not children for long in those days. *Should* she take Reuben with her? And it would tease Georges so that he should be there. And Reuben was so strong, so safe, so devoted. A sudden impulse of great affection for him, one of those impulses that were often all through her life to rise in her, straight, unalloyed, from her heart, influenced her now. She put her hand on his arm.

As she did so they both heard, quite clearly through the slashing and angry rain, a rap on the window. Her hand tightened on his arm and they turned. The rap came again, urgent, imperative. They stared and at first could see

nothing.   In any case there would have been only
a pale, fading light, but now with the storm all was
darkness.   Reuben hurried to the window and
pressing his face against the pane stared out.   He
could see a shadowy form.

' There is someone there,' he whispered to
Judith, then, hurrying through the little passage,
opened the outer door.   The wind almost blew
the door to, but holding it firmly he looked
out.

' Who's there? ' he called softly.

A moment later his fingers were grasped by a
cold hand, he had been drawn back into the
passage, a figure soaking with wet was pressed
close to him, and his brother Humphrey's voice
was in his ear, nay, at his very heart.

' Reuben . . . for God's sake—no sound. . . .'

' Humphrey! '

' Yes.   Is there anyone there? '

' Only Judith.'

But Judith, hearing the whispering voices, had
come into the passage.   Humphrey, pushing past
them, had peered into the little room, seen that
there was no one there, hastened to the door and
bolted it, then turned to them both:

' No one must know.   Not father nor mother.
No one.   Get me something to eat.   Oh, God, I
am so weary! '

He sank into the only chair in the room, murmuring again, ' Food.   Food, and secretly.'

Reuben didn't question.   It was, as it always
was with his brother, as though this were part of
himself, soaked with rain, fugitive, in some frantic

plight, hiding from the world. He moved as though hurrying to save himself, undid the bolt and was gone.

Judith bolted the door again. Her heart was moved at once to eager pity and a desire to help. When she had last seen Humphrey he had been so young, so handsome, so self-confident, so sure of himself and his ability to manage any situation in life; now another man was there, utterly weary, exhausted, his head back, the water dripping from the capes of his coat, his hair long and matted, his face pale, haggard, and his eyes that had been so gay and happy now restless, hunted, brimming with despair.

He seemed to her to be years older, older than himself, older than Reuben, and he seemed, beyond that, to be mysterious, a man from some world that she had never before realised, a man who should, by right, speak to her in a strange language.

He wasted no time, did not ask her why she was there, did not consider her except as an agent of assistance for him.

' I have been an age outside. I could not see clearly who was in the room. I had to risk something. Thank God, it was Reuben! '

His words came in gasps. His hands moved ceaselessly.

' I've had no food for two days. I have tramped from Kendal. . . .'

She was intensely practical, as she always was in a crisis. ' You must take off your coat. It is dripping. You must have dry things.'

He got up from the chair and she helped him to take off the shabby soiled riding-coat. His body was trembling; he was wet through to the skin. The thing that moved her most was that his eyes were never still, searching the globe, the powder-stand, the dull green portrait of some old Sunwood ancestor, the dark bulging window against whose panes the rain, falling now gently, pressed.

She did not stop to ask him why he was there, nor what catastrophe had plunged him into this disaster, but his fear infected her. She was not in the least afraid, but she listened, as he did, to any outside sound. She realised that whatever else happened his mother must not now see him. She did not know the reason, but she understood that he was bitterly ashamed to see his mother, that, beyond any other possible disaster, that was the one he dreaded.

Her sense of this made him still more mysterious to her and touched her heart yet more deeply. Towards anyone pursued she was always to be sympathetic, although there was some true Herries in her that placed her also on the side of justice. In herself she was to be always both pursued and pursuer.

Reuben scratched on the door and came in, not clumsy nor shy any more, but swift, silent, efficient. He was acting for the stronger part of himself. He closed the door very gently behind him, bolted it softly. He had half a cold mutton-pie, bread, cheese, ale.

Humphrey drew to the little table, devoured

the food frantically.   He seemed just then like an animal, his ears pricked, his eyes everywhere, his hand curved close about the meat.

'Mother is with father,' Reuben whispered, 'listening to his sermon.'

'He is wet to the skin,' Judith answered. 'He must change everything.'

Reuben went out again.   She stood by the door, letting him finish his food.   Life was like this.   She had seen it already countless times. Mrs. Osmaston's maid had stolen stockings, had fled and been caught in Keswick, jailed there; a pedlar had murdered a woman in Keswick for a shilling, he had been chased by a crowd of men and boys to Threlkeld and stoned there to death. . . .

'Yes,' said Humphrey, speaking quite clearly out of the half-light illumined only by one blowing candle.   'And now I must get to the coast.   I am so weary.   God, if I could sleep for twelve hours.'

'What is it?' she asked.   'What has happened?'

His face, pale, drawn, the hair shaggy on his forehead, looked up at her.   She felt as though he were her child.

'I killed a man in London.   Over cards.'

'Have you any money?' she asked him.

'Nothing—now.   It is all gone.'

She came over to him and stroked his hair back from his forehead.   With a gesture of infinite weariness he leaned his head, wet with rain as it was, back against her childish breast.

'I shall sleep,' he murmured.   'How soft your hand is!'

Reuben knocked; she unbolted the door. He came in with clothes on his arm. At once, as though a desperate hurry were now his accustomed state, Humphrey jumped up and stripped. Judith helped him. This was no time for maidenly modesty, and she had seen many a man naked before.

When he was finished he sat there holding Reuben's hand in his. The three of them began a quick whispered conversation. On the one thing he was determined, that his father and mother shouldn't know. Nothing would shake him in that. He told them very little of what had happened. Things had been going badly for a long while. Some fierce love-affair he had had with Nancy Bone: Pomfret had forbidden him the house. After that Judith had a picture of some dark underground London, gutters running with water, sudden flares of light, gambling, little rooms in crooked inns, life by the river, curious interludes of some great man like Mr. Fox or Mr. Burke, a struggle up again to larger rooms, then down again, fights in that same gutter, swinging shop-signs, a narrow street crowded with carriages, a woman looking from a window, a fight, some fat man with a wound in his breast, and all the while it seemed to be rain and fog. . . . She was to have this queer picture of London for years until the reality gave her another one.

But the one thing that stood out clearly was that he must escape from England. Some port . . . Whitehaven. . . . It was then that she had her idea. With a flash of inspiration she thought of

Georges Paris.   She had long known that young
Georges with other friends of Gauntry's had dealings with some sort of traffic on the Cumberland
coast.   Some kind of smuggling perhaps.   She
had been too much of a child for them to take her
into any kind of confidence, but her last time at
Stone Ends there had been a Captain Barnett,
a thin green-faced man like a nettle, who had
praised young Georges for his enterprise in some
Whitehaven or St. Bees expedition.

She did not doubt but that that was what
brought Georges into Cockermouth this afternoon.   He would do anything for her;   he
should help to get Humphrey out of the country.
Once again in a moment she took the situation
into her hands.   She acknowledged without a
tremor to Reuben that it had been this Georges
Paris whom she had been going to meet.   Was
he to be trusted?   Of course, he was to be trusted.
He was her friend.   She had known him for
years.   He would do anything that she told him.
They followed her.   What else?   Something had
to be done at once.   They must not stay in this
house.   There was no other plan.

Only Reuben said one thing that often afterwards she was to remember: ' If he does this for
you, are you under some obligation to him? '

Feverishly eager to be off, as she always was
when she had a plan, she tossed her head.   She
did not even answer, but almost pushed them both
in front of her, through the little passage and out
of the door.

That brief journey from the house to the

'Greyhound' was the most exciting thing that had yet happened in her life. She was in charge of the expedition; the men followed meekly. That sense of power, the strongest sense in her, drove her like a charm. Without her, Humphrey, all of them, would have been lost. Now she would direct the affair like God Himself. The rain had ceased; the little cobbled streets were gloomy and deserted. They left Humphrey in the shadow of the yard of the inn and went quickly up the wooden staircase to the parlour. No one was about. In the parlour, a small panelled room, a little sea-coal fire was smoking and two candles guttering. Someone came forward. It was Georges, almost hidden in the capes of his riding-coat. She saw at once that he was angry because she was not alone. She felt herself forty years of age at least as she took his hand, introduced Reuben. He had never seen her so beautiful. Indeed he had never thought her beautiful, only strange, unusual, in some antagonistic way appealing to his senses. Now, in the half-lit smoky room, in all her colour, her small hat with a feather, her hair, her little face ivory-coloured and in expression mischievous, kindly, proud, all together, she seemed to him for the first time a woman. He put his riding-whip on the table, clasped his hands behind him. He longed to kiss her. Who was this big clumsy oaf of a fellow with her?

Very quickly Judith explained, keeping him greatly at a distance, very lofty, commanding rather than requesting.

And she saw, a moment later, that he found
an opportunity in all this. It was the first real
request that she had ever made of him. He
asked no questions about Humphrey. A relation of hers in distress . . . He must get to sea
swiftly and quietly . . . Had he a friend? . . .
Was there a boat? . . .

By chance he had a friend. He paused and
looked at her oddly.

'If I do this for you——?' he broke off.
They had both, concerned in their own personal
drama, quite forgotten Reuben.

He forced her eyes. She would not be brow-
beaten by him, so stared proudly back at him, at
his dark eyes, black hair, thin, proud, restless face.

She said nothing. He, as though satisfied,
nodded his head.

'Where is the gentleman?'

They passed to the staircase. As they went
down she whispered to Reuben: 'Have you
any money?' He nodded his head: 'I had
thought of that.'

They found Humphrey in a panic of nervous
anxiety. How strange it was to Judith to see
what circumstances could do to a man! He
had been so easy, gay-hearted, confident. Her
whole being ached for him. She would have
liked to go with him, share his adventure wherever
it might be, see that he was not cold, hungry,
lonely. As they hurried down a dark side-
street, stumbling over gutters, holes in the road,
refuse, she put out a hand and caught his. For
a moment she held it, hot, dry, quivering. . . .

They stopped before a door below the pavement; a little flight of steps went down to it. Georges went ahead of them and knocked. While they waited, a man, swinging a lantern, passed them. He did not look at them, but Judith felt as though it were the whole town staring. Then the door opened a little way, a head peered out, some words were exchanged. They all went in. The place was a large cellar, a lantern hanging from a hook, some farming implements in corners, a pile of hay, and, seated on an overturned barrel, a man of an enormous corpulency. His coat was open at the neck to allow room for his three chins. His cheeks were purple above a yellow beard and his nose had been slightly flattened on one side in some fight, but his eyes were large, clear and merry. His hand was a roll of beef and his thighs so huge that it was a wonder any breeches could ever contain them. He rose to receive them, and standing, his legs wide, he was like a vast amiable monster at home in its cavern. He smelt of oil, fish and whisky, but it was plain that he admired Judith immediately, hanging over her with a merry possessive look as though at any moment he would pick her up and slip her into his deep coat-pocket.

It was clear also that he knew young Georges Paris very well and understood immediately what was wanted. He never looked at Humphrey, who had slipped into the shadow, nor addressed a word to him. His name, it seemed, was Captain Wix. His voice was deep, rolling, and had the same kindliness as his eyes. Those eyes scarcely left Judith. Straddling on his legs he kept looking at her while Georges quickly whispered. He nodded his head several times, took a great chequered handkerchief from his pocket and blew a blast on his nose.

'It will be good enough for charges,' he rumbled to Georges.

Judith, who was adoring this adventure, the dark close cellar, the straw, the swinging lantern, and the sense of having arranged the whole affair, spoke then and said that they had money with them.

'Keep it, lady,' growled Captain Wix. ''Tis no matter.' He became gallant and was inexpressibly comical. 'I have a ship,' he informed her, 'like a daisy. An you come for a trip in her you shall be as safe and trim as in your mama's parlour. I'll have the cabin done up special for you.' He bent towards her, beamed at her with the greatest kindliness: 'Now what do you say to a piece of fine lace? A present from a friend who knows the coast of France like his own hand. What do you say now to a little trip?'

But here Georges intervened. He drew the gigantic creature aside, speaking to him very seriously rather as a king speaks to his subject. The matter, it seemed, was concluded. They were to leave Humphrey in Captain Wix's charge.

Reuben went to his brother. When he rejoined them there were tears on his cheeks. Judith then kissed Humphrey.

He spoke with sudden desperation. ' My mother mustn't know. . . . I will beat them yet. . . .' Then fiercely, catching her hand: ' There's no God. . . . Naught but injustice, no mercy. . . . I shall find my way yet.'

Captain Wix kissed her hand.

When she went up the little steps again with Georges she felt suddenly helpless, very tired, six years old, and so cross with him that she did not thank him, only said ' Good night ' quickly and walked up the street.

Georges, before he went downstairs again, looked after her, smiling. He felt very important, very wise, a ruler of men.

DEATH OF DAVID

The July heat bathed the little town in its ardour, but breezes, stealing from the Lake, from the higher woods, from Skiddaw forest and Blencathra shallows, carried the scent of flowers everywhere. The town slept. Some sheep wandered dreamily down Main Street, the dust blew in little spirals between the hedges toward Crosthwaite Church, the post-chaise waited outside the 'Royal Oak,' two young men, with nothing whatever to do, lounged up against the wall of Mr. Crosthwaite's Museum. A little way up the street a small group waited for the arrival of the Good Intent post-coach from Kendal. It was five minutes past four of the afternoon, and nine out of every ten of Keswick's citizens were still discussing their good liquor and digesting the day's dinner.

Francis Herries came down the sunny street, riding from Penrith. He was, in this July of 1789, twenty-nine years of age and as handsome a bachelor as the counties of Cumberland and Westmorland contained. He was, however, as awe-inspiring as handsome. No young lady anywhere, not even the pretty daughters of Mrs. Herring of Bassenthwaite, reputed the most daring young women in the whole of the North of Eng-

land, had ever attempted a flirtation. He was
immensely clever, they said, was for ever reading.
It was true in any case that he had no close friend
—now, riding down Main Street, he seemed alone
with his own shadow.

He may have been half asleep, may have been
deeply lost in some speculation, when he felt a
hand laid on his bridle. He looked down and
saw little Mr. Summerson the Surgeon, short,
stout, very gay in a purple coat, looking up at him.

'Have you heard the news, Mr. Herries?' he
asked.

'No,' answered Francis. 'What news?'

'The Bastille in Paris has fallen.'

Francis straightened himself. 'The Bastille——?'

'Yes, sir. Fallen to the Revolutionaries. I
know no more. I had it from Mr. Jobling, who
has just ridden in from Kendal. The news is
quite certain.'

Francis smiled. 'Thank God, sir. Thank
God. This means a new world.'

Little Mr. Summerson looked as though he
were not so sure, but Francis did not wait to
hear what he had to say. His heart triumphant,
as though it were by his own agency that this
great deed had been brought about, he passed
along the road to Bassenthwaite now like a
conqueror.

The Bastille fallen! The Bastille fallen! It
must be true. Summerson had been certain of it,
and if it were indeed so, then all the secret wishes
of his heart were gratified. Secret indeed, for

F

there had been no one in whom he could con-
fide. The secret history of his mind had been born
with him perhaps; he had always, to his own
thinking, been different from all the others, but
its first real mature food had been the treatise of
Helvétius on 'Mind' and 'The System of Nature'
of Holbach. Holbach's work especially had
seemed to explain the whole of life to him; its
system of metaphysics had exactly suited his
speculative untrusting nature, his instinctive
cynicism, and its eloquent ardour for physical
science had become his ardour also.

Voltaire's scepticism and good sense, the
absence of all fanaticism and mysticism had carried
him yet farther. He delighted in his clear ideas,
his ironical banter, and his determination to make
the world a wiser place so that ultimately it might
become a better one.

His education had then been completed by
the influence of Rousseau. The *Contrat Social*
seemed to him the Bible of the new world. This
sentence of Rousseau's, 'The moment the Government usurps the sovereignty, the social compact is
broken, and all the simple citizens regaining by
right their natural liberty are forced, but not
morally obliged, to obey,' became his gospel.

Had his youth been spent in a larger and more
varied society much of the effects of these doctrines might have been worn away in contact with
older and more experienced minds. But there
had been few with whom he could discuss anything. His nature was in any case reserved;
some inherent shyness forbade confidences; his

father had views utterly divorced from these; his father was conservative absolutely in religion, politics, agriculture, everything. Will's mind was quite selfish and practical, his mother was not interested in ideas. Judith was only a child.

He made no friends among the gentlemen of the neighbourhood; there were very few gentlemen to make friends with. He knew that had any of them seen into his mind they would have regarded him as traitor to everything in which they believed.

At Penrith there was a certain Mr. Frederick Moore, an elderly man, a retired Army officer, who thought as he did, but went much farther. Mr. Moore was, indeed, a fanatic, and in that displeased the reasonableness of Francis' mind, a strange man, solitary, embittered, intensely dogmatic. But he lent Francis books and pamphlets, and they had many talks together.

Rousseau was Mr. Moore's god, and he very quickly became Francis' also. They would neither of them see that Rousseau himself recoiled from many of his own opinions and conclusions. Passionately they out-Rousseaued Rousseau. They disregarded such sentences as: 'If there were a people of gods, they would govern themselves as a democracy. So perfect a form of government is not suited for men' and 'The best and most natural order is, that the wise should govern the multitude, provided that one is sure that they govern it for the profit of the multitude and not for their own.'

But Francis, although he thought continually about Government, had only the simplest notions

of the matter. Had he been a fanatic like Mr.
Moore he would have gone farther, but just as his
nature held him back from extravagance so also
it prevented inspiration. He felt that he was
fortunate that he was born to be a citizen of a new
world, but in cruel fact he was neither the child
of the old world of reason nor of the new world of
feeling. He had the misfortune to sympathise
deeply with the unhappiness of a vast multitude
of human beings, who were only now growing
conscious of their rights, but he was an aristocrat
by instinct although a democrat by reason—and
was too reserved, too lonely, too self-suspicious
to venture into any kind of demonstrative action.

He had followed, as well as news-sheets,
pamphlets, books, and Mr. Moore permitted him,
every movement in France—the doctrines of the
Economists, who contended for the inviolability
of private property, the shameful consequences of
the stupid despotism of Louis XV., the iniquitous
taxes, the brutalities of the upper class, the exemp-
tion of the nobles from taxation, Necker's poor
attempts at reform in 1780, the monstrous sale of
offices, the increase of tyrannies that followed
Turgot's fall, Necker's failure in 1781, and after
that the growing incompetence of everybody and
everything: the luxury and ostentation of the
Court of Versailles, the unpopularity of the Queen,
the amiable weakness of the King, the Assembly of
Notables by Calonne, their dissolution—until at
last he had felt that he was almost a personal witness of the most dramatic of the recent events, the
coup d'État of May of last year, the convoking of the

States-General by Brienne, the strength of the Third Estate, the gradually rising tide of disorder, the flood of revolutionary pamphlets, the bad harvest of '88, and the fearful winter that succeeded it, the freezing of the Seine, the prominence of Mirabeau and Sieyès, of Barnave and Dupont and Bailly, the Oath of the Tennis Court on June 20.

The Oath of the Tennis Court was the last absolute news that he had had until to-day; for the last month he had been living in a ferment of expectation and feverish excitement. He could not understand that the men and women around him took so slight an interest in these events. If they spoke of outside affairs at all it was, at the most, in a late day, of the King's sickness, the possibility of a Regency, some new gambling scandal of Charles Fox or the eccentricities of Mr. Pitt. The small business of the countryside contented them all.

So he had moved, poor Francis, as though he carried a bomb in his breast. There were times when he thought that he would cross to France and take part in the great crisis that was developing there, but his self-distrust, his natural love of England and his home (cherished passionately in his heart, unguessed at by anyone save possibly Judith) held him where he was.

This great news to-day released him! The world was free! The strongholds of all the tyrants had fallen! This was to be a symbol that would stand to all the world for the new freedom!

These may seem empty phrases enough set down upon paper, but in Francis' heart they were

flames and torches.   In very truth as he rode now
under the July sun beside Bassenthwaite, he felt
as though every constriction, every doubt of himself, every shyness and stupid caution were now
released.

France would lead the way for all the world.
He saw Louis with his fat good-natured face,
Marie Antoinette with her gay beauty, seated
grandly on their thrones by the will of their people.
He could almost hear, beside these quiet sparkling
waters, the wild cheers, the frantic shouts of joy
that must fill the Paris streets.   And now all men
would hear them, and would be ashamed of their
lethargy, their shameful lazy injustice and indifference.

He was indeed ashamed of himself.   As he
rode along he felt born again; his life had been
most selfish.   It should be so no longer.   At any
cost to himself he would take part now in forward-
ing the new justice and uprightness that was come
into the world.   As he rode he could have sung
his happiness aloud.

He did not doubt but that his father, with all
other men, would see the grandeur of this event.
His father was a just man, although an obstinate.
He loved his father dearly (who could help but
love him?), although he was shy of him.   How
this new era in France would bring them together,
would bring all men together and would lead to
a new era in England also!   As he turned up the
lane to Fell House his eyes were dim with tears of
joy.

And at once, so characteristically, he was

checked by contact with his fellow human-beings. A maid, coming from the dairy, carrying buckets, Will's tutor seated reading on the lawn, his mother stepping down the staircase as he entered the house, all these drove him at once to silence.

His stout good-humoured sister met him at the turn of the stairs. He had nothing at all in common with Deborah. She had all the good-natured domesticity of a thoroughly contented Herries. So absolutely satisfied was she with herself, her family, all the little circumstances of her surroundings, that in all her twenty-six years she might be said never to have suffered an ache or a pain, whether of body or of soul. She was handsome in a large-boned Herries fashion, was never irritable, never excited, never curious about the nature of other people, always ready to do anything for anyone.

How ridiculous to say to her: 'Deb, the Bastille has fallen!' It would be to her exactly as though you had said: 'Deb, the cat has kittened!'

Having washed, brushed, changed his linen, he came downstairs again, walked into the garden and discovered Judith mocking the tutor. Mr. Langbridge was shortly leaving them. Will was now nineteen and did not need a tutor. Mr. Langbridge was long, gaunt, perpetually hungry, brilliantly founded in the classics (which was of no use at all to Will), hoping to be a clergyman, of a fanatically serious mind. He understood no sort of humour, and it delighted Judith to hold long conversations with him, asking him gravely

about his health, his studies and his home in
Dorset. For he detested the North, with its dark
clouds, its rain, the savagery of its people, its bare
strong hills. He was a perpetual exile. She
stood in front of him now, her hands behind her
back, her eyes twinkling, but her expression very
serious.

Francis, coming upon her, realised quite
suddenly that she was a woman. She was old for
her fifteen years in her self-possession, young in
her childish impulses. He knew that she adored
him, just as she had always done; it had been a
long faithful service on her part for which he had
made little return. There was something about
her small stature, pale face, and almost savage
unlikeness to the average Herries order that
frightened him, and yet he had long ago realised
that she was the only one in this family who ever
remotely understood him.

He realised it again now, for as she turned to
him he saw that she immediately recognised him
to be under the power of some very strong excitement. Mr. Langbridge pulled his long lanky body
together, rose, very solemnly bowed to Francis
and stalked away.

She looked at him, half roguishly, half with that
affection that she could never keep from her eyes
when she was with anyone of whom she was fond.

'Dear Francis,' she said, dancing about the
lawn on her very small feet, 'you have got a
secret. I can see that you have. And none of
the family is worthy of it.'

She turned towards the house and they both

saw David, followed by Will, coming towards
them.   The whole scene, the rosy brick house
with its chimneys and gables and pigeon-loft,
the dairy and stables behind it, the moor that was
like a heaving green curtain moved with the
intensity of the sun, the blue sky without cloud,
the lawn so brilliant in colour that it hurt the eye,
the trimmed hedge, the Gothic temple, the sprawling shadow of Skiddaw, the figures in their gay
clothes, David in purple, Judith in green, Francis
in silver, this moment of heat and colour would
be remembered by all of them for ever.

David, carrying a riding-whip, moved heavily.

'Well, Francis,' he said, 'what news in
Penrith?'

'Great news, sir,' Francis answered.

'What! has Pitt a fresh plan for the franch-
ise?' David asked with good-humoured scorn.
All Francis' notions seemed to him those of a
child.   But it was a half-sneer on Will's superior
face that drove Francis on.

'No, sir,' he answered.   'The Bastille has
fallen to the People in Paris.'

They all stayed, rigid, transfixed.   David
said at last:

'Where did you have the news?'

'Mr. Summerson told me in Keswick.   He
had it quite surely from Kendal.'

David raised his head and looked at everything, the buildings, the walls, the garden, as
though assuring himself that they were all still
there, safe and secure.   Then he said slowly: 'If
this is true it is terrible news.'

'I think,' Francis broke out, 'that it is the grandest news the world has ever had.'

Judith, who cared nothing for the fall of the Bastille in comparison with the immediate dangers of the scene, saw David's broad hand tremble about his riding-whip.

'Then you advocate rebellion,' he said slowly, 'murder, revolution. . . .'

'Yes,' Francis answered hotly, 'if these things are to bring justice back into the world.'

'Justice!' David's whole body trembled. 'Justice for the dirtiest mob of cut-throats that ever fouled a country. Justice for ingratitude, for disloyalty to a worthy King . . .' He half turned towards the house, then, his face swollen, it seemed, with anger, he came nearer to Francis. 'You are not my son if you find this foul rebellion glorious.'

'Then I am not your son,' Francis cried. 'I have long suspected it. For years I have watched your blindness to the way the world was going. For how much longer do you think a million men will suffer at the orders of one, and of one weaker, more selfish, more tyrannous than they could ever be? Thank God, men are to be free at last, free from tyrants, free. . . .'

'From tyrants like myself?' David cried, his anger now quite uncontrollable. 'A fine thing for a son. . . .'

'Take it as you will,' Francis answered, his words biting on the air. 'There is tyranny everywhere, here as well. . . .'

Some long accumulation of small persistent

differences, always unsettled, mingling with the heat of the July day and their deep love, always checked, always running into perverse courses, combined to produce in them both a furious anger.

'By God, for less than that . . .' David cried.

'If your pride is hit,' Francis answered, 'it is by your own will. It is time that your eyes were opened.'

'I'll have no rebellion here,' David shouted. 'No rebellion here. Your gutter-friends may for the moment have their way in Paris. I am yet master in this house.'

'No more!' Francis cried. 'Many masters are falling.'

David raised his riding - whip and struck Francis on the cheek. They were silent then, and the cooing of the pigeons ran like water through the air, the only sound. Francis bent his head. David dropped the whip.

'Francis,' he began in a thick low guttural, turned a step and fell, like a log, to the grass. He was carried in. It was a stroke. Mr. Summerson the Surgeon was fetched from Keswick. David was bled. Consciousness returned to him, but he could not speak, and his left side was paralysed.

Francis went about the place with his head up, his features cold and severe, and agony in his heart. No one, except Judith, knew that he felt anything. His mother would not speak to him. That moment, running out on to the sunlit lawn at the sound of a cry, had changed Sarah Herries from a cheerful normal woman of her world into

a creature of one impulse and one impulse only.
Nothing now was alive for her in the world save
David, her house meant nothing to her, her
children meant nothing to her, she meant nothing
at all to herself.   She would not speak to Francis.
She looked through him as though he were not
there.   She regarded none of them very in-
tently.   They were shadows to her.   She seemed
in one half-hour to become of a thinner, straighter
figure; the colour left her cheeks, her eyes held
a steely radiance, her voice a hard metallic ring.
Something masculine that had been perhaps always
in her personality came out now very queerly,
save when she was in David's room; there she
was soft, gentle, maternal.   David had always
been her child; now her love for him burnt with
twice the earlier intensity because he was altogether dependent on her.   He lay there, a huge
bulk, beneath the clothes, only his eyes moving.

Judith watched all this with an acute perception, but in the first weeks her thoughts were all
for Francis.   She longed to tell him what she
felt; at last she had her opportunity.

One evening, a cold wet August night drawing
on, at the turn of the stairs on the upper passage
beyond her room, she ran into him in the half
dusk.   His hands held her in the first shock of
their contact.   She could feel how they trembled.
And at once, deeply moved by that trembling,
she began, not weighing her words nor thinking
of anything but that she must comfort him:

'Don't go.   Don't go.   I have been wanting
to speak to you for these weeks past.   I know

that you have always a little mocked at my affection for you—indeed I have mocked at it a little myself—but it gives me a right, after all these years, to tell you that I am the only one in all this house who understands you. Don't grieve about him, Francis dear. It was not your fault, indeed, indeed it was not. You had to say what you believed that day, and I know that he admired you for that behind his anger. The stroke must have come in any case—Mr. Summerson says so. And his heart, too, has been weak these years past. So soon as he is better he will send for you and tell you that he loves you——'

'My mother will not allow me to see him,' Francis interrupted her.

'She cannot prevent you if he wishes it. As soon as he can speak he will ask for you. I know that now he is sorry and is grieving for you.'

His voice shook. 'No, I must go and never return. I have been a curse to this place. Only I can't go without a word from him. I am waiting only for that——'

'Yes. He is better to-day. Mr. Summerson thinks that in a week or so he will be able to speak a little. The paralysis is only on one side.'

They were in the dark together; neither could clearly see the face of the other, but Judith knew that Francis was crying. Half a child, she was greatly inclined to cry, but she only stood close to him, her hand on his arm.

'You have always been the best friend I have had here,' he said at last.

'And I will be,' she answered.

Afterwards she could not but reflect that she was always better with anyone who was in distress or desired her help.   She liked above everything to feel that she was needed, and yet she had a strong contempt for any weak-willed person who was for ever relying on others.   What she liked was to assist or direct those who normally were quite able to assist themselves.   What she would have done now to have helped Sarah had Sarah but invited her!   But Sarah needed no one's help, and least of all Judith's.   She allowed Deborah to do things for her, and very remarkably Deborah began to develop under this crisis, but Judith she completely disregarded.

This, again, was why Judith had no sort of contact with Will.   Will relied on no one but himself and took no one into his confidences.   He gave the impression that he was watching every move, every phase of the situation, weighing it all that he might turn it in the best way to his advantage.

The house very quickly suited itself to the new circumstances.   Everything turned now around the room where David was lying.   He had been always greatly popular with his servants; unlike many men of his time he had always seen them as separate individuals, was constantly inquiring about their families and circumstances, had a jolly, natural, healthy interest in all of them.   He had been the one of the family for whom they cared, who stabilised their loyalty.   His simple animal health and boyish pleasure in little things had always pleased them.   He had been an indulgent

but not a foolish master; they were very sorry now
for his misfortune.

David rose with infinite slowness and caution
from a sea of darkness.   Wearily he pushed aside
fold after fold of heavy clinging cloth that hindered
his sight.   Then, tired out, he lay back to resist
no longer, and saw swaying above his head a gold
rose set in a green cloud.   He heard, a little after,
from an infinite distance a voice speaking to him.
Someone touched him, and he sank instantly back
into the dark sea whose waters, smooth like oil,
lapped him round and lay upon his eyes and mouth.
Aeons later he saw again the gold rose on the green
ground, and once again heard the voice, and knew
that it was Sarah his wife who was speaking to him.

He raised very slowly his right hand and
touched the chill flesh of his breast beneath his
shirt.   Then he would raise his other hand, but
he had no other hand.   His perceptions moved
with infinite slowness.   After, as it seemed to
him, a lifetime of patient watching he realised that
the gold rose was fixed in its place above his head,
and that there were other gold roses.   Then, after
another infinity of time, he knew that these gold
roses belonged to the tester of the bed in which
he was lying.

His wife's voice was often in his ear.   She
made a noise like a bird, like a mouse; the noise
came and went and came again.   He was immensely susceptible to light.   A wave of light
would slowly sway in front of him, would be withdrawn and then return with greater intensity.

There came a time when he wished to speak

about this light, but he could not. He could speak no more than a dead man. But he was not dead at all. An urgent pulsing life began to beat within him. This life was connected with nothing that he saw or heard. It had a wild riotous time of its own within him: it laughed, it sang, it wept, it sighed, but it was imprisoned, and it longed to get out. His eyes began to take everything in— the room with the purple curtains, the piece of green tapestry, the crooked legs of the chairs, Sarah, Deborah, the maid, once and again Will. He saw and recognised them all, but he could not speak, nor had they anything to do with the wild life inside him. When he knew this he pitied himself and them; tears, helpless tears, rolled down his cheeks, and his wife wiped them away.

He knew now all the things that they did to him—the things the surgeon did, how it was when they turned him in bed (he was a very heavy man and it was not easy), and when they put a new shirt on him, washed his face. Sarah kissed him, and he touched her cheek with his right hand.

He was never by himself. At night candles were burning, and Sarah sat there, sometimes sewing, sometimes reading a book, her eyes continually going to meet his eyes. He was ashamed at some of the things she must do for him, but she was his wife, he had lain with her in his arms; he would lie there staring at the gold roses and think of how often he had buried his hands in her hair.

He was glad that she was always there, because he was lost in that wild turbulent life

within himself, and she was all that there was
to call him back.   Then one night he was far
away.   He was standing on a deserted beach
beside a lonely sea.   Someone was beside him, a
man, and quite suddenly this man raised a stick
to strike him.   He seized this stick, broke it in
half and flung it into the sea.   After that this man
never left him.   He was very tall, thin of face,
and he had a scar that ran from eye to lip.   The
man stood beside him on a green lawn, and this
time it was he who had the whip; he raised his
hand and struck; as he did so the man changed.
He was young, and after he was struck he bent his
head.

David lay there for a long while striving to
reconcile these two figures.   They were the same
and were not the same.   At one time they seemed
to be himself; then they were separate, then
together again.

One grey ghostly morning he awoke and knew
everything.   The man who had wished to strike
him was his father; the man whom he had struck
was his son.   He knew everything.   He had been
ill, and was lying now in his bed, while beyond the
window a bird sang, and near him the candles were
almost burnt out, and Sarah sat in a high chair, her
head forward, asleep.   He passed then, struggling
all alone, hours of terrible agony.   His left side
was dead; there was no feeling nor motion in it.
His heart bled for his son.   He could think of
nothing but that.   He must see his son.   He
must see his son.   He raised his right arm: he
tried to shout and to shout again.   No sound

would come. His father and his son. He must ask them both to forgive him; until he had done that there was no peace for him.

At last the door opened; someone came in, carrying something. Sarah woke and came to the bedside. His eyes besought her. He raised his hand. His agony of mind was terrible, for he could not reach her. How strange that he could not reach her! After all these years together, their love, their intercourse, their friendship. She was the mother of his children, and he could not reach her. Strange low mutterings came from his mouth. His eyes implored her, begged of her.

The light, grey, webbed, hung like a film about the room, and in this film she moved. At length she bent down to kiss him, and as she did so, his eyes were so near to hers that she must have seen the agony in them. He made sounds that seemed to him explicit prayers, but she could understand nothing.

It was three hours later that the surgeon understood sufficiently to send for a paper. Then David wrote in a large sprawling hand the word 'Francis.' Francis came. They were alone in the room together, and David spoke the first word since his illness. 'Forgive.' His voice was strange, cracked, with a slur in it, but Francis understood and knelt beside the bed. David, with his trembling right hand, stroked his hair.

After that he could not bear to have Francis out of the room, so that the two of them, Francis and Sarah, were there together. But Sarah would not speak to her son nor look at him if she could help

it.   David began then the slow business of seeing
that two and two make four.   There were some
things that he could not understand at all.   He
did not know why he had struck his son with a whip,
nor why he was sometimes there quite clearly in
the room with his wife beside him and at other
times he was in the little dark house in Borrowdale,
following his father, hearing his father's voice, and
behind the voice the wind rustling the tapestry,
and the noise of water falling down the rock.

He slept a great deal, and in his dreams he
climbed the rocks, ran across the springing turf
of the Fell, stood on the Pass with Sarah in his
arms, watching his enemy climb the road towards
him.

At times again he would be dreadfully unhappy.   Tears would roll down his cheeks; he
would wipe them feebly with his hand.   But why
he was so unhappy he could not tell.

But at these times an infinite pity for himself
overwhelmed him.   'Poor David.   Poor, poor
David.   Poor, poor David.'   Was there ever
anything so sad as poor David—and, from a great
distance away, he watched this poor David and
sympathised so deeply with his loneliness, his
helplessness, the injustice of his state.

After a time words came back to him.   He
could say 'Francis.   Sarah.   I don't want.
Good night.'   He mumbled them; his mouth
was twisted.

His brain conceived a new map of the world
for him.   There was the room where he lay.
Pieces of furniture became alive and personal to

him.   A china table, a tea-kettle stand, chairs with
faces.   He liked especially a ribband-back chair
covered with red morocco, a real friend of his,
that would smile and wave his leg at him.   The
tapestry on the wall, its subject Susanna and the
Elders, was also his friend.   He liked Susanna's
kindly breasts and her shining thighs.   He was
glad that he had not allowed Sarah to make the
house in the Gothic style, as she had once planned
to do, after Horace Walpole or some other London
absurdity.   He had an honest scorn for artists and
writers.   She had wanted a wallpaper printed
in perspective, windows with saints in painted
glass, and even arrows, long-bows and spears.

Poor Sarah!   What a good woman, how wonderful a wife she was to him!   He liked her to sit
beside the bed and be near to him.   He would smile
a crooked twisted smile and murmur her name.
Yes, all this was real enough.   Summerson with his
hour-glass, the basins and glasses, old Ballard the
man-servant with his handsome white wig, Will,
Judith, and, above all, Francis.   Deborah too,
good girl.   She had a genius for moving quietly,
big woman though she was: no hand so soft as
hers, and—best of all—she breathed good-humour.
He wanted no sad faces about him; in Sarah's
eyes he detected sometimes a look of terror, and
that he would not have because it made himself
afraid. . . .

Yes, all this was real enough.   But beyond the
room he could not be sure where he was.   The
landscape was the landscape of his young life,
and although in this room he was tied to the

heavy four-poster, once he was outside the room he could move where he wished. Every part of Borrowdale was open to him. All the old places: beloved Stonethwaite, with its tumbling stream, the springing turf of Stake Pass, the swinging birds above Honister, hundreds more; the wrestling bouts, the high room of old Peel's with its blazing fire and broad rafters, the taste of the dried salted beef and mutton, the oatmeal puddings, the bull-ring in Keswick, when on a grand day in the market-place you must sit on an adjoining roof to get a view, the shearing days with the chairing and the bell-ringing, Twelfth Night when the lighted holly tree was carried from inn to inn—all had departed from him so long, long ago, killed by the later modern times, but now he was back in them again, all his health and vigour were returned, he was the strongest man in all the valley, and every hill knew him, Glaramara smiled on him, Eagle Crag was his brother, Sprinkling Tarn his sister, Sea Fell his lover. . . .

He lay there, motionless, smiling, his blue eyes fixed on the gold rose. They thought that he was imprisoned there, a helpless hulk. Little they knew! He was free again, as he had not been for many a year.

His father now accompanied him everywhere. His father digging that intractable ground, riding with him to Ravenglass, sitting beside him at the old stone fireplace in Herries, his hand on his thigh, his father and Mirabell, his father and Deborah, his father who had been always closer to him than any other human being.

They wished to pull him back from this happiness, this freedom, this strength of body, and cold running air of the fells, smell of the bracken, sound never stilled of running water. The sheep moved, the sun glistening on their fleecy sides, the shepherd whistled to his dog, the clouds rushed out and covered the sun that yet escaped them, mocking them and flashing a shield of light upon the distant brow. . . .

'Hold on to me, father. They are dragging me back. I will catch your arm. They shall not separate us. . . .'

It was time for him to be washed, to be turned in his bed. The smell of the sick-room was there, the chair with the red morocco, Susanna with her breasts, Sarah's grave face and that look of terror in the eyes. Only Francis and Judith knew his father. That child with her pale face and red hair, hair like Mirabell's. Poor Mirabell . . . but no, she was not to be pitied, for she loved his father at the last. . . .

His mouth crookedly formed the word 'Judith.' She came to the bedside, not frightened like Sarah, smiling, standing on her toes to be level with the bed. He took her hand in his. It lay there warm and soft.

'Judith.' That was the last word that he spoke.

For he was swung away in a great torrent of light. He flew on the air, kicking his limbs free, his head up, his hair tugged at by the wind. Away and away, over Borrowdale and Stonethwaite, over Sea Fell and the Langdales, over

Waswater, black like ebony. . . . What freedom, what happiness!

He shouted; 'Oh, hoi! Oh, hoi! Oh, hoi!'
He came swinging down until the turf sprang
beneath his feet. He was leader in an immortal
chase. 'Oh, hoi! Oh, hoi! Away! Away!'
The scent of the bracken and the falling leaf, the
touch of the stone of the little running walls!
He had caught a cloud and swung into the
dazzling sun. Old Herries was at his side, the
moulded shoulders of the Tops were beneath his
hand, the ruffled water of the Lakes spun to the
swirl of his great strength.

'Follow! Follow! Away, away!'

His father and he, masters of the air, friends
of every hill, laughing with every twist of tarn
and river, raced towards the sun. . . .

Watching the bed, they saw his body lie
motionless: the eyes stared.

Sarah's scream brought Deborah running into
the room.

QUARREL AND FLIGHT

JUDITH awoke to a sudden consciousness of distress. She had been very happily asleep curled up in the corner of the settee with the green Chinese dragons. These dragons had pursued her very pleasantly in her dream, large amiable creatures with green scales; from their bodies flakes detached themselves (as they ambled along) and lay like green pennies on the hot dry sand.

It was so hot, this sandy country, that she woke with a start to find the warm spring sun shining in through the window on to her face. She looked about her, bewildered, on to the Sheffield-plated candlesticks and the blue and white china in the corner cupboard. With the final release from her dream she pushed a large, fat, beery, and most affectionate dragon away from her and sat up, listening. What she heard was Sarah, in the room across the hall, talking to herself.

Sarah was not talking to herself, she was talking to David. Judith knew exactly how it was; Sarah was walking quietly up and down the room and was begging David to return, was telling David that she could not endure life without him, was asking David how he could have left her.

These outbursts were becoming rarer with Sarah, but they were still constant enough to fill the house with uneasiness. She had been for years the happiest, most normal of women. One man's death had changed her from that into this suffering remote figure, who was battling, who had been battling for months, to recover her security. Soon she would be armoured again safely against life, but the old Sarah was dead, vanished for ever, and happiness was, for the time, gone from that house.

It was part of Judith's character that she had no patience at all with nerves or hysteria. It was a period when women enjoyed and fostered all the artificialities that might give them an important place in a world designed entirely for men. ' Vapours ' were the order of the day for the majority of God's females. If they could not rouse attention by one manœuvre they would rouse it by another.

Judith had never had the ' vapours ' nor would she ever have them. Nevertheless, she was near sixteen, and had the understanding, in many things, of a grown woman. Her education in life had been, thanks to Tom Gauntry and his friends, early and thorough. She realised that this was no nonsense nor affectation on Sarah's part. David's death had simply taken away from her all the ground on which for years she had been standing. She was fighting to regain her sure footing; she would regain it. Meanwhile she would allow no one to help her.

Now, as Judith listened to that murmuring

voice, she longed to go and help her. She knew, if she did go, the kind of treatment that she would receive. The only person in the world who could assist her now crossed the hall and went in to her. Deborah's soft comforting voice could be heard. A little later the two women passed out into the garden together.

It was one of Judith's deepest chagrins that in all this crisis she had been of no use at all. It was Deborah, of all people, who had saved the situation, stout dull Deborah who was suddenly the principal figure in the house, was kind and tactful with everyone, managed the servants, entertained the local gentry, kept the accounts, prevented Will (when at home) and Francis from open quarrel and understood Judith, it seemed, better than anyone had ever done. This had been that quiet woman's chance and she had seized it.

In the year that followed David's death the situation had demanded exactly such a woman as Deborah. She had always seemed slow, unobservant, uninterested; now it was apparent that she observed much and was never uninterested. She was greatly assisted by limiting her horizon to her own affairs. That France was in revolution, that her mother was in hysteria, these were not her business. She had loved her father as well, possibly, as any of them, but her father was dead, life must go on, the cows must be milked, intercourse with neighbours resumed. She quietly assumed direction of the house.

Had Will been there her domination might not have so quickly succeeded, but Will was in Liverpool, forming new contracts with Mr. Metcalfe. Francis also was away for days at a time. The house became the abode of the three women, and had it not been for Deborah, catastrophe would have rent it from attic to cellar. For Sarah, in the strange unnatural world that she now inhabited, had a fierce and unresting grudge against Judith. Judith's name had been the last word on David's lips, it was into Judith's eyes that David had looked before he turned his head on the pillow and passed. Judith was to Sarah still the strange unaccountable child that she had been ten years ago. At that time a girl of sixteen was often a mature woman, but Judith was for Sarah still a rebellious intriguing child, born of a gipsy. These things are mysteries, but beyond question there mingled now in Sarah's feelings about Judith something of her old uneasiness with Mirabell. Mirabell, Judith's mother, had never liked her, had indeed refused her kindliness and friendliness. Here was Mirabell born again.

But Judith was not Mirabell; she was fiercer, more readily hostile and resentful, far more dominating. She would not let Sarah hate her without making some return for it. It was not her fault that David had said her name before he died. If anyone wished to make a friend of her she was ready, but she was ready—oh, exceedingly ready—for anyone who wanted her as enemy.

Deborah disregarded all this. She was loving to Sarah, loving to Judith, loving to Francis, to whom even now, after these many months, his mother would not speak. Deborah took the situation and kept it, for the moment, safe. She could not keep it safe for long—it was charged with violence and danger—but what she could do she did. She indulged also her own fancy. Her fancy was, and had always been, for social amenities. She loved tea-drinkings, card-parties, evenings, when some neighbour ' put up ' four or six couples for a dance, expeditions of a moder-ate kind to some interesting site or historic building, and, above all, the chatter that circled around love-affairs and interesting engagements.

She had now entirely her own way in this, for Sarah was living altogether in her own world. When a decent interval had passed since David's death, neighbours came and went at Uldale with an easy frequency unknown for some time past. There were the Redlands of Thornthwaite, the Darlingtons from Whelpo, the Berrys of Roseley, the Carringtons of Forest Hall. It was suddenly a woman's world, and a world that seemed to Judith ridiculous in its obsession with trifles and incredible in its indifference to all outside events.

Deborah's principal friends were the Red-lands of Thornthwaite — Squire Redland, his stout pleasant wife, and the two handsome Miss Redlands — and the two Miss Berrys of Roseley. The elder Miss Berry was the great gossip of the district. She found everything amusing and left everything scandalous. The Miss Redlands, dark, big-boned, handsome women, were the flirts of the district. Their thought was only of men. Mrs. Redland had a genius for the arrangement, in other people's houses, of teas and suppers, parties at cards and little musical occasions.

Hours—and for Deborah most enchanting hours—would be spent in the discussion of social combinations and permutations. Mrs. Redland had the talent of making any house in which she happened to be visiting appear instantly as her own. She was massive, enjoyed bright colours and had a laugh like a trooper. She would arrange herself on the settee with the green dragons and instantly begin:

' But, my dear Miss Berry, we must not be too nice. Invite them all. Why not? They are a standing example of good humour and amiable intention, and I am sure Mr. Frank Fuller, although he may be the oddest creature in the world, is a gentleman, which cannot be said for Mr. Beaton, who has a store of underbred finery quite amazing.'

And little Miss Berry, with her sniff that suggested an eternal cold, would observe:

' Mr. Beaton is a coxcomb as everyone knows. But there is nothing to be ashamed of in being a coxcomb. What he enjoys the most is an evening of noisy entertainment, and for my part there are times when noisy entertainment is the thing. Ask Mr. Beaton by all means. That will make six couples exactly.'

'And this time,' Mrs. Redland would say, looking about her, ' we will make the dining-room of use by shifting the pianoforte. Last time there was not room for anyone to have real enjoyment.'

And Judith, listening, would wonder that Deborah had the patience to submit to these ladies who ordered the house as their own. But, indeed, she herself was not at all popular with them. They wondered why this sulky sarcastic girl was there. Was she ' out ' or was she not ' out '? Was it true that she was the love-child of some peasant courted in the ditch by that old ruffian of a Herries, who had died in a hut in Borrowdale?

David was only a year dead, and they were dancing in his house. But if Sarah made no objection to it had anyone else a right? Sarah's face was now a mask. She sat in her upstairs room, looking from her window. There were some days when no one came to the house at all, and then, so eerie was the silence, so threatening the atmosphere, that Judith understood why Deborah encouraged her sociabilities.

But with every week the inevitable crisis drew nearer. Francis was absent during all that summer. Will came and went, but in November, two days after Judith's sixteenth birthday, Francis returned—and life was permanently changed for them all for ever after.

His return was innocent and quiet enough. There was a storm of rain. Skiddaw was hid in purple shadow and over its head an ebony lake of cloud hung like a reflection. Beyond it, towards the sea, faint strips of blue sky showed that it was but a shower. The rain fell like thunder. Mrs. Redland and one of her daughters, the two Miss Berrys, Deborah and Judith sat in the parlour and waited for the rain to pass. A dance—arranged entirely by Mrs. Redland— was to take place in the following week at the Darlingtons'. The Darlingtons were lazy, but good-natured. They did not mind at all that Mrs. Redland should consider their house as hers so long as she did all the work for them. She was now in high feather. All the invitations had been successful. There were to be eight couples.

Mrs. Redland was pretending to be angry with Miss Berry's imitation of old Miss Clynes, whose teeth clicked in her head like castanets. 'For shame, Miss Berry, you shall not mimic her! And as to young Mr. Clynes, he is perfectly satisfied with his sheep and his farm.'

'Yes,' cried Miss Berry in an ecstasy of enjoyment at her own sense of fun and humour, 'and they say that coming in the dark into the house one day he took his aunt for one of his sheep that had been straying all the afternoon. "Shoo! Shoo! Shoo!" he cried. And you know how the good lady, when she is but half awake, baas for anyone who is close to her. . . . Well, well, I've no doubt but the young man will make a match of it with Jane Bastable. Poor thing. She missed the dancing-master last year, although she trudged into Keswick twice a week and oftener. . . . "Baa, baa!", and it wasn't until the young man lit a candle that he saw how things really were.'

Miss Berry's imitation was most lively, and they were all in a roar of laughter over it when the door burst open and Francis Herries, the capes of his riding-coat dripping with water, stood there, glared fiercely for a moment, and was gone.

Judith, who had been sitting by herself in the window watching the black cloud above Skiddaw shred into a dozen fish-tails, hating Mrs. Redland and Miss Berry, wondering what end all this unhappiness in the house could have, seeing him, sprang up and went out.

She saw him standing in the hall, that was dark with a kind of smoky reflection of the rain, as though bewildered. He looked at her, and without a word turned into the little room that had been always David's sanctum, a cold and cheerless little room now; here were cases with old books that David had never read, but his chair was there, a table with some of his papers and the prints of Derwentwater, Keswick, Borrowdale that he had dearly loved.

Judith followed Francis there. He had flung off his cloak and turned to her, his face working with anger and impatience.

'The house is changed,' he said bitterly. 'It is no home for either of us any more. . . . Where is my mother?'

'In her room. Oh, Francis, I am so glad that you have returned!'

'I have come back with a purpose. This cannot continue. My mother must speak to me for there are things that must be settled. This silence has lasted a year, and I will have no more of it.'

He looked so unhappy, so desolate, as he stood there that her heart ached for him, and the anger that had been piling up all these months at the treatment of both himself and her reached at that moment its crisis. She felt that the time had come for a settlement, and she was glad of it.

'Oh, Francis, isn't it the strangest thing! She loved you so. She was always so kind and so good. I have thought that it was a sickness that would pass, but you are right; it must be brought to an issue. . . .'

She recollected in that instant the scene in the cellar at Cockermouth, when Humphrey Sunwood, outcast and fugitive, had said farewell to her. Now she and Francis were outcast and fugitive: for no fault of theirs. She thought, standing in that room, of David's kindliness and benignity. Were his ghost with them now he must grieve at these circumstances. Oh, if he were only here, if he were only here!

'You do not know,' Francis went on rapidly, his voice trembling with emotion, 'that two weeks ago from Penrith I wrote to my mother. I said everything in that letter, of my love for my father, of my great unhappiness, that I was the cause of his sickness, that I would never, never, so long as I lived, forgive myself for that, but that I loved her too, that I loved her the more for my own fault, that I had borne patiently all these months her silence and that I had well deserved

G

it, but that this must have some limit because
I loved her, because I loved our home. . . .'
His voice broke. He turned, leaned his head on
his arms against the fireplace. For a little the
only sound in the room was the driving rain.
When he looked up and spoke again his voice
was stern and resolved.

'She did not answer my letter. I have waited
these two weeks. So now it must end. I must
know one way or another.'

'Yes, it must end,' Judith answered. 'For
all our sakes. . . .'

'I am going to her now.'

He left the room. She stood there, heard him
mount the stairs. In a little while the rain had
stopped. She heard the ladies come out, chatter,
laugh, depart. Deborah came past the open door,
but did not look in, and moved slowly into the
servants' part of the house. Still there was no
sound from upstairs. Then, quite sharply, Francis'
voice rang out, one word cutting the air like a
snapped stick. Judith, driven by an impulse that
was entirely beyond her governance, ran up the
stairs, stayed for a moment, then, her face harden-
ing into resolve, walked down the passage.

She pushed Sarah's door open and went in.
The room that Sarah had chosen for herself after
David's death was a small bare one. Over the
fireplace was a highly coloured, badly painted
picture of David. It had been done by some
travelling artist some ten years before, and showed
David complacent in full wig, a crimson coat and
flowered vest, red-cheeked, exceedingly amiable.

He grinned down at Sarah, his wife, who sat in a chair of crimson morocco; her hair, her face, grey, her dress black, a ghost of desperate anger and unhappiness. It was the unhappiness that Judith, standing in the doorway, first saw, then, a second later, she was engulfed in the anger as though she had to push up her head to avoid drowning in it. She closed the door.

'I will not speak either to him or to you!' Sarah cried, her hand trembling on her chair.

Francis, in entire command of himself, was by the window. He came forward.

'I am glad you have come, Judith,' he said. 'I would have a witness to this. After twelve months my mother has at length addressed me. . . .' He went close to her. His voice was tender and full of affection. 'I cried out at what you said, mother, but you have a right to say what you wish. You have told me to go and never to come back. I will go, but not before you have heard me.'

She did not look at him, but, half rising in her chair, spoke to Judith.

'I know that you are on his side,' she said, 'but that is no new thing. Ever since they brought you to this house as a baby you have made nothing but evil here. You have never belonged here, and it is quite fitting that you should take the part of the son who killed his father, leaving us all desolate.'

Even as her face was a mask hiding some real woman under it, so her voice was not her own. Judith had a queer perception of the old, rather tired, very quiet woman that Sarah would be after

this sickness was over, as unlike the woman that
she had once been as this present woman was unlike. She had a strange conviction, as though
someone spoke to her, that throughout this scene
she must keep that old tired woman in her mind,
so she would be kinder and more just.

No one could be more just or more decent
than Francis.

'Listen, mother,' he said. 'You *shall* attend
to me, for later when you look back you will be
glad that you heard me. You loved father.
God knows I did also. My love is something;
you cannot take it from me. But I could not deny
my nature, neither for you nor father nor anyone.
That nature has always put me by myself, alone.
I tell you now so that you may remember it after,
that I would change it, God knows how I would
change it, if I could. And is it not enough that
I must carry with me all my life the knowledge
that it was my insane obstinacy that killed father;
is not that some punishment for a man? Did he
not himself forgive me? Was he not the most
generous-hearted of men, and can we not now,
who both loved him, find some ground in his
generosity and make a peace? Mother——'

He approached her. She drew back violently,
almost pushing the chair over. Then she rose,
swept by him as though he were not there, and
went to the window.

'Very well,' she said, 'if you wish it you shall
hear me. I was a happy woman; you have made
me an unhappy. I had a home, a husband whom
I loved; I have nothing any more. You say it

was only your nature. Very well, I am an enemy of that nature. I was your mother. I am so no more. I do not know you. You may remain in this house if you will. You have the right. I believe the house is now yours. I will leave it if you wish. But understand, if you stay and I stay I do not know you. We remain as strangers.'

She beat her hand against her black dress, her fingers scraping the silk as though her control was almost exhausted. Yet her eyes, looking beyond them both into some mysterious distance, seemed to say: 'I am imprisoned here. These words are not mine. I do not know who is the speaker.'

Francis turned to Judith with a gesture as though of despair.

'No,' he said, 'I will not go like that. I am no stranger to you whatever I have done. You have borne me, suckled me. I have lain on your breast. Things cannot be ended. . . .'

'Listen then,' she interrupted quickly. 'I was once a girl, very unhappy. Your father came and rescued me, fought for me, married me. From the first moment that I saw him I worshipped him. I bore him three children. Now I have but two. Can you understand *that* then? That . . . That . . .'

But Judith, furious with what seemed to her the theatrical falseness of a woman hugging with a sort of selfish joy the self-inflicted tragedy, broke in:

'I have something to say in this. I am a woman, Sarah, as you are a woman. I am a child no longer. What right have you to fancy your grief is yours alone? For a year and more you have walked by yourself, hugging your wrongs, and you have hugged them so long that you are a comic figure, not real at all. We have all endured your nonsense long enough. Oh yes, you can order me to go. I know that I have no place here any more. I am going. But Francis is another matter. For a whole year, with absolute patience, he has endured your tantrums and bewailings. He is offering you now your last opportunity. Lose it, and when you come to your senses again you will whistle for him back and whistle to empty air. If I were your daughter I could show you something. You adore David, yes, but you allow the house to be filled with chattering women, and Mr. Finch comes with his fiddle from Keswick, and the pianoforte is moved to have room for another two couple, and——'

She paused for breath. She was in one of her rages, almost dancing on the Turkey carpet.

Sarah broke into her pause.

' No, you are right, Judith. You are no child of mine. Thank God for it. We, at least, have been strangers always. I see no kind of reason for you to intervene in this. Francis is the master here now. If he wishes you here I have no say. If you think me a comic figure, that also is of no importance. I did not ask you to come and wrangle here. I may be allowed, perhaps, another room where I may be by myself. When you have finished, if you wish to stay here, I will go.'

Then Francis turned to her, his face lit with a most noble generosity and kindness.

'Mother, listen. Why should you cut yourself off? You have been angry with me long enough. Were father here he would laugh at all of us. There are never so many in the world who are our own stock, our own flesh and blood, that we should separate ourselves from those we have. I have told you that all my life long I shall carry with me the burden of my father's death. But life is not over for that. Would my father wish us, because he is gone, to spoil our lives for him? He would be the last, the very last in the world, to tolerate it. He loved life, every piece of it, and he loved friendship and fellowship and the forgetting of injuries. He never grudged an injury his whole life long. You know that he did not. He has forgiven me, although I cannot forgive myself. Dear mother, in his name, forgive me too. Let me be your son again; come out and make this house real. I will be as true a son to you——'

She broke in: 'No. No. Never! You, both of you together, do you think I cannot see into your hearts? Do you think this treachery is a new thing to me? Make no mistake. I know you—and now, perhaps, you will allow me to find another room.'

Judith cried: 'You shall not go like that. Listen. You say that I have been false to you all my life long. I know that I haven't been good. I have always found discipline hard; not *your* discipline, Sarah. Any discipline. But I think, looking back, that you were always very kind to me. You never saw that I was always older than I should be, that I was disgraced by my own impulse to be for ever making new resolutions that I couldn't fulfil. There was no more evil in it than that. The greatest kindness you could ever show me was to let me have my own way that I might quickly discover how foolish my own way was. But there was no more wilfulness than that. I have always cared for you, Sarah, and now when I leave you, as I shall do this very night, I want you only to remember afterwards that I would tell you truths while I can and wish you well.

'And it is for that, because I wish you so well, that I beg you not to lose Francis. He is right. David's death is no reason for any separation. Keep him with you. His situation should secure your compassion, not your anger——'

Francis broke in: 'Judith, you are not to go.'

But Sarah was already at the door: 'Our worlds are separate, Francis,' she said, more quietly than she had hitherto spoken. 'You have thought me comic, Judith, in my selfishness. There you are doubtless right. Only I pray God that you may never know the unhappiness that I know. I did not think there could be such an unhappiness in the world and anyone live with it.'

She opened the door and went out.

Judith stared at the picture of the rubicund and complacent David.

'When he was alive,' she said, 'Sarah was quiet enough in her affections. She loved him, but not to any desperation. Francis, I hate women with their exaggeration and sentiment. There is something rotten here like a poison.'

He sighed wearily, stroking his forehead with his hand.

'No. There is a reality in it somewhere. I always knew that we were nothing to her compared with my father. He filled her whole vision, and now she is lost.'

'I will never be that for a man,' Judith answered sharply. 'Mark you that, Francis. Never, never, never!'

She went up to him, stood on tip-toe, kissed his forehead.

'Dear Francis, good night.'

He did not attempt to stop her, but stood there, lost in his own problem.

'Even he,' she thought, 'does not want me here.'

Indeed, when she reached her room, she felt more desolate than ever before in her life. She belonged now to exactly no one at all.

She must go at once, this very night, but she had no doubt at all as to what this going meant. She was going now once and for ever. This place was never again to be her home, or so at least she thought, being no witch to see in a glass her future.

She looked about her little room that had been the same ever since her babyhood. There was the oak-panelled arm-chair, the tallboy, the bed with the faded cherry-coloured hangings.

She got out of the drawer her childhood treasures: the fox's brush from Tom Gauntry, the book on cock-fighting, the china jar with the orange flowers, the two rag 'babies' and, best

G 2

loved of all, the Bible with the wood-cuts that
Reuben had given her.

She smiled when she looked at them, but smiled
quite without sentiment. Her childhood was
over, quite finally, for ever. And she was not
sorry. It had been a mischancy ill-fitting time.
Yes, that was one thing, but this sudden exile into
a vast uncanny world was quite another. Suppose
Tom Gauntry didn't want her? He was growing
old now and was uneasily under the domination
of his cook, Emma Furze. . . . Oh, well, if he
didn't want her, there were other places. She
could work; she wasn't afraid of anyone.

Then, quite unaccountably, she wanted to cry.
Indeed, indignantly, she brushed some tears from
her eyes. How she wished that Reuben was here!
He loved her, and only he in all the world. Poor
clumsy, fat-faced, kindly Reuben. She hadn't
seen him for six months. Deborah Sunwood,
too, was altered since Humphrey's troubles, not
the same bright tranquil woman as before, and
Reuben was so restless that he might be away
from Cockermouth any time.

Something had happened to them all, just as
it was happening to the larger, outside world,
breaking up all the old moulds, busily forming
new ones that would be, no doubt, very like the
old ones when they were settled.

But the thought of the change and of some
movement in the world very much larger than her
own little trivial affairs stirred her to action.
There were no tears any more. She would go to
Stone Ends to-night, and if they did not want her

there she would move on. What of London?
There were Herries there, who would help her.
After all she *was* a Herries, whatever they might
say. And at that she thought suddenly of
Georges Paris. She had seen him once and
heard from him twice since the adventure with
Humphrey in Cockermouth. The time she had
seen him had been at Stone Ends; they had not
been alone, had had few words, but there had been
something in a kind of mocking proprietary air
that he had had that had not altogether pleased her.
Nevertheless, he had grown extraordinarily handsome, slender, dark, with a sort of sword-like sharpness and brilliance. He shone among all those
befuddled squires and hunting men at Gauntry's
like a prince in disguise. Oh no, she was not
romantic about him. She knew his selfishness
and conceit and laziness well enough, but when he
was near to her, looked at her, touched her, he
stirred her blood, and she liked her blood to be
stirred. She liked anything, any risk, any danger,
rather than stagnation. That Georges Paris *was*
a danger she never disguised from herself for a
single moment.

Well, she must be moving. She wanted to
get away from the house, away from Sarah's sickness, from Francis' unhappiness, from Deborah's
chattering women, as quickly as might be.

She began to turn everything out, her possessions, clothes, hats and shoes, until they lay all
over the room. Then she decided to take nothing
with her. She would ride over on the cob to
Stone Ends and send for her things.

She smiled as she remembered the time when, years ago, after David's whipping her, she had climbed out of the window and ridden away.

It should not be so dramatic an exit this time.

But, in honest fact, when at last she walked out of the house she heard no sound, she met no one. It was as though she were going out of a dead house.

Out of a dead house into life.

MADAME PARIS

She went along on her horse—clop-clop, clop-clop—and with every ring of the road she was more surely leaving everything behind.

She saw nothing, thought of nothing outside herself. The separate strains fighting for order in her mind slowly, by a kind of reluctant agreement, as though they were obeying commands against their will, sulkily settled themselves.

' I have left everything behind me, and I am going out into nothing—or perhaps everything. Everyone with whom I have had to do has been showing Sensibility about something, even Will. But I wish to show Sensibility about nothing. I have only myself to consider. Even Francis does not need me. I am nearer to my dead father and mother than I am to anyone else. But there also I will not show Sensibility. They are dead and dead for always. I shall never see them or speak to them. I may have feeling in me that comes from them, but they cannot help me. They will not weep if I come to disaster. They will not answer if I call. Who is in my life? David is dead. Sarah has just thrown me out, Will and Francis think of themselves, Deborah is nothing, Deborah Sunwood has her husband and is grieving for Humphrey, Reuben thinks about God, Tom Gauntry to whom I am going is old and loves his cook, Georges—Georges wishes to kiss me when he sees me. Otherwise I am nothing to him. There is nobody at all who needs me. So far as I can tell, I have not a penny in the world, although Francis would, I suppose, give me some money if I asked him. I shall not ask him. I have no friends, no money, no work.

'I am sixteen years of age, with fine hair, a poor complexion, a nose too large, and ridiculously small stature. I have no especial intelligence, but I know when persons are speaking to me and I remember something of what they say. I have never been afraid of anybody or anything, but I have not as yet met anybody or anything to be afraid of.

'I have never had a lover, but am very ready to have one. I am curious about love. I expect that love itself is nothing very fine, but I could care for somebody very deeply. I would wish to have children that I might care for them. Is this Sensibility? I do not mind whether it be so or not.

'I know nothing as yet about the outside world, but I am extremely inquisitive concerning it, nor do I believe, like Mrs. Redland or Miss Berry or Deborah, that it spreads no farther than Kendal. I would be interested to see many countries, and the Revolution in France is a very exciting event. I would like to see Mr. Pitt and Mr. Fox and the King and Queen (although they do not appear to be interesting).

'I fancy that I have no very good Disposition.

I have a violent temper and dislike to be opposed
in anything, but when my affections are roused
there is nothing I will not do.   Is this Sensibility?
I fancy that it is.

'I am not a child any more but a woman.
When did this change come to me?   I think that
day in Cockermouth with Humphrey.   I had no
concern that day as to what happened.   I knew
that whatever happened I could master it.

'I love this part of England.   This is un-
doubtedly Sensibility, but I do not mind if it is.
I do not wish ever to live anywhere else, although
I wish to see other places.   I would like to marry
a man here, and have children here close to where
I was born. . . .

'Because of my father I am very proud to be
a Herries.   I would like to meet all the different
Herries, although I am sure that I should not wish
to be with most of them very long.   I find that
it is in my nature to hate people very much and to
love people very much, and also to laugh at everybody and also myself when I am very angry.

'I do not think that there is a God or that
Reuben saw Him on the road outside Tours.   If
there is one He is stupid, because He has so much
power and makes very little of it.   Neither
Francis nor Georges thinks there is a God.

'When I have some money I shall be very
good at managing it.   I am very good at managing anything if no one is in my way.   I am not
sorry for Sarah as I should be.   She likes to be
miserable, because she has never been miserable
before.   It is a new feeling for her.   I am sorry

for Francis, because he will remember all his life about David, which is a sad waste of time. I am resolved to make my life very amusing.'

With this she discovered that she was outside the gate of Stone Ends. The house was dead. A thin quarter moon hung like a wisp of pale rag over the end of a dirty silver-edged cloud, and, washed by ghostly mist, the house showed nothing human. She tied the horse to the gate and walked up the irregular stone path to the old worm-eaten door. At the sound of the banging knocker all the dogs in the house set up a fearful yelling and barking.

There was a pause, and Judith felt desperately cold and frightened. Suppose the old man didn't want her? He had been always good to her, but now he was aged and ailing, and under the thumb of his cook, people said. Suppose he didn't want her? And the wind, blowing sharply from Skiddaw, rustled all the plants in the weedy neglected garden in melancholy echo. One thing she noticed. The fountain was no longer playing. That had been Tom Gauntry's great pride, and his boast was that, however badly things went, he would always have enough water for the fountain. An owl hooted.

' You see,' said the owl, ' we haven't water enough any longer.'

There was a great unrasping of bolts from within, and then the door slowly opened. Old Tom Gauntry, holding a blowing candle, stood there, and a comical figure he looked. He was in a nightdress, black stockings and dingy slippers,

and he wore a very long nightcap with a red
worsted tip to it. Over his nightdress he had
flung an old riding-coat. He peered out, shivering, his old wrinkled face like an anxious monkey's.
When he saw who it was he gave a cry.

'Judy. By God, 'tis Judy!'

He looked so comical, with his nightcap, his
nose dripping, his unshaven chin, that she couldn't
help herself. She began to laugh, and then the
cold and her own most uncertain situation in some
strange way forcing her, once she had begun to
laugh she couldn't stop. She pushed past him,
to get in out of the cold, and then laughed and
laughed and laughed.

'Judy! For Almighty sake shut the damned
door. I've a cursed cold on me.'

'I must go and look after the horse first,' she
said. 'Where's Wull?'

He began calling 'Wull! Wull! You devil,
where are you? Wull! Wull!', and all the dogs
began to bark.

While she was standing there she could take
in the scene, which was certainly funny enough.
The old hall stank of dogs, drink, damp. Dogs
as usual were all about the place, scratching, sleeping, suddenly lifting up their heads and howling.
In the stone fireplace a great fire was roaring up
the chimney. In the ingle two old men, one in
an untidy wig, one bald-headed, were sitting.
On a table near them was a large bowl with a ladle
in it, and, her head resting on the table, slept
Emma Furze, a tall woman, snoring lustily.

'Hush!' said Judith. 'You'll wake her.'

'The last trump won't wake her,' cried Gauntry. He was rather drunken, but not badly so. 'Wull! Wull! Where the hell are you?'

Wull appeared, yawning, scratching his untidy head, his shirt hanging out over his breeches.

'Take Miss Judith's horse to the stable.' He put his old horny hand on her arm. 'Come to the fire and get warm, my pretty.'

She came to the fire and was introduced to the old men.

'This is my ancient friend, Mr. Jeremy Cards. He's a relation of yours. And this is Joe Twisset, he's a relation of none but the devil.' He kicked and cuffed the dogs, who, however, knew Judith and jumped about her, licking her hand. She went to the fire and stood in front of it roasting herself. She smiled on the two old men.

She was suddenly happy. She was at home here. The dogs, the smells, the old men, they were all right. She could manage it all very comfortably.

Gauntry was delighted to see her. She was, as he explained to the two old men, his especial pet, his pride, his joy. And although he was rather drunk he meant it all. The two old men were rather drunk too, but blinked their eyes in the firelight, rubbed their hands and looked happy.

'But why, my pretty, have you come so late? You should be abed, a child like you.' Sniff, sniff, sneeze, sneeze. 'I've a hell of a cold, a damnable hellish cold, and I'm not as young as I was.'

Judith explained that she had left Fell House

for ever. She said very little about it. She had taken off her hat, and her hair burnt in the firelight. The old men looked at it admiringly.

'Yoicks! Yoicks! Hurray for ever!' Gauntry was delighted. 'Didn't I know it was coming? "Wait a bit, you old devil," I said to myself. "She'll be coming to you. Just be patient a trifle." This is your cousin,' he added, pointing to the old man in the wig, 'and it's certain he's delighted to see you. Aren't you, Jeremy?' he shouted in the old man's ear. 'This is Judy Herries, daughter to Francis. She's your cousin, you old bastard!'

Old Jeremy Cards rose on his trembling legs and made a low bow.

'I knew your father, my dear, and a fine grand man he was. I was born in 1712, I was, and I'm seventy-eight years of age and got my full sight and everything, but my hearing's failing a trifle. My right ear's the one for you to speak into if you'll be so good. It was in 1763 I saw your father last in the town of Kendal, and I remember like yesterday. . . .'

'Well enough, well enough,' Gauntry broke in. 'You must drink something, my pretty, and then we'll find a bed for you. Before she wakes,' he added, suddenly dropping his voice. 'Better get settled before she wakes. Although I can manage her, mind you. She's afraid of me, she is, but she's a good soul when she's sober, and an old man like me can't be expecting young beauties at his time o' life. Down, Roger, get out of it, Trixie. . . . The dogs know you well

enough. So they should. This is your proper
home, my dear. Didn't I find you when you
were not a day born? By God and I did! Have
something to warm you, my pretty.'

She was glad enough of the hot strong drink.
Wull came in to say that the horse was stabled.
The old kitchen clock rivalled Mrs. Furze's
snores. All was cosy and comfortable.

Judith told the three old men about the scene
at Uldale, and they nodded their sympathy, but
old Jeremy Cards was galvanised to an extraordinary life by the very mention of the Herries
family. So David was dead! Aye, aye—a pity,
a pity! He'd known him as a fine young man
who could cross-buttock anyone in the country.
When would that be now? Aye, 1742, just
before the Jacobite troubles, he'd seen David
wrestle a man in Newlands, a great bullock of a
man he was too, but David was the prettiest lad
stripped—and there came before Judith's eyes a
David whom she had never known, young, fresh,
strong-limbed. Behind him were other Herries,
old Maria who had lived to be almost a hundred,
Pomfret and Jannice in Keswick, little Harcourt
at Ravenglass, and Jeremy's own people, his
father Humphrey, who had been born in 1687, and
his mother Charlotte, who loved dancing and was
a Beauty in the days of Queen Anne. The old
man went rambling on, putting his skinny finger
to his bare poll and wiping his eyes, that the smoke
made to run, with a large yellow handkerchief.
The logs fell to crimson ruin in the fire, and all the
dogs slept.

Old Jeremy sighed: ' All dead, buried, and the worms have eaten them. But the family goes on. I daresay there'll be Herries sitting in this same spot a hundred years from now.'

He seemed, Judith thought, a brave old man, because he was quite alone in the world and hadn't a penny. He stayed about in the district, in any house that would keep him. He didn't want much, a drink, a bite, and the fire to sit beside. As he told them, most of his days were now swallowed by dreaming. ' It's hard to tell what's a dream.' Yes, that was true. It was hard to tell.

It occurred to Gauntry that the girl might be hungry. She acknowledged that she was, and the old men all said that they were hungry as well, so the host scuttered off in his clop-clop slippers to find them some food. He returned with a mutton ham and a piece of a pie. Some of the dogs woke up and came sniffing round; then Emma Furze woke also. She raised her head slowly from the table, stretched her arms and yawned. Then she saw Judith and stared as though her eyes would burst from her.

' This is little Judy Herries, Emma,' said Tom Gauntry nervously.

She stood up. She was a big woman. She had large black eyes, a fine bosom, and she stood with her legs spread like a trooper.

The old man looked at her apprehensively.

' Oh, is it? ' she said.

Judith rose and held out her hand. But Mrs. Furze was uncertain as to whether she saw

two Judiths or three, so, to avoid any silly mistake,
she walked off a little unsteadily.

'She will be most agreeable,' said Gauntry,
'in the morning. She has a totally different
nature in the morning.'

The mutton ham was extremely good.

In the morning, indeed, Mrs. Furze shed tears
upon Judith's shoulder. She arrived in Judith's
room before Judith was awake and sat for a long
while moodily observing her. Judith, before
many weeks were out, was to know all Emma
Furze's history, was to know, too, that there was
much merit in her if also some melodrama.
Emma was to play an important part in Judith's
story. But for the moment Judith, after a most
healthy sleep, awoke to see this big woman
balanced on a small chair and tears rolling down
her nose. Tears, whether male or female, had
always an instant effect upon Judith's heart,
so now in a moment she was out of bed and,
in her thin shift, was kneeling on the bare
boards by Emma's side, imploring her to tell her
trouble.

What, now as ever, was not Emma's trouble!
At present it was difficult enough to disentangle.
Emma, as Judith soon heard, had been an actress,
and fine words were her pleasure. Words
poured from her like the water from Lodore after
heavy rains, and out of all the confusion nothing
was immediately to be gathered. There had
been a villain somewhere, 'a villain of unculti-
vated manners and corrupt heart'; there had

been 'a smiling innocent babe.' She had been 'tossed on the waves of a sea of sorrows' and so, 'washed up' on Tom Gauntry's 'shores,' had consented to be both his cook and his mistress.

Her tale was so lengthy, so incoherently mingled with tears, the boards of the floor were so hard, that Judith was compelled to rise, whereupon Emma also rose and, folding Judith to her bosom, embraced her very warmly, told her that she would 'worship her for ever' and, becoming instantly practical, asked her what she would have cooked, with what clothes she might supply her; stated that, in fact, she was her servant for life. She was very quickly of the utmost cheerfulness, laughing and plunging about the bare room It was thus, in this ridiculous manner, that Judith made one of the principal friendships of her life.

The next occurrence was, of all amazing things, the appearance of Will Herries. Two days after Judith's flight he appeared on a grand calm morning when the grass was still silver with frost and the scent of the Fell was stung with the breath of icy running water. The grass of the little tangled garden was crisp and crackling under Judith's heels. She looked up and saw Will, sitting there very stiff and reserved on a fine coal-black horse. She had not seen him for a long while. She thought he was in Liverpool. He looked older, thinner, better pleased with himself than ever, and he had all the pursed-up solemn air of a man who finds himself immensely important.

Their conversation was short. He did not

come down from his horse, but was quite friendly. She stood near him, her hand on the bridle, looking up at him and often smiling. He seemed to her so very pompous.

' Where are my things, Will? '

' Your things? '

' My handsome possessions, my marriage portion, my livelihood. There is a dress and a cap, two pairs of shoes, a cracked china jar, the brush of a fox, a Holy Bible. . . .'

He looked severe. ' You must ride back with me, Judith.'

She laughed. He couldn't but feel that she was a lively attractive little thing, standing there in the crisp morning air with the Fell and the old house for her background. He saw, too, with surprise that she had become in the course of a night or so a woman.

' Ride back? Is that your mother's wish? '

He leant over towards her confidentially. He always prided himself on his diplomatic gifts.

' Now, Judith. These are women's quarrels. You know well enough that my mother has been a sick woman since my father's death.' (He said *My* Mother and *My* Father as though they had been his own most especial private property.) ' A sick woman. . . . But it will pass. It is already passing.'

' Has she spoken of me? '

' No. She has kept to her room.'

' Has she spoken to Francis? '

Will's upper lip, that was thin and tight like whipcord, was sharp.

' Francis is greatly to blame. He is my brother, but I cannot acquit him of fault.' (He said *My* Brother as though, rather reluctantly this time, he owned him.)

Judith broke out fiercely:

' He is *not* to blame. . . . David's attack would have followed whether Francis were aggravating or no. You know well what the surgeon said. And after David's death Francis did everything that was possible. Sarah hugs her misfortune. She is not alone in losing a husband.'

Will said severely: ' You forget that she is my mother.'

' I forget nothing at all. Least of all do I forget that I never belonged at Uldale, Will. This is an old shabby place, and there are only old men in it, but it has always been my home more than the other. A poor taste, but my own. And so long as Sarah is living we can never be under the same roof. No, here is my place and here I stay.'

Will looked sternly about him as though he were making a quick business-like survey of the house, grounds, view, and found them of exactly no value at all.

' You know of Gauntry's bad repute?' he asked.

' Oh, Will,' she answered lightly, smiling at him. ' Who shall cast stones? There is not one of us without his detractor——'

This made Will uncomfortable. He looked for a moment as though he were going to ask Judith whether she had heard anything about

himself.   He had all the sensitiveness to personal
reputation that belongs to very selfish men.   However, all he said was:

'You yourself are a Herries, Judith, and in
this part of the country the Herries have a
reputation.'

She interrupted him laughing.   'There's
another Herries in the house here already—
Jeremy Cards.   He knew my father.'

Will's expression was as though he had smelt
some strong odour, which, indeed, as they were not
far from the midden, he might have done.

'I have heard of him.   A disreputable old
man. . . .'   He saw apparently that there was
nothing to be done.   He was relieved, perhaps,
that it was so.   'So you will not come?'

'No, Will.   I am happier here.'   She asked
him: 'Are things going well with you?'

He looked at her kindlily.   He liked anyone
who took an interest in his affairs.

'Well enough. . . . I am to go to London
very shortly.'   (He said London as though it
were *His* London, just purchased by him.)   'I'm
glad.   They say there's a deal of money there.'
He nodded very seriously.   'Liverpool is too
small a place,' he told her.

He shook her hand, was minded to pat her
head, but refrained.   Then he rode off, she calling
after him:

'Remember that my things must be sent.'

He turned in the saddle, nodded gravely and
disappeared.

She went in to find Tom Gauntry huddled in

an old bed-gown over a grumbling fire, dogs spread all around him. He looked up at her smiling, but his old face was wrinkled with pain. Her heart ached for him.

'That was Will Herries,' she said cheerfully. 'He asked me to return to Uldale. I say nay, like the girl in the ballad, and that is the end of that.'

'That is the end of that,' whispered the coal in the fire. 'Are you sure that you are wise?'

He put out his dry bony hand and took hers: 'Here has always been your home, and so long as I'm alive it shall be. But maybe that's not so long. My back aches and my head's like a turnip. There's a hunt to-day, Threlkeld way. Hunting's over for me. And I'll never be on a horse again neither. . . . Strange, strange! I've lived my life on horses. . . . But it's been a long life. Emma likes ye, my pretty. She's got a heart, Emma has, poor silly soul. She'd skin herself for anyone she's fond of—*has* skinned herself a hundred times, poor girl. It's mortal cold this morning. And yet I'm hot in the head, as though there were coals of fire blazing away. It's the devil to be an old man—better go while you're active.'

She nodded her head. 'I think,' she said, 'I could deal with whatever came. I feel that way on a fine crisp morning. Uncle Tom, what am I to do to-day? There are a thousand things— I'll ride over to Bassenthwaite village. There's a woman there a marvel with herbs. David had her once for his leg. . . .'

The old man rolled his head. ' Nay, nay, I'm past everything but dreaming, damn my bones. Don't you worry, my pretty. When you've had a pain in your leg a long while it's a kind of friend.' Then he added quite casually as though he were saying nothing at all: ' Georges may be riding over from Whitehaven to-day.'

Her heart began to hammer. ' Georges Paris?'

' Aye. He's grown a fine young man, but he'll burn his fingers one of these days. He's in with a lot o' rogues. I've told him, but he don't listen. Thinks he can manage them. Very confident young man is Georges.'

Before she could say anything or even reason with herself about her foolish excitement Emma Furze joined them. Judith saw that she had smartened herself. She had a black hoop and a silver band in her dark hair. She looked really handsome as she stood there. There was something both foolish and good in her face; her black eyes were large and always brimming with emotion; at the slightest excuse her breast would heave and swell. She looked at Judith with a childlike smile of pleasure.

' I saw a fine man on a horse and said to myself, " He's come to take her away." I was tortured by the anxiety, my dear.'

' You need be tortured no longer. No fine gentleman shall take me away.'

With a sigh of relief Emma sat down beside them. How pleasant it was for Judith in the fresh quietness of the morning, no sound in the house but the old clock ticking and a mouse scratching behind the wainscot!

Judith asked Emma some questions, and out her history tumbled in an overwhelming flood—some of it at least. As Judith was to discover, there were endless, endless chapters to it; she had led, it seemed, a thousand lives, and was yet, according to her own account, but two and thirty.

Her first part had been that of the Duke of York in *Richard the Third* at the Birmingham Theatre, then Cupid in *The Trip to Scotland*, then Prince Arthur in *King John*, then Bath, where Mr. Palmer gave her five shillings a night. Her first girl's part was Sukey Chitterling in *Harlequin's Invasion*. She drew from her bosom a packet of papers, yellow with age and greatly torn; she read to them with every possible dramatic gesture some of her notices.

' On Tuesday night Miss Pomeroy (" My name at that time, my dear ") made her appearance in *Isabella*; and, although the audience went with such strong prejudices in favour of the fashionable Melpomene, yet never did Mrs. Siddons draw more genuine tears from an audience. It is impossible to conceive what a high-finished picture this lady gave of Isabella's woes, and how nearly she arrived to nature in almost every scene. There were no studied pauses, to purchase, by vacancy of time, the approving hands of the audience, and yet the house echoed with repeated marks of approbation. Her shriek at the discovery of Biron had a good effect, but was rather that of terror without amazement, than of terror

and amazement mixed.   When the public consider that this Miss Pomeroy is that Miss Pomeroy
who performed Cowslip. . . .'

Old Jeremy came stealing down the stairs to
join them.   He was blinking his eyes and yawning, for he was only now awake, but Emma's
dramatic voice, the great rise in it as she came
to the word 'terror,' her sudden declamation of
Isabella's most moving lines, soon stirred him.
It was as good, he declared, as being at the Theatre
and with nothing to pay.   The dogs barked, Wull
came to the door and listened, and Judith, who had
never seen a play, was entranced.

Very early in the afternoon the light vanished
behind the hills, and the house was a place of
shadows.   Judith riding in from Caldbeck, and,
chilled to the bone, hurrying to the fire, saw
Georges Paris standing in the firelight.   No one
else was there.   It was the same as when they had
run, that first time, from the supper-room, and she
had smacked his cheek.

She would not smack his cheek now.   He had
grown a man, slim and tall in his riding-coat and
riding-boots, his black hair tied in a queue, his
handsome self-confident face bright with life, fun,
energy, adventure.

He saw, too, a changed Judith.   From the
child whom he had left there had grown a child-
woman, charming in her small buoyant independence, throwing her hat beside her and shaking her
red curls just as she used to do, holding out her
hand to him at once in their old friendship.

'How d'ye do, Georges?   I'm happy to see you again.'

'By heaven,' he thought, 'she's somebody. . . . I'm glad I came.'

For he had been in two minds about it.   Stone Ends was in no sort of way the place it had been. Gauntry was ill, only old men there, flea-bitten dogs, and the strange woman, half cook, half play-actress, in command.   Georges was profoundly convinced that he could live but once and must waste no time.   Had he been present when Gauntry needed he would have helped him to his last shilling, for he was impetuously generous, but he was happy in living for the moment and in finding the moment always exciting.

And now this Moment was Judith.   He had not expected to find her here and certainly not supposed that she would, at his very first glimpse of her, affect him so strongly.   He had thought of her, forgotten her, thought of her again.   He lived for excitement, and only accepted the things and people that could contribute to that.   Since he had seen her he had had adventures enough——on the Cumberland coast, on the Solway, in Holland, in London——to satisfy, he thought, any man.   What he did not recognise——as we never recognise the truest things about ourselves——was that all these adventures had been scattered with a thin second-rate dust, as though, with everything that he touched, he robbed it of a degree of fineness. He had first-rate moments and a great quality of happy fearless adventure when things went well, but he had second-rate ambitions, second-rate vision, second - rate reactions. He was a fine young man with a soul, through no fault of his own, inevitably shabby. Was it perhaps in Judith's power to raise him into a finer world? He did not think so, because he was convinced that no world could be finer than the one he was in; and she did not think so, because she never, all her life through, saw herself as a moral agent in anything. She never thought at all about moral qualities in the abstract.

At any rate, simply as a factor in the intricate course of Herries history, it must be recorded that on that afternoon, November 24 of the year 1790, Judith Herries and Georges Paris, standing beside the fire in the hall of Stone Ends, fell in love with one another.

Judith knew at once what had happened to her. She was always extremely clear-sighted about herself. Now if he attempted to kiss her she would not smack his cheek. But she did not intend that he should kiss her. She was in fact very cool to him indeed.

He had intended to stay the one night at Stone Ends and then ride on to Penrith, where he had business of an especially interesting nature. He was by present occupation a smuggler and just now a prosperous one. But his intention was to find a little place somewhere in the district, a rather remote place if possible, and make it his centre. This was not only a business ambition. He had a true love of the country, possibly the truest thing in him; he liked nothing better than

the old life of hunting, fishing and the rest that
he had had in the earlier days at Stone Ends.
Sensuous enough, he nevertheless vastly preferred
men to women as companions. He had long
pictured to himself a small farm somewhere that
could be the centre both of his business and his
pleasure. Now that he was in funds was the
time to purchase such a place. He certainly
would not be in funds for ever.

So, at the very first instant of seeing Judith
walk across the floor towards him, in a flash it had
come to him: 'Here is the woman you want.'
He had always considered her, even as a child,
a most sensible capable person. There was some
hard common sense in Judith that had always
roused his keenest admiration. She knew this
country and liked it. She would run a house well,
would manage men with authority. She had no
ties. She had pluck and courage and, he sur-
mised, would not trouble herself too deeply about
transgressions of the law. Now that he beheld
her again he remembered how greatly he had
been impressed in Cockermouth by her decision
and resolution. She was not strictly a beauty,
but there was something very attractive to the
senses.

When he wanted anything he always, in five
minutes, concluded that it was his. He wasted no
time at all; before they had been half an hour
together he was making ardent love to her.

Emma Furze was in her room that night imploring her to be careful.

'He is not for you — no, never, never!'

H

She held Judith's hand and spoke as though the
fate of nations were in danger.

'What have you against him, Emma?'

'He has no character, no fine feelings. I
have known men and been betrayed by them too.
They are all false, and this young man is French
as well.'

'They are not all false,' said Judith, thinking
of Francis and Reuben. 'But you must recollect,
Emma, that I am acquainted with Georges Paris
since I was a baby.'

'Yes, but now you are in love with him.
You were not and now you are. Love blinds
poor women. Men are never to be trusted for a
single instant. They are filled with cruelty and
caprice. On the most vain and frivolous pre-
texts, whenever their temper is in the least ruffled,
they cast you aside. They behave with propriety only when it is to their advantage.'

'Well, my dear, you need not fear. I know
myself.'

But did she? She lay in bed looking at the
moonlight washing the floor. She was in love
—and for the first time. Did she know that?
Her cheek was hot as she fell asleep. And her
dreams were of a fiery splendour and a happiness
that she had never touched before.

It was plain enough to everybody next day
that Georges remained at Stone Ends only because
of Judith. He carried on his courtship with an
impatient ardour that had a great deal of very
real passion in it. He was ruthlessly selfish
about everyone else. Gauntry he patronised,

the two old men he disregarded, Emma Furze
he detested. Like many sensual men nothing
exasperated him more than having to be in the
company of a woman who was most unattractive
to him. Emma exasperated him by her apparent
vagueness. She seemed to him to live entirely
in a world of make-believe. He declared that
she did not know where France was nor that
Paris was the capital of that country: neither
politics nor money meant anything to her at all.
She lived entirely in a world of the passions,
except when she was cooking. (She was a very
excellent cook.) She was vague and ignorant
and absent-minded except when someone for
whom she cared was in question; then she was
as sharp as a needle. He knew at once that she
was his enemy so far as Judith went, and he loved
her none the better for that knowledge.

So things moved swiftly. Judith was in a
strange state. He caught her when she was
isolated from all her claims and associations.
Everything played into his hands. When her
things arrived from Uldale, with them came a
letter from Reuben. It was very short.

DEAREST JUDITH—I am going with Humphrey to
France. There is the centre of all the movement for the
Betterment of Mankind. I shall learn there in that New
World how to help Mankind. I shall think of you so
often, dearest Judith. I love you with my whole Heart.
REUBEN SUNWOOD.

France! It had taken Reuben as it had taken
Francis. And now it seemed that it must take

her too. But what a different France hers!
For Georges seemed to care nothing for his
parents' country, save that he got lace and brandy
from it, nor did it concern him at all that there
was a Revolution there. What was Georges in
reality? Did she know him? Did she see him
as he was? Was Emma in the right about him?
But, as the days went on, she could not think
any more. She had never been in love before.
She had not known that it would be this strange
fiery heat, mist before the eyes, all the outside
world sounding dim to the ear.

The house, the old men, Emma, all grew
faint and unreal to her, and Georges was ever
more clear. He seemed to her most beautiful, and
now, because he also was in love, he was most
tender.

In these chill frosty December days he was at
his very best. There were in him somewhere
noble instincts; he wanted her so fiercely (as
he wanted anything withheld from him) that his
very desire brought him close to her and he
caught some of her fineness. He had been in
love again and again since he could remember,
but now three things were united that had perhaps
never been before—desire, perception of character,
and practical advantage. There was wisdom in
his choice of her, although the very thing that
now attracted him, the strong domination of her
will and purpose, would be, when passion had
died, the last thing that he would want in her.

She held out against him so long as she could,
but he was too strong for her. It seemed to her

that this had been foreshadowed since her sharp farewell to him in Cockermouth. He had looked at her then as though he knew that one day she would come to him.

But she was never less assured about him than at the moment before she submitted. Coming down the stairs she saw him standing in the hall that was lit by a blazing fire. He was dark black, standing motionless there, as though he were waiting for her. She paused on the stair, and the thought struck her heart: ' This man is my enemy.' Then she came down, and a moment later she was in his arms.

Afterwards he was speaking in all sincerity when he said:

' My dearest, I will care for you with my whole heart. You can make me noble and fine. This is a new beginning. There is nothing you cannot make of me.'

Lying in his arms she was wildly happy with that fierceness of intensity that was always hers in everything that she did. But she had never surrendered herself before to anyone save the ghost of her father. No one had held her and loved her and stroked her hair and kissed her with passion. She did not know that it could be so sweet. What vows she made of service and devotion! How she would work now that she had someone to work for!

She did not ask him where he would take her, whether he had money to keep her! She could work for them both; at what she did not inquire.

Her cheek against his, she stayed in a trance.
Perfect happiness had come. How could she
ever have thought that she did not know him?
She knew him utterly. She had always known
him as she knew herself.

She was so very young.

END OF PART I

PART II

WATENDLATH

FRANCIS RIDES OVER

This book is the history of a country, England (not, of course, the whole history); of a family, Herries (nor the whole history of that); and of certain members of that family especially— Judith Paris first, then, after her, of Reuben, Will and Francis (and not, of course, their whole history either).

But the Herries are English, and Judith, Reuben, Will and Francis are Herries. At the heart of this family there is a struggle and in each of these individuals a struggle. The history of that struggle is the history of this book, is the history, perhaps, of every book that has ever been written.

The history of any country and the history of any family is continually presenting strange underground movements of ebb and flow, and to these movements members of the country and of the family are for ever responding, although they may themselves be quite unconscious of it. Moreover, the actions of one individual will often permeate the whole body of which he or she is a part; even slender characteristics may affect it as the shape of Cleopatra's nose swung Egypt, Napoleon's passion for hot baths France, and Mrs. Fitzherbert's virtuous tenacity England.

So the determination of Will Herries' prominent chin affected just now the fortunes of the whole
family of Herries. They may be said to have
swung upwards upon it.

In 1791 Will Herries moved to London and
married there a Miss Christabel Carmichael, a
young woman with a fine waist, something of a
fortune, a doting father; against these benefits
must be set a slight cast in one eye and a rather
hysterical temper. Will cared nothing for the
first and soon dominated the second. He was
determined to get on, and, as in this life everyone
gets what he wants if only he wants it hard enough,
he did get on, and speedily.

He was soon known in the City as a man of
prudence and enterprise nicely commingled. His
business was especially in Indian trade, tea, silks
and spices. He had a pretty house in the village
of Chelsea, and in February 1792 Mrs. Will
Herries gave birth to a son, Walter, who, with
his opening shout to the world, proclaimed that
he also meant to get on and to waste no time in
doing so.

It would, however, be an exaggeration to say
that at this time any other members of the Herries
family were at all aware that they were about to
swing upwards on the point of Will's chin. As
was always the Herries characteristic, there was
perfect self-confidence everywhere until disin-
tegrating imagination broke in and threatened it.
The Family was at this moment divided, unlike
Gaul, into four parts. There were the Herries
of Uldale, Sarah and her children, Francis and

Deborah; the Pomfret Herries of Kensington, with whom poor Humphrey Sunwood once on a time visited; the Cards of Bournemouth, Prosper Cards who married Amelia Trent and had offspring, Jennifer, born in 1770, and Robert, born in 1771; and, fourthly (but in their own opinion absolutely firstly), Lord and Lady Rockage of Grosset Place in Wiltshire. Judith Herries, sister to Raiseley and first cousin to David, had, many years before, bewildered into matrimony the Honourable Ernest Bligh, who in his gout-ridden and exceedingly ill-tempered old age had become Lord Monyngham, then Viscount Rockage. Of them had been born three children, Frederick, who died, Carey in 1755 and Madeline in 1756. Carey, now Lord Rockage, had two offspring—Carey the younger, born in 1780, and Phyllis, born in 1782.

Lord and Lady Rockage, his sister Madeline, his children Carey and Phyllis, lived all in penniless grandeur at Grosset in Wiltshire, where the rain trickled through the roof, the trees creaked and wailed, and the cold of the stone passages carried rheumatism into the bones of all who suffered it.

Lest these family branches should seem confusing it may be said that the Uldale family stood for Country Life, Pomfret's family for London, the Cards in Bournemouth for Social Intercourse, and the Rockages for the Ruling Classes; yes, and more than that, for two strong elements of the Ruling Classes at the end of the eighteenth century in England, namely the arrogance of a dominating Aristocracy and the narrowness but courage of Methodism.

This book is not, however, in the main the history of the Rockage fortunes. There is a story there, in that odd proud group of the family, that should command a book of its own.

To have suggested to either the Rockages or the Cards of Bournemouth at this time that Will Herries was an important relation would have been to invite derision. But Will's time was approaching.

Possibly Francis, up in Uldale, had more fore-knowledge of it than any other. He knew his brother. Indeed, very often, Francis, who was without any personal conceit, felt that he knew everything about his own immediate relations, that he knew too much for anyone's happiness. He had in fact a very special quality of psychological penetration. He was now grown very handsome for those who did not find his figure too slender. His features were sharp but delicate, his colour fresh and gentle; he carried himself with a strongly reserved dignity, was always clothed with perfect simplicity but in absolute taste.

He wore an air of melancholy, no pose of the period, but very real indeed. These years were, in fact, very unhappy.

They might well be so. Uldale was, at this time, no cheerful place. He held himself there because he thought it his duty. A bailiff managed the farm, but Francis managed the bailiff—and everyone else as well. He had far more authority than cheerful stout David had ever had; he was the friend of no one, and would have been un-popular in his remoteness had there not been a

very proper pride in him.   He was the Aristocrat
of the district, and everyone was pleased that there
should be an Aristocrat.   His melancholy reserve
lent not only the house but all the district an air.
Unlike his sister Deborah, who was in and out of all
the houses of the neighbourhood with her giggle,
her two little dogs and her passion for gossip, he
went nowhere and entertained only with reluctance.

But it was on his relations with his mother that
the whole house hung.

Sarah Herries was now an aged and shrunken
woman.   In the spring of 1792 she was fifty-four
years of age, but she looked another ten.   Her
hair was white; she dressed always in the deepest
black, her shoulders a little bent as she walked
slowly, leaning on an ebony cane.   Her eyes were
scornful, as though she said always to the world:
' You took from me the only thing for which I ever
cared.   What do you expect of me now? '

Now that her features were more slender there
was a resemblance between herself and her son.
The stout and chattering Deborah seemed to have
no relationship with either of them.

Sarah had not, of course, forgiven Francis; she
would never forgive him.   She would never forgive him, but she surrendered to his influence.
She allowed him to do what he would with the
house and everyone in it.   She found indeed no
interest in either contemporary life or persons.
She sat, either in her own upstairs room or in the
temple in the garden on a fine day, staring in front
of her, at the bad blowzy painting of David or the
china figures or across the sunlit lawns to the

sweep of Skiddaw or the Scottish hills. Her lips moved; her thin pale hands beat together a little on her lap. She was in no way deranged. Any question asked of her she answered sharply and with a certain shivering impatience.

She allowed Deborah to chatter to her for so long as she would, and Deborah flattered herself that but for her jolly brightness and good-nature the house would fall into ruins. But Deborah also abandoned everything to Francis. She paid visits with increasing avidity among the neighbours. She was a great player of cards, a passionate gossip, surely a destined old maid. But Destiny does not always work to pattern.

Francis behaved to his mother with unfaltering courtesy and an unflinching patience. But it seemed to him that life could not continue for very much longer like this. His real life was imprisoned within him like a fire within an ivory bowl. The bowl would crack, and the fire burn the hand that held it.

He was thirty-two. His life was passing. And a day came when his endurance broke.

In the evening he sat opposite his mother in the China Room, while a thin coal fire whispered grumpily between them. The curtains, with their stamped pagodas and blue tilted bridges, were drawn. A small King Charles spaniel bitch lay at Francis' feet. He realised quite suddenly, with that premonition of coming events, always his special gift, that some crisis was approaching. Everything in the room seemed to share his knowledge.

On his lap, as he was always afterwards to remember, was a copy of Burke's *Reflections on the Revolution in France*. His mother spoke. She had a fashion, when they were alone together, of speaking, as it were, to herself, so that when he answered her it was as though he were addressing the wall behind her or a picture or a chair. But now she looked at him directly.

' Francis,' she said, and her eyes wandered over his face as though she were seeing him for the first time. ' Why do you stay here? It is not, I know, to give yourself pleasure.'

' Yes, ma'am,' he answered. ' I am happy here.'

' No, you are not. I know exactly why you stay. It is from a sense of duty. You think that you did me a wrong and repay it by this attention to us. That is your duty.'

He made no answer. His heart beat thickly.

' Well, it is no duty. You have your own life to be lived. Will is working in London, but there is money sufficient for you to travel. Herman is honest enough and will see that everything goes smoothly here.'

Herman was the bailiff. The reference to Will was no new one. The inference was that Will was working hard at making money in London while Francis idled. . . . No new inference.

But Francis, tried by much practice, only nodded his head.

' If you wish me to go, ma'am.'

' I wish! I wish! Who cares what I wish?

. . . I am a dead woman.' Then a surprising thing happened. She turned to him almost eagerly, as though they were, for an instant, friends. ' You didn't know, did you, that one person can die and quite another take her place within the same skin? That other woman would have long forgiven you had she lived. Besides, she was your mother. She was gay and happy, foolish possibly in her trust of events, but she was only a child, although she bore children. . . . But this other woman here is not your mother, was not even when she was alive. You have often felt her unjust, I know. . . .'

' No, ma'am,' he answered her.

' Oh, but you have, you have! And rightly. . . . Only I am not sorry at any injustice. That belonged to your mother.'

As always a strange mingling of irritation and pity rose in him. He hated a sort of melodrama and extravagance in her speech, and yet he knew that at the heart of the extravagance there was a real cankerous sickness.

He felt deeply sorry for them both, so gently he answered:

' I do not want to go, mother, unless you wish it.'

She got up, felt for her cane, walked towards the door, then turned and said roughly:

' I do wish it. We can have no life together, you and I.'

Then she went out.

He stayed there alone in a kind of impotent fury. So that was all he got for his years of faithful service! He had always had a sharp, keen sense of reality and also a kind of hunger for it. He felt now that ever since his father's death this house had been completely unreal, and it was his mother who had made it so.

To-night, his mother's last words in his ear, he was moved to a passionate sense of rebellion. He paced up and down the little parlour, the spaniel following his movement with soft anxious eyes. Yes, if she wished him to go he would do so! No word of thanks for all the drudgery of these years! Here he had lamed his life at its most active and promising period to serve her, and all he received was a contemptuous reference to Will. Will, who had never, in all his days, thought of anyone but himself or of anything but his own advantage!

Poor Francis was one of those who are confident about ideas but doubtful about the human race. That Liberty, Equality, Fraternity must ultimately flourish, he was convinced, but he was hurt, with pitiful ease, by any act of human injustice. He found it difficult to believe that human beings were egoistic, jealous, cruel, niggardly, and yet on every day of his life he was injured by proofs that they were.

He *could* not credit that all his years of service went for nothing. They did not go for nothing. Did he but know it, it was his mother's acute knowledge of her own injustice that aggravated her bitterness. But . . . 'Herman will do as well.' Herman, the stout, red-faced bailiff, who was honest only because he was stupid and faithful, only because he was without imagination.

To-morrow, then, he would go. He would show them— He stopped abruptly. Wiser councils were prevailing. First he would ride out to Watendlath and see little Judith. She would help him. She was now, he sighed, his only friend. The spaniel came to him as he sat down by the fire, put her paws on his knee and gazed into his face.

Next morning he rode out. He took a magnificent white mare, Juno, his especial favourite, who knew the country so well that she could find her way over almost trackless paths and climb precipitous hills like a young pony. He was a fine figure in his purple riding-coat with the high collar, his head up, like a king. But he didn't feel like a king. There was something surreptitious in his departure as he turned down over the fell towards Bassenthwaite.

He told no one where he was going. Mention of Judith to the Uldale household was a great deal worse than useless. He had seen her three times in the fifteen months since her marriage, once in Keswick, twice at Watendlath. Watendlath was an exceedingly remote little valley lying among the higher hills above Borrowdale. It could indeed be scarcely named a valley: rather it was a narrow strip of meadow and stream lying between the wooded hills, Armboth on the Grasmere side and King's How and Brund Fell on the other.

It was utterly remote, with some twenty dwellings, a dark tarn and Watendlath Beck that ran down the strath until it tumbled over the hill at Lodore.

Georges Paris had found here exactly the place that he wanted, an old house once a Statesman's but now belonging to a farmer, Ritson, who, owing to a ne'er-do-well son, now dead, was at money odds, but owned two farms. Paris bought one farm from him, but kept him there to maintain both. And there he deposited Judith, while himself, for much of the year, was engaged on all kinds of doubtful adventures on the coast, even in Holland and Scandinavia.

Francis had not seen Judith for some months, but at his last sight of her had been amazed by the happiness that radiated from her. He had regarded the marriage with that ragamuffin Frenchman as most certainly disastrous, had not had spirit even to contradict the self-congratulatory 'I-told-you-so's' of his mother and sister. When he heard that Judith had been banished to Watendlath, disaster seemed even more certain. But when he saw her he found her confident, assured, triumphant. It was true that it was then still the first year of her marriage and for most of that Georges had been away. But she had had six months in Watendlath alone—and had flourished on it. When he rode out there on the last occasion it had been veiled in rain and storm. It had seemed to him simply the end of the world. With the rain lashing his face and the gale tugging at his hair he had looked back to see that small indomitable creature laughing good-bye to him in the narrow doorway. Indomitable, yes! But the happiness was real. It was not assumed to reassure him. His heart was touched, and he loved her more than ever.

He thought, as he rode on this March morning of flushing sun and hovering cloud through Keswick and then beside the Lake water that now tumbled with a shiver of grey and then swam into straths of gold, that she was the only human being now in all the world whom he did love.

In old days, when she had been a child and told him insistently that she adored him, his own shyness and sensitiveness of taste had held him back, but, after his father's death and her flight to Gauntry's, he had realised to the full the courage, fidelity, warmth of feeling in her, yes, and her egotism and passion for power as well. How could that passion for power be satisfied in this lonely place where there were scarcely a hundred souls? He himself, who had no passion for power but only for justice, could not be quiet there. No, he thought, sighing, as he turned Juno away from the Lake up the Fell path, nor anywhere else.

Where in the world now was Equality, where was Freedom? He, who had killed his father with his joy over the fall of the Bastille, must now in this March of 1792 begin to tremble at the things that his Frenchmen were contemplating. After the Flight to Varennes his sympathies, always so easily swayed by human misfortune, had begun to turn towards that unhappy King and Queen. Then the news in December of the ultimatum to the Elector of Treves had moved him again towards this brave country beset by so many external, as well as internal enemies, but the latest news of the quarrels between Delessart and Brissot in the Assembly caused him the bitterest disappointment.

He was afterwards to recollect that it was on that March day of cold sunshine, riding out to Watendlath, that he foresaw something of the cruel confusion that led to the September Massacres.

As he rode into the higher air and crossed the little bridge above the running stream he shook his shoulders with a sort of indignant despair. He had never before felt his life to be so lonely, so aimless, such a failure. He looked about him, and as always the beauty of this beloved country fell on him like a balm. Only a few days before there had been a March snowstorm in the upper dales. He could not yet, riding among the trees, see the rising Fell, but he could scent the snow in the air. He knew that if the snowfall had been deep the shepherds would be anxious for the sheep. He felt suddenly a touch of their anxiety, and with that a kind of shame for bothering about unreal things like politics when there were such real things as sheep close at hand. Soon he would be clear of the trees for a while and see how the sheep were faring.

He had reached now the spot where Watendlath Beck tumbled into Lodore, and as always when he was here he must stop and breathe in deeply that perfect beauty. This was surely one of the loveliest places in all England—English, too, in its qualities of old imperturbable age, a kind of wistful tranquillity, a cosiness of beauty mingled with an almost fierce suggestion of force. Here Vikings had stood, here two hundred years later his descendants would stand, and at every time the cataract (when the rains had fallen) would fling clouds of mist above the turning flower-like whiteness of the water that leapt and fell and leapt again between the thin brown stones. The dark bare stems of the larch and oak stood sentinel on either side, and exactly framed by the delicate pattern Derwentwater lay, in colour now snow upon steel, a thin shadow of stainless white hovering over the silver grey. Skiddaw and Blencathra seemed to sway under the changing passing cloud. Every colour—white and grey and brown—although so delicate, seemed to hint at the coming Spring; there was the promise of saffron and primrose in the stems of the trees, in the leaping water of the Fall.

Francis felt for a moment that here was the answer to all his unrest. With his hand on Juno's back, his eyes leaping with the water, he swore to himself that he would be true to this fragment of English soil, and that so long as he was so no other disappointment, whether in God or man, could deeply touch him. Here was his proof that there was something lovely in the world that made this life worth while.

He rode then higher on to the Fell, Juno picking her way on an almost trackless path, and could see now the sheep gathered into dark groups feeding on the loads of hay that the farmers had sent to relieve them. The whole sweep of the Fell was flooded with thin sunshine, and little rocks stood out in it like islets of ebony. The snow, on the farther Fell, was more scattered and lay in streaks like marking on a tiger's back. The sheep moved in black sequence against the running stone walls. There was silence everywhere, except for the rhythm like a humming voice of the distant falls.

He rode on, through forest again. As he approached Watendlath in his purple coat on his great white horse, the distant white fells, like pummelled pillows, shining down on him, he might have been some knight-at-arms riding into the Forbidden Land. He seemed to be more and more withdrawn from the world. He was high up among the hills, and yet this meadow and stream had the quality of a mysterious valley that would later on be rich with flowers and enchanted with the voices of birds. But to-day ice and snow and rock ringed him inexorably round.

Soon, looking down, he saw the odd dumpy shape of John Green House, Judith's home. A queer little place indeed, crouched into the soil as though it feared a blow, its narrow windows peering blindly on to Armboth Fell that here was split to allow a beck to tumble down the hollow. There was the chattering of the beck, the bark of dogs, the lowing of a calf, but before he had reached the door Judith had seen him, had run out, had almost pulled him off his horse in her eagerness, flung her arms round his neck and dragged him into the house.

John Green House was L-shaped with a double porch. From the 'hallan' or passage there were three doors, one that led into the 'down-house,' now used for farm purposes, baking, brewings and the rest, the second that led to the garden, and the third to the 'house-place' or 'house,' a beautiful room with lovely views, surrendered now entirely to Judith; beyond this room was a smaller panelled one, Judith's bedroom. A small staircase led upstairs to rooms that had been formerly open to the rafters but that were now ceilinged.

Judith took Francis into the 'house-place,' shining now in the pale March sunlight. The walls were plastered. There was a stone mantelpiece over an open hearth; there was a settle, some carved chairs and a large oak table.

There were signs of Judith's passionate cleanliness everywhere. Everything gleamed and shone; china, candlesticks of beaten brass, an old spit with many hooks and a dripping - pan. Some early daffodils were in a china bowl on the oak table.

She stood back and stared at him.

' Now, let me look at you! Oh, how handsome you are, Francis! I had forgotten. You are more beautiful every day! ' She stood on tiptoe, pushing back the high hard collar of his riding-coat that she might see the white fall of his neck-cloth and the beech-coloured waistcoat with the stamped silver buttons.

' I always put on my best when I come out to

see you,' he said, laughing, and taking off his
riding-coat.

'That's more than I can do for you,' she
answered.

She was wearing the country clothes, an upper-
dress of undyed duffel like a man's and a skirt of
native wool woven into a sort of serge—wool of
the black sheep mixed with red and blue. Her
stockings were of blue homespun, and she had
clogs of uncurried leather. They were lined with
straw to keep her feet warm.

Francis thought she looked extremely well,
with her pale excited face and the pile of red-gold
hair on top of it. She was, as always, immaculate
from head to toe. She had an air of virginal
purity as though the wind, the rain, the unchecked
sun had cleansed her with an austerity of their
own. In fact she was neither austere nor remote.
She was wild with excitement at seeing him, could
not keep still, went dancing about the room, touching first one thing and then another, talking all
the time. Of course, she was yet a child, only
seventeen, while he was thirty-two. But it was
true what she said, suddenly turning to him and
crying: 'You know, Francis, I've always loved
you—from the moment that I was born!'

She had to have someone to love, and she had to
have someone to dominate too. It amused him
to see how at once she took charge of him, telling
him where he must go and what he must do. It
would soon be the dinner-hour, but first he must
see everything, and she danced in front of him,
taking him along the 'hallan' into the farmhouse of

the Ritsons. He was aware of a great fire roaring in the open fireplace, of a spit turning, of sacks of corn, hams and sides of bacon hanging, the oak settle screened by the 'heck,' the 'rannel-balk' or great wooden beam across the chimney, and a chain with hooks for cooking utensils hanging. The big room seemed filled with men and women, all busied with affairs, but he noticed in especial one magnificent old man with a snow-white beard like a patriarch. Judith introduced him. This was Robert Ritson, the head of the Ritson family, a man of seventy-four, who, in spite of his many troubles, financial and others, was yet above the world, above it and removed a little from it, with that touch of remoteness and austere reserve that is in all true Cumbrians.

Then they went out. She led him over the boulders and the foaming beck down the hill above the meadow to the Churn. The Churn was filled just now with water from the snow off the fells and toiled and tossed and seethed, an odd spot of turmoil above the quiet silence of the long meadow. Judith said a strange thing as they were looking into it.

'If Georges were to leave me I'd throw myself into it,' she said. Then laughing: 'No, I would not. I would stick a knife in his back.'

'Do you love him then so much?' asked Francis.

'I do.'

'And does he love you?'

'He loves no one at all but himself,' she answered.

Then they went and stood by the Tarn in front
of the stone wall of the house.   All was very grey
and silent.   The hills streaked with white, thick
with naked trees, looked down on them while
quilts of wadded cloud rolled heavily across the
sky.   Francis shivered.

'It's a black piece of water,' he said.

She told him that it could be every colour, that
it had so many moods that she could almost believe that it was alive, as Mother West, the witch,
said it was.

'Have you a witch then in this small place?'
he asked her.

They had, but a good and kindly one who gave
the girls love potions and the men cures for the
rheumatism.   'She is an immense woman, like
a whale.'   Then, as they walked back into the
house again, Judith told him about all the families
in the place, the Ritsons, the Wilsons, the Tysons,
the Morrows, the Blythwaites, the Gibsons, the
Robsons.

Judith knew everyone and, as Francis soon
perceived, governed everyone.   She was Mistress
of Watendlath, knew it and triumphed in it.

But it was not until after their dinner that they
truly talked.   For dinner they had oat-bread
baked on the girdle, a broth of onions and savoury
herbs, and a goose pie that had been made at
Christmas.   To drink there was ale brewed in
the 'down-house.'

When dinner was over they sat over the fire,
while the logs hissed and crackled and spat and
threw out tongues of flame against the blackened

stone. He asked her first whether she were happy. As she replied, telling him everything in her mind with her accustomed honesty, he watched her. She had changed but little, and he thought to himself that her real struggle with Georges was yet to come.

She had all the audacity and self-confidence that she had always had. Nothing in life had frightened her as yet then. She had a woman's knowledge and common sense.

' This Georges of yours,' he said. ' You'd stick a knife in his back if he left you. But he's always leaving you. How long has he been away this time? '

' He has to be away on his business.'

' What is his business? '

' Oh, smuggling, stealing, anything bad. But when he has made money he will settle down here.'

' Such a man settle down? '

' Oh yes. You cannot know him, of course. I often think no one knows him but myself.'

' How much has he been here in the fifteen months of your marriage? '

' Three months. Three months and a half. There was the first month—oh, that was grand! We did nothing but make love to one another. I was new to him. It couldn't stay. . . . One morning he knocked me down, and before I was myself again he was gone. But he wrote me a beautiful letter from Whitehaven. He was away then six months. He came back one forenoon without any warning and then we loved one another again —two weeks or more. Then he was away five

months, and the last time he was here we were
good company, not lovers.   He had a woman in
Whitehaven.'

'You knew all this,' he asked her, 'and didn't
care?'

She looked at him with bright eyes.   'Most
certainly I cared.   Night after night I cried myself sick; then if I made a noise he would go and
sleep with the farming men.   He has no heart.
He is quite cold.   When I saw that, I stopped
crying.'

'And you love such a man?' he asked, dis-
gusted.

'Certainly.   He wants me to love him.   And
I find him charming.   He is the most elegant
company in the world.   When he is here at home
we laugh and laugh for hours together.   If I am
in love with him and troublesome, he is either in
love, too, or he is drunk and doesn't care, or he
goes away.   He certainly cares for me more than
anyone in the world, but not for me very much.
He says it is the fault of his mother, who was a
bad woman and beat him.   Did I ever tell you,
Francis,' Judith dropped her voice a little, 'how
when I was little and ran away to Uncle Tom's I
looked through a door and saw Georges' mother
naked and a young man in his shirt kissing her
knees?'

'No,' said Francis, 'you never told me.'

'Well, that was the beginning of it.'

'The beginning of what?'

'Of my love for Georges.   I love him because
he is beautiful and witty and cares for nobody.

But one day I will make him think of me so that
he can never get me out of his mind.   It is almost
so now.   He is always writing to me . . . and
when he has stolen enough money from other
people, we shall go to London and steal some
more.'

Francis was aghast.

'But, good heavens, child, do you approve of
stealing?'

'I would not steal myself.   I wouldn't steal a
halfpenny.   But no one will ever stop Georges
from stealing.   It is in his blood.   He steals my
things all the while—and from the Ritsons too.
But one thing about Georges—he never tells a lie.
If I ask him whether he has had women in Whitehaven he always says Yes.   He tells me all about
the smuggling.   He tells me everything.   You
cannot change people's natures.   Isn't that what
your Mr. Rousseau said?   I have read the *Nouvelle
Héloïse* and find it too full of sentiment.   Well,
I love Georges and I cannot change him.   He
had a bad mother—so what would you?'

'And he beats you?'

'No longer.   After the last time I said next
time I would kill him.   Perhaps I would.   He
knows my father was mad and my mother a gipsy.
That is one thing he cannot understand—that I
am so *practical*.'   She said the word twice with
immense satisfaction.   'And on the other side
so wild.   I tell him that is the Herries blood;
what makes them so interesting a family.'

'But,' cried Francis, still greatly distressed,
'there will be some terrible scandal.   He will kill

someone or be killed or be put in gaol or be
hanged for a thief. . . .'

She nodded her head.   'Georges says he will
never die in his bed.   I would be for ever anxious
while he is away if I were not—what is it?—a
fatalist.   That's what I am, Francis, a fatalist.
What will be will be, and nothing shall beat
me.'

Then she went on eagerly.   'I want to go to
London.   London must be fine.   I want to see
all the Herries, my relations.   Will lives there
now, and they say his wife is as proud as a peacock
and has a cast in her eye.   Georges heard about
them.   And there is Pomfret, old Raiseley's
son. . . . Oh yes, and there are the Rockages in
Wiltshire.   It was the greatest fun, Emma Furze
saw them.'

'Who is Emma Furze?'

'She is my greatest friend.   She was Uncle
Tom's mistress, and after he died she went back to
the theatre again.   She had a season in Salisbury,
and Lady Rockage had a meeting about the
wickedness of the theatre.   Emma went, and she
says Lady Rockage is like an old pincushion and
has two children at her heels, and they have a house
always in the rain——'

'It can't always be raining,' Francis interrupted, laughing.   Then he asked: 'But how
can you endure it so long here alone?'

'I am never alone,' she answered indignantly.
'Never for a moment.   I shall prove it to you.   I
keep a Journal.'

She ran, pulled out the drawer of a cabinet and

brought back to him a book bound in dark-green leather with heavy clasps.

He opened it at random and read, in her sprawling childish hand, entries such as these: [1]

Nov. 3, 1791. Mrs. Ritson had a Haunch of Venison this morning from Mr. Crosthwaite of Keswick. Obliging of him but I think he has an eye on Mary Ritson. While I was in at Tom Blythwaite's this morning their cousin Nancy B. from Mardale was taken in Labour being only a quarter gone and had a Miscarriage. No doctor nearer than Grange and he not arriving till late afternoon.

Nov. 7, 1791. The Carrier, Ned Wilkinson from Keswick, round this forenoon. 2 Sauce Ladles pd twenty shillings. Poor Rate from Lady Day to Michlms pd 1.5.2½. Oh I forgot bought also of Ned Wilkinson a pair of Garters 0.1.0. To Poor Travelling Woman walking over from Grasmere 0.6.0. Mrs. Mary Robson's little Boy by me for an hour while his Mother baked.

Nov. 23, 1791. Mrs. Watson of High Head Grange sent us 2 Tubbs of Geneva. Very kind. The Robsons and Braithwaites—John, Hob, Anne, Henry, came in last evening and we had a Grand Feast. I gave them Pease Broth, boiled Leg of Mutton and Caper Sauce, Mince Pye. After supper we had Quadrille at which I lost 1d per fish—1.0.0.

Dec. 4, 1791. Mr. Bletson rode up from Rosthwaite— said he wished he could have driven up his new Curricle to show me. Very smart painted Green with Red lines. Walked down to Rosthwaite with him, he leading his horse. Walked back through Snowstorm. Very heavy over the Langdales. Fine Show of Sun betweenwhiles above Armboth. Pd 1.0. per yd for 6 yds of white Cotton for Lining.

[1] Judith Paris' *Journal* is still Herries property. See *An Old Border Family*, published by Houghley & Watson, 1894.

' Yes,' said Francis, looking up from the book to her eager face. ' You're not dull—and you *are* practical.'

' It is to show Georges,' she answered, ' if he were ever to ask where the money goes. But he never does. I have enough from the farm, even though,' her voice lowered, her face grew dark, ' Georges were never to return again.'

' Then you don't know . . . whether he comes, when he comes——? '

' No; even though he writes he never says. A while ago I had a letter, and from it you might fancy he would be here any moment. My eye is always on the road by the Tarn. One day without a word he will be coming along.'

She came closer to him, sitting curled up at his feet, her hand on his knee. ' I think so much of my father. I fancy that I am the only person left alive who gives him a thought. Already he has gone so far back for everyone else, but not for me. His house, you know, was just below here at Rosthwaite. It is tumbling down. Poor father! Everyone thought him too mad to be real, but I understand how he felt. He is alive in me still, Francis. Perhaps none of us ever die.'

' Better the dead than the living! ' Francis broke in so fiercely that Judith turned to stare at him. ' Put no trust in anyone alive, Judith— not in your Georges nor in me nor in your friends here. The dead are faithful, but the living change with every breath. What was my mother ten years back, Judith? You knew her. No one kinder or more generous ever breathed; but now, although I may break my heart serving her, she can only say that Will is making money in London or that the bailiff manages better than I . . . I am going away from Uldale. I can endure it no longer.'

She could feel his whole body heaving with his distress. She thought that in a moment he would break into tears.

' Nay, nay, it is not so bad. I mustn't speak of Sarah because, God forgive me, I never loved her, but it will be good for you, Francis, to go to London for a while. Perhaps I shall follow you with Georges.'

' Everything has left me,' he murmured. ' I am quite alone. I am not a man to make friends readily. Even Moore, with whom I had an intimacy, has gone too far for me in this French business. And now——my mother, my sister——'

She kissed him passionately. ' I will never, never leave you, Francis. After Georges I love you most in the world. Do you remember years ago when I crept in to look at Mrs. Monnasett after she was dead and your father beat me, how you came and comforted me? I ever *adored* you! '

' And do *you* remember,' he said, holding her close to him, ' one evening when there were fire-works on Keswick Lake, how we sat together— you and I, Will and Reuben—and talked of our future, how Will said that all he cared for was to make money, and I talked like a ninny, and Reuben——'

He broke off.

'And where is Reuben now? I have not seen him these two years. Someone told me he was an itinerant preacher.'

Judith nodded. 'Yes . . . He preaches in the hills to anyone who will listen. They throw stones and mud at him and set dogs on him from the villages, but he says that he is happy now, and so I hope he may be. Poor Reuben! Francis, will it not be terrible for him if there is no God, and when he is dead he has had all the stones and mud for nothing?'

'There can be no God,' Francis answered. 'This world is too unjust and bitter. No God could suffer Himself to witness it, an it is His own doing. . . . And yet I dream sometimes of a fine Heaven, all mercy and charity, where all men are free and there are no tyrants. . . .' He sighed, rubbing his eyes with his hands. 'Certainly a dream—farther from this world every day. . . . But you, Judith, Will, Reuben and I—we are a mixed lot of Herries. All Herries is in us together. From a study of all of us you would get the Herries quality. All obstinate, all proud, all English, but in nothing else alike. But you are right. You have told me what I came to ask. I will go to London. And yet I doubt that I will be happy there. I love this piece of country like none other in the world.'

She would have answered him, telling him, too, how she loved it; but he saw that she suddenly stiffened. She rose slowly from his feet, straightening her small body as though under a spell. Her eyes were fixed on the window.

He followed her gaze and saw coming on the rough path above the Tarn a group of people.

'It cannot be! It cannot be!' he heard Judith mutter, and then, a moment after, she had broken from him with a cry, had rushed from the room and, her red hair tumbling, had started down the path.

Standing at the window, he saw then a figure detach itself from the group and run ahead of the rest. The figure met Judith, raised her in the air, hugging her.

'This must be Georges,' thought Francis with a quick sensation of sadness and loneliness. It was right that Judith should run to him. It must be marvellous for her after so long an absence, but why must the fellow come just now and spoil the only happy hour that Francis had known for many months?

Judith cared for him, Francis, but at the sight of her husband she could forget him as though he had never been. So it was with him always. Everyone had someone else. He was first with no one. Well, what of it? Had he not courage enough for that rôle? He shrugged his shoulders and went out.

Standing in the little wind-swept garden, he could see that others had been attracted by the noise and had come to the doors. In front of a cottage not far from him stood an enormous woman, yes, like a whale. That must be the witch of whom Judith had spoken.

A wind blew up the little stream that tumbled from the Tarn. Some fat Herdwick sheep

wandered like sleep-walkers towards the Fell.
The group was near enough now for him to distinguish them. The leader was a slim, handsome, dark fellow, Georges Paris. He had an
arm round Judith, who was looking up, talking
eagerly. In the other he swung carelessly a gilt
bird-cage that contained a bright crimson bird.

Behind were two pack-horses laden with
boxes; there were sheep-dogs, some young men,
a stout laughing girl with a red ribbon in her hair.
Georges Paris was wearing a handsomely cut
riding-coat and a broad hat with a silver cord
round it. The colours of the gilt cage, the
crimson bird, the red ribbon, stood out sharply
against the dark Tarn ridged now with the wind
like a gridiron, the snow-streaked hills, the heavy
grey sky.

The air quivered with excitement; there were
the voices, dogs barking; everyone was laughing.
A group of the Ritsons came out eagerly from the
farm.

He felt that he could not bear to meet them.
He slipped away, found Juno and rode off. No
one noticed him. Within a week he had departed for London.

THE CRIMSON BIRD

GEORGES PARIS, running forward to meet Judith, did not know and would not have cared had he known that with those very steps he was influencing the future form and shape of branches of the Herries tree.

He was gay, he was honourably fatigued, he was hungry and thirsty, triumphant with physical health and money in his pocket. He hadn't seen his dear little Judith for many months. He was going to remain with her now and make her happy and make himself happy; but even as he greeted her he was able to notice that one of the Ritson girls, advancing now towards the little bridge, had grown uncommonly pretty while he was away and had exactly the figure that he preferred.

Judith, too, running forward to meet him, was unaware that she was running forward into the first chapter of her mature life, and that when he caught her up, putting the bird-cage for a moment on the stones, and hugged her and rubbed his cheek against hers, this was the opening of a battle that would form her nature and mould it, affecting through her the whole future stock and texture of the Herries family.

That moment when Judith was caught up and

felt Georges' arms about her and his mouth on
hers was her last of peace.   She did not at the
time realise that.   She was to have weeks now
of happiness.   But looking back long afterwards
she saw clearly that that was so.   The steps from
that were so gradual, so silent, but the movement
was sure.   So, to the end of her life, she remembered that heavy grey sky, the snow-flecked hills,
the ruffled water of the Tarn, the crimson bird
beating against the bars of the cage on the wet
shining stones, and that warm amused murmur of
Georges' voice.

' My little darling. . . . And is your hair still
so lovely? '

Afterwards she thought perhaps that she got
what she deserved, because in all her excitement
she forgot entirely Francis, never all that afternoon remembered him, sank into her husband's
arms that night without a thought of him.

It is of no use, however, to be too solemn about
it, for that day and many days after it were exceedingly happy for both Judith and Georges.
Georges wanted only for himself to be happy, and
if he was happy, why, then, he was charming to
everyone.   It was only when he began to be less
happy that others began to suffer.

And Judith wanted only that Georges should
be happy.   She could not have believed that the
world could be so lovely as it was in the weeks
after Georges' return.   They were still children,
both of them, in their capacity for happiness.
They could be happy at a moment's notice and
over nothing at all, a bird's cry, a gooseberry

pudding, a dance in the road, the sun on the Tarn.

The sun shone during those weeks. All the valley was illuminated. Nor was it ever a constant sun, whose glow can be wearisome. Not in this country. It was a sun attended by flights of happy clouds, and it shone upon all the running streams with the endearing tenderness of a passing hand, glittered in the heart of the bogs of peat and struck fire from the steaming rocks.

For the first weeks Judith had no conception but that she was going to be happy for ever. She knew that Georges was selfish, grabbing, thoughtless of others, a liar and a thief. On the other hand he was delightful to look at, a charming companion when he was pleased, and although a liar about his deeds, quite honest about himself. But beyond these things she loved him. She loved him with all her being, and when one says that of Judith one means it.

She loved him maternally, because she knew that he was an evil small boy, who had not reached any age of discretion. She loved him physically. She loved him as a comrade. She loved him quite selflessly, never thinking at all of her own advantage in anything, but in her heart she was determined one day to dominate him. She could not help that in herself. It was so in her with everyone whom she met. She must *want* to dominate them.

But she loved him behind and beyond these ways, as only women can love—that is as though she had made him herself. She did not like altogether some of the things in him that she had made, but it was her work. So she loved him with deep tenderness and care, but also with the proprietary pride that a craftsman has for his beautiful creation.

She knew that he did not love her in any sense of the word love as she understood it, but she did not want him to love her in *her* way. She wanted him simply as he was. Well, she got him as he was, and the first trouble came when he showed her a little of what he was. This was in March 1793.

The suddenness of that first trouble took her breath away. They had had a merry evening. They had had a 'rocking-night' in the Ritsons' great kitchen, the women spindling while everyone told tales. Wonderful stories were told, stories of the 'Wise Man' and 'Hobthross,' sovereign remedies against witchcraft, stories of the hunting of the 'hiding' men after the 'Forty-five.

Suddenly Judith was aware that no one there liked her husband. The Cumbrian can hide his true feeling better than any other of God's people; there is no sober reticence anywhere in the world so dignified, so impenetrable as his if he wishes. Judith knew these people; they were her friends; they had taken her in and made her one of them, and when the Cumbrian does that you are safe. They had not, however, taken Georges.

How did she know it? She could not tell, unless perhaps it were something that she saw in the bright unswerving eye of old Ritson, seated in the settle, his body high and taut, his white beard a prophet's. His eye rested on Georges, and Judith was suddenly frightened. They did not like Georges. They none of them liked him.

Later that night she was lying beside Georges in bed. They could hear the tumbling water beyond the house. No other sound. Driven by her queer uneasiness, she began to ask him questions, questions about his life in White-haven; he kept always a dark cloud over all his life away from her. It had always been under-stood between them that she left that alone. But if she asked him anything he must answer her truthfully. As his answers always hurt her she had learnt not to ask.

But to-night she was uneasy. Why did her friends here not like him? He felt strange to her, as though she had never touched him before nor heard his voice. She was very young and knew nothing yet about marriage.

So she said a very foolish thing.

'Next time that you go to Whitehaven, I shall come with you.'

He laughed gently. He put up his hand and buried it in her hair. 'Then I would kill you and throw you into the sea,' he said.

'But when you go to London you say you will take me with you.'

'Yes, I shall need you there.' He tugged at her hair.

'Don't, Georges. You hurt me. . . . But perhaps you need me in Whitehaven.'

' I neither need you nor think of you in Whitehaven.'

' You don't think of me? '

' But why should I?   I have quite another life there.'

' But you write letters to me.'

' Yes.   Suddenly you come into my mind. . . . Your smallness, your hair, how you laugh when you are amused.   Then I write.'

She sighed with satisfaction.

' Then you do belong to me.   I can make you do what I say.'

This was the instant of transformation.   He sat up in bed and shook her until her head was, it seemed, separated from her neck.   Then he pushed her out on to the floor.

She got up slowly, rubbing her hands in her eyes and staring at him in amazement.   Then he jumped out of bed and chased her out of that room into the next.   He caught her, dragged her by the hair and threw her on to the floor again. He was trembling with anger.   She could see him only dimly in a pale-green moonlight that shadowed the sky and the room.   But two stars quivered with laughter above the dark stern trees.

' Never you say that again! ' he shouted at her. ' I'll beat you!   That you own me!   Never you say that again!   You miserable!   I'll whip you. By God, I shall show you! '

He was dancing with rage.   She got up and stood against the wall, staring.   She was too angry to speak.   She sat all night in a chair under the green moonlight. She was bitterly cold. She couldn't think at all; she was so utterly surprised.

Early in the morning he came to her, kissed her feet and her hair, said that he was so sorry, so very, very sorry. Then he carried her to bed and warmed her cold body. She said not a word. She had never in all her life been so completely surprised.

All that day she was silent, going about her duties with a grave set face, and all day in her eyes there was that look of surprise. But she was not a fool, and she had the great gift that was to serve her again and again of seeing straight in difficult crises. When the situation was sentimental she was unsentimental, as indeed most women are. She was not in the least sentimental now, and when, in the evening of that day, Georges, made very uncomfortable by her silence, explained himself, she listened gravely, not thinking at all as to how she could snatch compensation from him for her wounded pride, but simply as to whether what he said really explained what had happened.

But, in the middle of the explanation, Judith, looking up, saw the crimson bird, a cockatoo, in the gilt cage hanging from a nail. The bird had its head on one side and, with its beady eyes shining, listened attentively to everything that Georges said.

'I am bad,' he began. 'I always told you that I was. I have never had—what do you say? —any fine sense of morality. I am not at all like

your Sir Charles Grandison. I despise the sentiments; they are for women. I have the devil
of a temper and I have never tried to check it.
My mother had it also. For myself I think that
if you understand my temper it is very agreeable.
It makes a change.'

'Do you love me?' asked Judith suddenly.
She asked not at all from sentiment, but because
whether he did or not was a practical question of
importance.

'No,' he said. 'No, Judith, I do not. I
love nobody. I don't know what it is to love
anybody if by love you mean to be in a fever, to
give up what you want, to run hurrying to the
feet of the beloved. I have never been in a fever
about any person except to sleep with a woman,
and then it is quickly over. No, I do not love
you.'

'I see,' said Judith.

'No, but you must understand. I do not
love you, but I care about you more than anyone
except myself. I am bad and worthless. Not
that I am ashamed. Why should I be? It is
the colour I was born, that is all. But I am nearer
having virtuous feelings when I am with you
than at any other time. I have always thought
that I had no heart as my mother had none.
The French people are not famous for their
heart. But at times I suspect that you are giving
me a little. For example, I have been unhappy
to-day because I hurt you, and I have never before
been unhappy about hurting anybody. I always
want to come back to you when I have gone away,

and I feel now that if ever I bring everything down about my head—as I shall one day—it is only you in the whole world that I want to come to. You are a wonderful woman, Judith. You have more strength and courage and sense than I have ever seen in a woman. I don't really care for women except for a moment. I prefer greatly men, and that is what I like, to be in danger, to be against the law. More than anything in life I like to be against the law. I cannot bear that anyone should say to me " Do this! " or " Go there! " I am like a bird in a cage. That was why last night, when you said that you could make me do what you wished, I hated you and wanted to kill you. I am no good, Judith, but I do not care. If I want to be in a rage I am in a rage, if I wish to steal I steal. Life is not important, not in the least. You and I are not important. No one is important.

' Only to break the law, to beat someone who plays against you, to take what isn't yours and make it yours, that for a short time is amusing. But I hope my life will not be long.'

After all this Judith nodded her head. ' I think I understand you,' she said. ' You are very honest with me, Georges, and it would be an easier matter if I did not love you. There is no reason for loving you that I can see, but I do. Only I must protect myself. You must not beat me nor drag me by the hair. That is stupid and sentimental. It is like Emma Furze acting in a play.'

He agreed that it was. They were reconciled and were good friends again.

But when two people live together, every struggle between them, however handsomely it is ended, alters the relationship. Judith was now on her guard. She watched Georges, even as the crimson bird watched her. Yes, the crimson bird was very like Georges. It was charming when it wished, and twisted its neck to be scratched and rubbed its beak against your finger. But it surrendered, for no very obvious reason, to the most frantic tempers, screaming its rage and rasping its claws against the cage; it was very proud of itself and its feathers, and its spirit was undaunted, which was also one of the fine qualities in Georges. Judith had no intention of surrendering to Georges; he should not dominate her, but he was now a little distance removed from her. She must be close to him without his knowing it. She thought that she was clever enough for that. But it is difficult for any woman who has a very tender heart and no sentimentality. She is for ever tempted into situations that seem to her foolish. And therefore she keeps back so much that she feels.

As the summer came nearer Georges began to grow very restless.

He was not restless with the place. In his fashion he cared for it almost as deeply as Judith did, and it did not worry him at all that the people did not like him. Ever since he had first come to Cumberland as a little boy, the Cumbrians had disliked and suspected him, and it had never

disturbed him at all. That it did not was one
of the things that in the old days amused Tom
Gauntry about him.

Watendlath was the wildest piece of land that
he had yet known. The fells towards the Langdales appeared endless, and in their mingling of
peat and heather, ancient rock, strange tumuli
in human shape, and sudden streams rushing
through the soil as though on some secret mission
enchanted his lawlessness. On the other side
there was Keswick. All England just then was
gambling crazy, and Keswick had its little
share.

Georges was a born gambler; one day he was
a genius at cards and at another he would be so
wild and reckless that he would lose all his advantage. Like Mr. Fox and the superior gentlemen in London he would bet on anything, the
fall of a leaf, the approach of a woman round the
corner, the wax of a guttering candle. There
were plenty of men, from gentlemen like Mr.
Osbaldistone and Mr. Kenrew down to ostlers
at the 'George' or broken-down wasters like Tom
Fawcett, who, in Keswick, would oblige him. At
first, after his return from Whitehaven, he was
well in funds. Then less and less so.

Judith sometimes rode with him into Keswick.
She had a few friends there, a Mrs. Pounder who
had come from Bath, a rather blowzy red-cheeked
lady, who knew Emma Furze, had a warm heart
but an uncertain moral code; a Mrs. Dunn and
her husband Henry Dunn, kindly people, crazy
about dogs and horses; one or two more. But

on the whole Judith did not care for Keswick and
would have given thirty of it for one of her beloved
Watendlath.   What really distressed her as the
weeks passed was that Georges might in a gambling fit rid himself of her adored farm.   That he
was capable of it, in one of his excitements, she
well knew.

For her own expenses she needed almost
nothing at Watendlath.   She shared with the
Ritsons food and shelter.   She was scrupulous in
her record of expenses, chronicling every penny;
Georges never looked at her laborious accounts.
At first he was ready to shower money on her.
He bought her scarves and dresses and shoes and
bonnets.   She didn't need them in the least.
Now he was less ready.   She didn't care.   There
would always be food and shelter for him at the
farm.

But if one night he should suddenly tell her
that the farm was gone?

On the other hand, she shared with him his
excitement about London.   She would like to
experience that adventure.   They were not so
cut off in the North as they had been.   There
was plenty of talk about the old King, the Regent,
Mrs. Fitzherbert and the rest.

Beyond this she had a strong Herries feeling.
The Pomfrets in Kensington, Will and his
ambitions, the Rockages in Wiltshire, she wanted
to see them all and maybe, herself, play some part
in the Herries fortunes.   Half of her was sober
Herries—she could understand Will's ambitions
—the other half was wild English, born of her

mother and father, belonging altogether to these
hills and lakes and streams. One half of her
looked at the other half of her, partly in mockery,
partly in wonder.

By the month of July, which was hot and
green with no wind, she knew that a crisis was
approaching. Even the crimson bird seemed to
know it, for it rapped its nails no longer on the
bars of the cage, nor fell into violent rages. It
perched, with its head on one side, and listened.

And the crisis came. But before it came, she
had a moment with Georges that she would never
forget, one of the happiest of her life.

He rode in from Keswick, up the little rough
path above the beck that was now thin and placid
like a child asleep. The evening sun was deep
and fair over all the landscape, and gold-dust was
in the air. He came and sat beside her in the
window-seat, took her hand, put his arm around
her and drew her to him. These gestures were
so rare in him that she knew that something
critical had happened.

She sat there, her heart trembling lest in his
next words he should tell her that he had gambled
the farm away. But he did not. He told her
nothing, and she, wise through much experience,
asked no questions.

They sat in the golden silence for a long time.
The little stream that ran down the break in
Armboth was only an amber line now after the
dry weather.

'Judy, you funny little thing, how can you
stay here month after month and be happy?'

'Because I love the place. My father lived
below the hill in Rosthwaite, and he was there
without moving for years and years.'

'Yes, but your father was crazed.'

'Maybe I'm crazed as well.'

'No, but you're not. You have more sense
than anyone in Keswick. I'm proud of you,
Judy.' Then after a pause he asked her: 'Do
you not hate me for riding into Keswick and
gambling, leaving the business in Whitehaven to
tumble?'

'No,' she answered. 'I could never hate
you.'

'Why not? Cannot you hate?'

'Oh yes, I can hate very well.'

'I could almost love you,' he said, 'if I were
quieter. Sometimes I dream of making a handsome fortune, and we have a big house with dogs
and horses, and you have all you want. . . .'

'I have all I want.'

He drew her closer, held to her as though
someone would tear her away. She did not dare
to let him see how happy she was. Wild ideas
ran through her head that perhaps always life
would be like this now. He would give up his
dangerous ventures, they would improve the farm,
sometimes they would go to London for a holiday,
perhaps there would be children. She would be
a hostess, as Sarah used to be in Uldale; on occasion she and Georges would escape from everyone
up into the hills, Eskdale or Patterdale, away from
everyone. . . .

'How old are you now, Judy?'

She told him.   Nineteen in November.

' I should not have married you so young. Indeed, I should never have married you at all.'

She drew his head close to her childish breasts. She sat on the window-seat clutching him to her. She saw her feet dangling.   How she wished she were taller!   Of course, he could not love her, so small and insignificant.   Then as she looked at his dark head and felt the warmth of his cheek against her thin dress she thought that she was as good as another, better than many.   But she would love him all her life long, even though she lived to be a hundred.   He was worn out.   ' He was playing cards all night,' she thought—and he slept there, his head on her breast.

It was her last quiet hour for many a day.

The crisis came a week later, and the cause of it was, of all people in the world, Reuben.   She had seen Reuben but thrice since her marriage, once at his mother's house in Cockermouth (little Mr. Sunwood had died a year and a half ago of a chill), once in Keswick, and had once listened to his preaching in Borrowdale beyond Rosthwaite. Poor Reuben!   On that last occasion her heart had ached for him.   He wandered, so she understood, from place to place, belonging to no especial ministry or sect, simply preaching Christ and His message.   Yes, simple enough in intention, but involved in every possible sort of loneliness, hostility, ostracism.   Reuben had not even, Judith thought, the gifts or personality of a preacher. He looked clumsy, ill-shapen, in his awkward, ill-fitting black coat, and he had what no public orator must have, lack of confidence in his own gifts, and so he bred lack of trust in his audience. He gazed anxiously around, and, save when he was caught up on the wings of his devotion and imagination, he hesitated for words and moved restlessly on his feet. On the day when she heard him there was a gathering of farmhands, women, boys, who listened, some with a mild, some with an angry, interest, and before the end he had been driven away with mud and stones. She had hurried after him, but had not found him.

Now, on a lovely summer's day, Mrs. Ritson ran in to say that there was an itinerant preacher on the nearer side of Brund Fell and that they were going to hear him. It might, Judith thought, be Reuben. Georges was away at a farm bargaining for a horse.

Indeed, it was Reuben. She saw him at once, standing in his black coat bathed in sun, while all about him the rough tumbled fell wore that rather sinister look that this country has in brilliant sunlight—something too naked and bold, as though the real country were only present in cloud and mist and had given way to some flaunting and scheming intruder. Reuben looked the more helpless, the more dishevelled in the glare, and Judith, her heart always instantly touched by anything at odds, longed to go and stand beside him. He had by now, however, his supporters. Since she had last seen him he had collected apparently a little band of strange and incongruous figures—a large stout

woman in a man's jacket and a bedraggled green
skirt, two rheumy old men who were so nervous
of their audience that they could scarcely stand
on their rickety legs, two girls and a boy. Reuben
was stouter of body, Judith thought, but younger
than ever in face, his eyes wide and anxious like
a baby's, his cheeks plump, his chin indeterminate.

A crowd had collected, it had followed him
from Seathwaite, Rosthwaite, Grange. It was
a rough-looking lot of men, women, children and
dogs, some there in evident sympathy, but for the
most they were, Judith thought, strangers to the
district. She had noticed of late a certain class
of foreigner in Keswick and surroundings. There
was much distress abroad. Food prices were
high, work in many parts scarce. Transporta-
tion, too, was so much easier than it had been.
This little world was no longer isolated from the
older one. The days of its extreme remoteness
were over for ever.

Reuben was speaking when Judith, Mrs.
Ritson, and two other women drew near. He
spoke with a shrill, rather piercing note that
dropped suddenly to a low bass. There was
something ludicrous about this that almost at once
set some of his audience laughing. As he talked
he waved his hands in the air and rolled his eyes.
Every once and again the little group round him
would break into singing with a wavering and
unsteady tone. Judith became with every moment
more uneasy. He began a passionate evocation
of the character of Jesus Christ, speaking of His
charity, His unselfishness, His courage. Behind

his uncertain voice there was a piercing sincerity, but he had not the power to evoke for others what he himself saw. Judith had the strange notion that the hills, the rocks, the peat seemed to understand him better than the people around him. She fancied that the sun was a little veiled, the colours a little milder. But he could not catch his audience; they were not fish that day for his net. Some of the more scornful men began to laugh. One of the dogs began a fight with another dog. When the quavering voices were raised other voices joined in derisively. And as the opposition grew, Reuben's voice was ever more shrill, and his eyes wandered more beseechingly to the heavens.

Then someone threw a stone, pretending that it was aimed at one of the dogs. Other stones followed. Two men had been drinking gin from a bottle and began to quarrel; a moment later they were rolling on the ground atop of one another. The dogs were barking, the women screaming, figures were running down the hill. Clods of peat were thrown, more stones; something cut Reuben's cheek. His little band clustered close together, and then, as the scene was wilder, the two old men and the stout woman started away quickly over the brow of the hill.

Reuben stood there, his hand on his bleeding cheek, as though he did not quite know what to do. Judith went up to him and put her hand on his arm.

' Reuben dear——' she said.

He started, at first seeming not to recognise her. The crowd was streaming away down the hill.

' Come and rest at the farm,' she said.

He followed her quite passively, like a child.
She felt his arm trembling under her hand. Then
when they had gone a little way he began to speak.

' They think it finer not to listen . . . to throw
mud . . . I cannot hold them. You may laugh,
all of you may laugh, but the day is coming when
the spirit of the Lord will descend upon me. . . .
Stay a moment, Judith, while I fasten my boot.'

He was wearing faded and stained green
breeches under his coat. He bent to tie the worn
string of his boot. When he raised his head
his forehead was bathed in perspiration and his
cheek was bleeding again. But he was smiling.

' God has but just spoken to me and told me
that I do well. He watcheth over me and will see
that I come to no harm.'

' Where are you living? ' she asked him; she
had to take many quick little steps to keep pace
with his almost running strides.

' Like the birds of the air——' Then he
shook his head. ' I cannot remember, but I must
always be talking in Bible phrases like the Methodists. But with you, Judith, that's folly. I live
nowhere. I have no home unless I go to mother.
You know,' he began more excitedly, ' now that
God is the only real thing in my life, roofs and
walls are constricting. I am happier in the open.'
She asked him to stay with them for a little while
and be rested, but he shook his head. ' No,
no . . . I must go on. There is so much to
be done.'

While he was sitting beside the big open fire,

she brought water, and he washed his face. He took off his coat and his shabby riding-boots and his soiled neckcloth. He opened his shirt and bathed his breast that was smooth white like a woman's. His hands, too, were soft.

He became more collected and told her of his brother's death in France, how he had joined the first ragged French army and almost at once had been killed in some squabble on the way to the frontier. As he spoke Judith saw again the desperate hunted man in Cockermouth. It had been, it seemed, since that day that both for her and Reuben active consciousness of life had begun. After his brother's death, he told her, he had been always restless, and at last had begun to preach up and down the country, simply by himself, attached to no creed. He didn't know whether he did any good; it seemed to him that he did not. But he must go on. He was the Bear, ordered to play his part. . . .

She realised that he had no great interest in her affairs. He put up his hand once and touched her hair, but he asked her no questions about herself, whether she were happy, how she lived here. . . . Once he broke out about women. They were his great temptation, the temptation of the Devil. He tried to lead his life without them, but they were always breaking in. Often he could not sleep at nights, and in the towns, in the taverns and inns. . . .

She kissed him. 'Reuben, stay here for a little. It is very pleasant here, and I will care for you———'

She broke off. Georges was standing in the doorway, looking at them. She realised at once the evil temper that he was in. Things had gone badly with him over the horse. Reuben rose. His coat and vest were on a chair-back, his long muddy riding-boots on the floor. He looked doubtfully at Reuben.

Judith said: ' Georges, this is Reuben.'

Georges began at once. ' Yes, and we want no canting preachers here. I have heard of your doings, sir. Whatever my wife may say, this is not the place for you.' He was in one of his black rages, trembling with anger.

Reuben at once hurried to pull on his boots, drag on his coat. He said nothing.

Judith burst out: ' Georges, you shall not. Reuben is my relation and my friend——'

' A fine relation. A canting humbugging preacher who steals the chickens and kisses the maids. A fox! A fox——'

But Reuben was clothed and stood for a moment with a very fine dignity. He kissed Judith's cheek. ' Good-bye, dear,' he said, then staying a moment before Georges, quite, as Judith was afterwards to remember, without any fear: ' Good-day, sir; I do not steal chickens, and that I am a preacher is true and is God's will.'

She ran forward with a cry. ' No, no, Reuben——'

But he was gone. She could see him walking swiftly, but still with dignity, along the little path by the Tarn.

She stayed, watching, until he was out of sight,

and then she was a proper termagant. Georges knew well that she had a temper, but he had never seen it like this, and had his own rage not been too fierce for him to be clear about anything he would have marvelled.

Although now they were close together, they shouted at one another as though they were at far ends of the valley.

' That is the last time! This is my place. He is my relation, like a brother. He came here weary, soiled——'

' A fine brother with his thieving.'

' You to talk of thieving——'

' Well, at least, I do it in the open. There's no hiding in women's cupboards.'

' You *shall* not! He is more noble than you can ever understand——'

' Well, go to him then! Tie a string to his tail and follow him round the countryside.'

She looked at him, then, moving back to the fireplace, drew her little body to its full height and in a small chill voice, speaking now very low, said:

' You are cruel. I have always known it, but how cruel, not until to-night.'

He came towards her, not for reconciliation. At that moment he hated her: to set up her will against his, and she had been bathing his cheek, that mean canting rat of a preacher—she—his wife—

' Aye,' he said slowly, ' when I have a ranting woman to discipline.'

' Now learn this,' she answered him, looking

him in the face as though she had struck him between the eyes.   In his rage he was not so angry
but that he could see some dignity of anger in her
that gave her a dominance he had never suspected
in her.   ' Learn this.   I am not your woman to
be disciplined.   Here was one who came to me,
my kinsman, weary, hungry, beset, and you drove
him out with a curse.   That I will never forget.'

' And I will never forget,' he answered as
fiercely, ' what you have been to me this day.   I
am master in this place.'

' You shall never be master of me,' she
answered.

' We shall see.'

He came towards her as though to strike her.
She never moved.   Then he remembered something.   He was held.   She was the elder at that
instant as he stood there like an angry boy, his
black hair ruffled and damp.   He had on still his
riding-coat, and he carried a whip in his hand.

They exchanged a long defiant look.   Then
he turned on his heel.

' I have had enough of this,' he said, and he
went up the winding stair.

She never moved.   Later—she had no sense
of time, but her anger bore her as though on a
horse with bright wings, timelessly, through dry
air—he came down, pulling after him a box.
It bumped on every stair.   He stood in the doorway, dark in an evening glow all saffron, with
faint blue light in the upper sky.

' I shall never return,' he said.

Still she did not move.   She heard him call

to young Jacob Ritson. She heard them lead the horse out and its sharp stamp on the stones, very clear on that summer evening. Then she saw him ride off, the box behind him. She saw him climb the Fell beyond the Tarn. And still her anger was so hot that it held her high in fiery space.

Many hours later, at some early morning time, she woke, and her brain was quite clear and her anger all gone. She did not at first realise that he was not there. Half awake, she turned as she was accustomed to do, to settle her small body inside the curve of his arm. She would lay her head on his breast, even in her sleep seeing that her hair was not in his eyes, then her hand would fold inside his palm.

She stretched out her hand and touched only the cold bed. Then she was fully awake. She sat up to hear some bird calling its cry like slipping water beyond the open window. There was a pale light, like stealing smoke over the room, and in her ear as though a voice had called it from over the hill: ' I shall never return.'

She waited weeks for a letter. None came. He was gone; and he meant, no doubt, what he had said. It would be like him. She saw now that she had never had any real hold on him. He did not love her; he had very often told her so. He liked to tell her. She knew nothing about his life without her. She envisaged White-haven and the sea as a strange town, the houses

running down to the sea-edge, figures moving
on the foreshore, bales loaded in darkness, the
firing of a pistol, or some woman, very opposite
to herself, tall and dark, coming softly in a
candle-lit room, drawing him towards her . . .
and outside these scenes a sea always angry, grey
and roaring, and some foreign coast, darkness
again, men moving on tiptoe.   That was what her
imagination did for her, and it was to this land
that he had returned. He would never come
back.

She had great courage.   She would show no
one that anything had occurred.   She went about
all her daily business, her head up, poking her
nose into every village affair, nothing too trivial
for her, deciding always what was best to be done,
hypnotising them into believing that she was a
woman, although she knew now that she was only
a child.

Her business now was to cut out all the outside world.   She would not think of Georges
nor of anything beyond Watendlath Beck.

All the souls of the village she brought
into her world and made them giant-size to fill
the space better——old man Ritson, patriarchal,
aloof, believing fiercely in God and His angels,
whom he expected to descend from the skies at
any moment, but practical, too, about money so
that he knew where every penny went to; young
Tom Ritson, deformed, with a crooked back, a
marvel at any job with his hands; Mary Ritson,
the beauty who loved some imaginary man of her
dreams and would wear a lost far-away look when

earthy young men courted her; Giles Braithwaite the wrestler, famous in all Borrowdale
already, though he was only twenty, later to be
famous through all Cumberland and the North,
at present a stupid young man who thought the
French lived over Ullswater way; James Wilson,
broad, brown-faced, kindly-eyed, the finest Cumbrian of them all, whose wife Jane gave him a
child every year so that he now had fourteen;
Mother West, the whale, the witch, perhaps at the
last, when all was said, Judith's warmest friend
in the place; the children, the babies, scattering
like ducks, like chickens, like puppies in and out
of the becks, the peat, the stony passages—all
Cumberland, if you liked, held in this small
space, among these few rocks and boulders.
Nor so changed from to-day when the Herdwick
sheep still pass from descendant to descendant,
and the children still go, day after day, rain or
shine, down the rocky path to school in Rosthwaite. They did not care that only a mile or two
away by the sea the new Industrial England was
beginning to show its dusky evil-stained face,
nor that there was an old mad King in London.
Here, between Armboth and Brund Fell, was,
and is, the whole heart of England.

Soon, though, it was not enough for Judith.
With all her resolve and courage, unhappiness
crept closer and closer to her. She began to
dread the waking moment of every day. She
began to watch, against her will, more and more
anxiously the path by which the carrier would
come on his old fat horse from Keswick.

She realised for the first time for many years how lonely she was. These friends of hers in Watendlath were not enough for her. Reuben, even if she could find him, was not enough. Francis was in London. Deborah, Reuben's mother, was a widow in Cockermouth. Judith thought sometimes of going to visit Deborah Sunwood, but she shrank from it because it was there that she had one of her liveliest memories of Georges. She began to see, with a vividness that appalled her, that she had staked her whole life on Georges. She had not cared so much when he was away, because she had always known that he would come back. Like many another she discovered that true love is irreplaceable. There may be other later experiences as fine, but never *that* one again. There was no one else like Georges. There never would be. His very selfishness, ill-temper, childish reckless independence gave him his colour. And the fact that she had lost him made him twice as precious. She was growing through all this knowledge. Life taught her more now in these few weeks than in years before, but we do not thank life for teaching us *while* we are being taught.

She became more and more miserable. Sleep forsook her. She lay for hours, watching for the light, and when it came she watched the road. One evening she went to Mother West's dark smoky room that smelt of herbs and bacon, and made her tell the cards.

But the cards told nothing. Then one

autumn afternoon her unhappiness was so deep that all her courage left her. She went out on to the peak of the Fell that looks down over Borrowdale and sat there, while the clouds rolled over Scafell in red and smoky splendour and all the bracken was gold. But she saw nothing. She sat there, her head in her hands, and cried her heart out. Only a stone's fall below her her father had lived, crazily alone for years.

'Oh, I cannot endure it any longer,' she cried as though to him. 'I cannot live without Georges. What am I to do?'

She dried her eyes and tried to be sensible. This was what she always despised others for doing, to have the vapours as the women in Keswick did, or to want a man who did not want them. Georges did not want her. Now, here on this hill, with only the sky about her, she must understand that he was never going to return. Her life with him was over, and she must make a new life for herself. 'No one can beat you but yourself.' She was young, strong, full of curiosity and eagerness to see the world.

Georges had never cared very much for her (but had he not always returned to her?), he was not a fine man (but was he not endearing with his dark hair and his sense of fun?), he was for ever in a temper (but was he not enchanting when things went well?), he would be hanged one day (would she not be proud to stand at his side when all the world was against him?), he was French, and the French were a bad nation (did she truly care *what* he was so long as he was with her?), she was

K

an independent woman (who would live her life in her own way whatever men did). Perhaps (for queerer things happen in this world than facts allow for) an old man with a scarred face stood beside her then, his arm about her, he looking down through rock and stone to a little house tumbling to ruin.

So she went back over the Fell with her head up, and the first thing that she heard was that there was a letter for her. On the one day that she had not watched!

It was scribbled on some rough tea-paper and ran:

DEAR LITTLE QUEEN JUDY—I have got a Fortune and We shall go to London to spend it. I am coming Home to fetch you.—Your loving husband,

GEORGES.

She allowed the letter to drop. She ran like a mad thing in to all the Ritsons, and she caught the Patriarch round the neck, crying, ' He's coming home! He's made a fortune! He's coming home! '

She danced like the child that she yet was, into the hallan and over the cobbles, and ran into the whale's parlour and danced all about between the stuffed birds and the snakes in spirits and the bottle with the baby's thumb.

The smoke blew out of the chimney, and old Mother West, smoking her pipe, nodded her head with pleasure, for she loved this child.

The crimson bird in the cage woke up and scraped with its talons on the wires.

HAPPINESS IN LONDON

THE only part of Georges Paris that was visible was his nightcap, white with a red tassel that lifted and fell above his nose with the rhythm of his breathing.

Through the open door in the larger room Judith Paris lay, also sunk in sleep, her hair loose about the pillow, and on her lips a happy smile, because she dreamt that she and Georges were alone in a chaise made of silver that drove swiftly through the clouds above Scafell.

All the cocks around Cheapside were crowing. Above London a heavy dark mantle was slowly lifted, and soon over all the mud and running water that clung to the toes of the red-bricked City the sun would ride with an especial triumph, because it had not been seen for so many days. It had rained for nearly a week, and Jackanapes Row and Blowbladder Street were running with water.

Had Georges looked out from his little window into the street below at that first cock-crowing hour, he would have encountered Cheapside at the single moment of either day or night when all life there was still, for the roisterers had roistered to their beds, the 'Charlies' had not yet started their policing day, the watchmen had completed

259

their happy and far-too-easy duties. The cocks, calling from St. Dunstan's in the West to the Strand, from Butchers' Row to the Poultry, were kings of the hour.

Then as the light grew stronger he might have seen one small figure, little Jack Robinson, youngest son of Mr. Jack Robinson, shoemaker, whose premises were on the ground floor under Georges and Judith. Mr. Robinson, senior, had four small boys, who worked on his behalf sixteen hours of the day, and twelve children, fruit of his own loins, so that he was accustomed to children. That Jack, his youngest, should at this moment be earning his wages as ' climbing boy ' seemed to him but right and proper, so that there he was with shovel, scraper and brush, and in his cap a brass plate with his master's name and address. He had had some bad chimneys that night, and was so sleepy that he had found his way home as it were blindfold, with chimneys dancing by his side all the way. His lungs were half-choked with soot, his knuckles were in his eyes, but he was home. In another five minutes he would have rolled under the blanket with six other young Robinsons, pushing in among them like a little bird. He was awake enough, though, to see that it was a fine day and to rejoice thereat, for there was to be a cockfight by Bath Street that afternoon, and there would be rich gentlemen to beg pennies of on a fine day.

You can almost see Cheapside sit up, rub its fists in its eyes, give a great yawn and, jumping out of bed, start shaking its rattle. A light air has sprung up with the sun. For days these piles of little red houses, lifted, like boats on a stormy sea, on heaving cobbles, open sewers, sudden little hills that run up and down in the middle of narrow thoroughfares simply for fun, have felt the mud rise higher and higher about their doors. But this is June, and even in Cheapside the country is not far away. You can smell hay and roses as well as sewage and stale cabbage and the offal of cows and dogs and horses. The river, too, is close at hand; you can hear the noise from the steam-engines in the factories of the soap- and oil-makers, the glass-makers and the boat-builders. Were you to stand on the roof above Georges' nightcap, you would see the Pool, a forest of masts, the ships at anchor, the lighters and the barges. . . .

But Cheapside has its own noises, and soon, its face rosy with pleasure, is waving its rattle like the infant that it is, while the sun grows stronger and stronger and the churches are ringing their bells.

The noise is now rocketing about Georges' room. He hears nothing because he is well accustomed. But soon it is ten in the morning, and Cheapside is going to make the best of the splendid day.

First there are the milkwomen, then the baker ringing his bell and calling out 'Hot Loaves,' then the water-cress men (three bunches for twopence), then the old lady (at this time there were two old ladies, one with a beard, who made Cheapside their headquarters every day from ten

to one) crying 'Baking or Boiling Apples,' char-
coal stove and barrow attending them.   And now
there is the man with bandboxes, carried on
either end of a pole (at this time in Cheapside
and the neighbourhood a giant negro), then the
brickdust man with his small sacks and his
donkey (the brickdust men are, after the lamp-
lighters, the great trainers of bulldogs).   There
are the rat - trap dealers and the bullock - livers
man, the basket man, the bellows man, the chair-
mender and the door-mat man.   All calling
together, they are answered by the opening of
high windows, the emptying of pots and pans,
the rumbling of the country wagons, the first
stir in the shops whose glass windows run round-
bellied above the cobbles, the barking of dogs,
the lowing of cows, the ringing of bells—such a
hubbub that, although it is not yet mid-day, a lady
with her servant meeting another lady with *her*
servant must step into Mr. Jordan's the silver-
smith's to exchange a word or two and, once there,
there are clocks to be seen and necklaces, and
there is a bull, they say, loose by St. Paul's and a
crowd running really for the fun of the thing,
because it is a June morning with the sun shining,
and here is an Italian with a peep-show and a
monkey, and a man caught robbing Mrs. Morris's
fruit-stall and no ' Charley ' anywhere to be seen
so that Mr. Benjamin Morris, fresh from a good
night's sleep and fit for anything, has given the
thief two between the eyes and he has tumbled
into the gutter, and the little Robinsons, thoroughly up and about now, throw choice pieces

of dirt at him, and the bull, they say, is really
mad, has trampled down two flower - stalls and
a Jew's clothes - basket, and in the distance
coming in veiled harmonies through the summer
air there are the strains of a band, strains that
mingle with the scent of the roses and new-mown
hay and make the young dandy in his blue and
silver, reading his paper in one of the Turk's
Head Coffee Houses, think of Apollo Gardens
and St. George's Spa.

All this before mid-day, and while Georges
and Judith are yet happy dreaming. The room
in which Judith was sleeping was a large one,
Georges' little more than a closet. A shabby
place, Judith's room. The bed in which she
was had over it a very heavy mustard-coloured
canopy, covered with faded red roses. The
mantelpiece was tall and narrow, surmount-
ing a wretched stove, semi-circular, with a flat
front. There was a bowed fender of perforated
sheet brass, a scarred table, and a large china jar
filled with roses. There were two cupboards,
a mean stand with a wash-hand basin. On one
of the stiff high-backed chairs some of Judith's
clothing. On another most of Georges'. The
crimson bird hung in a gilt cage by the window,
but there was now green baize cloth over his
head. The sun poured in through Georges'
room into Judith's, lighting up patterns of dust
and the bare boards of the floor and the bright
green silk jacket over the chair and the silver
sheen of Georges' white waistcoat with buttons
of emerald. There were lying on the floor two

masks, a child's drum painted brilliant red and
yellow, and a bunch of artificial flowers.

So they slept, but not for long.   A door burst
open.   A woman's voice (it was Mrs. Robinson's, who was at the moment stumbling down
rickety stairs, nursing a naked baby, devouring
a slice of bread and ham) screamed: ' You can
have it your own way, ma'am. . . . You can
have it your own way! '

In the doorway stood a lady of magnificent
proportions, tall as a grenadier, as broad as tall,
with a fine bosom, a grand impassioned eye, an
air of ruling the world.   How magnificently,
too, was she dressed!   Over her hair, arranged
'hedgehog' style and powdered a very light yellow,
she wore a high-brimmed hat of dark beaver
fur, adorned with splendid trimmings of purple
silk.   The dress that covered her noble form was
a long caraco jacket of brown striped silk, a
light corselet of black taffeta with white trimming.
She carried a cane with an ebony top.   She stood,
her head high, her large face rubicund and jolly,
her arm out resting on her stick in a fine theatrical
pose.

Her eyes took in the room.   Then she saw
the bed and moved nearer to it.   She stood
looking down on Judith, smiling, her eyes senti-
mentally soft, for she was a most sentimental
woman and had not seen her dear Judith for two
years.

Then after a while she tiptoed across the
room and looked in upon Georges, who was
snoring lustily now with his mouth wide open.

She looked out of window and had the pleasure to see a grand coach, wobbling along like a fat woman, stick in a rut between cobbles, little boys run up to the windows, a lady in a beaver hat very like her own push her head out, and a man have his fruit-barrow overturned in the general excitement.

After five minutes of this, back to the bedroom again and back to the bed. With a magnificent gesture that it was a thousand pities there was no one there to see, she bent forward and gave Judith a smacking kiss on the forehead.

Judith woke, sat up, pushed her hair from her eyes, then saw her visitor. With a cry she was out of bed and had her arms around the other's tremendous waist.

' Emma! my darling, darling Emma! '

' Emma it is, my love! Thy Emma, whom Fortune has constrained, but the Heart——'

She could say no more, for Judith kissed her again and again, while Emma's great arms enfolded her in her thin nightdress with the excited fervour of an amatory bear.

' Oh, Emma. Where *have* you been? I assure you I think it most ungrateful in you——'

But Emma would let her finish no sentence. Words poured from her. She had been in Ireland. She had been in Dublin. She had had the greatest success in the Irish theatres since Venus and Minerva took human form. Especially in *The Irish Widow* or, maybe yet more, in Dryden's *Rival Queens*. Tragedy, comedy or farce, as Judith knew, it all came the

K 2

same to her.   And there had been a gentleman
in Dublin . . . Oh, a gentleman in Dublin!
' Everyone who knew us spoke of marriage as a
speedy and certain affair, and I could have cried
myself into the vapours had I not Resolution and
Character. . . .'

' Well, and what prevented him? '

' An impudent little Toad with the morality
of a—but I shock you, my darling Judith.'

' Never fear,' cried Judith, jumping up and
down the floor in her bare feet and the greatest
excitement.   ' I have stood a good many shocks.'

' But how are you, my dear little love? and
how does Mr. Georges? '

' Very well.   Very well . . . we are all very
well.   But why have you been so long away from
me?   Two years. . . .'

All this in jerks, in exclamations, in frenzied
pauses while Judith laughs and Emma laughs.

' And he pursued me, the monstrous wretch,
through three streets and an alley-way until I was
forced to run into a toy-shop and hope to have the
fortune to meet with a chair! '

' But you are handsome now, Emma, so
handsome!   And so grand.   You have money.
You have wealth.'

' I have a little.   Just for the moment.   All
to spend upon you, my darling.   I am hoping
to have an engagement at Drury Lane.'

' Georges and I, we too have money, just for
the moment. . . .'

' Your Georges, he detests me.   I am terrified
of him.   He finds me impossible.'

' But Georges is changed, as you will discover. He is older, more serious. He has still some bad friends, but I have now a little influence, a very, very little influence. When he is not gambling at the " Salutation " or at Offley's he does very well with the money that he made two years ago; he started a business in Whitehaven with Captain Wix. You know Captain Wix? I forget. He is huge as a barrel, and his heart is as big as his belly. He is all heart. Even his liver is heart. But he is also shrewd, and they have made money. . . . Georges travels from London there and back again. . . . Yes, when he is away from his wicked friends, Mr. Charteris, Mr. Mandable, and there is a Whitehaven young man, Mr. Stane. I like him the least of them all. His father owns a ship that trades to Holland. Georges has a share in it. But Georges is good now. You will see that for a Frenchman he is very well. . . .'

' Oh, God, yes!' cried Emma, throwing her arms abroad in an ecstasy. ' I can see that you are the happiest of women.'

' I am indeed, indeed happy,' Judith cried, ' now that you are come.'

They settled down more quietly after that, and sat down together on the bed under the yellow canopy, Emma's arm around Judith, Judith's red head on Emma's bosom.

There was no insincerity in their affection; there was even a certain relief in their pleasure at being together again, for with neither of them had the success of their fortunes been quite so great as they gallantly pretended.

Emma had great qualities, and one of them was constancy to those whom she loved—for so long, at least, as they loved her! For Judith she had an especial care: there was something brave and reckless and good - humoured that exactly appealed to her. She liked a woman to have both spirit and heart, and a friendship with Judith that extended now over a number of years had proved her both dauntless and passionate.

When Emma had last seen the pair they had but lately descended on London, and their position was hazardous. She suspected, looking about the room, that it was still hazardous. Judith, she thought to herself, had been through something in these two years. She was prettier, her features were maturely formed, her assurance greater, her recklessness also, perhaps.

There was something individual in the dark flame and shadows of amber light of her hair. Emma had never seen any like it—and beneath it the pale vivacity of her small face was so sharply featured. Her body was lit with energy and independence. Covered as it was now with only the lightest of nightdresses, the June sun warming it, there was something virginal, untouched, in its fire and purity. Emma had once again the sense, that she had known before, that there was something in Judith remote and separate. And yet there could be no one more human, more normal in her passion for all the adventure, all the fun, all the experience that life chose to bring to her.

They had talked then, two years before, upon

the great things that were to come from the descent
upon the Herries relations. Well, what had come
of it? How were they all?

Judith jumped off the bed, caught Emma's
beaver hat, seized her cane. 'Look, Emma!
Look! Now I'll give you Will! He's very tall,
you know, very tall. Oh yes, extremely! And
he talks like a war-horse. "Oh yes! Ha, ha!
Well, well! Dear me! How are you, my dear?"'
(Here Judith bent forward, very grand, almost to
·the ground and shook hands solemnly with an
invisible midget.) 'Just as though, you know,
we hadn't been brought up as children together.
He's the City Man, but he's also moving up.
Oh yes, very much up indeed! He can tell you
all the latest about the Prince and his bride, and
what poor Mrs. Fitzherbert is doing, and why
Lady Jersey chose the Prince *such* a plain partner
and what Mr. Fox lost last night at cards. He
moves doubly, you know, Emma, darling. There's
the Will of the moment and the Will of ten years
hence—the Will there's going to be if he has any
luck. And Christabel. Oh, Christabel! She's
like this!' (Judith rolled her eyes, stood on tiptoe and made her face as vacant as a saucepan.)
'She's so stupid you can't believe it! She's for
ever running herself down that you shall run her
up! "I am but an old wife," she'll say. "I have
my principles but nobody cares to bother with
me!" And nobody does, you know. But she's
kind, poor Christabel. She has a heart. She's
all extravagances. "That's a *sweet* fellow," she
will say. "Oh, a *sweet* fellow."' (And Judith

gave her voice such a pitch of stupid ecstasy that
Emma roared with laughter.)

' And then there are the Herries from Kensington, Pomfret and Rose and dear James and sweet
Rodney. Pomfret's kind, but he loves the women,
and Rose is so busy catching him that she can
think of naught else. Pomfret's stout and
dresses grandly. He and Rose are socially finer
than Will and Christabel, but they haven't the
money. No Herries have as much money as Will,
and the house in Kensington costs a deal. I like
Pomfret. Georges and I found him the other
evening at Ranelagh, with a lady all simpers and
jewelry. Oh, it was the loveliest thing! They
had a chicken and a dish of ham between them,
and he was feeding her with the merrythought.
. . . Mr. James Herries puffs himself like a
bull when he walks. Like this.' (Here Judith
gave an admirable imitation.) ' His voice is all
falsetto. He's at the pimple stage.

' Then there are the Cards from Bournemouth.
They come every year to London for the Season.
Prosper and Amelia and the beautiful Jennifer,
their daughter. Prosper is nearly fifty years of
age and is most distinguished. He wears a full-
bottomed wig, although it's the fashion no longer,
and can tell you all about the virtues of Bournemouth. He's so grandly dignified that his knees
won't bend, and he has buckles on his shoes as
large as saucers. Amelia's a little woman like a
rabbit. But I like Amelia. She'd be happier in a
cottage with a sampler to work at. But Jennifer,
she's a beauty! She really is, Emma. Of the

dark kind! All cloudy splendour and proud as Helen of Troy.

' And then—oh, Emma darling, best of all there are the Rockages. I've stayed there down in Wiltshire. Yes, twice. Without Georges, you understand. Maria likes me—wherefore I can *not* understand! But she does! She thinks I have a soul to be saved, and so I don't doubt that I have. And what a place! They haven't a penny between them, and the family coach has rats in the straw, and they put buckets in the hall when it's raining to catch the water through the ceiling. But Carey—that's Rockage—must have everything as grand as grand, although the foot-men have holes in their stockings, and there isn't food to go round. The last time I stayed there I half died of discomfort. You know how it is in a country place where nothing is looked after. Here it was the *extravagance* of neglect! All day long it was nothing but pulling at bell-ropes that brought no answer or always the wrong servant, or a pair of rusty tongs that let slip a coal that is smaller than your head, or an asthmatic pair of bellows, the coals always out, all the pencils with their heads broken off, and *such* a mess of things in every room that was lived in—phials, fiddles, books and knick-knacks, and the rooms that weren't lived in as cold as tombs with all the family por-traits frowning from damp. And the gardens! Oh, Emma, the gardens! All laid out in the ancient taste. You know—a mile's length of clipped trees with spouting lions, fish-ponds as round as a wheel, with six or eight flights of neglected terraces and a summer-house, all broken-down windows and decayed bluebottles.

' And the religion. Oh, Emma, the religion! Early morning, all the maids and the footmen with their patched heels in air, while Carey read a sermon, and trampling through the Wiltshire mud with Maria delivering tracts on the villagers, and Madeline, Carey's sister, mad with enforced virginity, talking to herself in a cupboard. . . . And yet, Emma, it's there that I feel all Herries and want to feel so. Half of me is so Herries that I understand Will's ambition and Carey's pride and am proud of Jennifer's beauty because she's Herries like myself. But the other half of me . . . that's with Francis and Reuben and Georges and is lost in Cumberland peat. That's from my father, Emma, and I doubt it will ruin me in the end. But when I'm at Grosset or Kensington or Will's place I'm *all* Herries, and I would run all the establishment and see how the butter's used and where the beef-bones go to and how every penny fares. Were it not for Georges I'd be mistress of Will's place by now, and Comptroller at Grosset, but they're afraid of Georges. They think he may be hanged any day, and they don't want a hanging relation.'

' Well,' said Emma reflectively, ' I'm glad that there's plenty of money. Money! Money! Judy, my darling, I'd sell my heart and lungs for money. I've never enough.'

' To tell you truth, neither have we,' said Judith, dropping her voice. ' I was speaking a trifle out of order, maybe, when I said that Georges'

business was admirable. It might be if he'd
attend to it, but we've been put to some odd straits,
and it isn't twice or thrice only he's been in the
lock-up.'

'But not to-day!' cried Georges, laughing.
They looked up. He was standing in the doorway with his nightcap still on his head, a quilted
blue bed-gown wrapped around him, rubbing his
eyes and yawning.

This was an uneasy moment for Emma. In
spite of her size she was a deeply shy woman,
ready to burst into tears at any moment from
sensitiveness. In the bad old days Georges had
hated her; moreover, she was uneasy with anyone
who had known her in the raggle-taggle times
when she had been poor old Gauntry's mistress.
Two years ago Georges had been polite to her and
that was all.

Now, however, his regard was amiable. He
was stouter than he had been, she reflected, but
still very handsome. She was no trivial observer,
and at once she realised that Judith's influence
over him was now a very real one. Their relations had changed. He was more good-natured,
less self-willed, a little lazy, some of his earlier
energy dissipated. All this she realised in the
next half-hour, and with it her attitude to Judith
insensibly altered. Judith had a new power.
She was somebody now. Emma surrendered to her,
but resisted her too, a mixed attitude that Judith
would rouse out of many of her later companions.

They spent the happiest hour. Both Georges
and Judith were of a ravenous hunger. In the

cupboard there was a cold pie, a rice pudding, beer and cheese. They had everything out on the shabby table and ate as they were, Judith in a yellow jacket, her nightdress, and Emma's hat still on her head. Georges was kind to Emma. He had won money the night before over the contest between Battling Ginger and Monty Punt. He was right now for a day or two. He scattered his winnings on to the table among the pie and the rice pudding, and let Judith take what she wanted. Emma, encouraged, was able to come out with her project, which was that they should both accompany her to the ' Elephant and Castle ' at Newington for supper. She had, she told them, a young friend, a Mr. Audley, and the young friend had a coach, and he would drive the three of them, through the fields, to Newington. They should drive back under the moon with the hedges smelling of flowers; at the ' Elephant ' there were sheep and cows, and on a June night country-dances on the Green.

So they all gave themselves up to being happy. They had a fine natural capacity for happiness, all three of them, and being in one degree or another all adventurers, happiness brought no kind of obligation with it. Georges dressed there in front of Emma, and there was no false modesty on either side. The bells of St. Mary le Bow had struck three by the time that everyone was ready.

The usual dining hour was anything between three and four, but they would wait now until they could enjoy their supper under the trees of the ' Elephant.'

Georges, when dressed, was a dandy, and Emma sighed romantically, as she always did at thought or vision of a handsome man.

His stoutness, not yet pronounced, added to the impressiveness of his foreign good looks. He was a man now, not a boy, a man with a reckless air, a good-natured mouth, a roving and humorous eye. A man to be trusted? Emma thought not. A man for a woman to love? Of course. A man for Judy to love? Oh, Emma hoped so, but could not be sure. They made a fine pair. The colour of Georges' coat was dark cinnamon, no collar to it, single-breasted; the waistcoat fully seen, of light blue satin cut low under the pockets, under which, as well as down the front and at the bottom, was a border of rosebuds, jonquils and heart's-ease. He wore a lace frill, called a Chitterling, the ends of his white cravat trimmed with lace, and the ruffles at his wrists the same, his hair powdered, no curls, but brushed back from his face and hanging in a black bag with a rosette behind. Judith wore a jacquette of pale silver-coloured silk and the bodice and underdress were of dark wine colour. Her red hair was unpowdered and fell down behind with curled ends, and perched on it she wore a hat of light straw, also of pale silver. Her shoes had silver buckles.

Judith thought the clothes that she and Georges wore on this day important, for she describes them in her Journal minutely, and at the top of the page has written in a hand that is still very childish: 'The Happiest Day of My Life.'

Mr. Audley's chariot-chaise was to be met in

Holborn, so they engaged a hackney carriage and
drove there, Judith with her head out of window
for there was so much to see on this very fine
day. They rattled along with a great deal of
bumping, jerking in and out of holes, climbing
little hills and running down the other sides
again, along Blowbladder Street, past Butcher
Hall Lane, Bath Street—sacred to the memory
of Charles II.—Ivy Lane, where Dr. Johnson
had his Club, under the ancient gateway beside
Giltspur Street, up Snow Hill, past Cock Lane,
Cow Lane, Fleet Market, then a steep climb up
Holborn Hill, when they moved so slowly that
little boys looked in at the window, a gentleman
with silver rings in his ears wanted Judith to
buy a green parrot, the Bishop of Ely's Palace
with his gardens, Thavie's Inn, Staple Inn and
so to Holborn. Here, at a corner of Whetstone
Park, was Mr. Audley with his coach.

Judith had already asked Emma to tell her all
she could about Mr. Audley, but Emma could not
tell her very much. It seemed that Mr. Audley
was a young man with a very rich City father
(here it was Georges who pricked up his ears),
that he was a great admirer of Emma's (' A
passion for the Play, my dear. He was in
Salisbury at the time, buying a horse, and he
saw me in *Othello*. I am free to confess that
Emilia is not so splendid a rôle, most especially
in the version that we were playing, which was
one with music, and Othello, Mr. Barnstaple,
had a fine tenor and played the flute in the third
act, but I was wearing white satin, and poor little

Miss Huxley, who was playing Desdemona, was a chit of a thing that you could fit into a nutshell. To be honest, my dear, he liked my size. He was heard to say loudly in the pit that the Furze was his style and—well, we were friends very shortly after. He is a nice young fellow with most agreeable manners.')

He flushed with pleasure when he saw them. His coach was very smart, of a bright bay colour with silver ornaments on the harness. He was attended by a stout driver in a blue and yellow striped waistcoat who, as they approached, was engaged from the box in a sharp and apparently rather bitter discussion with two gentlemen and a fruit-barrow.

Everything and everyone was very lively, including the June sun, the shopmen standing in their doorways, the glittering glass of the shop-windows, an old man with a fiddle to whose tunes several children were dancing, a stout lady with a bell who was selling pinks and roses, and a church near by ringing peals as though it were mad with joy.

Mr. Audley was introduced, they all climbed in and started off. Judith gave herself up to complete enjoyment. Everything was as she would have it, except that she would have preferred a chaise to a coach, because in a chaise she could see more, but in a chaise there would not be room for them all.

Mr. Audley was exceedingly attentive to her, so attentive that she was afraid lest Emma should be jealous. His method of attention was to ask innumerable questions, to which, however, he appeared to expect no kind of answer. He had a foolish expressionless face, but his questions were for the most part educational, concerning literature and the drama. Judith soon conceived a feeling of maternal care for him, as though he were an infant or a puppy. He seemed to her so very eager, inexperienced and untutored.

'Pray, ma'am, you have read *Evelina*, of course. Do you not find the Branghtons too amusing? Is it not laughable where the Captain throws Madame Duval into a ditch? Is not the close inexpressibly touching? Is London not dull in June—no Covent Garden, only the Little Theatre? Pray, ma'am, have you been to the Tower lately? Are not the tigers and lions fine? I saw recently Foote's play *The Minor*. It is all against the Methodists. I laughed myself into hysterics. I was at the Pantheon the other evening. It is never the same since it was burnt. I was at a Masquerade there, as mean as ever you saw. But the fireworks at Marybone! Have you seen the fireworks at Marybone? I hope you find this coach easy. I have a phaeton, bought only last week, but Mrs. Furze told me that friends might accompany her. I trust you are comfortable.'

It was his way, she assured herself, of courtesy and politeness. She need not listen to his questions if she did not wish. She had, once and again, an uneasy feeling that Georges was watching Mr. Audley with a growing conviction that he would, a little later, be an easy friend to win money from. She pushed that from her. She did not care just now to consider that side of Georges' character. Yes, she surrendered herself completely to happiness. There had been many days in the last two years when she had been, it seemed to her, living on the very edge of irretrievable disaster. One touch and she and Georges would both tumble over into a bottomless pit, and no one in the world care that they had gone. She knew Georges so well now that the black side of the account of her life with him was fearfully familiar. But slowly, slowly she was influencing him. Month by month he was less drunken, attended more steadily to his Whitehaven business, submitted to her will.

By a constant good humour, a perpetual check on her fears and alarms, a refusal to be astonished at any sudden calamity, a trained restraint on her own nerves, temper, moods—by all these things she had gradually governed him, he not knowing that he was governed. The odd thing was that, although she knew now by heart all the iniquities of which he was capable, all his tempers, his violences, his infidelities, his shadinesses, she loved him more than ever. He was still her created work, although she was wise enough now never to show him that it was so. And there was, when all was said, somewhere in his strange character, a strain of sweetness, of loyalty, of liberality, of boyish candour, that made him to her, with reason, endearing. But, when all was said, she loved him, had always loved him, would always love him. There could be no one else for her.

It was enchanting when, after crossing the river, they left the town behind them and passed into the open fields. The blue sky was cloudless. Everything was painted with a shining lustre, and the trees were dark at the heart of their green foliage. They were at the 'Elephant' almost before they knew it.

Here, indeed, there was liveliness! In the centre was the stout sign-post with its four pointers, and round and about it all the world was on the move. There was a countryman on a donkey, driving two other donkeys in front of him, two shouting peasants with whip and dog, urging their stupid but amiable cows, two coaches drawn up at the inn door, and another, loaded with people, nearly riding down a little collection of barrows piled with flowers, fruit and vegetables. There was a private coach crammed with six people, and led by four horses, chariots, hackney-coaches, groups of country-people stood about enjoying the lovely afternoon, a party of very fine ladies and gentlemen, moving as though they were creatures of another planet, brilliant in their colours of red and purple, children outside the gardens playing at ball, dogs everywhere, and a superb solitary gentleman riding his horse, his servant riding behind him on another. Judith's heart beat with ecstasy when she saw all this life. She put her hand through Georges' arm and walked as proud as a duchess with him into the inn.

Here everything was in a bustle with the arrival of the two coaches, so, very soon, they crossed the road to the Gardens on the other side. These were simple Gardens, not like Marybone or Bagnigge Wells, but they were what Judith preferred. There were ‘Chinese’ benches, rough wooden tables, very childish amusements with a pillory for a gentleman to sit in until he was liberated by a kiss from a lady, a maze in which lovers might be lost and a peep-show rather the worse for wear and weather. But soon Judith was attending to none of these things, for sitting on the bench, her mouth open with excitement at all the things and people to see, her legs swinging, her eyes shining with delight, she was aware that Georges, of his own volition, had come to sit beside her, had his arm around her, was pressing her to him. All the world was forgotten in the heart-beating discovery of that moment. He had come of his own will, there in the public view, he who was so shy of demonstration, of anything that could attract general attention.

Wise from experience she showed no great responsiveness, only moved a little closer to him. But her heart was beating, and within herself she was thinking: ‘I must keep this in memory. Whatever comes in the future nothing can take this away!’

All she said aloud was: ‘Oh, how hungry I am! It is almost six, and we have eaten nothing all day long.’

‘There was the cold pie,’ he reminded her; then he whispered in her ear: ‘Judy, do you love me?’

'A little,' she answered.

'Are you happy?'

'Yes—but when I have eaten I shall be happier.'

'I think you are charming. I am seeing you to-day with fresh eyes.'

'Your old wife!' She turned round to him, her eyes dancing. 'After so many years you can find that she has charm?'

'You are better. You are vastly improved. You are a woman now and yet you are still a child. Life has taught you something.'

'Marriage with you has taught me something,' she answered, laughing. 'Striving to alter you——'

'I doubt your capacity to amend me,' he said. 'Nobody enjoys better spirits than I—at times. To-day when the sun is shining and my French blood is warmed and you, my little wife, are beside me, and we are in fine clothes and have money. . . . Then I think heigh-ho! how virtuous I could be! But soon it will be Mr. Moss and cold mutton and flying down side-streets to avoid creditors and the fog and rain——'

'Meanwhile,' she cried, 'let us be happy now. We have a happy day. We must enjoy it.'

'We must enjoy it,' he repeated after her. His eyes lighted as he saw Mr. Audley coming towards them.

'Sir,' he cried. 'I would have a wager with you. Guineas that the next person through that gate yonder is a female.'

Mr. Audley looked rather nervous. Judith saw that he was no gambler by nature.

'Why, surely,' he agreed in his silly fluttering voice. 'Guineas it is, sir.'

They watched the gate. Judith saw, with an odd mixture of tenderness and chagrin, that Georges was watching with an eager excitement worthy of some great hazard. His body was tingling with his suspense. For a moment no one came. Then a stout man in a high beaver hat, very solemn in his claret-coloured coat, marched in through the gate.

'Damn!' cried Georges. 'It is against me! But double or quits, Mr. Audley, that the next is a female.'

'No, no,' Judith broke in. 'For shame, Georges. I am famished. Food I must have. . . .'

She saw his brow clouding. He would, in another moment, have forgotten all his recent affection for her had not, fortunately, Emma been seen arriving and with her a serving-man.

She was now in her proper and most happy element, arranging ceremonies that had to do with food and drink. They were to have their meal under a large spreading chestnut. They would have veal cutlets, a small green-goose and asparagus, a damson pie. . . .

Judith was long afterwards to remember that scene, the soft warm air, the cool green benignity of the great tree, the children playing on the sward near to them, the noise of the coaches and the carriages, the voices, sheep bleating—all beyond the gate; the laughter of lovers happily lost in the maze near to them, her own happiness as she sat beside Georges, her hand once and again resting on his knee.

They were all so happy, Mr. Audley so proud of his entertaining, and Emma in her tall hat at almost bursting point with pleasure at the food, the cheerfulness, the general sense of security. Poor dear! Her life did not provide her with so many secure moments!

She complained, of course, of the cooking as in duty bound, being herself so great a connoisseur, but hugely nevertheless she enjoyed it. She shouted orders to the waiters, and herself, at one moment, hurried forward to inspect the green-goose on its way through the gate from the inn opposite.

Then, as the sun sank beyond the garden walls and everything was suffused with a pale shadow of gold, the dark friendly patterns growing lengthy on the grass, a silver star or two winking through the trees, a fiddler drew near and with him a woman, who had a strong sweet voice. She sang:

> ' Beauty clear and fair,
>   Where the air
> Rather like a perfume dwells:
> Where the violet and the rose
> Their blue veins and blush disclose
> And come to honour nothing else;
> Where to live near
> And planted there
> Is to live, and still live new;
> Where to gain a favour is
> More than light, perpetual bliss—
> Make me live by serving you!

> ' Dear, again back recall
>   To this light,
>   A stranger to himself and all!
>   But the wonder and the story
>   Shall be yours, and else the glory;
>   I am your servant and your thrall.
>
> ' Dear, again back recall
>   To this light! '

Oh, that this moment might last for ever, never to change. This voice, this shining light, enclosed in this garden. . . .

Georges, too, must have felt something of it for he rose impetuously and pressed money on the fiddler, then turned back to them a little shame-faced. But he kissed Judith before he sat down. The dusk came; candles were lit. There was dancing on the green.

But, alas, when it was time to go it was found that the coachman was perilously drunk. He greeted them all with a warm and most appreciatory affection. He would have embraced Emma, quarrelled with a little gentleman near by, who had, he fancied, insulted her.

Mr. Audley was greatly ashamed and not of much value in the situation. He twittered like a bird whose nest is in danger, looking at Emma as though to implore her not to like him the less for this accident. Georges was of excellent practical use. It was just the situation for his temperament. He helped to hoist the man on the box, frightened away the interested spectators, quieted the horses and threatened the coachman with such dire penalties were there an accident that for the moment he was sobered. So they started off down the road under the stars. There was a moon, and everywhere a radiant peace.

But not for long. After a while the coachman began to sing; the horses took fright; the coach rocked and rocked again. Georges attempted, with head out of the window, to bring the man to his senses. There he was with throat uplifted, singing to the moon. A moment later there was a fearful heave, and the coach was on its side in the ditch. Georges climbed through the broken door, ran to the horses' heads. The others, uninjured except for a shaking and a bruise or so, climbed painfully after him and sat in the hedge. The coachman, his singing silenced, was perched skywards, fallen almost on to the horses' backs, his thick legs dangling. Georges assisted him down, and he at once began to snivel, his fist in his eyes like a schoolboy's.

The shafts and one wheel were broken. The other wheel raised in mid-air made a fantastic gesture.

At length Mr. Audley and the coachman, still snivelling, set off for the nearest village to find some other conveyance. Emma, Judith and Georges sat in the hedge over a ditch, and a network of fiery stars shone down upon them. There might be highwaymen, an added adventure, but it seemed not; for the whole world was still, holding its breath under the moon.

In the shadow of the fantastic coach with its

clamant wheel Georges and Judith sat close together. He seemed to be, in the spirit of that
beneficent night, a transformed creature. He
declared his love as though this were the first
night that he had met her. She held her breath,
catching the divine moment that it might be with
her for ever.

'Judith, I love you to-night. I have never
told you that before.'

'No, never—and I have wanted it so.'

'It has grown in me. Through all my
vagaries it has been ever drawing closer to me.
You have been drawing closer to me.'

'And I love you, Georges. I always shall.'

'Perhaps this is the beginning of a new life
for us.'

She shook her head humorously.

'No. Things will be up and down again as
they have always been, but I am very happy for
this moment.'

She was in a transcendent happiness. The
two different strands of her life were suddenly
united in one common glory—her practical daily
Herries life, and the dream, that which separated
her from the rest of her kind. Love had for a
moment united them.

The fantastic wheel of the coach against the
sky seemed to promise her something:

'Trust this moment.'

And to threaten her something:

'This moment is already almost gone.'

'Oh, let me keep Georges!' was her unuttered
prayer. And if in the sequel her prayer was

denied her, it was also granted. Her whole nature in that half-hour was fulfilled.

In the hedge, bathed in the warm flower-scented air, for a brief while they were completely united.

THE HERRIES BALL

MAY 17, 1796

JUDITH went to the famous Masquerade at Will
Herries' house, given there in the month of May
of the year 1796, dressed as her mother.

She had never seen her mother, who had died
in giving birth to her. She had seen no picture
of her; nevertheless it was a link in the strange
sequence of events that once there should have
been a child sheltering in its mother's skirts at a
Christmas games in a Borrowdale farm, that then
there should have been a woman crying over her
lost lover in Carlisle streets, that again there should
have been a weary woman knocking at the door of
Herries in Rosthwaite, that now Judith, dressed
as a ragged gipsy, her red hair loose about her
head, should be waiting in an almost breathless
excitement for the coach to take her to another
Herries house.

There were to be many consequences from the
Masquerade on this night, consequences as important to the whole Herries family as the quarrel
that rose out of this occasion, consequences that
helped to make Judith's life afterwards what it
was, and from that to affect generations and

possibly the colour of England itself. For if, on that night, Judith had not been dressed as a gipsy, would the beautiful Jennifer have snapped the ivory stick of Mrs. Will's fan—that famous fan!

It is still in dispute as to whether the mandarins painted on it were clothed in blue or silver. A letter still extant, written on the day after the Masquerade by Rose, Pomfret's wife, speaks of ' Christabel's *blue* Fan.' On the other hand, in Judith's own Journal, there are these words: ' . . . And so, scarcely knowing what she did, so angry was she, she snapped one of the sticks of Christabel's Fan with the Silver Figures that had been lying on the Table at her side. . . .'

We may go back, too, and ask History whether if Francis Herries, senior, had not sold his mistress at a Keswick Fair, would Jennifer Cards have recollected the fable of old Maria and her spaniel, and, if she had not . . . Of all the things of which we are uncertain in this world—and there are more every day—we can at least be sure that History has for one of its subjects the ultimate importance of trifles. A coin rolled on a table, a verse by Mr. Pope, a cabbage grown in a stubborn garden, a foggy night in Carlisle, a players' booth in Penrith, scattered snow reflected like feathers in a lake—such things were the landmarks in the life of Francis Herries of Herries. Such things were to mark the life of his daughter also. And it is in the chronicle of such things that the history of the Herries family finds coherence.

Judith and Georges were ready dressed waiting for the hackney-coach, Judith as her mother and Georges as Mephistopheles. Four of the Robinson children, thumbs in their mouths, stood inside the doorway, wondering at the splendour, and a moment later there was Mrs. Robinson herself, a baby in her arms, to announce that the coach had arrived.

Georges was superb and was well aware of it. He wore scarlet shoes, black silk hose and doublet, a crimson cloak, a red peaked hat with a black feather. His costume, tight-fitting, displayed his figure to splendid advantage. He knew that his ankles, his thighs, his chest, could suffer any display. He would, if he did not take care, soon be too stout, but that was not yet.

Judith's dress was orange colour, trimmed with silver; it was ragged a little, showing her neck and arms. She had a wreath of flowers in her hair. She looked a child of ten; her excitement gave her a colour of eager expectation. But although her excitement was great, she was yet able to be practical. She had her anxieties. Georges was in one of his wild moods. They had, during the last three months, been living very precariously. She was not sure—he would not tell her—but she fancied that he had been losing heavily at cards. Young Mr. Stane (whom she hated) had arrived three days before from Whitehaven; in his sinister and complimentary politeness she had imagined threats and bad omens.

She was in the difficult position of attempting to protect Georges, but not knowing from what to

protect him.   He had been in his most cynical,
mocking, restless temper, treating her as though
she were a helpless child, assuming for himself an
air of profound wisdom (which was, as she well
knew, quite unjustified).   She could only control
or have any influence over him by asking him no
questions.   She would not ask Henry Stane anything.   The lovely intimacy of that wonderful
June day at Newington had never returned.   She
had been wise to tell herself that day that she must
treasure it, for there would not be many like it.
Her anxiety over him only made her love him the
more, but she was working in the dark, fearing she
knew not what, dreading some awful disaster.
She never saw Henry Stane without knowing her
fear increase.   And she was not yet twenty-two
years of age.

However, it was her nature to be concerned
with the happiness of everyone who came near to
her, and, before they started, she was busy with all
the Robinson children.   They were a dirty little
group, as, indeed, necessity forced them to be.
Judith, with her passion for cleanliness, had kept
her place as decent as she might, but the rest of the
house, although some of the rooms were let to
gentlemen of means, was a pig-sty.   Many of the
window-frames were black with soot, windows
were stuffed with paper and rag; in one room
eleven members of an Irish family slept in two
beds; a drunken tailor on the floor above Judith
kept a pig in his apartment.

Mrs. Robinson had enough to do with her
lodgers, her family and her husband's appren-

tices.   She was not a bad-natured woman, and she
had a deep admiration for Judith because she kept
her room so clean, was always in a sensible mood
and was connected with fine families.   She had
intended binding out her eldest girl Fanny, a child
of eleven, to a tambour - maker, but very reluctantly, for she knew well enough the cruelty
that these apprentice children must suffer.   And
Fanny was a bright, pretty child.   But Judith had
persuaded her to keep her at home, had even
herself employed the child and paid her a wage.
Then there was the little chimney-sweep (already
out on his work this evening), who was falling into
bad ways.   Judith had been looking after him a
little, letting him come into her room in the early
afternoon when he had had his sleep out and was
ready for any mischief.   He was a funny old little
boy and regarded Judith as just of his own age. . . .

So now she pinched the cheek of one child,
patted the verminous head of another, smiled at
the harassed mother and then, followed by her
splendid Mephistopheles, picked her way down
the filthy staircase.

Chelsea was a great distance in the coach, and
they had plenty of opportunity for conversation.
Avoiding any display of sentiment as she always
did when she wanted to get at the truth, she
challenged him at once as to the position: things
were bad?   He shrugged his shoulders.   He had
been unlucky.   He was always unlucky now.
Henry Stane had come down from Whitehaven with
his usual complaints.   Henry Stane—she shivered.
Why had he so much to do with everything now?

Well, he wanted to be a partner with Wix and
Georges. He was ambitious. Because his father
had once been a simple fisherman, he thought
it fine to have risen in the world as he had; now
he wanted to rise still further. Judith, trying
to think connectedly in the jolting coach, had an
impulse to implore Georges to free himself from
Stane, buy him out, do anything. She did not
know why she dreaded him as she did. Her mind
flew back to the night in Cockermouth when she
had helped to save Humphrey. That dark cellar,
the fugitive, they were connected in some way
with Stane and his ambitions. . . . But she said
nothing. After the night of that quarrel in Watendlath she had determined not to question Georges
about his Whitehaven affairs unless he wished.

' Don't sell the farm,' was all she murmured,
as much to herself as to him.

' The farm? '

' Watendlath. You said once that if all else
failed you could be happy there, in the life. . . .'

' By God, I could! It's strange, Judy, but
when you speak of it I could leave this London
and the coin and the stinking candles—all shut up,
closed—I'd give a fortune to see that water now
tumbling over the stones and watch those smutty-
nosed sheep pushing up under the stone wall. . . .'

She, too, had for a moment a vision—the cut
in Armboth Fell, the Tarn when the wind played
on it, the ridge of the Fell looking over Borrowdale.

But with his French impatience and eagerness for practical things he drove all that from
him. He had now an immense confidence in her

common sense and a respect for her judgement. It had grown in him through the years. So he began to outline the schemes that he had for making use of all the Herries connections. This was an old topic with him. He often blamed her for not making more of all her Herries family. They liked her. Those old Rockages would do anything for her. Will was like her own brother. Will Herries was becoming a very rich man. Everyone talked of him. Why could they not give up this hand-to-mouth existence? Why should she not get Georges some place in Will's City business? To-night would be a fine time to work something. Will would be in great feather at having so grand a Ball in his house. Judith would be able to do anything with him.

Judith sighed to herself. This was an old, old topic. Georges always raised it when things were going badly. When things went well he loudly despised Will and his business, said that he wouldn't be tied in the dirty City for all India's wealth. It was only when he was in a corner that he thought of it. Yes, Judith sighed. The omens were bad. Georges must be desperate. And she could not tell him what was the truth— that all the Herries family regarded Georges as a wild adventurer, almost as a vagabond. That they would not have Georges, this little gambling Frenchman from nowhere, into any intimate connection with them, not if you offered them all China! It was bad enough with the country crowded with French refugees as it was. . . .

Georges went on. How clever Will had been

about all this French War that was ruining so
many men, and he had managed to make his
profit out of it! There were rumours that he
had been lending the Prince money. Everything
that he touched seemed to turn to gold! And
Georges was just the man for him! They were
much of an age. Will could not be more than
twenty-six or so. So young a man must need
partners.

'He has partners,' Judith remarked. 'He is
the youngest in his firm.'

Well, young or not, he was the lively one.
What would he not be at forty? And he had
been in the City for so short a time! Georges
must make some association with him! Surely
Judith could manage it. Judith had an impulse
to turn to him: 'It's your own fault that I can't
—you with your tempers and sudden idleness
and bad company and gambling and the rest!'
But she might as well have said: 'You, Georges
Paris, because you were born Georges Paris.'

Their coach was going very slowly now, for
they were approaching Ranelagh and there was
much traffic. The road (that had been but a
few years before all country, but now buildings
were springing up) was crowded with chairs,
private coaches, hackneys, boys running with
lights, families walking—so much noise of wheels
and shouting that Georges and Judith could not
hear one another speak. Now, as always, she
surrendered at once to all the excitement. She
forgot all troubles, financial, domestic, thought
only of the Ball and all the fun there would be.

Will's house stood in its own ground. The whining purr of the violins could be heard coming, as it were, from the heart of the trees. Above the wide staircase the long ballroom glittered under the wavering flutter of the candles that blew gently in their hanging silver lustres.

Will had taken a bigger house than his present needs when, at a moment, Sir Frederick Cottenham must sell at a ridiculously low price because of a night's loss at cards. Servants were so cheap as to cost almost nothing, except for mouths to be fed, and although, because of the French War, food was more costly every day, here there seemed to be always an abundance. It came from somewhere, Christabel herself scarcely knew whence.

But the events of that strange evening began for Judith, not as she stood masked watching the fantastic medley of Turks, Nuns, Punchinellos, Italian Ladies of the Renaissance, Devils, Monks, Columbines and the rest, but rather at the sudden sight of Francis, disguised only by his mask, wearing otherwise a plain suit of black and silver. She would have moved at once to his side, but she must first speak to Will and Christabel. They were the only two unmasked in the room. There was something, Judith felt at once, a little pathetic in Will's sense of triumph. She had a divination (how utterly surprised he would be if he knew!) of what this glorious moment would mean to him, and of the jealousies, hatreds, contempts that his very success would rouse up against him.

L 2

Yes, even now, this very room would be seething with them! The Herries who were here would be resenting his power, but resolving to make use of it, and those who were not Herries would be scorning him for a City merchant who was pushing into Society. And yet the Herries were as ancient and well-rooted a family as any in England. But it was new, this pushing up-wards of the merchant by power of his wealth, this very Ball the symbol of the reluctant yielding of the old world to the new.

Will would have no sense of any of this. She realised, looking at his thin stiff body, marked with the sharp horse-bones of the Herries, his eyes lit with a cold, nevertheless animated pride, that he could feel nothing but his success. He might well be proud. Little more than a boy, he yet had arrived at this power. But Judith felt that in Christabel there was a real uneasiness. In an ugly dress of a pale yellow, her hair done too high for the present fashion, she seemed almost to be expecting sneers and insults. Judith saw that this evening had been both her proud ex-pectation and anxious dread for months before. She was in a state of nervous tension that might lead to anything. And, in fact, at this time moods, tempers, resentments, wild pleasures were very near the surface. There was in the London of that moment much social etiquette, but little social control. The world was turning over, and everyone's foothold was a little insecure.

Neither Will nor Christabel had at that moment very much time for Judith, and after a

while she was free to find Francis. A minuet
was in progress. The coloured masked figures
stirred in the candle-shine like fragments of a
pattern moving towards a perfect arrangement.
The moment when that arrangement was achieved
—would the world stop? But on every occasion
something prevented perfection. Tall high windows were covered with curtains of silver brocade.
On the distant gallery the musicians played.
Judith could see, above the clouded colour that
was veiled with a kind of dim smoke, one fiddler,
very thin, his arm raised like a stick, a sharp-
pointed nose that seemed almost to be directing
the whole room. . . .

She found Francis and touched his arm.

' Sir,' she said, ' a word with you,' as though
they were strangers. Then she laughed. They
stepped back into the curve of the window-
place. They had not seen one another for six
months.

Francis had, the year previous, made friends
with a Mr. Samuel Rogers. This gentleman was
a poet, who had become famous with a piece
entitled ' The Pleasures of Memory.' He lived
at Stoke Newington, and Francis had stayed with
him there. In January of this same year he had
been involved in some of the troubles connected
with what was known as the White Terror, the
suspicious and terrified reaction in England of the
Terror in France, and Francis had been able to
show him some assistance during this anxiety.
He was, from Francis' account, a sharp-tongued
little man, bitter in speech about everyone, but of

great active kindliness in deed.   Francis, at least,
seemed to understand him, and in his company
lately had met many interesting people.   Rogers
had London rooms in Paper Buildings, and
Francis had had wonderful evenings there with
men like Horne Tooke, Parr, Sheridan, and
even the great Mr. Fox himself.   Francis had
taken to a sort of sporadic journalism, the political variety.   He also had published essays in the
Gentleman's Magazine under the pseudonym of
Peter Mountain.

But he seemed to-night to have but little
interest in his own career.   He was making a new
life for himself; but Judith soon saw that it was no
more the life that he wanted than the earlier
Cumberland one had been.   He was as alone
here in this sounding, moving gaiety as he had
been beside the silence of the Watendlath Tarn.

He seized upon Judith with a kind of feverish
thirst.   His need to-night was for someone who
could give him some sort of reassurance.   Behind
his mask his loneliness seemed for a moment to
darken the candles, the coloured clothes, to put
out all the splendour.   She had her own excitements, her own anxieties, but as always when she
was with anyone whom she loved she forgot her
own life in her eagerness to benefit the other.

' Judith, let's escape together thousands of
miles away—to some island where there are no
people.'

' Only the savages,' she answered him, laughing.

' Well, we Herries are savages.   I hate us

in the mass.   Behind the masks you can scent
Herries a mile away.   There, in that silly black
costume, that's Maria Rockage, and near her in
the red and gold that's Rockage.   There to the
right, the Punchinello, that's Montague Cards;
there's Amelia, dressed as a Nun, dancing.   We
are a horrid family, so pleased with ourselves.
For ever casting someone into outer darkness.
" Oh, he's mad."   " She's lunatic."   " That's
an atheist."   And for what are we proud ?   Because we are English, because we are Herries, as
though you said: " Because I'm a cow."   Judy,
there was old Maria.   Have you ever heard of
Maria ?   She died in '45.   She lived almost to be
a hundred, within a month or two.   When she
failed her century Herries were angry all over
the country.   That is a record of the sort that
they value.   I have heard my father tell how
your father visited them in Keswick after old
Maria's funeral and found them all at odds.   But
her dog was there, the only thing that cared
for her, and your father said that the scorn of
them all in that dog's eyes . . .'   He broke off.
Looking at her half quizzically, he added: ' You
know you have no right here, you and Georges.
You are vagabonds.   And I am one also.'

' I know,' Judith answered.   ' And I had the
whim to dress as my mother.   I never saw her.
But I fancied her at this Ball.   What they would
all say, if she came in from Borrowdale with the
mud on her shoes!   But I feel Herries as well,
Francis.   I would like to be the head of the
family, very wealthy, telling them all what to

do.' Then, catching his arm: ' Why, see, that must be Jennifer! Did you ever see anyone so lovely? '

Francis turned, looking more closely into the room.

' Do you know,' he said, ' I have never seen Jennifer? My lovely cousin. . . .'

But he broke off. Quite close to them a beautiful girl was passing. Jennifer Cards was in that year when Francis first saw her twenty-six years of age. Francis Herries was thirty-six. That first sight of her was one of the more important moments of Herries history evolved on that eventful evening. She was dressed as Catherine de' Medici in a magnificent robe of slashed crimson, and behind her lovely head a stiff high collar of silver. Ropes of pearls were in her black hair. She was tall, carried herself superbly, her skin had the whiteness of a white rose. She walked lazily as though half asleep. Francis stared. He could not speak. It was as though, after all these years, his dream had been, by some favouring magician, created into fact for him.

' Her dress suits her nobly,' Judith said. But he did not hear her. He stood like a man lost.

Like a man lost! It was from that moment, perhaps, that Judith began to have the sense that this whole affair was a dream, and a dangerous dream too. Her excitement did not leave her, but the happy element in it. She began to feel that there was something evil in the air.

The dance had stopped, and the dancers broken up. A sort of wildness crept into the house. Not far away, in Ranelagh, down the dark alleys, couples were standing in the shadow, body strained against body in deep embrace. Although the music in the room had ceased it still seemed to linger in the trees, and little companies of wanderers gathered at the garden-gates, watching the house so brilliantly lit, heard the lean fiddler. Was he seated among the chimney-pots? Was it some strain from the Ranelagh musicians? Or an old beggar fiddling wildly down the road?

Judith saw that she had lost Francis. He cared no more what she said to him. And then she saw another thing. She saw that her own especial Mephistopheles was attracted just as Francis was. But he was more active. His eyes fixed on the lovely lady, Georges waited until he saw her a moment detached, alone. He went up to her and spoke. How exactly Judith knew what the tone of that voice would be, the softness, the charm! His mother's! She saw again, as she often did when she was with him, that moment of her childhood when in the bare room the young man had knelt to the naked woman! Mother and son. Ah, but he had charm when he spoke like that, when his body seemed to tremble behind his voice. She could fancy how his eyes would shine behind the mask! He spoke. Jennifer turned. She looked at him and laughed. He spoke again. She smiled, and they both moved away together, she leading, he following.

Judith shivered. She was cold there in the

window.　Francis and Georges, the two whom she loved best in the world, they would both leave her at any moment for a fine woman.　She had done so much for Georges, but at any instant he forgot her.　Indeed, it seemed that no one remembered her.　She seemed to be as alone in that crowd as though she were by herself on Brund Fell.　Her gipsy's dress, how shabby it was beside all these splendours!　And her mother would have been shabby, too, had she been here.　Once again she knew that sharp pang of alarm at her own insecurity in this harsh, indifferent world.　She had no one but herself.　Only her own pride to keep her.　No one would care if this moment she vanished for ever. Not Georges? No, not Georges.　Emma, perhaps, and at the thought of that large, comforting woman the tears stung her eyes, were damp behind the mask.　Then she pulled herself up.　What did it matter if she *were* alone in the world?　So her mother had been, so her father.　Oneself was enough.　She was aware then that a Mask, dressed as Punchinello, stood motionless at her side.　He had been there perhaps for a long while.　She turned, and as she did so he spoke:

'You would not expect to find me here,' he said.

She knew at once the voice.　It was young Stane.　How was young Stane here?　She thought he did not know Will.　Georges had not brought him.　He was always to her uncanny, and his presence now only increased her sense of the strange wildness of the evening.

She said coldly: 'I did not know that you were acquainted with Mr. Herries.'

'Yes. You would not know. I had said nothing to Georges. But I have known Mr. Herries—for some time.'

She might have guessed that he would. It was like him to make use of every advantage, but to tell no one of what he was doing. He would go far. He was not now more than twenty-five. Ten years back on naked feet he had been selling fish in Whitehaven. Georges had told her of his father, a huge man with a white beard, always reciting the Scriptures, who worshipped this his only child. She turned and looked at young Henry Stane. He had large black eyes behind the mask. He was black-haired, sallow like Georges, but tuned, she knew at once, to a far greater determination. He would eat Georges up! She saw at once how Georges' laziness, good-nature, bad temper, self-indulgence, all these would be simply easy material for Stane's advancement. He was an adventurer too, but he was resolved not to remain one.

Meanwhile she had never hated anyone so much; instinct, fear for Georges, and her own innate repulsion. She was not at her best when she hated anyone. She showed her feeling too readily. She showed it now.

'I congratulate you, Mr. Stane,' she said. She saw (and it was to explain very much to her afterwards) that his most maddening quality was his imperturbability. Nothing could touch him. That would infuriate Georges just as now it was

angering her. Then his next words amazed
her:

'Pardon me. I know how you regard me.
All is love or hatred with you. I admire so much
your sincerity. But although you dislike me so
very much, would you not perhaps allow me to
say a word about your husband?'

'No,' she answered.

'Very well. But you have much influence
with him.'

'What is it, then?'

'Only that he is making a great mistake to
neglect his business so constantly. It is a good
business, but it needs attention. He has a good
head, Georges, but no discipline.'

She hated the familiarity in his voice. From
behind her mask she looked at him.

'I know quite well what you feel about my
husband. You wait only to climb over him into
his place.'

'No, I assure you, madam——'

'Oh yes, I know very well——'

'Then there is nothing more to say. I
meant it civilly.'

As he went it was as though another little
Punchinello leapt out of him and sat on his
shoulder, its small, puckered, malicious face
laughing back at her. How insulting of him!
—but there was truth, too, in what he said.
And Georges was whispering somewhere in
Jennifer's ear.

She had not for many years felt so miserable,
so lonely, lost, deserted. Again and again the

hot tears gathered behind the mask, and she beat them back. She felt as though some influence separated her from everyone there. She had expected to be so happy, but now that sense of slipping on the very edge of some disaster frightened her so threateningly that all she could do was to start off in search of Georges, to be sure that he was safe. No, she did not care whether he were with Jennifer or no, so long as he were safe.

She was soon caught into the throng. She realised that everything was growing very wild. Couples whirled madly together, colliding with others. Both men and women were elated with their freedom. Many were unmasking. The fiddlers seemed to be playing mad, discordant tunes as though they were drunk.

She had an odd thought as some stout Cardinal tried to catch her by the arm. ' It's because in their hearts they despise Will that they do this. It would not be like this in a really grand house.' She suspected that any of the ' really grand people ' who had come had left already.

She was confirmed in her suspicions by having thrown almost into her arms poor Maria Rockage. Maria and Carey had, she knew, come to the Ball with a great sense of condescension. For one thing, Will was young enough to be their son; for another, he was a City man; for another, nothing in London anywhere was so fine and superior as Grosset. So they had come with condescension, with Methodist suspicion, and with kindliness of heart. Judith, young though she was, knew every motive in Maria Rockage's brain, her poverty, so that often at Grosset there was not food enough, her passion for her off-spring, her confused Methodism, her muddled benevolence and her real warmth of heart. It was on this last ground that the two of them met.

But now Maria was frightened. She could not find Carey. She *must* find him, for they must leave at once. Even the servants downstairs were drinking. There was a little black boy on the staircase eating pie out of a dish. The whole affair was tumbling out of control. She must find Carey and take him home, back to their rooms in Berkeley Square. As a matter of fact, Judith knew that the rooms were not in Berkeley Square, but up a mews in Brick Street. Young Phyllis (safely asleep at Grosset) was for ever betraying her mother's tactics. Maria's terror rose. She especially resented that Jennifer Cards should be the belle of the evening. She disliked and condemned the Bournemouth branch of the family. Moreover, her own rather shabby black dress had been, in intention, a Catherine de' Medici. It had a stiff high black collar. 'She paints shockingly high. How Amelia permits her . . . But Amelia wishes to sell her to the finest bidder, and for all they were so grand when Carey stayed at Bournemouth last year, the rain came into the coach and the straw was soaked . . . and I'm sure that Robert (Jennifer's brother) is an effeminate young man as you'd find among the silks and gauzes at a dressmaker's. Judith, *where* is

Carey? Oh, help me to find him! This is, indeed, pandemonium.'

Almost everyone now had unmasked, and the scene had a strange phantasmal beauty.

In the brilliant dusty light, figures moved now to country dances. One followed another, the 'top couple' always 'calling the dance.' There were *Chain Figure*, *Allemand*, *Triumph*, *Swing Corners*, *Poussette* and many more. The dancers kept their places, observed their decorum. It was beyond them, in the alcoves, up and down the stairs, in the hall, that the coloured figures, devils and monks, courtesans and milkmaids, Columbines and sea-captains tumbled and laughed, whispered and embraced. Silver and purple, cinnamon and orange, grey and crimson broke, melted, formed, as though from the gilt ceiling with the pink naked cherubs a figure solemn, sad-faced, remote, hiding a gigantic yawn, absent-mindedly pulled the strings.

In any case the Herries strings were pulled that night. By a kind of fate the little Herries figures were drawn together and with disastrous consequences.

For Christabel Herries the evening had become a torture. She was only a girl in years, although tall and gawky of figure. Will's wealth had come suddenly. Of the many persons invited she knew herself not half, and their masquerades made them only more mysterious to her.

At that time in London it was a very general complaint that many persons came to private Balls and Masquerades who were quite unknown to their hosts and hostesses. It was the increasing licence of these London seasons that led to the strict etiquette of Bath and other watering-places. With the divisions at Court, the uncertainty of the war with France, the consciousness of a lower class slowly but increasingly vocal, the new importance of the business man from the City, the advancing licence of Vauxhall, Marybone and the many lesser resorts, no hostess during the last years of that century but knew alarms and terrors that would have horrified her grandmother. No smaller hostess, in any case—and Christabel was a very new hostess indeed. It is an old and very true axiom that nothing can harm a party save the anxieties and alarm of the host and hostess themselves. All would have been well on this especial evening had Christabel been able to command herself. Unfortunately, when the crisis arrived, Will was elsewhere. He in fact saw nothing the matter with his Ball. It would have taken a great deal more than a few riotous spirits to upset his complacent equanimity. He had also enjoyed no small quantity of his own wine, which he thought excellent; he congratulated himself on acquiring it cheaply from a Jewish gentleman in the City. He was dancing the Triumph with a lady quite unknown to him, but, in his eyes, of an especial fascination, when Christabel so desperately needed his support. There were to be many occasions afterwards when he would have given half his wealth had he only been there that he might have prevented what occurred.

Many times in the records of any family it must seem that the stage has been set with especial and malicious purpose. Had Will's house not been an old one of Queen Anne's date there would not have been the small ante-room leading from the ballroom itself, and had there not been the small ante-room . . .

It happened that Rose Herries, Pomfret's wife, from Kensington, began the trouble. Rose Herries was a woman thinned and raddled by incessant jealousy. By birth the daughter of a small Worcestershire clergyman, she had been amazed when the handsome young Pomfret Herries had proposed for her in marriage. Pomfret's father, Sir Raiseley Herries, had married the sister of David, the son of old 'Rogue' Herries, but there had been an old boyhood feud between Raiseley and David that David's sister had certainly done nothing to heal. It was because of their proximity to David's family at Uldale that the Raiseley Herries had moved from Keswick to London. Raiseley, Pomfret's father, had always been delicate and ailing. When Pomfret had been around twenty-five years of age, Raiseley had moved for a summer into Worcestershire because of some doctor or other, taking his two children with him. It was here that one fine morning young Pomfret had seen the lovely Rose walking down a country lane. He had fallen in love with her on the spot. He had been often in love before, but never considered matrimony. Now he did consider it, and six months later was married.

Rose had never recovered from the shock of it. The most that she had ever expected was a local squire, but now to be a baronet's Lady, to have a grand house in Kensington and, above and beyond that, to be married to a man whose figure was everything that her most romantic imagination could have designed for her! Sir Pomfret was an amiable fellow, contented with all that came his way. He was as good a husband to her as was in his nature. But, after the first month, he was unfaithful, nor was he either then or later able to conceal his infidelities. And, so evilly does fortune arrange, Rose was designed to be jealous. She was made for it. The more jealous the more she loved, and the more she loved the more jealous. Pomfret learned, as all husbands learn, to conceal more skilfully his private life, but the less Rose knew the more she guessed. She was frankly a plague both to herself and to him. A Masquerade such as this was designed to torture her.

Sir Pomfret's stout figure (he had come to the Ball as Henry VIII.) soon escaped her vision. She told herself, as, poor woman, she had told herself a thousand times before, that ' she must permit him his pleasure.' For five minutes she knew a sort of unhappy nobility. She was being fine, generous, the true wife; but the five minutes were as long as a lifetime, and soon, her long thin neck craning (she was dressed in a watery green and considered herself a Naiad), she looked for him everywhere. She had come to the Ball happy and expectant; Pomfret would stay by her side, he would dance with her and then, very handsomely, she would say: ' Now be off. You don't want your old wife at hand all the evening.' But he had left her so quickly; he had given her nobility no opportunity.

It is another of the signs that Providence had its long finger crooked in this affair that the men were all of them absent, Will dancing, Rockage talking of his place in Wiltshire to an elderly baroness, Pomfret making love to a very young but very worldly Nun, and Georges . . . Well, Georges, his head singing with Jennifer's beauty, was betting with some young men on the staircase as to the number of young women's feet you could see moving across the ballroom floor.

So the men were away. This was a woman's affair. Rose Herries met Christabel by chance behind the bronze-coloured curtains that portioned off the ante-room from the ballroom. It was comparatively quiet here: the music, the voices came like water flowing up, ebbing away again. The room had been cleared of furniture; the walls had a blue and white paper recommended to Christabel within the last month as the very latest design. On it were depicted over and over again the sorrows of Werther, an elongated Werther watching a gigantic Lotte beside the spring.

It was unquestioned that Christabel did not, by this time, know what she was doing. It seemed to her that the whole thing was a devastating, world-shaking scandal. To-morrow all London would be speaking of it. She and

Will would be disgraced for ever. The scandalous Herries Ball . . . She had been always a
delicate woman. Child-bearing had but shaken
her nerves the further. Her stupid, wondering
features, pale but strangely streaked as though
with the marks of someone else's fingers, were
puckered and childishly distressed above her ill-
fitting yellow dress.

She had convinced herself that it was Jennifer
Cards who had disgraced the Ball. She had
always disliked Jennifer, always distrusted the
Cards branch of the family, who, she was well
aware, looked down upon Will and herself.
She did not like Rose and Pomfret, the Kensington branch, very much better. Little Judith
was the one she especially cared for. She would
have liked to have her always with her. It was
a thousand pities that she must live up in that
rough Cumberland and be married to a scamp
of a rascally Frenchman. Poor little Judith!
Christabel knew that she would come to some
catastrophe. But she liked her; Judith was kind
and considerate, despised no one, understood
one's troubles. How she wished that Judith
were here now! Then she saw her with Maria
Rockage and at the same moment Rose, in her
ugly green dress, peering about among the crowd.

The four women drew together as though by
instinct, standing just inside the ante-room as
bathers, soaked with the sea, gather together on
a rock for a moment's pause. They were all
nervous and uneasy—Christabel because of her
social anxiety, Rose because of her errant husband,

Maria because she could not find Carey, Judith because the whole evening had been a failure for her.

The big room was thinning. The candles were burning low. The music had lost its vigour. In the distance a crimson Cardinal pursued a Dairymaid, who ran with little screams of pleasure across the shining floor.

'That Baddeley,' said Rose Herries scornfully. 'There is some resemblance to mankind in him. That is as much as you can say. . . .' She was speaking of a Mr. James Baddeley, an acquaintance of Pomfret's.

'It is scandalous,' said Maria Rockage, 'that Jennifer should be so monstrously without a chaperon all the evening. When I was a girl, to leave one's chaperon for an instant, except to dance with an acceptable young man——' She broke off. She thought of her daughter Phyllis at Grosset, and how she could not afford to buy her the dresses . . . that flaunting crimson with the silver collar . . . 'But, of course, the looseness of these Masquerades. . . .'

Christabel felt at once that this was a criticism of her Ball. All over London to-morrow. . . . Her long fingers closed and unclosed about her fan. (The famous fan. Were the figures painted on it of blue or of silver? Who will ever know?)

'I admit . . . 'Tis a failure, a monstrous failure. . . . I am distracted. . . . And Will has assisted me in nothing at all. . . . I have had all the burden myself. . . .' She did not mind now what she said. She was on the verge of tears.

The others were surprised. They had not been thinking of the Ball. They had not thought it out of the way. Everyone knew what these Masquerades were. Once you wore a mask. . . .

'Why, Christabel,' Maria said amiably (for when she could rise above her own worries she was a kindly woman), 'the Ball is well enough. A very fine Ball. A Masquerade must always have a certain licence.' (But nevertheless she thought 'This is a pandemonium.')

Judith, who had been standing looking into the outer room, wondering where Georges was (she could not see with her small stature over the heads of the dancers), thinking that at least he might *once* that evening have sought her out, felt an instant desire to take Christabel in hand, to reassure her, to persuade her that everything was well, to make her happy again (and behind that she was still wondering about Georges, thinking that her love for him was a sort of poison in her blood, a poison that she would never, never be rid of).

'Yes, Jennifer has no modesty,' Rose said, bending her long neck. (Was *that* Pomfret laughing with that girl in white, there near the window in the farther corner?) 'Her father permits her to do as she pleases. Amelia has been playing cards instead of doing her duty. I never liked the girl: swollen with self-approval. They say that at Vauxhall the other week . . .' She broke off, for Maria Rockage's hand was on her arm. Jennifer was standing, quite close to them, alone, looking into the ante-room.

It must be understood that the girl was elated with her triumph. She had not been so very much in London, and Bournemouth's triumphs were not very satisfactory. This was her first *real* Ball, and, more than that, it was in the very heart of the family. Although the Rockages had been there, yes, and the Herries from Kensington, it was she who had been the evening's sensation. She knew that socially the High World had not been represented here. But Jennifer was true Herries in that. Although she disliked all the other Herries except her own family, yet she thought them as good as anyone in the world— as good as the Pope or the Prince or Queen Charlotte or Lady Jersey. She wanted nothing more than to be the acknowledged Herries Beauty, and that not at all for the outside world but simply for the Herries world.

So here she was, panting with triumph, her mask in her hand, her marvellous dark blue eyes glittering with success and pleasure, her magnificent bosom half bare above the crimson, her carriage superb, her youth, vitality, self-confidence all alive and shining—and she glanced for a moment into the ante-room to see whether her mother were there. She looked and saw the four women, three of them, to her, untidy old frumps, and the fourth that strange girl Judith Paris, whose force of personality she felt. The girl had marvellous hair. She had character too. She didn't like her.

She might in fact have passed on had Judith's gipsy dress in some odd way not challenged her.

Judith in her ragged dress with her unpowdered hair was unlike anyone else at the Ball. She had had, Jennifer knew, a vagabond for her mother and a vagabond for her father. Jennifer's grandfather had known ' Rogue ' Herries.

So Jennifer stayed. She had not intended to look scornful. She was too happy. But there was an element of cruelty in her. She looked at Christabel's pale face and ugly yellow, at Rose's thin bones and ill-chosen green, at Maria Rockage's untidy hair, and before she moved away, she smiled.

Then she asked:

' Is my mother at cards? '

The smile was, for Christabel, a statement of the whole evening's failure. Her voice trembling, she answered:

' No. But wherever she is, you should be with her.'

Jennifer came forward a little into the room. She wanted these old women to have a full sight of her youth and her beauty. Christabel was her own age, and yet how elderly, how worn, how awkward she seemed! And perhaps Christabel thought: ' This is what I should be! The Ball would have been a success to-night had I been! '

Jennifer stood there, swinging her mask between her fingers.

' Christabel,' she said, ' I must congratulate you on the evening.' She meant a compliment. She had no sense of irony there. But Christabel saw it as only ironical.

' I do not need your compliments,' she

answered, 'and least of all when they are not
intended.   I know what you have felt this evening.   I must tell you that you have failed entirely
if you wished to conceal your feelings.'

With a shock of surprise Jennifer realised that
Christabel was in a hysterical rage.   The three
girls were standing near to one another, the two
older women farther apart.   Maria, who wished
that everything should be peaceable, but that at
the same time she might satisfy a little her own
sense that her daughter had not fine clothes and
that the evening had lacked decorum, said: 'You
should have been more with your mother, Jennifer,
or your mother more with you.   Chaperons are
still in fashion, my child.   Yes, your mother is at
the card-table.   Pray give her my love.'

'Oh,' cried Jennifer, 'so that is what my
sweet relatives have been settling with one another.
That I need a chaperon!'   She curtsied to them,
and Judith thought that she had never in her
life before seen anyone so beautiful.   ('But,' she
also thought, 'what a temper!   My God, what
a temper!')

'But for my own part,' Jennifer went on,
addressing Christabel as though no one else were
there, 'it appears ridiculous ostentation to me!
At a Ball like this——'   She paused, staring
Christabel in the eyes.   She had always hated
Christabel, she thought, the mean pudding-faced
thing, proud only because her husband had made
money as a merchant, a vulgar City merchant.

'And what at a Ball like this?'   Christabel
whispered.   They had come close together as

though they were discussing some very intimate secret. Rose interrupted. She was aware that there was a very dangerous element here, something that threatened everyone's comfort. 'There!' she cried, laughing nervously. 'Why, I am certain that Jennifer meant nothing. The Ball is very fine. We have all enjoyed a most handsome evening. Jennifer had no intention——'

'But I had an intention,' Jennifer interrupted hotly, looking only at Christabel. 'If you fancy that I am to have my manners taught me—and my mother her manners also. There is a shabbiness here that one might have expected. Manners learnt from Great-Aunt Maria, I don't doubt, who learnt them at the Battle of Naseby. . . .'

'Manners!' cried Christabel, beside herself with weariness, hysterical exhaustion, jealousy, loneliness. 'Manners from you!'

She moved forward. Jennifer turned aside and, resting her hand on a small table beside her, without knowing what she did, picked up Christabel's fan that was lying there. She raised her head contemptuously; her fingers tightened about the fan, and one of the sticks broke with a little crack that sounded in Christabel's ears like a pistol shot. It was her favourite fan, one of her finest possessions.

She stepped forward and smacked Jennifer's face.

And this, exactly, was the true history of one of the most famous and momentous quarrels in all the Herries history, so long as events have been recorded.

THE HANGING

Judith sat facing old Montague Cards. He was not old in years, being but twenty-nine. He was the only son of Morgan, brother of Prosper and uncle of Jennifer, and was, therefore, the lovely Jennifer's cousin. He was a bachelor and plainly designed from the beginning for that character. He was thin to emaciation, never varied in his dress, a bag-wig, a suit of black silk. His nostrils constantly heaved in a sort of simpering protest, as though he were offended by a bad smell. But he was not. It was a sort of inner nasal irritation. His voice was affected and often rose to a shrill note, but behind these absurdities he was in reality a kindly, nervous, generous soul, who longed to be liked but did not know how to set about it. He had a horror of being made love to by women, although he liked their company, for he adored gossip.

He was tyrannised by his man-servant and his man-servant's wife. He had been, until Will's sudden rise, the wealthiest of all the Herries. His grandfather had left him money, and he, by careful investment, had increased it. He was very cautious and reputed to be miserly. This he quite certainly was not, but he found the reputation useful. Like all the other Herries he thought there was no other family in England so fine and so grand, but he quarrelled with individual members of it. He had not, for instance, spoken to either Carey or Maria Rockage for years until to-day. This cleavage was the result of the bursting of a damaged water-pipe upon him in the middle of a winter night when he was staying at Grosset. He complained that the Rockages thought it an honour to receive the contents of a burst water-pipe at any time, in any place, were it a Grosset water-pipe. He liked to stay with other Herries in the country. Visits saved expense. At once, however, on hearing of the family crisis, he had offered his rooms in Berkeley Square as an unprejudiced meeting-place. The Ball had not, as Christabel had feared, been the subject of any general scandal. It had in fact, in the outside world, made absolutely no mark whatever, but among the Herries themselves the effect had been terrific.

Judith, looking now at the various Herries seated in the fine brocaded chairs round Montague's panelled room, saw, from the barely concealed sentiments of pleasure in the various faces, that here at last was the family battle for which they had all for long been aching.

Carey Rockage, as someone outside the dispute and the titled head of the family, was in charge of the conference, and delighted he was. It had been no easy matter for the Rockages, economically, to be compelled to stay in London an additional week, but their rooms in the Mews were cheap, and young Carey and Phyllis would be living on short rations for many a week after their return to Grosset.

Rockage had a round baby face with dimples. His suit was rusty with age, his hair shabbily powdered, and one stocking had a hole above the heel. But he was a real Herries. There was dignity and discipline there. He could command men, and there was a certain sweetness in his nature, as there was also in his wife's, which had, in spite of their narrowness and Methodism, long ago drawn Judith to them. Maria, his wife, was sitting near to him, and in her excitement it was all that she could do not to be speaking all the time. She hated so intensely the beautiful Jennifer, jealous of her loveliness, the advantages she had over her own dear Phyllis, but in the main thinking, quite honestly, that the beautiful creature represented all the whoredoms of Babylon.

Jennifer herself was not present. It was thought more fitting that she should not be, but her father and mother, Prosper and Amelia Cards, were there in very truth; it would not be too much to say that their rage and sense of insult was as fine and pure an emotion as ever a Herries had known.

Prosper, in spite of his forty-eight years, was, by far, the finest figure in the room. His suit of crimson and silver, his elaborate wig of shining whiteness, the splendid ruffles at his throat and sleeves only served to emphasise his magnificent physique. He had the chest and neck of a bull, but his features were not common. They had, as Amelia was proud to emphasise, a classical correctness. He was not fleshy as Pomfret Herries was; his frame was gigantic. He carried on the Herries' physical tradition of David, Will's father. Curiously enough he was not proud of his beauty; he had been so, maybe, once, but now he had transferred it all to his lovely Jennifer and it was in her that the whole of his life—physical, material, mental—and his ambitions were centred. She was to marry a Duke. Nothing on this earth was too good for her. And that she should have been struck in the face. . . .

He sat there outwardly calm, his splendid legs in their silk stockings stretched in front of him. Outwardly calm. But, if he lived to a hundred, as he and all the other Herries felt it their right to do, he would never forget this insult. Amelia, his wife, in a dress of canary silk, seated at his side, had the subdued and colourless appearance of a woman who has, her life long, played second to a splendid husband. She was not, however, as he knew, so colourless.

The round shining table between them, on the farther side of the room sat Pomfret, fleshy, unserious, gay in spite of himself; Rose, his wife, thankful that she had Pomfret secure at her side for an hour at least, eagerly excited at the human possibilities of the situation; Will, very stiff, trying to be grand, feeling desperately young, aware at one moment that he was richer than them all, at another that his wife had slapped the face of a guest in her own house, trying to calculate the social and family consequences of the incident, rather as a financier will balance his probabilities. Christabel, gauche, awkward, knowing that the whole family, save possibly Judith, was against her, a sort of rough obstinacy rising to support her, warmed too by an almost frantic hatred of Jennifer; a little farther from them again Francis, elegant, aloof, looking out of window as though he were thinking of something else—and Judith.

She had not intended to come. It was only because Christabel herself, coming all the way to Judith's lodging in a coach, had persuaded her.

Christabel, bursting into tears, had protested that all the world was against her: even Will had scolded her, had told her that her temper had put back his affairs a dozen years at least. True, she had slapped Jennifer's face, but was she to endure impertinence from anyone who offered it her? Rose and Maria had been with her in that. But now—who knows? They were under the thumb of their husbands. . . . Judith must come and support her.

Judith had her own private troubles—worse, she could not but think, than anything that Christabel had to suffer. In the week since the Ball, disaster had crept nearer, and now, for these last two nights and days, Georges had not been home.

He was attempting (how well she knew it!) to repair desperate fortunes with some desperate remedy. At every occasion when he left her she did not know but that she might never see him again. Maybe he was even now at the

Thames bottom with his head battered or his throat cut. She thought, sitting in that room warm with the May heat, smelling the scent of the lilac bloom that came up from the Square below, hearing the cry of some vendor in melancholy tuneful cadence, ' Oh, if he would only come. Nothing else matters! It is strange how I love him! '

She had left word at the lodging if he should return there while she was away. Did any of those in this room love anyone as she loved Georges? She clasped her small hot hands together, smoothed her dress, and heard Prosper Cards' deep stern voice come to her as though from the heart of an abysmal pit:

' I am not indicting Mrs. William Herries for anything,' she heard him say. ' That is too strong a word. There must be, however, an apology in writing.'

' Come, come, Prosper, my friend,' Pomfret's easy genial voice interrupted. ' Is there not altogether too much ado about a trivial matter? Nay, nay—' (He raised a fat white hand.) ' We are all one family here. It is among relatives. Jennifer and Christabel are young, life is beginning for them, they had both an intemperate moment. For my part I like a little hot blood. . . .'

' Yes, Pomfret, we know that you do,' Prosper answered drily, crossing one splendid leg over the other. ' But I do not consider it a trivial matter, nor does my wife. We demand an apology in writing.'

Will's voice broke in. It trembled a little

and was more human than Judith had ever heard
it. 'If one apology is necessary, then so is
another. My wife has already agreed that her
action was hasty and undisciplined. The more
reason that the affair was under her own roof.
But what of the cause? Your daughter, sir,
used words of gross discourtesy and in her temper
destroyed one of my wife's most cherished
possessions. . . .'

'Cherished possessions!' broke in Amelia
Cards. 'Fiddlesticks! A fan, and no extraordinary one neither!'

'Fiddlesticks!' Will cried, now very hot and
red in the face. 'Is that a word for a lady . . .?'

But Rockage interrupted, the dimples on his
cheeks deepening so that he looked like a laughing cherub:

'Ladies! Ladies! Gentlemen! Gentlemen!
You have invited me to preside over this conversation, simply, it was understood from the first, a
friendly conversation that the little incident may
be closed finally. It was with the wish of everyone that we met. Let us all part friends. The
matter is surely clear enough. There was re-
grettable temper on both sides. The evidence
has proved it. Mrs. Will Herries has stated her
own regret. It only remains for my friend
Prosper on behalf of his daughter——'

'Not a whit! Not a whit!' answered Prosper,
slapping his silken thigh. 'I must have an
apology in writing. There is no evidence that
my daughter showed temper.'

'She did! She did!' broke in Christabel, on

the edge of tears. ' She spoke most insultingly, comparing me with old Great-Aunt Maria of Naseby Battle, and making a play of our entertainment, and all for no reason but her own vanity, because she thought that she was the beauty of the evening——'

' As indeed she was,' Prosper said with deep satisfaction. ' No one within a mile's race of her.'

The lilac, rich, warm, pungent, floated in through the open windows, bathing Judith's eyes with its lovely odour. Oh, why must they squabble about this silly business and her own life on the knife-edge of ruin ? She was here, a grown woman, to help her cousin, to aid in the family councils, but she did not feel like a grown woman. She felt like a little girl, shut in a dark room, expecting she knew not what terrible entry. What did they, these comfortable, well-fed Herries, know of the struggle that these last years had been for Judith and Georges, the scrapes for money, the taming of landladies, the corners of Coffee Houses, the night hours when Judith in her shift, her arm around Georges, had again and again persuaded him that all would yet be well? What did they know . . .?

Then Rose's introduction of her own name caught her attention.

' There can be no question about the impertinence offered. Ask Judith Paris.'

All eyes turned to her. Her head was confused. Her own personal anxiety pressed upon her heart like a hand closing down on it, and the hand seemed to crush lilac bloom in its fingers; lilac swinging through the sky, while the tops of the green trees in the Square flamed on the iridescent air.

She heard Prosper Cards' deep arrogant voice: ' Well, what has little Miss Judith to say? '

Years after, when she looked back and wondered at the sudden temper that she showed now (temper that had immense consequences), it seemed to her that everything rose together to influence her. Just as, had Christabel's fan not been on the table, there would have been no family crisis, so had there been no warm day, no lilac, no anxiety for Georges, nay, even no dimples in Carey Rockage's cheeks, and, most certainly, no ' little Miss Judith ' from Prosper, why then there would have been no temper, no such public taking of sides, binding her, she often afterwards felt, to a whole lifetime of consequences. ' Little Miss Judith ' indeed! There was certainly something insufferable about this Cards family!

She heard her own voice, rather shrill, not like her voice at all:

' I think that Christabel had aggravation. Contempt was shown for her Ball, not too civil in a guest who had been so kindly entertained. Christabel should not have slapped her face, maybe . . . but I would have slapped her. I would indeed. One's own guest . . . Oh, there was certainly cause! '

She realised with some satisfaction the surprise that everyone felt. For a moment she forgot even Georges, for she was doing what she loved to do,

M 2

influencing a situation, a group of persons, above all, a group of Herries! She could feel how Rose Herries was thinking, ' Well I never; who'd have thought it! ' and would wonder whether Judith's boldness might possibly titillate Pomfret's sensual side: how grateful Christabel would be, and even Will; how furious Amelia, Jennifer's mother; how scornful Prosper (but in his slow grandeur and handsome pride he would never forget it nor forgive it).

She stole a glance at Francis, who still was staring out of window, staring at the trees that shimmered like green glass in the sun. And what was *he* thinking of? She knew at once by a sort of inspired divination. He was thinking of the lovely, lovely Jennifer—had been thinking of her all day. Years later she was to know that her divination was true.

Meanwhile she had to fight to maintain her position. Prosper was regarding her through his large liquid brown eyes with a patronising indulgence.

' Come, come, Miss Judith,' he said. ' Why so unkind to my daughter? How has she offended you? '

' She *has* not offended me! ' (Judith thought— does he not know that I'm married, the great pompous ox? Oh, how once again she wished that she were larger, her legs longer, her brow more imposing!) ' I have nothing against your daughter, sir, but I was present, and must say what I think. In my advice it would be more seemly for nothing more to be said of the matter on either side. There was temper shown both ways. It was a late hour, and everyone was weary.' She was surprised at the firmness of her voice. Her personality counted; she knew that they were all impressed with it.

Perhaps Prosper felt that also, for he said, his voice a little more angered than it had been:

' Why do we waste our time? I should be in the country by now. My wife and I are not here for some child's play. I demand from Mrs. Will Herries an apology in writing.'

Will, his face pale with anger, the horse-bones of his cheeks emphasised with his passion, answered:

' It is clear enough from the evidence. . . . I also demand an apology in writing.'

Then everyone began to speak at once:

' No apology on either side.'

' Great rudeness.'

' For my part I'd have a public apology.'

' And what could you know of the matter? If you'd been beside your daughter as you should have been——'

' Most certainly she insulted me. She laughed at my entertainment and broke my fan——'

' I demand an apology in writing. . . .'

' After all, they are both young. Who should mind a slap in the face . . .?'

' I would call you out, Cousin Prosper, for less.'

' Call me out then. I'll make mincemeat out of you!'

' Pomfret! Pomfret!' (This, shrilly, from

Rose.) 'What are you about? And at your age. . . .'

And then a contribution from Cousin Montague, who had said no word until now, had been completely forgotten by everyone:

'The weather is so warm. There are refreshments in the parlour. The other room has a cooler outlook——'

Then from the hubbub, the decisive authority of Carey Rockage. Strange, the dominance of that shabby baby-faced man!

'Friends, friends! This is a family affair. About nothing so outrageous neither. Mrs. Will has agreed that she will offer an apology. As to writing, I am sure, Prosper, that your good-nature will insist——'

'Good-nature be damned!' Prosper interrupted. 'My daughter has had her face slapped and publicly. My wife is with me in this. For the hundredth time—there must be an apology in writing.'

'And I say there shall not!' cried Will, suddenly jumping up and tipping his chair over. 'This is our last and final word. My wife has expressed her regret for her hastiness. We expect the expression of similar regret from Miss Jennifer Cards. Otherwise there is an end to any possible intercourse between this branch of the family and the Bournemouth part of it. Greatly to be regretted—but this is final.'

The boy, for he was little more, glared across the room at the magnificent Prosper. It was a little, Judith thought, David defying Goliath.

But she was proud of him. She saw now—
perhaps for the first time—why it was that he
was making himself a solid figure in London.

Then came the real surprise of the occasion.
For Francis, who had hitherto been silent, spoke.
' I should wish to say,' he interjected, ' that I am
dissociated from my brother in this. I hold that
Miss Jennifer deserves an apology in writing.'

' Oh no, Francis—oh no,' Judith whispered
under her breath. She realised with an actual
pang of apprehension that this silly dispute about
so trivial an affair was going much deeper than
she had ever supposed. Her memory spread
before her in an instant of vision, scene after
scene—Uldale in the old years, Sarah and David,
Francis and Will; Francis hardly more than a
child, staring at Skiddaw, turning and picking
Will up from the long orchard grass, smoothing some fancied hurt; Francis and Will bathing
and running naked from the stream; Francis,
Will, Reuben, herself, watching the fireworks at
the Lake's edge. But Francis must be possessed
by this Jennifer! That he should so defy his
brother, so publicly. . . .

And it was the last straw for Will. He caught
Christabel by the arm, dragging her from her
chair.

' No apology!' he shouted; ' neither now
nor ever!' He shook his fist across the room.
' You can carry your Bournemouth manners back
with you! I wish you good day.' At the door
he turned. ' And your own betrayal of me,
Francis, I am not likely to forget.'

He pulled Christabel through the door with him. Everyone broke into confusion. Judith could hear Montague urging:

'It is the warm weather . . . refreshments . . . a cool parlour.' And Prosper's measured tones: 'Young puppy! I'd call him out for a penny!' And Maria Rockage: 'Oh dear, oh dear! . . . That's a pity, and Carey so wonderfully discreet.'

Well, the thing was done. Judith sighed, turning away from Francis, who stood with his back to the company, looking out of the window down into the Square. It seemed, Judith thought, as though the beautiful shadow of Jennifer hung over all the room.

A moment later she had forgotten them all, for there, standing just within the door, looking at them all, a half-defiant, half-apologetic smile on his face, was Georges!

He was neat and tidy, in a brown suit, holding his hat in his hand, but—she saw at once—infinitely weary. His round face was ashen. He held himself as though at any moment he might fall.

Rockage knew him. Rose and Pomfret spoke to him. A moment later Judith was tugging at his arm.

'Georges, you had my note. I have waited two days. . . . Where have you been . . .? What . . .?'

'I came to fetch you,' he said, looking at her with a great kindliness that caught at her heart. 'We shall talk better outside.'

She took his arm. He bowed to the assembled company. One last impression she had (that was

to seem to her afterwards like the closing note on all
her old life) of Francis, turning from the window
and very gravely regarding them both. Then
they were out of the room and down the stairs.

The Square was quite deserted and beautifully
still in the dusty golden sunlight of the hastening summer afternoon. They walked along, she
still holding his arm.

He spoke very rapidly, but still with a great
and considering kindness.

' Listen, Judy. . . . Everything is up. I have
been a fool these two days, just as I have been a
fool all my life. But worse now, much worse.
Listen to what I say. I must be off this instant.
There's a boat I know at Greenwich; away to-
night for Copenhagen——'

' But what have you done? '

' I've played two nights and a day. Once I
was handsomely to the good, then lost it all again.
But that's not the thing. There was a scuffle
this morning at Jonathan's. I stuck a ninny—
no, he's not dead—but they are out against me
and several more. London's closed to me for a
time at least.'

' And I? ' Her mind was active with a
thousand possibilities.

' Go back to Watendlath and wait for me.'

They stood at the Square corner, and now she
had actually just above her head a thick bush of
purple lilac that leaned towards her as though it
would brush her cheek. A negro boy, with a
silver turban and leading a spaniel by a thin chain,
passed them whistling.

He spoke to her most urgently. ' Judy, I know you are brave, and most sensible. I'm sorry indeed that I have brought you to this pass, the more that these years in London have made us friends. I have no friend in the world like you. You've tamed me because you caught my admiration and kept it. . . . Judy, I think I could love you for long now, were we quietly in Cumberland. . . .'

At the word ' Cumberland ' she broke out: ' Oh, why could we not go there? Both of us. No one would look for you in Watendlath.'

' No,' he answered sharply. ' I must be out of England. I've come to think that they hate me here. They turn on me and hunt me like dogs a hare if they have the slenderest reason. I'm a man of no country. I'd rather be on the sea than on the land anywhere. Except for you I'd go to sea and never touch land again. . . . But I always have to come back to you, and will come. Go to Watendlath. Be patient there. I shall write and send money if I have any. But you can manage in any case. You have a man's head on you. There's money enough in the lodging— the drawer by the fireplace. Here . . . the key. That will carry you North. I should pay the woman and leave to-night. Stay quietly there. Answer no questions if they ask you. One day, perhaps soon, you'll see me walk up the road. I *must* come back to you. There's no one and nothing else in the world draws me. . . .'

She asked no questions. She hated people who asked tiresome questions at an urgent crisis.

He caught her by the shoulders, as he sometimes did when he was pleased, lifting her a little
from her feet. He kissed her.

' Now—good-bye,' and he had turned the
corner swiftly and was gone.

She stood there, looking up into the lilac,
but not seeing it. Not from sentiment but
because she knew that in the future it would often
please her to remember, she repeated some of the
things that he had said.

' I think I could love you for long now. . . .
Except for you I'd go . . . You have a man's
head. . . .'

And so she had. She wanted to commit some
panicky folly like running down the street to
find him and then insisting that wherever he went
she would go with him, but she must be practical
and do exactly what he had asked her.

She was glad that she must leave London.
As though to be in tune with the urgency of her
own affairs, the day was clouding. Thunder
was behind the houses. She walked on, thinking
how, with ease, she could catch the night coach
to York. From there across country she might
share a post-chaise if she were lucky. The very
thought of Watendlath made her heart beat with
pleasure. The cool breeze slipping down the
mountain-side, the water, green-clear, tumbling
into the Punchbowl, the Tarn mirroring one
white cloud, while the Fell looked down to Rosthwaite; the Ritsons, the children, the dogs, the
smell of the peat, the dung, the Cumberland
bracken (now there would be new fresh fronds

springing up, curling above the stem) and, most lovely of all, the eternal running streams, so reassuring, so friendly. . . . Why had she left it? Although she was only a step from Berkeley Square all the members of the Herries family, with whom she had so lately been, seemed unreal and unalive.

She hurried on, for her mind was set now on the practical business of doing what Georges had told her—leaving London and catching the night coach.

Soon she was in the poorer streets that hung like spiderwebs about Charing Cross. The heavy day was dark now above her head, and the noise of the traffic on the street, the stench of the gutter, the projecting windows and the roughness of the cobbled road held and confused her.

When she stood it seemed that almost at once people closed in upon her. She was in a narrow street that opened out until it became almost a small cobbled square hemmed in with uneven and overhanging houses. She was aware then that her own thoughts had hindered her from noticing that some event was going forward. Before she knew it or could resist it she found that a mixed and very evil-smelling crowd was pushing her on; then, looking about her, saw that beside a butcher's shop that had above it a large swaying sign a platform had been erected and on the platform a gibbet.

The sight of the gibbet sickened her; it had in its very rough newness and sharp angles a sense of torture and pain about it. She turned as though to go back, but found now to her dismay that the crowd behind her was too thick for her to pass through.

She had heard at one time that malefactors were sometimes hanged by the place of their crime, and she supposed that unwittingly she had tumbled upon some such scene. The odd mixture of emotions in her breast at that moment—her passionate feeling of love for Georges, the excitement of the recent family squabble, the sense of the exceeding importance that she should do at once what Georges asked her—threw her into a special state of nervous apprehension. Her first thought was that she must at once get away from where she was. She realised that in her abstraction she had moved into a crowd that must have been waiting there for a considerable period. All the windows of the neighbourhood were open and were crowded with figures. Boys were clinging to the lamp-posts, and along one side of the street a platform of boards had been arranged on barrows and tubs, and this was thronged. Above the roofs the sky was dark, and she fancied that she could hear distant rumbles of thunder. Whatever happened she must escape, so she turned to go back the way that she had come, but she was at once obstructed by a large man carrying an empty tray round his middle, and a group of women who, so soon as they saw that she wanted to pass them, with laughter prevented her.

'No passage this way,' one woman, who had a huge bosom and her skirt tucked up almost to her knees, cried.

' I beg you,' Judith began. ' It is an urgent
matter—if you please.'

' If you please—if you please! ' the whole
street seemed to echo her. ' Only one thing
urgent here, and that is a jerk with the rope and,
lady or gentleman, it's all the same, we all go to
heaven! '

She was so small that she had no hope of
asserting herself. She looked about her to see
whether some face were likely to help her, but
she thought that she had never seen so many
coarse mouths, bright hard eyes. There was in
the look of everyone a flutter of the animal—the
animal allowed for an hour a little freedom, to
prowl into a larger cage and taste handsome food.
The sense that she had had for a long time in
London that times were changing, that the people
themselves were now more actively conscious
of possible power and were moving towards it,
held her now. For the first time in her life she
was afraid of people. She had never before been
aware of what a crowd was. Her individuality
was lost. If she were not careful she would be
trampled down, not her body but something much
more real and vivid than that.

She hated any public scene; her reserve and
dignity came to her rescue. She turned back
and found that she could move forward more
easily. She might escape at the broader street-
end. But when she had gone some way, jolted,
pushed, with much unpleasant contact with clothes
and hot breath, legs and arms, she came to a
stop again. She saw to her great distress that she

was almost under the platform where the gibbet
was. Here was a thick ring of people, mostly
women; she thought of France. It must have
been often like this in France, the women knitting
and singing, their ears straining for the rattle of
the tumbrils.

She felt faint with the heat and the smells and
the noise. Scarcely knowing what she did, she
caught at an arm to steady herself and found that
she was holding on to a little thin man in a large
hat and a rusty black suit. He smiled at her
kindly.

' Can you help me out of this, sir? ' she asked
gently.

He shook his head. ' I fear not, madam.
It is best to stay where you are. The crowd
grows thicker every moment.'

' Oh, but I don't wish to stay. I have a most
urgent appointment.'

He pointed with his finger. She looked and
saw that escape was now impossible. The crowd
had in the last five minutes flooded in. She
could see the shining hats of the ' Charlies ' at
the crowd's edge.

' Is someone to be hanged? ' she asked.

' A young man.'

' What had he done? '

' Stolen three shillings from his master's till—
the butcher's there.'

She was a woman of her time, she did not feel
the injustice of it as a woman of a later day would
do, but it was as though, in that moment, looking
anxiously into the little man's mild eye, pressed

in on every side, stirred perhaps by the drama
of her own personal circumstances, she received
some especial consciousness, ahead of her time,
a sense of cruelty and persecution that pierced
her very heart.

‘ Oh, poor boy . . . I don't want to see. . . .
Please cannot you assist me?　What are all these
people here for?　If he must die it should be by
himself alone.　Oh, help me, please ! . . .’

She saw herself the hopelessness of any escape.
He was very kind.　He put his arm very courte-
ously round her.　‘ There is no way out.　You
can see for yourself.　It will be over soon now.
It was to be at five o'clock.　We shall have a
storm if they are not quick.’

Something compelled her to look around her.
The people near her were decent enough, quiet,
grave-faced.　They waited indifferently, as though
it were a peep-show they had come for.　Two
women close to her were chatting about their own
affairs.　A hush spread slowly over the crowd, as
though a hand had been laid upon them all.　A
man, burly and broad, carrying a cane, mounted
the steps to the scaffold.　He went to the gibbet
and felt the rope.　A flock of pigeons flew from
one side of the street to the other, and a sudden
clap of thunder, as though someone had fired a
gun, startled them.　They rustled their wings like
a shower of falling paper.

It seemed to Judith that this was her own
personal tragedy, that all her life she would be
affected with her memory of it.　She was forced
now to watch ; indeed two opposite impulses

seemed to fight in her, one that she should hide her face, the other that she should see every slightest thing.

The crowd was very still in the vicinity of the scaffold, but beyond that, there were laughter and singing and beyond that, in a great distance, all the noisy traffic of the day. The atmosphere was strange, very dark above their heads, but pale beneath with the flat colour of sunlight. The shops were like pale faces staring from darkness, and the thunder muttered like an uncertain drum.

She saw all this with a sickness of anticipation. She really felt sick, as though it were Georges or Francis or Reuben—someone who was very close to her—who was going to suffer. The silence grew and seemed to spread to the farther distance. She saw individuals—a woman's face with a wart, an old gentleman in a shabby brown wig, a girl with a sharp nose who lifted a child that it might see better, a man, a foreigner surely, wearing a bright green turban—and all these individuals seemed to belong to her, to know all about her, and to have arranged to come with her to see this sight.

Then, as though obeying some signal, a little procession mounted the steps. There was the stout fellow with the cane, a long thin man bare-headed, three officers in uniform, a clergyman with parson's bands carrying a book, and, last, between the officers, a boy with his hands tied. At once she could not remove her eyes from the boy. He was broad and short and ruddy-faced, like any strong country boy. His hair was cropped, he had large blue staring eyes that, Judith saw, were now mad with an ununderstanding terror. But his mouth, which was a child's mouth, uncertain and tremulous, was trying to be resolved and manly.

She was, against her will, so terribly close that she was forced to see these things; she fancied then (she knew afterwards it could have been only fancy) that as soon as he was on the platform the boy's eyes were seeking hers. What he was doing was searching the crowd, the houses, the sky; a wild animal at bay looking for escape, although he knew that there was none. But Judith fancied that she could help him. Raising herself on her toes she nodded and smiled and nodded again; even (although she did not know it) her lips were forming words: 'Be brave! I'll help you! I want to help you! Be brave!'

Indeed he tried to be, poor lad. Things moved very quickly. The parson, who looked shabby and had mud on his stockings, read from a book. The boy came forward. He was in his shirt and breeches; the shirt, open, had slipped from one shoulder and showed his breast. His face was ruddy in spite of his fear; he looked as though he should have been caught robbing an orchard.

He came forward and began to speak bravely enough. Now an absolute silence froze the scene. Carts could be heard rattling on the Strand cobbles very far away.

'Good people,' he began (his voice was fresh and very young), 'I am told to bid you all farewell and to beg you to stay in peace with God. Good people, it is very true that I took the shillings from the till—I never for an instant denied it. I was tempted by the Devil, good people, for I am very weary of the Town and was hungering for the country again. It was but an instant's temptation, and here I am, so that, good people, all learn by me to resist——' He had begun bravely, held up, perhaps, by the importance of the attention given him by the listening crowd, but suddenly it seemed to come upon him that he was really going to die, that, in a few moments, he would be fighting for breath. . . .

He broke off, his voice rising to a shrill terror. 'No, no . . . I must not die . . . I must not die. . . .' He moved as though he would throw himself from the platform. The officers caught him, and then began a dreadful struggle. He was young and strong. The three officers wrestled with him all over the platform. His shirt was torn from him and he was bare to the waist. He cried again and again, 'No, no . . . I will not . . .' and other words that no one could distinguish, some private name that sounded like 'Nancy.' Then they had him. His arms were bound behind him; his naked chest, white and shining with sweat, pushed forward, his head, turning, twisting, turning like an animal's in the pen before execution. An agonised whisper came: 'Jesus! Oh, Jesus Christ!' Just before they had the rope round his neck his eyes seemed to find Judith's, blue, staring and asking some question.

Then he was swinging, his legs twisting as though with independent life. The body heaved, then his head hung and he was still.

' Now, madam,' said the little man from an infinite distance, ' I can assist you.'

Judith nodded her head. Reuben had been right. Until the Bear was safe from persecution nothing could be well in the world.

THE CLIPPING

Sarah Herries, widow of David Herries and mother of Francis, Deborah, and Will, died on the 3rd of July 1796, suddenly, at the age of fifty-eight.

She was walking in the garden with her daughter Deborah, wrapped in one of her strange and brooding silences, when she cried out suddenly in a proud and joyful voice: 'Davy! Davy!', ran forward, her arms outstretched, and fell down on the green sward.

Her heart had failed her, and she was mercifully relieved of a life that was only a torment and distress to her. Judith went from Watendlath to the funeral. Will and Francis naturally could not arrive from London. The distance was too great and the time too short. Deborah Sunwood, now an aged, white-haired, and very quiet little woman, long a widow and never the same since the death of her son Humphrey in France, came from Cockermouth, and she and Judith had a very loving meeting. Deborah Herries, a stout, large, rosy-faced, cheerful woman, was now left in sole charge of Uldale and its affairs. She begged Judith to come to her whenever she wished. They had a friendly regard for one another, but nothing whatever to say, and Judith knew that Deborah, who loved social events and decent behaviour, regarded Georges in her heart as a rogue and a vagabond, which indeed he was.

The night of her return from the funeral Judith had wild and fantastic dreams. It was a hot airless night, very still, and the streams, thin though they were, seemed to leap in through the open windows and chatter about the room. She had been sleeping badly for a long time past. Wise though she was and determined always to be sensible, a foreboding of distress and misfortune grew on her day by day, as though a cloud with every hour grew heavier and darker above her head. She had had one letter from Georges since he left her in London. It was addressed from Bergen in Norway, very short, sending his love, telling her that he was busy and would return when he could. She thought that she read between the lines a new sense of care and longing for her, but that, with her usual good sense, might be a willing imagination.

The nights were the bad times. During the day she was surrounded with friends in whose affairs she took ever a more active and dominating interest, but at night she was alone, and that part of herself that she could least easily control—her wild and restless part—seemed to have full power.

On this particular night she suffered especially from the thought of Sarah. Her loving heart could not endure that she had never been reconciled to Sarah. When she was a child she had not thought that she cared for Sarah at all, but as she

grew, so she perceived that there was some deep
loyalty and submission in her feeling.

She had always been too proud to go to Sarah
and ask her forgiveness; besides, she did not
think that Sarah had anything to forgive, but
she had supposed that some accidental meeting
would bring them together again. Now it would
never be.

At least, if there was another conscious life,
Sarah was now with David, was happy again and
understood everything. But this supposition, a
very doubtful one, as it seemed to Judith, was poor
comfort. She tortured herself, on the ride back
from Uldale, with the thought of all the lonely
years that Sarah had endured. She could never
bear that people could suffer, and especially that
they should suffer through her fault, and now
there occurred to her a thousand ways in which,
with a little courage, she might have approached
Sarah and done something for her.

Her dreams that night were wild, entangled
and desperate. She was again in the London
street, where the boy was to be hanged. Pressed
in, tossed about by a wild and revengeful crowd.
But it was Georges who was to be hanged. She
could do nothing to save him, but must stand
there helplessly and watch. The sky was black,
the houses ringed with flame, and from a high
window Christabel, Will's wife, leaned out and
cried that her fan was broken and Georges must
suffer for it. Then Georges came sailing towards
her in a little boat; waves, hot and angry, with cruel
white tongues, filled the street and beat about the

scaffolding. Young Stane was in the boat, and Georges suddenly caught him, held him in the air, then flung him into the waves while all the people cried.

She woke, trembling, damp with sweat. At first the deep quiet of the room with only the sound of the singing streams soothed her. She lay there and listened to her heart as it slowly diminished its terrible beating. How good that it had only been a dream! From her bed she could see, in the faint morning light, the shadows of the homely, familiar things, and beyond the open window the friendly breast of the rising hill.

She was in her own house with friends on every side of her. Since her return, although she had said very little to anyone, they had all understood, it seemed, that Georges was in some trouble. They did not like Georges, but with that wonderful silent sympathy that is perhaps the Cumbrian's finest gift, they had closed in around her, showing her their affection and loyalty. She had never been so near to them before as she was now.

Yes, but she wanted Georges. She wanted him with a fierce hunger that was an experience quite new to her. She was doing what he told her, staying here and filling her life with little daily interests, but, in the back of her mind, there was always the fear that after a while, if he did not return, waiting would be too hard for her, and she would run off to Whitehaven and search for news of him.

To conquer her desire for him she lay there, as the new light flowed about the room and a cluster of sharp steel-glittering stars faded out above the black hill line, saying over to herself, aloud, the names of places that she loved, and the names of people whom she loved. She said, as though she were addressing the shapes, with every moment less dim, in her room:

'Stonethwaite, Honister,
Gavel, Watendlath,
Rosthwaite, Uldale,
Bleaberry, High Seat,
Armboth, Grey Knotts,
Glaramara——'

They had sung her almost to sleep again, mingling with the streams that ran about the boards of her room when, with a sharp stab of awareness, she was conscious of an odd thing —that with every day she was becoming more frightened of leaving her own square of ground.

It was as though someone had told her that did she step over a certain line, something terrible would befall her. She had noticed at the funeral that she had to force herself to face people, even good friends like Deborah Sunwood. It was as though she expected that anyone at a moment's notice would cry: 'I have news for you. Georges——' The people here around her she could trust. They were her own people—the Ritsons, the Wilsons, all the children and the dogs. And her new great friend, Charlie Watson.

Watson had a farm, New Hope, towards Armboth. He had come there in the last year; he was from the village of Strands, near Wastwater.

He was a Cumbrian of the Cumbrians; that is, he was silent, often churlish, sharp, a marvellous shepherd and utterly loyal. She had met him one day coming up from Rosthwaite. He had two dogs with him. She had been startled by his looks, for he was broad and massive and his hair was of so jet a black, his cheeks of so warm a colour, that at first he seemed a foreigner. He had a short, sharply cut, black moustache that was not like the neighbours'. He was so broad of shoulder and thick of thigh that his height seemed moderate, but he was of good height nevertheless.

He would be thirty-five years of age. They began to talk. You would have said that all he thought of at that time was sheep, that or any time. He thought of other things later, though. He was proud, sensitive, suspicious, and hated foreigners till he knew them. He had worked in Liverpool five years in his youth. He was single; preferred sheep to women, he told Judith once. True enough then—not true later. On their first meeting he said little more than ' Aye! ' He looked at her as though he disliked her. He stood, his legs wide apart, striding the fells.

He told her that his sister looked after his comfort, that it was a dry month, that he didn't hold with politics—Regent or King, it was all the same to him, but we'd better not take after the Frenchies.

Judith said: ' My husband's French.'

He said: ' Aye,' looking at her meditatively and without a hint of apology. Then abruptly,

still looking at her, he remarked: ' You'll be Mrs.
Paris.   I mind hearing of you.'

' Nothing bad, I hope,' said Judith.

' For t'matter o' that—nay,' he said, suddenly
smiling a slow deep smile.   He strode away, not
looking back, his dogs after him.

After that first meeting they were always
encountering one another.   He was a friend of
old man Ritson's, but it seemed to her soon that
he came to the farm very much more often than
he had done.

Once or twice, without any conceit of self-
flattery, she wondered whether he were in love
with her.   He seemed to seek her out so directly,
with a simplicity that might elsewhere have
caused gossip.   But, in a week or two, she realised
that the Ritsons and the rest knew just what his
feeling for her was.   He was sorry for her, but
without hurting her pride.   They said of him
that he was mighty tender with all animals and
rough with women and off-hand with men.   It
seemed that he thought that she needed protection as an animal might.   He made himself her
protector.   There was no sentiment between
them.   They made a curious pair, he so large and
she so small, and she could have disappeared,
she used to fancy, into the outer pocket of his
coat.   He was an unusual man with his intense
depths of feeling unexpressed.   One day they
were standing together near the Tarn, and three
strangers, two ladies and a gentleman, rode
up on horses.   They were sightseers, the first
' tourists,' perhaps, that Watendlath ever beheld.

N

They called Watson ' my good fellow ' and, when he had given, very curtly, some information, the gentleman threw him a shilling. The ladies, very grand and speaking with affectation, looked at Judith, who was dressed like Mrs. Ritson or any of the people of the place. When they were gone Watson threw the shilling into the Tarn. He was trembling with anger.

' I'll tell them if 'tis t'right road. If they come again without biddin' they maun stay a bit . . . I'll settle him.'

She laughed and said that she supposed that anyone had a right to the place.

' Nay, they havena . . . the man's a lump of mutton off an auld tup.'

She didn't laugh any more, when she saw how deeply moved he was. It was as though these people had soiled the landscape for him.

Judith went one day and called on his sister. Then one evening, sitting in his kitchen, she told him everything: about her father and mother, her childhood in Uldale, her life at Stone Ends, her marriage with Georges, her time in London, her present distress and ever-growing anxiety, her love for Georges that seemed to grow ever deeper and deeper. He took her hand in his huge one.

' Aye, you want someone to look after you.'

From that evening it seemed to her that he was always at hand, although there were days when she didn't see him. Indeed he was a tremendous worker, had no time for idling with females. But he was behind her and beside her. The thought of him infinitely comforted her.

As, lying there, she considered him, his silence, his tenderness, her fears thinned away. It seemed that it was her fate to have these figures guarding her, protecting—Tom Gauntry, Emma, now Charlie Watson. The strange thing was that she did not want anyone to protect her. She was quite well able to protect herself. But she liked to have friends. She loved to be loved —that is, by the people whom she wanted to love her.

The sun flashed above the purple ridge of the hill. The sky was pale green like the wing of a young paroquet.

The Ritsons had their ' Clipping,' and it was a grand day. The hot weather had lasted for over a fortnight, and this was the hottest day of them all. The sheep panted fit to burst their sides. Armboth Fell shone like a brazen shield and was so slippery dry beneath the bracken that it was flaming ice to the feet. The Tarn was shadowed with an ebony mist under a sky clouded with heat.

The clipping was perhaps the grandest day of the year for the Ritsons. They were farmers in a small way, but very popular. Neighbours came from miles, first to help in the clipping, then to eat of the feast and dance in the Ritson kitchen.

Charlie Watson came. He was the best clipper in Cumberland maybe; a Master. Then there was Tommy Blunden of Smoke, Robert Tyndale of Cardale, Will Bennett of Axholme,

Roger Perry of Thunder. They, their wives, their children, their dogs.

Judith was happy again. The night was far behind her. But the thundery weather distressed her; it had been ominous to her ever since that last day in London, and now, in the middle of helping with the great joint of beef, with the huge pease-puddings, with the arranging of the long table, she would go to the porch and look out over the Tarn to the hills and listen. Perhaps it was Georges, also, for whom she was listening.

In the kitchen there was tremendous noise and confusion. Old man Ritson was too aged now to move about, the rheumatism had him fast, and sometimes the pain was so bad that someone inside him yelled loud enough to bring the roof down, but the yell never passed his inside. He sat, his grand head high, his gnarled hands on his knees, watching and saying nothing. His daughters, his grand-daughters and a great-grand-daughter (in a cradle by the window) were all around him. A sea of femininity. But he said nothing. He sat there thinking of his youth, of fighting a man bare-skin in Whitehaven and throttling him, of tending sheep on the hills above Coniston Water, of the fugitives in '45 from Butcher Cumberland and his father hiding one up the kitchen chimney, of sheep and sheep, cows and cows, fine weather and bad, of women whom he had loved, his children and their ways, Armboth and Brund Fell and Glaramara that were live creatures to him, Gods maybe, carrying on their gigantic forms the rocks and tarns and streams that were their splendid properties. Yes, he had plenty to think of. And he sat there, looking straight in front of him, while the pains at his hip made him bellow inside.

When the table was laid, Judith, to escape the kitchen heat, went out to watch the clippers.

As the weather was so grand the clipping could be in the open air instead of in the barn. All the sheep had been brought in. There were eight hundred sheep and five hundred lambs.

Beyond the house in a grand half-circle were fifteen clippers striding the sheep-stools, and each clipper held a sheep, shorn, half shorn, about to be shorn. There was a tremendous noise, for the gate of the farmyard was packed by five score of wooled sheep penned against it. They would be caught, one after another, by one of the boys, who, in a wild, excited pack, tumbled and fought and shouted, having the day of their lives. The sheep bleated and their lambs on the fell-side or in the fields bleated as well. The dogs barked and even horses neighed. It was strange to feel, beyond this excited whirlpool of sound, the glazen silence of the Tarn, the road, the hills, pulsating through the shimmering heat, but silent, as though holding their breath for the first peal of thunder that would release them from this spell.

Judith first looked for Charlie Watson, and a splendid sight he was. His shirt was open at the neck, and sweat beaded the thick black hair of his chest. His arms, red-brown to near the elbows then snow-white, bulged with muscle; his legs planted wide to hold the sheep between them seemed to be

rooted in the ground; every once and again his
head went up and his mouth parted, showing his
teeth white under the short thick black moustache.
(His perfect teeth were a phenomenon in the dale,
for most men lacked one or two.) His short, thick
hair had almost a metallic gleam in its blackness.

As always when at work, his dark eyes shone,
his parted lips seemed to cry aloud his energy, his
body worked in harmony with the fell, the running
water.   He worked with rhythm, as though the
whole of English nature and the wheel of the
brazen sky moved, back and forth, with the pulse
of his blood; and he handled the sheep as though
he loved them.

Tom Ritson was in charge of the clipping; an
old man called Benny Held—with two fierce
questioning white eyebrows and a face like a
wrinkled turnip—kept the pitch pan heated and
held the marking iron and the rudd stick.   Young
Roger Perry of Thunder, a lad nearly as thick and
broad as Watson, held the animals while old Benny
applied the marking.

Judith forgot her anxieties and trouble for the
while.   Now there came out in her all her passion
for management.   She could not be present at
a scene like this without burning to ' arrange
things.'

She looked fifteen years of age, with a high sun-
bonnet tied over her red hair and her legs bare as
the other women's were, stamping about in her
clogs.   Her cheeks were flushed, her eyes shining.
Her Cumberland blood exulted in the scene.   This
was the heart of England and so the heart of the

world. Everything was right for her—the scent
of the bracken, the still waiting expectancy of the
hills, the sun shining on the little stone walls that
ran up into the edge of the sky, the rough voices
that had a sort of grumbling humorous note in
them, the jokes and oaths and laughter, the bleating of lambs and sheep, the strange helpless whiteness of the sheep after they were shorn—knowing
that they were so different, so changed that their
own lambs did not recognise them—the life of this
little community centred here in this circle of fells,
so remote from the world but strong, independent,
asking nothing from any man (as for centuries they
had asked nothing, so for centuries more they
would ask nothing), and all of them looking at her,
speaking to her as though she were one of themselves (which, indeed, she was), the sun slipping
over the sky and, as the afternoon drew on, shadows
staining every hill with a different dye, Armboth
saffron as though sunlight had soaked into its very
heart, Brund Fell orange-red, then sinking, with
almost an audible sigh, into a gentle silver-grey,
and beyond them the farther hills, violet cloths
spread before a sky white with evening haze, and,
with the evening, a breeze springing that had
every scent of coolness in it, young grass, water
over shining stones, and the wet wavering mosses
that shadow the Tarn's edge. The sea also was
not far away.

Ale was brought out in pots, and there were
hunks of fruit pie. Then the sky was green, and
the first star winked at a silver moon half full.
The fleeces were tied in small bundles, the loft door

was closed on them, and everyone moved indoors
to the feast.

There were rounds of beef and oat - bread,
pease - puddings, gooseberry pies, puddings
' touched ' with rum. Soon everyone was very
merry. Benny Held had brought his fiddle.
Robert Tyndale, who had a fine tenor, sang Ewan
Clark's ' Happy Bachelor ':

> ' A bachelor life of all lives is the best;
>   No cares matrimonial disturb his calm rest;
>   No lectures called *Curtain* shake sleep from his eyes,
> When tir'd he can rest, and when tir'd he can rise.'

and ' Wey, Ned, Man! ':

> ' Wey, Ned, Man!   Thou luiks sae down-hearted,
>   Yen wad swear aw thy kindred were dead;
> For sixpence, thy Jean and thee's parted—
>   What then, Man, ne'er bodder thy head.'

Then, Charlie Watson, shy but determined, sang
in a deep bass: ' What charms has fair Chloe ':

> ' What charms has fair Chloe!
>   Her bosom's like snow!
>   Each feature
>   Is sweeter,
>   Proud Venus, than thine!
>   Her mind like her face is
>   Adorned with all graces,
>   Not Pallas possesses
>   A wit so divine.

> ' What crowds are a-bleeding
>   While Chloe's ne'er heeding:
>   All lying
>   A-dying
>   Thro' cruel disdain:

> Ye gods, deign to warm her
> Or quickly disarm her;
> While Chloe's a charmer,
>   Your temples are vain.'

He sang without any expression whatever, and a disdainful look on his face as though he despised the song and himself for singing it, but, when it was over, and the applause had been terrific, he flushed with pleasure and looked down the long table to see whether Judith had approved.

Then the tables were cleared, Benny Held struck up his fiddle and everyone was dancing. Stamp-stamp-stamp, clamp-clamp-clamp along the kitchen floor, the dust rising, faces flushed, bodies a little unsteady with the ale, whispers and pro-testing laughter, kissing and hugging, and old Ritson, sitting in his chair, looking straight before him, thinking of the time when he had taken the girl of his heart out of the hot room into the cold of the valley and wandering down to the Tarn's edge had kissed her for the first time. He fancied that now, although she had been dead so long, she was standing just behind the hallan, her eyes taunting him. . . .

Charlie Watson asked Judith to dance. He clamped round the room with her, staring over her head, saying nothing. He trod on her toes, bundled her about, and his arm held her like an iron rod.

They stayed by the door, and he was about to speak to her. Alice Ritson, the only unmarried Ritson girl remaining, for Mary had died two

N 2

years before, ran in from the garden path, waited
an instant, looking at the crowded room, then
went up to Judith, caught her arm and whispered:
' Judith, 'tis Mr. Georges. He's coom back.
He's there, in your own place.'

For a moment the room with its figures and
haze of heat swayed, in movement, almost it
seemed, to the fiddler's tune. She remembered
afterwards (looking back as she did so many, many
times) that Charlie Watson put out his arm and
for a moment held her. She felt (she knew afterwards, although at the time she did not notice
it) the beating of his heart against her cheek.
What an agony of joy, anticipation, and fear!

' It is my husband,' she said, looking up into
his face: then she ran out.

Georges was standing in their living-room,
near the staircase, down which he had once
bundled his box. She ran to him, and at once
knew by the way that he held her that something
terrible had happened to him. He had never
held her like that before, as though his only
safety lay in his contact with her.

' I thought that I would never be here,' he said.
He lifted her off her feet and looked into her eyes.
Then he put her down and went to the door, which
he closed, slowly, surely; then stood for a moment
with his back to it. They could hear through the
wall the scream of the fiddle and the tramp-tramp-
tramp of the dancing figures.

' Will you come down to the Tarn?' he asked
her.

' But you must eat.'

'I had food at Keswick.'

'Where's your horse?'

'I've tethered him. He had his corn. He can stay.'

'But here . . . You must be so weary. I can make all comfortable.'

'No, no, no. I must be outside. Away from the music.'

Taking his hand, looking up at him, she said: 'What is it? Are you in trouble?'

'Yes,' he answered. 'I'm in trouble.'

She nodded her head, asking him no more.

They went out together, and the evening was sweet with all the summer scents. One lamb in a fold bleated incessantly; as soon as they came down the hill the music faded to a murmur like a voice in the Fell. The Tarn had a broad path of moonlight that quivered with little shudders of gold.

'Will you be cold?' he asked her. 'If you've been at the dance.'

'No. The air is warm.'

He put his arm around her; she was pressed close against his thigh, and they walked up and down.

'Judy, I've murdered Stane.'

She shivered, and he held her close. When she could steady herself she thought, at once: 'Now he will need me. He shall want me always. He is mine to the end,' and directly afterwards: 'Are they searching for him? I must get him away.' It was odd, but she thought of Humphrey Sunwood and how sensible she had been then.

She asked him at once: ' Are they after you for it? ' She had always hated Stane. She didn't care that he was dead.

' No. It was two weeks back. Off Bergen. No one knows.'

' How was it? Was it in a fight? '

' No. Not a fight. I murdered him deliberately. I took him out in the boat to do it.'

' And no one saw? '

' It was evening. A storm got up. After I had drowned him I turned the boat over and swam to land. But do you not shrink from me? First, before all else, I must know that——'

' No. I love you. How could I shrink from you? '

' Because I shrink from myself. It was deliberate, Judy. Planned. Intended. Not a drunken scuffle, not a hand-to-hand struggle. I took him by the throat and squeezed it till I thought my fingers would break. Then I toppled him over. The rain was coming down in torrents, and there was a wild sea. I thought I should myself drown, and I would have been glad of it, but nothing can drown me nor hang me nor stab me. . . . I shall live for ever, Judy, with Stane around my neck—like a dead bird, clammy, with talons scratching my skin.'

His hand was fiery hot in hers. She remembered afterwards that in all her bewilderment, her determination to be sensible, her tenderness for him, her hatred of Stane, which seemed now to be double what it had been, was amazement at this new Georges. He was like a man whom she had never seen before; she loved him as deeply as the other Georges, nay more, because he needed her, which the other Georges had never done. But his French indifference, callous humour, self-sufficiency. . . . Where were they? Was this man a coward?

He seemed to know her thought. He drew a deep sigh of relief.

' Now it is better. If you are with me we will beat that damnable ghost. For he's been a ghost, Judy, keeping step with me all the way. Afterwards it was like a spell. In Bergen they believed every word. His body was beaten on to the rocks the day following, his face disfigured. It seemed natural that his neck was broken. Three days after I set back to Whitehaven. In Whitehaven I saw his father. . . .'

He broke off.

' His father—a giant old man with a beard to his waist. He had a mad worship for his son. You know it. I've told you. I thought that he must suspect, caring so much. . . . But no. He stood there without moving. He went blind, groping with his hands. Then he caught me round the neck and kissed me. He thought I was Stane's best friend. There was water lapping up against the room where we were and a man came in with a sword. I thought young Stane would slip from beside me, catch the sword and stab me with it. I would offer no resistance. But when later old Stane called his son, running up the staircase after him, shouting his name in the rooms, there was no one there.

'But he would not let me go. All night he sat there holding my hand.'

'But how did it come?' Judith asked. 'Stane's death, I mean. What made you do it?'

'You know how it was. You felt it as I did. Stane and I always hated one another. I've been bred in England, Judy. I speak like an Englishman, walk like one, in my behaviour am like one—is that not so?'

'Yes,' she said, but she knew in her heart that it was not so. He had never walked, talked or behaved like an Englishman.

'Yes, but there are times when I am French through and through, when I loathe England and the English. And some Englishmen I hate from the beginning. So I did Stane. So satisfied, arrogant *and* ignorant. That mixture of conceit and ignorance that is in all your relations, Judith—the most obvious thing in the English. And he was clever, too; he saw at once how I was, my laziness, excitement, that I was unable to stay with anything for long. He judged me well, truly—that was partly why I hated him. And he meant to supplant me. He saw that the others, Wix and the rest, were dissatisfied. He manœuvred me to London and then worked on them. . . . My God, Judy, he was clever! And I a fool! Holy Heaven, the fool I was!'

The words broke from him in a despairing cry such as she had never heard from him before. It seemed to be echoed from the hills. She was afraid lest someone should hear.

'Hush, hush!' she said, leaning up and strok-

ing his cheek as she might with a child. ' Not
too loud.   And then———?'

' Well, he came to London to work his way
into Will Herries' counsels.   You saw him at the
Ball that night.   He gave a black account of me
to Herries, worked promises out of him and then
returned to Whitehaven to show them that he
had power in the City, while I diced and drank.
. . . Oh, it was true enough!   Every word was
true. . . .

' Then when I had fled from London to
Christiania he knew all of it.   He must have been
spying into every corner.   I started some business
in Bergen.   Not much, but something.   It was
doing fairly, and I meant to return to Whitehaven,
show them my steadiness, make all well again.
For I knew Wix cared for me in his heart. . . . I
hadn't heard that Stane had told him all the
London affairs, my debts, the scuffle in the Coffee
House, everything.   He came over to Bergen,
Stane, I mean.   He pretended that it was an
accident, but I knew well what it was.

' We met in an inn-room above the sea.   He
was victorious.   He had a letter from Wix to say
that they were ended with me in Whitehaven,
that I had best never return to England.   Stane
was triumphant.   It was the moment for which
he had been working so long.   His face was lit
up.   He had a wart on his right eyelid.   Behind his head on the green wall there was a map
of China and the Indies.   I can tell you, Judith,
that I all but killed him there, drove his head
into that yellow map, there, just where China was.

But there were men about, a street with traffic, boats knocking with the tide against the wall.

'I waited. I waited two days. I was most friendly. I licked his hand, asked that I should be the clerk. Then he boasted, how his father had once been a common fisherman and he him-self had sold cockles barefoot. And he went further. He paid for my drink and told me how easy I had been, what a simpleton, and then he said something about you, Judy——'

'I always hated him,' she said.

'Yes, but he wanted you. You were his size, he said. He liked small women—and he was haunted by the wish to plunge his hands in your hair——'

She said nothing, only came closer to him.

'So I made my plan. I said I would row him across an inlet to a house where there were paid women—drink, women, dancing. He could be lascivious. Contemptuously he permitted me. As I strangled him he called out for his father thrice. That was his only decency. Physically he had no strength; I could have broken him anywhere.'

He stopped and said hoarsely: 'I have a fearful thirst. My mouth is dry every hour.'

'We will go home,' Judith said, laying her hand for an instant on his brow, 'and sleep.'

THE OLD MAN OF THE SEA

Judith woke, as now she was accustomed to do, to find Georges standing on the floor, wrestling in his sleep with his implacable enemy.

She could see only his shadow. The October night was dark; clouds hid the stars. The words came from him thick and fast: ' No, no. Leave me. I have done with you. That was to end it. Struggle then, and the water's cold. . . . Sharp, sharp. I'll not touch you again. Keep off me. No, no. I'll listen to no whisper. It is useless. Oh, God, keep me free ! '

The last was a whisper of intense and gasping weariness. He sank to his bare knees. She knew that he was kneeling on the floor, his head in his hands, while his body trembled.

She got out of their bed, went to him and very gently put her arms round him. He stayed there trembling against her. Then slowly he woke.

' Where am I ? ' he asked.

' Here with me.' She led him back to bed, he docile as a child. They lay down together, hand in hand. Almost at once he was asleep again. But she remained for a long time awake, wondering what it was best to do.

This was October. He had returned in

July—July, August, September, October, and
there seemed to be no end to it, no frightening
away of the ghosts, no helping him to overcome
them.　For the first time in her life she wished
that she were older—older and wiser.　In the
immediate weeks after his return her great fear
had been lest in an instant of indiscretion he
should confess to somebody what he had done.
He never rode into Keswick but she waited
in an agonised terror for his return.　She never
saw him talking to the Ritsons or walking with
Watson (for whom he had conceived a great
liking) but she expected the end of the talk or
the walk to be some terrible revelation.　But now,
especially when she was weary or lying awake
at that time of the early morning when fears are
most pressing, she sometimes wondered whether
it would not be better that he should confess
to someone.　The burden of sharing it alone
seemed often more than she could bear.

She was not subtle about it.　She was not
made for subtlety.　He had killed Stane, who had
tried to bring him to ruin.　That seemed to her
fair.　She would herself kill, if need be, anyone
who threatened Georges.　She would lie in bed,
clenching and unclenching her hot little hands,
with such a hatred of Stane in her heart that she
would almost swoon of it.　He had tried to kill
Georges, to kill in Georges' life everything that
was of any value in it: he would have taken
from Georges his livelihood, his friends, even his
wife.　Well, then — what crime had Georges
done?

No one had seen. No one guessed. It was over. What then possessed Georges? It was perhaps the hardest part of her task now that this Georges was another man from that careless, wild, courageous, casual Georges, whom she had married and loved. And yet they were the same! She saw dimly how the one had become the other. She could trace back a thousand times when, in the past, he had been afraid of his deeds and then, because he was afraid, had recklessly covered the old fault with the new one. He had never had any stability. He had refused to dig deep into life. She had seen that in him again and again, and now, when he had tumbled into reality, it had been *too* deep for him.

His kindly casualness had always made him live for the moment, but from his childhood— although he would never confess to it because of his pride—he had had an anticipation of fear like a child who is safe only while the lighted candle is in the room.

She did not analyse this. Women of her day did not analyse natures and motives, but she understood him at last.

The irony of it was that now at length she possessed him as she had always longed to do, but as so often when in life we are granted our desires, her gratification was tragic. For, although she possessed him, she could not help him. He relied on her now for everything. He did nothing without asking her. He hated that she should be out of his sight.

There in the half-dark, he uneasily sleeping at

her side, she was teased by the odd mixture of her feelings. If she had killed Stane she would see to it that she was not haunted by his ghost. Once done well done! There was impatience in her love for Georges. He must get some work to do: that would worry his ghosts! The farm was theirs and the next farm the Ritsons', both worked by the Ritsons. That just sufficed them for their immediate needs, but she could not endure to see Georges standing about, leaning against a stone wall watching the sheep or the clouds or walking on the uneven stone path beyond the farm outhouses, his hands behind his back, his head down, as though he were a prisoner. His only healthy days were those when he went off on the fells with Charlie Watson.

She was beginning to 'manage' him as she 'managed' old Ritson's rheumatism, Mrs. Ritson's bad clumsy sewing, Tom Ritson's carelessness about money, young Alice Ritson's love-affairs; and like all managing people she always a little despised those who succumbed to her management. It was part of Watson's power over her that she couldn't manage him anywhere.

But her real anxiety was that she did not herself know which way she would go. Part of her —her father's part—shared Georges' terrors to their depths. She knew how real that ghostly world was, how dark its valleys, how awful its inhabitants. But for the other part of her all ghosts were unreal, fantastic, just as her father had been altogether unreal and exaggerated for many people. As though, indeed, someone had said to her about her father: ' Fielding would not have drawn such a character.' No, but there were ghosts outside the books of Mr. Fielding and Mr. Richardson. But were there? Was it not merely the colic? How real were Georges' terrors? ' Very real,' whispered a shadow by Rosthwaite. ' I spent my life in fighting them.' ' Balderdash,' said Will Herries and all the Herries.

But if only she herself could go one way or another! At one moment she wanted to shake Georges by the shoulders, to wake him thoroughly from a silly dream; at another she had only to close her eyes, and young Stane, the wart on his eyelid, his mouth curled contemptuously, his clothes wringing wet, crawled from the Tarn and slipped up the field towards her. Two events showed her very sharply the division between her two worlds. One was an unexpected letter from Francis. He wrote from Bournemouth saying that he had intended to send her a letter ' weeks back ' but had been so closely occupied . . . Closely occupied in Bournemouth?

He was staying with Prosper and Amelia Cards. He had been there for some weeks. Judith, remembering the Ball, whispered to herself: ' Jennifer.'

. . . At first, dear Judith, I will be honest and confess that I found the country so desolate that I could have drowned myself. But there have been ameliorations, and now I find myself hanging on when the season is inclement and London calls. Moreover, my conscience tells me that I should come North and assist poor Deborah and see my darling Judith. Not that yourself are my conscience, dear Judith, but rather my pleasure. However, I am kept here and by what I will one day tell you.

('By whom rather,' thought Judith.)

The Town is a nest of old women who drink nauseous water and talk gossip by the bushel. We have also had a Menagerie with two Lions and a Bear. I tasted the waters but once. Do you remember how once for a punishment my poor mother gave us a pint basin of thin gruel with a spoonful of salt in it for a week and how it tasted? Well, that's for these waters. I fear that the Dispute that had its commencement with that accursed Ball of Will's shows no abatement but only an increase. Brother Will will have nothing to do with me, and there is indeed now a Division in our family starting with Brother Will and Cousin Prosper and spreading into many directions.

I am myself deeply sorry for it. What a stupid affair to start with a Broken Fan! I console myself with the friendliness of my relations here and especially with my cousin Jennifer.

I fear that yourself, dear Judith, are held here to have taken sides most decisively, and that Amelia, at least, is not to be reconciled to you. Cousin Prosper in his cups is reconciled to all the world, but out of them— well, he has enough family pride for Sir Charles Grandison. I have been entertained by Godwin's *Enquiry concerning Political Justice*. You should read it, for if we are going the way of France, which is none too unlikely, there are wise words for us here. I am myself engaged on a paper answering some points in Paine's *Age of Reason*. We were never, I am convinced, in all our National History, more at the parting of the ways than we now are. All Europe is in an uproar. The People's Voice is making itself felt everywhere and splendid extravagances at Brighthelmstone are not sufficient satisfaction for such a heavy rise in prices.

You know, Judith, that I was always more Dreamer
than anything. Now more than ever I dream my dreams.
I am thirty-six years of age and have done nothing with
my life. See Will, who is adding pound to pound with
every breath he draws. Dare I venture into matrimony,
little Judith? Is there any woman would be fool enough
to take me if I asked her . . .?

'Any woman?' thought Judith. 'Will Jennifer?'
The thought struck her with an added pang
of loneliness and difficulty. If Francis married
Jennifer, then he was lost to her, Judith, for ever.
And with Francis gone it seemed to her that she
would be, indeed, alone. But Jennifer would not
have him. She was to make a far finer match than
a poor North Country cousin ten years her elder.

Putting the letter down with a sigh, the world
contained in its pages slipped into incredi-
bility. How unreal, beside her present actual
trouble, seemed that little pasteboard quarrel of
the fan. Will's city life, Bournemouth's waters,
Paine's *Age of Reason*, Jennifer's beauty, Prosper's
pride and the rest. There *were* two worlds, and
the secret of living was to know both to be real!
But it was a problem. So she went out and
rubbed old Ritson's back with ointment, looked
at Tom Ritson's bull that he had bought in Keswick, advised Alice Ritson against young Humble-
thwath of Rosthwaite and stood, shading her eyes
against the October sun, to see Georges ride up
the path with Watson.

What she did see was incredible.

Georges was walking along the rocky path
leading his horse and beside him was walking

—Reuben! Reuben, as she could see, talking, gently, kindly, smiling, and Georges was smiling too.

At the first sight of them she had to recall that last time when she had seen Reuben, proud, master of himself, but driven from the house . . . and now, Georges was walking with him as though he loved him!

Reuben had been often in her mind. She was always thinking of him, but she had never seen him again since that day. Now, as she turned towards them, she loved him for being kind to Georges, and she loved Georges for being kind to Reuben. It was the first time she had had comfort since Georges' return. She met them and kissed them both. They stood there, the three of them, looking down at the Tarn, which was ruffled with little grey bird's feathers that ran in flocks under the pale sun, making the whole sheet of water quiver with life.

Reuben was different. He was far surer, more in command of himself and of everything. He was stouter but harder too. He was wearing black knee-breeches and stout black shoes and a broad black hat, but he was clean and neat; his white stock was clean and the white bands at his wrists. His voice was quiet and assured like his carriage. He moved and spoke like a man who had discovered how to rule himself.

They all went into the house. Reuben said that he would stay with them the night. He had come from Wasdale. To-morrow he had to preach in Mardale. He had walked from

Waswater over the Stye Head and up from Rosthwaite.

That evening they had a strange conversation that Judith was never to forget. Oddly now Reuben dominated them both. He had never dominated Judith before, he had always been subservient to her, but now, although he was as loving to her as ever, being with her as though they had never been separated, he had a new power that set him apart. Soon she knew where his power lay. He was no longer afraid of anybody or anything. She saw that Georges submitted to him like a child to an elder. They sat, the three of them, close together by the wood fire that blazed with a sharp exulting power in the hearth. Judith sat at Georges' feet, her head against his thigh. She caught his hand in hers and felt its pulse leap wildly against her palm.

She was always saying to him now with every movement, ' Don't be afraid, I'm here.'

Reuben had not very much to tell them about himself. He went about, just as before, preaching everywhere, anywhere.

' What do you preach? ' Georges asked suddenly.

' Jesus Christ,' Reuben said.

' I do not wish to be offensive,' Georges went on slowly. ' May I say what is in my mind with honesty? '

Reuben smiled. ' Yes. If you will.'

' Well, then, Christ is a figure to me who died long since. A Jewish rebel. The times needed a new religion. This was offered them and they took it. I cannot believe in any God, or that Christ was more than a brave man, mistaken. . . . This life is all that we have, and, by God, it is a poor one!' His hand trembled in Judith's.

'I do not think so,' said Reuben. 'I know Jesus Christ. I have talked with Him.'

'But these are words,' said Georges. 'My mother was heathen and her father before. My grandfather was an atheist, famous in his day, in the town of Toulouse. It is true that I was always taught that the Christian influence was a false one, but that has not formed my mind. I have observed men and their actions, and I find that there is no sign of a God in the world.'

'Then life is meaningless.'

'Yes, meaningless.'

'It is a question,' Reuben said quietly, 'that every man must decide by his own experience. Here we are, two men in the world. You are certain of your experience and I of mine. But if I had been to China and seen the Emperor and you had not, you would permit my right to my certainty, would you not?'

'Yes,' answered Georges impatiently. 'But the Emperor of China exists. Many people have seen him. The Christ is a fable.'

'You must permit me my experience. I know that God is in the world.'

'And I know that He is not.'

'Are you as certain,' asked Reuben, 'that He is not, as I that He is?'

Georges raised his eyes, haggard and restless, to Reuben's face.

' Then if He is, how can He permit this
cruelty, this pain . . .' He broke off. His
whole body was trembling.

' When I was a lad in Cockermouth,' Reuben
said, ' I saw one day a bear baited in the street. I
suffered torture from its helplessness. Now I
know from my own life that all experience adds
to one's riches. And pain possibly gives the
most.'

' Was the bear the richer? ' Georges broke out
passionately.

' If the bear knew his gain. This is not the
end,' Reuben said. ' Or so I believe. I have an
immortal part, and Jesus is my friend to show to
me that I have.'

' This world is enough,' Georges cried. ' A
vile world in which we have no chance and are
buffeted by a hidden enemy.'

Reuben was silent. He bent forward and
gazed into the fire.

' Ah, but I have two worlds,' he said at last,
' and there I am richer than you. I must deny
neither. I am citizen of both. In the one I am
very young, an infant, but with the Grace of God I
shall grow. In the other I eat my bread and pay
my tax, but my body dies, my tax is paid and I go
through the door, out of it, at any time.' Then
he added, smiling to himself: ' The great lesson
of life is patience.'

' Patience! ' Georges broke out He started
to his feet. ' I swear to God, if there be one, that
I have no patience. That I refuse to delay. I
want my judgement. For my sin . . . for my

crime. . . .' He stood over Reuben, bent forward, shaking the other's shoulder.

'Reuben! Your sins, if you've committed any, do they stay with you? In your other world that you speak of, will you be punished for ever? Will there be no release?'

Reuben nodded his head. 'Yes, there is release for sin—after repentance.'

'But I do not repent. I have done no wrong. He merited his death. He . . .' Georges broke off, seeing what he had admitted. There was an intense silence between the three of them. Judith, whose guard over Georges was constant, turned to Reuben with some of her old ferocity, as though she would defend Georges with her claws. But there was no need. Reuben looked down at the floor; then, glancing up, he said:

'What I tell you must seem like empty folly to you. I can only warrant you that nothing is final; there is no end to experience—and there is no sin too large to keep Christ Jesus from your life.'

He rose and went over to Georges and put his hand on his shoulder. 'Pay for your sin—good worthy coin. Then travel on.'

He went up to his bed.

After he was gone they sat close, hand in hand. Georges said desperately: 'Judith, there must be ghosts. It is true, although I never thought it. He will not leave me. At every corner I think to see him, and now it is months since I broke his neck and he drowned.'

Then after a little he added: 'There must be some end coming to this. I can *feel* it coming.

If I could fight someone with my hands, stand my trial, be hanged by the neck—yes, anything rather than this stealthy silence. I, all my life I have never cared what I did nor minded what I did, and I am young and have everything before me. And he's dead and no one knows. It is sentimental imagination, this fancy I have—but I can't be free of it. I can't! I can't! I can't!' He walked desperately about the room. Then he stopped sharp in front of Judith. ' Judith, do *you* think there's a God?'

' I don't know. No one knows.' (But she thought to herself: 'What he said about the two worlds is true. That is the way *my* life is going.')

But she rose and then, bending forward, said:

' I shall tell you what I think, Georges. That you are lazy. That you must go somewhere to work and forget Stane. Why should you think of him? If he were here and he had tried to hurt you as he did, and I were strong enough, I should strangle him with my two hands. He was our enemy, and you slew him fairly. Shake off your imagination! Go farming with Charlie Watson for a while. He'll teach you things. He has no business with ghosts——'

Georges looked above her head to the farther wall.

' Stane's father,' he said. ' His heart was broken.'

She herself felt a pang then. Yes, the consequences went, as always, beyond the act. But

she faced them. . . . Stane, his father, all his
relations—she'd face them all.   Let them attack
Georges and they attacked her too.   But to fight
for Georges, she now saw, needed more than
physical combat.

A week later Judith lost her temper in the good
old fashion of her childhood, and this loss of her
temper led to an incident.

There was a man just then, Larry Tod, who
was helping Tom Ritson with his cattle.   He was
a waster, this Larry, no good at all, and he wandered about the district doing odd jobs hither and
thither and not much good anywhere.   He was
famous, though, as a wrestler.   He was big,
carroty-haired, broken-nosed.   He liked to strip
to his shirt and drawers and show a chest like a
board, and, to quote the old description of the
famous French wrestler, Le Bœuf, ' a stomach
like a bale of wool.'   He was very proud of himself, very sly, up to any mean trick, the right sort
of figure for the villain in a wrestling bout.   And
that, on this occasion, because of Judith's temper
he was.

On this day, an October afternoon of driving
black cloud when the fells looked twice their
natural size, Judith coming into the yard saw Tod
bending down and twisting the tiny arm of young
Walter Ritson, who was yelling his loudest.

Tod straightened himself when he saw Judith.
He was always dirty with manure and mud and
the rest.   Now he wiped the back of his hand over
the flat of his broken nose and said something

about the child's laughing at him. Young Walter, the tears drying on his cheeks, stared up at them both in interested amazement.

Judith's temper was fine to see. She enjoyed it herself. She had been living in half-shadows with Georges for months back and she needed a change. Then she hated the huge oaf with the surly eyes, the tangled hair that seemed like a parody of her own. He was a sort of ogre personification of all that threatened Georges. She told him her notions about him. Slowly his brow darkened. What he would have said or done no one will ever tell, for Charlie Watson came by. Tod turned his rage in that direction. He hated Watson anyway.

A minute later Watson was stripping his coat. It was to be a wrestle. The news went round as though a bell had been rung. Everyone came flocking, and the match was moved to the green mound above the farm.

All the little village was there—men, women and children. A ring was formed, Watson and Larry Tod stripped to shirt and drawers. Both men were open at the neck.

It was to be the best of three throws. The little crowd held their breath, while the sky tossed cloud after cloud as though there were some giant juggler over the hill, and the Tarn, black as ink, lay insolently below them.

In the front of the ring, squatting on the grass, was young Walter Ritson, the cause of the trouble, with his mouth open. He hated Larry, but he feared him too, and if Larry won he fancied

that there would be trouble for him.   Perhaps
the others felt the same.   Larry Tod had been
prominent in the little place these last weeks, and
with every day he was becoming more sure of
himself and more insolent.   And for Judith and
Georges, also watching, although neither confessed it to the other, the result of this seemed like
an omen.   Let the red-haired ogre win, Georges
thought, and he was pushed a step farther into
his prison.

The men shook hands and got into holds.
Larry tried at once the back heel, the simplest
and oldest of all ' chips,' for all the wrestler has
to do is to lay his foot behind his antagonist's
heel and bend him over it.   But you must be
strong to do it.   Larry was strong, but so was
Watson, who at once slackened his hold and
moving his beautiful firm body with the most
delicate grace, turned his side.   Watson tried
then for a buttock, but Larry's immense strength
prevented him.   Watson tried to get under him
to lift him over his back.   Then, when that
failed, he stepped away and there they were again,
their arms at one another's necks.   They began
slowly to step round.   The little crowd drew
their breath.   This was to be an even match.

For Georges it was an agony.   In his strange,
over - nervous, harrassed state everything was
exaggerated.   The dark furry clouds hung low,
as though with an especial sinister message for
himself.   When the sun suddenly struck out
from them with bright splinter-like rays, flinging
the dry bracken into patches of amber light as

though there were a secret flame beneath the soil, that, too, seemed to point the finger at him. Why was he thus persecuted? Could he not bring his mind to order? It was true what Judith had said, that Stane deserved his death. It was only his imagination that dragged with him everywhere the accompanying scene, the rain hissing on to the boards of the boat, the sudden consciousness in Stane's eyes of Georges' intention, the cry lost in the storm, the whip, whip of the wind.

The women were shouting. Watson had tried the right - leg trip, making Larry swing sharply towards his left. With a mighty straining of muscle, his thighs and buttocks forced to their uttermost strength, he lifted Larry up, hoisting Larry's left leg up with his right and— to a great shout of all and sundry—landing the ogre with a fine bump on his back.

First throw to Watson.

The two men stayed a moment, wiping their brows. The crowd were silent. Did they feel, perhaps, that there was something concerned here more deeply than the personal encounter? The women were all on Watson's side, and yet he was aloof from them. He had never tried to make love to any of them. There was a little feeling that he was 'a bit above himself.' Larry, when he was dressed up and had washed his face, was a great figure of a man and knew what love-making was. One and all, though, in their hearts, they loathed him and perhaps, like little Wallie, feared him too.

At any rate he looked now a man to be feared.

O

As he stood there waiting, scowling between his sullen eyes, he looked as though he would kill Watson had he the chance.

When they came together again Larry tried the hitch-over, that is, he attempted to turn his left side to Watson, curl his left leg round Watson's right and, while Watson was standing on his left leg, cross-buttock him. But Watson was too quick for him, and soon they were moving round, slowly, cautiously, trying for some advantage.

You would not tell from looking at Georges, standing straight and grave, his rather round cheeks composed, his black eyes sombre and still, that his soul was in torment. If he had one! If he had one! That preacher, Reuben Sunwood, with his confidence in his Christ, his quiet happy assurance. . . . Ah well, that was not for Georges! His life had gone for nothing, one silly mistake and foolishness after another! He had begun life with a sense of adventure, with a kind of bravado, as though he could dare the world and bring it tumbling to his feet. But the world had snapped its fingers at him. He had got nothing out of it. Nothing save Judy!

He half turned and looked at her, standing on tiptoe, her mouth a little open, her hair blowing, all excitement like a child. A child! But how courageous and independent! How she had held by him—from the first, through everything, her loyalty never for a moment wavering. If he could but get rid of this present burden and dread he would show her that at last he realised her worth. He had been a long time coming to it, through slow selfish stages, but he knew it now, that he had had the luck of the devil to get her—yes, luck far better than he deserved.

He heard the deep indrawing breath of the women beside him and saw, with a beat of excitement, Larry Tod turning his back suddenly, getting right under Watson and, with a great heave that had also in it a lightning quickness, sending Watson flying over his back. He had buttocked him. Buttocked him, fair and square.

Second throw to Tod.

Then, indeed, Georges' whole life and purpose seemed to be in the match. Watson must win; he must, he must! The very sight of Larry Tod strutting about there like a flaming peacock, pushing out his chest, stroking his arms, throwing glances from his narrow eyes to heaven as though he expected the clouds to acclaim him, that was indeed too much. If Watson lost now all was lost. It was as though Tod with his coarseness and his evil had been sent as a messenger to Georges threatening him with some low, vile dominion for ever.

Watson stood there quietly, no expression in his eyes, waiting. Above them the clouds were stripping the sky, which began to be flooded with a white pale glow. The Tarn, beneath them, was white like the peeled inside skin of an orange; all the houses of the village were black.

The men took hold again. First Tod, setting his teeth, tried the swinging hips, but this, if it is to succeed, must be a swing of great quickness, and Watson was too strong for him.   Then Watson, in his turn, tried the chip, getting his knee behind his opponent's so that Larry might lose his balance.   It seemed that Watson would succeed.   Larry raised his head to the white sky, his teeth clenched, his eyes closed; you could feel that he thought that he was going.   But his strength was too much for Watson.   He escaped, and suddenly, a moment later, was clicking Watson's right leg with his own right and his left with Watson's left.   The struggle now was fearful.   Both men put out their uttermost.   Watson resorted to the outside click to save himself from falling, placing his leg as near the ground as possible.   The two men swung and strained; Watson's neck and upper chest were soaked with sweat.   Then Larry's little eyes were triumphant; he crossed both Watson's legs quickly with his own, cross-buttocking, and with a shout, his huge frame seeming to double its natural size, he had Watson on the ground.

He stood there, smiling.

Georges turned.   His fate was sealed then. He walked away down the hill.   Coming to the little rough bridge he saw someone standing there, someone with his back to him, a man of a great height, in a long dark-blue coat.   He knew, before the man turned, who it would be.   It was young Stane's father.

A few minutes later Judith noticed that Georges was not at her side.   She had been

absorbed by the incidents of the last bout, and
when she saw Watson beaten she felt, as Georges
had felt, that there was some personal omen, intended for them both. That was not like her.
She realised it herself, but these last weeks had
tried her. Yes, she wished she were older and
wiser and, in general, more patient. She wished
that she were not so easily excited—excited by
just anything, a piece of silk, a cloud in the sky
—and then by a man hanging! It was then that
she saw that Georges was not beside her and,
at once, apprehension seized her as it always
did now. It seemed to hover over her like a
black bird—yes, and the sky white behind the
bird, the Tarn dead white and all the bracken
dead.

Watson was walking slowly towards her, pulling on his coat. She had to speak to him.

' Next time, Charlie,' she said, smiling.

' Aye.' She could see that he was bitterly
disappointed. She was not sure that there were
not even tears in his eyes.

' I'll whack him—great oaf!' he said, half to
himself, half to her. She realised with a quick
sharpness of perception that he had done it all for
her, all from the first to the last. She put out
her hand and it lay in his hot one, damp and sweat-
ing from the tussle.

' I'll back you, Charlie Watson, against all the
world.' And yet, although she was so grateful
to him and friendly, the truth was that she was
scarcely aware of him.

Over and over again she was saying: ' Where's

Georges? What's he about? Why did he go
without telling me? '

She turned and ran down the hill. Pushing
open their door, she saw a strange sight. A giant
old man stood looking at her. He had long
white hair that fell to the blue collar of his long
heavy coat, and he had a white beard, like the
cleanest, most shining wool. Above his beard
a sharp pale nose and two pale-blue eyes. All
down his long blue coat were round brass buttons,
and he wore tall boots that gaitered him to the
thigh. He was so white and clean that he seemed
to be wrapped in some mask-like covering, and
Judith had the odd sense that with a gesture he
could throw off all of this—the hair, beard, face,
clothes—and that he would be then a thin naked
old man, sharp like a sword.

Another odd thing was that at once she knew
him. She did not need to hear Georges' voice:

' Mr. Stane, this is my wife. Judith, this is
poor Mr. Stane's father.'

She remembered always her sudden resent-
ment that Georges said ' Poor Mr. Stane.' There
was weakness and cowardice there. She would
never have said ' Poor Mr. Stane ' had a thousand
of his fathers been there!

She went forward, holding out her hand.

' How are you, sir? Will you not sit down?
You must be weary after your walk.' She saw
at once that the old man liked her and that, very
strangely, she liked him. It was always Judith's
way, her life through, to know in the first instant
whether she liked or disliked anyone.

The old man sat down. Georges had not moved from his place, standing against the wall, and Judith did not look at him. Rather she was compelled to notice everything about old Mr. Stane, how, with solemn, dignified, cautious steps, he moved to a chair; how he slowly sat down, spreading on either side of him the long heavy skirts of his coat; how he put up his hand and smoothed his white locks, pinched his white nose, then, very carefully, as though he were dealing with something extremely precious, laid his hands on his immense knees. It was then that she was struck with his great strength. His hands looked as though they could wring the neck of an ox.

' Mr. Stane,' Georges said, ' took a chaise to Keswick and walked from there to see us.'

' Aye,' said the old man. ' I was drawn like. My heart is aching for my son, madam, and your husband was the last to see him. It was a terrible accident and God's will. But he was all I had in the world.'

He spoke with very little accent in a soft mild tone. Then he went on: ' Whoso casteth a stone on high casteth it on his own head. He that worketh mischief, it shall fall on him, and he shall not know whence it cometh.'

Her heart beat wildly. He knew then? He had come here for some kind of vengeance? But he looked up and gave her a smile, so gentle, so friendly, so amiable that she could only smile back at him.

' The Scriptures, madam,' he said, ' have been a comfort to me all my days.'

'Yes,' she said, not knowing what to say.
'And now you must have some food.'

'Thank you kindly, madam. I could enjoy
a bit of food. Although I like a walk, you
understand.'

'Mr. Stane, Judith,' Georges said, 'will stay
here with us to-night.'

'Thank you kindly,' the old man answered,
pinching his nose. 'I wouldn't mind.'

He smiled on them both, then sighed a deep
heavy sigh.

TUMBLE DOWNSTAIRS

OLD STANE stood, as he liked to do, the blue skirts of his coat spread, before the fireplace.

Judith sat on the window - ledge, peeling potatoes from a large 'kist' on her lap, looking out of window at the gold smoke of the bracken that rolled in a low cloud up and up above the thin splintered blue of the Tarn. A late October afternoon, quite still, without a cloud in the sky, and the running everywhere of water, crystal clear.

Within the room, too, everything was sharp and clean; Judith, her lithe figure like a cut jewel, the flames of the fire like painted laths, old Stane's beard like the white of an egg, his blue coat without a spot, his long strong hands washed, you would say, with pumice-stone. Cleanest of all his long nose, always like the nose of a mask.

'Well, madam,' he said, 'I swore that my son should become a great man. I had myself sold fish with my feet bare on the Whitehaven cobbles, and the Lord thought it well for me to do so. My wife, ma'am, died in childbirth. She was a good woman, although with impulses not entirely Christian. When the Lord took her I accepted my rebuke that I could not have made

393   O 2

her more godly, and I offered my son, even as Abraham offered Isaac a sacrifice to the Lord——'

(' Young Stane,' thought Judith, ' a sacrifice to the Lord ! ' She could see his face, mean and ambitious, and his hands as they moved towards her . . . if she had allowed him——! She shuddered a little.)

' But as Abraham with Isaac, so with myself and my son. The Lord did not at that time demand the sacrifice. He knew His own good time. . . .'

Oh, when would he stop! She thought that in these last weeks he had managed to creep into her very being. She would never be rid of him again. He had done nothing but hang about the house. He never went farther than the steps beyond the door. He was always there. At night they could hear him move his great body in his bed, yes, although there were a thousand doors between themselves and him! He ate but little, drank only water, spoke to no one save Georges and herself. He was quite silent if they were not there. Sometimes he would talk to them, some-times only look at them. He would stare and stare over his long nose.

He had little movements that made her long to scream out. One was when he laid, slowly and almost sacramentally, his thick heavy hands on his thick heavy knees. Then he would stroke his beard with a purposeful meditation as though he were wondering whether, with a quick jerk, he would not tug it off and show it to be a disguise. He would raise a hand as though he would give a blessing. He was always gentle, kindly and

patient. She liked him behind her terror of
him. Had he not been young Stane's father
she might have been his friend.

As it was he must go—and as soon as might
be. But Georges would not let him go. He was
fascinated by him as the rabbit by the snake.

Two days before this, almost hysterical with
irritation (for it was absolutely against her character to be passive in this manner), in their room at
night she had attacked Georges.

' Tell him to go! '

' I cannot.'

' Why not? '

' This is the least I owe him.'

' You owe him nothing! Georges, tell him
to go! '

' You don't understand. . . . So long as he
wishes to remain he must.'

She could have shaken him until his head
rolled on his shoulder.

' Georges, wake up! You are dreaming. You
killed the man in self-defence. He would have
finished you. He wished to. Well, then. The
old man has no right over us.'

' I cannot tell him to go.'

' Then I will.'

' Tell him. You will see. Nothing will
happen.'

' But what *is* it? What spell has he laid on
you? '

' No spell. I cannot do otherwise.'

' But is he to be here with us always? '

' So long as he wishes.'

'But he makes you miserable. He reminds you always. If he went away you would forget.'

He came to her, put his arms round her.

'In this you *are* a child. You are too young to understand. It is not because I think I was wicked to kill Stane. I've done many worse things. But I'm not the same man since I did it. I feel that I must confess it to someone. Then it will be over.'

'But you have confessed it—to me.'

'You are part of myself or you have grown to be. We are both in this—as though you had been in the boat too.'

She stood up straight beside him, like man standing by man.

'Well, I shall tell him to go.'

And so, on this golden afternoon, she did.

She was not afraid to tell him; her earlier fear of him seemed to leave her as she spoke.

'Mr. Stane,' she said, coming quite close to him. 'When will you be leaving us?'

He didn't answer: he was pulling at his beard.

'I ask,' she said, smiling up at him, 'because I may have a guest. Mr. Francis Herries. He has written that he may be coming.'

The old man's nose seemed to probe into her, tickling her skin. As a fact he was bending down towards her.

'When you have no place for me,' he said, very gently stroking his beard and almost, it seemed to her, drawing her into the meshes of it, 'I may reside in the village. It is a pleasure for me to be

near your husband, who was so good a friend to
my son.'

She was on the verge of crying out: ' He was
not good to him.   They hated one another.'   It
was one of Mr. Stane's peculiarities that he
seemed to draw out of you your most secret
thoughts.

He smiled on her very affectionately as he
added:

' I am an old man, madam.   The Lord has
seen fit to take everything from me.   These, your
husband and yourself, are, it may be, the last
affections of my life.'

After that what could she say?

That night they lay awake hearing him walk
his room.   It was a heavy soft tread like an
animal's.   They heard him get into his bed at
last.   Then there was only an owl's cry.

They clung together that night like children.

' Georges, let us run away.'

' Where? '

' Anywhere.   London.   Paris.'

' He would come after us.'

' Georges, I *must* help you.   I must! I must!
I'm not a fool.   This is a ridiculous thing, to be
hemmed in by an old man.'

He sighed, holding her very closely.

' It matters very little.   I'm happy because
now I love you.   Judy, Judy, I love you so.'

' And I love you more and more.'

' But how can you when there is so little in me
to love?   I have never treated you well from the
beginning.'

'Georges, I shall never love anyone again. That is true. I know it absolutely. This is for all my life long.'

He stroked her hair. That, at least, he had loved from the very beginning.

'Judy, if we could be rid of this I know now what we would do. I could settle here now, I wouldn't wish to move. I would farm with Watson. I have lived out all my restlessness. We would have enough. Perhaps you would have children. If only we could be rid of this!'

'But we can, Georges!'

They were whispering as though the old man in his room could hear them.

'He must go, and then you will forget it all.'

'What did he say when you spoke?'

She did not answer.

'Did he say he would go?'

'No.'

'You see.'

'Oh, but I shan't be beaten by an old man.' Her voice rose. She dropped it to a whisper again without knowing that she did so.

'Judy, I love you! I love you! I love you!'

'Oh, Georges, I love you so! It has come at last, both of us loving one another—both of us.'

'Yes—both of us. . . .'

'It is very seldom that two people love with the same strength.'

'I did not know that I could love anyone for long. You have made me by being so good.'

They heard the old man in the other room rise from his bed. The boards creaked. They were silent, their hearts beating the one against the other.

But it was on that night that they both had terrible dreams. Georges dreamt that he was being hanged from a tree that was covered with white moss, and in that last moment before death the moss was alive with worms. Judith dreamt of a white horse that, plunging through dark water, leapt up the black hills beyond, and that, as it leapt, her father (she had never seen him, but she knew that it was her father) ran and jumped on to its back, calling to her to follow. But she could not, because Georges was struggling in the water and she trying to save him. The white horse vanished, a star fell from the sky into the water, and Georges was drowned.

In the dim musk-like shadow of dawn she waked and found Georges sleeping at her side. In her relief she laid her hand on his bare heart and felt its steady beat. Then she looked in his face and saw that he, too, was struggling in dreams.

She brushed his dark hair back from his forehead, kissed his eyes, stroked his breast, gently as a mother her child.

In the morning, however, all her sentiment was gone. They must be rid of this old man. The weather had changed. The sky was a fury of wind and rushing cloud. The clouds ran like messengers, and the sun struck like a whip on the hills, slashed and was gone. The bracken changed in an instant from dun to fire, from fire to sullen death. The clouds, after racing the sky, suddenly gathered into heavy bales of wool and then slipped down, enclosing Watendlath in mist. The rest of the world was shut away. Judith, in spite of her common sense, began to lose her wits, for now she, too, was conscious of a terrible impulse to catch the old man by the beard and tell him everything.

' Yes. It's true. I don't know whether you think it or not, but Georges killed your wretched son, and he deserved it. Now will you go? '

She had never felt any urge like this before. It was exactly as though someone were whispering in her ear. Their nights were broken. They were afraid to sleep because of their dreams. The old man stayed by the house, and they found that they, too, stayed there also. Charlie Watson was away in Carlisle. She did not seem to want to speak to anyone. She never went into the Ritsons' kitchen. The low wet clouds seemed to shut them off, the three of them, from all the rest of the world.

Judith sewed, cooked, sometimes walked to the Fell and looked down to Rosthwaite. That was the farthest she went. Georges sat, walked to the door and looked out, sat down again. It was as though they were both held by a spell. It could not, of course, continue like this. But what would happen? Old Mr. Stane seemed to be perfectly content. He talked much and always about himself and his son. He gave no trouble, stayed for the most part beside the fire.

' You may be sure that I appreciate your kindness. The Lord will not suffer a sparrow to fall to the ground. . . . My boy would have been wealthy had he lived. He had a fine head for business. Aye. Aye. All that I had, but it is the Lord's will, and His mercy must be great in our eyes. . . . But it is a grief to me that he should have perished in foreign waters. Your husband, ma'am, did all that he could, but it was beyond human power to save him. I know that. For an old man it is a hard blow, but it will not be long before the Lord will take me to Himself. . . .'

Nevertheless he did not give the impression of great sorrow, but rather of intent watchfulness. He watched with his nose, and when he stroked it with his thick slow finger it was as though finger and nose were communicating together.

One afternoon the rain came. It fell in hard relentless torrents. The country was blinded as though a hood had been drawn over its eyes. That night in the war of water and groaning trees Georges caught Judith's hands and told her that he could hold out no longer. He must tell the old man and be damned to him.

' When I have told him, I can take him by the neck and shove him from the door. He can take what revenge he pleases.'

For a moment she thought that perhaps this would be best. Then she saw what it would mean. Georges would be arrested and hanged. She told him that that would be the end of everything, of herself as well as of him.

' Well, maybe that would be best. Anything's better than this. He is strangling us as though he had a cord round our throats, and he knows it.'

She had a wild notion that they should start out then and there, run for their lives, on and on, reach some foreign country—China. . . . Even as she said it she knew that it was hopeless. He had strangled all her energy.

On the next night the rain had ceased, and a cold pale stillness lay over everything. They sat around the fire, and Mr. Stane told them about his home, his possessions, his clothes, his Bible, his intimacy with God as he had done a thousand times before. There never was such an egoist.

'The Lord giveth and the Lord taketh away. . . .'

Georges sprang from his seat by the fire, stood up against him, front to front.

'I killed your son. I killed your son. I threw him into the water and watched him drown. I hated him and hate him yet. . . . Now be damned to you both. . . . You and your son . . . both of you.'

It was as though the words had been spat out and then returned into him again. He put his hand to his throat. Judith rose with a startled cry. She came close to him, as though to protect him, so that they were all near together. In the silence she heard the owl's cry that had been haunting her for weeks.

At last, after this great pause, old Stane slowly lifted himself up from his chair, stood above them, then with his white hand pushed them, breaking through between them.

He looked at them, nodded his head.

'I knew it . . . a long time back. I wanted

confirmation from your own mouth. Bloody murderer of my son——'

'Well, he had been bent on my ruin for years. He wished to take my place.' Georges panted the words. 'It was an old feud between us. We hated one another from the beginning.'

Old Stane nodded his head. 'Aye—you hated him.'

'Now go!' Georges cried. 'Call in the Justice. I shan't run away.'

He seemed like a man liberated. Judith went to him and put her hand on his arm.

'We shan't run away,' she repeated.

But Stane did not move. Georges felt such a sickness of the sight of him, a sickness that involved himself, his deed, the whole world. He would never be free of all this until Stane was gone.

'Finish it,' he said, and went up the stairs.

Everything happened then with great swiftness. Georges had reached the upper landing, when old Stane turned and was after him. For so heavy a man he moved quickly, as though someone very young and vital were concealed in that bulk.

He was at the stairhead in a moment. Georges turned to face him and they stood close together as though in amity.

Stane shouted:

'I came for this! . . . I came for this! Down you go, murderer——'

His arms shot up, he hugged Georges close to his heart as though he loved him, lifted him

like a baby, then hurled him away from the stair,
over to the floor below.

He waited, looking down, then rushed down
the stair, bent for a moment over the huddled
figure, passed out through the door.

It had happened in a flash as lightning strikes
a house.   Judith had not stirred; now, liberated,
she ran to Georges, frantically, crying she knew
not what, knelt down beside him.

His head was bleeding and both his legs were
bent beneath him.   He was quite conscious and
he looked at her and smiled.

'My back is broken . . . he has done for me.'

'No.   No——' She lifted his head and placed
it against her breast.

'There's nothing to do, Judy, my darling.
I'll be gone in a moment.   The old devil was
strong. . . .'

She tried to be clear-headed and wise.   This
was the crisis of her whole life, something for
which she had been always preparing.   Her hand
was soaked in the blood from his wounded head,
but she could think of nothing save his eyes, which
stared into hers as though they would never let
her go.

'I must fetch someone.   They shall ride into
Rosthwaite. . . .'   She did not know what she
said.

'No.   Don't go.   Don't leave me.   Soon I
shan't see you.'

She began to cry.

' . . . It is just. . . . Now we had come to love

one another. Ugh, I can't speak. I am swimming in water. . . . Sinking. Hold my eyes, Judy. Oh, Judy, darling, how I love you!'

'And I you, Georges. Always. Oh, Christ, for help. Someone to help. . . .'

' Nothing to be done.' His head sank deep against her breast. His voice fell to a whisper.

' I love you—for ever——'

His hand touched hers and he was gone.

END OF PART II

PART III

THE BIRD OF BRIGHT PLUMAGE

FAMILY PAPERS

Letter from Judith Paris to Francis Herries, Esq.

22, WESTBOURNE PLACE, LONDON,
16*th of May*, 1800.

MY DEAREST FRANCIS—Dinner is over, Emma has gone out to visit a friend, the candles are properly trimmed and now is the time to do what I have for several days pledged myself to—write a proper and informing letter. You know well by this time, dear Francis, that I am never as informing as I would wish to be, but on this especial occasion I have real news for you—for, what do you think? I was actually present at Drury Lane Theatre last night when the poor King was shot at by a ruffian and had a most providential escape from death.

Mr. Ross with whom Emma has on several occasions acted at Drury Lane, had given her two tickets and, as you may well believe, we were all agog for we were promised that the King and Queen and all the Princesses would be present.

Now fancy the event! Scarcely had the King entered the box, before he had taken his seat and was yet bowing to the audience (myself and Emma were on the floor and had a most excellent view of it) when a wretch in the pit not far from us aimed at the poor King with a horse-pistol and fired.

You can imagine the sensation! Everyone was screaming. It was fortunate that there was not a panic. The King alone was calm, for he turned, said some words to an attendant, took his seat quite tranquilly and sat out the entertainment which was ' She Would and She Would Not ' and James Cobb's ' Humourist.'

It was terrible to see the people throw themselves upon the wretched would-be assassin, who was pulled over the spikes and hurried across the stage. Sir William Addington examined him in an adjoining apartment.

After a while up went the Curtain and we all—on the stage and off it—stood up and sang ' God Save the King.' Emma was crying like a child and I must confess that my own eyes were wet. Princess Mary fainted twice they say, but Princess Elizabeth was most brave and we could see how the Queen nodded to the Princesses that they should keep up their spirits.

They say to-day that the name of the man was James Hadfield and that the King was indeed lucky, for one of the slugs from the pistol was found only a foot to the left of the royal chair. The affair is the more mysterious it seems, in that only that same afternoon during his attendance at the field exercises of the Grenadier battalion at Hyde Park a Clerk in the Navy Office was shot while standing only a few feet from the King.   It

was thought at the time to be an accident but now
it looks otherwise.

What times we live in!   The whole world is
disturbed and the wretched Revolution in France
has been, I am convinced, the cause of it.   Gold
is scarce they say, and I know from my own experience how scarce food is.   Everyone is complaining but nothing is done and many well-informed
persons fear that we are on the verge of Revolution.   Well, after all this public news you will
wish to hear something more personal.

This is now my second year with Mrs. Dudeney and her children.   I go to her house in Meck-
lenburgh Square at nine every morning and am
there until six, save for Saturdays and Sundays.   I
take my dinner with them and often drive out
with Mrs. Dudeney or her sister Miss Chalpaine.

I must confess that I have grown attached to the
children.   They are good little things, even a trifle
too virtuous, for you know, dear Francis, I never
care sufficiently for those I can completely rule.

Poor Mrs. Dudeney misses her husband very
sadly and this that we have in common should
draw us closely together.   But something holds
me apart from everyone, even from Emma.   It is
as though my heart were indeed quite dead and,
although time has now passed, I live in a dream.
It seems to matter nothing where I am or what I
do.   My whole movement is external.   I speak
of this to no one else save yourself—even Emma
has no notion of it but thinks that I am well recovered from Georges' death.

But oh Francis, I am not!   Something has died

in me for ever. That condition of living when one existed only for another is gone never to return.

That catastrophe was a dream. Hunt though they did high and low for old Stane, he was never seen again. Was he imagined by Georges and myself? I sometimes think so. But it is not that I cherish any illusion about Georges. He was neither strong nor faithful; I loved him as he was—not as a Perfect Being, whom, in fact, I should have detested. Forgive these sentiments. You are the only one with whom I ever share them.

Emma has now abandoned the Theatre or possibly it would be more truth to say that the Theatre has at length abandoned her. She is a strange Creature, quite devoted to me until some man crosses her path, when she is for a while like a school-girl. She has still her Charms and is less stout than formerly and as good a woman as ever was known.

Our apartment here is pleasant and looks out to a Square with Trees. There are sparrows, a man with a clarinet, a Poodle that walks every morning in the Square and an Artist up the stairs who quizzes me at every opportunity.

Write soon and tell me all about dear Uldale. Is the Museum still there at Keswick and have there been any Balls? Give Deborah my greetings and nod to every stream, hedgerow and little hill in the neighbourhood. Do the clouds still dance above Skiddaw? How I wish that I were there!—Your loving

JUDITH.

Francis Herries, Esq., to Judith Paris.

ULDALE, 14*th of June*, 1800.

DEAREST JUDITH—I was delighted indeed to have a letter from you, for it was several months since I had heard and I was beginning to feel some anxiety. When I saw you last year in London you had not been sufficiently with Mrs. Dudeney to know how you would find her, and it is very gratifying indeed to discover that at least she is neither a bore nor a bully.

I cannot quite accommodate myself to the necessity of your earning a living in this manner, but quite honestly, dear Judith, I do not feel that it would be altogether wise for you to live with us while Deborah is here, nor would you yourself I think wish it.

Deborah is the best of women and the most kindly of sisters, but she must rule domestically any place where she is and will brook no rival. You also as you admit have a certain ruling capacity and when Greek meets Greek—!

Moreover remembering Georges still as you do, work is I do not doubt the most helpful of Panaceas, and I know that you are of the greatest value to Mrs. Dudeney and her family.

You do not say in your letter whether you have seen Brother Will. I hear that he is with every week a man of greater wealth and more important responsibility. I am told that they are to take a house in Mount Street (my information is from Bournemouth). I hear also that Christabel is no more in love with a grand life than she ever was, poor thing, and has in fact never recovered socially from the unhappy and now historic Ball.

Will will have no dealings with me and breathes fire and slaughter against his Bournemouth relations. Is this not foolish? But Will was always as filled with himself and his affairs as an egg with meat, and an insult to his wife is a snap of the finger in the face of the Almighty.

Nevertheless Will prospers and I do not. He is the other side of the Herries blanket from ourselves, dear Judith, and I think all the interest in our family's history must come from that, that men like Will are being for ever disgraced and made anxious by men like me. We break in upon their solid plans as a horse-thief breaks into their gold. So also on their side they break in upon our dreams. Where, I must ask myself, wandering among these fields and hills, do the two worlds join? Who may bring them together? Last week I rode up Borrowdale to Stonethwaite and wandered for an hour about the little overgrown court and garden of Herries where my grandfather and your father dug for so many years the hard and ungrateful soil. A shepherd, Wilson, now has it and lets it go as it will.

It was almost as though your father were at my elbow. I had forgot him but my father so frequently spoke of him that it is as though I had known him. I have only one memory of him, a tall gaunt black man with a scar on his face, riding up the white road to Uldale. I must confess to you that I was miserable enough that hour in that

garden.   All has gone wrong with me of late.
Deborah's little sociabilities, the neighbours, their
tea-parties, cards and small festivities I can take no
interest in.   My writing such as it was has failed
me; even my reading has little power over me.
The country seems to me on the verge of ruin, the
country people seething with discontent, the towns
no better, a crazy king on the throne and a Prince
—you do not need me to say anything there.

But you know what it is, dear Judith, that
drives me.   I am a man now of forty years and
should be past such madness and should be
master of such folly—but rather I am sunk in it
deeper than before.   Every breath I draw, waking
or sleeping, seems to drag me to Bournemouth.
They tell me that she is more beautiful than ever.
She should be indeed now in the full flower of
her loveliness.   I hear also, and this has possibly
given strength to my madness, that young
Beaminster, the Duke of Wrexe's eldest son, is
crazy for her.   What a match for her that would
be!   But if anyone in our age is fitted to be a
Duchess it is she!   What a triumph for the
Herries family if it should be so!   I hear too
that she is both proud and kind beyond ordinary
measure—and truly in every grace and virtue
she is over all others. . . .

I will not burden you more with this.   You
ask whether Skiddaw stands where it did.   Indeed it does.   This is a perfect month for this
country.   There is a spot by Portinskill bordering
the Keswick Lake where I love to be.   The trees
are now young flames and when the water is like

glass they burn in their reflections. Then a breeze ruffles that glass and the fire is suddenly in the sky carried on the breast of a cloud. Were she with me here to see this beauty I know that I could win her to love me. I know it, Judith, I *know* it! But what is the value of such vain dreams? If you should hear anything of young Beaminster being at Bournemouth or of their meeting in Town, pray let me know.—Your loving

FRANCIS.

Miss Jennifer Cards to the Hon. Angela Painter.

GROSSET PLACE, WILTSHIRE,
September 2, 1802.

MY DARLING ANGELA—Forgive this odious hand for I cannot find my own pen and all the writing-tables here are filled with birds' nests and bones for the dogs. I speak with the utmost literalness for you cannot conceive the disorder in which Maria Rockage loves to confuse everything. But I have told you of this odd Place before and there is no need to make a repetition save that it is truth itself that there is a Bason on the floor of my bedroom at this instant to catch the drops from a crack in the ceiling, for it has rained for twenty-four hours without ceasing and every room in the Place runs with water. Not that we any of us are disturbed in the slightest degree. We are all True Britons in this respect and discomfort is part of our Birthright. There are but three of us here at the moment, Rockage.

Maria and Phyllis, twenty last week and quite pretty in a milk-maid kind of style.

I fancy that she is the principal cause of my invitation here, for she had her Coming Out last Season and then must Go In again for they haven't a Penny amongst them and can make no sort of Show—while I, they suppose, have everyone in my Handkerchief from Mrs. Fitzherbert downwards. They fancy too that I can give the Child some kind of a ' ton,' but I am too amiable on the one side and too lazy on the other. And indeed she is not so bad in a simple kind of way.

But you know, dearest Angela, of what it is that I would write. Have you seen Beaminster since his return, have you spoken with him, if so did he mention me and what is his attitude now that he has seen China and all the Indies? Perhaps he has brought back with him a young Chinese Woman and I will not care if he has. But will I not? What is my mood? Upon my word it is hard to tell. How perverse is the world! Here am I, thirty-two years of age and still Single. And yet I have had every Element in my favour, have no aversion to Matrimony. At least I have told Beaminster a thousand times that I do not love him and would marry him only to be a Duchess. I like him at least sufficiently to be honest with him and as you know have refused him a hundred times. But now, time passes. It will not be long before I am a Withered Hag. What is Love, Angela? I swear I have never known it. My cousin, Francis Herries, swears that it is the Toothache of the Soul that no dentist can cure. I

P

can only say then that my Teeth have no need of a
Doctor.   But why are the Virtues and Qualities
of men so obstinately dissipated?   There is Francis
himself, the best and happiest of company, but
having nothing better than a small Place in Cumberland where it rains inordinately.   There is
young Stephen Hailes whose every breath showers
gold pieces, but he is so gross in his feeding and
thinks of nothing but Horses.   There is Beaminster (and I would adore to be a Duchess), but he
whines through his Nose like a Parson and cracks
at the knees.

And many another all of whom you know, dearest
Angela.   I'm not boasting that I tell you this, but
only that I may remind myself of my Vast Age
and how my Opportunities are slipping over me.

There is talk still everywhere of the Peace and
it is the fashion only to hasten to Paris.   Rockage
has heard that Charles Fox is on a visit to Bonaparte
and that Mrs. Fox is for the first time publicly
acknowledged.

I shall be soon returning to Bournemouth for
Wiltshire rusticity is softening my Wits.   Moreover there is shortly coming here little Judith
Paris whom you have seen I fancy in London.
Maria has an odd Affection for her.   She is a
quaint thing whose French husband was killed
some years back in a brawl in the North, since
when she must be a Governess or Companion as
he left her without a Penny.   She is as you will
remember, an Oddity, being but a few feet in
height and with hair of coarse flaming red.

Maria vows that she is a Noble Creature.   I

am not myself prepossessed too strongly in her favour as she supports the Will Herries part of the Family in that ridiculous squabble of which I have often told you and over which we have so frequently laughed together. In any case I prefer my Nobility over two foot and a quarter!

Write soon, dearest Angela, and relieve the Anxiety of Your loving Friend,   JENNIFER.

Francis Herries, Esq., to Judith Paris.

ULDALE, CUMBERLAND,
14*th of September*, 1802.

DEAREST JUDITH——I am following my letter of yesterday with this brief note that I may enclose this silver chain and cross. Last night rummaging in some old drawers, I came upon some effects of my father's, a packet or two of letters, a book or two, a riding-whip, this Chain and a small silver Box. The Box was the one of which he had often told me, decorated with the Picture of girls dancing round a Maypole and gentlemen hunting. It was given him when a Child by a Pedlar. The Chain also he had spoken of, and it seems that your Mother's Mother bequeathed it to your father for some Service he had one time done her.

The Chain then is by right your own and it pleases me greatly that I have discovered it, as also the silver Box by which I know my Father held considerable store.

I have no further news than that of yesterday.—— Your loving   FRANCIS.

Judith Paris to Mrs. Will Herries, of 48 Mount Street, London.

GROSSET PLACE, WILTS.,
December 3, 1802.

MY DEAR CHRISTABEL—It was most kind of you to write to me. I was most grateful. I have been here now for two months and have as yet no regrets at having left Mrs. Dudeney. Phyllis is a charming girl, modest and intelligent, with a sense of fun that enables her to see the Ludicrousness of much in her home and her Parents, and yet in no way impairs her Love for them.

They are indeed Lovable and yet most truly there is also something of the Ludicrous! Had you but now seen Carey peeping over the banisters, his nightcap nodding above his eyebrow, his nightshirt flapping at his bare ankles, shouting for Doggett, the man, because he heard that the sow had but just now littered! Indeed this is no place for early rising, for even now I was downstairs at ten o'clock to find such a confusion in the breakfast room, fender huddled two yards high, into the middle of the room, chairs, tables, shovel, poker, tongs anyhow, carpet thrown back, dust everywhere, dogs everywhere, bees-wax, rubber, brush, broom, mop, pail, and before a cheerless grate Maggie the girl on her knees. All the doors on this house have rusty refractory door-locks of which the hasp invariably flies backward, all chimneys smoke, going to bed the candle at once goes out with a whiff and a stink in the passage and you break your shins at every step, all the corks break and drop in fragments *inside* the bottles, all keys are lost to all drawers, room after room (there are dozens of unused ones) is piled with broken bricks, scattered chisels and hammers, battered trunks mildewed with neglect. No proper alliance is formed with any butcher, carrier or baker, no salt-cellars have their spoons, no knife its proper fork, every snuffer to every candlestick tilts off and drops its contents on the carpet, every bell-rope breaks, or if it rings, brings the wrong servant, every scissor pinches without cutting . . . and so on, and so on! Dear Christabel, I could continue this for an hour!

Into this chaos it is hoped that I shall bring some kind of order, and indeed I see a good ten years' work in front of me. But after all these are my own people and not strangers, and as I see Maria in an old silk Negligée padding around, her slippers flapping on the carpet, dogs sniffing at her heel, and that kindly amiable smile on her face, knowing that she loves me (as indeed I believe that she does), I must love her in return.

All this must seem terrible to you in your smart Mount Street Mansion, and you can understand what it must be to myself who have, as you know, a Passion for cleanliness, but I have no longer Energy to direct my own path and take what comes. Affection seems to me everything just at present.

Your beautiful Enemy, Miss Jennifer, was staying here in the summer. They report her

proud, matter-of-fact, worldly, not over intelligent
but kindly and not conceited. They were rather
relieved though, I fancy, at her departure. They
say that she has any number of times refused Lord
Beaminster and that now he, after a visit to the
East, is paying attention to Lord Garrison's girl,
but I do not know what truth there is in these
rumours.

Has Will still the same implacability about
Francis? The Monynghams have been here.
I dislike the name and am glad that Carey's father
after being Lord Monyngham became Viscount
Rockage—a far handsomer title!

What of Pomfret in Kensington? I hear that
he has been ill and that James, the monster, is
biting his thumb till he can be Baronet. Like
his grandfather Raiseley, whom Will's father
always so thoroughly hated, I never cared for
James.

Love to all in Mount Street and if Mrs.
Dudeney pay a call, as I fancy that she may, pray
be kind to her for my sake.—Your loving

JUDITH.

Francis Herries, Esq., to Judith Paris.
(Portion of letter only.)

ULDALE, *Jan.* 6, 1805.

. . . . You know what it was that I read in the
Gazette. And so she has surrendered! Well, it
will become her to be a Duchess although I hear

that he is sadly spindle-shanked and a dull dog. I will think no more of her.   I feel stronger now that the blow has at length fallen.   I must build my life on a sounder bottom.

One agreeable thing has occurred.   A Mr. and Mrs. Coleridge have for some time past lived at a Keswick house, Greta Hall, and now he is joined by another poet, Mr. Robert Southey, whose sister-in-law he had married.   I have met Mr. Southey and find him a most agreeable person of immense learning, but no haughtiness of manner.   Mr. Coleridge is an extraordinary man who lives for the most part in other worlds than ours.   He is often absent from Keswick and, so gossip says, is on no very easy terms with his wife, but the Southey family is excellent and very friendly towards myself.   I am even stirred once more to attempt something with my pen.   But more of this later. . . .

William Herries, Esq., of 48 Mount Street, to Judith Paris.

48 Mount Street, London,
Feb. 20, 1805.

Dear Judith—You must forgive the brevity of this letter.   I am but now returned from the City where I was consulted in certain important matters having no indirect connection with His Royal Highness's affairs.   Your enquiry on Carey's behalf concerning his City Investments

I will prosecute further and send you information when I have it.

The Budget of two days back causes some concern especially the extra 6d. per bushel of salt which will I imagine greatly hamper the curing of bacon and ham, but on the whole things might I consider be worse.

Have you heard how Jennifer's engagement to Lord Beaminster prospers? I can only say that I pity the foolish fellow from the bottom of my heart. He little knows the Tartar that he has taken to his bosom. After dancing round him for years she has condescended to be his future Duchess without I fancy intending him any return. He will discover his mistake in time. I must however admit that the Match is a fine one for our Family.

There is considerable anxiety in the City about the King's health. Stocks fluctuate accordingly. Christabel would I know send her love were she conscious that I was writing. She is lying in her room; she had a slight stomach affection to-day.

Pray give my regards to Maria and Carey. I am pleased to learn from Christabel that you find your stay with them agreeable. I must confess that I have little love for the Country save for our own Northern portion of it which however for family reasons of which you are well aware I am little likely to see again.

With kindest regards, dear Judith, I remain—
Yours most sincerely,

WILLIAM HERRIES.

Judith Paris to Francis Herries, Esq.

GROSSET PLACE, WILTS.,
Feb. 25, 1805.

DEAREST FRANCIS — I hesitated whether to
write after I had seen the news, but I feel that it
would not be friendly on my part did I not tell
you of my sympathy.   She has made her choice
and that she can prefer a marriage without love
because of its Social Splendour is only proof to
me of her unfitness for any marriage with a finer
man.

Put her utterly out of your Heart, dear Francis.
I do not doubt but that you have done so.   I
pity her for her unwise decision, for where there
is no love there can be neither companionship
nor respect.   So at least I feel.   I wish that I
were with you. I myself have often a longing for
the pressure of your hand.   You remember how
as a Child I loved you and how I would watch at
the window for hours to see if you came.   As it
was then so is it still, save that I am a woman now
and have learnt something of life and know what
it is to be alone.

Do not fancy, however, that they are not all
goodness to me here, for indeed they are.   I have
brought some discipline into affairs here, but the
real trouble is lack of means.   Poor Carey has
no mind for business and he cannot keep more than
one thing in his head at a time.

No sooner is he distressed by the loss of a silver

spoon than he is told that a dog has the Eczema, and some woman is up from the village to beg something of him, or Squire Somebody or Another has ridden over from Somewhere and must have a Bed.

The Guest Room is always in disorder, there are rats in the wainscot and a window-pane is broken. Still time passes and I am tranquil, refusing to lament over milk that is spilt or a fire that has died. Only maybe the fire is not dead and burns the more fiercely because no one perceives it. . . .

We have had a Visitor this last week and a pleasant one, Warren Forster of Alnwick. You recollect that he is the Grandson of Mrs. Dorothy Forster who used to visit at Keswick. He is a man of some thirty-five years and has been visited by incessant misfortunes. When a child he was kicked by one of his father's horses and has been slightly lame ever after.

He has also, I fear, some affection of the Heart. In addition to these things his wife to whom, as I understand, he had been some four years married, last year abandoned him and ran away to America with a theatrical gentleman and has never since been heard of.

In spite of these visitations he is a man of great Character and much tenderness of Heart, never complaining and always cheerful. Maria dotes upon him and I must confess that I myself have a warm Friendliness toward him. I can see you smile at this point, and prophesy me a second husband, but that will never be—Georges remains

with me as though he were yet living.   I must go
now as I hear Carey calling me.—Your loving

JUDITH.

Francis Herries, Esq., to Judith Paris.

ULDALE, *November* 9, 1805.

DEAREST JUDITH—By now you must be aware
that Jennifer has broken her engagement. Scarcely
had the glorious news of Trafalgar reached us and
we were in the midst of waving flags and hanging
lanterns, when I received a letter written by herself
informing me that she had broken off all relations
with Lord Beaminster.   She begged me to come
to Bournemouth and you will not be surprized to
learn that I am catching to-night's coach at
Kendal.

I will write from there.—Yours in haste,

FRANCIS.

Judith Paris to Mrs. Emma Furze.

GROSSET PLACE, WILTS.,
Dec. 8, 1805.

MY DEAREST DEAREST EMMA—Late though
it is and mean and drunken my candle, I am
scribbling a hurried word to you to tell you what I
have only myself this evening learnt—that my
dear Francis was married to his Jennifer secretly
in London three days ago.   I have only had the
barest word from Francis acquainting me with the

fact and that they have already set off for Cumber-land.   As I sit in this large bare room with the
wind howling down the chimney and the mice
scratching in the wainscot, it is hard not to be
melancholy.   How, how can this end?   Only
badly, I fear.   She has but accepted him on the
rebound from her trouble with Beaminster.   She
does not love him and even though she did, could
never endure the remoteness of our Cumberland
country.   I can see that they will move to London
and poor Uldale fall into the tea-party chatter of
Deborah's domination.   And yet I have heard
that Jennifer does not love London either and that
that is one of the first causes of her quarrel with
Beaminster.   You know, dearest Emma, that
yourself and Francis are now the two human beings
whom I love the most deeply and for Francis this
affection has existed from my earliest childhood.
He has been always a little remote from life and
interested in notions more than persons—always,
that is, until this passion seized him.   He is one
of the noblest of men, but reserved in the expression of his feeling.   She must be proud and selfish,
accustomed to adoration and her own way.   What
can come of this but disaster?   I have heard, too,
that she is lazy and idle and will sit for hours ad-
miring herself in the glass but this, I confess, comes
from Will Herries who detests her.

Where are you now—at Colchester or Notting-
ham?   Is Mr. Edwardes the Knight at Arms that
you fancied and is the care of his two little girls as
entertaining as you had anticipated?   There are
times when I am tempted once again towards

London and Mrs. Dudeney.   She would welcome me with open arms back again any while.

Only my affections hold me here, for try as I may I cannot bring any order into the Place. This Country is at its worst in the Winter, all muck and mist, so unlike my own beloved Cumberland where the Winter is the best, for the hedges sparkle with frost, the hills are powdered with snow and the air smells like wine.

Here, at Grosset, the Country is low and miry and one must walk in high, hard-bottomed fields not to be knee-deep at every step——one is like a frog kicking and sprawling through a welter of water.

My candle is at its last drunken nod and I must go to bed.——Your most loving

JUDITH.

Mrs. Cards of Macklin House, Bournemouth, to her daughter, Mrs. Francis Herries, of Uldale, Cumberland.

(*Portion of a letter.*)

MACKLIN HOUSE, BOURNEMOUTH,
June 8, 1807.

MY DEAR JENNIFER — Your father has requested me to say that we are both anxious at not having had news from you for so long a period. You must really, my dear daughter, try to oblige your loving father and mother more frequently in this respect.   It is not kind to continue any sort of grudge against your father because he did

not in the first place approve of your marriage.
A year and a half have passed since that event and
he has become as you know reconciled to it.　He
wishes only for your happiness and welfare and
you know well that there is no human being on
the face of the globe for whom he cares as he
does for you.　You know that it is our wish that
you should lie-in in Bournemouth and I have
written to Francis asking him his own feelings
in this matter.

I have not much News for you.　The talk is
only of the Princess, whose behaviour since the
return of her Champion, Mr. Perceval, into power,
has been, they say, outrageous.　At a Ball at
Mr. Hope's she was truly a sight if eye-witnesses
are to be trusted.　Her figure is now as round as
a drum and she paints monstrously.　Her conversation is so wild that she seems often like a
mad-woman and she is not ashamed to be seen
anywhere with her boy 'Billy Austin'.　The
Prince has broken entirely with the old Whigs
and his hatred of Grenville and Grey is fanatical.
Sheridan rules him in everything and in your
father's opinion is nothing but mischievous.

The London dresses are now so tight that it
is almost impossible to walk in them.　In my old-
fashioned eyes the 'robes en Caleçon' are quite
shameless, all the outline of the figure being
clearly seen beneath them.　Very often there is
nothing but a thin petticoat beneath and that is
sometimes omitted.　The skirt is now in two
pieces, a third piece sewn in diagonally as a lateral
gusset. . . .

Francis Herries, Esq., to Judith Paris.

ULDALE, *Dec.* 7, 1807.

MY DEAREST JUDITH—I wish you to be the first to know that last evening at seven-thirty of the clock Jennifer was delivered of a fine boy. They are both doing well and my happiness is beyond measure.   I am convinced that now with a child in the house all will go well.

I will write later at greater length.—Your loving,   FRANCIS, Father of John Herries.

Judith Paris to Francis Herries, Esq.

GROSSET PLACE,
March 29, 1808.

DEAREST FRANCIS—This is the first sign of Spring this year and so I write to ask you whether you are yet living or have changed into a Leprechaun or one of the Borrowdale Cuckoos? What I would give to see Keswick Lake or Newlands Valley or the Moor above Uldale on such a day as this—for at home the skies are ever changing and streams are running and the bracken is popping while here even on this Spring day all is Languid and barely stirs.

But do you know, Sir, that of late you have very gravely neglected your Half-Aunt or whatever is my true Relationship to you?   It is now some six weeks since I had any word from you and I am feeling very gravely neglected. Two Nights back I had a Dream about you and I awoke distressed, thinking that you had called to me and I could not go to you. Do pray write and tell me how you are and how Jennifer is and little John. I am uneasy in my mind.

At this especial Moment it is necessary that I should write to calm my Feelings, for this morning has witnessed one of my most celebrated Tempers. I fear I give vent to them more frequently than of old, whereas it should be the other way. This morning I stamped and shouted like a Fishwife. I think I had some reason though, and you shall judge. It was over young Carey, who is at home just now and doing no good here. He should have gone for the Navy, as was originally intended, instead of this foolish notion that he should superintend his father's estate. For that he has no more gift than his poor Father has, nor has he his Father's sweetness of nature. He is a thick heavy Oaf as I had the pleasure this morning of telling him, for I had but just, urged by the sweetness of the Spring sunshine, directed the clumsy Maggie to the proper cleaning of the Drawing and Breakfast Room when in Carey must come, knee-deep in mud, cracking a whip and followed by four huge dogs so that he breaks a China Ornament kissing Maggie (not knowing that I was present) and sets the dogs after the cat, crying 'Halloo! Halloo!' and riding the Chairs with all his lanes and bogs clinging to them.

I treated him to a pretty Scene and then, when

he laughed, boxed his Ears. Although he is twice my height that flummoxed him and while he stared I told him all I thought of him, that he was a selfish good-for-nothing nincompoop living on his father's Bounty and doing nothing but chase Foxes and set the Dogs on the Cats. And I fear, although I did not tell him so, that he does worse than this with the Girls in the Village and thinks it all Fine Sport.

Well, in upon this comes Maria, who thinks him the Paragon of all Wonders. He went off in a Sulk calling me a fine collection of names, and Maria was altogether at a loss for she loves me and thinks I can do no wrong. But I am sometimes deeply weary of this life here, dear Francis. There is something in me that aches for Cumberland, even though there are scenes there that I could never have the Courage to revisit. This is not my place nor are these in truth my people. But where is my place and where are my people? Like my father before me I have no Home and yet I am truly a domestic creature and could not live except for the affections of those of whom I am fond.

Warren Forster has been here visiting again and we are become the greatest of friends. I think his lonely situation touches me—not that we are melancholy together but rather laugh for most of the time.

Pray write to me soon and tell me how little John fares. In your last letter you mentioned that he was suffering with a Colic.

Francis Herries, Esq., to Judith Paris.

ULDALE, *June* 10*th*, 1808.

DEAREST JUDITH—I have not written frequently of late because I have not been in the
merriest of spirits—nothing specific but only a
Malaise that is, it seems, difficult for me to shake
myself free of.   But now I have two Items of
News that I must give you.   One is that Jennifer
will be lying-in again this November.   We hope
that this time it may be a girl.   She is well and
seems to have no fears of the event.   I am afraid
that she sometimes finds me a Dull Dog.

My second Item is that Sister Deborah is engaged—to a Squire Withering of Summerhays by
Carlisle.   As Deborah is now forty-six years you
can fancy that this event was most unexpected
but Withering is of her own age and has already
been twice married.   He is a jolly red-faced Ox,
whose interests are entirely bucolic, but he will I
think suit Deborah well, for her desires are as you
know of an exceeding Sociability, and now she may
entertain the Neighbourhood to her heart's desire.

Her relations with Jennifer have been, as I have
hinted to you before, of an armed friendliness and
I doubt whether there will be many tears shed on
either side at parting.

The Cotton Riots at Manchester have been
I understand of a serious nature, houses have
been broken into, managers burnt in effigy and
many rioters lodged in jail.   The People are
making themselves more and more felt and I must

admit that they and their Cause have increasingly my Sympathy.   Jennifer is an Aristocrat of the Old School and would have every Rioter burnt at a public Stake.——Your loving

FRANCIS.

I am becoming good Friends with Mr. and Mrs. Southey and frequently visit them.

Mrs. Francis Herries of Uldale, Cumberland, to Mrs. Judith Paris, at Grosset Place, Wilts.

ULDALE, *Nov.* 10, 1809.

DEAR JUDITH——You will I fancy feel some sur-prize at receiving a letter from me, but indeed I would have written sooner had we not all been so occupied with the Jubilee which for my part I am most thankful that it is safely over.   You would not, however, have recognized your little Keswick. We had grand Fireworks above the Lake, an ox roasted whole in the Market Place and many other Diversions.

It is not however of the Jubilee that I wish to write to you.   I am Laziness personified and to write a Letter is always an agony to me so I will come sharp to the point.

It is this——that both Francis and myself wish that you should come and live with us.   It is plain enough that Francis should wish it——he has always wished it——and therefore I write myself that you may believe in my own independent desire for it. In honesty I discover that, since the departure of Deborah, the two children and the management of the House are more than I can properly sustain. But beyond this I will admit that I consider that it will be of advantage both to Francis and myself that you should be with us. I have grown unaccountably sluggish of late and so I fancy has he. In addition to these things I have a real wish that you should love me—something that may at this present seem to you quite impossible, but juxtaposition and a Good Will may work wonders.—I am, Your sincere friend,

JENNIFER HERRIES.

Judith Paris to Francis Herries, Esq.

GROSSET PLACE,
Nov. 15, 1809.

DEAREST FRANCIS—I have but now received a Truly Extraordinary Letter from Jennifer which I have answered as honestly as I may. You doubtless know of it. But what am I to say?

Of course I wish to come to you and Uldale. I have wished it all these years when I have been in sober truth a real Exile from my own country. I have developed a fondness for Carey and Maria and Phyllis. I would leave them perhaps for no one else in the world, but you have always been —save for Georges—first in the world to me and I would go anywhere to serve you. Also it is a Happiness to think that I must have the Care in some part of your Children.

But does Jennifer truly wish me to come? Have you not pushed her into that Letter? I must know this before I give any Answer. I had fancied that she had in her Heart no affection for me. I am myself not easy, love to dominate where I am, am often in terrible Rages and am haunted by the past. But you know this, dear Francis, and you know your wife. It seems to me that if I come and things go ill I may imperil all our Happiness. Yet the House at Uldale calls me like a living person. I cannot refuse if you assure me that it is Jennifer's wish as well as your own.— Your loving

JUDITH.

Francis Herries, Esq., to Judith Paris.

ULDALE, *Nov.* 19, 1809.

DEAREST JUDITH—Come. It is Jennifer's wish most certainly. Things are not too Happy here. You can help us to understand one another. Come. —Your loving

FRANCIS.

Judith Paris to Mrs. Emma Furze.

(Portion of a letter.)

GROSSET PLACE, WILTS.,
Nov. 29, 1809.

. . . If you can meet the Coach I shall be most happy. Farewells here are of a quite Tragic Description. Even young Carey weeps down the Barrel of his gun.

Oh Emma to what Adventure am I going?

My Life is built on that piece of ground. I have tried to shake myself free of it, but how fruitless was that effort I now know as I feel the excited beatings of my Heart. It may be that I am committing the supreme Folly of my Life. . . .

ULDALE AGAIN

'Let us walk up the hill,' Judith said to Francis.

They got down from the chaise and allowed it to draw slowly ahead of them. She put her arm through Francis'.

She was not going to tell him how frightened she was. This scene so amazingly familiar to her, the trees bright and bare so that the winter sun seemed to be shining in the heart of their branches, the thick soft carpet of leaves, the fresh sharp air with a breath of approaching snow in its stillness, all these were the friendly accompaniments of countless old winters. Soon, at the turn, the first houses of the village would appear, the black-smith's, the little house with the round bottle-green windows, and beyond them the first comfortable shoulder of the moor. All so familiar that they were part of her own blood, and yet her heart was beating with an almost agonising apprehension.

She wished now that she had not come. Oh! how she wished it! She had been safe there in Wiltshire, safe even though she had not been alive. Now the pain was sharp, as when the blood returns to a limb that has been numb.

At once, on her first sight of Francis in Keswick,

she had been sure that he was not the same. She had seen him before he had seen her; he had stood in front of the inn, slim and dark, slapping his thigh with his whip, looking sternly out into a forbidding world.

She had instinctively drawn her shawl more closely about her and shrunk back as though she would prevent him from seeing her. He had kissed her, put his arm about her, given her a hot drink, seen to her baggage and, through the drive out of Keswick along the familiar Carlisle Road, had been infinitely kind. It had been her own fault that she had been so helplessly constrained. He did not know that with every step Georges was approaching more closely to her. Georges, Georges . . .

But that cowardice she had foreseen, and with every strength in her character she had beaten it back. Then, in place of it, as they turned away from the Lake into the heart of the woods, the thought of Jennifer increasingly possessed her. Why had she come? Jennifer did not want her. She *could* not want her. She had yielded to Francis' entreaties, and now she thought that Francis did not want her either. It was true, in fact, that for Francis, too, there had been a little shock. When he had last seen Judith she had been a girl; now she was a woman, and, with that exceptional sensitiveness that was his curse as well as his blessing, he felt, at first sight of her, that she had become a woman whom he did not know.

This resolute, solid little person almost hidden

under her shawl and pelisse, her small white face looking out at him from her rose-coloured bonnet with such seriousness, was very different from the fire and impetuosity of his own familiar Judith. He had good reasons—there had from the first been many—for doubting the wisdom of this experiment and now he suffered a sudden panic, foreseeing every kind of trouble and even disaster. He had, Heaven knew, enough already!

So, while they rode, a silence fell between them.   Then, as they started on foot up the hill, she stopped, laid her hand on his arm, looked up into his face.

' I am frightened, Francis,' she said.   ' I feel as though I cannot go on.'

' I am frightened also,' he confessed.

They looked at one another.   Then she laughed, and it was as though a screen were rolled away, the old Judith of all his life was back again.

' Do you remember once when your father beat me and I climbed out of the window? '

He nodded, smiling.

' I thought then that I could never be frightened at anything.   I am wiser now. . . . I am frightened of Jennifer.'

It was he now who put his arm through hers, drawing her close to him.   They marched now steadily up the hill.

' There's no need to be,' he said.   ' You can do so much for Jennifer, Judith.   And for myself as well.   We are in a tangle.   You must clear it.'

'Do you think she will like me? Because if she does not—I can do nothing with anyone who dislikes me.'

'You must make her like you,' he answered. 'Everything hangs on that. She is proud, she has been spoilt by much admiration, for which she does not really care. She *could* be happy here. You can make her so.'

'Are you yourself happy?' She stopped again, looking up into his face.

'I, my dear?' He shrugged his shoulders. 'Have I ever been happy save for a moment or two? But I love her very dearly. I am not a wise man,' he added, lowering his voice as though he were speaking to himself, 'I have never been wise all my life. I killed my father. My mother hated me. It is not natural that I should be more fortunate with my wife.'

'I have come into a pretty business,' she thought. 'This will not be easy.'

But they had found one another again. Her resolution, obstinacy and common sense were all active now that she realised that there was something to be done. The dusk had fallen when they reached the house. She could see it only as a white ghost. The lights in the hall confused her, and it was a moment before she could realise that Jennifer was greeting her. Then she was almost shocked by Jennifer's beauty. It was a woman of forty who confronted her, but age here had nothing to say. Jennifer's loveliness came from her superb richness of colour and form. Her hair was dark with the darkness of clouded fire, when the flame is imprisoned by black shadow. Her skin had warmth in its ivory softness. She was very tall, a height that was emphasised by her high close dress with its waist just below the breasts, but her body was moulded by her maturity to a perfect fitness. She stood, her head up, her lovely neck and arms bare, save for a thin Cashmere purple shawl, as though she were receiving a deputation of loyal subjects. Only her eyes were a little sleepy, heavily lidded.

Judith had never in her life before felt so small, so insignificant. It was as though she were a servant coming for a place. She was weary, too, crowded about with old memories, homesick for she knew not what. But it was not her way to be beaten. Only, as on so many other occasions, she wished passionately that she were taller.

The thought in Jennifer's mind as she bent down to kiss her was: ' Well, I need not be afraid of this little thing.'

Jennifer moved into the little parlour that was thick, for Judith, with pressing memories. She recognised at once gratefully that it was not changed. That was Francis' doing. But also, with a flash of intuition, she realised that Jennifer must be lazy. She would have altered things if she had had a mind for that. Here was the old spinet with the roses on its lid, the music-box with the King in his amber coat and the Queen in her green dress; there was the carpet with the pictures of the Battle, the leaping horses

and the cannon firing. For how many years had it
been there—and yet it looked even fresher than
in earlier days. Best of all, here was the China
wallpaper with the blue and white pagodas, the
bridges, flowers and temples.

Jennifer helped her to take off her jacket and
bonnet.

' You must be weary.'

' Oh no, thank you'; but she was. She sat
down on the old brown sofa that was covered
with a pattern of red leaves and little rosy apples.
Francis had gone to see about the horses. She
and Jennifer were alone.

' Did you have an agreeable journey? '

' Yes. The weather was fine. We had only
one storm before Kendal.'

' You must rest now and take your ease.
Life is very quiet here.'

Judith thought: ' She talks as though I had
never been here before. I knew it before she
did.' She was in that nervous state of weariness
and loneliness that can rouse, very quickly, the
Devil, but she had already faced the Devil so
often in her life that it was easy to say to him
now, as she did, ' Lie down! '

She smiled. She could not help it. Jennifer
was so very beautiful.

' What lovely hair you have,' Jennifer said.

' It is sadly tumbled.'

' No, but you will want to go to your room.
I will show you.'

They went up the staircase down whose
banisters Judith had many times slid. That

was something at least that Jennifer had never done.   Jennifer moved upwards like a queen.

' I hope you will like this room,' she said, throwing open the door.

Oh heaven! it was Mrs. Monnasett's room, the room where once she had crept up to the bed and touched the cold body, searching for the little box. . . .

' I trust that you will be comfortable here,' Jennifer said, staring with her sleepy eyes about her.   ' If you need anything pray tell me.'

' I have known this room,' Judith said, also looking about her, ' all my life.'

The two women looked at one another— one swift appraising glance—and at once Judith knew it was going to be a battle.

' She is going to let me be happy here,' she thought, ' if I do what she tells me.'   Then there was the further thought: ' You've never done what anyone told you—except Georges.'

But she was so weary that she could have cried if she had been a woman accustomed to crying.   She was not.

' Thank you, dear Jennifer,' she said.   ' You are very amiable.'   She knew that Jennifer was thinking: ' I can manage *this* little thing.'

For several years after Georges' death the terrible time had been the night.   If she slept, one horrible dream after another swept over her; if she were awake, loneliness and remorse weighed down her heart.   Loneliness because Georges was not there, remorse because again and again

she asked herself whether she might not have
done something to prevent the calamity. Why
had she not driven the old man from the house,
driven him, with whips and scorpions? How
was it that she had submitted to his presence
so passively? It was as though he had cast a
spell.

What could she have done? What? What?
She tormented herself day after day, night after
night. Then as the years had passed quiet sleep
had come back to her. She was not one to bewail
the past. She had her new life to make. But
during the years in London and Wiltshire there
had been no life. It had been as though she had
walked in her sleep. Now with one step into
the lighted hall to-night life had swept back to
her. Contact was made again.

She woke in old Mrs. Monnasett's four-poster
and looked about her trying to penetrate the
darkness. It seemed that she could. Georges
was alive again and at her side, and said with his
old reckless impudence: 'Soon we'll have this
house in our hand.'

So, leaning her head on his breast, she went
happily to sleep. In the morning she met the
two children, John aged two, Dorothy aged one,
in the charge of a fat beetle-browed woman, Mrs.
Ponder. Judith knew at once that this was a
bad, ill-disposed servant who was resolved to defy
her. John was a square-made, sturdy child with
the high Herries horse-bones and light blue eyes
that reminded her of David. There seemed to
be no nonsense about him at all. Dorothy was

small and dark and nervous.   She hid herself in
Mrs. Ponder's dress.

Judith loved children and had a swift power
over them, perhaps because she was herself little
and was amused by small things that seemed,
however, to her important.

For John the only thing that mattered on that
day when Judith first saw him was that Matt the
stableman had made a ship for him and would
take him later to the Tarn to sail it.   As soon as
he discovered that Judith also wished to see the
sailing of the ship, she became part of his world
and was never again outside it.   He did not as
yet talk a great deal, but expressed his emotions
with wriggles of the body and small stern
frowns.

'Pray, ma'am,' said Mrs. Ponder, 'do not
permit the child to be a worrit.'

'I care for children extremely,' answered
Judith quickly, looking straight at Mrs. Ponder's
black eyebrows.   'To be quite honest, I do not
think I can live without them.'

'That is very well, ma'am,' said Mrs. Ponder,
who was a woman of one idea at a time.   'But
he must not be a worrit.'

Dorothy was another matter.   Baby though
she was, she was already nervous, suspicious and
reserved.   Mrs. Ponder was her only haven.
When Judith came near to her she screamed,
which pleased Mrs. Ponder very much indeed.

Indeed everything that occurred on this first
day after Judith's arrival contained the signs and
portents of the struggle—a struggle that involved

the fates of all of them, and of many more beside them—that was to come. The prophecy of the walk up the hill had been a correct one.

Snow fell all day, snow most unusual for that time of the year, soft, feathery, gentle, at first not lying, then, as the day sharpened, lying with a silver radiance over all the world.

It always seemed to Judith afterwards that she gathered in her complete and final knowledge of Jennifer in that first winter afternoon. They sat after dinner in the parlour, drinking their tea, the two of them one on either side of the fire, where the logs crackled and hissed, the only sound save the gently whispering clock.

Jennifer sat very straight, working at a piece of silver embroidery. Erect, her splendid body, with its soft rounded arms, its swelling breasts, its crown of dark, slumbering hair, gave an odd impression of being on guard. Often Judith was in the future to notice that Jennifer's body seemed to have a life apart from the brain that directed it. Jennifer's brain, she was to discover, was not active. It moved very slowly from point to point and there stayed obstinately without stirring. It was not an animal brain at all— something quite other—but her body was entirely animal, wanted only to be cared for. That was why, perhaps, Jennifer was not conceited and minded nothing at all when her body was admired; why, too, men had deserted her at the moment of crisis.

But if she was not conceited she was intensely proud. She had all the pride of a woman who has no imagination, the most fundamental pride of all because the owner of it cannot look outside and make comparisons. Her pride had its origin in the fact that she was a Herries (though but a portion of one), and in the fact that she had a father and mother who thought her perfect.

She did not admire herself because they thought her perfect, but admired *them* for that reason, and her pride was all the greater.

There were things that Judith, as she sat by the fire on that first day, wanted to know. First how so gloriously beautiful a creature, who might (so Judith, rather simply and very modestly, thought) have had all London on its knees, could stay year after year in this little distant country place; secondly, whether or no Jennifer loved Francis; thirdly, why Jennifer had asked her, Judith, to come.

Before the hour by the fire was over, Judith had discovered the answer to the three questions. First—Jennifer liked the country better than the town because Herries were of more social value in the country, because she had always lived out of London and was a woman of habit, but in chief because she was lazy. The country demanded less energy than the town.

Second—she did not love Francis in any sense that Judith understood the word. But—she was lazy. That might explain it.

Third—she had asked Judith because, after Deborah was gone, there was too much to do. A housekeeper was impertinent. Judith, to whom, in Jennifer's judgement (she repeated this several times), Francis was quite devoted, would please

Q

Francis and keep him quiet. In short she had invited Judith because—she was lazy.

'Pray come nearer to the fire. It is monstrously cold.'

'Thank you. And is Deborah comfortable with her Squire?'

'I believe so indeed, as much as one may be comfortable in this world.'

She raised her slumbering eyes, lifted her white hand on which a great ring with a deep crimson stone glittered, to shield her face from the fire, and said: 'Are we to be friends, Judith?'

Judith bent forward, giving her glance for glance.

'I trust so. It is my own most earnest wish.'

'You will be on my side sometimes?'

'Your side?'

'Yes. You were not on my side in that most unseemly quarrel in London many years ago.'

'I was then quite unformed. . . . And Christabel was then my friend. You were not.'

'Yes, we were young then. I wonder. Is it wise—do you think—that we have met again?'

Judith answered gravely. 'It is for yourself to decide.'

Jennifer's body became more active. You could see the life stirring through it, as still water is suddenly moved by a breeze.

'Are you passionate?'

'I beg your pardon?'

'Are you passionate? With that hair you should be. I hear that you have a temper that

can be monstrously roused.   I should like to see
it.'

Judith laughed.

'There is time enough,' she said.   Moved by
a quick impulse and because she wished always
to be friends if it were possible (she could be an
enemy very easily if that was wanted), she went over
to Jennifer, bent across her chair and kissed her.
To her own surprise Jennifer put up her arm and
with her soft warm hand drew Judith closer,
kissing her again.

'It is by far more comfortable to be friends,'
she said.

But was it Jennifer's body that had kissed her—
or Jennifer?

That evening Jennifer, Judith and Francis sat
in the parlour.   The little clock with the china
dairymaid struck.   Jennifer rose, stretched her
arms, threw up her lovely head.   Her eyes were
almost closed.   She seemed to be tasting some
delicious food or smelling a marvellous scent.

'I am sleepy.   I shall go to bed.'   She moved,
slowly, majestically, to the door.   She turned towards them, showing a sleepy smile.   She yawned.

'Good-night,' she said.

After a little silence Francis said: 'I am so
happy that you are here, dear Judith.   Jennifer
likes you already.'

'Do you think so?   I am afraid that at first
I shall be needlessly troublesome.   In time things
will settle themselves.'

'Is it strange to you to come back here?'   He
looked at her with eyes of deep affection.   Now

he had regained his old Judith. It was true that on the outside this was almost a middle-aged woman who sat near to him, a woman, too, who had known the most bitter unhappiness, who had suffered years of the harshest loneliness, but there was there also the child with the light of humour in her eyes, with her pugnacity, eagerness and acceptance of adventure.

'Strange?' She looked into the fire. 'No. But, Francis, with what passion I love this house. I had not forgotten it—no, not a table nor a chair, not a print nor a carpet, and the garden, the high wall, every branch of every tree. But I had not known that I would be so touched by it, nor that it would lead me on into the country beyond it. *My* country. . . .' She laughed. 'Perhaps it will be wisest in me to check my feelings while I can; I am determined against too much enthusiasm. In an old woman it is an absurdity.'

'An old woman!' he said fondly. 'Why, Judith, you are not changed.'

'No,' said Judith. 'When I was in my room this evening after dinner and pressed my nose against the pane, standing a little on my toes, just as I did when I was a child, I could see nothing but the snow falling through the darkness. Nevertheless, the country crowded about me— Scarness, Bowscale, Calva, Blackhazel, Mungrisdale.' She said the names like a spell. 'And so leading to Watendlath, which I must face if I am ever to have any peace here. On the first fair day I shall ride over to Watendlath.'

'Why, Judith,' he said, 'you are a poet.'

'Part of me is a poet, and the other part, I fear, most unpoetical.'

He sighed and stretched his long, thin legs to the fire, rubbing his hands in his hair. 'I also. Part poet, and the useless part, the only part for which I have any care. We are a strange family. It seems that the Dreamer must always destroy the Man of Deeds, and so either way you fail. Your father let the practical go and was called a madman. My own father was ultimately all practical and faded spiritually away. Will has always been for the practical—he has never known a conflict and is become a money-bag. There is Reuben who has rejected the practical and is saved, maybe, by his Maker. And you and I, Judith—our fates are yet undecided. But it would be a subject for an Epic, this Herries struggle, with a changing England behind it. Which is real? Is there a soul? Are we for ever to be exiles from our true country? All my life I have been like a man wandering down a road that leads nowhere.'

'You should ask Mr. Southey these things. He is a poet.'

'I have asked him. He is sure of his destiny. His answer is in his books and his family. I never knew a man more confident. But his brother-in-law, Mr. Coleridge, has more genius, and so is more lost. . . .' He drove his fist on to his knee. 'Judith, I must lose myself in something greater than myself. That is the only answer.'

'And your marriage?' She asked at length the question that had been hovering between them all day.

'My marriage is a failure, a damnable, pernicious failure. How could it have been otherwise? Jennifer never loved me. She has never loved anyone. When she dismissed Beaminster she was frightened of her old age and she liked me better than the others. So she took me. And she has done her best with me. But there is a devil of selfishness in her. In a country life some sort of selfishness is, I conceive, a necessity. I also am selfish. But our selfishnesses—hers and mine—do not coincide.'

He stopped. Then went on eagerly, 'Judith, I say these things because all our lives we have been frank with one another, but also since you must live here you must understand what the situation is.'

'Yes,' she said. 'What is the situation?'

'I am as crazy for Jennifer as ever I was. She has a terrible physical spell over me. In a while you will feel it right through the house— the spell of her body. I care for her, too, in other ways; I have a great tenderness, sometimes an almost unspeakable longing to make her happy. And so long as she is comfortable she is happy, but let her comfort once be disturbed and the whole house is wretched.

'She is pure Herries, the unimaginative practical sort. Had she energy she would be the feminine Will of the family, turning everything to practical profit, but she has none and she wants none. She does not love me but she loves no one, not her parents nor her children. But she is proud of everything that is hers, myself as well.

She will quickly be proud of you if you serve her.
If you do not—'

' Yes—if I do not?'

' She will fight you until you do. And she
has many strange weapons. . . .' He went
on after a pause. ' I had thought when I asked
her to marry me that what she would not be able
to endure would be the quiet and silence here.
That she would be restless here, want people
that would entertain her, admire her. But that
has been the slightest of the trouble. She has
settled here like a cat by the fire so long as she is
comfortable.'

' Then why,' asked Judith slowly, ' did you
ask me here? If she is comfortable . . .'

' I had to have you, Judith. I had to. It is
turning me mad, this life here. It is not that
I have not much to do. I have learnt much of
the estate. I have grown a wise countryman.
Things are prosperous here. I buy land, sell
cattle. So far I have conquered my dreams.
But I love her and despise her. I love her and
despise myself. I know that she does not care
for me, that my children do not care for me. I
am in touch with no one here. And therefore
I had to send for you. For the last three years I
have had this longing, but beat it down. Now
it has been too strong for me.'

Judith felt her heart leap. She had loved
Francis all her life and at last her reward had
come. He needed her and had told her so.
This was perhaps the first moment of true happiness that she had had since Georges' death.

But she showed no emotion.

'Yes, but if we care for one another—brother and sister as we are, although, Francis, I am in reality your aunt, you know—what will Jennifer say?'

'There we must be on our guard. I do not know how it will affect Jennifer. If she is against it she will use every weapon to be rid of you.'

'She thinks,' said Judith, 'that I am a meek little thing. I saw it in her eyes to-night. But I am not. Francis, now that I have come, I cannot go again. Nothing can turn me out. I am resolved. This is my country, my home . . . even if Jennifer hates me.'

'You have no true realisation,' he said slowly, 'of Jennifer's obstinacy.'

But she was astonished at herself. She felt rising in her breast a resolved determination on power. That other self—not the self that at her window behind the falling snow had in the gloaming traced every rise and fall of the fell, the peaked line of Skiddaw, the thin haze of the Scottish hills; but the self that had conquered Georges and these last terrible thirteen years, this obstinate self—was moving her forward to this new conquest.

She would make them all love her, Jennifer, children, servants, even the dogs. But—if they would not love her—then they should obey her. But for Francis she felt an infinite tenderness. She got up and knelt in front of the fire by his chair. She did not touch him. She

would never again kneel by a man to embrace
him. That had been for Georges alone. But
she turned to him, looking at him with so much
sweetness that his heart was comforted as it had
never been since the day of his marriage.

'Francis,' she said, 'in the way of love I
shall never care for any man again, but in the way
of ourselves, of all our lives, I love you most
dearly. And I will win a victory here.'

He was about to put a hand to her. He
stopped and listened.

'Hush,' he said. 'I thought I heard a door
opening.'

But there was no sound. The door was fast
closed.

PAYING A CALL ON MRS. SOUTHEY

OPENING the door of her bedroom on a fine July afternoon, intending to prepare for her visit to Mrs. Southey, Judith stood frozen to the wall.

In the far corner of the room could be seen the broad, ill-shapen back of Mrs. Ponder, its calico covering spread to its utmost as she bent over the drawer of the little spindle-legged escritoire near the window. In these drawers were Judith's papers and personal odds and ends—old letters, legal documents, programmes of dances and concerts, ribbons and faded flowers.

Most of these were now scattered about the floor while Mrs. Ponder, in furious haste and grunting like a pig, burrowed ever deeper.

'Yes,' said Judith. 'Good afternoon.' She had always hated the woman; from the very first she had detested her, and now there was such a rage beating in her throat that she had a most childish impulse to rush across the room and seize the woman by the neck and shake her head off.

Mrs. Ponder's back jumped, then straightened itself; then Mrs. Ponder's pasty-faced, beetle-browed countenance turned round, terror braced by defiance appeared in it.

' Yes, Mrs. Ponder? ' Judith said again, her voice small and quivering in her anger.

' I was straightening things, ma'am,' the woman answered in her sulky, deep-toned voice, ' helping to keep your drawers tidy.'

' You are not paid, I think, to keep my drawers tidy.'

Mrs. Ponder was recovering her self-command. She had thought that she was safe enough, had just time enough. What ill luck that the little soft-footed, prying thing should come creeping up five minutes too soon! Oh well! she wasn't going to be put down by this red-haired left-over of a thief and a vagabond. She knew what she knew.

She put one hand on her hip.

' Excuse me, ma'am. I cannot say I am sure what I am paid for and what I am not paid for, only to do my duty, I should suppose.'

' And is it your duty to decipher my personal letters? '

' I do not know what you mean, ma'am, by deciphering. I was intending for the best.'

' You are very obliging, but it is a dangerous precedent, Mrs. Ponder, as I think you will find. Leave this room! It will not, I trust, be long before you leave this house.'

The woman came forward. She was half of a mind to have her say. It was a year and a bit since this French Madame (for Mrs. Ponder, like many another, confused facts when she wished to) had come to the house interfering and disturbing. She, Mrs. Ponder, had hated her from the first.

She would like to say now all the things that she knew and had picked up from gossip. What was she after all? The daughter of some road gipsy who had married a thief killed in a cheap scramble. If it were not for the Master, poor silly fool, she would not be here another day, with her red hair and standing on her toes to make herself taller! Mrs. Jennifer didn't want her, that was plain enough. And then she was alienating the children. The little boy had never been the same since her coming. . . . Mad she was, going off bareback with no hat on her head all the way to Caldbeck! Mad, as her rascal of a father had been, so she had heard, before her.

All these things Mrs. Ponder would have liked to say, but there was something about Judith, something both in her rage and her dignity, that frightened the woman against her will.

She was about to go through the door when Judith stopped her: ' Why did you do this? For what were you looking? '

' I, ma'am? Looking? . . . Why, for nothing, I assure you.'

' Nonsense. Of course you had some purpose.'

Judith stepped forward, and Mrs. Ponder, thinking she was going to strike her, retreated.

' No. I would not touch you. You are a bad servant. You have always been one. You will leave this house in the morning.'

' That is for my mistress to say.'

Yes. It was true. The woman was right.

But Jennifer would not hesitate. After such a thing as this!

'I cannot understand what it was that you wanted. Pray inform me.' The disgust in Judith's eyes was more insulting than the anger. Mrs. Ponder would not quickly forget it. But, for the moment, it would be better to withdraw. So she withdrew.

After she was gone Judith sat in her chair considering. They were to go to take tea with Mrs. Southey at Greta Hall, she, Jennifer and Francis. She had come up to put on her bonnet. But she must speak to Jennifer before they went. She could not calmly join in the social amenities of the Southeys while this was raging in her breast. To break open her drawer and read her letters! There were packets of letters from Georges there. . . . Oh, it was monstrous, it was impossible! The insolence of the woman. But she would go at once—that was one good thing. The affair would have a good issue, for the woman had been always impossible, and now there would be a fine reason for her dismissal. Jennifer would not hesitate. Of course, she would not. Judith's heart seemed to stop a beat. Jennifer was so strange a woman. They had been friendly enough during these twenty months. She had been delighted for Judith to take the house in her hands; she had given her free rein. But Judith knew her no better than on that first evening.

She could not any more now than then say whether it were War or Peace. The time had

gone so swiftly; there had been so much to do—
the house to order, the servants to watch, the
children to care for, Francis to make comfortable,
new neighbours to know, and sometimes—twice
or thrice—strange sudden expeditions into the
mountains, to Watendlath, to Newlands, once so
far as Ennerdale, when another life altogether
had stirred and moved, a life that was not dead,
although it was given so little freedom. The
time had gone, Judith had even been happy
because of Francis, because of the children, because the neighbours were kind, and chiefly
because this house and the little village and the
Moor were all hers. From Iredale to Caldbeck,
from Threlkeld to Mungrisdale it was hers.
And so, because of all these things, the central
situation, the pivot upon which everything else
turned, the relationship between herself and
Jennifer, had never been examined.

But it had been growing; all the while it was
growing. As she sat there, beside her bed,
looking at the dove-grey bonnet that lay upon
it, she suddenly shivered. *What* was Jennifer
thinking? Had Jennifer. . . ? And at the very
suspicion of that thought, she, to whom honesty
and cleanliness and fair dealing were the first
rules of life, sprang indignantly from her chair.
Oh no! that was monstrous. . . . Monstrous. . . .
But she must go, at once, *at once*, and speak to
Jennifer.

So down she went, and the first thing that
she saw was the fat, handsome, sensuous face of
Captain Fernyhirst in the hall. Captain Ferny-

hirst lived near Caldbeck.   He had bought, only
last year, old Uncle Tom's house, Stone Ends.
He had a pale, ill wife there and two lanky children.
And he was an admirer and friend of Jennifer's.

He was a fine upstanding man with a broad
back and stout legs.   His eyes were too small,
his nose a trifle too large, but he looked elegant
in his green coat, his hair curling above his ears,
his spurred heels spread, yes, as though he owned
the house and everything in it.

They were a handsome pair, a very handsome
pair.   He greeted Judith with the courteous
patronage that he always used to her.   He said
something about the weather, and went.   Jennifer was dressed in green and white, her lovely
hair falling in thick ringlets on her bare neck.
Very lovely, Judith thought, was her hair, parted
in the middle of her fair smooth forehead, combed
towards the sides, falling in curls that seemed to
hold in their dark shadows a strange, steely lustre.

'Very lovely hair,' thought Judith, 'but I
wonder whether Mrs. Ponder . . .'   She was in
fact too angry to wait, as she should have done,
for a more favourable opportunity, and in that
lost an important chance of commanding the
situation.

Impetuously she led the way into the parlour.

'Jennifer, I must speak to you.'

'My dear . . . but we are late, and Mrs. Southey
is most punctilious. . . .'

Slowly she followed Judith in.

'Jennifer, Mrs. Ponder must be dismissed.
At once.   To-night.'

' And why? '

' I caught her, now, five minutes back; I went to my room and she was searching my drawers. My papers were scattered about the floor.'

It was not Jennifer's way to speak quickly. It was as though slowly and with practised deliberation she sent a message through all her tall body that it must be prepared for a set of circumstances, that there was no haste required . . . plenty of time.

She sat down, put her hand to her hair, looked out of window.

' Well, Judith, I must inquire. Mrs. Ponder is an admirable servant. She was perhaps making tidy your effects.'

' Making tidy my effects? But who is she to make my things tidy? It is not her business. She had no place in my room. No, indeed. She was making nothing tidy. She was spying.'

' Spying? What is there for her to spy into? '

' Nothing, of course. I have nothing to hide.' Then amazement, increased by her anger, seized her. ' But, Jennifer—are you not yourself indignant? Do you understand what it is? She was *spying*! The woman was in my room, my letters were on the floor. Letters. Letters from my husband . . .' Her voice broke. She was very near to tears.

' Well, it shall be inquired into. I am convinced that you have judged too hastily. It *is* your weakness, Judith. You act too immediately on the impulse of the moment. . . .'

'*My* fault! My fault!' Judith broke in. 'But, Jennifer, I cannot understand! You appear to be blaming *me*! Do you hear what I said? That Mrs. Ponder was discovered by me tossing my private papers about the floor, her hands among my effects. She did not deny it. She could not. She was most insolent. She must go . . . must leave . . . at once, to-morrow morning. You must tell her so. A fine thing to have in the house, a servant who opens drawers and carries her secrets, I have no doubt, to the kitchen-maids and the grooms. You cannot hesitate. Francis would insist. . . .'

She pulled up. For her life she wished that she had not spoken those last words. Her rage had carried her away. The very thought of the woman's ugly thick back and the packets of Georges' letters. . . . But she should not have mentioned Francis. Was she never to learn?

In the short silence that followed, the place seemed to fill with the summer scents, the radiant sun floated the room with shadows of gold. Some man called to his horse, wheels creaked on the road. Then Jennifer spoke:

'Yes. . . . It was I who asked Ponder to search your drawer.'

She looked at Judith, and Judith looked back at her. Judith's pale face slowly flushed. This was an incredible thing. It was as though the spinet had leapt through the ceiling, or the little rosy apples on the sofa had rolled like little live bullets about the floor. An incredible thing. To Judith, in spite of the many events that had been her lot, the most astonishing, the most dumb-founding of them all.

'You . . . told her?'

'Yes. I wished to know what you were writing of me to London.'

'I . . . to London?'

'Indeed, yes. To dear Will and Christabel, who have so true an affection for me.'

'And so . . . you thought that such dishonest behaviour was in my character—that while I lived here and was your friend I would write . . .' She broke off. All words failed her. The sun had died from the room, which was grey in her eyes and chill.

'But why not? We must have common sense. When you first came here I hoped that we should form a friendship, but you had other ideas. You were determined to be mistress here. You alien-ated my husband, my children, my servants. I was well assured that your friends in London must have the benefit of your experience. Why not? If I had had your ambitions I should have doubtless done the same.'

'You thought that? I have been here for more than a year. All this while you have fancied me indulging in such treachery; you have known me so little that you suspected *such* things in my conduct? Why, then . . . why, then . . . if your mind has been of such a colour, you must have hated me! . . . And I thought that we were friends. For a year I have suspected nothing. And you have made your servant spy on me. . . .'

She was shaking, quivering with rage, astonishment, but also with a dreadful miserable unhappiness that seemed to strike deep into her very soul. All her life long, through every difficulty and distress, she had been supported always by her sense of her own integrity and the conviction that everyone thought her honest. She had not had pride in that, but it had been her comfort; whatever else went, that remained. And now—to be charged with such treachery and to be hated when she had thought that she was cared for.

Her lip quivered. If she wept now it would be a humiliation for which she would never forgive herself.

Steadying her voice she said quietly: ' I have never suffered any disloyalty to you, Jennifer, in myself or another. I had thought we were friends and so acted. You have wronged me,' and left the room.

Once in her own place any tendency to tears was gone. Tears! No, indeed! She walked the floor like a raging little animal in a cage. The letters, papers, ribbons were still scattered about, where Mrs. Ponder had left them. Mechanically, without knowing it, she bent down and put them back and closed the drawers. She remained, kneeling there, looking in front of her.

Her immediate impulse was, as it had always been in every crisis of her life, to take some dramatic action instantly—to find Francis, to tell him what had occurred, without either self-defence or accusation of anyone, and then to depart—to be, as swiftly as possible, as far from Jennifer as the world allowed her. But very quickly her temper

cooled. Her intelligence reasserted itself. There
was more in this than a vulgar quarrel. The
whole of her own past life was in it, her father, her
mother; the whole of the Herries family was in it,
for what she was meeting now in Jennifer was the
thing in the Herries blood that her father, herself,
Francis, Reuben, Georges had always been fighting
—the unimaginative, calm, self-assured obstinacy
and confidence.

At that she knew that she was herself now
calmer. She rose from her knees and, as she
looked about the room, realised something with
an absolute certainty of its truth, as though someone had whispered it in her ear. Jennifer had
intended this quarrel. She did not hate Judith.
Hatred was an emotion unknown to her sluggishness. She had decided—perhaps some while
back—that Judith made her uncomfortable and
that Judith must go. Francis would never allow
her to go, unless there were some very obstinate
reason or unless Judith herself was provoked to
it. She must provoke Judith or she must find a
reason. In all probability she was smiling now
quietly to herself, thinking that she had succeeded.

At that Judith flung up her head and swore
that whatever occurred she would not go. This
was her place, and here she would stay. She could
be as obstinate as Jennifer, yes, and more obstinate.

There was a knock on the door, and opening
it she found Francis there. The carriage was
ready. Jennifer was ready. He was smiling,
had no consciousness that there had been any
trouble. She looked at him and smiled too.

She was there to make Francis happy, and make him happy she would, Jennifer or no Jennifer. She put on her bonnet and shawl and went down with him.

' I like the grey bonnet,' he said.

' I had it in Carlisle,' she said, ' a month ago.'

Jennifer, in her fine green and white bombasine dress and an ostrich feather in her bonnet, stood by the carriage, the moors undulating in hummocks and pools of green on every side of her. She smiled as they came towards her.

' Dear Judith,' she said, ' what a charming bonnet!'

So it was all bonnets, and a more agreeable trio, sitting behind the immense back of Fred the coachman, could surely not be found in Keswick. Francis might complain that Will made the money and that he was a failure, but nevertheless things were very comfortable at Uldale. That land that they had bought towards Caldbeck was turning out very well, and, in spite of the unsettled times, the shares in the Liverpool shipping business were for ever improving. And, in a year, Judith had brought the house to a fine discipline. Mrs. Harper, the housekeeper, a widow from Carlisle, was an excellent woman. Jennifer herself was not at all extravagant. Whatever she wore seemed to be beautiful on her. She had no great taste for entertaining. An occasional little dinner with cards afterwards, a Ball at Christmas. No magnificence even then. Ten couples at the most. Yes, new bonnets could be afforded. They were very generous to Judith or, at least, Francis was. His allowance was most generous. She had never had so much in all her life before; never been so comfortable. . . . Comfortable? A glance across at Jennifer on the opposite seat, and it was as though everything sinister and destructive thickened the summer air.

To be charged with such malice and deceit, to be suspected of the basest treachery. . . .

'They say that Mr. Coleridge dislikes his wife extremely and will never again return to Keswick. He goes often, I believe, to visit Mr. Wordsworth in Grasmere. . . . How cool the woods are! . . . The Southeys always seem to me very pleasant people; Judith, my dear, if the sun is too hot you must change places with me. You know that I am never disturbed by the heat.'

She was not. She basked in it, or like a great bird of brilliant plumage bathed her feathers in it, letting the light strike gold and emerald and sapphire from her loveliness.

' Edith Southey,' said Francis, ' is a very pretty-behaved child, very pretty-behaved, indeed. And little Hartley, Coleridge's boy, is most unusual. But, of course, he is growing now. He must be fifteen, at least. He is at school at Ambleside. Yes, this is a most beautiful day; the air is exceptionally warm.'

Francis was happy to-day. He was always pleased when he was going to see Mr. Southey. That she should set her servant on to spy and then, without a tremor, admit it. . . . How lovely that rather selfish droop of her mouth and the faint warm glow of her cheek, and the softness of her eyes as they looked out so calmly under their heavy lids! . . . The falseness! That Judith had tried to alienate the children! John loved her. That was not Judith's fault. And he was uneasy with his mother. He knew, as children always know, that she did not in her heart care for him. Or did she care? Who could tell for whom she cared?

'Look, Judith, how blue the Lake is! There is not a ripple.'

Yes, she had thought that she had got her way, and that in a week Judith would be gone. She was wrong. As they approached Keswick the air was rich with the scent of the summer flowers. July and August are the bad months for this country. There is rain, everything is heavily green without variety. But days come like this one when all the trees, larch and birch and fir and oak, are so deeply shadowed and so highly lit that fire runs from stem to stem, melting into cloud and climbing into swift eddies of green smoke. If only there are clouds in the sky the hills lie waiting to receive the shadows that slip like birds from shoulder to shoulder. The clouds have a great richness in this month, so proudly filled with white light that they quiver with their intensity, throwing paths of ghostly radiance on to the Lakes that are blue, here and there ruffled darkly like tarnished silver. On such a day the richness of the English scene, when the hay burns in the nostrils and every cottage garden has the dusky odour of snapdragon and sweet-william, is immortal. One summer's day is enough for memory to be enriched for ever.

Keswick was so small a country town that in
the summer its gardens dominated all the rest.
Greta Hall is at the entrance to it from the Carlisle
side, and once they had crossed the little bridge
they were almost there, but Judith could smell the
flowers mingling with the soft friendliness of the
cut hay that lay on the open fields.

She could see the peace of the town, the
farmers' carts, Mr. Probus the Apothecary standing at his door enjoying the sun, two young
ladies laughing as they came out of Mrs. Gray's,
the bonnet shop, old Mr. Fordyce the anti-
quarian, who was said to sleep half the year on the
Roman Wall, with his snuff-coloured wig and
old-fashioned breeches. As the carriage turned
up the drive she thought: ' It will take more than
Jennifer's insults to drive me away from this.'

This was Judith's first visit to the Southeys.
Mrs. Coleridge and Mrs. Southey had been to
Uldale. They were quiet, comfortable women;
certainly Mrs. Southey was a comfortable woman.
About Mrs. Coleridge one could not be so sure;
there were lines of discomfort about her mouth,
restlessness in her eyes. You could see that they
were sisters and had lived for most of their lives
together.

Yes, the house was charming, a nursery garden
on the right as they climbed the hill; then you
could see an orchard with plum trees and apple
trees behind the house. They were admitted by
a cheerful motherly-looking woman, who con-
ducted them into the parlour on the left of the
passage. They waited in the parlour, gathered

together in a kind of attitude of defence as
people are when they are awaiting their hostess.

This was a charming room, with a large green
shaped like a horse-shoe in front of the window.
The room was comfortably furnished with old
furniture, shabby but friendly. There were
pictures on the wall—one really dreadful painting
of a staring doll-like Mrs. Coleridge.

Mrs. Southey came in. There were greetings
all round, words about the splendid weather,
about the hay, the crops, being tired, not being
tired, being hot, not being hot. But they must
all come upstairs to Mr. Southey's room. That
was where tea would be. So upstairs they all went.

Oh! this was a wonderful room, so light, so
well-proportioned, so airy! And the views were
fine. Were the views not fine? They were
indeed. The room had three windows. The
large one that looked down upon the green and
the flower-beds and away to the Lake and the
mountains, the two smaller ones whence you
could see the lower part of the town.

The room was lined with books, and there
were splendid volumes bound in vellum lying in
heaps on the floor. And the family portraits
on the wall; before long Judith knew who they
all were—Mr. and Mrs. Southey by Downman,
little Edith Southey and little Sara Coleridge
by that fine artist Mr. Nash; the other three
Southey children, Kate, Isabel and Bertha, also
by Mr. Nash.

Much good furniture, Mr. Southey's writing-
table piled with books and papers, a screen, a

desk. The room was decorated in quiet dignified tones, the curtains of French grey merino,
the furniture covered with some buff colour.
A noble room, the room of a poet, lit now with
the summer sun, and all the summer sounds
mingling beyond the open window.

It was, in fact, Mr. Southey himself who showed
Judith the portraits and then some of his books.
At first she thought him a little alarming with
his dark hair, his grave features, the dignified,
rather remote way he had of moving, a little as
though, she wickedly fancied, he were carrying
the offertory plate in church. He was at first
the official host, cold and ceremonial. He held
up his head as though he knew it was a fine one;
she thought that he certainly was aware that he
was an important personage. She fancied, too,
on their first arrival, that he had thrown an impatient glance or two at his writing-table, where
his papers lay, as though he wished his visitors
very far away. And he certainly had no idea as to
who she was; he took care to give her no name
lest he should be in error. She thought that he had
difficulty sometimes in seeing her at all and would
have spoken with the same grave courtesy if she
vanished; he would not know that she had gone.

And then, when they moved to the large
window, he became entirely another person.
When he spoke of this country, this country that
she loved as dearly as he, his voice thrilled, his
face was lit, his black hair flung back.

'You know it is hard for me to speak of these
things. When I first came to Keswick I assured

myself that I should never settle down without a
violet—no violet and no nightingale.   But now
I have long forgot those losses.   My brother
Tom was settled in the valley of Newlands, and
I would not like to confess to you how we have
been, the two of us, our childish behaviour.
And now with my own children there is no stone
or leaf of Walla Crag or Watendlath that we do
not know.'   (Watendlath—a quiver at the word
touched her and fled.)   'And with my books—
my books.   Are you yourself a bookworm?   If
so you see in front of you the most impassioned
of your clan.   Let me show you——'   He waved
his hand and, eagerly walking to the bookcase,
began to pull out volumes for her.   'Have you
been ever in Portugal?   Do you know Portugal?
What! you have never seen Cintra! . . .   And
is Verbeyst an unknown name to you?   Verbeyst
of Brussels.   He has three hundred thousand
volumes.   Do you know what it is to open a
chest of books?   What are you going to find?
. . . No, let me show you this—*The Revela-
tions of St. Bridget*.   See, not only are the initial
letters illuminated, but every capital through the
volume is coloured. . . . Fuller's *Church History*.
. . . Is not Sir Thomas Browne a favourite with
you? . . .' A small tortoise-shell cat came and
rubbed its back against his leg.

He was quivering now like a boy.   His
hands shook, his face was all smiles.   Then
ruefully laughing at himself: 'Ah, I am for ever
making collections.   It is foolish, is it not, for
who will read them if I do not, and they arrive

more swiftly than even I can peruse them.　Time!
Time!　Why are the days not twice as long and
the nights four times!　Come, I must not weary
you, but I can see that you have a fancy yourself
this way.　You have a fancy, have you not? you
have a library?　I hope that you have a library.'
He smiled at her so friendlily and his eyes were so
kind that she wished that they could be examining
books for ever.

At tea, seated in a half-circle, Mr. Southey,
Mrs. Coleridge, pretty Edith Southey, Mrs.
Southey behind the tea-table, they were all very
gay.　Judith had often noticed that when at
parties Jennifer was present, everything went
well.　People were delighted with her beauty.
Shadows and shapes of loveliness seemed to
radiate from her passivity and composure.　Then,
being so beautiful, people assumed that she would
be haughty and proud.　But when she was anywhere the first thing that she did was to secure
her comfort and, as she was always the most
beautiful person present, she was always the first
to be offered a seat, food, drink, whatever it
might be.　So, assured that she had all that
she needed, she was as amiable as anything,
listened with apparent attention to everyone's
stories (although Judith suspected that she never
heard a word of them).　There was, however,
always a sense of thunder behind the calm.
When suddenly out of her comfort she might,
Judith thought, snap something in her fingers,
even as on that old historic occasion she had
snapped Christabel's fan.

But on an afternoon like to-day's she was entirely at her ease. She had had a fight and, as she thought, won it. She had been increasingly uncomfortable during the last six months; now that cause of that discomfort would be removed. Then the weather was hot, which she greatly preferred. Then the Southeys were reputable people; she had herself never read any of Mr. Southey's long poems, but she knew that they were generally respected. What she liked was for the Herries to be gracious and condescending to families that were worthy of graciousness. The Southeys, she thought, were really worthy. Then Francis was happy here; he could here indulge his ridiculous passion for literature; and, although she only cared as to whether he were happy or no because when he was unhappy his sulkiness made her a little uncomfortable, yet, in warm weather like this, she preferred that everyone should pass a pleasant hour.

And lastly there was that little pushing nonentity Judith, who had been this very day told her place and at whom therefore it was agreeable, once and again, to look.

All in all, Jennifer that afternoon was very comfortable at the Southeys'. There would come a day when, looking back, she saw that warm, quiet afternoon as the beginning of all her trouble.

Mrs. Southey was the conversational one; Mrs. Coleridge had a tendency to peevishness (which you could understand, Jennifer lazily pondered, if it were true that her husband was always away from her and was a slave to opium . . .).

'Are you partial to evening visiting?' Mrs. Southey inquired. 'I must confess that we are not. Mr. Southey has so much work in the evening and the roads are so often floated by the rain. Not that I think this is a rainy district in reality. It is only that it seems very hard when it does come down. Does it not rain hard sometimes, Mr. Herries? I have never seen such hard rain anywhere.'

Mr. Southey, who was offering cake and bread and butter with a graciousness that almost demanded the accompaniment of music, answered with gravity: 'It is the rainy hours that give us the opportunity for all our reading. Is it not so, Edith? Or rather, in my little girl's case, the writing out of charades and riddles into our book. Come now, Edith. Confess. How many charades have you copied in to-day?'

'None at all, Papa. I have been in the town with Mama.'

What Judith liked in him, she thought, was the warmth of his affections. As he spoke to his daughter his eyes looked on her as though he would surrender the world for her sake. And, as she knew, there was his boy Herbert whom he loved even more dearly.

'That is what my friend Wordsworth will never do. Copy a charade for a lady. No, he bows and regards her sternly and slips out of door and takes a walk. Are you acquainted with Wordsworth, Mrs. Herries? The greatest man alive in England to-day. Yes, indeed, the greatest man in England, as the world will see

one of these times.   There has been a young man
in Keswick this last winter, a Mr. Shelley, with
his wife.   A most unusual young man.   I have
told him that when he is as old as I am he will
grant the truth of my prophecy about Wordsworth.   He, too, wishes to be a poet.   We are
all poets these days, Mrs. Herries. . . .   Well,
he is an unusual young man.   Just what I was
myself in '94.   What it was hard for him to
understand was that you may have Five Thousand
Pounds a year and yet be a good man; I fancy
that there are many young men like him to-day.
The Revolution in France is responsible, you
know.   But I set him upon a course of Berkeley.
That should do him good.   He does not realise
as yet that a man must put a bound upon his
desires and work within them. . . . Dear, dear,
how sententious I am becoming!   Pray, Mrs.
Herries, another of Mrs. Southey's tea - cakes.
They are quite famous in the neighbourhood, you
know.   John Wilson declares there are none
like them even in Scotland, which is the land of
tea-cakes.'

'Yes,' thought Judith.   'But will Francis
be on my side?   He must not know.   He *shall*
not know unless Jennifer herself tells him.   And
I believe that she will not.'

She had a horrible sense that the battle now
would be underground, that no one henceforth
would tell anyone anything, and that was so
against her own character that it was as though
she must twist her whole soul to conform to it.

'For my part,' Mrs. Coleridge was saying, 'I

would never encourage anyone to marry. There
can be so many blunders in matrimony. Although,
to be sure, young people must marry. 'Tis
only natural for them.'

It was now that Judith saw enter the room a
very extraordinary being. This was a boy of
some fifteen or sixteen years of age; he had a
small restless body dressed in clothes too young
for it, the short blue cloth jacket, the white
trousers and open frilled shirt of boys junior to
him. Dark hair strayed untidily over his forehead, but his eyes were the strangest part of him,
burning with intelligence and yet at the same
time lost, as he gazed about the room, in a kind
of abstract wonder. He saw them all seated
about the tea-table and smiled, came towards
them, stared at Jennifer as though he were
mesmerised, then, pulling himself back with a
jerk, nodded, still smiling, and stepped away to
the farther part of the room.

' Nay, Hartley,' said Mrs. Coleridge, ' you
must wish Mr. and Mrs. Herries good-day.'

He came back to them with an odd stepping
dancing movement as though he scarcely touched
the floor. Then he stood there, shook hands,
seemed as though at any moment he would break
into laughter. What was amusing him? It was
to Judith exactly as though he had sprung through
the wall, coming from another world. He was
no resident in this one. All his real life was
elsewhere, and as she watched him she became restless. She wanted to get up and run
away from all of them—to Watendlath, maybe,

find the old house, sit with the Ritsons by the great hearth and hear the lambs bleating beyond the window; then to pass into that other room and to stand watching that staircase, to see again that old man with the white beard as he turned to the stair. Georges would come in, wait beside her as he often did, take her and lift her, pressing her backwards against his breast. Oh, after all these years, after all these years . . . Was she never to be rid of it? If the battle were joined now between Jennifer and herself, it was also joined between the one world and the other. It was almost as though Georges were beside her, fighting Jennifer.

All this disturbance had come from that strange boy there, moving away again, flitting now here, now there, regarding no one and regarding everyone, humming (she fancied, although she could not be sure) some tune to himself. They had all moved away from the tea-table and so she found herself encountering Hartley. He was standing on one foot, one ankle curled around another, and staring at Jennifer. He greeted Judith as though he had known her all her life. Children often did so because she was small and independent.

'That is the most beautiful lady, ma'am, I have ever seen,' he said.

Jennifer was being shown books and manuscripts now by Mr. Southey.

'Yes,' said Judith. 'You are Mrs. Coleridge's boy?'

'Yes, ma'am; there are Derwent and Sara

R

and I. I go to a school at Ambleside. Mr.
Dawes is the Master.'

' And what do you learn there? '

(It was the strangest thing, as though behind
this outward talk they were conducting a quite
different conversation. As though he said to
her: ' I have just been with Georges and he told
me . . .' It was the boy's air of being not yet
awake, of suffering under some enchantment.)

His eyes were never still, nor his feet. He
looked at her with the most engaging friendliness.

' Oh, they try their best to teach me, but I
cannot learn any of the ordinary things. I shall
dream of that lady for weeks and write stories
about her. She shall be the Queen of Ejuxria.'

' Where? '

' Ejuxria. It is a country that I discovered
many years back. She shall be the next
Queen. Oh, ma'am, what a grand Queen she
will make.'

Oh yes, she will, and her servants will go
spying in the drawers of her Ladies-in-Waiting,
reading their letters, undoing the faded ribbons . . .

' Do you like to be here? ' she asked him.

' I like to be everywhere. It is all the same,
for if a place is ugly one can make one's own
picture of it, can one not, ma'am? '

How odd it was to see this small child, with
his restless, unexpected gestures (so that he would
crack his fingers or move three steps on one foot
as though he were playing hop-scotch, or swing
his little arms above his head), a child like none
other that she had ever seen, and feel that she had

so much in common with him. She felt no awkwardness. He understood her absolutely. His smile was the most bewitching part of him; it embraced and included her in his own delight.

' And what will you be when you grow up? ' she asked him.

' I shall be nothing,' he answered, twirling round on one foot. ' I shall never grow up, I should think. I cannot learn the things that help one to grow up, and I know such a number of things that one must not mention. I have a secret name for everything. What is your name, ma'am? '

' Judith—Judith Paris.'

' Judith—I shall call you Florindascantinopolis. One day I will show you where Ejuxria is.' Then he added quietly: ' And now I must go and do my Greek lesson. And then we are going to play cricket—when the others come back from the Lake.'

Yes, they were going. Farewells were being said. Good-bye, Good-bye. . . How warm it is! Is it not warm!

' Yes, the laurels are in great profusion here— but the kitchen-garden is not really too extensive. So beautiful at Uldale! So fine a view of the Scotch Hills. . . But certainly we will come . . . very much obliged . . . too kind of you . . . Good-bye. Good-bye.'

So they rode home.

' Most agreeable people,' Jennifer said. 'When you are in London, Judith, you must read Mr.

Southey's poems. They are all the thing in London.'

'London!' Francis cried. 'London! But Judith is not going to London.'

'No. I am not,' said Judith.

The two women looked at one another. Upon Jennifer's fine smooth white brow a small, a very small frown appeared, the first, Judith thought, that she had ever seen there.

'Of course not,' said Jennifer. 'But we cannot expect Judith never to wish to leave Uldale.'

'I am very happy at Uldale,' Judith said, smiling at Francis. 'You are so very good to me.'

But afterwards when Jennifer had gone up-stairs, slowly, majestically, like a green and white swan floating upwards, to take off her bonnet, Judith had a desperate, almost choking need of reassurance. She caught Francis by the broad lapels of his coat. He paused astonished. He was always shy of demonstrations, she knew. She looked up into his face and he saw that her eyes were filled with tears.

'Francis, you do want me here, do you not?'

'Want you!' He put his thin firm hand on her small one. 'Why, I will never let you go!'

She nodded and said in a low voice: 'I am glad. I wished you to tell me so.'

He added kindly, holding her hand more closely in his: 'You have altered everything here. The servants, the children all love you. And

the best of it is Jennifer has grown so attached.
I have never known her trust anyone so before.
She relies on you completely. I cannot thank
you sufficiently.'

'I am glad,' said Judith, moving towards the
stairs, 'that you are pleased.'

GONE TO EARTH

On a lovely October afternoon a post-chaise drew up outside Fell House and from it stepped a little short man in a brown hat.

He wore a dark brown 'carrick' with many capes, breeches of a light grey and very smart and shining top-boots. He was something of a dandy. He opened the gates, walked up the tiled path and pulled the bell-rope. He walked with a slight limp.

There was complete stillness round him. The thick, gold leaves of the trees in the garden, the little heads of amber chrysanthemums, never stirred in the blue air. Only the pigeons rustled in a flock above the pigeon-house at the sound of the bell, then settled again.

While he waited he sniffed the sharp beauty of the autumn weather and savoured the great spaces surrounding him on all sides. The edges of the hills were clear as though they had been cut out of paper. He could hear the sheep cropping on the moor beyond the garden wall.

A manservant opened the door and he inquired for Mrs. Paris. He was shown into the hall bathed in sun, then after a pause into the parlour, where he stood holding his hat and looking anxiously at the door.

A moment later it opened and Judith stood astonished. Then she ran forward, holding out both her hands.

' Warren ! ' she cried.

He laughed and was so glad to see her that his little grey eyes, bright and restless like a bird's, twinkled with pleasure. He had not seen her for four years.

' You are not changed in the least,' he said, holding both her hands in his.

' Why, of course not,' she said, leading him to the sofa. His limp made her seem protective towards him.   ' And why should I be? '

' I have thought at times,' he said, looking at her very closely, ' from your letters, that you were.'

' In which way? '

' Oh, more serious, more grave.'

' I am a most serious person,' she said.   ' You have never granted me that sufficiently.'

She was enchanted to see him. He was exactly what she was needing, an easy, good friend who cared for her, who was outside all the increasing perplexities and complications of this house and her position in it.

' But why are you here?   And where have you come from? '

' I have been in Keswick a week.'

' In Keswick a week and only just come ! '

' I had some business there and I would not come to see you until it was concluded.'

' But why not? '

' Because it concerns you.'

' Concerns me? '

' Yes.　Wait an instant until I have seen you.
I have been looking forward so impatiently to this
moment.'

He was holding her hand a little harder than
she wished.　Very gently she withdrew it.　He
must be her friend, nothing more.　But her
friend!　She had never in her life wanted a friend
so badly as she did just now.

His face was very charming, ugly because the
nose was too large and the mouth too small, but
eyes and mouth both were wrinkled and lined with
kindliness and humour.　His looks had also that
sense of strain common to everyone who has had
a life of pain and ill-health.　But he did not appear
a weakling.　His body was broad and sturdy, and
he was alert and active save for his limp.　He was
now forty-three years of age.

' Well, what is your great news?　I can tell
that you are bursting with it.'

' Yes.　You may not care for it when you
hear it.'

She was quickly apprehensive; recent events
had made her so.

' I had thought that you might have got wind
of it.'

She suddenly knew.　Of course! he was to be
married!　She was disappointed.

' I know—you are to be married! '

He looked straight into her eyes, so that she
dropped them.

' No . . . not yet,' he answered quietly.
' Nothing like that.　Will has bought Westaways
and I am to be manager of the estate.'

She drew back, erect with amazement.

' What! '

' Yes; Will has bought Westaways. The purchase was concluded last evening.'

Westaways was the house that old Pomfret, Raiseley's father and David Herries' uncle, Francis' and Will's great-uncle, had had built for him between Keswick and Crosthwaite Church. It was called Westaways because it was one of the best examples of the work of an old crazy genius of an architect who, a hundred years ago, had lived in Keswick. It had been built for Pomfret and his wife at great expense and it was a beautiful house. When Raiseley had moved with his wife, Mary, to London, he had sold the house to a Colonel Grant, who, however, had infrequently resided there. Six months earlier Colonel Grant had died in Spain and there had been much local speculation as to its next owner.

Will had bought Westaways! Will was coming here to live, eight miles from his brother with whom he was not on speaking terms! Will was coming back to Keswick. Will with his money and pride and scorn of everything outside London! Will . . . !

' Oh no, no! ' she broke out. ' It is impossible! Westaways and Will! Will and Keswick! '

' I know. But it is so. I have concluded the purchase myself.'

' And he is to live here? '

' He will come up occasionally. I fancy that Christabel and Walter will be here more frequently. She has not been well of late.

Young Walter loves the country. He is mad on horses.'

' How old is Walter now? '

' Twenty-one. He was born in 'Ninety-two. He will make as good a business man as his father. But different. He loves power even more than Will. I never saw a young man so arrogant. He must have his own way in everything.'

' But I cannot believe it. It is incredible. Does he mean to be reconciled with Francis? He will not find it so easy.'

' No. I am afraid not. He is very bitter against Francis, and young Walter carries on the feud.'

' Then——' Judith waited. Suddenly she cried: ' Oh, he is coming here to show off! To triumph over Uldale! I see it all. Oh! it is shameful, shameful! With his money he thinks that he will humiliate Francis! '

' Remember,' Warren said, ' Francis married Jennifer.'

Judith could not grasp it. The change in everything that it would make, the unpleasantness, the rivalries, jealousies, personalities! The difficulties for herself, a friend of Will's and Christabel's as she was. She could not cut herself off from poor Christabel. That would be a disloyalty that no one would command in her . . . but how otherwise was her life with Francis and Jennifer to be possible, difficult as it was already?

In her perplexities she burst out: ' Warren,

you should not have taken this. It is going to lead to nothing but hatred and ill-feeling——'

He nodded his head.

'Perhaps I should not. I hesitated, I will confess, but there was one thing that decided me.'

She said nothing. He went on.

'That you were here.'

'Oh no, Warren, please——'

He persisted.

'No, you have to hear me. I came to say this. From now we shall be living near to one another, and I do not care what you or any other may think. For four years I have tried to conquer my love for you, but it will not die. No, listen . . . listen . . . please do not send me away! No, Judith, please—please!'

She had risen and stood there looking at him: 'Warren, it is quite useless. You know that it is. We settled that four years ago. We were to be friends. You promised it.'

'I know, I know,' he answered. 'And so I intended it to be. But I cannot command it, try as I may. It is the last of my life. I shall have no more. My life has been always broken, everything has failed in it. This too will fail. I see that it must. But I am compelled to tell you.'

As she looked at him she longed to be kind to him, to give him anything that he wanted. What she had always desired, what she would always desire, was to give people what they wanted. And for seventeen years now no one had wanted anything very much. At Grosset it had been a carpet brushed, a window mended, a consoling word to Maria, a humorous word to Carey, and here it had been comfort for Francis, who after all was not comforted.

As she looked at Warren whom she liked so greatly, who was so courageous and bore pain without flinching, who never made complaint, she longed to give him anything. But how could she? She did not love him. He wanted passion, and she had no passion left for anyone in the world. And then it was absurd; she was thirty-nine.

'Dear Warren,' she said gently. 'I care for you very greatly. With Francis here you are the best friend I have. But love—love of the sort that you mean, I have none for anyone. It is true although it may sound fantastic, but I love Georges after all these years as dearly as I did when he was alive. Is that false, a senti-mentality? I think not. Or, if so, I am myself deceived. And then I am so old. I am near forty.'

He got up and stood beside her, but did not touch her.

'Yes, I know everything. Nothing has altered since we talked at Grosset. You are not old to me. Besides, I am not myself young. There is nothing to do—I did not ask you to do anything. But I could not come here to live and not show you that there is no change in my feeling. I shall not do anything but what you would wish.'

He kissed her hand, gave a little bow, and limped away out of the room. She heard the carriage rattle off down the road.

The light was failing, and the little room was shadowed with yellow dusk. She stood there, her hand on the lid of the spinet, looking at the dim garden and the white road beyond it. Her head whirled. Will coming to Keswick! Will only eight miles away! Will and his family hanging over Uldale and flicking Francis' sensitiveness, Jennifer's pride, with every hour that passed! Oh, but it was impossible! The situation was impossible!

The door opened, and Jennifer came in.

'Who was that who was here?' she asked. She was wearing a dress of deep crimson that fitted very close to her body. She walked wearily. During the last months Judith had seen that something was distressing her, something that had nothing to do with her comfort. A curious perception of life was slowly, slowly waking in her. One could see it tremble in her like a faint flutter in a white sky before dawn. Her battle with Judith continued, but this was not the cause of her disturbance. It was from some other direction.

'That was Warren Forster.'

'Warren Forster? Why did he not stay?'

'He had a piece of news——' Judith hesitated. This same news was going to shake Jennifer's placid laziness as nothing else could do. Judith longed to see that shaken; in part Judith hated Jennifer as she had never hated

anyone before. But, beyond that, there was
something further. Jennifer's anger would include
Francis' discomfort. They were all included
in this.

'Well,' Jennifer said slowly. 'Cautious little
Judith. You *are* cautious, are you not? With
your own plans and purposes——'

She always, now, when the two of them were
alone, tried any kind of irritation that seemed to
her clever, but like all unimaginative women she
could only think of the taunts and teasings that
would goad herself if someone applied them.
Quite different ones would be needed for Judith.

'No, I am not cautious!' Judith answered,
smiling. 'But this is rather astonishing news
that Warren brought. Prepare yourself for a
shock.'

Jennifer, who was standing, drawn to her full
height, looking out of window, had her mind
only half on Judith's words. She was watching
or waiting or listening. . . .

'Well, my dear? What is your great news?'

'Will has bought Westaways at Crosthwaite
and is coming to reside there with Christabel and
the family.'

Judith had her reward. Jennifer turned; her
eyes for once were wide and awake, her beautiful
mouth open, her whole body stung to attention.

'What? What do you say?'

'It is true. Warren has just completed the
purchase. He is to be Will's bailiff.'

At that same moment Francis came in. He
had been riding and looked immensely handsome

in his many-caped coat.   His face was splendid now, very sharp and set, thinner than it had ever been; his whole body was drawn fine and alert.

'Francis?   Do you hear?   It is impossible, fantastic.   Oh, no . . . he cannot . . . he would not dare.   No, no.   There must be a mistake.'

It was astonishing enough to see Jennifer pacing the room, her head up, waving her arms, in a flurry of agitation.

'Judith, what is it?   What's amiss?'

'Only that Warren Forster has been here and has told me that Will has bought Westaways and is to come there with Christabel.'

'Will!   Bought Westaways!'

'Yes.'

Jennifer turned sharply upon Judith.

'You knew of this.   You had heard of this already.   You knew this was coming.'

She was so frantically disturbed that for once she forgot the caution that she always kept before Francis.

He at once turned to her.   'Jennifer!   Certainly Judith did not know——'   He stared at her as though he were seeing something new.

'Well, then,' she cried, tossing up her head and moving towards the door, 'it is at least just what Judith would have.   Her dear friends, Will and Christabel, next door.   No one can wonder at her pleasure.'

Before she went, her voice shaking with rage, she said to Francis: 'You have brought me to this—to be humiliated before that City merchant and his chicken-faced wife, but I shall not sit under it patiently, you shall see.'

When she was gone he put his arm around Judith and drew her down in front of the fire.

' You are sure of this? '

' Quite sure.'

' Warren himself came to tell you? '

' Yes.'

' And of course you had not an idea of it? '

' Why, no—of course not.'

He sighed deeply, leaning his head on his hand, looking into the fire. He was still wearing his heavy coat. She slipped it off his shoulders.

At last he said: ' Will is doing it only to humiliate me. He could have no other purpose.'

She tried to reassure him. ' No. Why should you take it so? After all this is his home. He lived here all his childhood. He must care for it. He will come to make friends.'

Francis struck his knee with his hand, his favourite gesture when he was excited.

' Never, never. He hates me and Jennifer too. And besides—if he wished to be friends I would not agree. He has insulted Jennifer in every way, and now it only needs this——'

She said what she could, but what was there to say? It was quite true. She knew that there was only one reason why Will had bought Westaways.

Then quite suddenly Francis asked her a surprising question. Dropping his voice a little he said:

' Judith, has Fernyhirst been here this afternoon? '

'No. Why?'

'Oh, for no reason. I wondered. He seems to ride this way frequently.'   After another pause he asked her: 'Why did Jennifer speak to you like that?'

'Speak to me?'

'Yes, in that manner—unfriendly, angry. Is she offended with you?'

'Sometimes a little.'

'I have thought lately——'

After a while he said: 'Everything is turning wrongly.   I feel as though some great misfortune were coming.'

She must get away.   That, when she awoke the next morning, was her first and most dominating impulse.   This was no new passion for escape. It had been constant with her all her life long. She was for ever wanting to escape—but never in the end escaping!   That might be the just epitaph on her tomb were she ever to have one! Now she was going to escape almost exactly as she had escaped to Tom Gauntry's out of the window all those years ago after David Herries had beaten her.   Only now she would not escape out of the window!

No one in the house seemed astir.   It was as still as the lovely October morning around and above it.   She left a note for Francis, laying it on his table in his study.   She went round to the stables and brought out Peggy, who whinnied with delight at her approach.

Peggy was a small and very strong mare that

Francis had given her, a brown mare with a most human expression, for she could look wicked and evil at the approach of Jennifer and most affectionate and engaging when Judith was near.

As she turned the corner at the bottom of the hill, leaving the house and the village behind her, her spirits rose with every clatter of Peggy's hoofs. She had told Francis that she would be a night away in Watendlath; but now she thought that it would be very pleasant were she to extend the one night into two. She wished to wipe Uldale and everyone in it out of her mind, yes, even Francis.

For two days she would not be the woman of Uldale, but someone quite different—the woman of Watendlath.

As her spirits rose she was like a girl of twenty instead of a woman of almost forty. Peggy, who was also, by mares' standard, a middle-aged female, became a very conscienceless child, pricking up her ears at sounds of birds and rustlings in the trees, although she knew that they meant nothing at all, and striking the stones of the road with an especially youthful gaiety because this piece of freedom was quite unexpected and the thing that most of all she enjoyed.

Judith was once more reminded with especial clearness of that evening when she had climbed out of window and ridden to Tom Gauntry's. It seemed only yesterday, and she remembered how lively she had been, swearing in good strong Cumberland at the men in the road. It was as though nothing of any importance had occurred in her life between that ride and this, except Georges. And yet she was middle-aged, riding off like a girl. Something very ridiculous about that, but then she often found herself ridiculous! Women rode on horseback very much less than they had done when she was a child. They went now sedately in chaises or barouches; it was quite a common thing now to go to Edinburgh or even to London, whereas in her girlhood it had been quite an adventure.

And how formal and careful in these days the women of her age were! Mrs. Osmaston of Troutbeck (very far from sedate her old mother-in-law had been!), Mrs. Worcester from Threlkeld, Alice Sandon of Keswick and Mary Robertson of St. John's in the Vale, Mrs. Southey, Mrs. Coleridge—all stout, careful, sedate women who would never dream of riding on horseback from Uldale to Watendlath!

The matter with her, Judith, was that she was a trifle vulgar and common. It had always been so, always divided her from people. She had it, she supposed, from her mother. How enchanting it would be to see her mother appear suddenly now out from the hedge, with her hair about her face, her gay ragged clothes, her wild behaviour!

'I am your daughter,' Judith would say, jumping off Peggy, and then they would sit down in the hedge together and talk about everything. Judith would show her the silver chain that Francis had sent her; she always wore this under her clothes.

'Come away with me,' her mother would say.

And away at once they would go for ever! No question of a real escape then!

She had never been a proper lady; even Francis, she suspected, found it so. That was why she had been so easily friends with people like Georges and old Tom Gauntry, Emma Furze, Charlie Watson, who were not ladies and gentlemen either. If only she had looked a little different!—here Judith, in spite of herself, sighed. To be so small, to have such unimportant features—and now she was a little stouter and her hair had lost some of its lustre.

She could not understand how Warren Forster could be in love with her! Nobody had ever been in love with her for her looks; Georges had only come to love her through propinquity. But that was her greatest triumph, the triumph of her life!

But to return to the vulgarity of her nature, that was the reason, no doubt, of her struggle with Jennifer. Jennifer detested anyone who was not a lady. She had hoped that Judith was a lady, and then, when she found that she was not . . .

Well, Judith could not help it. She was not to worry her head on this beautiful morning about Jennifer. She bore Jennifer no kind of malice— only why was she, Judith, in that house at all? Some part of her was always dragging her back into Herries affairs. She did not want to go back. How splendid it would be if she could stay in Watendlath for ever—then her real life would begin!

She would not go through the town, but took the bridle-path at the back of it, along the lanes under Skiddaw until at last she joined the path that led up to the stream above Lodore.

Here at a clearing between the trees she was compelled to stop Peggy and watch, for a moment, the storm that struck the Lake. It had been, when she left Uldale, a perfect October morning, without one cloud to mar the pale delicate blue. But, with the dramatic splendour that makes these skies the most wonderful in the world, a rolling black cloud, like a great funnel of smoke, had rushed over from the sea, pouring over Cat Bells and Robinson like the issue of a conflagration. The Lake was yet blue, the hills still gold with their burnished bracken. But this cloud hurried with the gait of a drunken man. It had been a funnel of smoke, but now, even as Judith watched, it swung outwards as that same drunken man might wave his cloak in a gesture of defiance. Then it spread with ferocity, eating up the sky, frothing at its edge in spumes of grey vapour, its black heart catching a purple light, the stain of blackberries.

It ate the sun. The Lake shivered and fell into a trembling agitation of tones and circles; the hills, that had been so bright, raised their heads; they seemed before Judith's eyes to increase their stature, and shadowed gulfs of purple rent their sides. Around her still the bracken was gold, the sun beat upon her face. Then with a quick whirr of wind the raindrops fell. The woods sighed. Where, only a moment before, there had been gentle stillness, there was now a sibilation like the whisper of a thousand gossips.

Soon the rain was falling as though a huge bowl had been opened over her head, but already, above Robinson, a thin line of gold cut the black wedge; light, mysterious and lonely, fell on one of the small islands and lit it with an unearthly glow. The black cloud began to break.

This moment's storm seemed to mark her passage from one world into another. As she moved on up to the road above Lodore, she felt that all her other life was closed to her, and she was so happy that it was absurd to think that she had ever been otherwise.

It seemed a moment later that she was in the Ritsons' kitchen. What a welcome she had! She had been to Watendlath three times in the last two years, but only for very short visits. She had not slept a night there, and, on one occasion, Francis had been with her. Now she *was* to sleep a night there, maybe two, and she was quite alone. With all Cumbrians, when, after long years, much silent watchfulness and infinite caution, they decide that you may be trusted, the fidelity and affection is all the more fervent because of the earlier testing. But Judith was quite unique in the lives of the people of Watendlath. Her appearance, her history, her marriage with its extraordinary end, her long years with the ' Grand Folk ' down South, her character with its odd mixture of fiery temper and great patience, of humour and seriousness, of youth and old wisdom, half a lady, half anything but a lady, her character honoured them by being both so strange and yet so ordinary. In a way they took her quite for granted now after all those years with them, but in another way they never took her for granted. They were never sure what she would do next. And, in addition to all these things, most of them loved her (there are always grumblers everywhere who do not love anybody) because she made them laugh, because she washed dishes and scrubbed floors, because she was interested in everybody and everything, because she could talk the broadest Cumberland and often did, because she knew as much about sheep as anyone, because she could lose her temper with a man like any good woman, because her rascal of a husband (they had always hated Georges) neglected her, because she continued to be fond of him long after he was dead, because she had no pride and someone in one class was the same to her as someone in another, because she was shocked at nothing that they did, whether they were dirty, mean, lecherous, drunken, cruel, spiteful (and at times as with all other of God's creatures they were one or another of these things), because she was a plain-looking little woman but also unusual, so that you always looked at her twice—but chiefly they loved her because they trusted her, which, with a Cumbrian, is first and last the principal thing.   She kept her word; her heart was warm; she was not ' stuck on herself '.

Old Man Ritson had died two years back, his daughter-in-law last year; now Tom Ritson and Alice shared the farm.   Tom had married a girl from Cockermouth, a simple little woman who was a good cook, and Alice had married young Roger Perry of Thunder, who was so thick through,

broad across and short of leg, that he resembled
the small stone wall above the Tarn. He had a
round red freckled face and was a very silent man.
However, he liked Tom Ritson, loved Alice, had
three small boys who rolled about the kitchen
floor like little ninepins and was excellent with
cattle and sheep. The Ritsons were now a very
happy household.

They all rushed at Judith, even the three small
Perry boys, who had not the least notion as to
who she was, but, like puppies, felt that she was
part of a good and friendly world. Alice was
perhaps the best pleased of them all. She had an
almost reverential love for Judith. Although now
a quiet pale-faced woman who went about her
work with little comment, she saw further into
character than did the others. She understood
a little of what Judith's feeling for Georges had
been; he had not been for her merely the foreign
rogue and rascal that the others had thought
him.

As Judith sat down beside the huge open fireplace, realising with deep pleasure that all the
busy life of the kitchen was going on around her
just as though she were not there, the men stump-
ing in and out, the women in their clogs clattering
about, baking, working at the butter, going after
the chickens, shooing geese out of the doorway,
looking into the sunny yard to see whether the
men were coming for their dinner, Alice Perry
quietly watched her. She was anxious for her,
thinking of what none of the others would consider—for Judith had not slept the night here

since the night of her husband's death; more than that, she had never since then entered that room. Alice knew that now, this time, she would enter it.

Then, just as the men came clattering across the yard, hungry and thirsty, Charlie Watson rode in on his horse.

'It's Charlie!' Alice cried. 'Charlie Watson!'

Judith ran to the door and then out to meet him. He jumped off his horse and stood there, his legs spread, his mouth twisted in that strange, shy, almost angry smile so peculiarly his. It was as though he said: 'Well, it's a foolish thing to feel this pleasure and one is an idiot to set one's affections on anything but a sheep—still, I can't help myself.'

It was a year and a half since she had last seen him. He had stoutened, but otherwise was little changed from the man she had met on the road from Rosthwaite seventeen years ago. His skin was as clear, his teeth as white, his colour as ruddy, his body as strong—and his tongue as silent.

'Aye. 'Tis good to see ye. Lookin' fine.'

Then they walked into the kitchen together.

While they were all eating, Charlie sitting among the farm-hands and with one small Perry on his broad knee, she watched him with exceeding pleasure. She knew from all that she had heard in the last year that he was growing to be a very important person, not only in that neighbourhood but beyond, as far as Ravenglass on one side and Mardale on the other. One thing for which he was becoming famous was his fighting the cause of the farmers against the cattle-dealers. In those days, when there were no railways and few newspapers, cattle-dealers did much as they pleased, naming their own prices and seeing that they got what they demanded.

He was already beginning to buy cattle himself at fair prices, and send them to Liverpool. At present only in a small way; it was, later on, to become a famous thing. Then he was a great arbitrator in all local disputes. His scrupulous fairness, his evenness of judgement, made him ideal for the settling of boundaries, squabbles about sheep and cattle, even domestic troubles. He was himself growing wealthy, but lived always in the simplest fashion on his farm. Although he was older now he was still a great wrestler and player at any and every game. She had heard also that he refused to marry, laughing at every suggestion. Many liked him but he had no intimates; he seemed to prefer to be alone. He liked her, she knew, but she could not flatter herself that she knew him. She was even at times afraid of him.

But now as she sat there watching the October afternoon fall behind the kitchen windows, hearing all the sounds that she loved, sheep slipping like a flock of anxious old women up the path, water being drawn from the well, the soft crooning song of little Mrs. Perry as she rolled the dough on the long kitchen table, the screeching of the turkeys on the field above the farm, her own fear gathered about her.   Because she knew that she was soon to do that of which she was most in the world afraid.   The first time, after coming up from the South, that she had ridden over, she had intended to force her will, but Francis had been with her and that had been her excuse.   The second time Alice Perry had been sick, and that, she told herself, had been her excuse.   But to-day there was nothing to prevent her.

Her pale face grew weary and strained.   Her hands were clenched on her lap.   She answered Mrs. Perry's chatter without an idea of what she was saying.

Then she nodded her head as though something spoke to her, commanding, and she submitted. She got up and went out into the yard.   Watson stood there speaking to Perry.   She nodded to him, and he came across to her.

' Charlie, will you come with me? '

He seemed to know at once what she meant and walked off with her without another word.

The distance was nothing, but at the door she hesitated.

' I have never been inside — since it hap-pened.'

Gently he put his hand through her arm.

' Come in,' he said.

She felt as though she were leaving everything living behind her.   The air was suffused with a purple dusk, and she turned back to see the Tarn one blaze of fierce white light.   The hills seemed gigantic.   She heard, exactly as though she were leaving them all for ever, all the sounds of life, the animals, the human voices, the running water; then they went in together.

The room that had once been her sitting-room was used now for lumber, and one end of it was piled with sacks. An old kitchen table, rickety on three legs, was in the middle of the room and on it stood a large swinging mirror whose glass was cracked. The glass reflected the staircase. Some hens were rooting about on the floor. The place was dusky, but everything was as clear to her as though flooded with sun-light. And everything had happened yesterday, that night, only a few hours ago.

' Old Mr. Stane stood there in front of the fire. Suddenly Georges went up, as close as to touch him, and cried out: " I killed your son! I hated him! I killed him, I tell you, and you can do what you like." Then he went up the stair-case and the old man ran after him and caught him and threw him down. Then he ran down the stairs again and went out. I saw that Georges was dying. There was nothing to be done—nothing at all. But before he died he caught my hand and he told me he loved me. He died at once. There was nothing I could do. No one could have helped. It was too late.'

' Aye,' said Charlie. ' It must have been terrible for you.'

She began to cry, hiding her head in his coat, holding to him, and he put his arm round her. He stood looking over her into the cracked mirror.

At last she whispered, so faintly that he could

scarcely hear her: ' This is my home. . . . I shall never have any other.'

She cried on, then went and sat upon the stairs, looking all round at everything, taking every piece of it into her so that she need never fear to come again. And he stood gazing at her and knowing that she had altogether forgotten him.

They stayed so long without moving that the hens grew bold and scratched in the dirt at their very feet.

GHOSTLY IDYLL

BUT, as everyone knows, just when Fate seems to have a fine bouncing climax in his hand he shakes his head, changes his mind (which is not nearly so settled a one as people seem to think) and puts the climax back into his pocket again.

It was so with Judith now. She came back from her two nights in Watendlath happier than she had been for many a year. She had slept in her old room again. Whether she had truly slept or no she could not say, but, without either sentiment or nonsense, it had seemed to her that Georges kept her company. Therefore she returned to Uldale in a state of great happiness. She settled down into all the Uldale affairs again as though she were for a moment pitching her tent there. Very soon she would be back at Watendlath. Nothing should keep her. But everything kept her. It was to be months, and then even years, before she saw Watendlath once more. Members of the Herries family never escape so easily as that.

Her time now at Uldale was difficult, and it was the difficulties that kept her. Feeling that she must stay, she did not dare go even for an hour to Watendlath lest it should keep her for ever and her duty be broken. The first difficulty was Jennifer. Strange ! Can one be so secret a woman without being secret at all? For although Jennifer had now her mysterious preoccupation that caused her to twist her brows and bite her thumb, yet she was not really secret. She was wondering, Judith knew, whether to go further with Fernyhirst.

Judith suspected that Jennifer was moved, as a woman stirred by a man, for the first time in her life; that she was as uncomfortable, bewildered and disturbed as a child wakened up from a deep sleep by sunlight. She was finding one discomfort after another press in upon her. Always before she had been able to deal with discomfort. Now she could not. She had told Judith to depart, but she had not departed. She had tried to make Francis a convenient figure in her life and nothing more, but of late he had begun to frighten her. She had told Fernyhirst to cease to make love to her, and he had not ceased. She had told herself to be indifferent to him, but she was not indifferent. Even with Mrs. Ponder she was beginning to be uncomfortable, for Mrs. Ponder now was often insolent. Even with her children she was not comfortable, for they were growing and insisted on having lives and personalities of their own.

Because of all these unsettled discomforts Jennifer was at last beginning to live. Her eyes were no longer half-closed. She was often alert, as though she were listening for some sound.

One thing for which she was listening was

the arrival of Will and Christabel at Westaways; but the months passed, one year closed and another year opened. Still they did not come.

Warren Forster, who was often at Uldale, although Jennifer disliked him and showed it, said that This, That and the Other prevented them. . . . They would come. . . . Surely they would come. . . . A pity. . . . He had endeavoured to persuade Will to alter his mind. Westaways was not the house for him. But Will was obstinate. He did not know why he was so obstinate.

Francis, however, knew; Francis was an altered man. Biting, sarcastic, silent, even with men of his own mind, like Southey, he appeared to have lost all his sweetness.

' He's gone sour,' said Fernyhirst to Jennifer, and he stretched his broad chest and pinched his strong neck with a smile of satisfaction. It was a long business, this siege, but she was the hand-somest woman in the county and it was a fine occupation for a dull country life. It could have but one end to it. He was an extremely patient man, as his training of horses and dogs (for which, in the North, he was famous) showed.

Worst of all, Francis had now shut himself away from Judith. If he spoke his mind to her he must speak of Fernyhirst, and that he was resolved not to do. He was now entirely alone, even as his grandfather and namesake had been before him. He was going the same road.

It was on a winter morning towards the close

of '14 that family history took a stealthy step forward. Young John Herries, aged now seven, was the cause. He was a very typical Herries child, square and strong like his grandfather, rather sensitive, but with a more plentiful allowance of humour and less sentiment about his father than David had had about his.

In fact at this time he had no sentiment about either his father or his mother. His mother he quite honestly disliked. He knew that she did not care for him. He hated to be embraced by her. In his father he was more truly interested; but this was a bad period for anyone to be interested in Francis. John saw him as a thin, severe, august figure moving about the place giving orders. He admired his father, but was happier when his father was not present. For Dorothy, his sister, he had a feeling of mixed contempt and protection. She cried a great deal, and she clung to Mrs. Ponder, whom he, John, without extenuation or limitation, detested. No, he thought very little of Dorothy.

His whole heart was given to Judith, and had been ever since she had gone to the Tarn with him to sail his boat. He was very tenacious of ideas and affections. He loved Judith because he trusted her, because she talked to him like a human being, because she did not mess him about with embraces, because she was always so clean and neat (he was already fastidious about these things), because she thought the things in which he was interested important, because she considered the things funny that he considered

S

funny. He treated her as he would have treated another boy who was a friend of his (he had no boy friends). He never gave any sign that he was glad to see her. He would look at her, a little frown gathered between his eyebrows, and he would ask her opinion. When he was going to laugh, the laugh came first in his eyes, which would be twinkling with merriment while the rest of his face was quite grave. He liked to rub the flat of his hand up and down the side of his breeches. Another pleasure was to put on a sudden very deep bass voice which was supposed to be an imitation of Mrs. Ponder's.

'Boney's coming to eat you!' he would say out of his boots. It was her favourite threat, but instead of fearing he would chuckle with laughter.

He would walk up to Judith with great gravity and say, with his chin sunk into his neck so as to bring out his deep voice better: 'Boney's coming to eat you!'

It was John on this winter morning who made history. Judith had dressed and was ready for the day. She came out of her room on to the landing. On this landing the rooms of both Jennifer and Francis opened. Stairs led up to Mrs. Ponder's sacred chamber and attics; stairs led down to the main hall. Standing there for a moment before she descended, Judith thought of all that she had to do. She looked what at that instant she was, a very competent house-wife, with keys at her waist, a green apron, and a spotless lace cap on her head. She had much to do: there was Mrs. Harper, there were the kitchen-maids, there was the dairy. Mrs. Birket and some London friends of hers were coming to supper and cards. . . . She heard then, from a large ancient cupboard that had stood for many a day in a corner under the stairway, strange sniffs, and then—a most startling sneeze.

Opening the cupboard door she beheld an odd sight. Seated on the dusty floor was John, absorbed in the feeding of a large, and, it seemed, very greedy brown rabbit.

'Why, John——' she cried.

He jumped to his feet, catching the rabbit by its long ears. As always, in any situation, now or ever, he stood his ground, but he was very red in the face and his cheeks were marked with dust. The rabbit squirmed in terror.

'Oh, but, ma'am,' he said in his husky confidential voice, 'I was intending——'

She could see that he was really frightened. But why? She could not think that there was anything very terrible in feeding a rabbit. . . . But why a cupboard? Why this furtive secrecy? She asked him. He stepped out of the cupboard, holding the rabbit in his arms.

He dropped his voice so that it became even more husky.

'You see, ma'am, Mrs. Ponder had forbidden me to keep it. Yesterday. You see,' he dropped his voice yet lower, 'she has an exceptional distaste for rabbits. She ordered Jim to have it killed, and so I have been hiding it in this cupboard——'

' But why did you not tell your father? '

' Why, ma'am, he says that I must do as Mrs. Ponder orders. It is only,' he whispered, coming very near to her, ' for to-day. I have found a place in the field——' He broke off. She realised that he did not want her to know where the hiding-place was lest she should be inconvenienced by questions. She whispered back to him, smiling:

' My indulgence shall be given. I shall tell no one.'

Greatly relieved, he went back to the cupboard.

She remembered something in her room that she had forgotten, and, for a moment, was back there, opening and shutting a drawer. Before she had reached the door again she heard a clamour. A woman's voice, muffled as though she were endeavouring not to be overheard, but so passionate that it shook the air. Hastening out, she was horrified to see Mrs. Ponder, her face all black eyebrow, hurry across the floor and, with a vindictive gesture, fling open the window and throw the rabbit out. John gave a cry, then stood there, his face twisted with anguish. Not seeing Judith, Mrs. Ponder threw herself upon the boy and, in a convulsion of passion, dragged him by the hair towards the stairway. She moved so swiftly in her rage that she had knocked his knees against the lowest step before Judith could move. Then she was stopped by something else, for Francis had come out. Mrs. Ponder heard him and stayed. She let John go, and he, as though driven by a sort of wild fury, uttering little sobs, his eyes staring, ran past them all down the stairs.

'What is this?' Francis asked.

Judith had once heard him described by one of the ladies of the neighbourhood as 'a pleasant gentlemanlike man.' He had, she thought, never deserved the description less than at this moment. To speak in the terms of the author of *The Italian*, he was 'cold fury nobly seething.' Mrs. Ponder felt this, and for once in her courageous life was alarmed.

'Not at all, sir. Nothing, I mean. Master John has been disobedient.'

He moved towards her as though he would strike her. Judith remembered that she had once done the same. Mrs. Ponder appeared to have that effect on her critics.

He drew up and, looking at her as though she should, were he magician enough, change into a rat at his feet, said:

'You will leave this house within the morning.'

And she, recovering some of her confidence, answered, as once before she had answered Judith:

'That is for my mistress to say, sir.'

It happened then (for this landing was as public a place as that generally chosen in the theatre for intimate confidences) that Jennifer came from her room, looking very lovely in some loose garment of a rosy shade and a white cap with rosy ribbons covering her dark hair.

'Well, Ponder——' she said, and, seeing Francis and Judith, stopped.

'This woman,' Francis said, 'will leave the house to-day.'

Judith then saw Mrs. Ponder give Jennifer a very strange look.

Jennifer said: 'Why, what has she been doing?'

'She has been in a bestial temper and has dragged John by the hair.'

Mrs. Ponder folded her arms as much as to say: 'You have not the smallest chance of moving me.'

'And what has John been doing?' Jennifer asked.

'If you please, ma'am, he has been most disobedient. He had concealed a nasty filthy rabbit in the cupboard, and after my telling him that of all filthy animals and filled with diseases, and my doing all for the best, ma'am, as I always do——'

'She had thrown the rabbit,' Judith broke in, 'out of window and was beating John against the stair.'

It had been better, as usual, if she had not interfered.

Jennifer, looking only at Francis, said: 'Mrs. Ponder was in the right if John disobeyed her.'

'I have said what is to be done,' Francis answered, his face cold with disgust. 'The woman goes to-day.'

'I shall do what I think right,' Jennifer answered.

They looked at one another, a strange long look.   His unspoken words were: 'She has the command of you.   You do not dare to let her go.'

But he would have no scramble before servants.

At the top of the stairs he said again: 'She goes to-day,' and went down.

Mrs. Ponder began: 'I assure you, ma'am, I had no thought but for the best.   I would always do my duty——'

But Jennifer returned without a word into her room.

This little scene, so swift and so impromptu, was to have a deep and lasting effect on all the persons concerned in it, but on the life of Judith most of all.

After it the house was as silent as a valley in the moon.   The winter day was sharp and sunny. The hedge sparkled with crystal and the lawn was laced with silver frost.   A very fat robin at the parlour window sang.   He was the only live thing.   Francis rode out.   Jennifer stayed in her room.

Judith went about her work and felt very lonely.   What would happen?   Would Mrs. Ponder go?   Whatever happened she had for a long time to come lost Francis, who would now keep more within himself than ever, and John, whose look of terror and anguish as he ran down the stairs she would never forget.   Meanwhile the rabbit lay, with its back broken, on the stones below. . . .

While she was in the storeroom, marking in a book the jams, jellies and preserves while Mrs.

Harper, a small thin woman like an amiable radish, chattered along, she thought impatiently: ' I cannot endure this much longer. I can't stay in a house where nobody cares for me.' Although she was forty years of age she was as childish as that. But perhaps what she really meant was that she needed to be close to somebody, close in affection and sympathy. This house to-day was a prison.

So that when, an hour later, Warren Forster arrived on horseback, her reaction from that early morning scene was terrific. She had never before been so glad to see him. Had it not been for that early disturbance she would never have gone riding with him, and had she not gone riding with him everything in later Herries history would have been different.

As it was, she did not care. She was reckless that day, reckless through exasperation and a longing for someone who was not angry, was not hurt, was not deceitful.

Warren, his little figure so dapper on his large horse, was not angry nor hurt nor deceitful. He was enchanted to see Judith, who was kinder to him, more responsive to him, than she had ever been. The house was quite still. She looked around her and found nothing alive in it but the robin. The air was filled with distress and anger. So she gave the robin crumbs, took Peggy out of her stable and rode off with Warren.

Often, when afterwards she looked back upon this eventful day and tried to see how one step had so determinedly led to another, it seemed that it had all been planned. But it was not in reality so. Nothing was planned. They just rode into the cold and crystal air.

At first they talked lightly of general things: of how Napoleon had tumbled down at last, of the quarrels among the Allies at Vienna, and the clever man that Talleyrand was; that it looked as though France, Austria and England would soon be fighting Russia and Prussia; of Napoleon's exile on Elba, and whether he would be there for the remainder of his days. They talked of those things, but they did not really care any more than their descendants would care for similar figures and intrigues. Napoleon, Talleyrand, the Czar of Russia were as remote from them as they rode along the Cumberland lanes as figures on a Chinese screen. They talked about affairs in England: of the King and the Regent, and the high prices and the uncertainty of everything and everybody; of how the world was changing as it had never changed before; of how interesting it was to live in a time of transition, but also how unsettling; of how there were no great figures in the world any more, no great literature, although Mr. Wordsworth's poems were pleasant and *Childe Harold* had some fine writing (and was it true that Lord Byron was both so beautiful *and* so wicked, Judith asked), just as their descendants afterwards would talk. Warren said that Will Herries said that trade was going soon to recover and that everyone would be wealthy again, that there would be wonderful new industries, and that everyone

s 2

would soon be living in towns because the country was too dull.

'That would be a pity,' said Judith, looking about her at the grey hills, their tops scattered with snow like sifted sugar. 'There is nothing so beautiful as the country.'

'I think so also,' said Warren, looking at her. He was madly in love with her that day. He was never to know why his love for Judith was so much fiercer and more sharp than any other emotion of his life, his greatest happiness and his greatest distress.

It had been so from the first moment of his seeing her at Grosset, although that had not been a good occasion, for it had been a stormy wet afternoon and she had been standing in the hall rating a servant when he came in. Her voice had had a sharp and dominating note in it, as though she were telling all the world to go to Hades. The fire in the hall had been smoking, there were dogs all about the place and one of Maria Rockage's garments hanging up to dry. Judith had turned on him like a cross, exasperated child and had been anything but gracious. So perverse are men, and so beyond all rules is love, that he had liked her the better for her mood. He preferred, perhaps, women who were of the ruling kind. Then as he came to know her more truly he found that, although she wished to dominate, she could be led by her affections almost anywhere. She could not indeed be led to love him, but would do almost anything for him out of kindness.

He was a man of great courage, humour and spirit, and his pains, physical and other, had taught him patience. So he waited for a long time, and at last he had his reward.

They had no plan of direction, but they rode through Keswick (where Judith did a little shopping), then out, above the Lake, to the Grange Bridge and on into Borrowdale.

' My father lived here,' Judith said, ' all his life. They could not persuade him to move away. His house tumbled about his ears, but he died in it and I was born in it. Here,' she waved her whip to a broad bend of the little river, ' they drowned a witch. My father went before them all and took her out of the water and carried her away.'

The trees, bare above the chattering river, had a rosy edge to them in the cold air. The top of Castle Crag played with little wreaths of mist that crowned its head with a thin light, behind which the black rocks gleamed. His hopes began to rise, he knew not why. She was so friendly to-day. There seemed to be a new current of intimacy running behind her words. He did not know that he was indebted to a rabbit for his happiness.

' Would you have an objection,' she asked, ' if we paid a visit to that old house of my father's where I was born? I have not for a long while visited it. There is only a shepherd there. It must be bare and deserted.'

They turned off the road and across the little bridge.

In the little graveyard near here Georges had
been buried, and here her father and mother had
died.

The house that stood behind a little courtyard, defended by a rough stone wall, seemed
quite dead against the pale blue sky. It had
been, Warren thought, two houses; on the right
it was of some height, with latticed windows and
a gabled roof. From this attempt at grandeur
it fell away to a low rough place that had what
seemed to be farm buildings attached to it.

But all was now in utter desolation. As they
led their horses in through the gate, shabby and
broken, their feet struck the rime from the
stiffened grass. Birds rose in a whir of agitation from the thin stems of the bushes; a large
white cat with malevolent eyes slunk across the
fast disappearing stones. Yet it was a scene
of great beauty. Rosthwaite Fell and Glaramara
in further distance rose above the fields in purple
grandeur. Water ran in silver skeins down the
rocks, and its tumbling was the only sound.

Warren had got down from his horse to lead
it in, and now, standing in front of the old door,
he cried, ' Is anyone here? '

There was no answer. They heard some
animal stamping in a byre close by. They
pushed the door back and entered.

A musty odour of decay, straw, animal dung,
met them, but they persevered and, climbing the
stair, found themselves in a large room.

This, it appeared, was the place where the
shepherd was at home. A sort of couch made

from boxes, and a decayed chair that had great arms from which the stuffing protruded like a disease, had been arranged with cushions and a blanket before the wide stone fireplace. There were remains of a meal—a loaf, some cheese, a plate—on the table that was the only other piece of furniture there.

Judith stood looking about her. 'It is strange,' she said. 'It is as though I had lived here. I know where everything was. There are the marks on the wall yet where that picture hung. It was a picture of an old man of Elizabeth's time. It hangs in the house at Uldale now. When I was a small child he terrified me. Here they would sit, my father and mother, before the fire, and upstairs they died and I was born.'

'Ugh! It's cold,' said Warren, shivering. 'We will not stay.'

'We will make a fire,' Judith said. 'Why not? Perhaps we will bring their ghosts back with the warmth.'

He was eager to do anything that she asked. They climbed the rickety stairs, rotten now with holes, creaking at every step, into the upper storey. The rooms here were pitifully small, but had a more human air, for one of them was plainly used for sleeping by the shepherd and his wife.

'It was here I was born.' Judith stared about her. 'Uncle Tom has often told me. How he was riding through the snow and heard an infant crying. He came up here with all his dogs, and in the bed my mother lay dead, in a cradle myself, and on a chair the old woman asleep with drink. And in the next room my father dead. So he picked me up in his arms and rode off with me home.'

Warren would have wished to come close to her and put his arm around her. She looked so small and by herself. But he did not dare. In the next room they found a pile of logs. They carried some down and made a great fire in the open hearth.

They sat down near to it, close together, warming their hands. The house was filled with her father and mother. Georges seemed there too. Only dead people. And for that reason, because she could not get at the dead and her heart was so moved that she longed to be kind to the living, almost without knowing that she did it, she laid her hand on Warren's knee, and then, when she felt it throb in response, she did not care to take the hand away again.

It was the first demonstration that, unurged, she had ever made to him; after a little he, as though he were moving mountains or the heavens would fall, laid his hand on hers.

'The fire makes me sleepy—the fire and the cold air.' She took off her riding-hat and shook her red curls about her face. 'Warren,' she said, 'you look most solemn. Well, I should also feel solemn. Perhaps I do, but I have often noticed that whenever I feel most solemn I want to laugh.' She went on talking as though she would cover the emotion that she knew he was feeling. 'This house, deserted as it is, is better than Uldale just now. Everyone is at odds there, and I am weary of trying to make them better. I want a life of my own, Warren.'

'Come away with me, then,' he said.

'But that would be no life of my own. Since Uncle Tom carried me out of this place in his arms I have been for ever mixed with the lives of other people.'

'You can go to a nunnery,' he said, laughing. He came a little closer to her. The fire was burning with splendid energy and roaring up the chimney.

'No. I am mixed with other people because I want to be. I am not such a coxcomb as to suppose that I am inhuman. I am inquisitive; I must know just what their lives are, and then I must tell them what they ought to be. And yet I wish to be by myself. I am only happy in one place, and that is Watendlath.'

'Are you not happy now?'

'I shall soon be warm, and then, when I am, I will tell you whether I am happy.'

He put his arm around her; she did not move away. Why should she if it pleased him? And he was alive. His heart was beating against her breast. She was tired of anger and disappointment. Her heart ached to be kind.

She went on talking. At last he said (his hand was trembling under hers):

'Judith, I love you every day more. . . . What shall be done about it?'

In ordinary times she would have checked him, but now—what did it matter? Was she not too particular in guarding herself? After all, was she so important? She had only in all her life been important to one person, and that was to Georges, and even to him for only a little of a time. How much she was making of her life, considering herself this way and that way, when in reality she was nothing. The mother of no one, the lover of no one, scarcely the friend of anyone. . . . She was not pitying herself—rather laughing at herself—with a little interest and tenderness, because she knew herself better than she knew anyone else.

So she let him hold her hand, then tenderly kiss her cheek, then with great gentleness stroke her hair. The trembling of his body touched her infinitely. Warren, who had faced so many things with such courage, needed her now to help and befriend him.

'Oh, Warren!' She liked him close to her, the fire was very pleasant, and figures, friendly figures, seemed to be in the room. 'It is so long since Georges died. I wish I could let him go in peace. I shall not be a free woman until I can be friends with everyone and yet be independent. Does it make you happy to be sitting here, the two of us beside the fire?'

'Desperately happy.'

'I want you to be happy.'

Why not? Oh, in God's name why not? There was Reuben's bear, and the boy hanged on the gibbet, and Georges thrown down the stair, and John's rabbit. . . . Why not be kind while one may? So soon it is all over and nothing done, no kindness remembered, no indulgence or charity. She thought, looking into the fire and feeling perhaps the figures in the room gather more closely about her, that she had never been charitable enough. If this life had a purpose (which she gravely doubted), it was for us to learn charity. A dangerous lesson, because the more charitable we became the less free we became, and this desire for freedom was becoming with her a passion. But the bear danced in the Square, the rope swung on the gibbet, Georges lay with his back broken, little Hartley Coleridge was a prisoner, the rabbit was flung out of window, Warren had a bad leg, and his wife had left him, and he loved *her*, poor man—although why he loved her she couldn't conceive.

'I have never been happy until now,' he said, resting his head on her lap. It seemed as though Georges, and the child that she had never had, and maybe her mother and father whom she had never seen, were all represented in that little damaged body holding her as though she were its only hope.

She smiled, looking out above his head. Why should she be so proud of herself? Why should she not be kind? Why should she not give anything she could that would make him happy? She sighed, touched his cheek and then surrendered, giving him all he asked——

WILL HERRIES DINES AT WESTAWAYS

She knew early in February that she was to have a child. For some time she had been happy, and, when she was certain of this new circumstance, it was as though life beat up in her like a released fountain.

For years after Georges' death there had been no life, then slowly, slowly it had returned, always finding its source in Watendlath. Now she was going really to live again, and all she had to do was to fight for her freedom. That she had not yet secured, but she would secure it now that the child had come to help her.

She was beginning at last to understand something about life. A woman is made for the love and protection of someone or something else; this is the mainspring of her nature. But in order to employ this love and protection at its fullest she must be free of any bond that is simply a tyranny without love. All the women around Judith at this time were so bound—it would be generations before they would begin to be free—and Judith would have been held in the same way had it not been for the lives and natures of her father and mother whom she had never seen or known. The whole history of being a Herries is learning to be free.

She took things as they came. What was coming was her child. What was also coming was Will Herries to Westaways. What was also coming was some decisive crisis between Francis and Jennifer. And it seemed that all these things were arriving together.

Since the ride to Borrowdale, Forster had seen Judith less frequently. He was shy now and uncomfortable, for he had never realised so sharply that Judith did not and could not love him as at the moment of her surrender to him. He did not know that she was to have a child, but he did know that, on that day, she did not surrender to him but to her memories. She had begun by wishing to be kind to him, and then had recalled the voice and movements of a man who was dead. That hour had been filled with ghosts.

So, although he loved her with a fire that really ate into the very nerves of his small and ailing body, he came to visit her less often and, when he was with her, saw her as someone always just beyond reach.

She was resolved that he should not know about the child. It did not seem to her that it would be Forster's child at all, so filled had the ruined house been with others on that winter afternoon.

Passionately she wished that it should be born in Watendlath, in that room where Georges had died, but her practical mind saw beyond the sentiment of that desire. That her child should be born in Watendlath would involve too many others beside herself — the Ritsons, Charlie Watson, Jennifer, Francis. . . . She must go away, and the child must be born with only herself for its guardian. She did not know at present where she would go or what she would do.

There were more immediate necessities, for, in this same month, on a gusty evening of February 1815, Will Herries with his wife, his son and a vast deal of impedimenta arrived at Westaways.

On the morning after his arrival Judith and Francis had a talk.

Francis looked a man twenty years more than his real age. He was so thin that his facial bones, always prominent in the Herries fashion, gave shadows and lines to his cheeks and eyes. His dark, thick hair emphasised his pallor. He looked a man with his back to the wall. Judith knew that, besides his trouble with Jennifer, he was in great distress about the condition of the people around him. The long years of the French wars had brought hunger and unhappiness everywhere; in the agricultural parts of Cumberland and Westmorland, where life was largely self-supporting and where the narrow and remote valleys led to seclusion, the pinch was not so severe as in many parts of England, but in the last twenty years industrial life was beginning to make itself felt, a new phenomenon, and towns like Kendal, Whitehaven, Cockermouth knew something that was close to starvation.

He, who had been always on the side of the people against privilege, of the rebel, the underdog, found himself now a rich man with a fine house and a body of servants.   He would like to give away all that he had, but he was not free —he had a wife, children, dependants.   More than that he saw that this new growing England did not want his charity.   He was held to be an aristocrat, and to be responsible for taxes, bread prices and all the other evils.   Of his class he found no one in sympathy with his ideas. The squires and landholders round him thought that a sign of encouragement to a poor man meant that the poor man would rule, as he had been doing in France.   The French example was before every eye.   So Francis was once more alone, as all his life he had been.   But he was not only alone—he was inarticulate.   He had the great misfortune of seeing the justice of both sides. He, who had once proclaimed exultantly the fall of the Bastille, now feared any kind of revolution for his own country that he loved so dearly.

Until now there had been no riots in Cumberland, as in the Midlands and the South, but only a week or two ago rioters had burnt some ricks and stable-buildings of Osmaston's, and he himself had received several threatening anonymous letters.

If only, Judith thought, he would speak to me, say frankly all that was in his mind, as he used to do.   But it was years now since he had been honest with her.   Silence had grown upon him. He was shut up within himself.

But now to-day he began frankly enough.

'Judith,' he said at once, 'I want you not to avoid Will and Christabel because you are living here.'

That, unfortunately, produced a feeling of irritation in her—all in a moment when she had intended to be so kind and understanding. She was suddenly tired of the lot of them—Francis, Jennifer, Will, Christabel, all of them.

'What do you wish me to do, Francis?'

'Why . . . to go to Westaways . . . when you wish . . . as often as you prefer.'

'And Jennifer?'

He shook his head impatiently.

'What has that to do——' He broke off. 'I often think you hate Jennifer.'

She sat down, suddenly weary.

'Oh no—hate?—oh no, dear Francis. Perhaps I am a little tired. What would you say, Francis, if I went away altogether?'

'Went away!' His thin pale face was aghast. He put his hand up to his forehead in a movement of bewilderment.

'Oh no! You to desert us! It would be shameful!'

Then she was angry. There was the implied right here that had always irritated her in him, as though, if he decided that she was necessary for him, why, that was reason enough for anything. It was not selfishness but rather an obstinate preoccupation with his own ideas.

Her anger gave her the opportunity to say some things that had long been in her mind.

She looked up at him, and part of her thought, 'Oh, poor Francis, how weary and despondent he looks!' But the other part thought, 'How insensitive he is! I have endured this long enough.'

'Listen, Francis. I am going to say one or two things. One is that I have been here for over five years and have been a failure. Yes—don't protest—it's true. I have been a failure with you. Do you know that you have not spoken out your heart to me for three years? No, not once. I have loved you all my life. You are the only friend I have beside Emma and Reuben, whom I never see nor hear of, and one other. But of late you have shown me no friendship. You have never thought of me at all, never inquired how I did nor how things went with me. You have been filled with your own troubles. I have been the housekeeper here. Good enough.

'Then I have failed because Jennifer hates me. Oh yes, she does! When I first came she was too languid to hate anyone. But now she is not languid any more and is perfectly capable of hatred. Do you know that when I had been here a year or so I discovered Mrs. Ponder searching my drawer for my private letters? No, you did not know. But I begged Jennifer that Mrs. Ponder should depart. Mrs. Ponder did not depart. Later, *you* ordered that Mrs. Ponder should depart—but Mrs. Ponder is still here. I have not failed with the children—John loves me, I know, but even that has been an added

aggravation to Jennifer. Yet, although for five
years Jennifer and Mrs. Ponder have done all
that could be done to make me miserable (and
I am not happy, you know, when people near me
dislike me), I have stayed because I love you
and I love your children. Or no—maybe there
is too much sentiment in that. If I am strictly
truthful, I have stayed in part because I like to
make people do as I wish. I have stayed even
because Jennifer has wished me to go. I have
stayed, perhaps, because I would not be defeated
by a fat snake like Mrs. Ponder.

' But you, dear Francis, have never given these
things one thought. You have not asked yourself whether I were lonely or unhappy. In fact,
I am almost frantic for my freedom. There is
a place but a few miles from here where I could
be happy for ever. But, although it is so near
by, I do not seem to be able to reach it. My
father, by all that I hear, was the same. But he
was not a complacent female as I am.'

She smiled up at him then, feeling quite
friendly again now that she had said her mind.

But he, in a voice of horrified disgust, said:

' Mrs. Ponder searched your private papers.
You told Jennifer of it and yet Mrs. Ponder
stayed? '

' Well, but *you* told Jennifer about the
rabbit, and yet Mrs. Ponder stayed.'

She wanted then to rise and throw her arms
around his neck, so terribly unhappy did he look.

' You are right,' he said at last. ' Dreadfully
right. I have been most fearfully to blame.'

Then, of course, she repented of having said anything. She did not want to add to his distresses. What she *did* want, however, was to be free of them all and to have her life to herself!

She went on quietly: 'You see, Francis, I am the only one in this house who is friendly with Will and Christabel. What complications will come now from my being here! I cannot abandon Christabel, who was so good to me in London. And of course I cannot abandon you ! I think it shameful of Will to have come here, and so I shall tell him, but I shall be a shuttlecock between the two houses. I am nearly forty-one years of age, and that is too old for a shuttlecock!'

'You say you cannot abandon Christabel and you cannot abandon myself—but a moment ago you were implying that you wished to be free of all of us!'

'And so I do.' She shrugged her shoulders. 'And so I will. I am for ever promising myself. To-morrow—the day following . . .'

She had risen and, instinctively, they came together. He drew her to him and they exchanged a long embrace, the first of real intimacy for years.

'Judith,' he whispered, stroking her cheek, 'do not leave me, I beg you. I beg you. I am unhappy. No one understands——'

She thought of the child alive within her, and then she was so happy that she thought humorously, 'Was ever a woman in so many complications? But this is living—every moment has excitement.' At that instant she was so much a

child that she could have sat down at the spinet
and strummed any discordant noise. For she
loved Francis to love her. Never mind if she could
not be free just yet. Time for that! She *loved*
Francis to love her! He had not for so long!

'Oh, Francis, I love you!' she murmured.
What would he say if he knew that she was to
have a child, she who was, he thought, so faithful
to Georges' memory? Well, so she was. But
Georges would be glad for her to have a child.
Then she could not have Francis back again
without at once wanting to manage him. She
drew him down on to the sofa beside her, holding
his hand. She wanted at once, without delay, to
make him happy! Somehow to make him happy!
Her eyes were so glowing with life and eagerness
and vitality that she did not seem like a small,
round, middle-aged female in a grey spencer,
but rather she was the daughter of a gipsy,
telling fortunes.

She held his hand lightly.

'Now listen, Francis. Here is what you
must do——'

And at that moment Jennifer came in.

They were both silenced. They had nothing
whatever to say. Jennifer, brilliantly attired, stood
there and looked at them. She was dressed for
going out.

Francis thought, 'She is going to meet
Fernyhirst' and was at once miserable.

Judith thought, 'I really hate this woman
at last.' But did she? There was something
ignorant about Jennifer, as though with all her

beauty, her husband, admirers, children and the rest, she had never learnt anything about life at all. Just as you pity a selfish, wilful child because of the trouble that is in store for it, so Judith pitied Jennifer. And where you pity you cannot hate.

She was dressed in a crimson spencer with long sleeves that she wore open. It was lined with white fur. Over it she had a delicate Cashmere shawl and under it a long, tight-fitting dress of grey. On her head was a tiny crimson bonnet, close-fitting to the head, decorated with an upright ostrich feather. Her low boots, ankle high, showed the beautiful elegance of her little feet.

Remarkably, at this critical moment—for it was the only one at which the three of them together discussed the Westaways situation—scarcely a word was said.

Jennifer, looking at Judith as a bird of Paradise might look at a sparrow, said:

' So I hear that Will has arrived at Westaways. You know, Judith, that your visits there will inconvenience us in no way whatever. Pray visit there when you feel inclined.'

Judith got up and, simply because she knew that it would annoy Jennifer, rested her hand on Francis' shoulder.

' Thank you, Jennifer.'

Mrs. Ponder was in the doorway. ' Fred is there with the carriage, ma'am,' she said. She gave her two enemies, Francis and Judith, a dark look. Yes, she had stayed there although they had told her to go. And she would stay so long as she pleased.

Jennifer, her head high, her ostrich feather nodding, swung her way out.

When the door had closed, Francis said: 'Judith, do you think. . . ?' Then he stopped.

'And now,' said Judith, pointing to the sofa, 'I will tell you what you must do, Francis——'

The first occasion on which Judith dined at Westaways was on a wild, stormy afternoon in March. She was generously allowed the closed barouche by Jennifer, who was for ever making attempts to suggest that Judith was a sort of poor relation. (And indeed was she not just that in reality?)

'Dear Judith, I pray that you may have an entertaining evening. Do not encourage Christabel to call on us here.'

'I am sure that she will not wish to,' said Judith.

Jennifer looked at her closely. Was she beginning to suspect the child? Then Jennifer was clouded by a glance of apprehension. She looked back to the stairs as though to be sure that no one was there.

'Judith,' she said. 'If they talk scandal of me at Westaways—as of course they will—even though you dislike me, well, I am Francis' wife.'

'Scandal?' said Judith. 'What scandal?'

'There is always scandal in a country neighbourhood.' She looked most beautiful in the candle-light. Her dark ringlets gleamed on the soft orange texture of her Cashmere shawl.

Judith smiled, compelled by that beauty to which she was always surrendering wherever she saw it.

'How little even now you know me,' she said.

But as she climbed into the dark carriage she stubbed her shoe against the step. In the dark she nodded to herself. 'I cannot *endure* these people!' It was as though her mother, puzzled and bewildered at Herries fifty years earlier, had spoken.

But it was a most interesting evening. Judith stepped, in a moment, back into her old place. There was James, son of Pomfret and Rose, great-grandson of old Pomfret, who had built the house; he was a short, stubborn-looking fellow of thirty-six, very silent, and, everybody said, waiting for his father to die that he might succeed to the baronetcy. There was Montague Cards, in whose London rooms the famous arbitration had once taken place. He was now forty-eight, looked as though his cheeks were painted and wore most affected clothing. He spent as much of his time as possible in staying with relations free of charge. He planned to remain at Westaways longer than Will had any idea of. Carey Rockage, now sixty, was a splendid old fellow, wearing loose garments that seemed to have been made for someone else, most absent-minded but always finding something interesting and amusing to entertain him-

self with. Maria was now an old woman of
sixty-one and looked like a haystack on wheels.
She moved with a kind of rolling motion. She
had peculiar habits; she would whistle to herself
or, at table, make little pellets of bread and flick
them about. She was so untidy that no one of
her garments seemed to belong to any other.
Her hair was white and she wore a lace cap,
none too clean and set rakishly at an angle.
For Judith, who had such a passion for cleanliness,
her untidiness was an agony. She found herself,
before she had been at Westaways ten minutes,
running after Maria, picking up her handkerchief,
fastening a button, tying a ribbon.

Will Herries was not greatly changed, save
that he was a wealthy man now of forty-five,
and so had swollen in importance. Not physically swollen; he was as thin and stiff as a
water-pipe, and he spoke like Moses delivering
the Ten Commandments to the people of Israel.
Christabel also was now a middle-aged woman,
dressed better than of old, and was not so deeply
terrified of functions and ceremonies.

She was, however, one of those people whose
anticipation of catastrophe spoils every occasion.
And expectation of disaster attracts it as surely as
mountains attract rain.

Walter was now their only remaining child,
his sister having died some years previously of
smallpox.

Walter was terrific. He was, Judith thought,
the largest young man she had ever seen. Horse-
like as all the Herries were one way or another,

he resembled a charger for whom no general, however famous, could ever be grand enough. He had all the splendour of bone and muscle united to a supreme self-confidence and determination. He was the absolute symbol of Herries, blood, bone, and soul, all mingled together, engaged upon the same pursuit. He was neither dour nor aloof like his father. He laughed often, and his laughter, Judith thought, must make the inner confines of Borrowdale quake. His chest was the broadest, his legs the thickest, his neck the strongest, his arms the most muscular that she had ever seen. Set in all this splendour were very small eyes that had a strange meditative stare, even when he was most jolly. Later in the evening she was to perceive how instantly he could change from pleasure to business. She decided that he would become the most important of all the Herries family, and she was correct in her prophecy.

Already he dominated everyone there. He wore a huge stock, a vast purple coat and immense trousers, just then coming into fashion. His hair was a dark curly brown, and he had a snuff-box as big almost as a band-box.

He ordered the servants, arranged the details of the party as though he were master of the house. Two years previously he had married Agnes Bailey, daughter of a rich City merchant. She was not present this evening because she was expecting very shortly her first child. So Walter, roaring and laughing, informed Judith, adding that if the child were not a boy he would let his wife know of it! She was a little bit of a woman, he informed Judith, whom he could slip easily into his pocket. He spoke of her with all the pride that the Herries feel for any woman who has been wise enough to marry one of them. As always, when she was with anyone of great height, she was embarrassed by her own small-ness. But she soon recovered. He at once chaffed her.

' Why, you are the pocket Venus! ' he cried.

' Oh, Walter! ' cried Christabel. ' Pray, pray———'

But Judith laughed.

' How much brain is there in all that muscle, Cousin Walter? I've seen bullocks at a fair———'

He thought that immensely good. She found that he laughed at almost everything. She rather liked him. After the restraints of Uldale this was rather refreshing. She dis-covered very shortly that it was he who had per-suaded his father to come to Westaways. He was all for carrying on the family feud, partly from rancour and scorn of Francis, partly from pride and physical good health. And he had never been in Cumberland before, although it was his home. Of course it was his home. His grandfather had been the best fighter in the district, and his father had been born here. That was enough for him. She saw that he was determined to get Uldale into his hands before he had done.

She was happy at once when she saw how greatly pleased Christabel and Maria were to

see her. Then speedily also the light of battle
was in her eye. For she perceived that they were
all there, that everything was done, to impress
her. She was the spy from the enemy camp, and
the intention was that she should return and tell
them all at Uldale that they had no chance, that
they had better surrender at once, pack up and go.
Well, she was going to tell them nothing of the
kind. She was fond of Christabel, but she loved
Francis. Poor Francis, growing old now, with
nothing to show for life at all save his children,
who did not know him. Yes, she was on his side,
and so she would let that great hulking elephant
of a Walter know before the evening was over.

The house she had never been inside before.
She knew well its charming exterior; she had
often walked and ridden past it, its roof covered
with rosy tiles, the beautiful wrought ironwork,
the door with the fluted columns and the delicate
fanlight.

Within it was by far grander than Uldale,
with the pillared hall, and up the wide staircase to
the grand saloon that had been decorated by old
Westaway himself. The subject of the decorations was Paris awarding the apple, and there
were three fine, plump, rosy goddesses. In this
fine room, glittering and gleaming with the
candle-light and the swinging splendours of
the glass candelabra, they were all gathered.
Soon they went down to dinner.

Judith was seated between Walter Herries
and his father, who, his back erect, his thin neck
raised like a hen's, should have commanded the

T

assembly. He did not. Walter praised the food, guaranteed the liquor, chaffed old Maria, scolded and commanded the servants.

At the last moment Warren Forster slipped in and, with a nod and a smile to them all, took his place.

' You have nothing, I wager,' Walter said to her, ' like this at Uldale.'

Judith looked about her: a very grand room with a massive fireplace, the table piled with food, perfect organisation.

' I prefer Uldale.'

' You prefer Uldale? But, come now, Cousin. I may call you Cousin? What can you prefer? There is no space at Uldale, no light——'

' No light! We have all the light in the world! '

' Well, well—so has a barn. I know what I know. You shall have your Uldale.'

She looked at him with great calmness.

' You have come here, Cousin Walter, to crow over Uldale. Well, you shall not do it for me. I am old enough to be your mother, Cousin Walter, and there are one or two things I shall teach you before we are done.'

He looked at her with admiration. He liked her. He had heard that this little woman had spirit. What was she? Born in a barn-yard out of a gipsy? No matter. She had pluck.

' Is Jennifer as lovely as they say? '

' She is very lovely.'

' I would go a long way for a beautiful woman.

But Francis, now—he is vexed, is he not, at our taking Westaways?'

' He has other things to think of.'

' Ha, ha! . . . I warrant he has, and there will be more before long. Jennifer insulted my mother, you know . . . in a public place too.'

' That is an old story—and there are two sides to it.'

' Not so old that I have forgot it. And you would smack my face if there were cause, Cousin Judith. By gad, I believe you would too.'

' Certainly,' said Judith gravely, ' if there were cause.'

' Well, I drink your health, Cousin. We are to be friends.'

' I am in the other camp,' she said, smiling at him.

' It will be all one camp one day,' he answered her.

She heard Will saying with great gravity:

' I have heard my father tell many a time how as a small boy he came to this house. It was your great-grandfather Pomfret, James, who had it then, you know. Yes, and he sat there with my poor grandmother—she died shortly, poor thing—and stared and stared. For it was a grand house to him. He had never seen the like of it. And there were all the things in the room that are here yet. I will show them to you afterwards, Maria. We had them in London and brought them up with us. Out of the parlour window the fountain with the bird that has been

here from the beginning.   The screen with the
gold work on it, the clock with the sun and moon.
We had them in our London house.   You must
have seen them often, Maria.   But what frightened my father—he was only a small boy, you
know—was his great-aunt Maria, sitting there
with a spaniel on her lap.   He often told us
children of it.   She had a wig with flowers and
a hoop as large as a tent, a black patch on her
cheek, and her fingers covered with jewelry.
She was born in the year of the battle of Naseby,
you know.   So here we are back to the battle of
Naseby.'

   Will, Judith thought, was quite human all of
a sudden.   He was so proud of being here,
back in his rightful place.   Yes, she understood
him and sympathised with him.   Then he
looked at her, as though he would say: ' Here
we are, you see, and we shall remain.'   Then her
cheeks flushed.   So would Francis remain *and*
his children.   She would see to that while she
had breath left in her body.   (Odd that only an
hour or two ago, in the carriage, she had wanted
to be free of the lot of them!   Now she was in
the very middle of the battle, and glad to be!)

   More and more food appeared.   (They had
not dinners like this at Uldale.)   More and more
wine was drunk.   James began, in his stubborn
determined way, to talk of the present discontents.
He had nothing good to say of anyone—King,
Regent, Parliament, Army—but the villains of
every piece were the working-classes.   Oh! these
working-classes!   What was it they wanted,

the dirty dogs? Why were they *never* content?
They complained of the price of food. Well,
let them work harder and earn more. They
said that their homes were not fit to live in!
What did they expect? Palaces?

Nearly everyone joined in. At Manchester
and at Liverpool there were disorders every day.
Of course it would be right enough now that
Napoleon was safe in Elba. But would it be?
Someone said that we would be fighting Russia
next. . . . Wars were endless. One led to another. And while there were so many wars,
of course trade would be bad. . . . At the
word 'trade' Will lifted up his sharp blue-
tinted chin and told them all what he thought
about Trade.

Money would be in the towns — Birmingham, Liverpool, Manchester. . . . This new
machinery. . . . The country would be a dead
place in another thirty years. Cotton? Had any
of them thought about cotton? Well, he had.
India and the East were all very well, but wise
men were turning their attention to home pro-
ducts. Now that Napoleon was shut up and
the Allies were in Vienna. . . . In another
thirty years there would be no country in England,
no *true* country.

Why, when his grandfather had come first to
Keswick his father, as a little boy, had ridden into
Borrowdale on horseback as though you were
riding into China. His father had often told
him. Why, nothing on wheels had ever been
seen in Borrowdale a hundred years ago, and now

he wouldn't be surprised but that one day they
would be driving carriages with steam. He
looked at them all grimly, just like an angry and
emaciated Moses.

'They'd better look out,' he seemed to say,
'or they would have the surprise of their life!'
For a brief moment he dominated all of them;
even Walter disappeared.

Old Maria Rockage, on his other side,
listened to him and thought what nonsense he
was talking. She had drunk some wine—not
her customary habit—and her head was a little
fuddled. To tell the truth, she was homesick
for Grosset. Oh yes, she knew that this was all
fine, with the fountain in the garden, and the
painting of the naked women upstairs and all the
shining candles. Everything was very orderly,
the servants moved most quietly. There was
enough food to feed the village at Grosset for a
week (and that when all the countryside was
starving!), but she wasn't really comfortable
here. She didn't care for that big shouting
Walter, and Will wasn't kind to Christabel, and
the large four-poster that enshrouded herself
and Carey at night was not truly a *friendly* bed,
and she missed her children; even though Carey
the Younger *was* fond of doing nothing, she would
rather have him than this hulk of a Walter,
and Phyllis was a *sweet* child. . . . She began
to feel very melancholy indeed. A tear fell into
the goose on her plate. Then she looked up and
changed a smile with Judith.

She felt better. What a pity that Judith

had ever left them! They had all been very happy together! And now she heard the strangest things about Jennifer. Judith surely was not happy there. But the child (for although Judith was over forty, Maria thought of her as a child) *looked* happy. She had grown stouter. What a sensible woman! Grosset had been in pieces ever since she had left them! And it was neither nice nor kind of Will to come here simply to triumph over Francis, all because years ago Christabel had slapped Jennifer's face. Not that she had ever liked Jennifer, beautiful though she was. And they said that Francis was most unhappy. . . . It was not as though he were a boy any longer. . . . He must be fifty-five or so, and had done nothing with his life, poor man. . . . She piled up little pellets of bread beside her plate.

Behind the wall of talk and laughter they were moving on their secret ways. Will was stiff with triumph. This was a grand dinner. He would show brother Francis at Uldale. . . . Christabel longed to have a real talk with Judith. She wanted that somehow, in one way or another, they should understand at Uldale that she was not their enemy. . . . In her heart she would rejoice to have a reconciliation with Jennifer.

Walter was hot and thick and turbulent with the pride of life. He saw himself as a conqueror. Of what? Of whom? It did not matter. James had in his heart contempt for all these country bumpkins, the grand Walter included. The old-maidish bachelor with the painted cheeks was enjoying the food and the wine. Here was the place for him! He would stay . . . one month, two, three? Old Carey was thinking of a dog of his, Pluto, who was as game a dog . . .

Warren Forster, who had scarcely spoken, sat, his eyes secretly fixed on Judith. Judith, placed so demurely there, once in his arms while the logs crackled in the stone fireplace. Judith, the passion of his whole life. . . .

And Judith herself began to wish to escape. She felt unwell, some great uneasiness at her heart. She *was* in the camp of the enemy! It was as though she could foretell in some secret way all the consequences that were to come out of this move into Westaways, a move made from vanity and vainglory. She had sympathised with Will, but now she felt that he was there only that he might snub Francis. And as for his son! He seemed to be more overbearing with every minute that passed, as the room grew more heated, the food more grossly devoured, the wine more carelessly drunk, the lights more brilliant. He seemed to grow and hang over her in a vast imposing shadow. He had drunk great quantities of wine, but it had not affected him. Will's speech was already clouded, poor old Carey was waving his glass with uncertain hands, Monty Cards was calling for a song in a shrill high tone, James scowled. . . . It was time for the ladies to be gone.

They rose. Walter got up, bowed, then kissed her hand.

' Adieu, Cousin Judith ! '

His purple coat with its high collar strained across his tremendous shoulders, his stock seemed scarcely to confine the muscles of his neck—but his eyes were very small. She looked up at him, glance to glance. What she would give for a few more inches! But his little eyes closed before hers. In a majestic procession the ladies left the room.

Upstairs, seated beneath the rosy goddesses, Christabel at once drew Judith aside. From where Judith sat, under the swinging glittering glass on the gilt sofa, she could look out through the curtains that were not yet drawn, to the Lake darkening now in the gathering dusk. Its bosom was shaken with trembling; its surface was crossed with paths of pale opalescent light, and one rosy shadow hung on to the green skirts of the hill. It moved Judith most strangely to see how the Lake was trembling; however, in another moment she was looking about the room and thinking how she would arrange it were it hers. That cabinet would be best in the corner and the large clock with the marble pillars. . . .

' And so, Judith,' Christabel was saying in that hushed anxious voice of hers, while old Maria nodded her head, jumped awake and then fell off again, ' you must understand that I have no animosity. Bygones must be bygones.'

' No, *you* have no animosity,' said Judith, nodding her head and swinging her legs as well as she could in her long gown (for the sofa was a trifle high). ' Of course *you* have none, dear Christabel. But what of Will and Walter? '

'Oh! yes!' Christabel admitted, her brow wrinkling with anxiety. 'Should not the curtains be drawn? It is almost dark. Ah, here comes Wiggins with the tea.—I am half afraid of Wiggins. We brought him from London. Monty found him for us!'

Judith looked at Wiggins, who was almost as mountainous as his master, Walter. Poor Christabel—to be crushed among all these huge men! But she would like to have the managing of Wiggins. He would be child's play beside Mrs. Ponder.

'Yes, Wiggins. Here, if you please. You understand, Judith, that men look upon these things quite differently. Walter regards it as a sort of a game. He does indeed, and he is very chivalrous about any insult to myself. . . . And Jennifer *was* rude to me, you know. . . .'

'So long ago!' said Judith scornfully. (Yes, and the spinet would be better nearer the window. What a lovely pattern of flowers and leaves on its cover! And then you could have the sofa. . . . Sofas were still rare and this was one of the finest Judith had ever seen.) What a lot of money Will must be making! Well, it was what he had always wanted. . . .

'At least,' Christabel went on, 'you will not leave me, dear Judith. I must see you sometimes. I must indeed. It was my only comfort in coming here. You must not hate me because Jennifer does!'

'Hate you! Dear Christabel!' Touched as always by any appeal to her affection, she

leaned forward and kissed Christabel's dry cheek.
' Alas, I hate nobody!   Hatred is so difficult to
sustain.   Even Mrs. Ponder——'

   ' Who is Mrs. Ponder? '

   ' An odious female.'

   ' And Jennifer? ' Christabel looked to see that
Wiggins was gone and Maria fast asleep.   ' They
are saying very odd things about Jennifer,
Judith.'

   ' What things? '

   ' Is there not a Captain Fernyhirst?   And they
say that Francis——'

   ' I suppose Walter brings you this gossip,'
Judith broke in indignantly.   ' Remember,
Christabel, that I love Francis more than anyone
in the world.   I will not hear a word against
him——'

   ' No, no,' Christabel cried, frightened of
offending Judith.   ' It is only that it is common
talk——'

   ' There is always common talk,' said Judith.
' In every country place they talk.'

   She was thinking : ' Well, there you are, now
it has all begun.   Christabel is different already,
sniffing out things about Uldale.   And soon
Jennifer will be saying things about Christabel.'
She saw Walter on a huge horse riding deliberately past Uldale and making rude gestures,
mocking the smallness of the place and the bare-
ness of the garden.   Oh! it would be impossible!
She had an impulse to rise there and then and
run for her life.

   Indeed, she did shortly run, but not before

she had heard some astonishing news. The door burst open; all the men were there, Walter in front of them. They were shouting and crying out. Old Maria woke up, Christabel thought the house was on fire, Judith wondered whether Walter's wife upstairs was suddenly delivered of a child. But no! Walter was roaring out:

' What do you think? What do you think? Boney has escaped from Elba! Escaped from Elba, by God! He's in Paris, and the French are with him to a man! Esthwaite has looked in to tell us. There's news for you! Boney escaped from Elba! Whoop! Whoop! . . . What a fellow! By gad, I admire him! Escaped from Elba, by gad!'

They were all in a frantic excitement, even James, and Monty Cards was crying out like a woman:

' He'll be in London yet! We shall all be French before the year's out.'

Judith, standing by herself, beside the window, felt the news run inside her like wine. That marvellous fat little man, whose corpulent shadow had hung over them, almost all their lives as it now seemed, had done it again! Yes, it was wonderful. He was a wonder. She could see, looking through the haze of the candles, all Europe in a hurry and a scurry, hastening like ants, hither, thither, everywhere. Stiff and conceited Talleyrand, and the sentimental weak Russian, their own mountain of flesh, the Regent, the old mad King, all the bourses and the shops and the theatres, the country lanes, cottages, mountains, lakes—all suddenly quivering again under the shadow of that little indomitable monster!

The others in the room had for the moment forgotten her. They were all talking together; in the doorway Wiggins and another man-servant stood listening.

Bonaparte free again! You could hear the cry from China to Peru! Well, if Napoleon could free himself so easily why should not she?

The news and a sudden glimpse of Warren Forster's anxious, pale face (even in the excitement he did not forget her) made her almost mad with eagerness to get away. Away! Anywhere. . . . To have her child somewhere by herself. No Herries. No relations or duties or scandals. Napoleon had done it. She had as strong a will.

Moved by an irresistible impulse she was out of the room and had slipped down the stairs. They were not thinking of her. She felt as though she had the energy to escape down the road just as she was, and in a moment she would be in Paris! Well, why not? Anything to escape. However, she found her bonnet and shawl, ran out into the garden, and then in the courtyard at the back discovered Fred. She told him that she wanted the carriage. At once! At once!

While she waited for him she smiled up at the stars that were beginning to break into the sky.

If Napoleon had done it she could! And it was as though the child in her womb laughed its approval.

JUDITH IN PARIS

This time Judith escaped some distance; she ran from Westaways to Paris.

In June the battle of Waterloo was fought and Napoleon's escape was concluded.

Judith told Francis and Jennifer that she would take a little holiday. She was going to stay with Emma Furze in London. Jennifer was kind to her and kissed her good-bye. Judith did not know whether she was aware of the increase in her figure or no. No one else seemed to notice anything. Francis was grave and reserved again. All he said was:

'It is not for long, Judith. Have you sufficient money?'

'Yes, thank you. . . . No, it is not for long,' she answered him. She did not know whether she were lying or no. It might be for ever.

But John made a scene. Quiet as he usually was, on this occasion he made a scene. He cried himself into being sick and scratched Mrs. Ponder's cheek. Then, two hours after Judith's departure, he ran away. He was found on the road to Bassenthwaite in a hedge, fast asleep. . . .

On a very hot summer afternoon, in the middle

of the Café des Mille Colonnes, sat La Belle Limonadière, dressed in crimson velvet and covered with jewels, serenely looking down on her hundreds of clients, like an empress, but very accurate in the change that she gave to the waiters. Spread before her were dozens of portions of broken sugar, five or six pieces in each portion, arranged in little silver saucers like wine-funnel stands. This was the remnant of the respect for sugar induced by the period when Napoleon closed Europe against English commerce. There were at this moment no sugar-basins in Paris.

La Belle Limonadière, although perhaps her best time was now over, was indeed a brilliant creature. A contemporary—a gentleman certainly to be trusted—describes her as having a complexion of Parian marble. He goes on (his letter is in the Herries' archives): "Her black hair and eyes were in striking contrast with her complexion. The usual aids of colour to the cheeks were not forgotten, but quite what the French call *au naturel*—a word merely meaning something less artificial than the last stage of artifice. *La Belle* has an air and expression of great good nature; and, what most amused me, a most solemn attitude of correctest propriety. Nobody presumes to address her without previous formal presentation, and it is found impossible to give any coffee orders to her majesty except through the medium of a gentleman-in-waiting!"

To Judith and Emma, sitting almost under her nose, this brilliant, black-haired, crimson-clad creature was infinitely fascinating. They could not take their eyes off her! She reminded Judith a little of Jennifer, only that she was not so beautiful. She always afterwards seemed to Judith to be the symbol, the decorated figure-head of this strange Paris adventure—to have the colour, the audacity and also the sordidness and underground thunder of this fantastic Paris scene. During all that followed in these exciting weeks, La Belle Limonadière was marching just in front, the presiding deity of this affair.

On this especial afternoon she was very gracious to a noble-looking gentleman (plainly not a Frenchman) who sat with some friends near to her, eating an ice and smiling up at the queen's throne. This gentleman, someone confided to Emma, was no other than Mr. Walter Scott, the famous poet. Judith looked at him with all her eyes, and loved him at once for his grand high forehead, his eyes beaming with kindness under their shaggy eyebrows, the courtesy of his mien. He was like a very noble sort of sheep-dog. When he got up and, limping on his stick, passed down the hall, she felt as though all were indeed well with this strange world, which was neither so fantastic nor so threatening as she had thought it.

For although she was greatly enjoying it all she was also rather frightened. For one thing they had not very much money, she and Emma, for another she was not very well, she who had always been so strong and so healthy. And then she was taken with strange waves of homesickness, wondering whether Francis were in health, whether the meals at Uldale were served properly, whether John missed her and what the clouds were doing to Skiddaw.

However you cannot, as she was for ever discovering, both have your cake and eat it, and this was most truly a fascinating scene. Paris was now a hotch-potch of all the nations of the world. This splendid hall, mirrored all round, divided by fluted Corinthian pillars, made the company seem innumerably multiplied. Here were English officers, then Highlanders with their plumed bonnets, now Prussian hussars, and again Brunswickers in their sombre uniforms. The French ladies, in their walking dresses and in high-crowned, plume-covered bonnets and shawls, were attended by their beaux, who were as gay, lively and noisy as though there had been no revolutions, no devastating wars, and as though their country were not at the moment occupied by the triumphant foe.

But how dazzling this scene, thought Judith, and how unreal the figure of the strange crimson hostess, her figure, solemn, correct, almost austere, multiplied in all these mirrors, herself entrenched with peaches, sugar and nosegays of flowers!

Beneath all the gaiety and sparkle you felt that the ground trembled. The English were popular, but the Prussians were hated. She saw on every side of her the Prussian arrogance. She had heard that when Wellington had protested about some outrageous piece of conduct,

Blücher had replied: ' Yes, but remember—
the French were never in England.' The very
fact that the French found it so difficult to submit
to the domination of a people whom they had so
long despised, caused those people to be more
arrogant. In the cafés their behaviour made
Judith, who, when the English were not in
question, was, because of Georges, more French
than the French, tremble with indignation.
And the whole public life of the French, so that
they seemed to be never at home but spent their
whole time in the cafés, the theatres, or on the
boulevards, made this trouble with the Prussians
the more prominent.

But then, as she by this time thoroughly
realised, the French themselves were scarcely,
as yet, disciplined. They had not suffered a
revolution in their country so long a while for
nothing. The French boys in the street, for
instance, were insolent beyond belief, and she
and Emma were for ever encountering both men
and women who seemed to them like dangerous
animals just let loose from their cages.

She found evidence enough of it in the lodgings; they were in the Rue Vivienne. They had
two rooms in the apartment of Monsieur and
Madame Dufresne. Little M. Dufresne, thin
as a stick, with a funny black toupee and a tiny
black moustache, had suffered some terror in his
earlier years from which he seemed to find it
impossible ever to escape. His chief pleasure
was in animals, so that he had in his room a
cockatoo, a monkey, three dogs, two cats and a

tortoise. For animals he had, it would seem, a very special gift, but for human beings no gift at all. His wife, on the other hand, was a large brawny woman, whom Judith could well imagine knitting in front of the scaffold while the tumbrils rolled up. Her great muscular arms were always bared to the elbow and she had a deep bass voice like a man's. They were a pair who led their own lives—they interfered with neither Judith nor Emma in any way, but at night one could hear the thick, low rumble of Madame's voice through the wall; it seemed to threaten every sort of vengeance.

However, here they were in the Café des Mille Colonnes and enjoying every moment of it. For Emma, indeed, this stay in Paradise was simply heaven. She had her darling Judith to look after and care for, and there rolled all around her the very life that Fate should have designed for her. She was now a woman between fifty and sixty, handsomer than she had ever been, for her figure, tall and majestic, had thinned, and her grey hair, her sparkling eager eyes, her vitality attracted attention wherever she went.

She was more ready now to be spectator than actor, but the sight of almost any man stirred her blood and excited her curiosity. And had ever a city in the world's history been so grandly filled with splendid men as was Paris at this moment? Glorious men, and most especially the Highlanders, who, in their intriguing costume, simply had the French ladies at their feet!

She was always on the move, for ever seeing

the sights. They went to the Opera, saw the King, a most benevolent-looking gentleman, the Emperor of Austria and the Duke of Wellington. They witnessed a ballet in which some of the performers were dressed as Highlanders, and heard the building ring with cries of '*Vivent les Écossais!*'—a glorious moment. There were constant processions, and one morning they saw pass no less than thirty thousand Russian soldiers. They went to the Théâtre des Variétés and saw 'Jean Bool' most amusingly caricatured. Best of all, perhaps, were their visits to the encampment of the English troops—the 95th Rifles, 52nd Light Infantry, and 71st Highlanders—in the Champs Elysées. This was one of the sights of Paris and immensely Emma enjoyed it. The world seemed only to exist to provide handsome military forms and fine ladies to gaze upon them.

She would, in fact, have known perfect happiness had it not been for a certain anxiety about Judith. Judith had been the one constant and unchanging devotion of her life. She would never have claimed for herself that she had a constant nature. She had not one herself, nor did she, any longer, expect constancy of others. She knew, she said, human nature too well.

But Judith was changed. You must expect it, of course. Judith was over forty and the child coming. It was no light matter to have your first child when you were over forty. But there was more in it than this. In the first place, Emma could not understand Judith's devotion to Georges. No, she certainly could not! It was

true that Georges had never really liked her,
but it was not that she was prejudiced.   She could
never have fallen in love with Georges herself;
but one of the things that life taught one was that
everyone must have, and be permitted to have,
their own taste!

No, but Georges had not been good to Judith;
he had been a thoroughly worthless, selfish fellow;
and here she still was, after all these years, adoring
him as though he had been a paragon!

But she was filled with contradictions.   She
adored Georges' memory, but some other man was
father of her child.   She had always seemed to
Emma one of the most virtuous of women,
possessing in fact a virtue that poor Emma herself
could never hope to command.   And yet she had
apparently given herself to a man for whom she
did not greatly care, simply from an impulse of
kindness.   Emma herself was kind, but she was
also passionate, even now when she was nearing
sixty.   But Judith was passionate only in relation
to Georges.   And how ironical that she had
offered all that love to Georges, who was never
to give her a child, but that now, when she was
almost past child-bearing, a chance moment with
someone whom she did not love should accom-
plish everything!   But life was like that.   Emma
herself could remember . . .

Beyond her nostalgia for Georges there was a
deeper nostalgia, and this Emma could not understand at all.   For it seemed from Judith's brief
and broken confidences—Judith talked very little
about herself even to Emma—that she thought

that could she only get away to Watendlath,
leave for ever all her Herries relations, and hide
herself in the hills for the rest of her days, all
would be well.

'Surely then,' cried Emma, 'in heaven's
name, go! You are your own mistress!'

But that, it seemed, was exactly what Judith
was not. She was for ever being dragged back
into Herries affairs.

'But you are not so weak!' cried Emma.

'But don't you see,' Judith answered, 'it is
a struggle inside myself. And one day it will be
too late. I shall be compelled to choose, and
shall make the wrong choice. And then I shall
be inside the Herries for the rest of my days.
And the worst of it will be that I shall like it—
and I shall have lost all my real life for ever.'

Not that Judith often talked like this. But
she was brooding, Emma knew, too much within
herself. If Emma made a fool of herself, which
she often did, she burst into a rage or a flood of
tears and it was all over. But Judith took things
to heart. And then of course you did brood
when you were having your first child. Poor
women! What a time they had! And then
Emma would see a Highlander pass by, with a
great swing of the haunches, and be glad indeed
that she was a woman!

On this particular afternoon Judith was in the
highest spirits. They came out into the Palais-
Royal, chattering and laughing. Judith was
full of Mr. Walter Scott—what fine eyes, how
kindly an expression, how interesting his limp

made him! Emma had never read one of his poems—they looked so very long—but she was prepared to find anyone noble whom Judith thought to be so.

The Palais-Royal was a place of enchantment. Under the hot afternoon sun it glittered and glowed with its life and splendour. It was a little city in itself. In shape an oblong quadrangle with piazzas completely around it, a garden planted with rows of trees, laid with gravel, with flowers and grass plots enclosed. Under the piazzas were countless shops, far more brilliant, as it seemed to Judith and Emma, than the shops of London. On the ground-floor, coffee-houses and restaurants; on the principal floor upstairs, coffee-houses, gaming-houses, exhibitions; higher up again, what a Herries traveller of the period calls in his Journal 'the abodes of vice and profligacy.' (This is from the Journal of Rodney Herries, the very pious younger brother of James, who in middle life took orders, and was ultimately Archdeacon of Polchester.) He goes on: 'The attics are inhabited by filth, misery, and crime, in endless variety and in a manner that renders it much safer to take that fact on hearsay than on actual reconnaissance. I should have mentioned,' he piously continues, 'that below the pavement are places much corresponding in character to the attics, though many of them are only cheap cafés, traiteurs, or pastry-cooks, of fair respectability.' He ends in a passage of particular eloquence by calling the Palais-Royal 'This immense gangrene.'

It was for Judith wonderful in all its mingled life, its wealth and poverty, fine ladies and scoundrels, triumphant soldiers and washer-women, ordinary quiet Frenchmen and ruffians almost in rags, clerics and flower-sellers, tourists and solemn officials. They had been in it so often, Emma and she, that she wondered why it seemed to-day to have some special significance for her.

She stood for a moment under the burning sun, jostled on every side, trying to define her impression. She was being reminded of some-thing. The broad space around her seemed to narrow. The dazzling sunlight on the white walls darkened. She was suddenly chilled. The movement was frozen. She heard a voice in her ear: 'No, madam, I fear the crowd is too great. . . . Yes, he stole from his master's till . . . a butcher . . .'

She caught Emma's arm. 'Let us go home, Emma. We must rest before this evening.'

'Why, my dear, you are pale. You are un-well.'

'No, but I was reminded of something.'

Afterwards, in the dark little room in the Rue Vivienne, she said to Emma:

'Emma, I am sure that something will happen to us in the Palais-Royal. I shall not return there.'

And Emma thought to herself: 'It is begin-ning. These fancies that women get at such a time!'

She made her lie down, and sat beside her,

telling her lively improper stories of her own past life. Through the wall they heard the odd plaintive chatter of M. Dufresne's monkey. It chattered like a child, then broke into an angry scream. Then the dogs barked. Then could be heard the deep menacing rumble of Madame Dufresne.

Their window was open because of the heat, and from far below them came the rattle of carriages, the crying of wares, the distant dreamy cadence of a band. In the air was the smell of Paris, the scent of carnations, the tang of baking bread, the hot touch of the iron trellises before the balconies, the sniff of crumpled paper, dry almost to burning-point. Judith was almost asleep. Once opening her eyes, looking at Emma, she said: 'I saw a boy hanged once in London. I thought of it to-day.'

'I know; you have told me of it often,' said Emma composedly. 'What is a hanging? You are too sensitive, my darling.'

'Perhaps I shall die when the child is born.'

'Nonsense. Nonsense. Die! I never heard such folly!'

'I know how cool it is now up Newlands, and how the breeze blows above the turf of Maiden Moor. . . . I rode once, but only once, with Francis to Hawkshead, and then up the hill to where the two little tarns lie. Oh, Emma, you never saw a thing so quiet and so cool when a great white cloud floats overhead and Fair-field and Helvellyn watch over you. . . . Oh, how hot it is, and how sorry I am for Monsieur

Dufresne's monkey. . . . Madame Dufresne will murder us one night in our beds. She hates us for Waterloo. And she will hide our bodies in that vast cupboard with the creaking door. I am sure there are rats in the wainscot. . . . Emma I *know* that something will happen to us in the Palais-Royal, and that great woman with the black hair and the crimson dress will sit above us and watch us torn to pieces while she arranges pieces of sugar. . . . I wonder how Francis is, and whether he has that blackberry preserve that he loves. They are always forgetting to have it on the table unless I am there. . . . I wonder if you can see the Scottish hills clearly to-day, and what they are doing at Westaways. . . . That crimson woman has Jennifer's air. . . . Jennifer would be fine in a café with mirrors multiplying her. . . . How I wish I knew Mr. Scott! He has stayed, I know, with Mr. Southey. Francis may have met him. . . .'

She dropped away to sleep while Emma, her eyes full of devotion, watched her and listened to M. Dufresne's monkey.

That evening they went to the Tivoli Gardens. Judith, after a long sleep, had recovered all her spirits and was ready for any amusement. Here there was plenty. They had quite agreed that the place could not compare with Vauxhall for size and splendour; but the summer evening was so lovely, the crowd so diverse and so intent upon enjoyment, that it was impossible not to be merry. There was a great crowd on this especial night, for it was said that the King and the

Duchesse d'Angoulême were to be present to see the floating of an illuminated balloon. Emma had said that the Duchess would not be there, because she was so devout that she considered all amusement harmful. In fact no Crowned Heads were present, nor could they persuade the balloon to rise, although a great many people paid five francs to stand within the ropes to see it do so.

There were all the regular diversions. One of the principal of them was to guess who were French officers; for in spite of Blücher's order that any discovered should be at once apprehended and treated as prisoners of war, Paris was filled with them. Then there was the gaiety of going around in a circle—the gentlemen on wooden horses, the ladies in chairs—in order to carry off with a small sword a ring hung out upon a post for the purpose; or you might get into a boat and ride about on a small artificial pond scarcely larger than the boat; or you might watch Mlle. Sachi, elevated sixty feet on a tight-rope; or there were the fireworks, *quite* as good as Vauxhall; or you might simply laugh at the costume of the French ladies, which seemed to Judith and Emma very ugly, with the high head-dress, the hair drawn tight from the temples and forehead over a coif, or hid with a high-crowned bonnet covered with feathers, no perceptible waist, but a loose robe hanging like a sack from the throat to the ankles, carefully collected about the wrists, and a shawl worn three-corner-wise. Emma and Judith thought these styles most absurd and laughed together a great deal.

However, the grand feature of the Tivoli, as of every other place of entertainment in Paris, was the dancing.

Everyone formed a circle round the dancers, who did everything possible to be as widely observed as might be. One gentleman was pirouetting round on his wooden leg and vastly enjoying it.

Soon a grave French gentleman with a square black beard invited Emma to dance, and, old though she was, she eagerly agreed, giving Judith a nod and a wink and setting off into the middle of the ring as though she were not a day more than twenty.

Judith was tired and sat down on a little wooden bench. The green of the trees was as brilliant as fresh paint under the illuminations, and between the leaves the evening sky showed, soft and delicate and tender. She loved to see people happy, to hear their cries of pleasure, to see the children running, to watch the sturdy simple faces of the English soldiers as they walked about in pairs, gravely considering the French girls, to catch the quick coloured flash of the fireworks, blue and green and red, above the dark water of the little pond. . . . She was tranquil. She was waiting for the delivery of her child. She felt at peace with all the world; she owed no one a grudge. When she thought of how hazardous and desolate had been her entrance into the world she was fortunate indeed to have had so full and adventurous a life. When her child came she would see that it had all that she could give it. Poor Warren! She thought of him with warm kindliness and affection. She was glad that he did not know what had happened to her.

She heard a familiar voice say 'Judith,' looked up and saw Warren Forster standing in front of her.

At once she cried: 'Oh, Warren, how ill you look! Sit down. Sit down here beside me!'

That was at first all that she could think about. He did look very ill. His sharp face, always strained with the memory of past suffering, was grey and haggard. He was so frail that, although when she began to think of all that his being there in Paris would mean, she would be intensely aggravated, she wanted now to put her arm around him and protect him. He sat down beside her. She patted his knee. He thought, as he looked at her, Had she any idea of what his finding her meant to him, of what burning dizzy happiness it was to him to look at her small child-like face with its honest eyes, its rather sharp ironical mouth, its clear smooth brow, the whole energy of her sturdy compact body, the independence, courage, humour that her poise always implied? No, she did not know. Had she known she would not have had the heart to leave him without a word.

'Well, Warren. What are you doing in Paris?'

'I have been searching for you for a whole fortnight, every day, all the time——'

'But how did you know that I was in Paris?'

'Francis told me.'

'Francis!—but he did not know my address.'

'No; that is why I have been searching for a fortnight. I have been looking everywhere. I had a feeling that to-day I should find you.'

'But what did you want to find me for?'

'Oh, Judith, you should not have left England without telling me! That was not kind of you. And the other also was not kind.'

'What other?'

'I know everything. Jennifer told me. . . . Yes. I went one day to Uldale. I had not seen you for three weeks. I must see you, so I went to Uldale. Jennifer was in a temper. She had been furious. When I stood in the hall, asking for you, she leaned over the stair and said, quite loud, anyone could have heard, "Judith has run away because she is going to have a child!"'

'Oh!' cried Judith. 'Did she?'

'Yes. And so I then at once understood everything. How could I have been so blind, so selfish?'

'So now they all know,' said Judith slowly. 'Well—it does not matter.'

'I was crazy with anger at myself. All these months and I had never thought! I went to Francis and demanded to know where you were. All he could tell me was that you were in Paris.'

'Poor Warren,' said Judith, patting his knee with her gloved hand. 'You look so very unwell.'

'So then I went to Will Herries and said that I must be permitted a holiday. He made some demur, but Walter said that it would be right. It did not matter. Walter is staying at Westaways through the summer. So then I came to Paris.'

'But why do you look so ill, Warren?' she asked again. 'What have you been doing to yourself?'

'It is my heart—nothing at all. I have been so anxious about you. Oh, Judith, you should not have gone without saying anything to me!'

'Why not? It was no one's affair.'

'No one's affair! It is my child as well as yours. And I love you so. Ah, let me say that once again. For a whole fortnight I have been searching for you. I deserve to be allowed to tell you that I love you. And now you are going to be mother to my child. That is so wonderful that I cannot believe it is true.'

'It is true enough.' She sighed. Here she was—caught again! But he looked so unwell that she could think of nothing else. She would take any trouble now, when he looked so unwell, not to hurt him. She began to be very practical.

'Now listen, Warren. I am here with a friend—Emma Furze. You have heard me speak of her. We are in lodgings in the Rue Vivienne together.'

' I am in a hotel near the Palais-Royal.'

' Near the Palais-Royal. Very good. Then to-morrow morning——'

' Oh, not to-morrow morning! ' he broke in. ' I have been two weeks looking for you. Allow me to stay with you for a little while this evening.'

' Our rooms are very small.'

' I do not mind what they are. I must see that you are comfortable. You must have better rooms. You must allow me——'

' Nonsense, Warren. Everything is very nice where we are.'

A moment later Emma arrived, very heated. She smiled at the square-bearded gentleman, who bowed significantly, as though they had agreed on a further meeting, and went away.

' Oh, such a charming man! And he speaks perfect English! He is a Professor of Languages, and his wife has been dead five years. He has a——'

' Emma, this is a friend of mine from England. Mr. Warren Forster.'

So this is the father of Judith's child, thought Emma, this little pale insignificant man!

She was inclined to be resentful, because he had provided all this trouble for Judith, but when she saw how ill he looked her heart was melted and she was as eager as was Judith that he should be comfortable.

They hailed a carriage and drove to the Rue Vivienne. Oh, dear! thought Emma, how he does love her, poor man! For he continued to look at her as a dog looks at its mistress, a fashion

that always irritated Judith, who thought that
everyone should be equal.

Warren insisted that he should pay the
carriage. That Judith permitted him. Then
they went through the courtyard, climbed the
dark and smelling stairs.

In the close little sitting-room Warren said:
' What is that? '

' It is the monkey and the cockatoo in the
next room.'

Emma was very tactful and went away. She
knew that they would want to talk to one another.
There were only two chairs. He insisted that
Judith should take the larger. So she sat there,
her hands behind her head. She felt her child
move beneath her heart, her child and his. He
sat very erect in the stiff-backed chair, leaning
forward, his thin fragile hands tightly clasped
together.

' Oh, I am so glad that I have found you! '
he said. ' If you knew how happy it makes me.
And that you are to be the mother of my child—
that is the proudest thing that has ever happened
to me! ' Then as he saw that she was going
to speak: ' No, don't say anything yet—pray,
pray do not. I know that you do not love me,
that you have never loved me. But you have
given me such great kindness, and now that we
are to have a child, I do not know—I do not
know——' He broke off, twisting his hands
nervously together. He looked up at her,
smiling like a child asking a favour. ' It is a
bond.'

U

But that was exactly what she would not have it. How was she to be honest with him without hurting him?

'No—Warren. I must be free. I am bound to no one, and the child will not be bound either.' She got off the chair and came to him and stood close to him. She put her arm round him, and he, like a child with its mother, bent his head against her.

'You know, Warren, I have told you before. I have only touched life deeply once. I have only once loved and I never shall again. At that time I was so young that I did not know that that would be the only time. But I could not have valued it more highly even if I had known. And at the end when he was dying and said that he loved me . . . No, no,' she broke off, her hand trembling on his shoulder. 'That was my real life. Nothing, my dear friend, has been quite real to me since. And I came to France because I wished my child to be born in Georges' country, and if I have been unfair to you, forgive me. I did not mean it——'

'No, no,' he broke in, 'never unfair. You have been only good.'

He bent forward and kissed her. She went on eagerly:

'We will make you comfortable, Emma and I. We will all be together. I was wrong, Warren dear, not to see you more frequently in England. That was most reprehensible, but now we will make you well. We will all be so happy together——'

For he looked so ill, poor little man.   He had
sunk against the hard back of his chair.   His
fingers clutched her hand.   His face was the
colour of ash.   His lips were purple.

'Yes . . .' he murmured.   'I am ill . . .
my heart. . . . In my coat . . . drops.'

She rushed to his carriage-coat that he had
flung off when he came in.   In a pocket she
found a little bottle.   He murmured directions.
She thought that he was going to die.   There
seemed nothing so important in all her life as
to save him.   Little by little he came to himself.   His lips were less blue.   He even smiled
a timid nervous smile.

'The pain,' he murmured.   'The pain is
very terrible.'

'Oh, you must remain here!'

She knelt by him, stroking his hair, holding
him close to her.

'Are you better?   Are you better now?'

'Yes, I am better now.'

'Of course, you must remain.'

She thought what she could do.   One of the
beds must be moved out of the other room.
She and Emma could sleep together.   Reassuring him that she would return in a moment
she went out to find Madame Dufresne, and
behold that woman, who had been so fierce and
so sinister, was now the very soul of kindness.

Emma also was there.   All together they
moved the bed.   Then alone Judith helped
Warren to undress, as a mother her son.   She
gave him one of her own nightdresses.   Very

small and wan he looked lying there, never taking his eyes from her face. The doctor had been sent for.

She sat down beside the bed, sewing at something for the child.

She could hear very faintly the street noises. The candle flickered and threw great shadows on the wall. He put his hand out, took hers and kissed it.

' Now, now . . . you are to sleep. That is what you are to do.'

But she bent forward, leaned over the bed and kissed his forehead. He closed his eyes as though in an ecstasy of happiness. She continued quietly to sew, to listen for the doctor. She felt the child move in her womb. How strange life was! That she should be sitting here in Paris, waiting for her child to be born, Warren in bed in her room!

How strange, incongruous, foolish and touching! She felt a strong pride as though she had her hand on life, a mettlesome steed, restive under her touch, restive but obedient!

PALAIS-ROYAL

' SON ALTESSE LE PRINCE DE BENEVENTO ! '

' That is Talleyrand,' whispered Emma, who was in so frantic a state of excitement that the feather in her head-dress wobbled like a live thing.

Oh! thought Judith, how I wish they were all here to see us—Will, Christabel, Walter, Pomfret, Rose, Maria, Carey, Francis, Jennifer and the children, John and Dorothy. How they would adore it—the brilliant colours of the uniforms, the flash of the decorations, the silks, satins, shawls, diamonds of the ladies!

It was not Judith's natural disposition to want to show off, even to the members of her family whom she disliked most; but this was one of the great Balls of History!

How was it that they were there at all? Well, Warren had encountered (on the first day that he was able to go out after his recovery from his heart attack) a business friend of Will's, a Monsieur Rakonitz of the famous Viennese jewellers, and he knew everyone: had supped with Blücher and shown rubies to the King of Prussia, and sold a bracelet to Fouché. He had suggested that he could find three tickets for Warren.

In all probability he had some deal with Will in hand, or wanted Will's influence for something. In any case, he was a grand jolly fellow, with a big beard and his hat cocked on one side. Then, unlike so many men with their hats cocked on one side, he had remembered his promise, and Warren had had his tickets.

So here they were, as merry and excited as three children. Judith was very near her time, and, in consideration of her age and that this was her first child, it had been wiser of her perhaps not to have come, but she could not resist it. She could never refuse to have fun, nor could she refuse to be kind to anyone, and she knew that Warren's evening would be nothing were she not there with him.

Not so Emma. She was devoted to Judith; but whether Judith were there or no she would enjoy herself. Her purple gown, her splendid turban, gave her a fine dramatic air, as of a prophetess given to acting tragic rôles at occasional moments. This was her pose while she remembered, but when she forgot she was simply a tall jolly libertine, ready to smile at anything and eager for every kind of attention, with a heart that Warren, who did not really like her, described as ' incredibly open.'

Judith stood beside her, insignificant in the white gown that hid her figure, a little, very ordinary, middle-aged woman, but to Warren more magnificent and splendid than any one there.

They stood against the wall under a huge

galaxy of candelabra, and Warren told them who everyone was.

Talleyrand was an old, powdered, old-fashioned gentleman.   He might have been any card-playing, gently-flirting, fussy-about-his-food-and-his-bottle, old gentleman—one of the milder, politer Herries, Judith thought.   But when you looked at him more closely (and they had an excellent opportunity, for he stood near to them, smiling, bowing, his sharp eyes ceaselessly darting now into this face, now on to that stubborn back, now beyond the other ingratiating desire for recognition) you could see an elaborate calm, a dangerous mildness. . . .

' *Le Duc d'Otrante !* '

Fouché, the villain of the piece, the super-policeman, sly devil, malicious tyrant, admirable teller of indecent stories. . . .

'*Sa Majesté le Roi de Prusse—leurs Altesses Royales les Princes Royaux de Prusse—le Duc de Mecklembourg.*'

The Prince of Orange, pale from his recent wound, Lady Castlereagh, General Alava, the Prussian King, plain, kindly, stout, melancholy, the princes his boys, also melancholy. . . . Oh yes, it would be agreeable to have Francis here, *dear* Francis whom, now that one was away from him, one loved as deeply as ever . . . he would enjoy this and would look so distinguished and for a moment would forget Jennifer . . . and oh! if Jennifer suddenly entered how startled everyone would be!   What a wonderful entrance she would make, moving lazily like a queen,

ever so slightly smiling in her consciousness of
the great beauty that she was, and Talleyrand
would bend his little figure forward and inquire
of Lady Castlereagh, and Fouché would turn his
sharp eyes, and the Prussian King would stroke
his melancholy cheek. Yes, Jennifer should
have been a queen in some country where everyone admired her, where there would be little
work. . . .

And then followed the great thrill of the
evening. An important body of officers and
aides-de-camp, a rather aged, not very interesting
officer at their head, and the announcement:

' *Son Altesse Sérénissime—le Prince Blücher.*'

Everyone pushed forward to stare at him,
and then what a moment! half-way down the
salon, Wellington moved forward and, meeting with smiles, the two great heroes shook
hands.

But for Judith even that was not the final
climax, for, just behind her, she heard a voice
say ' Look at that—a few weeks ago those two
men delivered Europe '—and, half turning, saw
standing quite close to her, whom but Mr. Walter
Scott?

His expression was one of rapt and intense
fervour. His eyes, from under their heavy eyebrows, glittered with emotion. She thought
there were tears in them. As he leaned forward,
his high-domed forehead rising into an odd peak,
his strong shoulders set, the nobility of his
mouth speaking of all the kindness (and yet
firmness and stiff obstinacy too) that a Scottish

gentleman is capable of, she felt that she *must* speak to him, wisdom, folly, or no.

'Is it not wonderful to be present at such a moment?'

He turned and saw a modest, stout little body in a white gown. As he greatly preferred modest and simple people to any other, he smiled like a brother and gave a little bow.

'It is indeed, madame.'

He turned his eyes back to Wellington and Blücher. She did not venture any more, but she pulled Warren away to a little distance and whispered in a voice husky with excitement:

'I have just spoken with Mr. Walter Scott.'

She was so happy and Warren was so happy that they were united in this hour more than they had ever been. For some weeks she had been looking after him, and he had needed her so; she had grown as a sister, as a mother, fonder and fonder of him. And he *was* someone to be fond of. She had not known that he had so tender and gentle a nature, one so honest and sincere. And in knowing him better she perceived a new and a better side of the Herries character, something more generous, easy, and kind. Francis had had that strain, Maria and Carey had some of it, even Pomfret and Rose. If only their wretched ridiculous family quarrels did not obscure it!

She said to Warren one day:

'Although you are but *quarter* Herries you are the *right* quarter! You are what we all ought to be!'

He flushed with pleasure.

'You can say that when yourself——'

'Oh no, I am all wrong. I shall turn into the most awful old woman if I live. Always grab, grab at people, and they will all run—and then I shall blame them and not myself.'

So to-night they both forgot Emma (who was quite capable of entertaining herself) and wandered about in blissful excitement together. Every once and again, laying her hand on his arm, she would say: 'Are you certain that you are quite well? You feel nothing? You are sure?'

And he would answer radiantly: 'I am too happy to feel ill.'

His features were very pale, she thought, but otherwise he had filled out again. His body was sturdy and firmly set once more.

They saw many interesting things. They saw a portrait of Napoleon resting against the wall, the stern fixed eyes gazing out upon this scene that emphasised his defeat. They saw in the ante-chamber of the great supper-room Wellington himself slip across to a small supper-table and join Lady Castlereagh and Mr. Scott. They were all very gay and merry, Lady Castlereagh indeed screaming like a peahen.

They themselves went out into the gardens, where long supper-tables were laid and hundreds of people were supping. They sat down at a table under the trees from which lights were shimmering. Everywhere there was a flood of noise like the sea, multitudinous voices, laughter, knives, forks, plates, the popping of corks, the rhythm and pattern of the distant band.

'Oh, Warren, I feel as though something wonderful were going to happen with the birth of our child. Will it, do you think? Am I cheating myself? I have not been so happy since I was with Georges. You know I came to Paris because of Georges, do you not? You are not angry, are you? Because now I am so glad that you came. I wasn't glad at first. I was so *sickened* of Herries. All quarrels and temper, and no one caring for anyone. I wanted to be rid of it all. But now you are yourself, dear Warren. We are splendid friends. I care for you so much. I am glad that it is your child. Is it not ridiculous that it cannot be always like this, you and I and the child? I don't *want* to go back to all the Herries character. It will catch me up, and I shall like it and become a managing, *nasty* old woman, and be too old to know that I am. . . . You must save me from that, Warren.'

He put his hand on hers. 'You are so good, Judith. . . .'

'No, I am *not* good. I have never done anyone good. Emma said that the other day, and that when I met her first she was drunken and lost. But Emma would never be lost. She has too great a vitality. And I did Georges no good neither. But now perhaps, if I choose rightly and stay outside the Herries family——'

'You must eat some of this chicken,' said Warren. 'This chicken is excellent.' Then added inconsequently: 'I have not long to live.

Another attack like that last one will finish me.
But I want you to know, Judith, that you have
given me the happiest days of my life.   I did not
know I could be so happy. . . .'

'Yes, is not this chicken excellent?   It would
be nice to have Francis here, and Maria——'

'Ah, now you want others——'

'No.   It is beautiful as it is.   But I want
everyone to be happy to-night.   Imagine!   All
the Kings eating chicken only a yard away!
And I spoke to Mr. Scott, and I heard the Duke
say "Damnation."   Would it not be funny,
Warren, if I suddenly had my baby here on the
grass, in a corner under the tree?   And then we
would ask Mr. Scott to be its godfather.   I do
hope that it is a boy.   What shall we name him?
Some new name.   Not a Herries name, like
Francis or Pomfret.'

She sucked a chicken-bone, holding it in her
fingers.

There was a '*grimacier*' entertaining a crowd
on the lawn away from the tables.   At his side
were the long windows flooded with light, phantasmal figures moving within, beyond him; behind him shadows pooled with dancing candle-
shine, and into the pools figures moved with
white, excited, laughing faces.   The King of
Prussia's two boys were there, laughing at his
antics.   He was a long cadaverous man and
wore a sheepskin cap.   He made the most
extraordinary faces, pulling his chin down,
wrinkling his forehead, closing his eyes.   He
imitated the English, did a Highlander making

love to a French girl, ' Jean Bool ' and his wife eating at a restaurant, Napoleon running from Waterloo, Mlle. George singing a song.

Judith began to laugh.

' He is so clever. Is he not clever? Oh, Warren, see—look what he does with his cap! Is not that marvellous? '

She laughed till she cried. They stood close together and then hand in hand, while Emma, in another part of the garden, told a stout Frenchman how comic he was; and Fouché took the leg of a chicken in his fingers and cracked the bones with his teeth as though they were so many condemned criminals.

Then came the fearful day, never to be forgotten by Judith as long as she lived, September 4, 1815.

On the early afternoon of that day they walked, the three of them, to view the site of the famous Bastille. At first they had all been in the highest spirits. Judith had, in the last few days, been feeling almost incredibly weary, but heavy though her body was, her heart was light. Since the day of the famous Ball she had known a new relationship with Warren, a deeper intimacy. They were now like brother and sister; she could care for him, watch over him without any falseness on her side or irritation on his. On these days he poured out everything from his heart, talked and talked as though he could never tell her enough, and she loved to listen. It was all thrilling and exciting to her as though she had shared in it.   Emma, occupied with many romances of her own, left them much to themselves.

Then, early on this morning of the Fourth of September, Judith awoke in a panic.   She lay on her bed, feeling the child kick in her womb, wondering whether it were a bad dream that she had.   Some figure seemed to be in the room with her, now it was young Hartley Coleridge twisting one leg round the other, now Reuben, now young Stane, and now, more definitely, La Belle Limonadière from the Palais-Royal with her black hair and crimson dress, arranging the lumps of sugar.

The figures faded as the light in the room grew clearer.   There was no one there.   The panic remained.

They started to walk in the afternoon, but it was very hot, and they called a carriage.   Little light silver clouds flecked the sky, the buildings were pigeon-colour, the air full of the scent of flowers, there was the echo of bands, distant as though from behind closed doors.

They crossed the bridge of Austerlitz, drove gently along the boulevards and then came to the site.   Here they got out, dismissed the carriage and walked about, seeing, from every angle, where the famous attacks of 1789 had been made.   For Judith this was an event of poignant memories.   She could see now David advancing across the bright shining grass of the Uldale lawn to meet Francis, then the talk, the quarrel, the uplifted stick.   If David had lived, had

Sarah not ' gone crazy ' . . . Ah well, what was
the use of that kind of memory? Every link
in the chain must be there; she would not be
here now had she not ridden over to Stone Ends
and struck a small boy because he loved her
hair; she would not be the woman she was had
she not rescued Reuben's brother in Cockermouth, had she not. . . .

She dragged herself wearily after the other
two (how tired she was, how hot the day, how
heavy the child within her!), but she smiled when
Emma, who was being very dramatic over the
Revolution, turned to her; she put her hand
through Warren's arm, and was interested in
everything.

What they especially were interested in was
an immense wooden shed, in the middle of the
site, and a half-finished colonnaded tower of
freestone. This was enclosed with a wooden
paling and had a gate. Inside the gate on a
stool was sitting a slim, pale-faced, elderly woman,
one of whose cheeks had a painful twitch. Her
eyes were sad and staring, as though she were
looking for something that she could not find.
She was clothed very decently with a shawl over
her thin shoulders.

She begged them to enter and see the ' Elephant.'

' The elephant?' said Warren. ' Pray, what
elephant? This is not the *Jardin des Plantes*.'

But it seemed that Napoleon had determined
to erect a huge fountain on the Bastille site that
its waters might wash away the memory of the

awful events that had occurred there. This fountain was to spout its waters through the trunk of a great elephant. The melancholy woman, her eyes staring far beyond them while she spoke, pressed them to enter. Judith did not want to go; she did not know why, but she did not want to go.

However, Emma was all for seeing everything, so in they went.

The model was built of clay, indurated and whitened, exactly in figure and size what the bronze was intended to be, and it stood at the tremendous height of sixty feet. It had been intended that it should be placed on a stone pedestal and that then the water should pour out of its trunk into a succession of basins all round.

The woman, in a dreary unhappy voice, said that the English intended to finish this work, so she had heard.

' They have a number of other things to finish first,' said Warren laughing. But nothing at all seemed to amuse the woman.

She asked them gravely, as though she were accusing them personally:

' What have *you* done with the Emperor? '

' He is in charge of the Allies.'

' Will he ever return? '

' Never! . . . Never! '

' *Tant mieux! Mais l'Éléphant!* '

For some reason this huge white towering beast affected Judith with nausea. It looked so bare, so savage, so revengeful. With its great trunk it seemed to be ready to catch them, throw them up, and then, when they had fallen at its feet, riotously trample on them. In the hot quivering summer air it appeared to move, there was life in its vast body. The woman became more sinister, her cheek twitching, her hands moving; they would be prevented from escaping and the elephant would pursue them, trumpeting, within the palings. The air was so close that it was stifling.

She felt that in a moment she would be hysterical.

'Quickly. I cannot endure it. It is horrible. It is moving, cannot you see that it is moving?'

'Why, Judith——'

'No, no. I must get out. I cannot endure it.'

In a moment she would be laughing and screaming. She ran out into the street.

They followed her, wondering what the matter was.

'No. It is nothing. The heat was terrible. And the elephant . . . its trunk . . . And the woman hated us. Could you not see? Of course, she hated us.'

They sat down at a little table on the boulevard and ordered coffee. Judith was surprised to discover that she was trembling.

'But did you not feel it? I cannot understand why you did not. The elephant was alive. Oh yes, I know. . . . But it *was* alive. In another moment . . .'

She drank her coffee, feeling that she had been

too foolish for anything. She to give way to nerves! So that when they suggested that they should go to the Palais-Royal, although she hated to do so, she agreed.

Arrived there, they sat at a little table beneath a wide awning and watched the scene. The ladies with their high hats, their long sumptuous dresses, some of them with canes, all of them painted, vivacious and, it seemed, without a care in life, smiled at the men as anglers throw their baited hooks. The shops glittered, the sun shone down relentlessly; the moving crowds were like players in a game where something has to be found, now suddenly hurrying forwards as though the scent were ' hot ', now hesitating, halting, the scent lost.

Judith's uneasiness increased. It was the heat, it was the noise, it was the smell of hot iron and dried dung and clothes. The long stretches of the square shone like glass. Some toy balloons, red and green and yellow, were floating like swollen puff-balls in the air. In one place a ' *grimacier* ' held a little crowd, throwing on and off his headgear, changing his coat, dancing, bending backwards. Nearer her there was a Punch and Judy, and from within the little coloured box came the sharp rasping cry and the quick bark of the little frilled dog.

It seemed to her that everyone was hostile, and this was not all her imagination, for at this time in Paris, behind the gaiety and laughter, all nerves were taut, no one knew what was to happen next, no one could trust his neighbour.

There was great hostility to the Prussians. French officers in disguise were everywhere waiting to pick a quarrel. One of the means was to sit in a public place with your feet stretched and trip up a Prussian. Duels were fought every day. Two Prussians had been murdered the night before in a dark street behind the Opéra.

Judith sat there wondering what was the matter. She was not exactly ill, but felt a deep apprehension. Was her time imminent? Perhaps she had best go home, but she did not wish to spoil Warren's pleasure. She knew that he would insist on going with her.

She looked at him while he talked to Emma; how fond she had become of him, what good companions they were! She liked to be fond of people, especially when they were not weak and yet did what she advised. The pleasantest people in the world were the selfish ones who were also kindly, so that in the middle of their selfishness they thought of you and did something for you. Unselfish people who were always eager to do something for you were so irritating. . . .

A group of French people, eagerly laughing and talking, came out of the restaurant behind Judith and, not noticing her, bumped against her and almost knocked her chair over. She felt her heart leap, the shops and chairs and coloured clothes danced before her eyes. She could not drive that horrible white elephant out of her mind. It would not surprise her to see

it come trumpeting and trampling, the crowd
running before it. She would not be able to
move; she would be held in her place as one is
in a nightmare. Something had warned her not
to come to the Palais-Royal.

Then she noticed sitting near to her a young
Prussian officer, quite alone. He had large
melancholy eyes and was little more than a boy.
He stared out into the pageant with unseeing
gaze. What was it? Was he sick for home?
Was he thinking of someone he loved and wishing that she were with him, wondering what he
did there?

Warren turned to her smiling. He was
watching the 'Punch,' laughing at the little dog.
Always after she would remember every detail
of the next few minutes. A tall very handsome
lady, in a high green fur hat, was leaning across
her little table, gazing into the eyes of a stout
frog-faced gentleman choked by a huge stock.
Some band was coming nearer, the music grew
louder and louder as though a door were opening.
Two more crimson balloons floated into the air;
a small poodle, ridiculously naked, ran forward
into the crowd, lost, and a shrill feminine voice
cried ' Dédé . . . Dédé! ' It heard the voice
and eagerly ran back again.

Emma was exclaiming: ' But the air was so
ravishing that I could not endure to return, so
I waved my hand and he came, running, such
ecstasy painted on his features. . . .'

Then everything happened in a moment.
The band just entered with a blare of sound,

someone laughed, the lady in green pinched the gentleman's chin. . . .

A young Frenchman with a black moustache and sharp beady eyes moved against the chair in which the young Prussian was sitting; a glass fell with a clash, the Prussian was almost tumbled from his seat. The Prussian started up, his hand on his sword. The two faced one another. A pistol-shot cracked; the young Prussian, his legs bent oddly beneath him, lay huddled against the iron legs of the table.

At the sound of the shot the sky seemed to swing, the buildings to bend forward.

Everyone came out running from the restaurant. There were shouts and cries. Two officers in Uhlan uniform approached the Frenchman.

Judith saw him struggling with them. She was quite near to him, and could observe how, although his face was white, he expressed a rage that was like a mad cat's. He repeated, in a shrill treble voice, over and over again the word ' *L'Empereur!* '

He pushed back the men who were attacking him, turned with a swing of his body and looked straight into Judith's eyes—without of course seeing her, but, in the fiery meeting of sun, sky, roofs, and floor that seemed now to whirl in a wheel of flame before her, she saw the face of the hanging boy from London.

She felt herself now, just as she had done then, sick from a kind of claustrophobia, the crowd shutting her in. She had lost sight of both

Emma and Warren. She was alone, as she always seemed to be in every crisis.

Then the young Frenchman, brushing his cheek with one hand, as though a fly had bothered him, flung out the other, and again a pistol-shot crashed like a stone flung through glass.

At that it was as though the Palais-Royal had been a plate in a second tilted forward, spilling its contents downwards into some abyss. The screams and shouts were detached. One shout was deep like a drum, another was shrill like the knock on a high gong.

Judith, struggling to escape from chairs and tables, saw Warren endeavouring to push through an absurd clump of bodies that clung together like plants in a storm. Behind them the whole Palais-Royal, still tilted, swarmed with figures as unreal as puppets worked by strings.

He called ' Judith! Judith! ' He beat the bodies in front of him frantically aside with his arms. He reached her, fell against her. Horses were rising. A horse, mounted by a soldier, came charging through fallen furniture. Glass fell with a crash. A dog barked, and on that bark she caught Warren in her arms, for his face was purple. He could not speak. He dropped limp against her, so that she stumbled to the ground.

Kneeling there, her arms around him, she saw that he was dead, heard a bell ring just above her head, saw the horse (shaped like an elephant) go charging into the sun.

A wave of pain caught her, so frightful that

some other person broken to pieces inside herself screamed.   Everything was black,

She sank down on a descending shaft of pain.
She slowly mounted again, to find that she was
quite clear-sighted, was lying on a hard, dry sofa,
her head on a pillow that smelt of cheese.   She
hated the smell, but also the row of lofty shining
mirrors that reflected again and again the long
room with empty tables, chairs piled high.

Somewhere in the distance shouting fell
against the mirrors and died on the floor.   She
felt the sweat tumble into her eyes, wiped it
away, and saw a vast Emma towering above
her.

' Warren is dead,' Judith murmured.

A little stout man with two chins, who seemed
also to smell of cheese, advanced to her.   She
saw that he was greatly agitated.   A big silver
ring trembled as his hand trembled.   She heard
him say:

' A screen!   A screen! . . . Where is a
screen!'

Then she had one more absolute moment
of clear vision.

Warren was dead.   Her child was being
born.   She would die also, and history would
repeat itself, for even as she had been born at the
instant of her parents' death, so now would her
child be born of their death.

The little man leaned over her.   She saw
the silver ring tremble.   A cascade of pain
hovered in the air—but before it broke over her

she screamed out, ' I will not die! . . . I will not die! '

' It is a boy,' said the doctor to Emma, quarter of an hour later.

They were bringing the bodies of the wounded into the restaurant and laying them in the shadow where the room was coolest.

END OF PART III

PART IV

MOTHER AND SON

THE HILLS

WALTER HERRIES rode up the hill from Hawkshead one fine summer's evening to get some air before spending the evening with his friend, Squire Thistleton, at High Grange. He had come over from Grasmere more swiftly than he had intended, having already eaten his dinner with the Bordens there, not wishing to invade High Grange before nightfall. Squire Thistleton's lady bored him most desperately: stay the night with Thistleton he must, for he had important business matters to discuss with him, but be bored by Mrs. Thistleton he would not. Although he was so genial, for ever laughing at the jokes of others, yes, roaring and slapping his vast thigh at them, yet, like all very self-centred men, he had a watchful eye. If he must suffer at the jokes of others there must be excellent reason for it. He did nothing at all without an admirable reason. Immense in build though he was, he was not yet corpulent for his twenty-eight years. He looked exceedingly handsome in his green riding-coat as the white horse picked its way carefully up the rough stone-strewn path. The summer is the worst time of the year in which to see this country: the naked blue sky does not suit its shape and size; the hills dwindle beneath the sun; the green carpet of field and brow has neither shade nor variety. But to-night fragments of orange cloud floated across a blue so faint as to be almost without colour, and the hills were so clearly outlined that they forced themselves, dark rocks of a mysterious country, out of a sea with no ripple.

Walter had no eyes for scenery; he left that to the romantic writers, now ever more numerous. But, pausing on the brow, and looking down to the left where the waters of Coniston lay bronzed and still, he felt all the pride of one who owns a fine property. For he had come now to feel that he, and he alone, possessed the whole of this charming and fruitful land. It was a natural and happy evolution of circumstance. He was at this moment well beyond his own actual territory, which was not as yet a very large one, but he felt himself to be so infinitely the most important person alive in the combined counties of Cumberland and Westmorland, and what he felt himself to be, that he was.

It was now over three years since Will Herries, his father, had departed back to London. He was to be seen very seldom at Westaways. It had been made clear to him (Walter had assisted in the demonstration) that the City was the place for him. For one thing, there was nothing in life so pleasant for Will as the making of money, and although now much of his wealth had its richest foundations in Manchester and the Midlands, London was inevitably the heart of affairs.

For another, Walter had helped him to perceive that, although Cumberland society did not object to wealth, it still objected to the City. The time was coming when a City man, granted that he had retired and had pocketed plenty of gold before retiring, would be admitted into good company, but that time was not quite yet. Moreover, Will had no intention whatever of retiring. He was now only fifty years of age and in excellent health. Business had never been so interesting as now when it was beginning to rouse itself, in the promise of so much fresh industrialism, out of the depression that followed the French Wars. The chimneys of the Midlands were gallantly smoking, and Will must be there to see that they were properly supplied.

Walter's ambitions were quite other. He disclaimed now all connection with business. With his handsome person, his geniality, his ruthless selfishness, his happy disregard of the interests of any but his own, his fine place (but he already felt Westaways far too small for him) and, above all, his almost insane pride in the Herries name, he was excellently placed to dominate his country world. The men and women around him, he would say, had judged of Herries by the miserable specimens hitherto offered to them. *He* would show them what a Herries really was. Indeed, his earlier scorn of Francis and Jennifer had by now grown to an irritated and festering hatred. He would never dominate this country properly until Uldale and its occupants were wiped from the face of the land.

They had not a chance against him; Francis weak and idle, Jennifer dull and scandalous. Only in their children could they rival him. At that thought, which constantly peered up at him out of the dark recesses of his mind like a malicious stinging animal, his whole body would tremble. For, in the spring of 1815, his wife had presented him with twins, a boy and a girl, and the boy was a weak and ailing cripple. Moreover, his wife would give him no more children, and, unless she died, Uhland must be his only son.

In his disgust at the puny and deformed baby he had not cared what they called him, and Mrs. Herries, moved perhaps by the increasing wave of German Romanticism, or hoping, it may be, that the child thus named might make some escape from the Herries nature, had had this outlandish fancy. The boy was Uhland, marked in this way, as in all others, from the common kind.

And Francis' children, John and Dorothy, were healthy and strong. Elizabeth and Uhland —John and Dorothy. He was beset by the contrast.

The horse moved forward. He turned down the hill to the two small pools that lay, in blue translucent stillness, under the dark guardianship of the wood. Behind the trees Helvellyn and Fairfield kept sleepy tolerant guard.

The day had been hot; their purple shadows slumbered.

There was perfect stillness all about Walter Herries as he sat on his horse and looked into the pool. There were other little things that had exasperated him to-day. He had been slowly riding by Grasmere Lake when he encountered that crazy old poet, William Wordsworth, and his mad sister as they walked along.

Walter, with his accustomed geniality, had stopped his horse to speak to them, as a king might to his subjects. Everyone knew that Wordsworth as a poet was a mock and a derision, and his sister, Dorothy, was as mad as a hatter. Wordsworth wrote poems about donkeys and daffodils. He was a joke to the neighbourhood, and that little sister of his, with her shabby clothes and fiery eye . . . And yet, speaking to them with all courtesy, he had been in some way rebuked. The comical pair! Wordsworth was going fishing; his sister said something about a bird on a tree. They did not seem at all gratified that he had spoken to them.

'Good day to you, Mr. Herries . . . Good day to you,' Wordsworth had said, as though he were impatient to be gone, and his sister had wandered about the road, following some bird with her glittering eye. . . . Oh, mad, mad both of them! But mad or no they should have been impressed by his greeting.

Another vexation had been a queer one. As he left home that morning little Uhland, five years old, had limped to wish him farewell. He had felt a sudden pride in his heart at sight of him. Proud of that white-faced bony little cripple! But it was pride that he had felt; he had been moved; he had bent down to embrace him. That was an absurd emotion—although, after all, when all was done, the child *was* a Herries . . . his only heir. . . . In spite of himself he sighed, rested his hand on his great thigh and looked about him, breathing-in the sweet-scented summer air.

At that same moment there rushed past him, out of the wood, the most astonishing figure, a small naked child. It was a boy, and, straight in front of Herries' horse, he splashed into the pool. Another moment and he was swimming vigorously, tossing his head and uttering cries of delight. The pool was deep—the two pools would be a fine small lake one later day—and this midge of a boy, screaming like a little shrill bird, dived, appeared a moment later at the pool's edge, and then sprang out, dancing about and waving his arms in front of Herries' horse.

The horse, alarmed by this unusual adventure, reared, and Herries, in anger, snapped his whip, catching the child's bare leg. The child laughed and plunged into the pool again; a moment later a peasant woman appeared at the wood's edge, then ran down to Herries.

' What are you doing, whipping a baby! Have you nothing better——'

She broke off. They had recognised one another. This woman was Judith. She was dressed like a peasant in some rough material of red and green. On her red hair she wore no covering. On her bare feet she had wooden shoes. She stood, her small body set, her little face grinning.

'Why, Cousin Walter, I did not know that it was you. . . . It is a long time since we met.'

So it was. Years and years. He had not set eyes on her since that night in '15, when she had dinner with him, and they had heard of Napoleon's flight from Elba. None of them had seen her. She had been living in the hills with her bastard child. She had gone back to her origin.

'Well, well. Cousin Judith.' He took off his hat.

'Yes, and don't you whip my son or I shall have something to say.'

She was laughing, and he felt that in some way she was mocking him.

'Your son?'

'Yes. Adam, Adam, come here!'

The child seemed to spring from nowhere and stood, naked and dripping, by the horse. Yes, this would be her child. It would not be a day more than five, born in the same year as his own. He saw, with satisfaction, that the boy was ugly. The small body was brown with sun, the hair—that lay thick and matted above his eyes—jet black. He had a short snub nose and a large grinning mouth, a strong sturdy body, but the legs and arms were too long. Yes, an ugly and common-looking child. He did not seem to feel cold, but Judith drew him to her, put her green shawl over him and her arm around him. He leant against her, wet as he was. She did not seem to care.

'This is Mr. Walter Herries, a relation of ours,' she said to him.

X

How strong and sturdy the woman seemed!
She must be between forty and fifty now.   What
a queer pair they made.

At that he recovered his self-command which,
for a moment, he seemed to have lost.   He
leaned lazily toward her, resting one hand on
his hip.   The horse shifted a little and, bending
down, began to pluck the grass.   The stillness
was exquisite.   A cloud, like a bronze chrysan-
themum, jagged at its edges, floated over the wood
and darkened, like a hand, the little pool.

'Where have you been all these years?' he
asked her, friendly and patronising.

'You know well enough.'

What clear bright eyes she has! he thought,
and wondered whether there were specks of dust
on his clothes.   His hand moved down the lapel
of his coat.

'And when will you return to civilisation?'

'It is quite civilised enough where I am.'

'Have you seen Francis and Jennifer lately?'

'Francis has come to see me at Watendlath.'

'Well, I must be off to my supper.'   He
looked at the infant, and the infant looked back at
him.   'So your name is Adam, young man?'

The child grinned up at him, looking at him
fearlessly.

'Adam Paris,' he said.   Then he added most
unexpectedly: 'I could make your horse jump
more if I tried.'

'You try—that's all!' said Walter, suddenly
angry again.

'Now you leave the child alone, Cousin Walter,' said Judith. 'He is not afraid of you nor of anything else in the world. But I will give you something to be afraid of if you touch him with your whip.'

He had a sharp consciousness (which he was to recall one day) of the force and vitality of her personality. Whenever he encountered her she compelled him to remember it, small though she was. While she was away he created, if he thought of her at all, his own picture of her as an insignificant sort of poor-relation-governess. But when he was with her it was another matter. And now he suddenly thought: 'I had forgotten *her*! Suppose that she should come back to Uldale!'

However, all that he did was to be gracious again. He took off his hat, bowed, invited her to bring her boy to see them at Westaways.

Judith was not ungracious. She always returned courtesy for courtesy. 'Yes, I will come one day, Cousin Walter. I hope Mrs. Herries is well.'

'Oh yes. Well enough.'

Then Walter rode away, his figure for a moment gigantic at the top of the bend against the soft glow of the milk-white sky. Judith, her hand in her son's, started along the little path that skirted the pool. Adam was wrapped up entirely in the shawl; the end of it trailed on the ground behind him. He danced along.

'What a fat man!' he said.

'That is your Uncle Walter.'

' In truth my uncle? '

' Near enough.'

' I could have made his horse jump.' He skipped a few paces and nearly tumbled. But she did not move to catch him nor did she ask him whether he were cold, as any other child would have been.

' Was the water agreeable? '

He wrinkled his nose like a little dog. ' I can smell the fire burning.' He shouted and cried aloud with happiness. The shawl fell off him, and bare as a young foal he ran towards the wood. Judith walked soberly after him. She was thinking deeply about Walter.

A small nondescript dog ran out to meet them. This was a mongrel dog who, coming from no-where, had attached himself to them. He first ran eagerly towards Adam, moving awkwardly on legs that were longer than they should have been, but with eager excited joy. Then, just before he reached Adam, it occurred to him that he might not perhaps be so popular as he had hoped, so he crawled on all fours, dragging himself along with a bright supplicating eye.

' Dog! Dog!' Adam cried, and picked him up and ran into the wood, hugging the animal to his bare stomach; the dog's tail wagged in an ecstasy of happiness.

Just inside the wood a bright fire was burning, and on the other side of the fire sat a stout man in black, reading a book, and with an absent-minded hand once and again stirring with a stick the pot that hung over the fire.

Adam, who was now almost dry, flung himself, dog and all, into the stout man's lap.

' Uncle Reuben, a fat man on a horse tried to whip me, but he could not.   Can we eat now? '

' You must dress yourself,' Reuben said, putting his book down and reaching out to a pile of minute clothes near to him.

Adam stood up on Reuben's thighs, putting his hands round Reuben's neck.   Reuben clasped him round his small naked body, holding him lest he should fall.

' And who was this fat man? ' he asked, moving his face a little; the small dog, when he saw what Adam was doing, was trying the same with the addition that he would lick Reuben's cheeks.   The fire threw a shining colour on Adam's body.   He seemed to be surrounded with a nimbus of light.

' Mother said he was my Uncle Walter. . . . Can we not eat now? '

He jumped suddenly off Reuben's thigh and had scuffled into a shirt and a pair of diminutive blue trousers.   His legs were bare.

' Mother, can we not eat now? '   He ran towards Judith, who stopped to look into the pot.

' Whom do you think I have seen? ' she asked Reuben.

' I know.   Adam told me.'

He spread his black riding-coat for her and she sat down, leaning her head against his knee. She looked up and could see the dark fans and wheels of the trees flecked with cool shell-white sky.

' Yes, Walter.   After all these years.   He

looked huge and mightily satisfied. Do you
know what he said to himself as he looked at me,
Reuben?'

'No.'

'Here is slattern Judith and her bastard.
. . . Adam laughed at him. . . .' She pushed
Walter away for a moment and went on: 'You
had a grand meeting this noon. The grandest
I've seen.'

'Yes, praise the Lord!'

'But Reuben, you talked more of political
things than religious. You were trying to make
them discontented.'

'They are discontented already. They have
been starving for years and now their masters
will bring in machinery and they work in the dark
like slaves.'

Judith shook her head.

'No. Not here. They are farmers and
shepherds. There is no discontent in Kendal
or Keswick.'

'No, but a little way out—at Whitehaven,
Cockermouth. . . .'

She looked up at him and put up her hand.
He took it in his.

'I like it better when you talk about God.
Although I do not believe in Him I like others
to. At least . . . believe or not . . . I haven't
the wits to be so certain. But I like to hear you
speak of Him. You bring Him so close. You
are so sure of yourself now, Reuben, and yet
as kind and good as ever you were. I had rather
people were kind than anything else. Yet I

detest a fool, and so many kind people are half-witted.' She let herself run on, looking up and seeing that a little evening breeze moved, as a tiny boat moves on a pond, through the trees. She looked down and saw that Adam was playing with the dog.

'Reuben, are you still bothered with women?'
He laughed. 'No. I am too old.'
'Nonsense. You are not sixty. When did they cease to torment you?'
'I will tell you. It was in Kendal some ten years ago. It was in the winter-time and I had been preaching out on the hills. It was perilously cold, and in the inn after supper a large red-faced girl invited me to her room. Then, to be warm and to be comforted by someone (for I was much alone at that time) I went into bed with her. And she had but just blown out the candle when I saw the Lord, a young man in silver armour standing on the floor. The fire shone on him and he was glorious. He cried to me, "Reuben, the pleasure is not worth the pain." And I answered "Nay, Lord, I was so cold." And he came to the bed and touched my forehead with his hand. I lay by the girl all night but neither of us was harmed.'

'And do you truly think it was the Lord?' asked Judith.
'Who else could it have been?' said Reuben.
'No, no one else.'
'Well, then——'
'But maybe you were already asleep——'
'Not before embracing the girl. No. It

was the Lord. I have seen him in such armour at other times too——'

'And women are nothing to you since then?'

'I like women,' he said. 'But the temptation is over.'

'What are your temptations still?'

He answered gravely, counting on his fingers. 'One, I am a coward; two, I am greedy; three, I like a warm bed; four, I tell tales; five, I hate the Methodist preacher at Cockermouth; six, I am lazy—I can sleep all day——'

She interrupted him. 'Look up. There is a red cloud like a crimson bird that Georges once had, hanging between two trees.'

But it was one of Reuben's defects that natural scenery meant nothing to him. Any human thing, but a tree, a cloud, a mountain—nothing. The pot was boiling. Judith commanded the whole situation. The three of them and the dog sat and had a splendid meal.

'We will go up the hill and see the sunrise as you promised?' Judith asked.

'Yes,' Reuben said, but in spite of himself he yawned behind his hand.

She had an impulse to be cross, as she always had when things were not to be as she wished them. Then she conquered her crossness. She had been expecting for months this evening with Reuben. About twice a year they spent a night together. Once before they had ridden up into the Langdales and seen the sunrise. And now he was sleepy. His head was nodding. It had been a grand meeting and must have wearied him, but she had been looking forward passionately to a long talk with him. It was so seldom now that she could talk with her own kind, and to-night, most especially, she wanted his advice, for she was about to pay a visit to Uldale again for the first time since her return from France. She was taking Adam with her. The sudden vision of Walter had been like an omen. She was not frightened, but she needed help and only Reuben could give it her. And now Reuben was sleepy. Only Adam was not. He was dancing about with the dog, eager for the next adventure now that his hunger was satisfied.

Reuben turned round, knelt on the grass and said his prayers. Then he leaned against a tree-trunk and in another moment was asleep.

' He's asleep,' said Adam, laughing.

The night was so warm and the scent of the trees so comforting, the uncertain flicker of the fading fire so bewitching that, standing there, she felt that she was under a spell.

She was in magnificent health because of the life that she had been leading since coming to Watend-lath, the life of a peasant, harvesting, digging, helping with the sheep, riding off with Watson for a whole day on the fells, ploughing for hours through the quagmires at the top of the Fell after a lost or strayed lamb—and always in perfect content. That was the life to which part of her temperament entirely responded; but the other part would not have been content had she not had Adam. Adam now was her whole life, her soul, her body, her past, her future, her God and her destiny.

She had been waiting always for some such passion as this. Her love for Georges had possessed her, but it had not been returned until the last and, say what one may, a love that is not returned is only half a love.

Moreover, although she had not known it, she was a woman to whom motherhood was the only possible complete fulfilment. Her love for Georges, her affection for Reuben, Francis, Maria, Warren, Emma Furze, Watson, had been in its impulse maternal. But they had not been her own. Now she had something that was her own, and anyone watching her might have been frightened of the fiery, possessive, passionate element at the heart of her love for her son.

But she was not a fool. She kept her love in control as yet. And Adam was not at present difficult. His mother was his companion; he knew none other as good. He loved her quite naturally without thinking of it. He was independent but warm-hearted and, at present, he had no feeling that she threatened his liberty. There was as yet no cloud on his sky. The first five years of his life, two in France, three at Watendlath, had known no blemish. She had been able to give him all he wanted, because when Warren's will was read it was found that he had left her all his own small means—not much, but enough for her needs. The boy was of amazing health, and, so long as he was not shut up in a room for too long, asked for no attention. He trusted everyone as a puppy trusts everyone before his first betrayal. He was fearless, truthful and gay, the three best things a small boy can be. He would defend his mother against anyone or anything; he was obedient so long as she did not hamper his liberty. Once, for some small crime, she had locked him in a room; he had broken the window and disappeared until nightfall. She understood that because she had once climbed out of a window herself.

Their relationship was, at present, perfect.

Now as the light faded and the stars came out she tried to persuade him to sleep. She would not wake Reuben. She would walk up the hill and see the sunrise by herself. But she almost hesitated to speak because the silence was so glorious, broken only by the running water that is to be heard everywhere in this country, the gentle friendly crackle of the burning wood as it fell into crimson embers, the occasional movement of the horses behind her.

Adam, too, seemed to feel the silence, for he stood without moving, his legs spread, looking up.

' Now you must sleep, Adam.'

He shook his head, not saying anything.

' Oh no. . . .' He looked at her, smiling. ' There's the moon.'

And there it was, sailing very calmly with a sort of smiling conceit between the trees.

She knew that he wouldn't sleep. ' Come. And we shall see the sunrise.'

So he took her hand and they started off, the small dog following. Adam was never very talkative. To be out at night was no very new

thing to him. They left the little wood behind
them and started to climb. They were now
on the open moor. The Langdale Pikes, Fairfield, Helvellyn were beyond, and across Yewdale
loomed the hump of the Old Man. The light
about and around him was diffused as though
shed by the multitude of stars. The pools of
shadow, neither brown nor grey, lay below them
like lakes of sleeping water. Fairfield and Helvellyn were marked with crags and precipices like
the tearing made by some giant's fingers. How
black, how black the hills against the luminous
sky! A little higher on the moor and they were
suddenly staring into the moon's face. They
could see now the two little pools which seemed
to blaze with moon-silver among the surrounding
vapour. No wind stirred; somewhere some sheep
were moving and the air was warm like the
breath of a flower.

They sat down against a gigantic boulder;
the stones around them rose in that moonshine
like monolithic sacrificial monuments. As they
sat in that stillness the hills seemed to approach
them. Helvellyn, always a beneficent hill, leaned
towards them, Fairfield embraced them, the pools
below smiled at them. Somewhere in that wood
Reuben was lying against a tree snoring with his
mouth open. Adam curled in against Judith's
side, the little dog curled in against Adam.

With her arm around her son Judith sat
staring into the moon. She did not often think
of the past, but to-night it came crowding towards
her, figures issuing from the hills, events stealing

up from the mist—the day that she had looked at Mrs. Monnasett and David had beaten her, the moment when she had seen Georges' mother, the night of the fireworks when Will and Francis and Reuben had talked, the escape of Reuben's brother, David's stroke and death, Sarah's passion —and then all her life with Georges, from the first week (what a baby then she had been!) to the last awful scene with Stane's father! And then the dead quiescence of the years at Grosset, the semi-life with Jennifer and Francis, Will's coming to Westaways, the friendship with Warren leading to the drama in Paris—drama of death, drama, thank God, of life.

She did not believe in God, but she did feel to-night that every event, every character, had led her to this—this question that was now the dramatic crisis of her whole life—which world was she to choose, the world of Uldale or the world of Watendlath?

She had thought that it was settled. Only a month or two ago she had said to Charlie Watson that her Herries life was finished for ever; she would not leave Watendlath until Adam was grown. Then he should choose for himself, but she would remain.

She had thought that it was settled. Then came a letter from Francis. He implored her to come to Uldale. He gave no reasons. She was to come, if only for a night, and bring Adam with her. The most touching thing was that Jennifer had scrawled at the bottom of the page: ' The two of us need you.'

Well, she would go, but only for a few nights, only to show them that she was out of Herries affairs for ever. But was she? The invitation had stirred her. She wanted to see Uldale again—the dairy, the housekeeping, the servants. She was sure that it would be in a mess. And Jennifer, John, Dorothy. . . . She was too proud to come to see them, after all the scandal about her, without an invitation . . . but if they asked her. . . . For a brief moment Watendlath had seemed small, shut in, her domination there a poor thing, even her beloved Charlie a rough ignorant farmer. . . . Then she had been ashamed, and in a day or two her true nature had recovered itself. For she knew that this was her true nature, the nature that she derived from her mother, the nature that outlawed her from the Herries blood.

Had she not written to Francis and said that she would come she would now have refused his appeal. But she had given her word.

Then the sight of Walter Herries this evening had revived all the struggle again. How proud and conceited he had been! It was thus, seated on his horse, gigantic against the skyline, that he remained for her, and, at the thought of him, her whole proud obstinate passion for dominating returned.

It was thus that he meant to wipe out Francis and Jennifer, John and Dorothy. She saw them helpless and cowering under his whip. She knew suddenly why Francis had sent that letter to her. How amusing to return to Uldale—she, the outlaw with her bastard boy—and fight Walter, make Adam—illegitimate though he was—head of all the Herries! Her heart beat triumphantly; she drew her arm more closely about him; he was sleeping.

She looked up at the stars as though to defy them. And the answer came back without question. 'Here is your country. Here is your place.'

But why? All the rebels were killed or disgraced. Georges had been murdered, Warren killed, Francis humiliated, her father an outcast, Reuben — well, Reuben talked more of social things now than of God. What of the bear, the boy hanged, young Hartley Coleridge? She was not sentimental about outlawry, but it seemed that if you fought against the laws of the House —if you broke the windows, rushed downstairs with no clothes on, rang the bells in the belfry, refused the common food or drink, brought the mongrel dog into the parlour—they all together, with one loud cry, threw you into the street; and then, how were you better?

For three years in Watendlath she and her boy had been outlawed; and how was she better?

'You *are* better,' the little dog, the cherry-faced moon, the scar like a sword on Helvellyn's flank answered her. 'You have never been at peace before. *This* is your world, not the other.'

But she was practical and not given to hearing voices. To beat Walter, to dominate all the Herries, to place Adam at the head of them.

He would have, she was sure, all Will's genius for money, all Walter's physical strength, all Francis' brains. . . .

Which way was she going? Her whole life led to this crisis—or so she fancied, as we like to fancy that there is a line and a course and a climax, when it may not be so at all.

She remembered the way that the hens scratched in the room when she had first returned to it after Georges' death, the elephant in Paris, and that woman bending over, searching among her letters, and Adam trailing in the shawl, Reuben licking his fingers after the meal from the pot. . . .

Perhaps there is no line, only a gesture here, a leaf falling, the sheep huddling up the path outside the farm. But there was Adam. . . . She was responsible for the life that he would have. Would he be like Charlie Watson, blowing on his fingers for the cold, or Will sitting in his counting-house, or Walter at the head of his table, or Francis waiting for his wife's lover and pretending not to see . . .? No, not that. Adam, even now, was as brave as a lion. Poor Francis. . . .

But before she fell asleep she was aware that the decision that she would make must affect many lives, much Herries history. She knew what she could do if she tried. She had never as yet tried with her whole heart. She had always been divided. Her son had united her. She saw him, as her eyes closed, reaching up with his hand, catching the stars and joining, with the light that streamed from them, her divided heart.

She woke to see one bright bar of gold above the ridge. The edge of the bar sparkled and quivered. Behind it a fleet of tiny pink clouds trembled, hovered, then merged into a fan-shaped shadow of rosy light.

She bent down and kissed Adam. ' Wake up,' she said, ' and see the sun.'

He looked up, rubbed his eyes with his knuckles, then jumped to his feet, caught her by the hand and pulled her to a higher ridge of the moor.

Little winds, little fingers passing over an instrument, blew against their faces. The sky was beyond depth, without end, but was flecked now with fire. Thick white mist lay like water beneath them, but this soon was touched and lightened, thinned; the rocks and the spear-tops of the trees rent and tore it. They, too, caught the gold, and Helvellyn was, as though it had rolled its shoulder towards the light, purple.

The mist broke everywhere, and the sky was showered with flecks of gold. The cloven mist streamed down the hills like rain. Light was everywhere. The valleys ran with sun.

' Now I'll race you!' Adam shouted, and started tearing down to the little wood.

JUDITH RETURNS TO ULDALE

When Judith stood again in the so-familiar hall at Uldale she was deeply excited. It was her nature to be excited, and that nature had not changed although she was forty-six years of age.

A stranger would have seen only a little ordinary pale-faced, middle-aged woman, bewildered perhaps by the sudden light, dressed in bonnet and shawl, faded but scrupulously clean, holding by the hand a very small, rather ugly boy. No romance there. Nevertheless the situation was romantic, for Judith was returning to the home of her childhood, after behaviour so scandalous that it should have ostracised her for ever, holding her illegitimate child by the hand—and she was there by invitation! She would not, she proudly assured herself, be there in any other way!

Her emotions were mixed and confused: she could never enter this house without a hundred memories crowding upon her, but it was characteristic of her that the first thing that interested her was that there were signs of neglect and untidiness everywhere. She saw that at once, and her fingers itched to put everything to rights.

For a moment the only person who greeted her was the very decent woman who opened the door. She knew that her ancient enemy, Mrs. Ponder, had been dead now three years of a fever. She gave the woman a quick friendly glance.

' Thank you,' she said, smiling.

Then her very next move, instinctive, almost unknown to herself, was to step forward, still holding Adam by the hand, and put a picture that hung crooked on the wall straight again.

' That's better,' she said.

It was an old picture that she knew well, of a huntsman leaping a little ditch. She gave it a friendly little pat.

Then Jennifer came out from the parlour. ' Judith!   I didn't know——' she cried; but even then she came forward a little slowly, a little lazily, as though she were but half awake.

She was not as handsome as she had been; she was middle-aged now, as Judith was, but she was still a very remarkable woman, carrying herself with the same old dignity and grandeur, and her hair, untouched with grey, was of the same superb darkness. She was wearing a coloured bodice of orange over a white skirt. The orange sleeves, puffed and slashed, were very fine. But Judith saw at once that the dress was a little slatternly, and that her cheeks were painted. Her eyes, too, were weary, not with quite the old affectation of sleepiness. There was real fatigue, disappointment, unhappiness there.

She towered over Judith and the little boy. She bent down and kissed Judith.

'Is this Adam?'

'Yes. This is Adam.'

She kissed him, and he returned the kiss
with fervour. She was quite the most beautiful
lady he had ever seen, as this was the most
beautiful house he had ever been in. He
stared at the wallpaper with its Chinamen and
castles, at the silver candlesticks, at the broad
staircase, at the tall grand lady with the wonderful
orange sleeves. From that first moment he and
Jennifer were friends.

'Here is Francis! Francis, Francis, Judith
is come!'

Francis was coming down the stairs, and
Judith, looking up at him, felt a shock of dismay.
He had been over to Watendlath to see her a
year ago, and she had thought then that he
looked old and ill, but now—how thin he was,
how tired he seemed; he was an old man, and yet
he was not more than sixty!

In a way he was more handsome than he had
ever been. His extreme thinness suited him;
his high collar, frilled shirt, and dark blue trousers
showed his figure to the greatest advantage.

Judith was proud of him and deeply sorry for
him; she longed to put her arms around him and
mother him. He took both her hands in his.

'Judith, this is famous! . . . After all this
time! And is this Adam? How do you do,
Adam?'

'Very well, I thank you, sir,' said Adam in
his shrill piping voice that was apt to end in a
squeak.

They all laughed to relieve the tension of the meeting. There was a bustle about the baggage.

Judith went out into the dark garden. Charlie Watson had driven them out from Keswick. He leaned over and held her hand. For a moment she clung to his touch. All Watendlath seemed to be personified by him.

'Good-bye, Charlie,' she said, raising herself on tiptoe. 'We shall soon be back.'

'I am not so sure about leaving you.'

'Nonsense.' His face was close to hers. She let her hand rest for a moment on his rough coat and thick strong arm.

'Watendlath is not far away.'

''Tis a world away,' he answered her gruffly, and at once drove off.

She went back into the house. Her thought was, before everything, of Adam. He must go to bed. They had left Watendlath early that morning and, wild with excitement, he had been awake at four. Then, too, putting him to bed would give her some excuse to be alone a little before coming down.

On the landing they met the two children. John was now thirteen and Dorothy twelve. John was oddly like his father in face, but would be broader and thicker in body. Judith knew that he had a most charming character, kindly, affectionate, loyal — a little weak perhaps, a little dreamy like father and great-grandfather before him. How strange! John's great-grandfather had been her father! She thought of it as she kissed him. Dorothy was good-natured, obedient and conventional, something like her Aunt Deborah, fair-haired, at present plump, at the moment conscious of her 'panta-lettes,' which were only fastened with tapes above her knee and gave her much anxiety. Such things were always to make her anxious.

Both children were delighted to see their Aunt Judith as they had always called her. Life at home had not been too pleasant of late; now that Aunt Judith had come it would be more gay.

They were exceedingly interested to see Adam. He was at once at his ease with them. He was always at his ease with everyone, because he trusted everyone.

He threw off his little riding-coat, letting it be where it fell, and showed John how the horse that Charlie Watson was driving had thrown up its head and snorted, but in the middle of this exhibition he was excited by the sight of the room where he and his mother would sleep. He had been too young during those first years in France to notice or remember things, and since then the farm at Watendlath had been all that he had known.

Certainly the room at the Keswick Inn to-day had been grand, but that had been a public place with men drinking and a man playing a harp, and there had been a dog with a lame leg. This was *his* room and his mother's!

He ran round and round it, shouting cries of joy. For Judith it was strange enough. For,

once again it was her old room, the room where
Mrs. Monnasett had died.

'I thought you would wish to be in the
same room,' said Jennifer, standing in the
doorway.

It was indeed the same room! In all these
years the wallpaper had not been changed.
Still there were those blue pagodas, there was
the tallboy that had seemed to her as a baby
so infinitely high, over the bed the blue tester
hangings and overlay, the bed itself with the
columns fluted and reeded and so charmingly
carved with acanthus leaves. There Mrs. Monnasett, with her yellow face, had lain, the candles
flickering in the breeze, her lips fixed in a sar-
donic smile. . . . The room of all Judith's life.
Nothing had occurred. Only yesterday she had
bent forward to find the little box. . . .

'I will leave you,' said Jennifer. 'Come,
children. Aunt Judith will soon come down.'
There was a new note in Jennifer's voice,
as though behind her words she was pleading
for something.

But Judith now could think only of Adam.
She undressed him and washed him. He would
hardly keep still. She held him naked in her
arms and kissed him. He lay back against her
watching the leaping flames of the fire. His
small dark head against her breast (he was quite
suddenly sleepy), he asked her questions.

'Is that gentleman my uncle?'

'Yes, dear.' Impossible to explain now why
and how he was not!

' Was my father like him? '

' No; your father was not so tall nor so old.'

' This gentleman is very, very old.'

' No. Not truly. He will not appear old when you know him.'

' Is that boy called John? '

' Yes.'

He yawned a huge yawn.

' I like him. . . .' Then he added, blinking his eyes at the fire: ' Is the beautiful lady his mother? '

' Yes.'

' But he called her ma'am.'

' Many boys and girls call their mother ma'am and their father sir.'

He thought about this. ' I cannot call my father sir because I haven't one, and I have never called you ma'am.'

' No, and you never will,' said Judith resolutely. She put on his shirt and carried him to the big four-poster.

He looked so small in it that she laughed. Then they both laughed. The touch of the cool sheets woke him up again and he rolled all over the bed. Then he lay still, watching her with wide-open eyes while she changed her dress, washed her face and hands, brushed her hair.

' This is a very grand house,' he said at last.

' Yes. I lived in it when I was a little girl, younger than you are.'

But the strangeness of it! In that bed, where her small son was lying, old Mrs. Monnasett had

once lain! She looked at him, her heart bursting
with love, but her voice was quite severe when
she said:

'Now go to sleep, Adam. Are you hungry?'

He could not be. He had eaten a tremendous
dinner at Keswick.

'Yes, yes. I am! I am!' he cried, although
until his mother had mentioned it he had not
thought of it. But how wonderful he thought
her in her evening dress! The colours of her
gown were rose and lavender grey, and she had
a turban with a plume of feathers.

When she bent down to kiss him he hugged
her and pinched her nose, a favourite game of
theirs.

'If I do not eat soon I shall be asleep,' he
answered, grinning at her. Yes, he was ugly as
proper standards went, but she would not alter
him by a hair's breadth.

'Do I look fine?' she asked him.

He nodded and watched her with all his eyes
until she was out of the door.

But she did not feel fine at supper. They had
dined at three in the afternoon but she at five in
the Keswick Inn, so they were hungry and she
was not. It seemed very natural that Jennifer
should enjoy her food. However severe the
crisis her appetite was strong.

Judith was strongly conscious of her clothes.
That was not like her, but for three years the
rose-lavender dress and the turban had lain in
a box under the stair at John Green House.
Fashions had changed. Evening dresses were

shorter and had a padded 'rouleau' at the bottom. Waistbands were directly above the hips. Nevertheless, although she was in fashion, Jennifer was not smart. She looked as though she had put on her clothes in her sleep. Jennifer was untidy, Judith was dowdy; that's what they were. Francis was the grand one, seated gravely at the end of the table, his head thin now, as though carved of a fine stone. The ruffles at his neck were of a peerless whiteness.

Their talk was stiff and awkward. They spoke of general affairs. People were still discussing the Cato Street business, although it was eight months since its occurrence. Judith noticed at once with what feverish excitement Francis spoke, as though ignorant desperadoes like Thistlewood and Edwards were in every town, hiding down every lane, concealed in every corner.

She noticed, too, that when he went on in this exaggerated sensational strain Jennifer's lips stiffened and her eyes were scornful. She looked at Judith once, as though to say: ' You see now what he has come to. Can you wonder if I despise this man?' and Judith thought again that there was an appeal for help there.

Matters became even more personal when they discussed the Coronation that was to be celebrated in the following year, the King's efforts for a divorce, and the Queen's eccentric behaviour.

Francis, who had been drinking, Judith saw, very much more than was his habit in the old

days, broke into a demonstrative, emotional defence of the Queen. The King was a blackguard; he did not care who heard him say it.
He was surely old enough now to say what he
pleased. Besides, everyone knew what the King
was. It was disgraceful that the country should
have to suffer under such a man. And the poor
Queen — well, she had been, perhaps, a little
imprudent at times. She was eccentric, emotional. But who had driven her to her eccentricities? Brougham was a hero. He would drink
to Brougham. They must all drink to Brougham.
Judith noticed then Jennifer's irritation. She
saw that such scenes as these were part of every
evening's programme. Jennifer, looking across
the table at Francis scornfully, praised the King,
said that he had been much calumniated. At
least he was no prig nor Methodist. For her
part she liked a jolly fellow, a man who knew what
life was and lived it to the full . . . not a half-
alive pedant who skulked about the house. . . .
She stopped abruptly. Then smiled at Francis.

'I am fortunate,' she said softly, 'to have a
husband who strikes the mean. Judith, do you
not think that Francis is looking well?'

'Very well,' said Judith, and she put out her
hand and touched his. He looked at her with a
glance that had in it so much of apology and
unhappiness that her heart was wrung.

The food was badly cooked and warm when
it should have been hot. The meal dragged on
interminably. No allusion was made to anyone's
private affairs. At last they sat there in silence

while the candles trembled and the old clock ticked like a miser counting his money.

What was the matter with the house? There was more in this than the relations of Francis and Jennifer, more than Jennifer's infidelity, more than Francis' self-disgust. An air of apprehension was everywhere. She had detected it, even in the faces of the two children.

When at last they got up to move into the parlour, Judith thought of Watendlath with a longing that was almost irresistible. She had an impulse to run out into the dark cool garden. She would be closer to the hills there and would hear water running somewhere. She felt the touch of her hand on Charlie Watson's strong arm. Oh, there everything was so simple, so happy!

In the hall she stopped for an instant to hear whether there was any sound from Adam. No, he would be sleeping quietly. She was comforted again.

In the parlour the three of them sat like images. The outburst was soon coming, but until it did they must be silent. Judith herself was affected by the stillness that was so vocal. Seated with her back to the window she had a sudden fancy that Walter Herries was standing outside, watching them, peering in. It was all that she could do not to get up and see.

Then Jennifer rose, said that she was going to bed, kissed Judith and went out, her eyes half closed, yawning a little, just as she had used to do.

' Well, Judith,' said Francis.

' Well, Francis.'

He got up with a quick impetuous movement and came to where she was sitting. He knelt down by her chair, put his arms around her, rested his head on her breast.

' Oh, I am so weary, so weary,' he murmured.

She thought of the time when she was a baby and had adored him, when David had whipped her, and she had not cared so long as Francis loved her. She smiled a little wryly above his head. Poor Francis!

Then to her distress he began to weep. He seemed to be completely broken down. He wept as though all his control must be abandoned or he would die. She had never seen Francis cry. She could not bear it.

' Oh no, Francis. No. . . . No, no! '

Then at last he looked up at her, his cheeks stained with tears.

' Forgive me, my dear. It is many years since I wept last. I am not given to weeping. But seeing you come back to-night, after all this time, the same, so familiar, the only friend I have left—it has been too much for me. Truly, Judith, I am desperate. I don't know which way to turn.'

' Now sit here beside me.' She motioned to a place on the sofa. ' Let us talk over things quietly. They are never so urgent when one talks over them quietly. We will discuss everything just as we have always done.'

He came and sat beside her.

' But you are going to stay now that you are

here, are you not? . . . You are not going away?'

'For a few days. Of course, we will stay for a few days.'

'For a few days? Oh, but that is nothing. Judith, you must live here again—for a while at least—you and your boy. . . .'

'Live here?' She laughed. 'Francis, do you not realise that I am now a scandalous person? I have had a child out of wedlock as everyone knows. With Jennifer and the children——'

'Scandalous!' he broke out. 'We are all scandalous now! Yes, I will say anything to-night. I have held myself in long enough. Jennifer has been that man's mistress for years now—quite an old family affair. As soon as I am away at Kendal or Carlisle he comes here, and everyone knows it. Everyone knows it, I tell you. It is the common joke! Walter sees to that. . . . And all these years I have done nothing. I, the fine Francis who started the world with such grand ideas. I have done nothing, nothing at all.

'I have skulked in corners, taken his hand, offered him drink, while he makes my wife a common whore. . . . Oh, my God, my God, I am the most despicable man on this earth, the most despicable and the most unhappy!'

She tried to calm him. He was trembling from head to foot.

'She hates me. She despises me. And, God forgive me, I love her yet. It is because I

love her that I have been able to do nothing,
because with my cursed nature I have always
seen two sides of everything.   She never loved
me.   I forced her into marriage.   Why should
I have denied her all opportunity of love? '

He caught her hand.

' Judith, do you remember that Ball all those
years ago, the Ball when Jennifer broke Christabel's fan?   Of course, you do.   It all started from
that.   It has all come from that.   You remember that I was talking to you when she first came
by!   How lovely she was that night!   Do you
remember?   Catherine de' Medici with the collar
of pearls and her white neck and the crimson
dress?   Her excitement at the Ball—do you
remember? . . .

' And after—the meeting in Berkeley Square.
Do you remember?   When I sat in the window
and it was so hot and the scent of the lilac came
up from the street.   I sat in the window thinking of Jennifer, and then do you remember how
I broke in upon Will and how angry he was?
Our separation dated from that.'

Did she not remember?   And how, a moment
after, Georges stood there in the doorway,
Georges in his brown suit, spent and done . . . ?

' Before that,' Francis went on eagerly, ' everything had been well—for all of us and for the
country too, I think.   What a good old country
it was when I was a child, so quiet and so cosy!
Everyone drank ale, and there was " oat clap
bread," and no one came to disturb us.   The
children would help in the spinning or drive the

sheep on the fells. Everyone was happy together. But now there are visitors peering and
fingering, and in the towns children of six and
seven years work in the dark, and the machines
have come to take the bread out of men's mouths.
The sky is blackening with smoke, we have a
King too drunk to sit on the throne, and class is
against class. . . .'

He broke off. ' No, by God, what do I care
for the country any more? There was a time
when I cared. Did I not kill my own father and
cause my mother to hate me, because the Bastille
fell? '

He laughed bitterly, striking his knee with
his hand.

' But now what should a cuckold think of his
country—a cuckold plain to all his neighbours,
and any who do not know of it kind Cousin
Walter will tell them of it.'

She tried to calm him. He was so dreadfully
excited that she thought that at any moment he
might raise the house.

' Dear Francis, the country is well enough.
This is a time of transition, and such times always
seem hard to those who are in them. There is a
grand new world coming. . . .'

' And I don't care if there is! ' he interrupted
her. ' You can have your fine new world! If
I could but get my fingers round dear Walter's
large throat! ' He stopped himself with a
tremendous effort. ' You see how it is with me
to-night, my dear. I am excited at seeing you
again. For you are the only one I have left,

the only one who understands me. I killed my father. My mother hated me. My brother and wife hate me yet. God knows but my children hate me too. But I ask for no pity. It is all my own doing. You and I, my dear, are misfits; and to be a misfit in the Herries family is to be slain.'

'We are neither of us slain,' she said, looking up at him quickly. 'It is perhaps true that we are misfits. But it is the misfits, I fancy, who give the value to the world. What would the Herries family be without us? A dull, poor lot. We are the ones who understand and because we suffer have charity. We can see into both worlds. We travel into strange countries where the others cannot go, and bring back the news.' She laughed. 'I am turning very poetical,' she said. 'It is not my ordinary fashion. But I must tell you, Francis, that if I am a misfit I am a very happy one. And so may you be too if you will. I am certain that Jennifer does not hate you. She must be long weary of that other affair. All will soon be forgotten. . . .'

'Forgotten!' he broke in. 'Not with Walter Herries there! Ah, you do not yet know the villain of the piece!'

'Walter?' she asked. 'What can he do?'

'What can he do? What has he not done? He hates us, has always done, because, firstly, he says Jennifer insulted his mother, secondly, he must be king of the castle here and wants no other Herries round, and, thirdly, he has a deformed son, and my children make him mad. . . .'

Y

'But he can do nothing.'

'Do nothing? He can do everything. He is my perpetual enemy and has been these five years. He is so proud that he will burst his skin one of these days. He has all the neighbourhood in his pocket.'

He calmed himself that he might give the value to his words. 'Do you know what for five years he has been doing? There are spies all around me, and every small action of mine is repeated to him. It has been so for five years now. Fancy to yourself what it would be if a good friend of yours, who had known you well for a long while, drew a caricature of you in a book, using all your external habits, your tricks of speech, your eccentricities, and then, with a diabolic cleverness, twisted them all to mean and sordid motives? You would be yourself bewildered. You would say yes, that it was true; you had done this and that, you wore your hair so, you laughed thus, and like all men you had your weaknesses, your follies. Was this perhaps a true picture? And if you saw it as partly true how much more would others, who know you but externally, judge of your true self? And you would begin to doubt yourself and to suspect every movement, every gesture. I tell you, Judith, that my neighbours here who have known me all my life long take rather Walter's picture of me now than their own. There is nothing goes on in this house that he does not know, nothing that he does not use. . . .'

Yes, he would be like that. She knew in-

stinctively that what Francis said was true. She
felt, even here in the warm safe room, the force
and danger of his overbearing vitality.

But she answered firmly:

' Listen, Francis. No one can traduce you
but yourself. Even your bitterest enemy knows
that a satire is a satire. Its very exaggeration
must make him consider the opposite. One is
alone in this world. No one knows one save
oneself, and then it is only a glimpse of the truth
that one has. Forget Walter, and if you cannot
forget Walter fight him! '

She jumped to her feet.

' I could fight him! He should have enough
of his spying and traducing if I got at him! '

' Yes, yes,' he cried eagerly. ' You must
stay, Judith. Remain here. With you to help
me I can be another man. Although I am old—'
His voice faltered. ' Sixty is an age. . . .'

She had had enough. She was infinitely
weary. Francis' request that she should stay
gave her a sudden flick of terror. She did not
want to stay. She must get back to Watendlath. She and Adam safe in Watendlath, away
from all these Herries. . . .

She kissed him.

' Good-night, Francis, dear. All will come
right.'

But as she climbed slowly the stair she thought,
in spite of herself, ' But how *could* he not have
challenged Fernyhirst? How *could* he let it go
on as he has—all these years? ' But she was
too weary to consider it further. However, her

evening was not yet done with. As she passed
Jennifer's door a voice called her.

She went in.

Jennifer was sitting on her bed in her shift,
her long white legs dangling to the floor. Her
room was in a disorder. Clothes were flung
about the floor, drawers were pulled open, the
curtains were roughly drawn, a lamp by the
bed was smoking to the ceiling.

Judith closed the door.

'What has he been saying?'

'Oh, it is so late!' Judith sighed. 'Dear
Jennifer——'

'No, I must know.'

'He has been saying nothing, only that he is
unhappy——'

Jennifer put out a long white arm and drew
Judith to the bed.

'I am unhappy too! Oh, so dreadfully unhappy! It is all his fault. I hate him. . . . I
have hated him for years. Why was I such a
fool as to marry him? He has been speaking to
you of Edward.'

'Edward?'

'Fernyhirst. But that is all finished.
Finished long ago. I hate him too.'

Judith looked at her, and again her tiresome
maternal impulse that was for ever preventing
her real action interfered. But what was she
to do? This poor, tired, aged woman! And
once there had been that brilliant happy girl,
radiant with beauty and success, in the crimson
dress, the collar with the pearls?

But she had still lovely legs and feet! How different might Judith's own story have been had she had such wonderful feet and ankles! She put her arm round her, but how she longed for her bed!

'Francis spoke for the most part of Walter!'

'That devil! He is determined to ruin us, Judith, all of us—my poor children—' and even then, when she should have wept, she yawned, kicking her feet a little, looking at her silver slippers. And in that yawn Judith saw once and for ever exactly what she was. She was true Herries. She had no imagination, none whatever. Had she had any she would never have married Francis, never have lived in Cumberland, never have suffered an intrigue with Fernyhirst, never have stayed here for years, doing nothing, understanding nothing, seeing nothing! And it was against the Herries in her that Francis had beaten in vain! Had she been of an age it was Walter that she should have married. They would have suited one another to perfection.

It was from that moment of comprehension that Judith's complete domination of Jennifer began.

'Dear Judith. You are such a consolation. There was a time when I was jealous of you. I know how shockingly I behaved. You need not tell me of my behaviour. But now I would do anything for you—and Francis too. It is the one point on which we are agreed. You must stay for a long, long while.'

Judith smiled and shook her head.

' I am an abandoned woman, Jennifer—myself and my little bastard. We do not belong to good society any more.'

' What foolishness! I am sure that an illegitimate child is nothing. Everyone is so free in these days. And I am as bad as you. Everyone knows about Edward. Certainly you must stay.'

' I have grown unused to society. I am a peasant, digging and ditching, watching the sheep. You cannot think how strange these clothes seemed to me to-night.'

Jennifer, looking at her naked legs with approval, answered:

' I am sure that is a very good costume. But we are two old women. What does it matter what we wear? My legs are still fine, although there is no one who cares any more. Nor do I wish there to be. Love is the most wearying thing I know.'

Judith said good-night.

' Then you will stay?'

' For a day or two at least.'

' No, for always. The children worship you, and little Adam is a love.' She stood up in her shift that fell in folds to her silver slippers. For a moment there was something genuine and touching in her fine eyes that looked out above her painted cheeks in a true and human appeal.

She said what Francis had said:

' You are my only friend.'

Judith undressed and lay down beside Adam.

She stared into the dark. She *would* not, no, she *would* not be caught by these two. She *would* not come back into these Herries affairs. . . . But they were so alone. Francis had no one—Jennifer only her brother, who was a fat careless bachelor in Bournemouth. Both Prosper and Amelia were dead.

But she *would* not be caught. . . . She seemed to hear beyond the window the water of Watendlath. She could see the Tarn lying in ebony silence under the stars. The sheep were pressing up the road, the cows were to be milked; here came Tyson, his arms loaded with hay for the cattle. Armboth touched the stars. . . .

She was near to tears; she was so homesick.

She was too old, too settled in her quieter life to take up these quarrels again. Ah, but Walter, riding his white horse, striking at Adam with his whip. . . .

With a gesture of protection she stretched out her arm and drew Adam to her. He was deep in sleep but he grunted like a little pig and nestled into her side.

ROUND OF THE MOON

THE house was bathed in sunlight and ladders of dust quivered in the air. No room had been swept for months; the kitchen was a disgrace; the dairy—ah, how beautiful it had once been with its gleaming cleanliness, the stone floor like a mirror—and now! In the stables there were but three horses, two of them fit for little but to drag the carriage at a funeral pace along the rocky, uneven roads.

Judith swept through the place like a whirlwind. Mrs. Quinney, the housekeeper, Martha Hodgson, the woman who had opened the door on Judith's arrival (she was cook and maid both), Doris, a stupid country girl, and Mr. Winch, the thin cadaverous little tutor, were, in addition to Bennett the coachman and Jack the stable-boy, all the servants. Very different from David's day, different even from Jennifer's early day, but Judith must make the best of it. And make the best of it she did. In no time she had them all at her call, all save Mr. Winch, of whom more in a moment.

She summed them up instantly. Mrs. Quinney was lazy, greedy, gossipy, weak, amiable, gossipy, greedy and lazy. Martha was earnest, plain, silent, faithful, opinionated and earnest. Doris was little, if anything, removed from the beasts of the field and like them was hungry, obedient, and responsive to overtures of love from the opposite sex. Bennett had always reminded her a little of her dear Charlie. She liked him because of that. He was stouter, less intelligent, had far less personality, but was a man —that is, he was a Cumberland man and therefore silent, suspicious, obstinate, faithful and courageous.

Jack the stable-boy pleased her best of all. He was only a lad and had come from the depths beyond Mardale, but he had the makings of a grand gentleman. He, from the first, would do anything for her.

There they were, ready to her hand. For years they had been neglected. Francis had scarcely spoken to them, Jennifer had let them do as they would. Before the week was out the house looked a different place, the floors shone, the silver glittered, the food came hot to the table, the horses trotted, Caesar the dog barked at night when he heard a strange step, the spiders were broomed away, the carpets were dusted, the grass of the lawn was cut, a dead cat was removed from the Gothic temple, a mouse was found in the chaise, chrysanthemums, bronze and orange, lighted the parlour, the drawers in Jennifer's bedroom were tidied, Dorothy had fresh ribbons to her dress, and the holes in John's stockings were mended.

Judith was to stay only a day or two. It was

Y 2

nearly Christmas before she had the house entirely to her liking.

Then, one winter's day when the sun like a swollen red penny rolled between shifting orange clouds over Skiddaw, she looked out through the bottle-green glass of the parlour window and saw Mr. Winch creeping round the corner of the house toward the stables.

Creeping he was. His thin lanky body was bent almost to all-fours. There was a moment when in actual fact he knelt on the path and looked ludicrous enough in that position.

Abruptly round the corner came Francis, his head bent, his arms behind his back, and almost stepped on Mr. Winch, who was diligently brushing his trousers. Francis said a word to him and came on, lost in thought as he always was in these days.

Now what had Mr. Winch been doing? With her accustomed impetuosity Judith had disliked him from the first moment of meeting him, and, it is to be feared, for no better reason than that his hands were damp. Afterwards there were other reasons. Whence had he come? He had been in the house for four years and yet both Francis and Jennifer were exceedingly vague about him. He had tutored Lord Somebody's son once somewhere; he said himself that he came from Warwickshire; Jennifer disliked him and behaved as though he were not there. Francis talked to him on a day, and then on another day disregarded him. It seemed that he taught the children something. John at

least said that he did. Judith disliked him
increasingly, and the more she disliked him the
more obsequious he became. His appearance
was most certainly not prepossessing, for his
narrow grey eyes were so placed that you could
not be sure whether he had a squint or no, his
suit was always a shiny black and he was for ever
blowing his nose.

This vision out of the window woke Judith to
life. She had been alive indeed all these weeks,
engaged on a business that she adored, but the
house had swallowed her. She had not seen
outside its affairs. Except in one matter, and
that was the emotion that never left her, night
or day, her love for her son, Adam. She
was suffering for the first time in her life from
jealousy.

For Adam, when he had been in the house two
days, fell in love with John. He was in love so
completely and absolutely that he forgot his
mother altogether. For five years she had
been everything to him, and now she was, in the
flash of an instant, it seemed, nothing to him at
all. Of course it was not so. It was simply
that he was at the age when he could not think
of two things at the same time. He had never,
as yet, in his life had an older boy for companion,
and he found it simply enchanting.

John was kind, amiable and easy. He had
not had in these last years a happy life. The
house had been smoky with unhappiness. The
two children had been quite neglected. He had
followed the hounds at a time, but then the

horse had been sold. He went out shooting rabbits with Bennett. He witnessed an occasional wrestling or cock-fight. But he was ' soft ' for his time. He hated cruelty of any kind. It made him sick. It was hard to say at present what he cared for. He was not a student like his father, he did not roam the country. He liked to stay at home, work in the garden, read stories. Although he was no student he could read tales and poetry to himself by the hour. He would sit curled up in a corner somewhere and pray that he would not be noticed. He had always detested Mangnall's *Questions* and Butler's *Guide to Useful Knowledge*—for such things he had no use whatever, but Gold-smith's *History of England* he devoured in all its four volumes because of the thrilling detail in it. Then there was Vicesimus Knox's *Elegant Extracts in Prose and Verse*, then *Marmion, The Lay*, the Waverleys, *The Parents' Assistant, The Fairchild Family* and, secretly, obtained from some of the Forresters who lived in Bassen-thwaite, many volumes of the Minerva Press, *The Mysterious Hand, The Demon of Society* and the rest.

He read, he dreamed, his life was intensely solitary. It was an amazing thing for him when this ugly baby, so fearless, so interested and so happy, came into it. The two great characteristics of Adam Paris, then and always, were his interest and his happiness. In later years he was to exasperate many persons by these two qualities, for most human beings quite naturally call extensive interests selfishness, and happiness complacency.

John had not known much happiness yet in his life, and few persons had cared very actively whether he were happy or no. He was shy of his father as his father was shy of him, and afraid of his mother. Dorothy was a girl. Mr. Winch was nothing. Only Bennett was his friend, and Bennett had never much to say. Now this small boy came and worshipped, thought him a god, believed everything that John told him, trusted him utterly. Soon they were inseparable.

Adam did not forget his mother, but she was always there, while John was something new and showed him everything that he wanted to see.

When Judith realised that she was jealous she was amazed at herself. She liked John and trusted him; Adam could not be with anyone better. But her jealousy would not let her alone. She showed it to no one, but something told her that the first stage of her life with her son was over. She would never again have him so completely her own as she had had him during those first five years. She was alone again. It seemed to be the one lesson that life was for ever teaching her. Alone she was; alone she must ever be. She did not yet realise that it was the lesson that every other human being was also, with exasperated tears and helpless gestures, learning.

The fire of her love for Adam burnt her heart, it seemed to her. She stood listening for him.

She called softly, then louder, then louder again. At last he would appear at the stairhead or at the stable door, John beside him. She would smile and wave to him and go away.

At night she had him. He would dance into bed, ask her one question after another on the wonders of the past day, and then instantly fall asleep. Then her time came. She would fold his small body in her arms and, with his head against her breast, would tell him how she loved him, how he was everything to her, how he was all that she had, how she loved him as no mother had ever loved her son, and the shadows of the fire would leap ironically on the wall and Adam would breathe softly in his sleep, lost to her even then.

But he was not really lost to her. In the depth of her being she knew it and was comforted. Meanwhile the discovery of Mr. Winch on all-fours on the garden path woke her to important issues.

Having the house now tidied and disciplined, she was aware that, in spite of herself, Walter Herries' shadow was hanging over her as it was over the others. Not so grimly perhaps, nor so tragically, for she still maintained to herself with all her energy that her stay here was only temporary and that in another fortnight—after Christmas for certain—she would be free, in Watendlath, of the pack of them, never to return. She was not very sensitive as to her social position —she had never been sensitive—but she was aware that the visitors to Uldale in these last

months had all regarded her with a very lively
curiosity, and she thought that, behind their
politeness, there was a kindly ostracism.   They
did not, she was aware, invite her to their houses,
but that might have been as easily because of
Jennifer's scandal as her own.

Only good, kind Mrs. Southey invited her.
She went with the secret hope that she would
see again that strange boy Hartley.   But Hartley
was not there.   None of the children were present.   Mr. Southey was very kind and a little
distant.

Of Walter himself and his family she had seen
nothing.   The two households were cut off from
one another as though they were as remote as
China from Spain.   But, rightly or wrongly,
she heard the loud voice and saw the broad
back of Walter behind everything and, in spite
of her own good common sense, began to catch
something of the superstition that Francis and
Jennifer had of him—as a sort of malicious devil,
horns on his head, hoofs instead of feet, and an
eye in the middle of his back.

Seeing Mr. Winch, one thing at least became
plain to her: Mr. Winch was Walter's spy.
Assured of that, she was, in a moment, alive to a
whole blazing bundle of circumstances, as suddenly bright and crackling as though she had
seen it burst into flame before her eyes.

On looking back afterwards it appeared to
her that everything and everyone sprang into
action from that moment when she saw Mr.
Winch on all-fours.   It was, in any case, very soon

after that day that some of the worst and un-
happiest moments of her life confronted her.

The awful day opened for her quietly enough.
It was a fortnight before Christmas, and in the
morning the sky was a bright shrill blue, the
tops had a powdering of snow and the roads
were hard with frost.

Adam was to go on some grand Christmas
expedition into Keswick with John and Dorothy.
She accompanied them, riding her own sturdy
little mare, Phyllis, that she had brought with
her from Watendlath. She thought that after
she had seen them safely into the town she would
ride on into Borrowdale and have a glimpse of
Herries again. She had woken that morning
with her head full of Warren. She could not
tell why. She had not thought of him, she was
ashamed to confess to herself, for months. But
now, without warning, he had returned as the
dead do unexpectedly return.

They had an agreeable ride into Keswick,
passing many enchanting things on the way—a
pedlar, a blind man with a trumpet, two drunken
men fighting, a flock of sheep and a herd of
cows. Adam had had his eyes and nose pressed
to the windows of the chaise and was asking
questions as fast as he could breathe, not waiting for any answers. The vast broad back of
Bennett bobbed up and down on the box outside,
the inside smelt of straw and mice, and Judith
tried to feel no jealousy as she watched John
holding Adam that he should not fall.

Then she rode on into Borrowdale. The

road was still wild and uneven and unfit for a carriage, although carriages often used it, for it was the thing now to tour the Lakes and see 'the horrid precipices' and 'the thunderous waterfalls' that had so terribly frightened Mr. Gray. To-day, however, Judith had the scene to herself. Not a human being did she see, save an old man gathering sticks in a field. The Lake embraced the blue sky with a little tremor of excitement, and very lovely were the reflections of the snow-sprinkled hills in that blue water, hill-tops trembling like shadows in a swaying mirror.

The village of Grange was dead, and when at last she came to the Herries house, that was dead also. As before, when she had been with Warren, no one was there, but there were the remains of a meal on the table and a crumbling fire in the kitchen.

She sat on the old mildewed couch in the upper room for a while. Here she and Warren had sat . . . how long, long ago! Had they not sat there that day Adam would not be sucking lollipops (as she was sure that he was doing) in Keswick at this moment. Once again she asked herself why she had surrendered to Warren? For love of Georges' shadow?—and then with a sharp pang she realised for the first time how swiftly Georges was now fading from her mind. All the pain of losing him was gone. She did not miss him any more! Adam had taken his place.

She was not a sentimentalist. Facts were facts, and Georges, who had always wanted everyone else to be happy so long as he himself was not uncomfortable, would be glad. But Adam! She stood before the dead stone fireplace and pressed her hands before her eyes. Her passion of possession was terrific. She must govern it, guard it. Adam as he grew must be free. Looking into darkness, seeing into the future, she was afraid of herself.

The house dripped with damp and was of a fearful cold. She listened. Were there ghosts about? No; to-day Adam had slain them all. Father, mother, husband—one crick of her son's finger and they were fled.

She visited Georges' grave, then stopped at one of the cottages in Rosthwaite and ate and drank there. She knew every man, woman and child in Rosthwaite. It needed all her control not to push Phyllis up the well-known track. She was so near to Watendlath that, had Adam been with her, she must have gone—and then never have come down again! It was just over her head! If she listened she could hear Mrs. Ritson calling and Molly the cow lowing for her calf!

She would not come this way again. It was dangerous. But she would not need to come, for in a fortnight Christmas would be here, and directly after Christmas she and Adam would leave Uldale for ever.

She started homewards and saw that the weather was changing. She looked back and beheld how over Scafell and the Gavel great black clouds were climbing. They were piling up as though out of a vast vat. The blue sky above her head seemed to tremble in anticipation of its destruction. The clouds had a sort of boiling rage and fury in their blackness. She turned on her horse to watch as though at some show or pageant. Then she saw a small white cloud, like a puff of smoke from a cannon, spring above the hill and start to fly from the enemy. The little white cloud spread across the blue, and the black clouds pursued it. She could almost hear them roaring in their fury. ' I hope it will escape! I hope it will escape,' she could fancy the bare trees around her, that were all beginning to tremble, were saying. But of course the little cloud had no escape. The vanguard of the black army put out an ebony feeler, as an octopus might do, and the little white cloud was instantly swallowed. The landscape around her went dead as though a hand had struck it. The trees were shaking violently. A drop of rain smacked her cheek. She whipped Phyllis up and ran for it. By Grange she was caught. The rain slapped the earth like a woman beating a carpet. The drops danced on the ground with exultant joy. There was an empty outhouse off the road opposite the bridge. Pulling Phyllis after her, she ran in—and found Walter Herries filling the little place with his bulk!

They were at first very polite. His eyes twinkled with amusement. The noise of the rain on the roof was so loud that they had to shout. Then, quite suddenly, she sprang in.

' Walter Herries, you should know that shortly

I intend to wring the neck of your shabby little spy and throw him into the stable.'

'My spy!'

'Nasty Mr. Winch.'

He laughed, throwing his great head back and slapping his thigh.

'Cousin Judith, come and stay at Westaways for a little. Food and drink are better than at Uldale.'

She looked at him contemptuously.

'I would marry Mr. Winch sooner than sleep under your roof.'

'I am not inviting you to share my bed, Cousin Judith.'

She flushed.

'That was worthy of you,' she said. 'But remember you cannot touch *me* anywhere. It may be in the end I can harm *you* the more.'

He seemed contrite. 'I said a dirty thing. For once you see me ashamed. Make the most of it.'

She looked at him with a quiet inspection that made him, she saw, uncomfortable.

'I believe I could be your match if I cared, but I have done with all the Herries affairs. I never was in truth part of them and I never will be. But you must understand that I have loved Francis all my life, and something will come of your persecution of him.'

They had to shout, and there was something very ludicrous in that. In spite of herself, and although she was feeling exceedingly angry and had never hated him more, she smiled. He smiled too.

'I think we could be very good friends,' he said.

'Never! Never!' she answered passionately. 'I hope very much I can do you some harm before I die.' Then, to her great vexation, she smiled again, for a little trickle of rain, coming in from the roof, fell down his cheek and made him look absurd.

'Why do you persecute Francis? It is a very small game and not at all worth all the energy you put into it.'

'Jennifer insulted my mother,' he said like a sulky schoolboy.

'What! You are going back all that way— because years ago at a stupid Ball Jennifer broke your mother's fan?'

'They can leave Uldale and go elsewhere. Francis is doing no good there. Jennifer is the countryside scandal. They do the Herries name harm.'

'The Herries name! And what good do *you* do the Herries name?'

That touched him. He started up.

'By God! I do the Herries name more good than your rascally father, or *his* miserable puling grandson.' He grew calm again, came near to her and would have taken her arm had she not moved away.

'Now listen, Judith. I have but begun. I am a young man, strong and healthy. I shall wipe your Uldale family out as though they had never been. I have wealth and power, but nothing at all in comparison with what I shall

have. I am here for ever—I and my son after
me.'

'I have not seen your children,' she said
quietly.

It was cruel of her. She touched him there.
His stout red face grew more crimson. For a
moment she felt almost kindly towards him.

'Never mind,' he said, so low that she scarcely
caught the words. 'My son has one leg that
is shorter than the other, but he will have a head-
piece that Francis' boy will one day fear.'

'So you carry the feud into a later generation,'
she said scornfully.

'Not if they leave Uldale. Let them go
South. I will not bother them.'

'I see!' She looked him in the eyes. They
were now very close together and she could smell
the stuff of his handsome brown riding-coat.

'Had I not other plans for myself I should
like to stay and fight you, Cousin Walter. . . . I,
too, have a son, you know. His father was
Herries, even though distantly.'

'Yes. Poor Warren.' He laughed contemptuously. 'An illegitimate Herries, my
dear.'

'But Herries blood,' she answered.

He caught her arm then, whether she liked it
or no.

'We should be friends, Judith. We are of
the same sort.'

'But we are enemies, Cousin Walter,' she
answered. 'Good, sound, rock-bottom enemies.
Good-day to you.'

The rain had almost ceased. She mounted Phyllis and rode away. It was nearly dark when she reached Keswick, but the sky had cleared again. There were a few stars already and a fine frosty tang in the air. Soon there would be a grand full moon. The thought of the moon stayed her. There would be plenty of light to ride home by if she returned later. Francis had gone to Cockermouth for the night on a piece of business and she shrank from an evening quite alone with Jennifer. There was nothing more dreary, for Jennifer would either yawn and say nothing, or seek to abuse Francis, when Judith must stop her, or retrace the by now desperately familiar path of her affair with Fernyhirst, her weariness of him, the unfairness of everything and what would Judith advise her to do?

When Francis was present things were better, but without him—no, she could not endure it! Moreover, she was herself tired. She was not so young as she had been. It had been a long ride to Borrowdale; the visit to Herries, the encounter with Walter had for the moment exhausted her.

So she stepped in to see the only two friends that she had now in Keswick. They were a quaint pair, Miss West and Miss Pennyfeather. They were one of the scandals of Keswick, and about them Keswick was never weary of talking. They lived in a very small house in Main Street, next to a smithy. They were indeed an eccentric pair, devoted, original, entirely indifferent to public opinion, clever and sarcastic.

Miss West dressed as near a man as to be no matter. She wore a powdered wig and a coat with brass buttons. It was said that in the evening in her parlour she wore trousers. She drank and, it was rumoured, smoked a long clay pipe. She had a thin dried face with a long nose and very bright keen eyes. Miss Pennyfeather was very feminine, round and plump, pink and white. But she was even more sarcastic and cruel than Miss West in a quiet soft way. In reality they were neither of them cruel, but gave much in charity. They hated men and would not, it was said, have one in the house. They liked Judith greatly and would have seen much of her had she wished it. She liked them also, but was not in Keswick sufficiently.

She knocked on the door, was admitted by their little maid Betty, and found them by the fire in the parlour, Miss West reading to Miss Pennyfeather from one of the novels of Mrs. Cuthbertson.

They were enchanted to see Judith.

Miss West threw Mrs. Cuthbertson on to the floor, crying in a deep bass voice: ' This is Stuff! '

Then they had supper off cold chicken, rhubarb pie and cheese and, after that, played cards very frivolously. Miss West told some scandalous stories about the curate of Crosthwaite, about the wife of a coal-merchant who had recently come into money and set up his carriage, and a French poodle owned by the eccentric Mrs. Mason, a widow. They all laughed very much

and Miss West imitated the Crosthwaite curate
looking for his handkerchief in the middle of his
sermon.

When Judith at last departed she wondered
what had happened to her lately. It seemed
so long since she had last laughed with real
abandon.

Phyllis was thinking of her stable and under
a full moon trotted with enthusiasm. It was
late. The Crosthwaite Church struck the hour
of eleven as they turned into the Carlisle road.

As she went along she was happy and confident. ' Three old women! Never mind. We
know how we can enjoy ourselves without the
men—and I stood up to Walter. I enjoy
standing up to Walter. I shall do it again.'
She would tempt Miss West and Miss Pennyfeather up to Watendlath after Christmas. They
were great riders. They should stay a day or
two with her at the farm. They would enjoy
the Ritsons. . . .

When she reached the house it was five
minutes to twelve by the round-faced clock above
the stables. The moon shone with such brightness that the whole world of hill, fell and dead
white road was recreated into unreality. The
stars were fiery—all else was icy cold and like
a dried bone in colour.

She put Phyllis into her box, patted her nose
and then, almost startled by the sound of her own
steps on the cobbles in the still world, crossed
over to the house.

She let herself in and with soft tread went

straight to her room.   The stair was flooded with moonlight.

She lit the candles and, with one raised in her hand, went over to see that Adam was sleeping.   With his cheek on his hand, his mouth a little open, he looked so entirely hers and hers alone that she gave a little gasp of happiness, put down the candle and sat on the bed-edge gazing at him.

She blew out the candle, drew back the curtain and let the moonlight spread a pool of liquid shadow about the carpet.   She did not feel sleepy.   She was immensely content.   She sat at the window looking at the frosted slope of Skiddaw, the friend of her life.

She was thus idly watching and had listened to the clocks tell the half-hour when, muffled by the window but sharp on the frosted road, she heard the hoofs of a horse.   She bent forward and saw, to her amazement, the horse stop at the gate and a heavily-cloaked rider, whom she quickly knew to be Francis, dismount.   Francis! Here!   Now!   She stood up, her hand at her heart.   Something told her at once that there was trouble.   She saw him open the gate and lead the horse round to the stable.

Driven by some instinct, unreasoning but imperative, she softly went from her room on to the landing, and, as she did so, at the same moment Jennifer's door opened and she appeared, in her nightdress, her ringlets about her shoulders, a candle in her hand, and on her feet her silver slippers.

' What was that? ' she said, her finger to her lip.

' Francis is returned.'

' Oh, my God! '

Even as she breathed that they heard the outer door of the house open. Jennifer seized Judith's wrist. She never spoke, but pushed Judith into her room.

Six candles were blazing, a table with wine and the remains of a chicken was near the bed, which was tumbled and in disorder, and Fernyhirst in his shirt and trousers, his shirt open at the neck, his rather long grey hair untidily over his forehead, sat sprawling in a large crimson chair.

' What is it? ' he asked, looking up; then saw Judith and his mouth stayed open. She thought that she had never seen a more unattractive creature, purple-veined, double-chinned, with a heavy stomach and thick unwieldy legs. Her disgust with both of them was so intense that for a moment it covered everything else. That they should thus—these two elderly lovers—have been philandering in the room next to her sleeping son seemed to her a foul thing. That Jennifer should thus have gone back on her word—

But beyond her personal sense of affront she knew at once there was something more important. Francis must not find them there. He must not. And once this hateful discovery of hers was passed she would see to it that Fernyhirst came to the house no more.

But they remained, frozen into silence. The room seemed chilled by an icy wind from the cold world outside, although the fire blazed in the grate. They waited, the two women standing where they were, Fernyhirst sitting up in his chair.

Jennifer only whispered once: ' He always goes to his room.'

They heard nothing, for the door was closed: then, as though the house crashed about their ears, the door opened and he stood there.

Judith saw at once from his face that he had known what he would find. Instantly he flung himself across the room and fell upon Fernyhirst, pulling at his shirt, beating his face with his hand and crying:

' At last! At last! . . . You bloody rat. . . . You whoring, filthy . . .'

Jennifer ran to them, pulled feebly at Francis' coat and screamed. The table with the chicken and wine fell over, making a terrible crash.

Judith ran in among them.

' Francis! Francis! Listen! . . . Be quiet! Be still! The house must not hear, it must not wake . . . Francis! Francis! '

Francis seemed to hear her, for he stopped clawing at Fernyhirst and walked away, trembling from head to foot, his breath coming with a strange shrill sob.

The scene indeed was very quickly over, for Fernyhirst, silent and, it seemed, unmoved, rose, felt the blood that trickled on his cheek, put on very calmly his waistcoat and coat, picked up from the chair his hat and riding-coat and walked to the door.

There he turned and, looking at Francis, said heavily, ' You shall answer me for this.'   He seemed not at all disturbed, and even looked at the decanter on the floor as though he had half a mind to pick it up.   Then he went out.

Francis came forward, and, speaking very rapidly and, Judith thought, as though he had made up his speech in his head beforehand, addressed Jennifer, who was now sitting on the bed and crying very wildly.

' I go now,' he said, ' and I shall never return. Thank God I have seen the last of you. . . . I shall attend to your lover. . . .'

He stammered, as though he would say something to Judith, but suddenly hung his head and went swiftly out of the room.

He dragged his horse out of the stable and clattered up the road in pursuit of Fernyhirst, who was but a little ahead of him.   He had but paused to take two rapiers from the corner of his room—the small room behind the parlour that was cluttered with guns, fishing-tackle, books, papers, swords and these rapiers.   No one had touched them for many a year.

As he rode he did not feel the cold; he was rather bathed in a damp heat that was also dry, so that, although his forehead was wet with sweat, his hands had no moisture.   That afternoon, walking along the street in Cockermouth to see some fellow on a land transaction, he had been touched on the elbow by a ragged man with a black patch over one eye, who had given him a dirty piece of paper. On this was scrawled in a rough unfamiliar hand: ' The Captain is with your wife to - night and don't leave till morning.'

Reading it, he walked on mechanically until he was almost out of the town without knowing it. He was no longer Francis Herries—that weak, lily-livered creature was gone for ever. He was a fiery man of action, but cautious withal, a crafty vengeful devil, murderous in intent, brilliant in device. This sly fiery devil waited until night at the Cockermouth inn, sitting in a room there, with a plate before him, but not eating. Once and again he held scornful converse with the pitiful Francis, who was imprisoned in a cage and could not get out.

' Let me out! ' cried Francis.

But the fiery devil only grinned, while his hand trembled on the table and his eyes were blind.

Later he found them just as the dirty piece of paper had said, and now he was going to kill Fernyhirst.

He came upon him a quarter of the way to Stone Ends. He rode past him at a gallop and then turned and faced him. There was bare moor on either side and the moon cynically observant. Everything was as bright as day, and the smoke from the horses' nostrils clouded the air.

' Off your horse, Fernyhirst,' Francis said. ' We will finish this here.'

'Let me pass, you blackguard,' Fernyhirst cried. But he was a coward at a pinch, had always been. He did not know whether Francis had not a pistol. He climbed off his horse and began blustering.

Francis showed him the rapiers.

'We will fight here and now,' he said.

'This is monstrous,' Fernyhirst said. 'No seconds. No arrangements. I protest. I refuse——'

'We will fight here and now,' Francis repeated.

Perhaps it occurred to Fernyhirst that here would be a good opportunity to teach this puling husband a lesson, for although a coward he had been a skilled duellist in younger days, and the rapier was his favourite weapon. He knew, too, that this business would be scandalous if he let it go on. The quickest over the less said.

His hesitation swung to bluster.

'If you wish it,' he said scornfully. 'You are a poor husband, Herries, and poor husbands always make shabby fighters.'

Herries said not a word.

They drew the horses up the moor and over the ridge to a hollow where they could not be seen from the road. They fought in their shirts, although the cold was intense. Francis was a good swordsman, but it was years since he had had any practice. He fought in what was known as the Neapolitan style, with straight arm and straight back, his knees bent. Fernyhirst fought with a flourish, sweeping his rapier in the air. He knew instantly that Francis was a good swordsman, and cursed his own lack of condition, for he was fat and had been drinking heavily that same night. The scene was strange enough. Sheep came up the moor and stood bewildered. The two horses cropped the grass, and across a cloudless sky the full moon proudly sailed. The hills cut the sky sharply in the frosty air and seemed to bend their brows in attention.

They fought for a while without advantage to either side; then suddenly Francis, lowering his rapier a little, pressed upon his enemy. Fernyhirst retreated a step or two, then Francis made a short lunge in tierce. Fernyhirst backed again, but, after some clever feints, came forward and himself began to challenge Francis.

This extra exertion told on him. His breathing distressed him, and soon two moons circled in his vision, swinging about the shining length of Francis' weapon. Was he to be killed? In this bitter air with no witness? A sudden fear of Francis' intensity caught him. He lunged, his breath coming in pants, but he could not find Francis' body. Everywhere that stiff wall of steel met him. His legs were trembling, the ground rocking. The fear of death, of imminent and dreadful death, leapt at his throat like an animal from the moon.

He gave a yell that made the sheep scatter down the slope, turned and fled for his life. Panting, he flung himself on his horse, threw the rapier away from him and rode off as though all the Furies were beside him.

And Francis stood under the moon without

moving. This had been the creature to whom for all these years he had surrendered his wife.

The agonised bitterness of a self-contempt that now would never find a cure stole slowly, quietly down upon him.

Gently his head bent; he went towards his horse.

FRANCIS IN LONDON

Spring 1821

FROM the window of his little lodging off St. James' Street Francis could see a pale green sky floating between the clouds of two smoking chimneys, a curricle waiting outside the bow-window of Ashton's, the hosier's, and a very elegant dandy picking his way through the puddles as though his life depended on the dryness of his boots. Both before and behind him spouts, charged with the rain that the flat roofs had collected, were pouring out their floods. He had navigated one. Now he paused before the other as though collecting all his resources. Soon the lamps on the little elevated posts that dotted the street would be lighted. The sun was almost set. One star, freshly washed, so bright it was, by the recent rain, hovered in the green sky. So agreeable was the spring air that Francis had his window open. He could hear the rattle of the carriage-wheels on the cobbles of St. James', could smell the damp and soot and sea-coal and the cooking that was going on in Mrs. Morland's room downstairs.

In his melancholy depressed mood, to watch the dandy gave him some occupation. The man in his light pantaloons (surely his calves were padded!) his absurdly exaggerated hat, his ridiculous collar *à la guillotine*, his monstrous waist (he was wearing beyond question Cumberland corsets), seemed scarcely human.

As he paused, looking at the water-spout, raising first one foot and then another, Francis, in spite of his dejection, could scarcely forbear to laugh. Then there hurried past, his coat up to his ears, a little man with a pile of books under his arm, who, Francis fancied, might be Mr. Lamb, to whose house his friend Daintry, the water-colour painter, had one evening taken him. Francis thought, for a wild moment, that Mr. Lamb might be coming to pay him a call. Why not? He had been most pleasant to him, talked to him of old plays and actors, asked him whether he had thought of play-writing, had appeared to be interested, had inquired his address . . . but no, it was not Mr. Lamb. Of course not. No one ever came to visit him.

The green sky faded, the old lamp-lighter whom Francis knew so well by now, with his funny step that was a kind of dot-and-carry walk, passed down the street. Francis closed the window, drew the curtains, lit the candles, went to the table, drew out his papers; he was writing an article on Malthus which he hoped (very faintly) that the *Evening Chronicle* might look upon kindly. He wrote a few lines and threw down his pen. It was no good; the thing was a farce. He sat there, his head between his hands, muttering to himself that the end had come.

He had taken of late to talking to himself, for indeed he had for the most part no one else to talk to. Mrs. Morland told Morland that the poor old gentleman was wrong in his head; she hoped he would do no one a mischief. Morland, who was a coal merchant by trade and as kind-hearted as any man in London, shook his head and said that he thought that Mr. Herries had lived too long in the country. He had lost touch with the Town. 'London's a big wild place these days, Maria, and not good for a gentleman who has no friends seemingly and is accustomed to country fields.' This was perhaps true. Francis *had* lost touch with the Town. He had been here now for nearly five months. After the wretched farcical fight with Fernyhirst he had ridden to Penrith, slept the night there and taken the London coach on the following day.

He had found rooms with the Morlands, and for a week or two had fancied that he might begin a new life. He had written a brief letter to Jennifer, saying that he would never return, but that proper provision would be made for her and the children. He had sought out some of his old friends, avoiding, however, any possible contact with any Herries relations. His principal success here had been with his old acquaintance, Samuel Rogers, who, only a year or two younger than Francis, welcomed him with the warm kind-

liness and good heart that that crabbed old poet
hid under his sneers and oddities.

He welcomed Francis to his famous house in
St. James's Place, with its view of the Green Park,
its collections of prints, its Etruscan vases.
Here Francis could have found exactly the
society suited to his taste, and many happy con-
tacts might have come of it. He had real
literary feeling, could talk excellently when he
was in the mood. He had, however, developed
an almost crazy spirit of suspicion and self-
detraction. It seemed to him that everyone must
know of the disgrace and misery that weighed so
heavily upon him. No one knew and no one
cared; but, after a few visits, some fancied slights,
some momentary irritations on the part of old
Rogers, he slipped away and hugged his loneliness. He had thought that writing would be
his great recourse. He thought that now at last
he had the freedom and independence. But
always his own wretched thoughts broke into
his imagination and shattered it.

He walked mile upon mile of London streets,
but here, too, he was unhappy, for the old London
that he had known was gone or going. The
stucco of Mr. Nash was rapidly covering with
its pallid cloak the red and brown and grey of the
earlier houses. A passion for building seemed
to have sprung upon the town, and the suburbs
were eating fields and lanes and trees as fast as
they could be devoured. This was a busier,
more serious London than he had known, and it
seemed to have no place for him. Everywhere

new shops were opening, no one appeared to have leisure any more, all were thinking of making a fortune or seeing some new invention. House-building, experiments with machinery, expeditions to America, a visit to Paris and back, a tour on the Continent—all these were everyday adventures. It was a world in which he was lost. He was altogether a lost man; he had no foothold anywhere any more. On the little ink-stained desk near the window lay a pile of letters from Judith unopened. He had not read one of them; he did not dare to. She would implore him to return, would tell him of John and Dorothy, of himself and, worst of all, of Jennifer.

The awful thing, the poison that in his loneliness devoured him, was that he still loved Jennifer. He loved her as ardently and as hopelessly as at the beginning, yes, as madly as on that first occasion when he had seen her at the Herries Ball. The thing that had ruined him, apart from his own indecision of character, was that his love had never been returned. That had not been Jennifer's fault—she had been honest with him—but from that misery of tantalisation he had died. For now he was as good as dead. Had he once captured her he would have found, likely enough, that the thing captured was neither interesting nor valuable, but he had been able neither to catch her nor leave her, neither to admire her nor despise her, neither to fight for nor against her; she had completed the ruin that his own miserable weakness had begun. As he sat there he did not pity himself nor curse himself. He did

not feel that he was altogether to blame. He
was a piece of pottery in whom the potter had
carelessly set a flaw.

He might be, as Judith had said, one of the
hopes of the Herries; but they had been too strong
for him and the hope was lost. From the very
beginning he had been frightened of Will's
efficiency, a rebel against his father, acquiescent
in things as they were, a slave to his mother's
melodrama, subservient again to his wife's lazy
indifference. The Herries had beaten him every
time. He might have been a success in any
other family. Judith alone had understood
him. Judith . . . dear, darling Judith . . . so
kind, so wise, so brave, so friendly and true. . . .

He got up, made a step towards the desk.
He had almost those letters in his hand. But
no, he must not. If he read them he would
return and there would begin again that wretched
half-life, with Walter's spying and bullying. . . .

Walter! He called the name aloud as though
he were challenging it. He could see that swollen,
red-faced, confident boaster. . . . There was a
knock on the door. Mrs. Morland looked in.

' A lady to see you, sir,' she said.

' A lady? ' He turned back, smoothing his
hair that had grown too long and tumbled over
his forehead. His heart beat nervously, as it did
now when anyone approached him. There was
a pause, and then who should come in? Who
but old Maria Rockage?

He was so greatly surprised that he could not
speak, but could only stare at her with his mouth

open. She was an odd enough figure. She
must be, he thought, nearly seventy. She was
wearing a black, rather faded costume of a fashion
quite ten years earlier, all in one piece, tied with
a band of ribbon immediately under her ample
breasts. Her shoes were muddy and she had a
black poke-bonnet. Her face wore its accustomed expression of anxiety, nervousness, kindliness and assurance.

Her nervousness was for the actual moment,
her assurance for her general state. But, as
always, kindliness was the predominating note.
As a matter of fact, she was not so old as Francis
thought her—she was sixty-six—and she felt
a great deal younger than that.

' Cousin Maria! . . . But I never expected.
. . . Pray come in. . . . I am delighted. . . .
But how did you know my lodging? '

She smiled at him with great beneficence.

' Mr. Rogers told me. Carey and I were at
a party in St. James's Place the other evening, a
very fine party . . .' (The odd thought came to
him that, in spite of her Methodist proclivities, she
was ever going to parties.) ' I had Phyllis and
Carey with me. Literature and the Arts. . . .
And then Judith wrote to me. She begged me to
search you out. She is so greatly distressed——'

She was looking at him, and biting the fingers
of her worn gloves, and putting up her hand to
pat the hair under her bonnet, and screwing her
mouth round in a strange way that she had.
What a funny old thing she was!

He cleared the papers away and sat her down

at the table. Of course, he said to himself, she
was looking around her and seeing how shabby
everything was. She would tell Will and Christabel, and everyone would know. How was he
certain that she had not come to spy out for
Walter? She had but recently been staying at
Westaways. Tiresome old thing! And then,
to his amazement, he saw that tears were trick-
ling down her cheeks! When he saw that, it was
all that he could do not to cry himself, so tired
and wan and miserable he was. She began to
chatter with little gulps and stammers.

' Francis, we have never known each other
very well. We are almost of an age. I fear it
is an impertinence my coming like this and
intruding on your privacy. But I had to come.
The Lord told me to come; and although I know
that you think me foolish about my religion,
still we are both old people now and can be
tolerant about one another. I have not come
to interfere in any way, dear Francis. Indeed
I have not. But I could not bear to think of
your being all alone and away from Jennifer and
your lovely children—although I have never
quite agreed with Jennifer, yet she is no longer
as young as she was neither, and the pomps and
vanities of our life fade away, leaving us often
much alone. I know that, although I have the
best husband in the world and dear Carey and
dear Phyllis, I know what it is to be lonely and
have only the Lord to depend upon——' She
broke off and looked at him with mild kindly
eyes, beseeching him not to be rude to her.

She smiled at him over her handkerchief, a watery but encouraging smile. He wished to be kind—but what was he to say?

'Dear Cousin Maria, this is very good of you. I fear I have no hospitality to offer you.'

'Oh,' she broke in, 'I want nothing. I want nothing at all, I assure you. Too good of you—and your room is very cosy, very cosy indeed. And right on the street, so that you have people passing. I always say that if you have people passing you cannot really be lonely. Always something going on—a carriage accident or a fire or a Punch and Judy. I would go any-where myself to see a Punch and Judy. Carey is for ever laughing at me for it. "Why, Maria," he says, "I believe you'd run down the street if there were a Punch and Judy about"—and I believe I would, you know. So very amusing. . . . One never tires. . . .' She broke off and then said abruptly: 'And when was the last time you heard from dear Judith?'

'I haven't heard,' he said in a very low voice, 'for quite a while.'

She put out her gloved hand and laid it on his.

'Francis,' she said, 'go home. Think of your dear children. Forgive Jennifer and go home. We must all forgive one another. I am certain that Carey and I have forgiven one another a hundred times. Go home, Francis.'

He caught his hands one within another and looked straight in front of him.

'I cannot, Cousin Maria. I cannot. You do not know——'

She came closer to him, putting her hand on his arm.

'No, of course I do not know, but I cannot endure to see you looking so unhappy. We are not young any longer, Francis, you and I; and when we are old it is not at all easy to be alone. No, it is not easy. Carey and I miss one another if we are apart a day. What will you do here in this lodging alone? Come to us at Grosset for a while if that will assist you. And then go home. Jennifer means very well. She means very well indeed. She had a selfish upbringing. Poor Rose never had a notion of how to bring up a family. She is the mother of your children, Francis.'

He was deeply touched. Her sincerity and true longing to be good to him were beyond any question. But he wished that she would go. No one could help him any more. He smiled at her and laid his hand on hers.

'Thank you, Cousin Maria. You are exceeding kind. But I must shoulder my own troubles. What you say is very true. We are growing old, and nothing is of very much importance any more. Thank you, Cousin Maria, but indeed I must stand on my own feet.'

There was something in his face that told her that it was so.

She hesitated, stammered, then broke out: 'Well, then—would it trouble you. . . . You would not laugh, I am sure . . . but it might be a help to you. The Lord is always nigh. If I offered a prayer. . . .'

Her eyes gazed at him with the eager moisture in them of a puppy begging for a biscuit.

'Certainly, Cousin Maria. It is good of you——'

At once she knelt down on the floor beside him and, her bonnet falling back a little from her head, her gloved hands clasped, prayed.

'Oh Lord God, I pray Thee to look down on this Thy servant who has been sore troubled and in deep distress. Thou knowest what are our faults and failures, but there is in Thy heart an infinite patience and an all-preserving Wisdom. Take this Thy servant into Thy care and show him the way that he may find once again those whom he best loves and be restored into their company. Thou knowest what is best for him, and Thy will be done. In the name of Thy Son who was crucified for us on the Cross and whose Divine Example we would eternally follow. Amen.'

She waited a moment, her head between her hands, then she rose. There was thick dust on her black gown, but she did not notice. She stroked her nose with her hand.

'And now I must really be off,' she said briskly. 'Phyllis and I am to spend a little evening alone together. We are reading *The Task*. Remember, pray, Cousin Francis, that we are most eager to have you with us at Grosset, if you care to come. You have only to send us word. Yes, we shall all be delighted to see you.'

She bent and kissed him on the forehead;

then murmuring something to the effect that she did hope that it was not raining, she gave him a smile at the door and went out.

He sat on, lost in thought. In what was he lost? The candles flickered, the shadows leapt on the wall, carriages rumbled beyond the window, steps hurried by, voices rose and fell, but he was engulfed in his sense of utter disaster. Good old woman! She had wished to help him, but it would need more than Maria Rockage to help him now.

At last he rose, found his hat and coat and went out. He walked up St. James' Street and into Piccadilly. He did not know why he was walking nor whither, but it seemed to him that a figure was at his side, keeping pace with him, murmuring in his ears: ' This is your farewell to the world. Soon, when the lights have dazzled your eyes sufficiently, you will return into your dark house.'

In the nervous state in which he was, it seemed to him that there was a babel of sound all about him. The lamps were lit, but there was still a great deal of traffic and business, and the fine spring evening after the rainy afternoon encouraged everyone to be out. London, although it was so rapidly growing in size and energy, had still something of the village about it. In this central part at least there was much recognising of acquaintances, the cheerful intimacy of shopmen who knew their customers and, only a yard away, big houses, silent squares with lawns and gardens, the grandeur of the great mansions on the Park, footmen standing on door-steps, coachmen from the boxes of their carriages looking down upon this world as though they commanded, shopmen filling their doorways, their legs spread, their noses sniffing the fresh evening.

To all this Francis was a stranger; he passed like a shadow, hurrying nowhere. At every moment something occurred to infuriate him. For some while a cart accompanied him. It contained, it seemed, a thousand iron bars that rattled and rumbled and screamed above the cobbles. A drunken sailor, rolling by, ejected a shoot of tobacco and missed his shoes by an inch: an odour of meat seemed everywhere; the hackney coaches rattled his brains to pieces.

Infuriated by the noise, but still, as it seemed to him, driven on by this companion at his side, he turned up a side street hoping to find quiet, but first on a doorstep a footman was practising ' Paddy Whack ' on a small fife, execrably out of tune, a headlong butcher's boy rushed by uttering a shrill cat-call; in a room just above his head there was a dancing lesson being held. The window was open and he could hear the ' One — Two — Three ' and then ' Now then — Left — Right,' and the shrill discordant wail of a fiddle. . . .

Despairing of freeing himself from all these miseries, he turned back, found Piccadilly again and ventured into Mr. Hatchard's bookshop; there would be silence, the friendliness of books, the courtesy of good Mr. Sumner who, although he looked like a prize-fighter, had all the delicacy and sensitiveness of one who knew Byron and Scott and Coleridge, and had often, under Mr. Sheridan's direction, supplied the Prince, in earlier days, with the best literature.

So Francis stepped in—and there was old Mr. Rogers!

Yes, old Mr. Rogers, the very last man in the world whom he wished to see. Nor was he alone. He was attended by a stout thick-set young man, badly dressed, with an untidy neckcloth and a very supercilious air.

Mr. Rogers gave him a finger and introduced him to his friend.

'This is Mr. Macaulay, who is at Cambridge and soon will be having the world at his feet. Come, come, Macaulay. You know you will. You know you will. You are as confident of it as I am.'

The thick-set untidy youth raised a pair of very remarkable piercing eyes and began to talk with great eloquence and volubility. It was clear that he did not suffer from shyness.

Francis meanwhile hated the confident young man and hated Rogers. He was sure that they were mocking him; indeed, that everyone in the shop was mocking him. It was true enough, perhaps, that Rogers was not over-pleasant, because he had gone out of his way to be kind to this fellow who, of late, had treated him casually.

'Well, Mr. Herries,' he said in his sharp restless voice, 'it is well met and farewell, for

I am shortly taking a sister and niece with me on to the Continent—Switzerland and Italy. I have been trying to persuade Tom Macaulay here to accompany me, but he has better things to concern himself with. . . . Well, well, Mr. Herries—good-day to ye. Good-day to ye.'

The loquacious young man had already forgotten him and was talking eagerly to Sumner about a book that he held in his hand. Sumner also (who was, as a rule, so courteous) had not noticed him. In a tumult of irritation Francis left the shop. So Rogers had had enough of him? Even Sumner did not care to speak with him, and so old and insignificant was he that an untidy young man from Cambridge could turn his back on him. It was true enough. He was old and shabby. He had no place in the world any longer.

At the corner of St. James' Street he met a man whom he slightly knew, an effeminate bore, and this fellow would not let him go, but with one finger on his coat must, in a shrill piping voice, talk about the coming Coronation. It was all that anyone was thinking of, it was the finest and grandest the world had ever seen, no expense was to be spared, and they said that the Queen, poor thing— At last Francis broke away. As he hastened down the street he fancied that the man was looking after him, wondering what madness had taken possession of him. Well, he was mad if they liked. He had no place in this absurd world any longer—this absurd, monstrous crazy world.

When he entered his little room again and lit the candles once more, a sense of disgust took him. What a mean little place it was, with its smell of soot and cooking food! How grimy and foul the world had grown!

He went into his little bedroom, filled his basin with water, stripped, washed from head to foot, put on clean linen and another suit. Then he returned to his table, took out paper and pen and began to write:

DEAREST JUDITH——You have all your life forgiven me for my many faults and failings; once again—and this is the last time that I shall ask you—you must forgive me. For many weeks your letters arrived here and now they are lying in a pile on a table near me unopened. For it is only a part of my general weakness that I have not opened them. I did not dare, for I know that if I had done so you would have tempted me back. But I must not go back, dear Judith. Were you not so noble and generous to me you would be honest with me and tell me what I know well to be the truth —that I must never come back again. You have known me all my life long and once when you were a baby you loved me. Perhaps you love me still, for your heart is so generous that it can pass over all weaknesses and all mistakes. But I myself cannot pass them over. In these last weeks I have learnt to face myself and to see what is there. You will think that there is too much self-pity in what I have written, but it is not so. I have never pitied myself. I have had every chance to make something of life and I have thrown every chance away.

When I was a young man and you were a child I used to talk to you about all the things that I intended to do. I had great faith in myself, and because I have none any more is not a reason for pity, but rather for acceptance. I have failed everyone—my father, my mother, my wife, my children and my ideals.

I think that there are other men in like case. Men of our time have some of them been unfortunate because they have lived in an age of transition. The Great Time was behind them. The Great Time is coming again—but some of us have had our faith taken from us and have not been given, or have not found, a new one. I thought once that all men would be free now. I thought once that the poor man would have Justice. But the poor man is more a slave than before, and we are all of us in prison. I cannot write clearly; I see everything darkly, but I know that for myself I took the wrong path.

I am writing this only because you must not, *you must not*, dearest Judith, take the wrong path also. Return to your own life, take your boy, have nothing to do with the fortunes of our family. For such as you and I there can never be any happiness in Herries affairs. They are ruin and damnation to us. They deprive us of all that our souls need. I have been no good friend to you. I have not given you assistance when you sorely needed it. I have left you alone when you were most lonely. In this as in everything else I have betrayed myself. But now I am speaking truth from the heart. Your life is not with Will and Walter and Jennifer and the rest. They are strangers to you and you to them. Because I married a stranger and, God help me, love her now as dearly as I ever did, I have worked my own Destruction.

I know that you will be good to Jennifer and my children, but they are provided for, and *you must not stay with them*. Be true to yourself. You know well enough what you should do. . . . Go back to Watendlath. I can see the light over the hill, hear the streams running . . . the streams running. My hand shakes. Tell Jennifer that I love her, I love her, just as I did . . . as I always . . . Embrace the children. John

will be a fine boy . . . and your Adam. Go back
to the light over the hill. There is so terrible a noise
in this town. Dear Judith, think of me kindly, but
better to forget me. I could not find a Balance I
was always fearful of Action. God be with you, but
there is no God—none for me. Nothing. . . .

He broke off; his pen rattled on to the table.
He sat there for a long while, his head buried in
his hands. Then he got up, folded the letter
and addressed it. He went to the window,
pulled back the blind and looked out. Two
ladies were talking, laughing. A little dog came
sniffing up to the lamp-post. Another dog saw
him from the other side of the street and came
slowly across. A boy, carrying some parcels,
stood idly and watched them.

Francis went to the drawer of his little ink-
stained desk and took from it a pistol.

He crossed to the mirror, cracked and seamed
with age. He saw with great clearness the faded
green paper, the print of the fight between Gully
and the Chicken, the copy of Drayton's Poems,
that he had been reading, on the table. Then
he put the pistol to his mouth.

Mrs. Morland, fancying that she heard someone tumble or the distant firing of a gun or the
collision of two carriages, went to her window
and looked out. But no: in the street there
was nothing to be seen but two ladies laughing
together and the cautious intimacies of a New-
foundland and a King Charles.

MONEY

'WILL you not come in and pay us a visit, Cousin Judith?' Walter Herries asked. He was standing at the high pillared entrance to Westaways. The wind was blowing with a kind of innocent child-like caprice and turning back the leaves of a giant beech to a duller chillier gold. Judith, with Adam beside her, felt the wind tugging at her big velvet-lined feathered hat. Her hands were warm inside their muff. Her face for once was rosy; the sharp air, the wild sky, the scudding fragments of blue and the harp-like swing of the wind across the bare fields, the ridges of snow on the brown range of fell, all exhilarated her.

Moreover, it was four days before Christmas and directly Christmas was past she was returning with Adam to Watendlath—yes, for ever and ever!

She had passed Westaways as she had done a thousand times before, walking from Crosthwaite to Keswick. The carriage was in Keswick for the day; Jennifer was paying visits and after their three o'clock dinner at the inn they would drive home.

It was now mid-day. The Crosthwaite Church clock had but just told the hour. She had intended to take Adam to show to her friends, Miss West and Miss Pennyfeather. The last thing that she had expected or wished was to be caught by Walter Herries.

Westaways looked gleaming and polished in the wet windy sunlight. On the eastern corner there were ladders and men working. Walter was for ever doing something to the place.

'Do come inside now, Cousin Judith, and taste a glass of sherry.'

She knew that he had a family party for Christmas—Will, Christabel, old Monty Cards, Rodney, the pious second son of Pomfret and Rose from Kensington, old Pomfret himself and his ancient old-maid sister Cynthia, and best of all, Maria's Phyllis with her husband, Mr. Stephen Newmark, and two of their children; Phyllis had been married in 1818 and had already three babies!

It was Phyllis whom she would like to see; Christabel too, Will even. But she shrank from the crowd of them, all gathered in the parlour, talking scandal, most of it of the family order. In she would march with Adam, and Will's neck would tighten in its collar, and fat, over-decorated, 'Regency' old Pomfret would wink at her (she could bet on it!), and silly kind old Monty would stroke his powdered cheek while his corsets creaked, pious Rodney would look down his nose—only dear Phyllis, untidy like her mother, with some of the Grosset disorder clinging to her, only Phyllis would really welcome her, would be enchanted to see her. She had a curiosity, too, to behold Phyllis' husband,

Mr. Stephen Newmark. Maria, in letters, had informed her that he was a very fine man indeed, a wealthy religious landowner from Warwickshire. Wealthy *and* religious—not a very promising combination!

There was the other temptation, too, that this was her last opportunity for spying out Westaways. Was it not absurd, perhaps, to say that, when Watendlath was only a mile or two away? But Watendlath was more than a mile or two away, it was a world away. As poor Francis had said in that last despairing letter.

Strange to pass from the thought of that letter to that great brilliantly-coloured body straddling there in the gateway! But, looking at him, she suddenly wondered whether he were not already a trifle old-fashioned? The thought gave her a malicious pleasure. He was certainly over-dressed for the present times, with his billowing stock and its jewelled pin, his claret-coloured coat with the exaggerated waist (he was corseted—and what immense corsets they must be!), the fawn-shaded pantaloons fitting so tightly over the calves. There were rings on his fingers. And yet he was a man! Do Walter all the injustice in the world, but you could never name him effeminate. He was the prize bull of the stock. Already, young as he was, there was a purple tinge to his cheek, but his eyes were hard and clear and his mouth firmly and confidently set.

' Come inside and drink a glass of sherry with us, Cousin Judith.'

She looked up at him from under her broad-brimmed hat with that air of humorous impertinent defiance that they seemed always to use to one another.

' I have Christmas shopping and calls to pay. Have we not, Adam? '

Adam, who was holding a little toy whip, had never taken his eyes from Walter since he had first seen him.

' Why, young man, you have some clothes on at last, I see.'

' Yes, sir.'

' And how old are you since I saw you last? '

' Six, sir.'

' Six, are you? Well, your mother shall bring you in out of the wind. Not too young for a glass of sherry, are you? '

' Of course he is, Walter. A glass of sherry indeed! '

' Why, I was drinking sherry before I was weaned, and look at me! Come along in! Come along in! '

So Judith went and Adam also, his eyes still following Walter's back as though he had never before seen anything like it.

She knew that he had been doing things to the house, and when she stood in the hall her astonishment was vivid at the changes that he had made. Everywhere were riches. On the wall facing the front door a great piece of purple tapestry showing Diana hunting, on either side of the door pieces of sculpture, one of a Pan playing his flute, another of a stout naked goddess

drinking. (What, oh, what would Maria Rockage say to this paganism?)

At the stairhead, over the door of the saloon,
was a sumptuous painting of a French king
(Louis XIV. perhaps) dining with his ladies, and,
beside the door, a silver pedestal with a black
bust of some Roman Emperor—and Walter,
as he walked slowly up the stairs, gave the impression even in his back-view that it was he and
no one else who had wrought all these splendours.

They were gathered about a blazing fire in the
saloon—Will, Christabel, Monty Cards, Rodney
and his father, Phyllis, Carey her brother, and a
thin upright man with a hooked nose who must
be her husband, Mr. Newmark.

As Judith crossed the long shining slippery
floor, holding Adam by the hand, she felt that
both herself and her son were midgets. She was
not frightened but she could feel their intense
interest as they all turned towards her. She was
helped by Adam's absolute confidence. He nearly
tripped and fell as he bent his head back to
look at the gods and goddesses in their brilliant
nakedness. He feared no one.

Christabel and Phyllis rose with cries of
pleasure to greet her. Everyone made a display over Adam. Old Pomfret (still a very gay
and brightly set-up dog in spite of his years)
was the most pleased with him. He took him
between his knees and looked into his ugly little
face with a very lively interest. He asked him
questions, and Adam, in his funny high voice,
answered them all instantly.

Judith, sitting with her hand in Phyllis', thought: 'This grows grander every month. Up, up, up. And at Uldale we go down, down, down! Never mind. The battle is not ended yet. . . . Yes, Adam is ugly. His mouth is too large by far—but he charms everyone. . . .' That strange pang at her heart again! He charms everyone! He always will—and I shall be left. . . . 'But I *wish* him to charm everyone, to be happy and honest and brave as he is now—always.' And then, following quickly on this, cutting across the self-sufficient tones of Rodney, who would be one day Archdeacon of Polchester and patroniser of the very Black Bishop, came this thought:

'In ten days we shall be in Watendlath, eating food with the Ritsons, and Adam will be mine, mine, mine!'

She could almost hear the sheep shuffling with the noise of the rustle of leaves across this shining floor. She could see the sun strike the flint in those rocks until they shone like spear-heads, dulling the painted goddesses. 'Oh, if anything should hinder my reaching there! But nothing can, now surely nothing can!' It was as though she were planning to get as far as China!

They were still discussing that now so wearily worn topic, the Coronation and the Queen's beating on the Westminster doors. Will, who was strangely aged now and thinner than ever, so that he looked like a stork standing on one leg and protecting his nest (only his eggs were money-bags), was all for upholding the Crown.

'What we want,' he said with his usual air of delivering judgement, 'is stable conditions. To counteract the lower classes. Relax, and we shall have another Peterloo. . . . But the country is recovering its Balance. I am glad to be able to say that the country is recovering its Balance.'

Everyone looked greatly relieved. It was pleasant to hear from Will, who must know, that all was well.

Adam was passed round from hand to hand. They were all kind to him although he was a little bastard. But Judith knew that it was for the moment only, and that her presence made them uncomfortable, yes, even poor Christabel, who was restless under the eye of her lord and master. The thought came to her as she saw Rodney's eyes meditatively resting upon her: 'Oh, if Adam could grow into the master of them all, rule the pack of them! He could. He has even now twice their spirit. . . .' But she was going to Watendlath, and Adam with her, leaving the Herries behind them for ever, and Adam would be a farmer like Charlie Watson, and one day he would come down into Keswick, driving his sheep, and he would encounter Walter's children in their fine carriage, and the coachman would shout to him to clear his sheep from the road. . . . And after Adam would return, riding up the road to see the Tarn shining with the evening sun, and he would call to his dog, and the fields would smile up at him, the hills look kindly down. . . .

'Well, my little friend,' said Rodney Herries to Adam (he spoke as though to a little black child newly rescued from the heathen), 'and what is the game you enjoy the most?'

'To cut men out of wood,' said Adam with complete assurance, but his eyes wandering a little. 'I have cut Mr. Noah and the Duke of Wellington and Mr. Winch.'

'Very praiseworthy. Very praiseworthy indeed,' said Rodney, looking, however, bewildered.

'He is commencing,' said Judith, 'to carve figures. He has a true disposition towards carving.'

'Yes,' went on Adam eagerly, looking at everyone with an enthusiastic smile. 'And I colour them also. And Bennett gives me the wood. He says——'

'Hush, Adam, hush,' said Judith, drawing him towards her. He came to her, but with one last look round him and pointing at old Cynthia Herries, Pomfret's sister, who had a nose like a door-knocker:

'That old lady would be very fine for cutting.'

His manners, Judith could see them deciding, were not at all of the best, but what could you expect when his mother . . . ?

Then Walter came forward.

'Judith, you must see my improvements. Forgive me for taking you away an instant. I must show you the improvements.'

She knew that he wished to speak to her alone. She had known it all the time. The drama of the scene, the implication of it all, had been

rising in her with increasing force.   Poor Francis
was dead, Jennifer bewildered, like a woman lost
in a wood, the children helpless—and this power,
this force, destructive and remorseless, hung over
them.   And something told her that she was the
only one whom Walter feared; it had always
been so.   And it might be that she was the only
one whom, of all that company, Walter respected.

    She looked back and saw that Adam was safe
with Phyllis' arm around him.   Then she followed Walter out.

    He preceded her into a little parlour off
the saloon, a room so small that, when he had
motioned her into a red morocco chair and himself stood, with his legs straddled, in front of the
fire, the two of them filled it.   There was nothing in the room save a Chippendale cabinet on
which was a bowl of Christmas roses.   They
were full-blown and wore that look of patient
expectancy that precedes death.

    Walter began at once:

    ' Judith—how long will you remain at
Uldale? '

    ' I cannot see that that is any business of
yours, Cousin Walter,' she answered sharply.
She had retained her white fur muff, and her
fingers in it clasped one another with self-con-
gratulation.   What was it in her that made her
love a battle?   She was at the moment perfectly
happy, all her faculties widely awake, her eyes
on the rich panelling, the Christmas roses, and
the brilliant person of Mr. Walter Herries.

    ' No business of mine,' he went on.   ' Well,

perhaps not. And yet because I have a regard for you, Cousin Judith, I would wish you out of Uldale. That place and all in it are doomed.' He said this, a little swell of importance rising in his great chest.

' Really! That is exceedingly interesting. And by whom are they doomed, pray? '

' By myself.'

' Are you so powerful? ' He was, she reflected, like a giant schoolboy fallen from some star where everyone was twice as big as nature.

' I am indeed,' he answered. ' And growing more powerful every day. It is my father's wish that our family should be the chief figures in this country. Natural enough, when you think of it. He was born here, and his father lived here till the end of his life. He has developed an affection for the place.'

' An affection so deep,' interrupted Judith, ' that he never comes near it save on Saints' Days and Festivals! No, no, Cousin Walter,' she went on, ' there are the two of us alone here, and we may be frank. I belong to this country far more than you ever can. My mother may not have been of the country, but at least for generation upon generation my ancestors have lived and thieved here, stolen cattle and ladies only too ready to be stolen. I love this country, and so will my son after me. I love it because it is dark and full of storms and rains every other day, and smells of bracken and sheep and cow-dung. But you have none of these reasons. You love it because you wish to impress it, and I can tell you, Cousin

Walter, it is not so easily impressed. What
have you got? You have one thing—money.
Nothing else. You are not especial clever that
I have heard; you are too stout to be beautiful;
you are a bully of those weaker than yourself;
you are as conceited as a peacock. I am almost
old enough to be your mother, Walter. In fact,
in Eastern countries I believe I might have been
—so forgive me for my frankness.'

'Go on,' he said, smiling at her.

There were moments when she thought that
she rather liked him. Hatred would make everything easier.

'Very well, then, I will. You have nothing
but money. At Uldale they have much. Poor
Francis, who took his life because he had so much
more perception and understanding than you,
loved this country with all his heart. He made
an unhappy marriage. Oh! I am not blaming
Jennifer. There was a time when I hated her,
but it is hard to hate anybody long. It was not
her fault that she could not love him. Now
that is all over, and there are two very fine children
who are *not* doomed, dear Walter, however much
you may say it. They have more right to this
country than you have. Money can't beat them,
and don't you think it.'

Walter nodded.

'Very well, then. We know where we are.
You have said nothing, though, of the scandals
that we have all suffered for years past. It may
be foolish' (again his immense chest swelled),
' but if I am proud of one thing in this world it is

of being an Englishman and a Herries. I have
as much right as yourself to any part of England,
Cousin Judith, even though your ancestors *were*
cattle-thieves. How agreeable has it been to us,
do you think, that for years past, under our very
noses, we should have a Herries who is too weak
to challenge his wife's lover, who allows adultery
any day or night under his roof; a woman so
lost to shame that she receives her lover in the
room next to her children; a man so lily-livered
that he challenges that same lover, and then before
the duel is fought runs to London——?'

' I do not believe that,' Judith broke in, her eyes
flashing. ' We have only the word of that miserable oaf whom everyone knows for a coward——'

'Yes; and what about Uncle Francis for a
coward, who let such things be year after year?'

' And who are you,' she broke in hotly, ' to
be so virtuous? How have you treated *your* wife
all these years? And what of milkmaids in
Keswick and loose women in Kendal? Do you
suppose that you are so sacred that no. one talks
of you?'

He threw his head back and laughed.

' I am no hypocrite, Cousin Judith. Nor are
you. I am as other men. You had your little
come-by-chance in Paris. But I have not
allowed my wife a lover, nor have you blown off
the top of your head with a pistol. But come
. . . that is not the point. You may say that
there is no power in money. But I say there is.
And more. Money is going to be powerful in
England as it has never been before. I am no

such fool as I look, Judith.   In spite of my size
I have a trifle of my father's brains.   But the
long and short of it is just this.   They must
leave Uldale.   It is my obsession that they should.
I hate Jennifer, for she was rude to my mother;
but beyond that they are a blot on the Herries
name.   I will pay them a good price for the house,
but they must quit this part of the country!'

'Never!'   cried   Judith,   springing   up.
'Never! Never! Never!'

'Now come, Judith.   Why should you care?
What are they to you?   You loved Uncle Francis.
Good.   I have nothing against it.   But he is gone.
Jennifer is a dull, heavy, stupid woman.   You have
never liked her.   What is all this to you?'

'It is this to me!   These are Francis' children.   You would bully them out of existence.
Well, you shall not.'

'What will you do to prevent it?'

'Never mind.   You shall not.'

He shrugged his great shoulders.

'It may be true that I am a bully,' he said
slowly.   'I hate the weak.   They have no place
here if they cannot stand up for themselves.
You are the only one whom I admire, and you
have put yourself out of court with your little
bastard.   Not that I have anything against
bastards; but you are a little public with yours,
are you not?   It was worth seeing just now
the way that prig Rodney's nose curved down his
cheek.   So leave them alone, Judith!   Be quiet
with your boy in some place and we will be good
friends.   But leave Uldale alone.'

It was on the edge of her tongue to tell him
that he need not be disturbed, for in ten days
she would be in Watendlath and free of him for
ever. But she did not speak. As she faced
him the dominating part of her longed to oppose
him, to fight him, and beat him, to defend John
and Dorothy, to show him that the little bastard
was not so negligible as he pretended. She
could fight him! And what a fight that would be!

Meanwhile there was Watendlath. She almost sighed as she turned away and saw a smooth
white petal of the Christmas roses flutter to the
ground.

' Good friends? ' she repeated. ' Not if you
touch Uldale.'

' Well I *shall* touch Uldale,' he said, moving
towards the door. ' I have told you. And now,
come up and see the children. Bring your boy
with you.'

But at the door she paused.

' This is not a game, Cousin Walter.'

He stood over her.

' No. I have told you. It is a chapter in
family history.'

' What have you ever done,' she asked scornfully, ' to be so proud of our family history? '

' *Non mi ricordo*,' he answered in the phrase
that had been the popular catchword ever since
Majocchi's evidence in the Queen's trial. He
was determined to be amiable.

But, with her hand on the door, and with a
passion that in these days she rarely showed, she
burst out: ' I tell you, Walter, you must leave

Jennifer and the children alone'; and he, smiling, murmured lightly that popular epigram:

> Most gracious Queen, we thee implore
> To go away, and sin no more;
> But if that effort be too great,
> To go away, at any rate.

They looked into the saloon and found Adam diving into old Pomfret's pockets and producing treasures—a gold snuff-box, some seals and a small watch set with diamonds. The old man was watching him with delighted pleasure, and Judith at once forgave him all his pomposities, sensualities, infidelities to Rose, every other crime or weakness.

Adam came at once running when she called him. He turned when he was half-way to the door and waved his hand to the figures at the fire. Pomfret and Christabel waved back. Phyllis got up from her chair.

'Are you going up to see the children? You shall see my babies too.'

Judith knew how deeply intrigued they all were. What had Walter been saying to her? How much part did she play now in family affairs? She knew that Will was regarding her with secret alarm. She had always been a signal of danger to him, representing everything that was lawless and unsanctified. And she had been always Francis' ally. Perhaps he thought now of that old scene in Monty Cards' house when Francis had defied him . . . lured by Jennifer's beauty. . . . Well, he had never been

lured by anyone's beauty, and he was glad of it.
But this pain in his leg was vexatious. This
Northern air did not suit him. He was truly
well only in the City. But she knew by this
time that she was in the camp of the enemy and,
as she went out of the room with her head up
and trying not to slip ignominiously on the
polished floor, her hand went quietly to the silver
chain, her father's, that she always wore beneath
her clothes.

So the four of them went upstairs, Walter
leading. It was a fine high room where the
children were. Almost a hundred years ago
old Pomfret's children, Raiseley and Anabel and
Judith, had sat there, the girls with boards down
their backs to keep them straight, learning their
Latin. But much had been done to the room
since then. The windows were fine and high,
with a great view over the Lake and Scafell,
and the Gavel grouped handsomely at the end of
it. The waves were running across it now as
though in a race, and the woods by Manesty were
black as jet.

Inside the room everything was warm and
cosy—a great fire roaring, a decent-looking elderly
woman sitting beside it sewing. On the carpet
Elizabeth, one of Walter's twins, was playing
with Phyllis' two babies; Uhland, the other, was
sitting on a small chair by himself, his face absorbed as he pulled the hair out of the tail of a
painted wooden horse.

Many, many times afterwards she was to look
back to this moment when she first saw Uhland.

(Poor child, that he should be burdened his life long with so outlandish a name!) How characteristic that he should be sitting gravely by himself pulling something to pieces! But, at the moment, she felt nothing but pity. He had already, although he was but six years old, the face of an old man, the high forehead lined and the corners of the mouth bitter, and those strange grey penetrating eyes. His legs were dangling over the chair, but she noticed immediately that, absorbed as he was, at once, when he heard someone enter, he drew them up so that no one should observe their inequality. His body was too small for his head; his hands, she saw, were very beautiful, and, later, when she had reason to know how proud he was of them, she was interested to remember how quickly she had perceived them.

What followed touched her deeply. Walter, in his magnificent claret coat and resplendent pantaloons, hurried forward to his son, caught him up in his arms and held him close to his breast. The child seemed unmoved. His face did not change. Only one hand rested on his father's big one. Walter kissed him many times, oblivious of everyone else there.

' You must say How do you do?' he commanded him, and brought him to Judith. The child's cold grey eyes rested on her and, she fancied, with an expression of instant dislike.

' How do you do, ma'am?' he said in a small, remote voice. She bent forward and kissed his cheek, which was chill and dry. It was odd to touch that pallid, small face and feel Walter's great red one just above it. Walter took him back to his chair and, kneeling on the floor beside him, talked to him about the horse.

Walter had shown no attention to his daughter Elizabeth. This was a charming child with fragile, delicate features and pale flaxen hair.

She glanced once at her father as though she would have liked his attention, but she did not seem at all unhappy; she talked eagerly, made friends with Adam, played games with the babies, who already, Judith thought, bore, both of them, resemblance to Mr. Newmark.

After a little while they came away, but Judith saw that, as they left the room, Uhland stood up and gazed after them with an almost frightening intensity.

Judith, with Adam holding tightly to her hand, walked into Keswick. Even the road was alive with the stir of Christmas, but she moved for some while with unseeing eyes; she had a sense of danger—as though did she let Adam out of her sight for an instant Walter would get him.

The touch of his warm little hand in hers comforted her; but that was not enough. In one hand she held her muff, but with the other arm, had it not been so public a place, she would have encircled him that she might be the more secure.

He meanwhile had observed everything and had a hundred questions to ask. Why did no one wear any clothes in the pictures? Why was the floor so slippery? Who was the old gentle-

man with the diamond watch? The little boy
upstairs had one leg longer than another. Why
was the big man who had tried to hit him with
the whip so red in the face? Why. . . . Why.
. . . Why . . . ?

Then suddenly he was aware, with the perception that came from their long-continued
intimacy together, that she was disturbed and
wanted his help. He always knew when she
needed him, although he might not understand
what it was that she needed. Even at the time
of his greatest intimacy with John (he was as
deeply devoted to John as ever, but the novelty
was gone) he would look up and run off to find
her, although he could not himself tell why.

She walked more slowly. She wanted him
to understand something:

' Adam, would you wish to live in a house like
Uncle Walter's, so grand and rich, with everything you could need?'

He put out his tongue at two small boys who
were mocking him from the hedge, then he
applied his whole intelligence to the question.

'I would like that rocking-horse,' he said at last.

'Yes. But besides——' Her step was slower.
So soon she would be in Keswick, and there would
be Jennifer and gossip and the outside world.
At this moment she felt for him so overpowering
a love that it was as though she were saying good-
bye to him before he departed to America or the
incredible South Sea Islands.

' Besides—would you wish to live there—
always?'

'Would you come and John and Dorothy and Bennett, and might I cut things?'

'No. We would not come.'

He considered it.

'I should *like* the rocking-horse,' he said slowly. 'But, *of course*, you would be in the house.'

'No, I would not.'

'But you will be everywhere I am always.'

'No.' She shook her head. 'No.'

He laughed, for the two little boys were running along in the hedge making faces at him, and one of them, not being able to see in two places at once, fell down.

'The boy fell down,' he said, screwing his head round to see better.

She stopped at the little stream that was now coffee and now a froth of foam.

'Listen, Adam. I wish you to hear this. No one will ever love you as your mother does now. No one can take you from me. No one. We will soon be in Watendlath with Charlie and Mrs. Perry again. I could make you a fine man in a grand house, and everyone would do what you say, but I am going to make you a farmer like Watson, and when you are in the road with your sheep, the carriage that you should have ridden in will order you to clear the way. You will be walking and you might have been riding. You will be rough and poor and you could have been grand and rich.

'But we will be happy, you and I and Charlie and Alice; but the little sick boy will be rich and powerful, and you will be poor and nobody.'

He did not mind at all. He was looking to see a fish jump in the river.

But she put her hand under his chin and looked into his eyes.

' I want you to remember this, because all my life I have been making this choice. You cannot understand now, but one day you will look back and perhaps be angry with me.'

He knew that she was wanting him to understand something, so he screwed his forehead into a hundred wrinkles and did his best.

' Would you prefer that you were Charlie Watson or big Uncle Walter? ' she said.

He laughed at the thought of being Uncle Walter and, then and there, puffed out his cheeks, swelled out his chest, and began to strut about. Then his face was grave. He turned, looking back down the road.

' If he hits me with his whip again,' he said, ' I'll *beat* him.'

The change was so swift that she was astonished.

' But you like Uncle Walter,' she said. ' He was very kind to you.'

' Why does the little boy have one leg bigger than the other? '

' He was born like that.'

His mind seemed to jump.

' It's Christmas! It's Christmas! ' he cried, and began to run down the road in front of her. She walked after him. He turned back to meet her.

' Boneyparte was beat at Waterloo, Mr. Winch

says,' he remarked very gaily, dancing about.
Then catching her hand again and dragging her
along he shouted:

'And I will beat Uncle Walter when I am
bigger!'

He ran, pulling her hand, calling like a song:

'And I love you better than everybody—
better than John, better than Dorothy, better
than Bennett, better than Jack, better than——'

But even as the litany continued, something
caught his attention, a goat dragged along by a
cord, and a very small girl in charge of it.   He
pulled his hand away and ran on to see this
phenomenon, but as he ran he chanted in a
high absent-minded refrain:

'Better than Bennett.   Better than Jack.
Better than——'

And she, feeling that it was an omen, followed
after.

JUDITH in a state half sleep, half wakening, heard a voice say: ' Dig deep here. The deeper you may dig the richer the loam.' She recognised that she had a choice either to stay in that square of country, hemmed in by hills, and dig down and down—for what? treasure perhaps—or to fasten to her shoulders a pair of very elegant gold wings and fly the country over, but, of course, be for ever on the surface. She had to make a choice, and she made it without hesitation. With a sense of great relief and satisfaction she shouldered a spade, and as she did so saw the pair of wings be drawn up on a gold wire through the dark sky.

With confused notions of Mrs. Radcliffe, a novel that the night before she had been reading, *The Last Step; or The History of Mrs. Brudenal*, Rousseau's *Confessions*, and *Isabella; or The Rewards of Good Nature*, she woke to see the thin January light covering the floor with a sort of pale mildew and to realise that Adam, having thrown off the clothes, was sleeping upside down with his feet on her breast. She turned him round, heard him sigh happily in his sleep, and staring up at the bed-hangings, thought: 'He—— She—— It was right. She must dig and remain faithful to the——' To what? That question woke her.   She realised that the crisis of her life had come.

How often before it had seemed to be upon her—when David had beaten her, when Georges had married her, when old Stane had robbed her, when Jennifer had insulted her, when Warren had kissed her, when Adam had kicked his way out of her, when Francis had called her back to Uldale, when Francis had written a last letter to her, when Walter had challenged her—but now at last the crisis had truly come, for to-day she must make Jennifer realise that within a week she was positively and for ever departing and that no prayers, no beseechings could alter her resolve.

She moved restlessly on the bed as she thought of it.   No wonder that she had woken early with this in front of her!   Again and again in the last year she had attempted the break; but first there had been poor Francis alive, and then there had been poor Francis dead, and then Jennifer had kept to her bed for weeks, and when at last she had been driven out of her bedroom had refused to attend to her affairs, refused to see Mr. Bertram, the solicitor from Keswick, refused to do anything unless Judith were there to force her to do it.

During the last three months it had come to this.   Again and again she had said:

' Well, Jennifer, I will do this for you' (speak to Mr. Winch or Bennett, or talk business with Mr. Bertram, or write to London about some shares or discuss with Mrs. Quinney the fare for the coming week). 'But you had far better yourself, you know, for a week after Christmas I am off, and you will have to manage it all then.'

' Oh, a week after Christmas—besides, you will change your mind.'

' I shall not change my mind.'

After the discovery of Fernyhirst (who had never put in another appearance), Francis' refusal to return, and then his suicide, Jennifer's sluggishness had swallowed all the rest of her. Once she had been lazy because she was proud; now she was lazy because she was humiliated. She tumbled into a slattern over whom Judi.. had absolute command. Judith had seen her as lovely girl, proud and overbearing wife, self-satisfied mistress, betrayed beauty (her attitude after Francis' departure), and now she was humble, but yawning, slattern. Poor Jennifer! Parents who had adored her too deeply to educate her or to force her to anything that she avoided had begun her ruin. Her lazy and stupid in-difference completed it. She cared now only for her food, an occasional fine gown, and sometimes to dress Dorothy up and take her into Keswick. (But when there always fancied that she was in-sulted, and returned in a state of indignation and confused panic.)

She went to bed of an evening ever earlier and earlier; the time would surely come when she would never rise at all.

She had, however, one increasing terror, and that was of Walter Herries. He had assumed now quite gigantic proportions for her. He could do, she was convinced, any horrible thing that he chose. He was bent on her destruction. And in that last she was perfectly correct.

Poor Jennifer! She might have been, Judith thought, a brilliant, successful beauty at an earlier time. She was born too late for her period. Like many of her contemporaries, she was the victim of a transition world.

She would, however, now be forced to action. When Judith was gone, Mrs. Quinney, horrid little Mr. Winch, kindly but saturnine Bennett, would do as they pleased. And then John would grow and take his place. He was now fourteen years of age and as nice a boy as you could find— gentle and kind, thoughtful for others, but manly also; more resolute in character than his father. He was reticent; no one had ever known what were his real feelings about his father's suicide, or how much he knew about the scandal in the house. Judith suspected that he had suffered with intensity. She fancied, too, that he had a sort of irritated pity for his mother.

But John against Walter? That was the only thought that gave her obstinate departure a touch of treachery.

To-day she must tell Jennifer that the matter was final, and, three days from now, she would be safe with Adam in Watendlath.

It was a kind of fate, as things developed, that before mid-day she should encounter Watson.

He stopped his horse by the Uldale gate. He would not come in. She came out to him.

Why did her heart beat so when she saw him? She was not in love with him. She had never been. He was a fine thick figure of a man, but it was not his figure that made her heart beat. Did a shadow pass? Behind him the hollows under Skiddaw filled like wine in a jade bowl— but it was not the hollow valleys. He did not love her, or at least had never given her reason to think that he did. They were two elderly people now, she nearing fifty, he over sixty. Was it their friendship and mutual trust that made her heart beat? But when she put her hand in his all the nonsense was over. He never had much to say. She had many things to do and could not waste precious time standing there in the cold.

Besides, after three days, she would be seeing him six times a week! There was a joy! It was so intense that she burst out:

'Now there's no need, Charlie, to keep me in the cold. I am busy this morning—and in three days I shall be in Watendlath, for good.'

'Truly, you're coming?'

'Truly, I'm coming.'

'Aye, but you've said it so many times. . . .' Then he added, smiling, speaking his broadest, as he did when he was happy: 'I willn't believe tha, not without thou'll swear 't.'

'Oh, I'll swear it. In three days.'

'Aye, I'm glad!'

This was too much emotion for both of them,

so she asked him what he was doing so early in their direction. He could give no connected account of himself, mumbled something about visiting for an account in Caldbeck, but she was aware instantly that he was troubled and had come to tell her something. He talked on about agricultural distresses—the old grievance of cash payments, the abundant harvest of '20 that had led to over-supply, the wet autumn of '21 that had destroyed the crops, the new contemplated Corn Law, Huskisson's speech in the House of Commons, all uninteresting enough to her with the wind driving down the road in icy gusts. Then at last he came out with:

'There's trouble about.'

'Trouble?'

'Aye. They burnt Squire Forrester's ricks last night over at Deddon.'

'Who did?'

'Oh, some of t'wild lads and men with no work, and others egging them on!'

'Poor Mr. Forrester!'

'Aye. 'Hope they'll hev a long wait in gaol. Well, I must be moving. 'Tis true you're coming in three days?'

'Yes—true enough. And never going away again. Adam is to be a farmer like yourself, Charlie.'

'Reet.' He smiled a tremendous smile, his teeth as white and perfect as they had been twenty years before. 'I'll gang down and mak' all ready for him.' He gave her one of his long protecting looks as though he thought she was

only safe when he had his eyes upon her; then
he lifted his hat and rode away.

All day she remained troubled. Charlie was
so cautious that you had to guess from one spoken
word the twenty that he had intended. But the
remark about Forrester's could have no applica-
tion to them. No one would want to burn *their*
barns. Nevertheless she knew that this was a
day of fate. She set back her shoulders as
though a shadow had warned her that before
nightfall she would need all her endurance.

In any case, without any shadowy whispers, she
needed all her endurance for her talk with Jennifer. All her life she had detested scenes, but
she was aware that Jennifer fell into them and
out of them as easily as she washed her hands.
A scene there would be—but it would be good
to have it behind her, and, although there would
be, in all probability, three days of silence and sulks,
after that—liberty!

She chose her time well—six o'clock in the
parlour, following an excellent dinner, the curtains drawn, Jennifer languidly —with a painted
hand-screen to shade her face—before the fire,
thinking of her food and the handsome flock-
gauze gown that she was wearing.

'Jennifer,' said Judith, 'I think that you
should realise that in three days Adam and I
will be gone.'

'Oh dear,' Jennifer, stifling a yawn, answered.
'Not this evening, Judith, pray. You are for
ever speaking of going. 'Jennifer, to-morrow I
am going—the day after to-morrow I shall be

gone, Jennifer,' but, thank Heaven, it is only a bagatelle like Mr. Hume and his grey top-hat.'

Judith sighed. This would be indeed a tiresome affair.

' This time it is no bagatelle. It has been one often enough. I had intended to go a year and a half back, and I have remained on and on until I do not wonder that you hesitate to believe me. But this time it is true and certain.'

' But you cannot go in three days. Mr. Bertram is coming from Keswick next Wednesday.'

' Well, it will be practice for you in something you will have to do very often—talk business with Mr. Bertram.'

' Oh, but it is absurd! Of course I cannot talk business with Mr. Bertram.'

' Really, Jennifer. A woman of your age and unable to talk business.'

Jennifer smiled and put her hand on to Judith's arm.

' Oh well, you do it so very much better than ever I can. You are made for business, Judith. Why, only last Tuesday——'

This would be interminable. She rose from her chair and stood between Jennifer and the fire.

' I am very serious. You *must* understand. I am going to Watendlath in three days' time to *live*. This was always temporary—my stay here. You have been very good. I have been happy here; but it is not, it has never been, my real life. I have been running away from this house since I was a baby, since I can remember, and I am for

ever returning to it. Now I am running away
for the last time.'

Something in Judith's grave serious gaze,
something in the determined set of her small
body, caused Jennifer to put down her screen and
move her head uncomfortably.

'It grows wearisome, Judith, this everlasting
talk about Watendlath. What you should want
to go to the place for at all I cannot conceive;
but if you *must* go—for a visit, to see your farmers
and their wives—well, I cannot prevent you.
Only, pray return as soon as may be.'

Judith stamped her foot with irritation.

'Jennifer, listen! I am going to Watendlath in three days and I am not returning. I am
not returning. Now, do you understand?'

'You will leave me?'

'Yes, yes, yes. I have told you a hundred
times.'

'Leave me?' The screen fell to the ground.
Her big blue eyes widened, her hand began to
beat on her dress. 'Leave us? Oh, but, Judith,
you cannot! You cannot indeed!'

The note of terror was there. Jennifer was
awake to reality; fright was the only thing that
awoke her. Judith was suddenly compassionate.
She put her arm around the large trembling
woman:

'Listen, Jennifer. I have been trying to
escape from this house ever since I was a baby,
and I am now a woman of middle age and *still*
I haven't succeeded! From the house, not from
Francis or you or John. I have never been per-

mitted to lead a life of my own. When I was
with Georges I was devoured with love for him,
so that I was not myself. Now I have Adam,
and Adam shall not lead this false life, nor will I
any longer.'

But Jennifer did not understand a word of it.
She had no imagination, and she saw only things
that concerned herself.

' False life? But this is not a false life here.'

' No,' said Judith, striving to be patient.
' The tables and curtains and chairs are real,
but it is a false life to me, nevertheless, occupied
with fears and ambitions that do not matter.
You see, Jennifer, I am only half Herries. My
mother was a gipsy. And even that Herries
half is wild. You know what my father was.
So now I am going away where there are no
Herries, and I shall take my son with me.'

But Jennifer had not heard a word of it.
Slowly, while Judith was speaking, her brain had
been taking in this fact—that Judith was going
away and that she would be alone and defenceless.

She gripped Judith's arm and cried out, her
body trembling again and her cheek white where
it was not painted.

' No, no . . . you are going away, to leave
me and my children to Walter Herries! You
cannot. . . . You must not!'

Now the terror was real enough, and the strange
thing was that Judith felt it also. She looked for
an instant at the darkened window-pane. She
had been troubled all day. She was, in her
final resources, alone in this house with this

crying, hysterical woman. Of course Walter
could do nothing, nor did he wish to. He was
at this moment kneeling on the nursery floor
embracing his pale little boy. Nevertheless. . . .

'Now, Jennifer. Come, this is absurd. Walter
can do nothing. You have Walter Herries on
the brain. Everything is well here. There is
money enough, you have Mr. Bertram in Keswick, you have most devoted servants, John is
growing a fine boy. You cannot wish me to
stay here and cosset you for ever. Besides, I
am blown on. Everyone knows that I have an
illegitimate child and that poor Warren was its
father. What good can that do you? You will
discover when I am really gone that it is much
better so.'

But Jennifer, in full realisation now that
Judith meant what she said, was past all control.
She clung to Judith, holding her with a frantic
grasp.

'What can you mean? You cannot be so
cruel. You were never cruel even when I was
stiff with you in the old days. Walter is a devil.
You have seen it for yourself. All the scandal
about me everywhere is his doing. He will
poison my children and——'

'Jennifer, don't be so absurd.'

'No, but it is not absurd. I am certain he
will poison all the water here before he is done.
I see him at every turn. I dare not walk out
unless I should see him. I am quite alone here.
I have not a friend but you. Everyone hates me.
Walter sees to it that they do. He is everywhere

whispering. . . . If you go, Judith, I shall kill
myself and then you will have to come and see
to my poor children, my poor deserted children.
I know that Walter forced Francis to kill himself.
I am sure of it. He wrote him a letter or something, and only because years ago I broke his
mother's cheap little fan. Oh! how I wish
that I had never left my dear father and mother.
There has never been anything but unhappiness
since I left Bournemouth. But I will not be
alone in this house. . . . If you go I kill myself. . . .'

'Come, come, Jennifer. You must not be so
foolish. You are like a child.'

Jennifer was now in floods of tears. She
waved her hands, beat with her feet on the
ground and behaved like a madwoman. Part
of this was stupid and lazy histrionics, but part
of it was the true bewildered apprehension of
a slow, but not evilly intentioned, woman who
might, had she married a rich warm husband in a
safe comfortable place, never have been exposed.
It was because Judith knew this and by now
understood her so well that she was touched.

'Come, Jennifer. Come upstairs and lie
down.' (Always the recipe for Jennifer's distresses.) 'We will talk quietly. There is
nothing for you to be so distressed over. Nothing at all. You have an obsession about Walter.
He can do you no harm. Come and lie down.'

She surrendered as though hypnotised. Judith
led her away.

On the stairs she said:

' Well, but you were only laughing at me, Judith.   You are not going away? '

Judith patted her shoulder.

' You will see in the morning it does not look so terrible.   After all it is only a few miles.   I shall be close at hand.'

But when at last Jennifer had been laid down and petted and quietened and she, Judith, stood in the still hall with the clock ticking the only sound:

' Phew! ' she said to herself.   ' *That* was something.'   But she was resolute.   Nothing now could turn her.   However, half an hour later she had to suffer another attack.   There was a knock on the parlour door and John appeared.

He looked at her shyly.   Of late she had noticed in herself a certain embarrassment which she was for ever trying not to show him.   Was she not going to desert him?   A look that he had of his father, although he was more firmly built, a look of delicate sensitiveness and courtesy, deeply touched her.   Then there was his love for Adam.

He had fair hair, blue eyes, a very white skin and a proud mobile mouth.   His worst fault was his modesty and his lack of self-assurance.   Perhaps the unhappy history of his parents had encouraged that.   She knew that his sense of honour was so scrupulous that decisions, their rights and wrongs, were often an agony to him.

' John,' she said.   ' Come in.'

He came in and stood near her, twisting and untwisting his hands.

'Aunt Judith, mother is crying. She says that you are going away.'

'John, dear, come here,' Judith said, drawing him to the sofa where so often she had sat with his father. He sat close to her, very erect, his thin white hands resting on his knees. She looked at him and loved him dearly. In that one look the foolish childish jealousy that she had had because Adam loved him too vanished altogether.

'I want you to understand. Adam and I are going away because it is best for you all that we should. I have managed everything for too long here. I am a managing old woman, you know. I cannot see a thing without wishing to arrange it. Now you are growing into a man, and this is your position, not mine. And then—' she hesitated for a moment, 'you know that I was not married to Adam's father, and people gossip. So—it is better for me to go.'

He gave a small gulp in his throat, staring into the fire.

'Yes, Aunt Judith.'

'You do understand, do you not?'

It was harder than she had expected.

'Yes, Aunt Judith. . . . But will you never come back any more?'

'You and Dorothy will come to visit us—only we shall be farmers, you know.'

'Yes.' He hesitated, then said: 'You and Adam are my best friends. I know Mr. Winch says that I am not one that others can like very much——'

' What does Mr. Winch say? ' she burst out indignantly.

'Oh, he means it very well. And it is true. I like to be by myself unless it is someone I understand. And I do understand you and Adam. So—if you go——'

And then to her utter dismay he broke into tears, hid his head in his hands and sobbed most bitterly. She put her arms around him (a thing that she seemed to be doing to everyone to-day). He leaned against her for a little, then looked up, deeply ashamed and rubbing his eyes with his knuckles.

' I never cry,' he said. ' I don't know why now. . . . Mother was so unhappy . . . and she is afraid of Uncle Walter. She says that if you go he will destroy us . . . and I am not very old yet. . . .'

' John, John. Listen to me. Uncle Walter can do nothing to you. You are here to care for your mother and sister. You are on guard over them. There is nothing to fear, and Adam and I will only be a few miles——'

She was interrupted by a loud banging at the door, a furious, impatient knocking.

They both started up, and she was never to forget that John put out his hand on to her arm as though he intended to begin, at once, to guard her from danger.

The knocking was repeated, more impatiently than before. She hurried out and opened the

door.   There was a figure against the dark, and
then as he moved forward she saw who it was—
it was Reuben.

'Reuben!' she cried, astonished.   Then she
saw that he was in the very greatest agitation.
He closed the door behind him.   Mrs. Quinney
was coming towards him.

'Quick, Judith,' he said, 'I must see you
alone.'

She drew him into the dining-room, something
in her saying: 'This is what you have been expecting all day long.'

When the door was closed she caught his arm.
'Reuben, what is it?   I thought you were at
Whitehaven.'

There was perspiration on his forehead, and
his breath came in gasps until he was calmer.

'Have you not heard anything?'

'Heard anything?   No, of course not.   What
is it?'

'I have ridden as swiftly as I could.   I got
away only in time. . . . My own men. . . . My
own people. . . . They would not listen to me.
They knocked me down, threw things at me.   I
tell you, Judith, they have thrown me over and it is
because I have deserted God.   I have been drawn
more and more into earthly things, politics,
money . . . and now——'

He was incoherent, staring about him;
scarcely, it seemed to her, recognising her
at all.

'No, but, Reuben, what *is* it?   Please,
please. . . .'

' Yes, you are right. I scarcely know what
I am saying. Listen, Judith; they are on their
way now to burn this place down. I had dinner
in Cockermouth and it was there that by chance
I learnt of it. Holroyd, Atkinson, Bell, Wood—
no, but of course their names mean nothing to
you. There is a mob of them on their way now.
Someone had put them up to it. They have been
out of hand the last month. Last night some
of them burnt Squire Forrester's ricks. . . .'

' Yes, yes, I know. But why here? We
have done nothing.'

' No. No. I don't understand.' He wiped
the sweat from his forehead. ' It was about
Jennifer—some vastly improper things that they
were saying.'

' Jennifer? '

' Yes—and Fernyhirst.' He seemed to waken
then to the sense of the urgency. ' No, but no
matter. They can be only a mile or so away.
A good hundred of them. What are you going
to do? What have you here in the way of
servants? '

He stood staring about him. Then he went
on quickly: ' Someone should ride for one of the
Magistrates. Mr. Fox at Holtby is the nearest.
He is old but courageous. Only last year he
wished to have me whipped off his grounds. Is
there anyone can go? He should be there in an
hour.'

' Yes. Jack. He's a brave boy. He'll go.'

She seemed to be transformed. This was a
situation that she could understand. No tears

and vapours and horror of some vague unknown danger.   Something definite.

'We must have all the servants in '—and from that spoken word until the end of the affair she was in absolute command.   She went out into the hall and found John and Mrs. Quinney there, wondering.

'John—will you do a thing for me?'

'Anything,' and she knew that he too was glad that action had come at last.

'Go up to your mother.   Sit beside her bed. Read to her.   Anything.   She must be kept quiet and tranquil in her room for the next hour.'

He gave her one look, asked no questions, and went.

'Now, Mrs. Quinney, I want all the servants. Everyone.   In here.   I have something to say to them.   Will you fetch them, please?'

Mrs. Quinney went.   Judith returned to Reuben.

'Reuben, you must have something to eat and drink.'

He nodded.   He was sitting down and in his eyes was a look of utter dejection.   Once again she was carried back to that day when she had given succour to his brother.   The same incident —the same command.   She brought him bread and meat and ale, and he ate and drank eagerly.

'But I cannot understand,' she repeated. 'Why here?   Why Jennifer?   Jennifer has done no one any harm but herself, poor thing.'

'Oh, they are mad.   They have been so for months—indeed for years.   This is only a little sequel to Peterloo, and there will be many another before all is done. But the wretchedness of this is that it is I who have been urging them to it. . . Oh no, not here, of course, nor to any violence. I have preached peace, but of late I have been filled with their material harshness and have forgot their souls. You yourself saw it when we were at Hawkshead. You spoke to me of it. And now to-day they would not listen to a single word from me. Bell and Holroyd are the worst. And only a year back Holroyd would have done anything for me.'

The door opened and they came in: Mr. Winch, Mrs. Quinney, Martha Hodgson, Doris, Jack Turner, Bennett.

At the sight of Bennett Judith's heart warmed. With his broad thick bulk, his utterly unperturbed air, his kindly protective eyes (just as Charlie Watson was protective), he would be the man for her now.

They stood in a group together, Mr. Winch, with his pallor and nervous shifting eyes, a little apart from the others.

'Listen!' she said, smiling to reassure them. 'Mr. Sunwood has ridden on to tell us that some rioters are on their way here from Cockermouth. It seems they mean mischief. Well, they shall find us ready for them. Jack, I want you to take Peggy and ride off at once to Squire Fox at Holtby. He is a Magistrate. Ask him to come as speedily as possible. You should be back with him in two hours. You know his place?'

Jack nodded.

'Well, go then.   Be as quick as you can.'

With another nod he was off.

'Fred' (this was Bennett), 'have we any fire-arms?'

'There's two guns and an old pistol.   I don't know if 'tis firing yet.'

'Good.   Get anything you can.   So soon as we hear them we will make the whole house dark.   Do not disturb Mrs. Herries or the children until we must.   It should be an hour or more yet before they are here.   They may not come at all.   Now, Mrs. Quinney, Martha, Doris, no fuss, now.   At the worst it is only a few rough boys and men.   Mr. Fox will be here as soon as they—that is, if they come at all.   You be quiet in the back of the house, will you?'

They smiled and nodded proudly.   They were Cumbrian women and not lightly disturbed. Nor were they garrulous.   They showed no agitation at all.   Bennett remained alone with Judith and Reuben.

'Dusta think,' he asked, 'there'll be many of them?'

'A good few, I reckon,' said Reuben.

'Aye,' said Bennett slowly.   'T' height of wickedness.   And they'll suffer.'   Then he added: 'Foreigners likely.'   That was his principal sentiment—that he was shocked.   He did not know, as he was often fond of declaring, what had come to the country.   However, he was really only unhappy when he was puzzled as

to which way he should act. It was the fear of
his life that he should act the wrong way and look
a fool. Happily in this present case his duty and
his pleasure were clear.

He went off to the stables.

Reuben looked at her admiringly. This was
how he liked to see her.

'Judith, you should be the Captain of a
pirate.'

She laughed. 'Perhaps they will not come
after all, Reuben.'

'Oh yes,' he said. 'They will come.'

'Let us go out and listen.'

They went into the garden and then on to the
road. Then up on the moor. It was a fine
night now, with a thin moon and quivering sheets
of dim smoky stars. On the ridge of the moor
the frosty air stung. Hills and valleys lay,
under the deep shadows of the moon, in up-and-
down disorder like a quilt shaped by the limbs
of a recumbent giant. They listened, but there
was only the thin whistle of the wind, smell of
earth and sheep and rabbits, and the peaceful
sleeping land.

'Maybe they will not come.'

'Oh, they will come. Not a doubt of it.
Holroyd shouted filth at me; I had lost all touch
with him. Do you remember one night when I
came to Watendlath and Georges asked me about
God? I was in touch then. It was as though I
had Him under my cloak; but the world tempted
me again, and I lost Him. First, when I was a
boy, it was my fear of being a fool; then it was

women; then I climbed over that and saw God
as plainly as I see you; then their politics
tempted me, and I lost Him.   So I lose them as
well.'

'You have done a good, kind thing coming to
tell us, Reuben.   God will be pleased with that.
For myself, if there is a God, I will be grateful
one moment and defy Him the next.   It is no
use to be always on your knees.'

She was talking to cover her own fears.   She
was thinking at that moment only of Adam.
Her heart was wild with fear for him.   Had she
not been ashamed she would have snatched him
out of bed, caught him up in her arms and run
away with him out of the back door.   When she
was in the house and there was plenty to be done
it was one thing, but out here in the cold and
silence quite another.   An owl hooted.   A little
wind pulled at their feet.   The anaemic moon
was enveloped by a thin cloud of gauze, and the
world was veiled.

'Hark!   Can you not hear something?'

She caught his arm.   They both listened.
The breeze rose and fell; a church bell from a
great distance could be heard echoing the half-
hour.   On the wind for a moment there seemed
to be the crack of horses.   But it died.

'No.   That was the church clock.'

They listened again.   It seemed as though all
the landscape were listening with them.

'Yes.   I am certain I hear something.'

She stood close to him.   He put his arm
around her.   The breeze came up the slope

again and the moon rode out, her light stroking Skiddaw's shoulder.

' Yes. Listen. Listen.'

Then above the beating of their hearts they heard it beyond any question, the strike of horses' hoofs on the winter road.

' Quick! Quick! Back to the house! '

They ran down the fell, along the road and through the gate. As Judith turned in she saw a figure come out of one of the village houses; the black shadow stood looking down the hill. It was beyond doubt now, a clatter of horses, laughter and voices.

She ran into the house and up the stairs. First she went into Jennifer's room. It was in darkness. John came towards her.

' She is asleep.'

She went to the bed and shook Jennifer's shoulder.

' Jennifer! Jennifer! Wake up! '

When she was awake she told her as quickly as possible.

' Now, Jennifer, it is nothing. Only some drunken boys. But you must stay here. Don't move from here. It will be soon over.'

' Drunken boys? . . . But what do they want? '

' Reuben is here, and Bennett has a gun, and Mr. Fox of Holtby is coming over.'

' Oh dear. Oh dear. . . .'

But she had no time for Jennifer's ' Oh dears! '

' John, you remain with your mother. Adam and Dorothy had best be here as well. I will bring them.'

When she went into her own room her heart for a moment failed her. Adam was lying, his head on his arm, fast asleep. She woke him, wrapped him in a blanket so that he looked a young bewildered Indian, and told him quietly:

' Adam, there are some noisy men in the garden. If they shout and throw stones, it is no matter. Mother is here and Bennett and Mr. Winch and Uncle Reuben. You stay with John, darling, in Aunt Jennifer's room.'

He nodded his head, yawning and rubbing his eyes with his knuckles. ' Where will you be? ' he asked.

' I shall return very soon. Now, go to John, darling.'

' Can't I see the men throwing stones? '

' No. Not now. Be a good boy.'

He was always a good boy if his mother thought that it was serious. He saw that she thought that this was serious, and obeyed. She took him into the next room, saw that Dorothy was also there, and Jennifer sitting up in bed and asking John questions. She gave Adam to John and left them.

When she came downstairs another world had already burst upon them. The house was in darkness, save for the candles in Jennifer's room. The women were in the kitchen. Bennett and Reuben, each with a gun, were in the hall. They all three moved into the parlour.

She looked between the curtains and almost cried out at the scene. At least a hundred men, women and boys were gathered in the road,

dark and shadowy in the moonlight, but some
of them carried torches whose flames, leaping
in the wind, jumped from shadow to shadow.
About a dozen men were on horseback.

She recognised at once a number of villagers
among them. Since Francis' death the men and
women of the village had held aloof from Jennifer,
whom in fact they had always disliked.

There was the strangest contrast between the
black silence of the house and the shouts, laughter,
cries that came from the crowd. She saw that
one of them, a long thin bearded man on a white
horse, was their leader.

' That is Holroyd! ' Reuben whispered to her.
The crowd moved backwards and forwards as
though stirred by some impetus within themselves.
Through the closed window she could not hear
what they were crying. White faces leapt into
torchlight and out again. Arms rose and fell.
Suddenly the gates swung back and they all
tumbled pell-mell into the garden. Then there
was a pause and silence. They stood transfixed,
as though a spell had been cast on them, staring at
the house.

That was queer—to stand behind the curtains
with that familiar room all about her, to look out
and see that multitude, faces like fish-scales in the
moonlight, all still and waiting. All for no reason!
These were familiar things, the furniture, the
walls, the pictures, and yet these strangers had
the impertinence to break through the gate, to
trample on the garden, to insult the shadows of
David, of Francis, of Sarah—perhaps to frighten

the spirit of her own son, Adam! A furious indignation began to rise within her.

The silence cracked. A stone was flung and smashed through the parlour window, missing Judith by a breath.

'Take care!' Reuben whispered, pulling her back.

The throwing of that stone released them. They all began to shout at once. More stones were thrown. Figures were running down the lawn, others towards the stables. Meanwhile the thin man with a beard sat motionless on his horse.

'I must go out to them!' Reuben said.

'No. No. They will throw stones. Wait——'

'No. I cannot wait.'

He went out. She heard him open the door of the hall, and, before he shut it, a roar of voices reached her, like a sudden ripple of thunder. What had she better do? Her impulse was to go with him. The parlour door had closed, but now it opened to show the meagre black figure of Mr. Winch, who entered with a lighted candle.

'Blow out that candle!' she ordered him sharply.

But he could not. He stood there, his mouth open, his eyes shifting from place to place, the candle shaking in his hand. He was in a sweat of terror. Indignantly she snatched the candle from him and blew it out, saying:

'No one will harm *you*, Mr. Winch. Your place is with the children upstairs.' She heard him slip away.

From the intervals where the curtains were not drawn the glare of the torches, falling and rising, lit the room—the coloured top of the spinet, the crimson chair, the sofa with the red apples. She could also hear now through the break in the window that the stone had made. Reuben's voice came across to her, and it seemed that they were listening:

'. . . and if I had done so you might have charged me with a fault, but for many years now I have had only your interests at heart. What others could I ever have had? Have I not given my whole life to your friendship? . . .' She lost it again. Then it returned. '. . . and this house has never harmed you. It has not starved you as some have done, nor ill-treated your children as some have done, nor thrown you out of employment like some. But even though it had, this would not be your Court of Appeal. Violence of this sort has never won anyone any good, and well you know it. Cruelty to women and children has never been our Cumberland way. . . .'

'A little too much of the orator,' she thought. '*I'd* speak to them!'

But he was not to speak much longer. She caught the words: '. . . and be for ever ashamed of as dastardly an action. . . .'

Perhaps someone was stirring up trouble from the road. In any case, there was a sudden rush from the rear of the crowd, shouts and screams, and someone threw a lighted torch, whirling through the dark until it fell with a hiss on the lawn and lay there blazing. The man on the horse made as though he would ride on to Reuben and so past him into the house; but, in spite of his furious movement, his voice was sharp and controlled as he cried:

' Enough words, Sunwood! Back to the stables, lad. And we'll see them blaze!'

' Shall I fire? Shall I fire?'

Judith heard a voice in her ear, and putting out a hand felt Bennett's breast and his heart beating like a clock.

' No. . . . Wait, Fred. Oh, the devils! I cannot endure this. And with the children upstairs. Oh, when will Mr. Fox come? I must go out to them! I cannot endure this here!'

' No, no, ma'am. Stay where you are!'

' No. I must go.' She tore herself from Bennett's hand and ran from the room, he following her. She could never quite clearly remember afterwards what occurred in that outside pandemonium. The air was cold and yet the heat seemed intense. There was smoke in her nostrils. Reuben was shouting. She saw that his forehead was bleeding, and that seemed to loose a fury inside her. She never knew what she cried, but she drove into the middle of them; then, nearly stumbling over a mounting-block by the door, she climbed on to it.

' Be ashamed of yourselves. Attacking women and children who have done you no harm. Go back to your homes, you bullies. . . .'

The ineffectiveness of her words enraged her yet more. They swept past her and around her, not

2 B 2

even seeing her, shouting, some of them singing, the horses rising in the moonlight like white sea-horses. Then, as though it were a banner unfurled, a shuddering, quivering flame leapt up into the sky from the stables. The fire lit the whole scene; all faces were white, the house like a black wall with the pale glass squares of the windows. A woman's cry came from inside the house.

'The horses! The horses!' Judith cried, and began to push and fight through the mob, who, at sight of the fire, seemed dimmed and quieted as though they sank from the scene. Some man struck her in the breast. She turned, gasping for breath, and saw Bennett behind her, his gun raised.

'You shall have it then!' he cried, and fired.

Holroyd on his horse half turned, raised an arm, shivered and slowly fell. Reuben sprang forward, was for a moment illuminated by the fire; a shot rang from the road, and he too jumped as though, with arms lifted, he would touch the moon, and collapsed on the horse-steps.

The two shots, the crackle and gesture of the fire, the riderless horse plunging, seemed in a moment to change the scene. Men and women all turned. They fled through the gate.

A woman, her hair loose, turned and shouted in a shrill broken voice: 'Curse you . . .' and something more about Jezebel and vengeance.

Then panic had caught them all, for they were flying down the road—horses, men, women—the white moonlit stretch was black with fleeing figures. . . . Then, save for Reuben's huddled body on the steps, there was nothing in the garden. Only the flames of the stable chattered, hissed, rose and fell as though they were busy with their own private important business.

Judith, with Reuben's head in her lap, looked desperately around her.

' Quick, quick, Fred. Someone fetch Doctor Borden from the village. He'll be hiding in his house. Tell him ' (her voice was fierce and bitter) ' that it is safe now. He must come. The women must get buckets for the fire. . . .' She caught sight of some slinking figures in the gateway. Villagers who, now that the riot was over, had crept out. ' Force them. They must help. The house must not burn.'

Bennett answered. ' The house is safe. It is only the outside sheds. The fire is burning itself out. Oh, Mr. Reuben, are you hurt, sir? Are you hurt? '

' He's dying, Fred.' She bent over him. His eyes were open, looking at her. He smiled.

' Good-bye, Judith. I did my best.'

She knew that he was dead. Her hands were soaked in blood. She stared out above him to the quiet sky and the stables lit by fire. She felt a hand on her shoulder and looked up. It was Mrs. Quinney.

' He is dead,' she said quietly. ' Help me to carry him in.'

THE CHOICE

REUBEN was buried five days later in Ireby Churchyard. As Judith drove in the carriage, away back to the house again, she was so weary that the whole world was quite unreal.

A great crowd had been at the funeral. Men and women had come from all parts, for Reuben was in general much beloved, and the riot, the disorder and his death had made the greatest possible stir. Nothing else was talked of. Holroyd (who had only a flesh-wound in the arm) and Bell were in Kendal gaol; other arrests were expected to be made.

All of this could do poor Reuben very little good; but Judith was aware as, a lonely little black figure, she moved through the courtyard gate into her carriage, that she was surrounded with sympathy. She had known already that Uldale village was properly ashamed and anxious to make amends. She did not care. Reuben was gone—and, very soon, oh, very, very soon, she would be away from them all, safe with Adam in Watendlath.

It was a most curious day, she thought, as she drove up the road. For three days and nights there had been unceasing rain, and as, night after night, she had lain awake the rain had seemed to shroud her in as though it were weaving for her a great suit of silver armour, and in this she could live, safe and protected, for ever after.

But this rain in the valleys had meant snow on the hills. They were more thickly covered than they had been for many years. To-day the landscape was shrouded in mist. There seemed to be three veils, one upon another, and these were always shifting. The middle veil was faintly radiant and orange in colour, for it held the sun, sunlight enfolded and shrouded. The farthest veil was of a very dim blue, cold, with snow in it. The first veil was almost transparent, of the thinnest gauze.

All the land moved in mystery behind these veils, for it was the land that appeared to be moving as the veils shifted. Everything was on the edge of discovery, but nothing was clear, only the stones under your feet, trunks of birch and larch and oak at your hand. In the corner of a field leaves were burning, a blazing fire in smoke.

So, sitting in the carriage, only half-awake, in this shrouded world, it did not seem strange to her that the forms of her four friends, all dead from violence, should be sitting beside her—Francis, Georges, Warren, Reuben—one of whom she had loved and still loved, one the father of her son, two the friends of her lifetime.

They none of them, she thought, looked at her with any reproach. She had in a way been the cause of death in all of them—at least she had been in the minds and hearts of all of them when they died. But, unsentimental as ever, she did not intend in any way to reproach herself. She had been honest with them all, and she knew that they wished her well. They had all died fighting—Georges fighting discipline, Francis his own soul, Warren convention, Reuben fighting his way back to God. They had all, in fact, been fighting Herries one way or another—if you took Herries for fact against fancy, as she did.

However, she was too weary to do more than smile upon them and assure them that they need not look at her with such anxiety. She and her little son were on the very point of escaping. The Herries would not get her, try as hard as they might. Nevertheless, she knew that when she was alive again she would discover that the unfair savage death of Reuben had placed something hard and bitter in her heart that had never been there before.

When she had taken off her bonnet and cloak, washed her face and brushed her hair, she thought that she would finish the thing once and for all. Jennifer was down in the parlour looking at the mist that trailed past the window. A small block of wood had been placed where the stone had crashed; they would come very shortly from Keswick and mend the window. Indeed, very little damage had been done: two windows broken, a shed or two destroyed—that was all there was to show for the flaring torches, the flaming sky, the shouts and curses and Reuben's death.

Jennifer looked very fine in her black gown. There was no paint on her face, and her magnificent black hair gave her to-day some nobility. But the shock of that night had done something to her. She was more properly controlled than she had been for years.

' There is a letter come for you,' she said.

Judith took it and saw that it was from Emma Furze. Emma! As she read it her heart glowed. And then, when she found that Emma was in London, was well and happy and gay, and wished to come up and spread some of her happiness around the Watendlath farm, it was as if the sun had broken into the room. She should, indeed she should. In another week Judith and Adam would be there. Then there would be Emma and Charlie and Alice Perry. . . .

' Were there many at the funeral, Judith dear? ' Jennifer asked.

Judith told her of the funeral.

Jennifer nodded to all the details.

' I am glad that I did not go. I am very unrestrained at funerals. And I do not know that I shall ever have the courage to go out again. Do you not know what they were calling . . . some of the women. . . ? Doris heard them. " Jezebel." One woman wanted to burn me in the stable.'

' Nonsense, Jennifer. You must not think of it. They are very kindly disposed to us. They are ready to do anything.'

' To us? To you, you mean. So long as you

are here we are safe. But I want to tell you.
I have been thinking deeply and I see how weak
and wretched I have been. I am terribly
ashamed. And I mean to be a help to you,
Judith, in the future as I have never been. And
to John and Dorothy too. Yes, I am most
wretchedly ashamed, and John, that evening,
was so brave and so good. I am sure no boy
of his age anywhere is so brave. You will find,
Judith, that I shall be quite another woman——'

'Well, that is excellent,' said Judith cheerfully. 'It is what I have always told you,
Jennifer. You have been frightened by shadows.'
Then she went on more gently, but with great
firmness. 'Next week Adam and I are going.
My mind is quite made up. You will find everyone here as kind as possible—everyone in the
village. Eager to make friends.'

'Oh no,' said Jennifer in a voice so low that
Judith could scarcely hear her. 'Oh, please
Judith—it will kill me if you go away.'

They had had it out already so many times.
There was to be no more discussion of it. But
as she bent to kiss Jennifer's cheek she had an
appalling sense of weakness.

Oh, let her waste no time! Let her slip out
now, this moment! Jennifer was harder to
resist now that she was so quiet, and there was
John who had been so brave and Dorothy who,
on that awful night, had been so good to Adam,
telling him stories. As she kissed Jennifer and
felt the cold touch of her hands she cared for her
as she had never done before.

Another moment and she would surrender, moved and softened as she had been by the funeral. She would surrender and be lost, all hope of her happiness gone! She murmured something and hastened out, almost expecting to find Walter Herries barring the door of the house with his huge body, defying her to escape.

But in the hall, instead of Walter Herries, she found Mr. Winch.

'May I speak to you a moment, madam?' he said.

'Yes, Mr. Winch,' she said. She had a new gravity. She had noticed it herself. She did not dislike it so long as she was in Uldale. It would not do at all for Watendlath. She led the way into the small room that had been Francis'. Mr. Winch, very pale, his hands clasped, his head up, looked at her.

'Well, Mr. Winch?'

'I thought I should tell you. . . .' He hesitated. ' . . . I wish to resign my duties here.'

She felt a relief. It would be easy to find some far better tutor, someone who did not go down on his knees on the gravel path. Indeed, had she had her way he would have gone long ago. Jennifer had some weakness for him. He read Minerva Press novels to her.

'But why?' she asked. In spite of herself she was scornful. 'Have the rioters been too much for you? You remained safely in the back of the house for the greater part.'

'I know,' he stammered. 'You must despise me—and rightly. But you do not know all. If . . .'

Then to her amazement he burst into sobs, threw himself down on his knees, held up his hands.

' Mr. Winch! ' she exclaimed, stepping back, thinking he must be out of his senses, that the fear of the other night had unsettled his wits.

' No, no. Listen to me. I have been miserable for a very long time, and this terrible catastrophe, with the death of Mr. Sunwood, has destroyed me. I was his murderer.'

' You! ' She could have laughed at the little figure in the shiny black with the rather grubby hands. But his distress was real, his fear was real. She saw that this was a matter of importance.

' Please rise,' she said. ' Please get up. You cannot be Mr. Reuben Sunwood's murderer, for I myself saw the shot fired that killed him.'

He was sobbing. He buried his head in his hands.

' I cannot speak to you unless you get up.'

He rose. He composed himself. His head bent a little, as though he were making a confession, he went on:

' No, not in positive fact his murderer. I did not fire the gun. But in everything else— Mrs. Paris, ever since I came to you I have been spying upon everyone in this house. Mr. Walter Herries of Westaways has paid me for that odious business.'

' I know it,' she said quietly.

' You knew it? '

' I saw you one day on your knees in the garden spying on Mr. Francis.'

' You knew it and you did nothing? '

' I did nothing because, once I knew it, you were safer than someone I did not know.'

He went on a little more confidently.

' I have no excuse.   None.   I did not need the money.   All my life I have avoided shabby actions.   But Mr. Walter Herries had a strange power over me.   He could do anything with me that he pleased.   I do not urge that in my defence; there is no defence.   But so it was. He overtook me one day walking to Keswick and from the first I was his slave.   I brought him news of everything that happened at Uldale —everything.   It was I who found a man that should carry the note to Mr. Francis when he was in Cockermouth, telling him that Captain Ferny-hirst was here that night.'

' You did that? '   He thought she would strike him and he moved back, but she had not stirred.

' Yes, I.   It was Mr. Walter Herries' plot, entirely arranged by him.'

Her face was so terrible that he could not look at it.   He turned away.

' Yes.   And so with everything here.   Every day he had news.   It was he, by my agency, who brought the rioters here.'

' Yes,' she said (but she was not addressing him).   ' I understand.'

' He intended, I think, only to give you a fright.   I was in Cockermouth and saw Holroyd and Bell and the others.   They were given money. There was to be no real damage to life or property.

But they had drink on that afternoon. They went further than they intended.'

'Yes,' she said. 'They went far.'

'I have been very miserable ever since I have been here. Again and again I have gone to him to tell him that I would do his work no longer but when I saw him . . . I cannot explain. . . . He had a power. . . .'

He was trembling.

'Forgive me,' he said. 'I must sit.' He sat down, his head so bent that she could scarcely catch his words. 'Again and again I have tried to say to you that I must go. Something prevented me. And at the beginning of this week when I knew what was in hand I was in hell. I could not sleep nor eat. A hundred times I was on the edge of breaking it to you. But his presence seemed always behind me. I thought that he would kill me if I betrayed him. He has often said, in his jolly laughing way, that he would. But he did not mean it to be murder. I did not intend. . . . But it is too late. You may give me up to the Justice, Mrs. Paris. You may indeed. I would be happier. . . .'

'You!' She turned to the window. Francis and Reuben both killed by Walter!

Her stomach was sick. Her knees trembled. She also sat down, but with her back to him. For a long while there was silence. Could she bring the thing home to Walter? She half turned, as though she would speak, but turned back again. No! there was no help there.

He would have seen to it that nothing could be carried to him. Who would believe a creature like Winch? Walter's power . . . ! And suddenly she saw him, as though he were there with them in the room, vast, blazing with colour and jewels, laughing, but so bent from conceit and arrogance on his purpose that nothing was too terrible for him, too mean, too cruel. And yet he was a jolly man and loved his son even as she loved hers. She got up.

'Pray go away, Mr. Winch,' she said. 'Go away in the morning. What is due to you will be sent to you. I would be happier not to see you again.'

Without a word he got up, and, head still bent, went out.

Very slowly she went upstairs to her room. No one was there. She looked out. Behind the mist the moon of five nights ago was now full, but it was like a flat stone ridged with light and wrapped in wool.

She had been caught. Now she had no doubt. She could not go. She had been able to defeat everything but this. Now a hard determined anger such as she had never felt had come and would abide. Francis . . . Reuben . . . killed by that laughing man. How could she now leave Jennifer and John and Dorothy defenceless?

Oh, but the other life! Watson was expecting her. In the Ritson kitchen Alice at this moment perhaps would be speaking of her. And her home, the room where Georges had died.

And Adam to be a farmer, to grow up knowing nothing of this world of money, deceit, jealousy, unkindness. The Tarn, wrapped in mist, would be waiting for the moon to break. Or, perhaps, there was no mist there to-night and the slopes of the fells, snow-clad, glittered.

' I cannot . . . I cannot. . . .'

She turned, possessed by some strange madness, pulled drawers open, found a box beneath the bed, began, on her knees, to cram it.

Adam came running in. He was shouting and dancing.

' Jack says there will be a new barn. They will begin to-morrow, and the windows——'

He stopped, seeing what she was doing. She shook her head as though the battle were hopeless. Once as a little girl she had climbed out of window, but now—to leave them, Jennifer weak, John, Dorothy, so young, to that determined remorseless purpose. . . .

' They are doomed, you know,' Walter had said, and even as he said it, he was aware that he had killed Francis, was planning this.

She got up from her knees and went to the window again. As she looked the moon broke the mist. Skiddaw started up in dazzling white. Like a white rose, like a glorious white rose from heaven, she lifted her head, and the mist sank to lie in waves across the valley.

She looked and she wept. The tears blinded her. She said farewell.

She came and sat down by the bed and drew Adam to her. She had command of herself.

'Tell me something,' he said. 'Tell me about Uncle Tom.'

It was his favourite story. While her mind was fiercely working on her future, hers and his, mechanically she went on with the familiar words:

'Although it had snowed so bitterly Uncle Tom got off his horse because he heard the baby crying, and he rode over the little bridge——'

'Don't forget the dogs! Don't forget the dogs!' Adam cried.

'Yes. They were all there and they followed him solemnly over the courtyard and into the house. And they went up the stairs. And they went into a room, the dogs sat down by the door, the old woman was sleeping——'

Oh, who was moving in the hills? What Rogue was wandering, calling for her, telling her that here was her home? The dry bones of the dead were alive. They were calling for her, those two old ghosts, and she could not come. . . .

She had now complete command of herself. She drew him closer.

'Adam, I want you to listen. You may not understand, but do you remember that one day going to Keswick I talked to you about being a farmer?'

'Yes,' he said. He drew himself up very straight because she was reposing a confidence in him and he was proud. He stood up straight with all the pride of a very small boy, that pride that is perhaps the small boy's most lovely quality.

'Now everything is changed. I have had
to make the most important decision of my life
—a decision for you also. You and I are to
fight, Adam. I had thought that it would all
be quiet and at peace, but now we are going to
fight.'

'Who will we fight?' Adam asked with great
interest. 'Uncle Walter?'

'You are too young to understand, but later
you will see that I could do nothing else than this.
We have to be very strong, you and I, and very
wise, Adam. We will beat them all, and you
shall be the head of them. No, you cannot
understand now. But you must trust me.'

He threw his arms round her neck. She was
small, and it was easy for him to draw her head
down; he could kiss her and lay his cheek against
hers. Now, if she wished to fight someone, he
would help her. He thought that perhaps she
was sorry that she had made him stay in Aunt
Jennifer's room when they came to burn the
stables. Now, this next time, he would go with
her and help her.

While he hugged her, her pride was rising.
Her pride, her deep and unchangeable hatred of
Walter Herries. In that hour the second half
of her life began.

She got up. Now she would take command.
A fierce bright delight flowed in her veins.
She would make Adam the master of them all.
Walter's boy. . . . She saw him in his little
chair, his deformity, his old, pale face, and the
big man kneeling at his side. She caught Adam

to her, kissing him passionately.   Adam should
be King.

With her head up, as though she already commanded a kingdom, she stepped downstairs.

She opened the parlour door.   Jennifer was
standing at the window.   When she heard the
door open she turned.   She looked and saw a
short pale woman in a plain black gown.   But
she saw also a woman on fire with determination,
with pride and an almost fanatical purpose.

' Why, Judith——! ' she began.

' All is well,' Judith said quietly, coming
forward and stroking the red apples of the sofa.
' I shall not leave you, Jennifer.   It is better I
remain.'

THE END

NOTE

The sequel to
JUDITH PARIS
is entitled
THE FORTRESS

Printed in Great Britain by R. & R. CLARK, LIMITED, *Edinburgh.*

By HUGH WALPOLE

HERRIES
A FAMILY CHRONICLE

(1)
ROGUE HERRIES
10s. 6d. net. Leather, 15s. net.
Cheaper Edition 5s. net.

"The canvas is huge, but something is happening, there is movement, colour, life, in every square inch of it. There is not one tired, listless page. . . . It is thunderingly alive. . . . *Rogue Herries* is a grand tale, a real full-time man's job in fiction, and everybody should read it. . . . It is fiction running on all six cylinders and of a staggering horse-power."—J. B. PRIESTLEY in the *Graphic*.

(2)
JUDITH PARIS
10s. 6d. net. Leather, 15s. net.
Cheaper Edition 5s. net.

"Mr. Walpole has achieved a triumph in his new novel. He has created a fascinating character in Judith. . . . Her experiences from childhood to middle age are of absorbing interest. . . . Judith is the most delightful of Mr. Walpole's heroines."—E. G. HAWKE in the *Daily Telegraph*.

(3)
THE FORTRESS
10s. 6d. net. Leather, 15s. net.

"Mr. Walpole leads us with rare brilliancy of description through the Victorian scene. . . . But his pictures of the Lake country, the home of the Herries, remain the most beautiful he has to offer, and supply the real atmosphere of this moving chronicle."—*The Times*.

(4)
VANESSA.   *August* 1933

LONDON : MACMILLAN AND CO., LTD.

1

THE NOVELS OF

HUGH WALPOLE

Pocket Edition. 3s. 6d. net. Leather, 5s. net each.
Uniform Edition. 3s. 6d. net each.

Above the Dark Circus
The Captives
The Cathedral
The Dark Forest
The Duchess of Wrexe
Farthing Hall (with J. B. Priestley)
Fortitude
The Golden Scarecrow
The Green Mirror
Hans Frost
Harmer John
Jeremy
Jeremy at Crale
Jeremy and Hamlet
Maradick at Forty
Mr. Perrin and Mr. Traill
The Old Ladies
Portrait of a Man with Red Hair
The Prelude to Adventure
The Secret City
The Silver Thorn
The Thirteen Travellers
Wintersmoon
The Wooden Horse
The Young Enchanted

All Souls' Night : A Book of Stories. 7s. 6d. net.
Four Fantastic Tales : Maradick at Forty, Prelude to
    Adventure, A Man with Red Hair, Above the Dark
    Circus. 936 pages. 7s. 6d. net.

LONDON : MACMILLAN AND CO., LTD.

SCOT-LAND

SOLWAY FIRTH

Brampton

Stanwix

Carlisle

Wigton

Caldbeck

Uldale

CUMBERLAND

Penrith

R. Derwent
Cockermouth

Bassenthwaite
Water

Skiddaw

Eden

R.

Keswick

Sockbridge

Derwent
Water

Ullswater

Appleby

Whitehaven

Crummock
Water

Borrowdale

Rosthwaite

Patterdale

Shap

Ennerdale
Water

Mardale

WESTMORLAND

Gosforth

Wast
Water

Seatoller

Santon Br.

Seascale

Ennerdale
Water

R. Irt.

R. Esk.

Long Sleddale

Rydal

Muncaster
Castle

R. Mite
Eskdale

Coniston
Old Man

Hawkshead

Miles

0   5   10

Ravenglass

LANCS.

Kendal

Loweswater

Loweswater

Whitehaven

Crummock
Water

Butt

Ennerdale
Water

Map of Borrowdale
and surrounding Country
Scale of Miles

0   1   2   3   4   5

Haycock

Seatallan

Middle Fell

Wast

Wast

Emery Walker Ltd. del. et sc.